J. M. Sherwood

Memoirs of Rev. David Brainerd, missionary to the Indians of North America

J. M. Sherwood

Memoirs of Rev. David Brainerd, missionary to the Indians of North America

ISBN/EAN: 9783744677554

Printed in Europe, USA, Canada, Australia, Japan

Cover: Foto ©Raphael Reischuk / pixelio.de

More available books at **www.hansebooks.com**

MEMOIRS OF

Rev. DAVID BRAINERD,

Missionary to the Indians of North America.

BASED ON THE LIFE OF BRAINERD PREPARED
By JONATHAN EDWARDS, D. D., AND AFTERWARDS REVISED
AND ENLARGED BY SERENO E. DWIGHT, D.D.

EDITED

By J. M. SHERWOOD

Author of "The History of the Cross."

WITH AN INTRODUCTION ON

THE LIFE AND CHARACTER OF DAVID BRAINERD

By THE EDITOR.

ALSO AN ESSAY ON

GOD'S HAND IN MISSIONS,

By ARTHUR T. PIERSON, D. D.

———◆———

FUNK & WAGNALLS COMPANY

TORONTO   1891   LONDON

NEW YORK

TABLE OF CONTENTS.

CONTENTS.

PRESIDENT EDWARD'S PREFACE TO THE ORIGINAL EDITION.

THERE are two ways of recommending true religion and virtue to the world ; the one, by doctrine and precept, the other by history and example. Both are abundantly used in the holy Scriptures. Not only are the grounds, nature, design, and importance of religion clearly exhibited in the doctrines of scripture—its exercise and practise plainly delineated and abundantly enforced in its commands and counsels—but there we have many excellent examples of religion, and its power and practice set before us in the histories both of the Old and New Testament.

JESUS CHRIST, the great Prophet of God, when he came to be " the light of the world,"—to teach and enforce true religion, in a greater degree than ever had been done before—made use of both these methods. In his doctrine, he not only declared more fully the mind and will of God—the nature and properties of that virtue which becomes creatures of our constitution, and in our circumstances, and more powerfully enforced it by exhibiting the obligations and inducements to holiness ; but he also in his own practice gave a most perfect example of the virtue which he taught. He exhibited to the world such an illustrious pattern of humility, divine love, discreet zeal, self-denial, obedience, patience, resignation, fortitude, meekness, forgiveness, compassion, benevolence, and universal holiness, as neither men nor angels ever saw before.

God also in his providence, has been wont to make use of both these methods to hold forth light to mankind, and inducements to their duty, in all ages. He

has from time to time raised up eminent teachers, to ex-
hibit and bear testimony to the truth by their doctrine,
and to oppose the errors, darkness, and wickedness of
the world ; and he has also raised up some eminent persons who have set bright examples of that religion which
is taught and prescribed in the word of God ; whose examples have, in the course of divine providence, been set
forth to public view.   These have a great tendency both
to engage the attention of men to the doctrines and
rules taught, and also to confirm and enforce them ; especially when these bright examples have been exhibited
in the same persons who have been eminent teachers.
Hereby the world has had opportunity to see a confirmation of the truth, efficacy, and amiableness of the religion taught, in the practice of the same persons who
have most clearly and forcibly taught it ; and above all,
when these bright examples have been set by eminent
teachers, a variety of unusual circumstances of remarkable trial ; and when God has withal remarkably distinguished them with wonderful success in their instructions and labors.

Such an instance we have in the excellent person
whose life is published in the following pages.   His example is attended with a great variety of circumstances
calculated to engage the attention of religious people,
especially in America.   He was a man of distinguished
talents, as all are sensible who knew him.   As a minister
of the gospel, he was called to unusual services in that
work ; and his ministry was attended with very remarkable and unusual events.   His course of religion began
before the late times of extraordinary religious commotion ; yet he was not an idle spectator, but had a near
concern in many things that passed at that time.   He
had a very extensive acquaintance with those who have
been the subjects of the late religious operations, in
places far distant, in people of different nations, education, manners, and customs.   He had a peculiar opportunity of acquaintance with the false appearances and
counterfeits of religion ; was the instrument of a most
remarkable awakening, a wonderful and abiding altera-

tion and moral transformation of subjects, who peculiarly render the charge rare and astonishing.

In the following account, the reader will have an opportunity to see, not only what were the external circumstances and remarkable incidents of the life of this person, and how he spent his time from day to day, as to his external behavior, but also what passed in his own heart. Here he will see the wonderful change he experienced in his mind and disposition ; the manner in which that change was brought to pass; how it continued ; and what were its consequences in his inward frames, thoughts, affections, and secret exercises, through many vicissitudes and trials, for more than eight years.

He will also see his sentiments, frame, and behavior, during a long season of the gradual and sensible approach of death ; and what were the effects of his religion in the last stages of his illness. The account being written, the reader may have opportunity at his leisure to compare the various parts of the story, and deliberately to view and weigh the whole, and consider how far what is related, is agreeable to the dictates of reason, and the Word of God.

I am far from supposing, that Brainerd's inward exercises or his external conduct, were free from all imperfections. The example of Jesus Christ is the only perfect example that ever existed in human nature. It is, therefore, a rule by which to try all other examples ; and the dispositions, frames, and practices of others, must be commended and followed no further than they were followers of Christ.

There is one thing in Brainerd, easily discernible by the following account of his life, which may be called an imperfection in him, which, though not properly an imperfection of a moral nature, yet may possibly be made an objection against the extraordinary appearances of religion and devotion in him, by such as seek for objections against everything that can be produced in favor of true, vital religion ; I refer to the fact, that he was, by his constitution and natural temper, so prone to melancholy, and dejection of spirit. There are some who think that all religion is a melancholy thing ; and that what is called Christian experience is little else besides melancholy vapors, disturbing the brain, and exciting enthusiastic imaginations. But that Brainerd's temper or constitution inclined him to despondency, is no just ground to suspect his extraordinary devotion to have been only the fruit of a warm imagination. All who have well observed mankind, will readily grant that many of those who by their natural constitution or temper, are most disposed to dejection, are not the most susceptive of lively and strong impressions on their imagination, or the most subject to those vehement affections, which are the fruits of such impressions. Many who are of a very gay and sanguine natural temper are vastly more so ; and if their affections are turned into a religious channel, are much more exposed to enthusiasm than many of the former.

As to Brainerd, notwithstanding his inclination to despondency, he was evidently one of those who usually are the farthest from a teeming imagination ; being of a penetrating genius, of clear thought, of close reasoning, and a very exact judgment ; as all know who knew him. As he had a great insight into human nature, and was very discerning and judicious in general ; so he excelled in his judgment and knowledge in divinity, but especially in experimental religion. He most accurately distinguished between real solid piety, and enthusiasm ; between those affections that are rational and scriptural—having their foundation in light and judgment—and those that are founded in whimsical conceits, strong impressions on the imagination, and vehement emotions of the animal spirits. He was exceedingly sensible of men's exposedness to these things ; how much they had prevailed, and what multitudes had been deceived by them ; of their pernicious consequences and the fearful mischief they had done in the Christian world. He greatly abhorred such a religion, and was abundant in bearing testimony against it, living and dying ; and was quick to discern when anything of that nature arose ; though in its first buddings, and appearing under the most fair and plausible disguises. He had a talent for describing the various workings of this imaginary enthusiastic religion—evincing its falseness and vanity, and demonstrating the great difference between this, and true spiritual devotion — which I scarcely ever knew equalled in any person.

His judiciousness did not only appear in distinguishing among the experiences of others, but also among the various exercises of his own mind ; particularly in discerning what within himself was to be laid to the score of melancholy in which he exceeded all melancholy persons that ever I was acquainted with. This was doubtless owing to a peculiar strength in his judgment, for it is a rare thing indeed, that melancholy people are sensible of their own disease, and convinced that such things are to be ascribed to it, as are its genuine operations and fruits. Brainerd did not obtain that degree of skill at once, but gradually ; as the reader may discern by the following account of his life. In the former part of his religious course, he imputed much of that kind of gloominess of mind, and those dark thoughts to spiritual desertion, which in the latter part of his life he was abundantly sensible were owing to the disease of melancholy ; accordingly he often expressly speaks of them in his diary, as arising from this cause. He often in conversation spoke of the difference between melancholy and godly sorrow, true humiliation and spiritual discretion, and the great danger of mistaking the one for the other, and the very hurtful nature of melancholy ; discoursing with great judgment upon it, and doubtless much more judiciously for what he knew by his own experience.

But not to argue from Brainerd's strength of judgment merely, it is apparent in fact, that he was not a person of a warm imagination. His inward experiences, whether in his convictions or his conversion, and his religious views and impressions through the course of his life, were not excited by strong and lively images formed in his imagination ; nothing at all appears of it in his diary from beginning to end. He told me on his

death-bed, that although once, when he was very young
in years and experience, he was deceived into a high
opinion of such things—looking on them as superior attainments in religion, beyond what he had ever arrived
at—was ambitious of them, and earnestly sought them ;
yet he never could attain them. He moreover declared,
that he never in his life had a strong impression on his
imagination, of any outward form, external glory, or any
thing of that nature ; which kind of impressions abound
among enthusiastic people.

As Brainerd's religious impressions, views, and affections in their nature were vastly different from enthusiasm ; so were their effects in him as contrary to it as
possible. Nothing, like enthusiasm, puffs men up with
a high conceit of their own wisdom, holiness, eminence,
and sufficiency ; and makes them so bold, forward as-
suming, and arrogant. But the reader will see that
Brainerd's religion constantly disposed him to a most
humble estimation of himself, an abasing sense of his
own sinfulness, unprofitableness, and ignorance ; looking
on himself as worse than others ; disposing him to universal benevolence and meekness ; in honor to prefer
others, and to treat all with kindness and respect. And
when melancholy prevailed, and though the effects of it
were very prejudicial to him, yet it had not the effects of
enthusiasm ; but operated by dark and discouraging
thoughts of himself, as ignorant, wicked, and wholly unfit for the work of the ministry, or even to be among
mankind. Indeed, at the time just mentioned, when he
had not learned well to distinguish between enthusiasm
and solid religion, he joined, and kept company with some
who were tinged with no small degree of the former. For
a season, he partook with them in a degree, of their dispositions and behaviors ; though, as was observed before,
he could not obtain those things wherein their enthusiasm
itself consisted, and so could not become like them in
that respect, however he erroneously desired and sought
it. But certainly it is not at all to be wondered at, that a
youth, a young convert, one who had his heart so swallowed up in religion, and who so earnestly desired its flourish-

ing state—and who had so little opportunity for reading, observation, and experience—should for a while be dazzled and deceived with the glaring appearances of mistaken devotion and zeal; especially, considering the extraordinary circumstances of that day.   He told me on his death-bed, that while he was in these circumstances, he was out of his element, and did violence to himself, while complying in his conduct with persons of a fierce and imprudent zeal, from his great veneration of some whom he looked upon as better than himself. So that it would be very unreasonable that his error at that time should nevertheless be esteemed a just ground of prejudice against the whole of his religion, and his character in general; especially considering how greatly his mind was soon changed, and how exceedingly he afterwards lamented his error, and abhorred himself for his imprudent zeal and misconduct at that time, even to the breaking of his heart, and almost to the overbearing of his natural strength; and how much of a Christian spirit he showed, in condemning himself for that misconduct, as the reader will see.

What has now been mentioned of Brainerd, is so far from being a just ground of prejudice against what is related in the following account of his life, that, if duly considered, it will render the history the more serviceable. For by his thus joining for a season with enthusiasts, he had a more full and intimate acquaintance with what belonged to that sort of religion; and so was under better advantages to judge of the difference between that and what he finally approved, and strove to his utmost to promote, in opposition to it.   In his testimony against it, and the spirit and behavior of those who are influenced by it, he also speaks from impartial conviction, and not from prejudice; because he thus openly condemns his own former opinions and conduct, on account of which he had greatly suffered from his opposers and for which some continued to reproach him as long as he lived.

Another imperfection in Brainerd, which may be observed in the following account of his life, was his being *excessive in his labors*; not taking due care to pro-

portion his fatigues to his strength. Indeed, the case
was very often such, by the seeming calls of Providence,
as made it extremely difficult for him to avoid doing more
than his strength would well admit of ; yea, his circumstances, and the business of his mission among the Indians, were such, that great fatigues and hardships were
inevitable. However, he was finally convinced, that he
had erred in this matter, and that he ought to have taken
more thorough care, and been more resolute to withstand
temptation to such degrees of labor as injured his
health ; and accordingly warned his brother, who suc-
ceeds him in his mission, to be careful to avoid this
error.

Besides the imperfections already mentioned, it is
readily allowed that there were some imperfections
which ran through his whole life, and were mixed with
all his religious affections and exercises : some mixture
of what was natural, with that which was spiritual ; as it
evermore is in the best saints in this world. Doubtless
natural temper had some influence in the religious exercises and experiences of Brainerd, as it most apparently
had in those of David and Peter, of John and Paul
There was undoubtedly very often some mixture of melancholy with true godly sorrow, and real Christian humility ; some mixture of the natural fire of youth
with his holy zeal for God ; and some influence of
natural principles, mixed with grace in various other
respects, as it ever was and ever will be with the
saints, while on this side heaven. Perhaps none were
more sensible of Brainerd's imperfections than himself;
or could distinguish more accurately than he, between
what was natural, and what was spiritual. It is easy for the
judicious reader to observe, that his graces ripened, that
the religious exercises of his heart became more and more
pure, and he more and more distinguishing in his judgment, the longer he lived. He had much to teach and
purify him, and he failed not to make his advantage.

Notwithstanding all these imperfections every pious
and judicious reader will readily acknowledge, that what
is here set before him, is a remarkable instance of true

and eminent piety, in heart and practice—tending greatly to confirm the reality of vital religion, and the power of godliness ;—that is most worthy of imitation, and in many ways calculated to promote the spiritual benefit of the careful observer.

The reader should be aware, that what Brainerd wrote in his *diary*, out of which the following account of his life is chiefly taken, was written only for his own private use ; and not to obtain honor and applause in the world, nor with any design that the world should ever see it, either while he lived, or after his death ; except a few things which he wrote in a dying state, after he had been persuaded with difficulty, not entirely to suppress all his private writings. He showed himself almost invincibly averse to the publishing of any part of his diary after his death ; and when he was thought to be dying at Boston, gave the most strict peremptory orders to the contrary. But being, by some of his friends there, prevailed upon to withdraw so strict and absolute a prohibition, he was finally pleased to yield so far, as that " his papers should be left in my hands, that I might dispose of them as I thought would be most for God's glory, and the interest of religion."

But a few days before his death, he ordered some part of his diary to be destroyed, which renders the account of his life the less complete. And there are some parts of his diary here, left out for brevity's sake, which would, I am sensible, have been a great advantage to the history, if they had been inserted; particularly the account of his wonderful success among the Indians ; which for substance, is the same in his private diary with that which has already been made public in the journal he kept by order of the society in Scotland, for their information. That account, I am of opinion, would be more entertaining and more profitable, if it were published as it is written in his diary, in connexion with his secret religion, and the inward exercises of his mind, and also with the preceding and following parts of the story of his life. But because that account has been published already, I have therefore omitted that part.   However, this defect may in a great measure be made up to the reader by the public journal.*   But it is time to end this preface that the reader may be no longer detained from the history itself.

JONATHAN EDWARDS.

* [The extracts from the Journal here referred to, were for the first time incorporated with the Diary in Dwight's New Haven edition, published in 1822, which forms the basis of the present edition.—J. M. S.]

PREFACE TO THE PRESENT EDITION.

THE beginning of the eighteenth century was an epoch in the history of modern missions. The Danish Mission to India was organized in 1714, and continued to do efficient work until the close of the century, when Rationalism undermined its roots. The Moravians, or United Brethren, also began early in the century their wonderful missionary career, and have not ceased their energetic efforts down to the present day. They have sent out nearly 2,300 missionaries, of whom more than 600 are still in the field. In Germany and England the good work was also begun quite early in the century. In England the Society for the Propagation of the Gospel in Foreign Parts was founded in 1701, but did very little until the opening of the present century. It gave some attention to the Indians and the Negroes of the American Colonies. The Society for Promoting Christian Knowledge was more active. Collections for it were taken up even at court, and George I showed his interest in the work by writing a cordial letter to Zieyenbalg and Gründler, leading missionaries. In Edinburgh a Scotch Society for Promoting Christian Knowledge was founded in 1709, and also a Corporation for the Propagation of the Gospel in New England. It was the former of these Scotch societies that employed David Brainerd and several other missionaries to labor among the Indian tribes of this New World; and the latter aided in the support of Jonathan Edwards among the Stockbridge Indians.

About the year 1740, several distinguished ministers in the city of New York and its vicinity, among them, Ebenezer Pemberton, of New York, Aaron Burr, of Newark, and Jonathan Dickinson, of Elizabethtown, communicated to this society "the deplorable and perishing state of the Indians in the provinces of New York, New Jersey, and Pennsylvania." In consequence of this representation, the society agreed to maintain two missionaries among them, to convert them to Christianity; and in pursuance of this design sent those gentlemen, and some others—both clergymen and laymen, a Commission to act as their Commissioners, or Correspondents, "in providing, directing, and inspecting the said Mission."

Thus empowered, these Commissioners immediately looked out for two candidates for the ministry, whose zeal for the interests of the Redeemer's kingdom and compassion for perishing souls would prompt them to such an exceedingly difficult and self-denying undertaking. They first prevailed with Mr. Azariah Horton to relinquish a call to an encoruaging parish, and to devote himself to the Indian service. He was directed to Long Island in August, 1741, at the east end of which there were two small towns of Indians; and, from the east to the west end of the island, lesser companies settled at a few miles distance from one another, for the distance of about one hundred miles. At his first arrival he was well received by most, and cordially welcomed by some of them. Those at the east end of the Island, especially, gave diligent and serious attention to his instructions; and many of them were led to ask the solemn inquiry, "What they should do to be saved?" A general reformation of manners was soon observable among most of these Indians. The spiritual results of his ministry were truly remarkable. Just how long he labored among them, and what were the total fruits, we have no authentic record.

"It was some time after this, before the Correspondents could obtain another missionary. At length they prevailed upon David Brainerd to refuse several invitations to places where he had a promising prospect of a comfortable settlement, to encounter the fatigues and perils which must attend his carrying the Gospel of Christ to these poor, miserable savages."* Brainerd was examined and approved as a missionary by this Commission in the city of New York, and assigned to his field of labor. He began his work at Kaunaumeek, an Indian settlement between Stockbridge and Albany, and subsequently labored among the Indians of New Jersey and Pennsylvania.

At the request of the Society in Scotland, he regularly forwarded to them a copy of his journal, which contained a succinct account of his missionary work. That society published extracts from this journal in two parts; the First in 1746, commencing with his residence at Crossweeksung (June 19, 1745, and ending Nov. 4, 1745), under the title:

"*Mirabilia Dei inter Indicos;* or the rise and Progress of a remarkable Work of Grace, among a number of Indians, in the Provinces of New Jersey and Pennsylvania: justly represented in a Journal, kept by order of the Honorable Society in Scotland for Propagating Christian Knowledge, with some General Remarks; by

---

* Preface of the "Correspondents" to Brainerd's Letter to Pemberton.

David Brainerd, Minister of the Gospel, and Missionary from the said Society."

The second part (Nov. 24, 1745 to June 19, 1746) was published in the latter part of that year ; and was entitled :

"Divine Grace Displayed ; or the Continuance and Progress of a remarkable Work of Grace among some of the Indians belonging to the Provinces of New Jersey and Pennsylvania ; justly represented in a Journal, kept by order of the Honorable Society in Scotland for Propagating Christian Knowledge ; with some General Remarks ; by David Brainerd, Minister of the Gospel, and Missionary from the said Society."

These two parts have always been called "Brainerd's Journal ; " and were published during his life.

Brainerd died at the house of Dr. Jonathan Edwards, at Northampton, Mass., October 9, 1747, leaving all his papers in his hands (a portion of his diary he had previously destroyed) "that he might dispose of them as he thought would be most for God's glory and the interest of religion." Of these the most valuable was the account of his early life, which we give entire, and the original copy of his diary. From these authentic records President Edwards prepared a Life of Brainerd—chiefly in Brainerd's own words—which was published in Boston in 1749, with the following title :

"An account of the Life of the Late Rev. David Brainerd, Missionary to the Indians, from the Hon. Society in Scotland for the Propagation of Christian Knowledge ; and Pastor of a Church of Christian Indians in New Jersey ; who died at Northampton, October 9th, 1747, in the 30th year of his age.

"Chiefly taken from his own Diary, and other private writings, written for his own use; and now published by Jonathan Edwards, A. M., Minister of the Gospel at Northampton."

Edwards' Life of Brainerd did not include his " Journal," which had already been published abroad, in two parts, under the auspices of the Scottish Society which employed and supported him.

In 1822, a new memoir was prepared by the Rev. Sereno E. Dwight, D. D., a great-grandson of Jonathan Edwards, embracing, in addition to the matter contained in the original " Life," the whole of Brainerd's " Journal," together with his Letters and other writings, and Reflections on his Memoirs, by President Edwards. This "complete" Memoir was published at New Haven, in 1822, and afterwards included in the works of President Edwards, in ten octavo volumes, edited by the same author, and published in New York in 1830.

This complete Memoir is now entirely out of print, and is accessible only in Public Libraries, and in connection with the ten volume edition of Edwards' works.

The present edition is based on Dwight's edition, and is equally full and complete, except that it omits the Sermons of Pemberton and Edwards (except that which bears directly on Brainerd), and occasional lines thrown in by the Biographer, where he omitted some entries in the Diary, to indicate the fact and the drift of the omitted parts. Portions of the Memoir have been slightly revised and condensed by the present Editor, chiefly for literary reasons ; a few Notes have been added on points of historic interest, and also an Introductory Chapter on the Life and Character of Brainerd. And, in addition, likewise, a stirring Essay on God's Hand in Missions, written at our special request by the Rev. Arthur T. Pierson, D. D., whose vigorous and eloquent pen has often done efficient work in the great Missionary enterprise of the nineteenth century.

The whole is commended to the blessing of the Great Head of the Church, with the earnest prayer that this humble effort to elevate the standard of personal consecration to Christ, and to revive and extend an interest in that Cause which is "The Glory of the Age," may not be wholly in vain. If the reader shall find that intense interest and spiritual quickening in reading these Memoirs that the writer has experienced in revising them (having first read them forty years ago), he will thank him for calling attention to them and making them again accessible.

JAMES M. SHERWOOD.

BROOKLYN, *June,* 1884.

INTRODUCTION.

THE

LIFE AND CHARACTER

OF

DAVID BRAINERD.

By

J. M. SHERWOOD.

LIFE AND CHARACTER OF BRAINERD.

As the lives of men are written down in human History and estimated by the world, the life of DAVID BRAINERD was singularly uneventful and insignificant—an infinitesimal factor in human existence. Born in a little hamlet in New England, living in the period of our colonial dependence and obscurity, modest and humble in disposition, educated in a very quiet fashion, without worldly ambition, devoting his brief life to the welfare of a few Indians scattered over the wilderness districts of New York, New Jersey, and Pennsylvania, and dying in his thirtieth year—there was nothing in the outward events of his life to attract attention, or make his life in any respect noteworthy in the eyes of mankind.

He was not a genius, nor an orator. His scholarship was not very remarkable. He laid no foundations of empire. He made no discoveries. He achieved no literary fame. And yet young BRAINERD had that in him of which heroes and martyrs are made. He was a representative man of the truest and noblest type. His is a character of such saintliness, of such lofty aims and principles, of such intense loyalty to "Christ and him crucified," and of such all-absorbing love for souls and desire for God's glory, that it has left a lasting impression on the Christian Church, and his name will travel down the centuries, hallowed in the memory of the good, and regarded as one of the brightest stars in the constellation of Christian worthies.

DAVID BRAINERD is a household name to-day wherever exalted piety is revered, or moral worth is cherished, or a heroic and self-sacrificing spirit is honored. Although his life was brief, it was long enough to take on an immortal impress; to develop a character, a purpose, a richness of experience, a fervor of spirit, and a longing after holiness and usefulness, as grand and majestic, as rare and glorious. The gift he laid upon Christ's altar was a priceless gift; and the Divine Master has honored and blessed it, to enrich the faith, and stimulate the zeal of those who came after him. The short life of the "Missionary of the Wilderness," spent in teaching a few ignorant savages the way of life, has already borne abundant fruit to the glory of God, and will continue to do so to the end of time, as few lives have done or will do. "*Being dead he yet speaketh.*" Through the silence of nearly one hundred and fifty years he is speaking to-day, with trumpet tongue, words of almost matchless power; speaking also by example, by his "Diary," and "Journal," and "Letters," recording in simple words his religious experiences from day to day—his hopes and fears, his joys and trials, his self-reproaches and longings after a higher life—speaking to our young men in college and seminary and in the several professions, and to those just entering upon life's work in the gospel ministry—speaking indeed to the Church at large, urging the claims of dying millions, and the obligations of redeeming love.

Little did the solitary, and often lonely and desponding missionary, ruminating in his wigwam or log hut in the forest, which his own hands had built, sleeping on his pallet of straw, or on the floor, or out in the woods, living on poor and scanty food, often sick and suffering, with "none to converse with but poor rude, ignorant Indians"; wrestling with God and with his own heart day and night, and writing down in his journal an account of his inner life and daily work ;—little did he dream that that life, whose surroundings were so unpromising, whose scene of labor was so secluded, and whose errors and shortcomings cost him so many regrets and bitter tears, would carry light and conviction and stimulus all over Christendom and down the centuries. But so it has proved. BRAIN-ERD's Memoirs have been read and wept over for almost one hundred and fifty years, by Christians of all lands and creeds and conditions ; and they are as full of Christian life and power to-day as when Jonathan Edwards gave them to the press in 1749. It is certainly one of the most wonderful auto-biographies extant. No better manual of Christian experience has ever been given to the world, bating the vein of morbid melancholy which runs through it. No loftier example of Christian heroism and conse-cration to the work and purpose of Christianity has been held up since the apostolic age. His life has been a potent force in the grand missionary movement of mo-dern times. Reading the life of BRAINERD decided Henry Martyn to become a missionary and "imitate his example." William Carey likewise received a powerful inspiration from the same source. Jonathan Edwards, the greatest theologian of his times, had never appeared in the rôle of a " missionary to the Stockbridge Indians," had he not come into intimate contact with the seraphic spirit of this missionary apostle and martyr, for such he truly was. Thousands and tens of thousands of Chris-tians in America and Europe, and all over the mission-ary world, have had their piety deepened, their faith quickened, and their spirit of consecration fanned into a flame, by reading the wondrous record of this man's life and Christian experience, whose brief ministry was spent among the Indians of the American wilderness.

Let us study carefully the brief life, and analyze the remarkable character of BRAINERD, that we may learn the secret of his great power and abiding life in the Church ; learn what there was in his religious character and experience which lifted him immeasurably above his age and surroundings, the conditions and incidents of his being, and identified him with the conflicts and triumphs of the Church in all times, and placed him among the foremost characters in religious history.

As we have already intimated, the annals of his life were few and simple. He was born of pious and respectable parents ; of good Puritan stock. He was left an orphan at fourteen. He was cared for by kind Christian friends. He entered Yale College, but was expelled after two years and before graduation, for a trifling offence. We shall notice this further on, for it was an act of cruel injustice, and had a marked influence on his character and whole future life. He pursued his theological studies in a private way with a pastor, as theological seminaries were not yet established. He was licensed to preach at the age of twenty-six. Declining several urgent invitations to settle in New England, and a highly flattering one from Long Island, he deliberately and solemnly devoted himself to missionary work among the Indians, scattered among the several colonies. And having once put his hand to the plow, he looked not back, but gave himself, heart, and soul, and mind, and strength, to his chosen mission, with unfaltering purpose, with apostolic zeal, with a heroic faith that feared no danger and surmounted every obstacle, and with an earnestness of mind that wrought wonders on savage lives and whole communities, but which in four years broke down his health and consigned him to an early grave.

We cannot *appreciate the choice he made*, the kind of life he lived, or the work he accomplished, unless we look at the times and the circumstances in which he lived and wrought.

It calls for no great sacrifices, in our day, to be a missionary to the heathen world. There is now a widespread and grand missionary spirit and sentiment existing in the Church. Thousands have gone forth to labor in distant fields. The eyes of the Christian world are upon them, the sympathies and prayers of the great Christian brotherhood follow them. They go for the most part in groups, and carry home, and Christian society, and civilization, with them. They know that behind them, watching and deeply interested in them, sustaining them, and praying for them, are great National Societies, thus giving dignity, character and importance to their missionary work.

But how different was the case with reference to BRAINARD and his times. It was before the birth of modern missions. Christian missions had then no standing in the American Church. There was little or no faith in them, No prayers were offered for them, either in public or in the closet. There was no public sentiment calling for missions to the heathen and pagan world. Not a dollar was contributed or pledged to the support of missionaries. The few hundreds necessary to BRAINERD'S support in the mission which he undertook, came from over the sea. It was a little foreign society, organized in Edinburgh, Scotland,—too far away to extend effective sympathy to its distant missionary—that undertook to "hold the ropes" while he made the venture. So little missionary interest existed in this country that even seventy years afterward when the first American missionaries were sent out to foreign parts, the money needed to defray expenses was sought in England.

And then BRAINERD had to undertake and carry on the work literally *alone ;* he had no associate or helper. Although authorized by the Society to employ "two missionaries," the Commission, which acted for it, could find but *one*—so little interest was then felt in such a work. One young man, solitary and unsupported, went forth into the wilderness, in obedience to the Saviour's great command ; and there with his single hands laid the foundation of Christ's kingdom in that field ! It was an act of sublime heroism ! He touchingly alludes, at times, to his "loneliness"—only Indians to associate with—no one to speak to in English, or commune with —wholly destitute of the comforts of civilized life—the only white in a community of savage Indians, and many days' journey remote from a white settlement. His only mode of travel was on horseback, through dense and trackless forests ; often obliged to "sleep out in the woods," exposed to dangers and hardships of every kind, often weary and sick, dejected and cast down. But never wavering in his purpose, never regretting his choice ; incessantly at work, preaching, catechizing the Indians, moving among them like an angel of light, pleading with them in the name of Christ, and pleading their cause against greedy and unprincipled whites, who sought to corrupt and rob them (as is so often done in our time) as he had opportunity, and ceasing not his arduous and self-sacrificing labors for their temporal and spiritual welfare, until his strength was finally ex-

hausted and his life worn out. Then, by slow and painful journeys, he made his way back to his native New
England to die !

Surely, whatever may be the case at present, there
was no "romance" in missionary life in such an age, among
such a people, in such surroundings, amidst such repul-
sive scenes and conditions of physical and social life.

His, then, was not the dream of a visionary enthusiast.
Had it been, his zeal would quickly have abated, and the
enterprise been abandoned. But instead of being dis-
gusted or disheartened by the terrible experiences which
he encountered, he rose superior to them all, and prosecuted his mission with the zeal of a Paul, and made his
life a " living oblation." His work grew in interest and
love and dignity to the last. And when, finally, health
and strength utterly failed him, under a constant strain
upon his physical and mental energies amidst severe privations and hardships, it cost him the bitterest pangs to
cease his work and turn his back upon his " dear Indians "
and abandon the field. And he ceased not his prayers
and efforts in their behalf, so long as life remained in
him. Through the subsequent months of severe sickness, and while lying on his death bed, his Indian mission was continually on his mind. Again and again was
he heard to plead with God for its continued prosperity.
His efforts also to interest his friends in it were unceas-
ing ; and he would not rest until he had induced his
brother John, whom he " loved the best of any being on
earth," to take his place and prosecute the great work
which he had been compelled in the providence of God
to relinquish.

That BRAINARD rose above the spirit of his age—for
the spirit of Evangelism is the measure of the Church's

life—and taking his life in his hands, alone and single-handed, went forth into the wilderness to preach Christ to savage tribes, and was permitted to witness among and upon them astonishing displays of God's converting grace—demonstrates the high order of his faith in God, and of his consecration to the great work of the world's salvation.

No eulogy can exalt such a man. The simple story of his life proves him to be one of the most illustrious characters of modern times, as well as the foremost missionary whom God has raised up in the American Church —one whose example of zeal, self-denial and Christian heroism has probably done more to develop and mould the spirit of modern missions and to fire the heart of the Church in these latter days, than that of any other man since the apostolic age. One such personage, one such character, is a greater power in human history than a finite mind can calculate.

His Character.

An analysis of his character it is not difficult to make, for the leading traits or qualities of the man stand out in bold relief and challenge our observation and admiration.

The first thing that impresses the reader of BRAINERD's life is *the genuineness and depth and thoroughness of his personal piety.* We see at once that there is nothing superficial, transient, doubtful, half-hearted about it. We are brought into contact with a Christian character, and a Christian experience, and a Christian life, most rare and extraordinary in many of their elements and features. There is something startling and awe-inspiring in the depth and intensity of his religious "frames" and "exercises," as recorded so frankly and faithfully in his diary, running through several years, with no expectation that any eye save his own and God's would ever read them. " He belongs to a class of men," as one has well said, "who seem to be chosen of Heaven to illustrate the sublime possibilities of Christian attainment—men of seraphic fervor of devotion, and whose one, overmastering passion is to win souls for Christ, and to become wholly like him themselves."

The Law made thorough work with him. His sense of the evil, guilt, and awfulness of sin, of his own deep moral corruption and desert of God's wrath, his personal unworthiness, and entire dependence on Divine grace, and his constant need of the Holy Spirit to cleanse, enlighten and sanctify, was most profound and ever present with him. He could not find language strong enough to express his hatred of sin and desire to be entirely and forever cleansed and delivered from it. He longed and strove after holiness, after complete victory over sin and the world and the devil, after entire conformity to the will and likeness of Christ, with a strength and intensity of soul that seems almost superhuman.

2 *His consecration to the Master's service was, seemingly, entire and sublime.* Not since the apostolic age has the Church produced a grander illustration of the power of the Gospel to subdue human selfishness, and the love of ease and pleasure and self-indulgence, and to make Jesus Christ supreme, " all and in all," in the affections and life of the soul. Like Paul, he made a total surrender of every faculty and power of body, soul and spirit, to the Divine Son of God, and at the same time an unreserved, absolute consecration of his life and being to His service. He could not love and serve God enough. He was jealous of his own heart and life, lest he should not render

every day and hour a full measure of love and labor. He kept nothing back. From the time he gave himself to Christ, he devoted his life and strength and attainments and acquirements and opportunities to the work of saving souls, without recreation, without cessation, sparing him-self in no particular ; serving God to the full extent of his ability, and even beyond. The amount of work he did was almost incredible. He broke down his consti-tution in four short years, by exposure, privation, and labors of every kind ; literally wore his life away in the cause of his blessed Master. It is affecting in the highest degree, to read the entries in his journal from day to day, of what he did, what he attempted, what he longed to accomplish ; and, in the midst of his incessant labors, to hear him bemoan his shortcomings, his bar-renness of spirit, his unfruitfulness, and pray God to forgive him his unfaithfulness and grant him a new bap-tism of love and zeal. Here is a specimen :—

"Here I am, Lord, send me: send me to the ends of the earth ; send me to the rough, the savage pagans of the wilderness ; send me from all that is called comfort in the earth ; send me even to death itself if it be but in thy service and to promote thy kingdom."

And it was no ascetic or misanthrope that wrote thus, for he adds :—

"At the same time I had as quick and lively a sense of the value of earthly blessings as I ever had, but only saw them infinitely overmatched by the worth of Christ's kingdom. Farewell friends and earthly comforts, the dearest of them all ; the very dearest, if the Lord calls for it : adieu, adieu ; I will spend my life, to my latest moments, in caves and dens of the earth, if the kingdom of God may thereby be advanced.

He was affianced, as is well known, to a youthful saint, of rare gifts, the youngest daughter of Jonathan Edwards ; and such a pure, intelligent and sensitive nature as his, would have enjoyed, in an eminent degree, the felicity of domestic life. But he sacrificed even this.

and plunged alone into the wilderness and passed his
years with savages, that he might win them to
Christ. The little patrimony left him, he also devoted to
the education of a poor and promising young man for the
ministry, soon after entering upon his missionary work.

3. *His love for souls amounted to a passion, which
nothing could cool or conquer.* No miser ever clung to
his treasure as he grasped this idea and made it an ever
present and supreme object with him. No matter where
he went, or what were his surroundings, the ruling bent
of his soul was manifest. In health and in sickness, in
his wigwam among the Indians, on his numerous and
solitary journeys, from settlement to settlement in the
wilderness, and in his occasional visits to New England,
his supreme desire was to convert souls; and no occasion, no opportunity, did he fail to improve, however
weary or racked with pain, or weak or broken down from
disease. This intense, ever burning passion often finds
expression, as when he writes in his diary :

"O how I longed that God should be glorified on earth. Bodily pains
I cared not for, though I was then in extremity. I never felt easier; I felt
willing to glorify God in that state of bodily distress, so long as he pleased
I should continue in it. The grave appeared really sweet, and I longed
to lodge my weary bones in it: but O that God might be glorified! this
was the burden of all my cry. O to love and praise God more, to please
him forever! this my soul panted after, and even now pants for while I
write, O that God might be glorified in the whole earth! Lord let
thy kingdom come! . . . O the blessedness of living to God! . . . Spent
two hours in secret duties, and was enabled to agonize for immortal souls,
though it was early in the morning and the sun scarcely shone, yet
my body was quite wet with sweat. . . With what reluctance did I feel myself obliged to consume time in sleep! I longed to be a flame of fire, continually glowing in the divine service, and building up Christ's kingdom to
my latest, my dying moment."

Is it any marvel that many souls—even the souls of
such ignorant and degraded savages—were given to

him? And he never regretted his devotion and self-sacrificing zeal in this work. Read his thrilling words, as he hung over eternity while in Boston. "I declare now I am dying, I would not have spent my life otherwise for the whole world."

4. *His humility and spirit of self-denial and cheerful submission to deprivations and hardships for the Gospel's sake,* are touchingly illustrated in his life. According to President Edwards' testimony, he was a young man of "distinguished talents;" "had extraordinary knowledge of men and things;" had "rare conversational powers;" "excelled in his knowledge of theology, and was truly, for one so young, an extraordinary divine, and especially in all matters relating to experimental religion." "I never knew his equal of his age and standing, for clear and accurate notions of the nature and essence of true religion." His "manner in prayer was almost inimitable, such as I have very rarely known equalled." He "had a very extensive acquaintance, and engaged the attention of religious people in a remarkable degree." He had also many invitations to settle in his own New England, and an urgent and oft-renewed call to "East Hampton—the fairest, pleasantest town on Long Island, and one of its largest and wealthiest parishes." So that he did not give himself to the missionary work, as is often, though unjustly, said of other missionaries in these days, because he could not succeed at home. His talents, gifts, and Christian attainments made him the peer of New England's most gifted preachers, with few exceptions.

But he put from him all these tempting offers, and all considerations of a merely personal and temporal nature, and gave his whole self for life to the work of teaching the poor American Indians the way of salvation. And he had no thought that he was doing anything wonderful, or that he was degrading himself, or throwing away his talents and life by so doing. On the contrary, he evidently felt that God had greatly honored him in calling him to such a service; and he consecrated his heart and soul and mind and strength and life to it, with as much heartiness and enthusiasm and ambition as though he were ministering to a highly cultured people in some conspicuous and wealthy parish.

So real and great was his humility that he often expressed his surprise that he was called to such a noble service; that the Indians should have any respect for him, or show him any attention, or that any good should come from his labors. His *privations and hardships* likewise were such as few missionaries have ever experienced. An extract or two will serve to introduce the reader to his mode of life:

"My diet consists mostly of hasty-pudding, boiled corn, and bread baked in the ashes, and sometimes a little meat and butter. My lodging is a little heap of straw, laid upon some boards a little way from the ground, for it is a log room without any floor, that I lodge in . . . I have now rode more than 3,000 miles [on horseback] since the beginning of March [8 months] . . . Frequently got lost in the woods . . . At night lodged in the open woods . . . crept into a little crib made for corn and slept there on the poles."

And yet not one word of complaint do we hear. Even in his times of extreme melancholy and dejection, and they were frequent; when sick and racked with pain; when lonely and disconsolate, not one breath of murmur rises to Heaven. His forest home was often a "Bochim," or as the "valley of Baca," as it respected the outward man and his surroundings. And, yet, even then and there, like Jesus after the temptation of the wilderness, angels comforted him and his soul often exulted, while he magnified the God of his salvation, "who giveth songs in the night."

5. *He exemplified the law of Christian meekness and forgiveness in a preëminent degree.* The unusual attention which his extraordinary career and saintly character attracted, at home and abroad; the sympathy and interest manifested in him by many of the most eminent ministers of his day, among whom were Jonathan Edwards, Bellamy, the Tennants, Pemberton, Aaron Burr, and Jonathan Dickinson, and the high esteem in which he was held by the Christian world, especially towards the close of his life, did not tend in the least to elate him. On the contrary—as in all cases of real and eminent worth and superiority—it only tended to make him more humble; it induced Christian meekness, and filled him with a profound sense of his unworthiness. The expressions of this feeling in his journal are frequent, emphatic, and evidently sincere.

In all the annals of human life and experience, excepting those of the God-Man, we have no more striking example of *Christian forgiveness than the life of* BRAINERD *furnishes.* Take a single particular.

He was *wronged ;* wronged as few men in similar circumstances, ever were wronged. He was wronged by a public institution ; wronged before the world ; nay, it is not uncharitable to say that he was persecuted, insulted, outraged—and all redress refused, and that against the united, solemn, and earnest protest of such men as President Edwards, Burr, Dickinson, Pemberton, and many others of the most distinguished men of the times. He was wronged in a way to mortify and humiliate and injure a young man of his ambition, and talent and genuine manliness and high Christian character and standing, to the utmost possible extent. The wrong was *persisted* in, with iron determination and relentless severity, even after he had made the most manly and Christian acknowledgment and confession that it was possible for the college authorities to exact, or a gentleman, respecting his own manhood, truth and righteousness, could consistently make.

And that he *felt* the wrong exquisitely, and smarted under it, and carried the memory and the scar of it to his grave, his diary affords abundant and affecting proof. This ill treatment, at his tender years, had much to do with his dejection at times. It preyed upon his sensitive nature. He felt as if a brand was placed upon his forehead. Most of all he mourned over it, because he thought *religion suffered* in consequence of it. No one can read the entries made in his journal during his visit to New Haven a year after his expulsion, at the time when he would have graduated but for that unjust procedure—afraid to show himself in the town for "fear of imprisonment"—hiding away in the house of a friend in the outskirts of the town, as if "guilty of some open and notorious crime," and there spending commencement day in prayer and sweet converse with Christian friends—and not feel his heart rise in rebellion against that stern and unrighteous decree which on that occasion crushed his last hope of redress ! Earnest application was made on his behalf to the authorities of the college by a "council of ministers at Hartford," and by Edwards, Burr, and many other distinguished men in the various colonies, that he might be allowed to take his degree with his class. But all in vain. Yet here is the entry he made in his diary in this bitter hour of disappointment :

"*Sept 14.* This day I ought to have taken my degree ; [this being Commencement day] but God sees fit to deny it to me. And though I was greatly afraid of being overwhelmed with perplexity and confusion, when

I should see my classmates take theirs; yet, at the very time, God enabled me with calmness and resignation to say, ' the will of the Lord be done.' Indeed, through divine goodness, I have scarcely felt my mind so calm, sedate, and comfortable, for some time. I have long feared this season, and expected my humility, meekness, patience, and resignation, would be much tried ; * but found much more pleasure and divine comfort, than I expected. Felt spiritually serious, tender and affectionate in private prayer with a dear Christian friend to-day."

But notwithstanding the wrong done him was so great, and was so obstinately persisted in to the last ; notwithstanding he suffered in his feelings as only a man of such exquisite natural and moral sensibilities could suffer, not once was he known to speak harshly or unkindly of those who had committed the injury. Not a line is found in his diary alluding to the matter that breathes other than a spirit of Christlike charity and forgiveness ; while he was fervent and frequent in his prayers in behalf of those who had "so ill used him." The same spirit that cried out from the cross, " Father, forgive them, for thy know not what they do," animated the heart of this youthful disciple while living, and to-day encircles his brow with a halo of Christlike glory.

6. But the *crowning excellency of* BRAINERD *was the large measure of the spirit of Prayer which characterized his life.* Prayer was his chief reliance, and the secret of his remarkable success. Much of his time was spent in prayer. Days and nights were thus passed ; and he grieved when anything interfered to keep him from his knees in solitary and prolonged intercession and communion with God. Closely in this respect did he follow in the footsteps of Jesus. Prayer was his solace, his inspiration, his strength. No part of his diary or journal is of more thrilling interest to any and every Christian

---

* Had he been allowed to graduate, he would have been at the *head* of his class, and that class the largest that had ever graduated at that college.

worker, either in the home or the foreign field, than the
numerous entries in relation to his seasons of secret
prayer. Few saints, this side of heaven, ever got so
near to the throne of God in prayer; ever so "wrestled
with the angel of the covenant;" ever experienced such
communion with the Father of spirits until his soul exulted and overflowed with the fulness of "ineffable comforts."—Read a specimen or two :—

"Had the most ardent longings after God, which I ever felt in my
life. At noon, in my secret retirement, I could do nothing but tell my
dear Lord, in a sweet calm, that he knew I desired nothing but himself,
nothing but holiness ; that he had given me these desires, and he only
could give me the things desired. I never seemed to be so unhinged from
myself, and to be so wholly devoted to God. My heart was swallowed up
in God most of the day . . . Felt much comfort and devotedness to God
this day. At night, it was refreshing to get alone with God, and pour out
my soul. Oh, who can conceive of the sweetness of communion with the
blessed God, but those who have experience of it ! Glory to God for
ever, that I may taste heaven below . . . Retired early for secret devotion,
and in prayer God was pleased to pour such ineffable comforts into my
soul that I could no nothing for some time but say over and over, O my
sweet Saviour ! O my sweet Saviour ! whom have I in heaven but thee,
and there is none upon earth that I desire beside thee. If I had a thousand lives, my soul would gladly have laid them all down at once to have
been with Christ . . . My soul was this day at turns sweetly set on God;
I longed to be with him, that I might behold his glory. I felt sweetly disposed to commit all to him, even my dearest friends, my dearest flock, my
absent brother, and all my concerns for time and eternity. O, that his
kingdom might come in the world, that they might all love and glorify
him for what he is in himself, and that the blessed Redeemer might 'see
of the travail of his soul, and be satisfied ! Oh come, Lord Jesus, come
quickly ! Amen."

Is it wonderful that such a habit of prayer, and such
experiences in prayer in the closet, should have made his
social and public prayers edifying and striking in a remarkable degree? President Edwards' testimony on
this point is very explicit and noteworthy : "*I know not
that I ever so much as heard him ask a blessing or return*

thanks at table, but there was something remarkable to be observed both in the matter and manner of the performance." Prayer, in secret and personal communion with God, will temper the whole spirit of a Christian, and put its impress upon his social and public habits. If you witness habitual fervency, and fullness, and power, and a wrestling spirit in prayer, on the part of any disciple, you may be sure the habit has been acquired in secret intercourse with God upon his knees. Prayer is not so much a gift as a grace, implanted, nourished and matured in long and intimate communion with the Hearer of prayer.

The end of such a life, as we might anticipate, was peace and joy —peace in fullness of measure, and "joy unspeakable and full of glory." A glance in his dying chamber reveals the fact that it was "quite on the verge of heaven." Says President Edwards:—

"On Tuesday, Oct. 6, he lay for a considerable time, as if he were dying. At which time he was heard to utter, in broken whispers, such expressions as these : 'He will come, he will not tarry. I shall soon be in glory. I shall soon glorify God with the angels.' . . . The extraordinary frame he was in that evening could not be hid. His mouth spake out of the abundance of his heart, expressing in a very affecting manner much the same things as are written in his diary. Among very many other extraordinary expressions which he then uttered, were such as these : 'My heaven is to please God and glorify him, and to give all to him and to be wholly devoted to his glory; that is the heaven I long for—that is my religion, and that is my happiness, and always was ever since I suppose I had any religion: I do not go to heaven to be advanced but to give honor to God. It is no matter where I shall be stationed in heaven—whether I have a high or a low seat there, but to love and please and glorify God is all; if I had a thousand souls, if they were worth any thing, I would give them all to God.

It only remains that we touch upon the matter of young BRAINERD's expulsion from Yale College and vindicate his memory from the aspersion cast upon his good name by that high-handed measure. Sure we are that no unprejudiced mind, possessed of the facts of the case on which the act was based, as carefully stated by President Edwards, and also by BRAINERD himself, in his journal and letters, can come to any other conclusion than that the College authorities erred in expelling him in the first instance, for so slight an offence—erred in inflicting the severest academical punishment. in their power for a word spoken in confidence to two or three college mates and intimate religious friends, with no malicious intent ; that they erred again in refusing to accept his very humble and penitent confession, and restore him to his standing ; erred the third time by their strange and relentless persistency in refusing the request of a large number of the most distinguished clergymen in the col onies, that BRAINERD might be allowed to take his degree with the class from which he was expelled the year before. Had his alleged offence been tenfold more serious than it was, we cannot see how their conduct in this instance could be justified, especially in view of the peculiar circumstances of the case, and the fact that the offending party had made a prompt and manly acknowledgment.

But the offence in fact was a *trifling* one, and one that the offended tutor and the faculty of the college ought not to have laid to heart or made a serious fuss over. If the authorities of Yale, or of any other college in the land *to day*, should expel a student for such an offence, a cry of shame and indignation would ring throughout the land.

The offence consisted of two particulars : The first a hasty and foolish remark, reflecting on the piety of one of the tutors, made in private to two or three fellow students, and overheard and reported by another student who happened to overhear it. The other item was in going to a religious meeting in the town when the college had forbidden attendance on such meetings. *That was the whole of the offence.* It seems scarcely credible to us in these days. The *last* item must be ruled out. For no college rulers had a right, legal or moral, to enact such a rule. It was a high-handed assumption of power, and was a fling at the promoters of the great religious revival which then agitated and divided New Haven, and many other parts of New England. And whether the other offence—the words applied to tutor Whittlesey—were true or false, there was, as all must admit, a great deal to excuse or palliate the offence in the spirit and occurrences in the life around him at the time.

A great religious movement was then on foot. Whitefield, and other apostles of the New Evangelism, had fired the hearts of multitudes. Excitement ran high. The revival had shaken the town of New-Haven, and the mass of college students had come under its power, BRAINERD among the rest, who entered into the work with all the intensity of his earnest nature. " Ministers of long standing," and churches without number, were divided in regard to these " New Lights," as they were called. Extravagancies and evils, according to President Edwards' testimony, mixed with much that was good. A censorious spirit was rampant. Whitefield himself publicly judged and denounced ministers of standing and experience, and many leading churches, also for their supineness or opposition ; so much so that the pastor of Northampton, while sympathizing with the movement and throwing the great weight of his example and preaching in favor of it, deplored the excesses of intemperate zeal, and specially exposed and condemned the censorious and self-righteous spirit which character-ized a portion of its promoters: even Whitefield him-self he censured and personally rebuked!

Surely, when old and staid ministers, ministers of learning and piety and recognized standing in the country, were led away for the time being from the meekness and sweet gentleness of Christ, and in speech and manner, in preaching and praying, implied that all who were not of their way of preaching, and praying—all who cast not out devils after their fashion—all who failed to enter heartily into their measures, or who dared to oppose them,—were hypocrites or graceless professors, the young, inexperienced and zealous sophomore, who had caught the contagion and entered into the excitement, and who took an active part in the revival, which changed the character of the college and numbered many of its students among its converts, might have been pardoned the hot, thoughtless words spoken in private concerning the lack of piety in one of the tutors, who had just been "pathetically" praying before the students! What college law was broken? What was there in the nature and extent of the offence to call for college discipline? Were there not many palliating considerations in the times and in the circumstances of the case? Would not a reprimand have been all that the offence called for? On what principle of justice or fairness could they visit upon him, a student too of blameless virtue and exemplary piety, condign punishment and blast his future prospects and consign him to disgrace, so far at least as their ac-tion had effect? Fortunately it did not seriously injure the character of Brainerd, even at the time, or lessen the high esteem in which he was held by his friends; while it served to rally to his support many of the most eminent ministers of his time, and called forth great sympathy and interest in his career, not only over all New England, but also in New York, New Jersey, and Pennsylvania. And God so overruled the matter, that, beyond all question, it was one of the chief causes which led to the establishment of Princeton College.

There is one point suggested by these memoirs that is worthy of careful consideration by all the friends of missions at the present time : it relates to the *methods and the machinery of missionary operations.* I do not propose to discuss this important and vital question here, but simply to note the example of this eminent Christian and missionary, and the results of his labors.

Brainerd literally obeyed the ascended Lord. He went forth with the Bible only in his hands. He gave himself to prayer, and to the preaching of the word of God, to catechetical instruction, to direct efforts to convert souls and train them for Christ. He at once began to *preach* to these untutored, uncivilized, degraded barbarians, the central truth of Christianity, the cardinal doctrines of the Christian system—the very same doctrines which Jonathan Edwards then preached in Northampton, and which Dr. John Hall preaches to-day on Fifth Avenue in New York City : and he preached them with the same distinctness, and discrimination, and directness, and urgency, and application; and the same results followed ! He had to preach through an interpreter. He labored under a thousand disadvantages. But he honored God's word, God's method of saving sinners; and he preached and prayed with faith in the efficacy of the Gospel and the Holy Spirit's power ; and the effect, the fruit, was the same at Kaunaumeek, and Crossweeksung, and at the Forks of the Delaware, as at Northampton, and in New York City, and in primitive times.

Have we not, in these days of weak faith and decay of spiritual life, departed quite too far from the *apostolic idea and practice*, in our missionary endeavors? Are we not making organizations, schools, civilizing influences, machinery, and merely human devices, altogether too prominent? Is not the natural, if not the inevitable tendency of such a policy, to unduly exalt the *human* element, at the expense of the *Divine?* And is not the effect to weaken our hold on God ; to lessen the felt necessity of prayer and the Holy Spirit's omnipotent energy? Is not precious time lost ? are not energies wasted ? and is not the time of harvest delayed ?

Christ understood perfectly the conditions and necessities of the case, and the nature and adaptability of the Gospel to its end, when he commissioned the disciples to go and teach all nations. And we know how the disciples understood his message, and how they obeyed it ; their one uniform and universal method among Jews and Greeks and Romans, alike among barbarians, and in civilized communities, was to preach Christ and him crucified, and to organize and gather the converts into Christian churches on the simple basis of the Gospel. They knew nothing about our modern theories, and accessories. We do not find the slightest trace of any of these modes or machinery in the primitive Church's effort to evangelize the world. And human nature is the same to-day ; and the condition of the heathen world is essentially the same. And yet we have drifted into a totally different method. We have come virtually to put civilization, education, preparation, before and in place of the Gospel. It is not "the *foolishness of preaching*," so much as it is the perfection of appliances, and constructive agencies, and civilizing forces,

that is the Church's main reliance to-day for the evangelization of the world, both nominally Christian and
heathen.

The Indians to whom BRAINERD ministered, were
exceedingly ignorant ; their social and moral condition
was of the lowest order. They were simply savages.
And yet, the Gospel, as preached and expounded to
them by this single young isolated missionary, whose
heart was all aflame with the love of God, and who spent
hours every day on his knees in prayer, was made
mighty unto God for their salvation. The grace of
God achieved in four short years among that degraded
race, as signal and as glorious a triumph as it achieved
under Whitefield and Edwards among the civilized and
educated whites. No one can trace the history of God's
converting and transforming grace at Kaunaumeek and
Crossweeksung—note the operation of Gospel truth and
of the Holy Spirit's influence on these ignorant and degraded sinners—and especially such manifestations of
power and grace as are recorded in chapter ten of these
memoirs, and doubt for one moment the sufficiency of
the Gospel in the hands of the Spirit of God, when
wisely and faithfully preached, in faith and with importunate prayer, to transform and elevate any people, however depraved and degraded. O for the simplicity, the
faith, the whole-heartedness, the reliance on the teach-
ings of Christ and " the witness of the Spirit," which characterized the early Christians, and characterized the life
of BRAINERD ! *The Church must yet come to this,* or the
" millenial " age, for which she has prayed and waited
so long, will prove only a pleasing dream. May a
renewed study of the life and example and achievements
of this illustrious missionary help to bring it about !

BRAINERD, and his co-workers on the same field—
Eliot, Horton, Sergeant and Edwards—really *solved
for us the Indian problem*, and we have been almost a
century and a half finding it out ! Had the work which
they began among and in behalf of the aboriginal tribes
of North America, been continued and prosecuted to its
legitimate end ; had the policy which they clearly
marked out and inaugurated in their treatment of the Indian race—viz., honest dealing, evangelization, education,
teaching the industrial arts ; had this Christian policy
been recognized and pursued by the United States in
their subsequent dealings with them—what untold
millions of treasure had been saved the nation ! what
bloody wars and frightful massacres had been averted !
The long dark record of injustice, cruelty, perfidy, treaty-
breaking—the strong oppressing the weak, high-handed
unrighteousness in the sight of Heaven and the civilized world—had not been written ! At length the truth,
which these missionary pioneers clearly perceived and
exemplified in their teaching and lives, begins to dawn
upon the American mind ! The Gospel of Jesus Christ,
the church, the ministry, the school, Christian society
and civilization, are coming at length to be recognized
as the only forces and methods to settle this perplexing
question, which has so long overmatched alike the wisdom
of statesmanship, the resources of military genius and
power, and the humanities of philanthropy.

We bless God to-day for such a noble life, for such a
saintly character, and for such an example of Christlike sacrifice and toil in the glorious cause of human redemption ! That life, that character, that example, are
calling to us to-day—-calling by the printed page
which perpetuates his wondrous, burning testimony—

calling by those earnest soul-wrestlings and prayers, which God witnessed and heard in the American wilderness five generations ago—calling by those displays of Almighty and regenerating grace which he was the occasion and the instrument of displaying among the heathen and savage tribes of this new world—calling by the tongues of prophets long dead ; by the sacrifices and the triumphs of modern missions, and by the hopes and expectations of the Church of God, to awake out of sleep and take hold of the work of the world's conversion in dead earnest. The appeal is made to *us*, of this generation, as truly as though an angel were flying through the midst of heaven, summoning the sacramental host of God's elect to be up and doing ; to go up and possess the land ; to thrust in the sickle and reap ; to "stand and see the salvation of God." The prayer of the Church for more than eighteen hundred years has been : "Thy kingdom come, Thy will be done, on earth as it is in heaven." And the apocalyptic angel has joined in the grand chorus, "Even so come, Lord Jesus ! Amen." The souls under the altar, that were slain for the word of God, are crying : "How long, O Lord, holy and true ? " The earth groaneth and travaileth in pain for her redemption hour. The nations which sit in darkness stretch forth their hands unto us and are struggling upward toward the light. There are signs, too, in the heavens, and commotions on the earth, and stately steppings of Almighty power and regenerating grace in the providential world, which plainly indicate that Christ the Lord is speedily coming to take to himself his great power and assert his kingship over all and establish his millenial reign on the earth.

The preparation of long ages is now complete.

Prophecy has closed its testimony. The promises are world-embracing. Discipline, waiting, training, developing, laying foundations, have had their day and done their assigned work. The time for ACTION has now fully come—the time for a combined assault on the Kingdom of Darkness—the time for a grand aggressive movement all along the line. The trumpet is sounding to the charge! In the name of the Lord of Hosts, lift up the banner of Righteousness and fling to the breeze the all-conquering standard of our Immanuel. Long since the Church had her marching orders: "Go ye into all the world and preach the gospel to every creature!" Why hesitate? Why wait for other manifestations?

Young men and maidens! can you look on the stirring scenes which this world presents to you to-day—the world in which the Eternal Son of God has planted the Cross, the symbol of Omnipotent Love and Divine Sacrifice, by which He is to conquer and reign over a redeemed universe—can you view these scenes and events and not long to participate in the glorious struggle and the glorious conquest? Ye Brainerds, and Henry Martyns, and Careys, and Judsons, and Livingstones—ye Harriet Newells and Mrs. Judsons—this is the day for such as you to come to the front and assert your mission, and fire the heart of the sacred brotherhood with flaming zeal and holy enthusiasm and a self-denying spirit—the day to emulate the faith, the heroic spirit, and the sublime self-sacrifice of Paul and Peter and John and the other primitive disciples.

We are approaching the close of the nineteenth century, and what a century it has been, especially the latter half of it, in the way of change, development, progress, achievement! Stirring events are transpiring before us every day. Divine providence is writing history with a rapidity and on a scale of magnitude unparalleled in the past. And have these things no significance? Have you no personal interest in them? Is not God speaking in them all, to you, to me, to every disciple, with loud and solemn voice? Are not especially the *young men* of this generation " brought to the kingdom " at a momentous crisis in the world's history? Is not human life to day, measured by its opportunities, its responsibilities, its possibilities, worth a hundred lives in ages gone by? Did ever a generation have such opportunities to distinguish itself in the grand march of human events? Was ever such a cry heard from so many lands, and from the isles of the sea—from India and from Africa, from China and Japan and Mexico—from so many races and nations and peoples and tongues—saying, " Come over and help us," as now resounds throughout Christendom?

If we will not respond to these wondrous Providential calls—these calls of the Spirit of God, these calls of a groaning and perishing world, going up day and night to heaven like the sound of many waters—we shall be thrust aside, and the kingdom, the work, the honor, and the victory, will be given to another. For, CONVERTED TO THE LORD JESUS CHRIST, this world will be. The Eternal God has purposed it. Prophecy has proclaimed it with a thousand tongues. Divine promises without number are the pledges of it. All the instrumentalities and facilities necessary to its accomplishment have been made ready. All over the earth prayer is ascending for the hastening of the work. Christianity was never such a living power in the world as it is to day, despite the unbelief and wickedness of the times. The Anglo-Saxon race— the race of progress and dominion, the custodian of Christianity—which numbered but 7,000,000 when the

Pilgrim Fathers replanted Christianity on these desolate shores, numbers to-day 100,000,000, and is marching on to universal supremacy; while the achievements of the last seventy years in the missionary field, are on a scale of grandeur unparalleled in the history of the Church, not excepting even the apostolic period. A few decades of years will decide the momentous issue; will flood the earth with supernal glory, or witness the going down of the sun of human hopes in a night of darkness that shall have no morning !

GOD'S HAND IN

MISSIONS.

By

ARTHUR T. PIERSON, D.D.

GOD'S HAND IN MISSIONS.

By the Rev. Arthur T. Pierson, D. D.

Science, as nature's interpreter, can show us no greater wonders than the crystal and the cell; one the miracle of inorganic symmetry, the other the mystery of organic life. But when God's Spirit reveals to us the wonders of Grace, he shows us holy lives, which combine the beauty of the crystal with the energy of the cell; not a cold, imprisoned luster, but a radiance that shines with the living light of God.

"History is philosophy teaching by examples," said Dionysius of Halicarnassus. David Brainerd is a luminous example of the spirit of missions, and of its transfiguring power in human character; and he is alphabetically at the head of a noble army of martyrs, illustrious in missionary history. His name is inseparably linked with those of Burns, Bushnell, Carey, Dober, Duff, Eliot, Ellis, Edwards, Fiske, Grant, Gutzlaff, Gulick, Goodell, Henderson, Judson, Jessup, Livingstone, Lindley, Martyn, Milne, Moffat, Morrison, Mayhew, Newell, Perkins, Riggs, Rhea, Stoddard, Scudder, Schwartz, Turner, Williams, Wolfe, and a host of others, whose biographies read like new chapters in the acts of the apostles, and the logic of whose lives both demonstrates and illustrates this great truth, that the spirit of missions is the spirit of the Master.

To those who feel the force of the scripture appeal,

all further argument for a world-wide Evangelism is needless. The Iron Duke called those last words of our Lord, "the marching orders of the Church," to be promptly and implicitly obeyed. But, when the positive precept of the Holy Scripture is buttressed by considerations of every sort, personal and social, temporal and spiritual; when events add their unanswerable logic; when the Pillar of God moves before the Church; what true disciple can longer hesitate! The mind must be overwhelmed with conviction, and the heart inspired with enthusiasm, in witnessing to a lost world!

Facts are the fingers of God. Although indifference is not always born of ignorance, there will be little zeal without knowledge. To awaken a deep passion for the universal and immediate spread of gospel tidings, believers must be brought face to face with those grand facts, which make the march of modern missions the miracle of these latter days.

The watchword of every Christian life is, "the obedience of faith," and such obedience depends upon knowledge of God's will. His direct command and the voice of an enlightened conscience are two permanent and perpetual sources of that knowledge; but in the leadings of his providence and the teaching of his Spirit, we shall find two more sources, supernatural and confirmatory of the others, All of these combine and concentrate, as in one burning focal point of power, urging us onward to the outposts of civilization and the limits of human habitation, with the Word of life!

The Gospel is God's economy of grace for the ruined race of man. Back of human sin is one fall; and the second Adam brings to man, as man, one rising again, one divine remedy, one generic redemption. Between those lost souls and that great salvation, there is one living link, the witnessing lips and lives of believers. Here then is the glorious work for the Church to do: being one with Christ by faith, love is so to link us to the lost as to make us a bond between him and them.

What altar ever before so sanctified the gift! The widow's mites, laid on that altar, are magnified and glorified as well as sanctified : they grow into shekels of the sanctuary, precious as gold, pellucid as crystal. And when self is laid on that altar of missions, those fires of God come down, which, instead of consuming, transfigure with celestial glory.

In these days, out of the midst of the cloud, the vocal, moving Pillar of God's providence, sounds as loud a call as was ever heard by his people. It is the clarion voice of command, for an advance all along the lines. Not only do the precept and promise of our ascending Lord inspire us to service and sacrifice, but the trumpet signals of prophecy are echoed, enforced, emphasized by a new voice sounding in our ears, louder and clearer, every day, bidding us " go forward ;" while the Pillar itself *moves*, and marks its course by actual conquest, advancing in the face of gigantic foes and obstacles. and leading on to complete triumph the little missionary band that have the faith and fortitude to follow.

Our Lord's last command was joined to a promise of supernatural signs, a promise sealed by actual fullfilment in the early history of the Church. Because those signs ceased in their fullness and frequency, it has been assumed that they were limited in purpose as well as period. The Scriptures hint no such limits, and the notion of such limitation was an *after thought*, an apology for their cessation.

We need not go so far to account for the disappearance of those early signs. If they were to be our Lord's seal and sanction upon the universal preaching of the Gospel, their decline may be sufficiently accounted for by the decay of evangelical faith, and especially of evangelistic zeal. Will it be said that there is no need now of marked Divine interpositions? The primitive saints plead with God to grant them "boldness in speaking his word, by stretching forth his hand to heal" and doing "signs and wonders in the name of Jesus." There was never a day, when constant and convincing proofs of the supernatural were more needed than *now*, to embolden us to meet worldliness and wickedness, materialism and naturalism! And we believe that such supernatural signs abound in exact proportion to the measure of the response we yield to the command, "Go ye into all the world and preach the gospel to every creature." To prove and illustrate this, is the object of this paper. Professor Christlieb unhesitatingly affirms that in the history of modern missions, "we find many wonderful occurrences which unmistakably remind us of the apostolic age." This statement is confirmed by the observation and experience of all who themselves fall into this grand march of missions, and keep abreast of these advancing lines. They have such a sense of Divine presence and guidance, as makes the pillar of cloud vivid and almost visible; they feel the inspiration of an Almighty Power, co-working with human weakness, and they seem at times to catch glimpses of the very Shekinah.

Whatever may be said or thought of the genuineness of "modern miracles," one "everlasting sign" remains which, according to prophecy, "shall never be cut off."

Isaiah says, "instead of the thorn shall come up the fir-tree, and instead of the brier, the myrtle-tree." The power of husbandry is shown in displacing noxious and offensive growths, by fair, fragrant, useful plants and trees. So God gives this unfailing sign and proof of supernatural power, that in the soil of the human soul and the broader fields of human society, he is now and always displacing hateful and hurtful opinions, motives and practices, by the lovely and glorious products of his gracious culture.

To this everlasting sign, then, as well as to the plain proofs of his moulding hand in the history of missionary advance, we may constantly and confidently appeal. Transformations of personal character, and of entire peoples, by the power of his Gospel and Spirit, constitute the everlasting sign of divine, supernatural energy, at work in this world,—a sign as convincing and conclusive as the restoration of sight to the blind, hearing to the deaf, or life to the dead !

When we add to these spiritual transformations, the rapid opening of doors, great and effectual, in the face of many adversaries; the effecting of entrance to the very heart and center of the Pagan, Papal and Moslem world ; the steady onward movement of a feeble mission band, undismayed by the giant Anakim with their formidable fortresses and engines of war, we have, to a discerning spiritual eye, as satisfactory proof that God is moving in modern missions, and by his pillar of cloud and fire goes before his people, as was furnished when the Red Sea heaped up its waves, Jordan drove back its waters, or Jericho's walls fell flat ? In a word, we affirm that the results of the labors of the present era of missions present a problem which cannot be solved without the Divine Factor.

This great field might be viewed from many points on the horizon, and the whole march of the Lord's hosts is marked by his own golden footsteps. But for brevity of statement, and unity of impression, we select a few of the conspicuous proofs of Divine interposition.

1. The removal of barriers, opening doors of access, and flooding of lands with the Gospel.

2. The direct transformation of individual character and of entire communities.

3. The indirect results in the modification of existing evils, and the elevation of society.

4. The reflex influences on the workers themselves and on the churches which sustain them.

I. First, there has been *a progress in missions* during the last century, which would have been impossible without the intervention of a higher power.

It is scarcely sixty years ago when the Church as a body took up the work of evangelizing the world. At that time obstacles, like mountains, stood in the way. When this century began, *Ten* great barriers, to human view insurmountable, interposed between the Church and the fullfilment of the Lord's command. We may group them into four classes.

1. *Obstacles to approach:* Many great peoples were not accessible.

In the pagan world, China was walled about ; Japan's ports had stood shut and sealed, even against merchant ships, for three centuries ; India was held by an English power, really hostile to missions ; Africa was impenetrable even to the explorer ; and the isles of the sea, crowded with cannibals, were more to be dreaded than the hungry jaws of an angry ocean.

In the Moslem world, blind bigotry crushed all freedom of speech or thought as with the iron flail of Talus, and the death penalty, like the sword of Damocles, overhung every Mohammedan who dared look from the crescent towards the cross.

In the Papal world, though nominally Christian, there was less hope of doing evangelistic work than among the cannibals of Fiji. The Waldenses found that to those who sought even to *keep* the pure faith, the Vatican was an Olympus for its gods, a Sinai for its thunders, and a Calvary for its blood. Even travelers visiting the eternal city had to leave their Bibles outside, and no Protestant chapel was tolerated within its limits.

Secondly, *obstacles to intercourse :*

Even where there was outward approach, there was often no real access. Serious hindrances to communication existed. Slow methods of transportation made travel so tedious as to make even neighbors seem foreigners ; languages, strange and hard to master, offered no mould in which to cast spiritual ideas, and at least sixty of them must be reduced to writing, having no literature or even lexicon or grammar ; woman was hopelessly shut up in seraglios, zenanas and harems ; degraded into a beast of burden, little above the cattle for which she was bartered, or the donkeys with which she was associated ; denied not only any social status, but even a *soul,* "unwelcome at birth, untaught in childhood, enslaved when married, accursed as widow, unlamented when dead." And to all these obstacles to intercourse we must add that most gigantic foe, *caste,* which seemed to make alike impossible, conversion, or communion among converts.

Thirdly, *obstacles to impression :*

The unevangelized world was divisible into two classes: first those races which seemed too low to be reached and elevated by the Gospel; and secondly those which seemed too high to feel any need of its uplifting power. In some the image of God seemed not only defaced but effaced; in whom even the image of man could scarcely be discerned, who for shamelessness were dumb beasts, and for ferocity wild beasts, savage, brutal, bestial, beyond all hope of being moulded anew; not only dehumanized but demonized.

Others, like the two hundred millions of India, or the twice two hundred millions of China, boasted hoary civilization and faiths, high culture, and a social morality that might compare favorably with that of many Christian communities, while they were under the sway of a subtle, sophistical priesthood, and entrenched in self-complacence and self-sufficiency. What could the Gospel do, in confronting nations, proud of antiquity and aristocracy, where apostasy was counted a sin against God and a crime against the State, admitting no apology, and having no forgiveness here or hereafter?

Fourthly, *obstacles to action :*

In the Christian Church itself, some of the worst hindrances existed. Disgraceful iniquities and immoralities in Christian lands, with which the Church was complicated, made the very Gospel itself a stench, where it should have been a sweet savor, to the pagan world. China cannot forget that England forced opium upon her, even at the cannon's mouth; Africa remembers that the very nations that now bring missionaries to her coast, not long since stole slaves from those same shores; and the Hawaiians caught the consuming leprosy of lust from the trading ships of Christian lands, as the North American Indians took the infection of drunkenness from contact with our higher " civilization." An awful shadow hung in advance over our mission work, when intercourse with Christendom had proved already a greater calamity than complete isolation! Think of the missionary landing on foreign shores, only to bewail the fact that the shuttle of commerce had already woven a band of contact with the Christian people whom he came to represent!

Worse than all, apathy and lethargy reigned in the Church. Ignorance of God's work, and of man's need, made the prevailing indifference the more hopeless. Some professed disciples were not only without sympathy, or full of apathy, but showed absolute antipathy towards missions; while sectarian strife and jealousy checked effort and cooled ardor, wasting energies that, if harmoniously united and concentrated, would have multiplied present results many fold. The zeal that at times seemed to be enkindled flashed into the flame of temporary excitement and then died away, leaving no lasting results in self-sacrifice. Dr. Judson said his hand was nearly shaken off, and his hair shorn off for mementoes, by those who would willingly let missions die : and Dr. Bushnell declared that no obstacle abroad was so disheartening to him as the churches at home, one half of which give nothing, and the other half give little and pray less. How could missionaries go down into the awful depths of heathenism with no one " to hold the rope."

Such are a few of the representative obstacles that, within the memory of men still living, defied all human wisdom and power. To-day, if they are not all gone, they are down like Jericho's walls, and we climb over their ruins to take the strongholds of Satan!

It is vain to hope to pack into a few paragraphs the immense mass of facts, which no candid disciple can superficially survey without becoming a convert to missions. We see God's angel going before the missionary band, till within a century their lines reach round the world. Land after land opens its two-leaved gates to admit the heralds of the cross, till every people becomes accessible. What were rallying points for gospel efforts in 1820, in 1870 were radiating centres for gospel light to lands yet in the death-shade. Converts multiply and churches are gathered, in the most discouraging fields, till India becomes a starry firmament of mission stations; Turkey is planted with crosses, from the Golden Horn to the Tigris; Syria sends Arabic Testaments to the bounds of the Moslem world; Japan takes giant strides toward a Christian civilization; Polynesia's isles lift church-spires, thousands in number, toward the sky; Africa is crossed with a chain of gospel outposts;—and even Papal lands welcome the open Bible and the Prot-testant preacher!

He who studies history piously and prayerfully, not only sees the Hand of God in these recent developments, but traces the moving Pillar far back in the centuries, while as yet even the eyes of disciples were holden that they saw it not. From the day when the Morning Star of the Reformation rose, God has been unconsciously pre-paring his church for the world-wide preaching of the Word. By the double reformation in philosophy and re-

ligion, he laid the basis for a purer and more primitive
faith and life, gave the Bible to the people in their own
tongue, made less distinct the dividing line between
clergy and laity, struck a blow at priestcraft, and by reviving evangelical piety led the way to evangelistic
activity. Eyes, long blinded to the true character of
God, and the real destitution of man, now felt the touch
of partial restoration, and began dimly to see that a
lost world had a claim upon the saved for the Gospel.

Step by step of this marvellous preparation for the
modern era of missions followed in quick succession.
That triad of inventions, the mariner's compass, printing-
press, and steam navigation, made all nations neighbors,
and helped us to give wings to the word of God and to
the herald of the cross. But still the Church seemed
deaf, if not dead, to all sense of debt or love to a dying
world, and the proposal of missions to the heathen met
with sneers of ridicule. Dr. Ryland bade Carey " sit
down " and leave God to take care of a pagan world ; the
Scotch Assembly branded the idea of universal missions
as fanatical, dangerous and revolutionary, and stirred up
old John Erskine to pour into them hot shot and shell ;
and the Massachusetts Association timidly let a few
pioneers sail for the lands beyond the sea, half doubtful
whether the scheme of preaching the Gospel throughout
the world were not impracticable and visionary. And
all this within the last hundred years !

Over against this hesitating Church of Christ stood
a compact phalanx of foes, Herod and Pilate friends together in opposing Christ. Every Oriental empire
positively hostile to approach ; Mohammedanism and
Paganism visiting apostasy with death ; and oriental
churches with nothing but the empty shell of formalism,

bent on persecution just as systematic and intolerant. The fact is, however, that through these iron gates of Pagan hostility and Christian apathy, a way has been made for the chariot of our God, and the manner in which this has been done compels us to say, like Pharaoh's magicians, " This is the Finger of God."

Not to go back further, for four hundred years we can trace signal providences casting up this broad, level highway between the centers of Christendom and Pagandom. Near the close of the sixteenth century a new route to the golden Indies by way of the Cape of Good Hope led to the chartering of the East India Company a few years later ; and so, while the Pilgrims were sowing the seeds of this Christian Republic beneath the setting sun, Protestant England planted an Empire toward the sunrise and in the very heart of the Pagan Orient. Unconsciously the leading nation of the Protestant Christian world was reaching out one hand eastward and the other westward to lay the foundations for a world wide Church. Subsequent conflicts in America and India settled the question that in both hemispheres the cross was to displace both the crescent and the crucifix.

By the middle of the eighteenth century, America and Asia are respectively held by the two foremost Protestant powers of the world. England has a firm foothold in the critical centre of oriental missions, and in her hands holds the keys of the kingdoms of the East. This makes necessary, as a line of communication, an open highway for travel and traffic between the mother country and her eastern possessions. If Britain had any right in India, she had a right to a safe and peaceful road thither ; and this political necessity was used of God ultimately to shape the attitude of every nation along that highway. Had England not held that highway to the Indies, the destinies of Europe and Asia might have been changed. Turkey would probably have been devoured by Russia, or divided between Russia and France; the Greek and Roman churches, crossing the mountains, might have swayed all Asia and kept out Protestant missions. Behold the hand of God, using English arms and diplomacy to hold Popes, Czars and Sultans in check, to shield converts from persecution by Turkish Armenians, Persian Nestorians, Syrian Moslems, or Indian Brahmins; and giving Britain a casting vote in the affairs of the Sublime Porte!

What means this Providential establishment of British empire in India! It is an entering wedge, driven into the heart of Asia,—a wedge, the direction of whose cleavage is still eastward, splitting in twain these gnarled and knotted trunks of mossgrown empires!

Meanwhile, from seed sown at Plymouth, develops another mighty, evangelizing power. The Protestant Republic of America strides from Atlantic to Pacific, and, planting foot on the western shores, moves toward the eastern coasts of Asia, as though there were no more sea. Here is God's counterforce, moving from the opposite direction to meet England and oppose her entering wedge with the resistance of co-operation, as anvil opposes sledge hammer! In other words another irrepressible conflict has come. Commerce will have her highway round the world, and knocks imperatively at the sealed ports and barred gates of exclusive Oriental empires.

Our Republic leads the way. In 1853, Commodore Perry sails into the bay of Yeddo, spreads the Star Spangled Banner over the capstan, and the open Bible upon the flag, and without firing a gun or shedding a drop of blood, peacefully opens the ports of Japan to the world. Five years later, four leading nations knock loudly at the gates of China, and the walled kingdom opens her doors ; expressly stipulating by treaty that " any person, whether citizen of the country with which the treaty is made, or Chinese convert to the faith of the Protestant or Roman Catholic churches, who, according to these tenets peaceably teaches and practices the principles of Christianity, shall in no case be *interfered with or molested !* " This one edict of toleration gave religious liberty to one third of the population of the globe.

At one titanic blow, God levels an obstacle as high as the Himalayas, and opens the way from the Bosphorus to the China sea, through the heart of Asia.

Passing by all other providential interpositions, let us emphasize the recent unveiling of Africa. In August, 1877, after 999 days from Zanzibar, Stanley, emerging at the mouth of the Congo, completes the transit of the Dark Continent. The dying cry of Jesus has rent the last veil in twain, and the missionary has only to follow the footsteps of the explorer !

The same providence that opens the doors, prepares the forces of his Church for the crusade.

The missionary advance of this century is directly traceable to answered prayer. Since Luther nailed up his theses, there has been no historic hour so dark as the first half of the eighteenth century. Even England was, as Isaac Taylor said, in " virtual heathenism," with a lascivious literature, an infidel society, a worldly Church and a deistic theology. Blackstone heard every clergyman of note in London, but not one discourse had more

Christianity in it than the orations of Cicero, or showed
whether the preacher was a disciple of Confucius, Ma-
homet or Christ. In America, Samuel Blaine declared
that " Religion lay a dying." In France, Voltaire,
Rousseau, and Madame de Pompadour, led society ; and
in Germany, Frederick the Great made his court the
Olympus of infidels.

If Collins and Tyndal denounced Christianity as
priestcraft, Whiston called Bible miracles grand imposi-
tions, and Woolston treated them as allegories ; if Clark
and Priestly openly taught the heresies of Arius and
Socinus, and even morality was trampled under foot,
what missionary activity could there be ? To diffuse
such 'Christianity' would be disaster ; but happily such
a type of piety has no diffusive tendency or power ; if it
has any divine fire left, it has not a coal or even a spark
to spare to light a blaze elsewhere !

The only hope of missions lay in a *Revival* of Religion, widespread, deep-reaching ; and God gave that to
his Church through a wonderful constellation of Evan-
gelists. Whitefield, the Wesleys, Grimshaw, Romaine,
Rowlands, Berridge, Venn, Walker, Hervey, Toplady,
Fletcher—these Bishop Ryle names as twelve of the
apostles of that new Reformation, which, between 1735
and 1785 woke not only England but the Protestant
world from the awful apostasy of irreligion and infidelity.
At first even the Church resisted all efforts to revive her
dying life. Whitefield found Scotch ministers opposing
him by set days of fasting and prayer ; and church doors
shut against himself and Wesley, compelled that open
air preaching which was the great stride of the century
toward the reaching of the masses.

But the Spirit of God was breathing on the dry

bones. The fires, slowly kindled at first, burned brighter and hotter, caught here and there, spread far and wide, till even America, across the sea, was aflame. Within fifty years from Whitefield's first sermon at Gloucester, all Protestant Christendom thrilled with a revived evangelical faith, and as evangelistic zeal is sure always to follow, out of these Pentecostal outpourings came the flaming tongues of witness. The Church, from her silver trumpets pealed forth her summons to prayer, for the effusion of the Spirit upon all disciples, and upon the whole habitable earth. Praying bands answered the trumpet peal in all parts of Britain, and from American shores came the echo in 1747 of Jonathan Edwards' bugle "call to concerted prayer." The tidal wave of revival rose higher and moved with greater momentum, under the Haldanes, Andrew Fuller, Sutcliffe, Rowland Hill and others.

In 1792 the Warwick Association formally made the first Monday of each month a "monthly concert of prayer" for the world's evangelization. No sooner did the revived Church, after this awful period of drought, begin to pray for a great rain, than a cloud like a man's hand appeared on the horizon ; and in that same year, 1792, the first Foreign Missionary Society was formed in England, and the next year sent to India its first missionary, William Carey, who within the thirty years following secured the translation of the Scriptures into forty tongues, and the circulation of two hundred thousand copies. Thus the revival of evangelical faith, and of concerted prayer, are the two pillars on which rests the arch of Modern Missions.

How fast that little cloud has grown, till the heaven is overspread, and there is a sound of the abundance of rain ! During these eighty years, the number of trans- lations of the Word has increased *fivefold*, from fifty to two hundred and fifty ; of Protestant mission societies, *tenfold*, from seven to seventy ; of male missionaries, *fifteenfold*, from one hundred and seventy to twenty- four hundred ; of moneys contributed *twenty-fivefold*, from two hundred and fifty thousand to six and a quar- ter million dollars : of converts, *thirty-fivefold*, from fifty thousand to one million six hundred and fifty thousand ; and of mission schools, *one hundred and seventy fold*, from seventy to twelve thousand !

The whole tide of thought has turned in the Church, since William Carey first offered to go and meet the giant of heathenism. The wave, at its lowest ebb a century ago, now touches a flood mark never before reached, and is still rising. Sydney Smith would no longer dare to sneer at the "pious shoemaker" of Paulersburg, or characterize his schemes as "the dreams of a dreamer who dreams that he has been dreaming." England is prouder of Carey than Athens was of Pericles, or Rome of Cicero, and lifts the statue of Livingstone to its lofty pedestal in the metropolis of the world, to inspire Christian colonies to push into the heart of the dark continent. American churches hurl their columns against the ranks of pagan and papal su- perstition, and erect missionary lectureships in the foremost institutions of learning to train youth to imi- tate the devotion of David Brainerd, Henry Martyn, and Alexander Duff.

In fact, the whole history of Modern Missions is a Burning Bush, whose every twig is aflame with the Divine presence : we are standing on holy ground ; many and marked are the divine interpositions ; we see the iron gates open of their own accord, obstacles suddenly sinking, continents unveiling their secrets, and missionary exploration going forward so rapidly that the maps of yesterday are out of date to-day!

II. The Divine Hand is also seen in the direct transformation of character, both individual and national. The fiercest, hardest, rudest of heathen have been subdued, softened, refined by the Gospel. Africaner, that monster of cruelty, who would kill an innocent man to make a drinking cup of his skull and a drumhead of his skin, was, at the touch of that Gospel, turned from a lion into a lamb. Guergis, the ferocious Koord, who would have killed his own daughter as she prayed for him, was struck by it into penitence, as bitter as Peter's and as potent. He laid aside gun and dagger for Testament and hymn book, and made the mountains echo with the story of his great sins and great Saviour, shouting with dying breath, " Free grace!" Even Fidelia Fiske could scarcely believe she saw the miracle of such a conversion. Sau Quala, the Karen, was by that same Gospel changed into an apostolic worker. He aided the missionaries in the translation of the Word, guided them for fifteen years through the jungles; then himself began to preach and plant churches—within three years gathering nearly twenty-five hundred converts into more than thirty congregations: and refusing a tempting government position, rather than mix up God's work with secular labor, though his poverty forced him to leave his lovely wife in loneliness.

So has the Gospel transformed whole communities. In 1878, the Ko Thah Byu Memorial Hall was consecrated, commemorating the fiftieth anniversary of the first Karen convert, whose name it bears. Karens built it at a cost of fifteen thousand dollars. It represented twenty thousand living disciples converted from demon worship, maintaining their own churches and schools, beside twenty thousand more who had died in the faith of Jesus. That hall confronts Shway Mote Tau Pagoda, with its shrines and fanes on an opposing hill,—the double monument of what the Karens *were* and *are*.

The story of the Gospel in the South Seas should be written in starlight. John Williams, the blacksmith's boy, and the apostle of Polynesia, found idolatry of the most degraded type, and savages of the lowest grade. Yet his progress was one rapid career of conquest. Churches and schools grew, he knew not how. A lawless people adopt a code of laws and trial by jury. Printing presses scatter their leaves like the tree of life ; and even a missionary society is formed with King Pomare as its president, and twenty-five hundred dollars as its first year's contribution. Within a year after he landed at Raratonga, the whole Hervey group, with a population of seven thousand, have thrown away their idols, and a church-building is going up, six hundred feet long. He turns to the Samoa group, and shortly has the whole people, sixty thousand, in Christian schools.

The tale of Fiji is not less wonderful. These cannibals built the very huts of their chiefs upon the bodies of living human beings, buried alive, and they launched their canoes upon living bodies as rollers ; they slew infants, and strangled widows. Human language has no terms to describe the abasement of this people, or their atrocious customs. Such deeds of darkness should be written in blood and recorded in hell. The Fijians are now a Christian people. In 1835 missionary labor began among them ; seven years later the island of Ono had not one heathen left on it, and became the centre of Gospel light to the whole group. To-day every village has its Christian homes and schools, and there are nine hundred churches on those islands.

So was it with the new Hebrides. It was written as Dr. Geddie's Epitaph, that "when he came to Aneityum, there were no Christians; when he left, there were no heathens." These are but a few representative cases. Madagascar was so hopeless a field that the French governor of the island of Bourbon told the pioneer missionaries that they might as well try to convert cattle as the Malagasy. Yet the Gospel barely got a foothold there when it took such root that twenty-five years of fire and blood failed to burn out or blot out its impression. And now a Christian church stands on the court grounds, and on the coronation table together lie the Laws of the Realm and the Bible, as the Higher Law of Madagascar, "that crown of the London Missionary society."

The American Board, however, in 1879, declared at Syracuse, that the previous seven years in Japan furnish the most remarkable chapter in the history of the world, eclipsing not only Madagascar, but the early triumphs of Christianity. The "Lonestar" mission among the Teloogoos, almost abandoned as both hopeless and fruitless in 1853, in 1878 blazed forth with a brilliancy like that of Sirius; within forty days nearly ten thousand converts were baptized. The experiences of Powell at Nanumaga, Duncan at Columbia, Judson in Burmah, Wheeler in Turkey, Johnson in Sierra Leone, Grant in Persia, Scudder in India, Wolfe in China, Mc'All in France, and David Brainerd in New Jersey, besides many more which we have not space to mention, furnish unanswerable proof that the hand of God is in this work of missions.

While looking at the marvels of this missionary history, we must not forget how the subsidence of opposing systems has prepared the way for gospel triumphs. When the first seventeen missionaries landed at Hawaii, God had gone before them, the old king was dead, the idols burned, the old pagan faith cast away as worthless, and the first death blow struck at the tabu system. The isles were waiting for his law. When Mc'All crossed the English Channel, the fields of France were already white for the sickle. Bouchard, Reveillaud, and others, had already forsaken Romanism, as the ally of ignorance and superstition; and a whole people were ready for a grand insurrection of thought and resurrection of conscience. Tired of feeding on the ashes of Atheism and priestcraft. they hunger for the bread of life. God has let down the continent below the sea-level. It is not so much a rising tide as a sinking land. But is his hand any the less conspicuous when he thus floods the continents with the Gospel!

III.—At least a rapid glance should be given to the indirect influences of the Gospel. As Sir Bartle Frere says, wherever the Gospel has gone, it has promoted the "Dignity of labor, the Sanctity of marriage, and the Brotherhood of man." Where it does not convert, it checks and controls; where it does not renew, it refines; where it does not sanctify, it softens and subdues. Resultant motion is the diagonal of direction followed by a body on which two forces act, at right angles. So missions, acting in an opposite direction from paganism, modify and change even the society they do not wholly transform. Statistics, therefore, rather understate than

overstate results, which cannot be estimated numerically.
Each church and missionary station represents a *community*, closely identified with Christianity, a center of
light, radiating holy influence on every side. Two million
converts represent two hundred million, drawn into more
or less sympathy with the Christian faith and life, con-
fronted with the standing proofs of the superiority of
Christian teaching, individual character, and family life.
All this is like the honeycombing of rocks at Hellgate,
preparatory to a sudden and widespread destruction of
those obstacles to navigation : pagan society, with its false
faiths and iniquitous customs, is being undermined and,
as Sheshadrai says, " God works according to a higher
arithmetic of his own ;" it will be no surprising thing,
if, in his good time, all India shall suddenly be evan-
gelized, and it will then be seen there, as elsewhere, that
in the absence of positive and visible results, the preparation has been going on for a final and glorious consum-
mation.

IV. One more grand fact remains to be considered
briefly, viz : the reflex influence of missions upon all who
earnestly engage in them.

It is inconceivable that any work which is not su-
premely owned of God should develop such *character in
the worker*. The seal and sanction of God is upon missions,
for the very vanguard of the Church is found in the
heroic, self-sacrificing souls who represent us in front of
the citadels of heathenism. These men and women are
the foremost disciples of Christ ; some of them seem
both to lift mortals up and to bring angels down ; they
realize to us the day of heaven upon earth, in the sanctity of their lives and the ideality of their unselfish
services.

We see the Moravians going into the lazar house, and entering the leper villages of Africa, cheerfully isolating themselves from the "clean," and identifying themselves with the "unclean," for life, that they may point the accursed victims of loathsome disease to him who can cleanse the leprosy of the soul. We hear Dober and his co-laborers at St. Thomas, when told that they could not preach to those ignorant slaves, resolutely reply, "then we will sell ourselves as slaves, and preach while we work by their side!" We follow John Eliot, "the apostle of the Indians," spending twelve years in learning their difficult language, reducing it to a written form, publishing a grammar, and writing on its title page that holy maxim which has since passed into the uninspired scriptures of the church, "Prayer and pains, through faith in Christ, will do anything;" we look at him patiently translating the Bible into the Indian tongue, gathering those rude children of the forest into Christian settlements, and closing his fifty years of toil for their salvation by expending his dying breath in teaching a little Indian child to read. We trace the pathetically beautiful career of Adoniram Judson in Burmah, his lofty devotion to principle, and his entire consecration to Christ and to souls, and we do not wonder that even Theodore Parker should declare that "if modern missionary enterprise had done no more than produce one Adoniram Judson it were worth all it cost."

We need not look beyond the subject of this memoir for a shining illustration of the transfiguring power of the spirit of missions. It may be doubted whether in all Christian history the spirit of a seraph has ever burned in a human body more certainly than in David Brainerd. Dying in his thirtieth year, a long life of holy toil was condensed into the *four years* of his apostolic life. We see him, in the solitude of the forest, praying for the red man ; in his lonely log hut, barring his door to keep out wolf and bear, seated near his lighted torch, after a wearisome day, that he may read the Word of God, or record the Lord's dealings with him ; suffering pangs of hunger, exposing his delicate frame to night chills and stormy winds, sleeping on the ground, or climbing a tree for safety from wild beasts ; and through all this experience only exclaiming, " Oh that I were a flame of fire in the Lord's service ! Oh that I were spirit that I might be more active for God ! " We look at such lives as these, and we are compelled to feel that a work that demands such consecration, and develops such Christlike devotion and heroism, must be especially the work of God.

The more disciples, at home and abroad, become pervaded with this spirit of missions, the more is all the glory of the apostolic Church again revived. This holy labor for souls develops apostolic unity : for as Macaulay well observes " Where men worship a cow, the differences between evangelical Christians dwindle into insignificance." Sectarian lines disappear as, in presence of a united and gigantic army of foes, the ranks of disciples draw closely together for one onset in solid column to pierce the very center of the enemy and turn their staggering wings.

Even the churches at home feel the reaction of missionary effort. The Revivals of the last century gave birth to missionary societies, and the missionary labors of this century have stimulated revivals. It might be thought that Foreign missions would draw away funds and energies from home work ; on the contrary, organized efforts for the home fields have actually followed the others, and been quickened by them. There were no Sunday-schools till just before the spirit of missions was kindled, and they have multiplied with incredible rapidity since. When relapse into barbarism threatened the converted Hawaiians, they had to resort to missions to the still pagan groups near by to keep from practical apostasy ; and this was the actual origin of the mission to the Marquesas isles !

And so, side by side with the culture of the spirit of world-wide missions and their zealous prosecution, we find the culture of charity, unity, and apostolic piety at home, and the prosecution of all work in the regions immediately about us. The old Arab proverb is illustrated,—"the water poured on the roots of the cocoanut tree comes back to us in the sweetened milk of the cocoanut that falls from the top." The streams poured into the arid desert field of missions return on the churches in heavenly showers.

But we have no adequate space for the further expansion of this thrilling theme. The fullness of the times has surely come for the last great crusade against the powers of darkness. Everything is providentially ripe and ready. Nearly fourscore missionary societies enclose the globe in their golden network. The walls of nations lie flat, and challenge us to move from every quarter, and move together and at once, and take the very capitals and centers of Satan's dominion. The word of God may be had in every leading tongue, and the miracle of Babel is reversed, and the miracle of Pentecost crystallizes into permanence! The coffers of disciples contain wealth so vast that a tithe of it would furnish all the funds for a world's evangelization ; and the numbers of disciples are so vast that a tithe of them would give one missionary to every one hundred of the population of the globe! Time and space are practically annihilated and all nations are neighbors. And in addition to all, from out the shining pillar of a luminous and leading Providence rings out the trumpet voice of God, bidding us "*go forward!*"

What opportunity and what inspiration! We need only organization and consecration to carry dismay and defeat to the allied powers of hell. Wm. Carey's grand motto of 1792 should be emblazoned on the banners of a Church that gathers all her hosts for one overwhelming charge: "Expect great things from God! Attempt great things for God!" All around the horizon the signs are appearing, which indicate to him who watches, that a more momentous era is at hand than historic pen ever chronicled or artistic pencil ever illustrated.

Dr. Anderson said, with sadness, "the grand defect in the practical Christianity of our age is, that it does not respond as it should to the call of God's Providence." Let us roll away that stone of reproach, and it shall be our privilege to behold, issuing forth from the sepulchre of old but dead faiths, nations now hopelessly entombed; we shall see them, at the sound of the Word of Life, come forth to cast off the cerements of idolatry and superstition for the white robe of the saints!

MEMOIRS

OF

DAVID BRAINERD.

———✦———

CHAPTER I.

His Early Life—First Religious Impressions—His own written Account of his Conversion and Religious Experiences until he began his Studies for the Gospel Ministry.—President Edward's account of the Great Revival in New England, and of the Circumstances connected with Brainerd's Dismissal from College.

[DAVID BRAINERD was born in Haddam, Connecticut, April 20, 1718, and died at Northampton, Massachusetts, October 9, 1747, in the thirtieth year of his age. His father was Hezekiah Brainerd, one of His Majesty's Council for that colony, and his maternal grandfather was the son of Rev. Peter Hobart, the first minister of the Gospel at Hingham, in England, and who, owing to the persecution of the Puritans in the mother country, came over to New England and was settled in the ministry at Hingham, Massachusetts. David was the third son of his parents. Two of his brothers likewise devoted their lives to the Gospel Ministry—Nehemiah, who settled at Eastbury, Connecticut, and who died before David—and John, who succeeded David among the Indians of New Jersey, and afterward labored as a home missionary among the whites, and was also for many years a trustee of the College of New Jersey.

David was left an orphan at the early age of fourteen. He seems to have been a very sober youth. He was thoughtful beyond his years, of a melancholy temperament, and somewhat inclined to a morbid conscientiousness. His religious exercises were quite marked when he was but seven or eight years of age; but his serious impressions wore off, and he had no further special convictions of sin or concern for his salvation, until he was about thirteen years of age, when they returned upon him with increased power, and resulted, as he evidently believed at the time, in his conversion to God. Under his severe self-scrutiny, however, he afterward questioned the genuineness of these experiences and thought that he was relying upon his own righteousness. But the careful reader of his life will be disposed to believe that at this early period he was really a subject of Divine Grace. When about twenty he was visited with new light and power from on high—with an intensity of feeling, a depth of conviction, in relation to sin and his undone condition, and a fulness of peace and rejoicing very unusual in one so young, and one who had always led a strictly moral, and, in some respects, a religious life. This new baptism stirred his soul to its profoundest depths, and was the starting point in a most extraordinary career of Christian attainment and personal consecration.

It is not surprising that Brainerd should date his conversion from this period of his life, so profound and so remarkable were his spiritual exercises and experiences. His own account of himself, during and preceding this eventful period— the operations of his mind and heart while the Holy Spirit of God was searching him, and trying him, and making thorough work with him, that he might be eminently fitted for the mission to which the Master had appointed him—is so intensely interesting and instructive, that we shall leave him to relate it in his own simple yet graphic words. Fortunately such a record exists.—J. M. S.]

BRAINERD'S OWN ACCOUNT OF HIS EARLY LIFE AND CONVERSION.

"I was from my youth somewhat sober, and inclined to melancholy; but do not remember anything of conviction of sin, worthy of remark, till I was seven or eight years of age. Then I became concerned for my soul, and terrified at the thoughts of death ; and was driven to the performance of religious duties; but it appeared a melancholy business, that destroyed my eagerness for play. And though, alas ! this religious concern was but short-lived, I sometimes attended secret prayer ; and thus lived 'at ease in Zion, without God in the world,' and without much concern, as I remember, till I was above thirteen years of age. In the winter of 1732, I was roused out of this carnal security, by I scarce know what means at first ; but was much excited by the prevalence of a mortal sickness in Haddam. I was frequent, constant, and somewhat fervent in prayer ; and took delight in reading, especially Mr. Janeway's *Token for Children.* I felt sometimes much melted in the duties of religion, took great delight in the performance of them, and sometimes hoped that I was converted, or at least in a good and hopeful way for heaven and happiness ; not knowing what conversion was. The Spirit of God at this time proceeded far with me. I was remarkably dead to the world ; my thoughts were almost wholly employed about my soul's concerns ; and I may indeed say, Almost I was persuaded to be a Christian. I was also exceedingly distressed and melancholy at the death of my mother, in March, 1732. But afterwards my religious concern began to decline, and by degrees I fell back into a considerable degree of security, though I still attended secret prayer.

"In *April* 1733, I removed from my father's house to East-Haddam, where I spent four years ; but still 'without God in the world,' though, for the most part, I went a round of secret duty. I was not much addicted to the company and amusements of the young ; but this I know, that when I did go into such company, I never returned with so good a conscience as when I went. It always added new guilt, made me afraid to come to the throne of grace, and spoiled those good frames with which I was wont sometimes to please myself. But, alas ! all my good frames were but self-righteousness, not founded on a desire for the glory of God.

"In *April*, 1737, being nineteen years of age, I removed to Durham, to work on my farm, and so continued about one year ; frequently longing, from mere natural principles, after a liberal education. When about twenty years of age I applied myself to study ; and was now engaged more than ever in the duties of religion. I became very strict and watchful over my thoughts, words, and actions ; concluded that I must be sober indeed, because I designed to devote myself to the ministry and imagined that I did dedicate myself to the Lord.

"In *April*, 1738, I went to Mr. Fiske's, the pastor of the church in Haddam, and lived with him during his life. He advised me wholly to abandon young company, and associate myself with grave elderly people : which counsel I followed. My manner of life was now wholly regular, and full of religion, such as it was ; for I read my Bible more than twice through in less than a year, spent much time every day in prayer and other secret duties, gave great attention to the word preached, and endeavored to my utmost to retain it. So much concerned was I about religion, that I agreed with some young persons to meet privately on Sabbath evenings for religious exercises, and I thought myself sincere in these duties ; and after our meeting was ended I used to repeat the discourses of the day to myself; recollecting what I could, though sometimes very late at night. I used occasionally on Monday mornings to recollect the same sermons ; experienced a considerable degree of enjoyment in prayer, and had many thoughts of joining the church. In short, I had a very . good outside, and rested entirely on my duties ; though I was not sensible of it.

"After Mr. Fiske's death, I proceeded in my studies with my brother ; was still very constant in religious duties, often wondered at the levity of professors, and lamented their carelessness in religious matters. Thus I proceeded a considerable length on a self-righteous foundation, and should have been entirely lost and undone, had not the mere mercy of God prevented.

"In the winter of 1738, it pleased God, one Sabbath morning as I was walking out for prayer, to give me on a sudden such a sense of my danger, and the wrath of God, that I stood amazed, and my former good frames presently vanished. From the view which I had of my sin and vileness, I was much distressed all that day, fearing that the vengeance of God would soon overtake me. I was much dejected ; kept much alone ; and sometimes envied the birds and beasts their happiness, because they were not exposed to eternal misery, as I evidently saw that I was. Thus I lived from day to day, being frequently in great distress : sometimes there appeared mountains before me to obstruct my hopes of mercy ; and the work of conversion appeared so great, that I thought I should never be the subject of it. I used, however, to pray and cry to God, and perform other duties with great earnestness, and thus hoped by some means to make the case better. Hundreds of times I renounced all pretences of any worth in my duties, as I thought, even while performing them, and often confessed to God that I deserved nothing for the very best of them, but eternal condemnation ; yet still I had a secret hope of recommending myself to God by my religious duties. When I prayed affectionately, and my heart seemed in some measure to melt, I hoped that God would be thereby moved to pity me. My prayers then looked with some appearance of goodness in them, and I seemed to mourn for sin. Then I could in some measure venture on the mercy of God in Christ, as I thought ; though the preponderating thought, the foundation of my hope, was some imagination of goodness in my meltings of heart, the warmth of my affections, and my extraordinary enlargements in prayer. Though at times the gate appeared so very strait, that it looked next to impossible to enter; yet, at other times, I flattered myself that it was not so very difficult, and hoped I should by diligence and watchfulness soon gain the point. Sometimes after enlargement in duty and considerable affection, I hoped I had made a good step towards heaven; and imagined that God was affected as I was, and would hear such sincere cries, as I called them. And so sometimes, when I withdrew for secret prayer in great distress, I returned comfortable; and thus healed myself with my duties.

" In *February*, 1739, I set apart a day for secret fasting and prayer, and spent the day in almost incessant cries to God for mercy, that he would open my eyes to see the evil of sin, and the way of life by Jesus Christ. God was pleased that day to make considerable discoveries of my heart to me. Still I trusted in all the duties I performed, though there was no manner of goodness in them; there being in them no respect to the glory of God, nor any such principle in my heart. Yet God was pleased to make my endeavors, that day, a means to show me my helplessness in some measure.

" Sometimes I was greatly encouraged, and imagined that God loved me, and was pleased with me,—and thought I should soon be fully reconciled to God. But the whole was founded on mere presumption, arising from enlargement in duty, or warmth of affections, or some good resolutions, or the like. And when, at times, great distress began to arise, on a sight of my vileness, and inability to deliver myself from a sovereign God, I used to put off the discovery, as what I could not bear. Once, I remember, a terrible pang of distress seized me; and the thought of renouncing myself, and standing naked before God, stripped of all goodness, was so dreadful to me, that I was ready to say to it, as Felix to Paul, ' Go thy way for this time.' Thus, though I daily longed for greater conviction of sin; supposing that I must see more of my dreadful state in order to a remedy; yet, when the discoveries of my vile, wicked heart were made to me, the sight was so dreadful, and showed me so plainly my exposedness to damnation, that I could not endure it. I constantly strove after whatever qualifications I imagine others obtained before the reception of Christ, in order to recommend me to his favor. Sometimes I felt the power of a hard heart, and supposed it must be softened before Christ would accept of me; and when I felt any meltings of heart, I hoped now the work was almost done. Hence, when my distress still remained, I was wont to murmur at God's dealings with me; and thought, when others felt their hearts softened, God showed them mercy; but my distress remained still.

" At times I grew remiss and sluggish, without any great convictions of sin, for a considerable time together; but after such a season, convictions seized me more violently. One night I remember in particular, when I was walking solitarily abroad, I had opened to me such a view of my sin, that I feared the ground would cleave asunder under my feet, and become my grave; and would send my soul quick into hell, before I could get home. Though I was forced to go to bed, lest my distress should be discovered by others, which I much feared; yet I scarcely durst sleep at all, for I thought it would be a great wonder if I should be out of hell in the morning. And though my distress was sometimes thus great, yet I greatly dreaded the loss of convictions, and returning back to a state of carnal security, and to my former insensibility of impending wrath; which made me exceedingly exact in my behavior, lest I should stifle the motions of God's Holy Spirit. When at any time I took a view of my convictions, and thought the degree of them to be considerable, I was wont to trust in them; but this confidence, and the hopes of soon making some notable advances towards deliverance, would ease my mind, and I soon become more senseless and remiss. Again, when I discerned my convictions to grow languid, and thought them about to leave me, this immediately alarmed and distressed me. Sometimes I expected to take a large step, and get very far towards conversion, by some particular opportunity or means I had in view.

"The many disappointments, great distresses and perplexity which I experienced, put me into a most horrible frame of contesting with the Almighty; with an inward vehemence and virulence, finding fault with his ways of dealing with mankind. I found great fault with the imputation of Adam's sin to his posterity; and my wicked heart often wished for some other way of salvation than by Jesus Christ. Being like the troubled sea, my thoughts confused, I used to contrive to escape the wrath of God by some other means. I had strange projects, full of atheism, contriving to disappoint God's designs and decrees concerning me, or to escape his notice, and hide myself from him. But when, upon reflection, I saw these projects were vain, and would not serve me, and that I could contrive nothing for my own relief; this would throw my mind into the most horrid frame, to wish there was no God, or to wish there were some other God that could control him. These thoughts and desires were the secret inclinations of my heart, frequently acting before I was aware; but, alas! they were mine, although I was frightened when I came to reflect on them. When I considered, it distressed me to think, that my heart was so full of enmity against God; and it made me tremble, lest his vengeance should suddenly fall upon me. I used before to imagine, that my heart was not so bad as the scriptures and some other books represented it. Sometimes I used to take much pains to work it up into a good frame, a humble submissive disposition; and hoped there was then some goodness in me. But, on a sudden, the thoughts of the strictness of the law, or the sovereignity of God, would so irritate the corruption of my heart, that I had so watched over, and hoped I had brought to a good frame, that it would break over all bounds, and burst forth on all sides, like floods of waters when they break down their dams.

"Being sensible of the necessity of deep humiliation in order to a saving interest in Christ, I used to set myself to produce in my own heart the convictions requisite in such a humiliation ; as, a conviction that God would be just, if he cast me off for ever; that if ever God should bestow mercy on me, it would be mere grace, though I should be in distress many years first, and be never so much engaged in duty ; and that God was not in the least obliged to pity me the more for all past duties, cries and tears. I strove to my utmost to bring myself to a firm belief of these things and a hearty assent to them ; and hoped that now I was brought off from myself, truly humbled, and that I bowed to the divine sovereignty. I was wont to tell God in my prayers, that now I had those very dispositions of soul which he required, and on which he showed mercy to others, and thereupon to beg and plead for mercy to me. But when I found no relief, and was still oppressed with guilt, and fears of wrath, my soul was in tumult, and my heart rose against God, as dealing hardly with me. Yet then my conscience flew in my face, putting me in mind of my late confession to God of his justice in my condemnation. This, giving me a sight of the badness of my heart, threw me again into distress ; and I wished that I had watched my heart more narrowly, to keep it from breaking out against God's dealings with me. I even wished that I had not pleaded for mercy on account of my humiliation ; because thereby I had lost all my seeming goodness. Thus, scores of times, I vainly imagined myself humbled and prepared for saving mercy. While I was in this distressed, bewildered, and tumultuous state of mind, the corruption of my heart was especially irritated with the following things :—

1. "The strictness of the divine Law. For I found it was impossible for me, after my utmost pains, to answer its demands. I often made new resolutions, and as often broke them. I imputed the whole to carelessness, and the want of being more watchful, and used to call myself a fool for my negligence. But when, upon a stronger resolution, and greater endeavors, and close application to fasting and prayer, I found all attempts fail ; then I quarrelled with the law of God, as unreasonably rigid. I thought, if it extended only to my outward actions and behaviors, that I could bear with it ; but I found that it condemned me for my evil thoughts, and sins of my heart, which I could not possibly prevent. I was extremely loth to own my utter helplessness in this matter; but after repeated disappointments, thought that, rather than perish, I could do a little more still ; especially if such and such circumstances might but attend my endeavors and strivings. I hoped, that I should strive more earnestly than ever, if the matter came to extremity, though I never could

find the time to do my utmost, in the manner I intended. This hope of future more favorable circumstances, and of doing something great hereafter, kept me from utter despair in myself, and from seeing myself fallen into the hands of a sovereign God, and dependent on nothing but free and boundless grace.

2. " That faith alone was the condition of salvation ; that God would not come down to lower terms ; and that he would not promise life and salvation upon my sincere and hearty prayers and endeavors. That word, (Mark xvi. 16,) 'He that believeth not, shall be damned,' cut off all hope there. I found that faith was the sovereign gift of God : that I could not get it as of myself ; and could not oblige God to bestow it upon me, by any of my performances. (Eph. ii. 1. 8.) This, I was ready to say, is a hard saying, who can hear it ? I could not bear that all I had done should stand for mere nothing ; as I had been very conscientious in duty, had been exceeding religious a great while, and had, as I thought, done much more than many others who had obtained mercy. I confessed indeed the vileness of my duties; but then, what made them at that time seem vile, was my wandering thoughts in them ; not because I was all over defiled like a devil, and the principle corrupt from whence they flowed so that I could not possibly do anything that was good. Hence I called what I did by the name of honest faithful endeavors ; and could not bear it, that God had made no promises of salvation to them.

3. " That I could not find out what faith was ; or what it was to believe and come to Christ. I read the calls of Christ to the weary and heavy laden ; but could find no way that he directed them to come in. I thought I would gladly come, if I knew how; though the path of duty were never so difficult. I read Stoddard's *Guide to Christ*, (which I trust was, in the hand of God, the happy means of my conversion,) and my heart rose against the author ; for though he told me my very heart all along under convictions, and seemed to be very beneficial to me in his directions ; yet here he failed ; he did not tell me anything I could do that would bring me to Christ, but left me as it were with a great gulf between, without any direction to get through. For I was not yet effectually and experimentally taught, that there could be no way prescribed, whereby a natural man could, of his own strength, obtain that which is supernatural, and which the highest angel cannot give.

4. " The sovereignity of God. I could not bear, that it should be wholly at God's pleasure, to save or damn me, just as he would. That passage, (Rom. ix. 11—23.) was a constant vexation to me, especially verse 21. Reading or meditating on this, always destroyed my seeming good frames : for when I thought I was almost humbled, and almost resigned, this passage would make my enmity against the sovereignity of God appear. When I came to reflect on the inward enmity and blas-

phemy, which arose on this occasion, I was the more afraid of God, and driven further from any hopes of reconciliation with him. It gave me a dreadful view of myself; I dreaded more than ever to see myself in God's hands, at his sovereign disposal; and it made me more opposite than ever to submit to his sovereignty ; for I thought God designed my damnation.

"All this time the Spirit of God was powerfully at work with me; and I was inwardly pressed to relinquish all self-confidence, all hopes of ever helping myself by any means whatsoever. The conviction of my lost estate was sometimes so clear and manifest before my eyes, that it was as if it had been declared to me in so many words, 'It is done, it is done, it is for ever impossible to deliver yourself.' For about three or four days my soul was thus greatly distressed. At some turns, for a few moments, I seemed to myself lost and undone ; but then would shrink back immediately from the sight, because I dared not venture myself into the hands of God, as wholly helpless, and at the disposal of his sovereign pleasure. I dared not see that important truth concerning myself, that I was dead in trespasses and sins. But when I had, as it were, thrust away these views of myself at any time, I felt distressed to have the same discoveries of myself again ; for I greatly feared being given over of God to final stupidity. When I thought of putting it off to a more convenient season, the conviction was so close and powerful, with regard to the present time, that it was the best, and probably the only time, that I dared not put it off.

"It was the sight of truth concerning myself, truth respecting my state, as a creature fallen and alienated from God, and that consequently could make no demands on God for mercy, but must subscribe to the absolute sovereignty of the divine Being ; the sight of the truth, I say, my soul shrank away from, and trembled to think of beholding. Thus, he that doth evil, as all unregenerate men continually do, hates the light of truth, neither cares to come to it, because it will reprove his deeds, and show him his just deserts, (John iii. 26.) Some time before, I had taken much pains, as I thought, to submit to the sovereignty of God; yet I mistook the thing,—and did not once imagine, that seeing and being made experimentally sensible of this truth, which my soul now so much dreaded and trembled at, was the frame of soul which I had so earnestly desired. I had ever hoped, that when I had attained to that humiliation, which I supposed necessary to precede faith, then it would not be fair for God to cast me off ; but now I saw it was so far from any goodness in me, to own myself spiritually dead, and destitute of all goodness, that, on the contrary, my mouth would be for ever stopped by it ; and it looked as dreadful to me, to see myself, and the relation I stood in to God—I a sinner and criminal, and he a great Judge and Sovereign—as it would be to a poor trembling creature, to venture off some high precipice. Hence I put it off for a minute or two, and tried for better circumstances to do it in ; either I must read a passage or two, or pray first, or something of the like nature or else put off my submission to God's sovereignty with an objection, that I did not know how to submit. But the truth was I could see no safety in owing myself in the hands of a sovereign God, and could lay no claim to anything better than damnation.*

' After a considerable time spent in similar exercises and distresses, one morning, while I was walking in a solitary place, as usual, I at once saw that all my contrivances and projects to effect or procure deliverance and salvation for myself, were utterly in vain ; I was brought quite to a stand, as finding myself totally lost. I had thought many times before, that the difficulties in my way were very great; but now I saw, in another and very different light, that it was for ever impossible for me to do anything towards helping or delivering myself. I then thought of blaming myself, that I had not done more, and been more engaged, while I had opportunity—for it seemed now as if the season of doing was for ever over and gone—but I instantly saw, that let me have done what I would, it would no more have tended to my helping myself, than what I had done ; that I had made all the pleas I ever could have made to all eternity ; and that all my pleas were vain. The tumult that had been before in my mind, was now quieted ; and I was somewhat eased of that

---

* About this period Brainerd wrote the following fragment, found among his MSS, entitled :—

"SOME GLOOMY AND DESPONDING THOUGHTS OF A SOUL UNDER CONVICTIONS OF SIN AND CONCERN FOR ITS ETERNAL SALVATION.

1. " I believe my case is singular, that none ever had so many strange and different thoughts and feelings as I.

2. " I have been concerned much longer than many others I have known, or concerning whom I had read, who have been savingly converted, and yet I am left.

3. " I have withstood the power of convictions a long time; and therefore I fear I shall be finally left of God.

4. " I never shall be converted without stronger convictions and greater terrors of conscience.

5. " I do not aim at the glory of God in anything I do, and therefore I cannot hope for mercy.

6. " I do not see the evil nature of sin, nor the sin of my nature ; and therefore I am discouraged.

7. " The more I strive, the more blind and hard my heart is, and the worse I grow continually.

8 " I fear that God never showed mercy to one so vile as I.

9. " I fear that I am not elected, and therefore must perish.

10. " I fear that the day of grace is past with me.

11. " I fear that I have committed the unpardonable sin.

12. " I am an old sinner: and if God had designed mercy for me, he would have called me home to himself before now."

distress which I felt while struggling against a sight of myself, and of the divine sovereignty. I had the greatest certainty, that my state was forever miserable, for all that I could do; and wondered that I had never been sensible of it before.

" While I remained in this state, my notions respecting my duties were quite different from what I had ever entertained in times past. Before this, the more I did in duty, the more hard I thought it would be for God to cast me off; though at the same time I confessed, and thought I saw, that there was no goodness or merit in my duties; but now, the more I did in prayer or any other duty, the more I saw that I was indebted to God for allowing me to ask for mercy; for I saw that self-interest had led me to pray, and that I had never once prayed from any respect to the glory of God. Now I saw that there was no necessary connexion between my prayers and the bestowment of divine mercy; that they laid not the least obligation upon God to bestow his grace upon me; and that there was no more virtue or goodness in them, than there would be in my paddling with my hand in the water, (which was the comparison I had then in my mind;) and this because they were not performed from any love or regard to God. I saw that I had been heaping up my devotions before God, fasting, praying, pretending, and indeed really thinking sometimes, that I was aiming at the glory of God; whereas I never once truly intended it, but only my own happiness. I saw that as I had never done anything for God, I had no claim on anything from him, but perdition, on account of my hypocrisy and mockery. Oh, how different did my duties now appear from what they used to do! I used to charge them with sin and imperfection; but this was only on account of the wanderings and vain thoughts attending them, and not because I had no regard to God in them; for this I thought I had. But when I saw evidently that I had regard to nothing but self-interest; then they appeared a vile mockery of God, self-worship, and a continual course of lies. I saw that something worse had attended my duties than barely a few wanderings; for the whole was nothing but self-worship, and a horrid abuse of God.

" I continued, in this state of mind till the Sabbath evening following, when I was walking again in the same solitary place, where I was brought to see myself lost and helpless, as before mentioned. Here, in a mournful melancholy state, I was attempting to pray; but found no heart to engage in that or any other duty; my former concern, exercise, and religious affections were now gone. I thought that the Spirit of God had quite left me; but still was not distressed; yet disconsolate, as if there was nothing in heaven or earth could make me happy. Having been thus endeavoring to pray—though, as I thought, very stupid and senseless—for near half an hour; then, as I was walking in a dark thick grove, unspeakable glory seemed to open to the view and apprehension of my soul. I do not mean any external brightness, for I saw no such thing; nor do I intend any imagination of a body of light, somewhere in the third heavens, or anything of that nature; but it was a new inward apprehension or view that I had of God, such as I never had before, nor anything which had the least resemblance of it. I stood still; wondered; and admired! I knew that I never had seen before anything comparable to it for excellency and beauty; it was widely different from all the conceptions that ever I had of God, or things divine. I had no particular apprehension of any one person in the Trinity, either the Father, the Son, or the Holy Ghost; but it appeared to be Divine glory. My soul rejoiced with joy unspeakable, to see such a God, such a glorious divine Being; and I was inwardly pleased and satisfied that he should be God over all for ever and ever. My soul was so captivated and delighted with the excellency, loveliness, greatness, and other perfections of God, that I was even swallowed up in him; at least to that degree, that I had no thought (as I remember) at first, about my own salvation, and scarce reflected that there was such a creature as myself.

"Thus God, I trust, brought me to a hearty disposition to exalt him, and set him on the throne, and principally and ultimately to aim at his honor and glory, as King of the universe. I continued in this state of inward joy, peace, and astonishment, till near dark, without any sensible abatement; and then began to think and examine what I had seen; and felt sweetly composed in my mind all the evening following. I felt myself in a new world, and everything about me appeared with a different aspect from what it was wont to do. At this time, the way of salvation opened to me with such infinite wisdom, suitableness, and excellency, that I wondered I should ever think of any other way of salvation; was amazed that I had not dropped my own contrivances, and complied with this lovely, blessed, and excellent way before. If I could have been saved by my own duties, or any other way that I had formerly contrived, my whole soul would now have refused it. I wondered that all the world did not see and comply with this way of salvation, entirely by the righteousness of Christ.

"The sweet relish of what I then felt, continued with me for several days, almost constantly, in a greater or less degree. I could not but sweetly rejoice in God, lying down and rising up. The next Lord's day I felt something of the same kind, though not so powerful as before. But not long after I was again involved in thick darkness, and under great distress; yet not of the same kind with my distress under convictions. I was guilty, afraid and ashamed to come before God; was exceedingly pressed with a sense of guilt: but it was not long before I felt, I trust, true repentance and joy in God. The latter end of August, I again fell under great darkness ; it seemed as if the presence of God was clean gone forever ; though I was not so much distressed about my spiritual state, as I was at my being shut out from God's presence, as I then sensibly was. But it pleased the Lord to return graciously to me not long after.*

" In *September* I entered Yale College ; but with some degree of reluctancy, fearing lest I should not be able to lead a life of strict religion, in the midst of so many temptations. After this, in the vacancy, before I went to tarry at college, it pleased God to visit my soul with clearer manifestations of himself and his grace. I was spending some time in prayer and self-examination, when the Lord, by his grace, so shined into my heart, that I enjoyed full assurance of his favor, for that time; and my soul was unspeakably refreshed with divine and heavenly enjoyments. At this time especially, as well as some others, sundry passages of God's word opened to my soul with divine clearness, power, and sweetness, so as to appear exceeding precious, and with clear and certain evidence of its being the word of God. I enjoyed considerable sweetness in religion all the winter following.

" In *Jan.* 1740, the measles spread much in college ; and I, having taken the distemper, went home to Haddam. But some days before I was taken sick, I seemed to be greatly deserted, and my soul mourned the absence of the Comforter exceedingly. It seemed to me, that all comfort was forever gone. I prayed and cried to God for help, yet found no present comfort or relief. But through divine goodness, a night or two before I was taken ill, while I was walking alone in a very retired place, and engaged in meditation and prayer, I enjoyed a sweet refreshing visit, as I trust, from above ; so that my soul was raised far above

---

* It was probably at this time that the following fragment was written, entitled " Some signs of Godliness. The distinguishing marks of a true Christian, taken from one of my old manuscripts ; where I wrote as I felt and experienced, and not from any considerable degree of doctrinal knowledge, or acquaintance with the sentiments of others in this point."

1. " He has a true knowledge of the glory and excellency of God, that he is most worthy to be loved and praised for his own divine perfections. Psal. cxlv. 3.

2. "God is his portion, Psal. lxxiii. 25. And God's glory, his great concern, Matt. vi. 22.

3. " Holiness is his delight ; nothing he so much longs for as to be holy, as God is holy. Phil. iii. 9—12.

4. " Sin is his greatest enemy. This he hates, for its own nature, for what it is in itself, being contrary to a holy God, Jer. ii. 1. And consequently he hates all sin, Rom. vii. 24. 1 John iii. 9.

5. " The laws of God also are his delight, Psal. cxix. 97. Rom. vii. 22. These he observes, not out of constraint, from a servile fear of hell ; but they are his choice, Psal. cxix. 30. The strict observance of them is not his bondage, but his greatest liberty, ver, 45."

the fears of death. Indeed, I rather longed for death than feared it. Oh, how much more refreshing this one season was, than all the pleasures and delights that earth can afford! After a day or two I was taken with the measles, and was very ill indeed, so that I almost despaired of life; but had no distressing fears of death at all. Through divine goodness, I soon recovered; yet, owing to hard study, and to my being much exposed on account of my freshmanship, as I had but little time for spiritual duties, my soul often mourned for want of more time and opportunity to be alone with God. In the spring and summer following, I had better advantages for retirement, and enjoyed more comfort in religion. My ambition in my studies greatly wronged the activity and vigor of my spiritual life; yet, usually, "in the multitude of my thoughts within me, God's comforts principally delighted my soul." These were my greatest consolations day by day.

"One day, I think it was in June, 1740, I walked to a considerable distance from college, in the fields alone, at noon and in prayer found such unspeakable sweetness and delight in God, that I thought, if I must continue still in this evil world, I wanted always to be there, to behold God's glory. My soul dearly loved all mankind, and longed exceedingly that they should enjoy what I enjoyed. It seemed to be a little resemblance of heaven.—On Lord's Day, June 6, being sacrament-day, I found some divine life and spiritual refreshment in that holy ordinance. When I came from the Lord's table, I wondered how my fellow-students could live as I was sensible most did.—Next Lord's day, July 13, I had some special sweetness in religion.—Again, Lord's day, July 20, my soul was in a sweet and precious frame.

"Some time in August following, I became so weakly and disordered, by too close application to my studies, that I was advised by my tutor to go home, and disengage my mind from study as much as I could; for I was grown so weak, that I began to spit blood. I took his advice, and endeavored to lay aside my studies. But being brought very low I looked death in the face more steadfastly; and the Lord was pleased to give me renewedly a sweet sense and relish of divine things; and particularly October 13, I found divine help and consolation in the precious duties of secret prayer and self-examination, and my soul took delight in the blessed God; so likewise on the 17th of October

"*Oct.* 18. In my morning devotions, my soul was exceedingly melted, and bitterly mourned over my great sinfulness and vileness. I never before had felt so pungent and deep a sense of the odious nature of sin, as at this time. My soul was then unusually carried forth in love to God, and had a lively sense of God's love to me. And this love and hope, at that time, cast out fear. Both morning and evening I spent some time in self-examination, to find the truth of grace, as also my fitness to approach

God at his table the next day ; and through infinite grace, found the holy Spirit influencing my soul with love to God, as a witness within myself.

" *Lord's day, Oct.* 19. In the morning I felt my soul hungering and thirsting after righteousness. In the forenoon, while I was looking on the sacramental elements, and thinking that Jesus Christ would soon be ' set forth crucified before me,' my soul was filled with light and love, so that I was almost in an ecstacy ; my body was so weak, I could scarcely stand. I felt at the same time an exceeding tenderness and most fervent love towards all mankind, so that my soul and all the powers of it seemed, as it were, to melt into softness and sweetness. But during the communion, there was some abatement of this life and fervor. This love and joy cast out fear ; and my soul longed for perfect grace and glory. This frame continued till the evening, when my soul was sweetly spiritual in secret duties.

" *Oct.* 20. I again found the assistance of the Holy Spirit in secret duties, both morning and evening, and life and comfort in religion through the whole day.—Oct. 21. I had likewise experience of the goodness of God in ' shedding abroad his love in my heart,' and giving me delight and consolation in religious duties ; and all the remaining part of the week my soul seemed to be taken up with divine things, I now so longed after God, and to be freed from sin, that when I felt myself recovering, and thought I must return to college again, which had proved so hurtful to my spiritual interest the year past, I could not but be grieved, and thought I had much rather have died ; for it distressed me to think of getting away from God. But before I went, I enjoyed several other sweet and precious seasons of communion with God, (particularly Oct. 30, and Nov. 4,) wherein my soul enjoyed unspeakable comfort.

" I returned to college about Nov. 6. and, through the goodness of God, felt the power of religion almost daily, for the space of six weeks. —Nov. 28. In my evening devotion, I enjoyed precious discoveries of God, and was unspeakably refreshed with that passage, Heb. xii. 22-24. My soul longed to wing away to the paradise of God; I longed to be conformed to God in all things. A day or two after, I enjoyed much of the light of God's countenance, most of the day ; and my soul rested in God.

" *Dec.* 9. I was in a comfortable frame of soul most of the day; but especially in evening devotions, when God was pleased wonderfully to assist and strengthen me ; so that I thought nothing should ever move me from the love of God in Christ Jesus my Lord,—Oh ! one hour with God infinitely exceeds all the pleasures and delights of this lower world.

" Towards the latter end of January, 1741, I grew more cold and dull in religion, by means of my old temptation, viz. ambition in my studies. But through divine goodness, a great and general awakening spread itself over

the college, about the latter end of February, in which I was much quickened, and more abundantly engaged in religion."

[The following reference to a time of great religious excitement, into which Brainerd actively entered, and which
was intimately connected with the offence which led to his
expulsion from college, should be read with special care.
This " Great Religious Awakening " began in 1739, and continued with varying power until 1745. Whitefield took an
active part in it, and was sometimes more zealous than discreet. Edwards himself was one of the chief instruments in
promoting this Revival, which had a marked effect on the
future religious history of New England. He gives a highly
interesting account of its rise, and progress and fruits, as well
as of its excesses, in his published works. His candid and
particular account of the circumstances connected with Brainerd's dismissal from college—an event which had a great
influence on his whole after-life—should be carefully noted,
as we shall have occasion to refer to it again. Justice to his
memory demands a thorough understanding of the circumstances here particularly narrated by one familiar with the
facts of the case. J. M. S.]

This awakening was at the beginning of that extraordinary
religious commotion, through the land, which is fresh in every
one's memory. It was for a time very great and general at
New Haven; and the college had no small share in it. That
society was greatly reformed; the students, in general, became serious, many of them remarkably so, and much engaged
in the concerns of their eternal salvation. However undesirable the issue of the awakenings of that day have appeared
in many others, there have been manifestly happy and abiding
effects of the impressions then made on the minds of many
of the members of that college. By all that I can learn concerning Brainerd, there can be no reason to doubt but that
he had much of God's gracious presence, and of the lively
actings of true grace, at that time; yet he was afterwards
abundantly sensible, that his religious experiences and affec-

tions at that time were not free from a corrupt mixture, nor
his conduct to be acquitted from many things that were imprudent and blameable ; which he greatly lamented himself,
and was desirous that others should not make an ill use of
such an example. Hence, although at the time he kept a
constant diary, containing a very particular account of what
passed from day to day, for the next thirteen months, from
the latter end of Jan. 1741, forementioned, in two small books,
which he called the two first volumes of his diary, next following the account before given of his convictions, conversion,
and consequent comforts ; yet, when he lay on his deathbed,
he gave orders (unknown to me till after his death) that these
two volumes should be destroyed ; and in the beginning of
the third book of his diary, he wrote thus (by the hand of
another, he not being able to write himself), " The two preceding volumes, immediately following the account of the
author's conversion, are lost. If any are desirous to know
how the author lived, in general, during that space of time,
let them read the first thirty pages of this volume ; where
they will find somewhat of a specimen of his ordinary manner
of living, through that whole space of time, which was about
thirteen months ; except that here he was more refined from
some imprudences and indecent heats, than there ; but the
spirit of devotion running through the whole, was the same."

It could not be otherwise than that one whose heart had
been so prepared and drawn to God, as Brainerd's had been,
should be mightily enlarged, animated, and engaged at the
sight of such an alteration made in the college, the town, and
country ; and so great an appearance of men reforming
their lives, and turning from their profaneness and immor-
ality, to seriousness and concern for their salvation, and of
religion reviving and flourishing almost everywhere. But as an
intemperate imprudent zeal, and a degree of enthusiasm soon
crept in, and mingled itself with that revival of religion ; and
so great and general an awakening being quite a new thing
in the land, at least as to all the living inhabitants of it ;

neither people nor ministers had learned thoroughly to distinguish between solid religion and its delusive counterfeits.
Even many ministers of the gospel, of long standing and the
best reputation, were for a time overpowered with the glaring
appearances of the latter; and, therefore, surely it was not to
be wondered at, that young Brainerd, but a sophomore at college, should be so; who was not only young in years, but
very young in religion and experience. He had enjoyed but
little advantage for the study of divinity, and still less for
observing the circumstances and events of such an extraordinary state of things. To think it strange, a man must di-
vest himself of all reason. In these disadvantageous circumstances, Brainerd had the unhappiness to have a tincture of
that intemperate, indiscreet zeal, which was at that time too
prevalent; and was led, from his high opinion of others whom
he looked upon as better than himself, into such errors as
were really contrary to the habitual temper of his mind. One
instance of his misconduct at that time, gave great offence to
the rulers of the college, even to that degree that they expelled
him; which it is necessary should be here particularly related,
with its circumstances.

During the awakening at college, there were several
religious students who associated together for mutual conversation and assistance in spiritual things. These were wont
freely to open themselves one to another, as special and intimate friends; Brainerd was one of this company. And it
once happened, that he and two or three more of these intimate friends were in the hall together, after Mr. Whittelsey,
one of the tutors, had engaged in prayer with the scholars;
no other person now remaining in the hall but Brainerd and
his companions. Mr. Whittelsey having been unusually pathetic in his prayer, one of Brainerd's friends on this occasion
asked him what he thought of Mr. Whittelsey; he made answer, " He has no more grace than this chair." One of the
freshmen happening at that time to be near the hall (though
not in the room), overheard these words. This person, though

he heard no name mentioned, and knew not who was thus censured, informed a certain woman in the town, without telling her his own suspicion, viz., that he believed Brainerd had said this of some one or other of the rulers of the college. Whereupon she went and informed the Rector, who sent for this freshman and examined him. He told the Rector the words which he heard Brainerd utter; and informed him who were in the room with him at that time. Upon this the Rector sent for them. They were very backward to inform against their friend respecting what they looked upon as private conversation; especially as none but they had heard or knew of whom he had uttered those words; yet the Rector compelled them to declare what he said, and of whom he said it. Brainerd looked on himself as very ill used in the management of this affair, and thought that it was injuriously extorted from his friends, and then injuriously required of him—as if he had been guilty of some open, notorious crime—to make a public confession, and to humble himself before the whole college in the hall, for what he had said only in private conversation. He not complying with this demand, and having gone once to the separate meeting at New Haven, when forbidden by the Rector; and also having been accused by one person of saying concerning the Rector, "that he wondered he did not expect to drop down dead for fining the scholars who followed Mr. Tennent to Milford," though there was no proof of it (and Brainerd ever professed that he did not remember saying anything to that purpose); for these things he was expelled the college.

How far the circumstances and exigencies of that day might justify such great severity in the governors of the college, I will not undertake to determine; it being my aim, not to bring reproach on the authority of the college, but only to do justice to the memory of a person who was eminently one of those whose memory is blessed. The reader will see, in the sequel of Brainerd's life—particularly under date Sept. 14, 1743—what his own thoughts afterwards were of his

behavior in these things, and in how Christian a manner he
conducted himself, with respect to this affair; though he ever,
as long as he lived, supposed himself ill used in the management of it, and in what he suffered. His expulsion was in
the winter of 1742, while in his third year at college.

CHAPTER II.

His Education for the Christian Ministry.—Licensed to Preach the Gospel.

IN the spring of 1742, Brainerd went to live with the Rev.
Mr. Mills of Ripton, to pursue his studies with him, for the
work of the ministry. Here he spent the greater part of the
time until the Association licensed him to preach; but frequently rode to visit the neighboring ministers, particularly
Mr. Cooke of Stratford, Mr. Graham of Southbury, and Mr.
Bellamy of Bethlehem. While with Mr. Mills, he began the
third book of his diary in which the account he wrote of himself, is as follows :—

"*April* 1, 1742. I seem to be declining, with respect to my life and
warmth in divine things; and have had not so free access to God in
prayer, as usual of late. O that God would humble me deeply in the dust
before him! I deserve hell every day, for not loving my Lord more, who
has, I trust, loved me and given himself for me; and every time I am
enabled to exercise any grace renewedly I am renewedly indebted to the
God of all grace for special assistance. Where then is boasting? Surely
it is excluded when we think how we are dependent on God for the existence and every act of grace. O if ever I get to heaven, it will be because
God pleases and nothing else; for I never did anything of myself, but
get away from God! My soul will be astonished at the unsearchable
riches of divine grace, when I arrive at the mansions, which the blessed
Saviour is gone before to prepare.

" *April* 2. In the afternoon, I felt in secret prayer, much resigned,
calm and serene. What are all the storms of this lower world, if Jesus
by his Spirit does but come walking on the seas! Some time past, I had
much pleasure in the prospect of the Heathen being brought home to
Christ, and desired that the Lord would employ me in that work: but
now my soul more frequently desires to die, to be with Christ. O that
my soul were wrapt up in divine love, and my longing desires after God
increased! In the evening, was refreshed in prayer, with the hopes of
the advancement of Christ's kingdom in the world.

"*April* 3. Was very much amiss this morning, and had a bad night.

I thought, if God would take me to himself now, my soul would exceed-ingly rejoice. O that I may be always humble and resigned to God, that he would cause my soul to be more fixed on himself, that I may be more fitted both for doing and suffering.

" *Lord's day, April* 4. My heart was wandering and lifeless. In the evening God gave me faith in prayer, made my soul melt in some mea-sure, and gave me to taste a divine sweetness. O my blessed God! Let me climb up near to him, and love, and long, and plead, and wrestle, and stretch after him, and for deliverance from the body of sin and death. Alas! my soul mourned to think I should ever lose sight of its beloved again. " O come, Lord Jesus, Amen."

The next day, he complains that he seemed to be void of all relish of divine things, felt much of the prevalence of corruption, and saw in himself a disposition to all manner of sin ; which brought a very great gloom on his mind, and cast him down into the depths of melancholy; so that he speaks of himself as amazed, having no comfort, but filled with horror, seeing no comfort in heaven or earth.

" *April* 6. I walked out this morning to the same place where I was last night, and felt as I did then; but was somewhat relieved by reading some passages in my diary, and seemed to feel as if I might pray to the great God again with freedom; but was suddenly struck with a damp, from the sense I had of my own vileness. Then I cried to God to cleanse me from my exceeding filthiness, to give me repentance and pardon. I then began to find it sweet to pray and could think of under-going the greatest sufferings in the cause of Christ, with pleasure and found my-self willing, if God should so order it, to suffer banishment from my na-tive land, among the Heathen, that I might do something for their salva-tion, in distresses and deaths of any kind. Then God gave me to wrestle earnestly for others, for the kingdom of Christ in the world, and for dear Christian friends. I felt weaned from the world, and from my own repu-tation amongst men, willing to be despised, and to be a gazing stock for the world to behold. It is impossible for me to express how I then felt : I had not much joy, but some sense of the majesty of God, which made me as it were tremble ; I saw myself mean and vile, which made me more willing that God should do what he would with me; it was all infinitely reasonable.

" *April* 7. I had not so much fervency, but felt somewhat as I did yesterday morning, in prayer. At noon I spent some time in secret, with some fervency, but scarce any sweetness ; and felt very dull in the even-ing.—April 8. Had raised hopes to-day respecting the Heathen. Oh that God would bring in great numbers of them to Jesus Christ! I cannot but hope that I shall see that glorious day. Everything in this world seems exceeding vile and little to me; I look so on myself. I had some little dawn of comfort to-day in prayer; but especially to-night, I think I had some faith and power of intercession with God. I was enabled to plead with God for the growth of grace in myself; and many of the dear children of God then lay with weight upon my soul. Blessed be the Lord! It is good to wrestle for divine blessings.

"*April* 9. Most of my time in morning devotion was spent without sensible sweetness, yet I had one delightful prospect of arriving at the heavenly world. I am more amazed than ever at such thoughts; for I see myself infinitely vile and unworthy. I feel very heartless and dull; and though I long for the presence of God, and seem constantly to reach towards God in desires: yet I cannot feel that divine and heavenly sweetness that I used to enjoy. No poor creature stands in need of divine grace more than I, and none abuse it more than I have done, and still do.

"*April* 10. Spent much time in secret prayer this morning, not without some comfort in divine things, and hope I had some faith in exercise; but am so low, and feel so little of the sensible presence of God, that I hardly know what to call faith, and am made to possess the sins of my youth, and the dreadful sin of my nature. I am all sin; I cannot think nor act, but every motion is sin. I feel some faint hopes, that God will, of his infinite mercy, return again with showers of converting grace to poor gospel-abusing sinners; and my hopes of being employed in the cause of God, which of late have been almost extinct, seem now a little revived. O that all my late distresses and awful apprehensions, might prove but Christ's school, to make me fit for greater service, by teaching me the great lesson of humility!

"*Lord's Day, April* 11. In the morning I felt but little life, except that my heart was somewhat drawn out in thankfulness to God, for his amazing grace and condescension to me, in past influences and assistances of his spirit. Afterwards, I had some sweetness in the thoughts of arriving at the heavenly world. O for the happy day! After public worship, God gave me special assistance in prayer; I wrestled with my dear Lord with much sweetness; and intercession was made a delightful employment to me. In the evening, as I was viewing the light in the north, I was delighted in contemplation on the glorious morning of the Resurrection.

"*April* 12. This morning the Lord was pleased to lift up the light of his countenance upon me in secret prayer, and made the season very precious to my soul. Though I have been so depressed of late, respecting my hopes of future serviceableness in the cause of God; yet now I had much encouragement respecting that matter. I was especially assisted to intercede and plead for poor souls, and for the enlargement of Christ's kingdom in the world, and for special grace for myself, to fit me for special services. I felt exceedingly calm, and quite resigned to God, respecting my future employment, when and where he pleased. My faith lifted me above the world, and removed all those mountains over which of late I could not look. I wanted not the favor of man to lean upon ; for I knew that Christ's favor was infinitely better, and that it was no matter when nor where nor how Christ should send me, nor what trials he should still exercise me with, if I might be prepared for his work and will. I now found revived in my mind, the wonderful discovery of infinite wisdom in all the dispensations of God towards me, which I had, a little before I met with my great trial at college ; everything appeared full of divine wisdom.

"*April* 13. I saw myself to be very mean and vile ; and wondered at those who showed me respect. Afterwards I was somewhat comforted in secret retirement, and assisted to wrestle with God with some power, spirituality, and sweetness. Blessed be the Lord, he is never unmindful of me, but always sends me needed supplies ; and from time to time, when I am like one dead, he raises me to life. O that I may never distrust Infinite goodness !

"*April* 14. My soul longed for communion with Christ, and for the mortification of indwelling corruption, especially spiritual pride. O, there is a sweet day coming, wherein the weary will be at rest ! My soul has enjoyed much sweetness this day, in the hopes of its speedy arrival. —April 15. My desires apparently centered in God ; and I found a sensible attraction of soul after him sundry times to-day. I know that I long for God, and a conformity to his will, in inward purity and holiness, ten thousand times more than for anything here below.—April 16 and 17. "I seldom prayed without some sensible joy in the Lord. Sometimes I longed much to be dissolved and to be with Christ. O that God would enable me to grow in grace every day! Alas ! my barrenness is such that God might well say, Cut it down. I am afraid of a dead heart on the Sabbath now begun. O that God would quicken me by his grace !

"*Lora's day*, *April* 18. I retired early this morning into the woods for prayer; had the assistance of God's Spirit, and faith in exercise; and was enabled to plead with fervency for the advancement of Christ's kingdom in the world, and to intercede for dear, absent friends. At noon, God enabled me to wrestle with him, and to feel, as I trust, the power of divine love, in prayer. At night I saw myself infinitely indebted to God, and had a view of my failures in duty. It seemed to me, that I had done, as it were, nothing for God, and that I never had lived to him but a few hours of my life.

"*April* 19. I set apart this day for fasting and prayer to God for his grace; especially to prepare me for the work of the ministry; to give me divine aid and direction, in my preparations for that great work; and in his own time to send me into his harvest. Accordingly, in the morning, I endeavored to plead for the divine presence for the day, and not without some life. In the forenoon, I felt the power of intercession for precious, immortal souls; for the advancement of the kingdom of my dear Lord and Saviour in the world; and withal, a most sweet resignation, and even consolation and joy, in the thoughts of suffering hardships, distresses, and even death itself, in the promotion of it, and had peculiar enlargement in pleading for the enlightening and conversion of the poor Heathen. In the afternoon, God was with me of a truth. O, it was blessed company indeed! God enabled me so to agonize in prayer, that I was quite wet with perspiration, though in the shade, and the cool wind. My soul was drawn out very much from the world, for multitudes of souls. I think I had more enlargement for sinners, than for the children of God, though I felt as if I could spend my life in cries for both. I enjoyed great sweetness in communion with my dear Saviour. I think I never in my life felt such an entire weanedness from this world and so much resigned to God in everything. O that I may always live to and upon my blessed God! Amen, Amen.

"*April* 20. This day, I am twenty-four years of age. O how much mercy have I received the year past! How often has God caused his goodness to pass before me! And how poorly have I answered the vows I made this time twelvemonth, to be wholly the Lord's, to be forever devoted to his service! The Lord help me to live more to his glory for the time to come. This has been a sweet, a happy day to me; blessed be God. I think my soul was never so drawn out in intercession for others, as it has been this night. Had a most fervent wrestle with the Lord to-night for my enemies; and I hardly ever so longed to live to God and to be altogether devoted to him; I wanted to wear out my life in his service, and for his glory.

"*April* 21. Felt much calmness and resignation; and God again enabled me to wrestle for numbers of souls, and had much fervency in the sweet duty of intercession. I enjoyed of late more sweetness in intercession for others, than in any other part of prayer. My blessed Lord really let me come near to him and plead with him.

"*Lord's day, April* 25. This morning, I spent about two hours in secret duties, and was enabled, more than ordinarily, to agonize for immortal souls; though it was early in the morning, and the sun scarcely shone at all, yet my body was quite wet with sweat. I felt much pressed now, as frequently of late, to plead for the meekness and calmness of the Lamb of God in my soul; and through divine goodness, felt much of it this morning. O it is a sweet disposition, heartily to forgive all injuries done us; to wish our greatest enemies as well as we do our own souls! Blessed Jesus, may I daily be more and more conformed to thee! At night, I was exceedingly melted with divine love, and had some feeling sense of the blessedness of the upper world. Those words hung upon me, with much divine sweetness, Psal. lxxxiv. 7. They go from strength to strength, every one of them in Zion appeareth before God: O the near access that God sometimes gives us in our addresses to him! This may well be termed appearing before God: it is so indeed, in the true spiritual sense, and in the sweetest sense. I think that I have not had such power of intercession these many months, both for God's children, and for dead sinners, as I have had this evening. I wished and longed for the coming of my dear Lord: I longed to join the angelic host in praises, wholly free from imperfection. O, the blessed moment hastens! All I want is to be more holy, more like my dear Lord. O for sanctification! My very soul pants for the complete restoration of the blessed image of my Saviour; that I may be fit for the blessed enjoyments and employments of the heavenly world.

> " Farewell, vain world; my soul can bid adieu;
> Your Saviour taught me to abandon you.
> Your charms may gratify a sensual mind;
> But cannot please a soul for God design'd,
> Forbear t' entice, cease then my soul to call;
> 'Tis fixed through grace; my God shall be my all.
> While he thus lets me heavenly glories view,
> Your beauties fade, my heart's no room for you."

" The Lord refreshed my soul with many sweet passages of his word. O the New Jerusalem! my soul longed for it. O the song of Moses and the Lamb! And that blessed song that no man can learn, but they who are redeemed from the earth! and the glorious white robes, that were given to the souls under the altar!

> " Lord, I'm a stranger here alone;
> Earth no true comforts can afford:
> Yet, absent from my dearest one,
> My soul delights to cry ' My Lord ! '
> Jesus, my Lord, my only love,
> Possess my soul, nor thence depart:
> Grant me kind visits, heavenly dove;
> My God shall then have all my heart."

" *April* 26. Continued in a sweet frame of mind; but in the afternoon, felt somewhat of spiritual pride stirring. God was pleased to make it a humbling season at first; though afterwards he gave me sweetness. O my soul exceedingly longs for that blessed state of perfect deliverance from all sin! At night, God enabled me to give my soul up to him, to cast myself upon him, to be ordered and disposed of according to his sovereign pleasure ; and I enjoyed great peace and consolation in so doing. My soul took sweet delight in God; my thoughts freely and sweetly centered in him. O that I could spend every moment of my life to his glory !

April 27. I retired early for secret devotions; and in prayer, God was pleased to pour such ineffable comforts into my soul, that I could do nothing for some time but say over and over, " O my sweet Saviour ! O my sweet Saviour ! " whom have I in heaven but thee ? and there is none upon earth that I desire beside thee." If I had had a thousand lives, my soul would gladly have laid them all down at once, to have been with Christ. My soul never enjoyed so much of heaven before ; it was the most refined and most spiritual season of communion with God I ever yet felt I never felt so great a degree of resignation in my life. In the afternoon, I withdrew, to meet with my God, but found myself myself much declined, and God made it a humbling season to my soul. I mourned over the body of death that is in me. It grieved me exceedingly, that I could not pray to and praise God with my heart full of divine heavenly love. O that my soul might never offer any dead, cold services to my God ! In the evening had not so much divine love, as in the morning ; but had a sweet season of fervent intercession.

" *April* 28. I withdrew to my usual place of retirement, in great peace and tranquility, spent about two hours in secret duties, and felt much as I did yesterday morning, only weaker, and more overcome. I seemed to depend wholly on my dear Lord ; wholly weaned from all other dependencies. I knew not what to say to my God, but only lean on his bosom, as it were, and breathe out my desires after a perfect conformity to him in all things. Thirsting desires, and insatiable longings, possessed my soul, after perfect holiness. God was so precious to my soul. that the world, with all its enjoyments, was infinitely vile. I had no more value for the favor of men, than for pebbles. The Lord was my all, and that he over-ruled all, greatly delighted me. I think that my faith and dependence on God scarce ever rose so high. I saw him such a Fountain of goodness, that it seemed impossible I should distrust him again, or be any way anxious about anything that should happen to me. I now enjoyed great sweetness in praying for absent friends, and for the enlargement of Christ's kingdom in the world. Much of the power of these divine enjoyments remained with me through the day. In the evening, my heart seemed to melt, and I trust was really humbled for indwelling corruption, and I mourned like a dove. I felt that all my unhappiness arose from my being a sinner. With resignation, I could bid welcome to all other trials ; but sin hung heavy upon me; for God discovered to me the corruption of my heart. I went to bed with a heavy heart, because I was a sinner : though I did not in the least doubt of

God's love. O that God would purge away my dross, and take away my tin, and make me ten times refined !

April 29. I was kept off at a distance from God; but had some enlargement in intercession for precious souls.—April 30. I was some-what dejected in spirit: nothing grieves me so much, as that I cannot live constantly to God's glory.   I could bear any desertion or spiritual conflicts, if I could but have my heart all the while burning within me with love to God and desires of his glory.   But this is impossible; for when I feel these, I cannot be dejected in my soul, but only rejoice in my Saviour, who has delivered me from the reigning power, and will shortly deliver me from the indwelling of sin.

" *May* 1. I was enabled to cry to God with fervency for ministerial qualifications, that he would appear for the advancement of his own kingdom, and that he would bring in the Heathen.   Had much assistance in my studies.   This has been a profitable week to me; I have enjoyed many communications of the blessed Spirit in my soul.

" *Lord's day, May* 2. God was pleased this morning to give me such a sight of myself, as made me appear very vile in my own eyes.   I felt corruption stirring in my heart, which I could by no means suppress; felt more and more deserted; was exceeding weak, and almost sick with my inward trials.—May 3. Had a sense of vile ingratitude.   In the morning I withdrew to my usual place of retirement, and mourned for my abuse of my dear Lord; spent the day in fasting and prayer.   God gave me much power of wrestling for his cause and kingdom; and it was a happy day to my soul.   God was with me all the day; and I was more above the world, than ever in my life.

" *Lord's day, May* 9. I think I never felt so much of the cursed pride of my heart, as well as the stubbornness of my will before.   O dreadful ! what a vile wretch I am !   I could submit to be nothing, and to lie down in the dust.   O that God would humble me in the dust!   I felt myself such a sinner, all day, that I had scarce any comfort.   O, when shall I be delivered from the body of this death !   I greatly feared, lest through stupidity and carelessness I should lose the benefit of these trials.   O that they might be sanctified to my soul!   Nothing seemed to touch me but only this, that I was a sinner.   Had fervency and refreshment in social prayer in the evening.

" *May* 10. I rode to New-Haven; saw some Christian friends there; and had comfort in joining in prayer with them, and hearing of the goodness of God to them, since I last saw them.—May 11. " I rode from New-Haven to Wethersfield; was very dull most of the day; had little spirituality in this journey, though I often longed to be alone with God; was much perplexed with vile thoughts; was sometimes afraid of everything :

but God was my Helper. Caught a little time for retirement in the evening, to my comfort and rejoicing, Alas! I cannot live in the midst of a
tumult. I long to enjoy God alone.—May 12. I had a distressing view
of the pride, enmity and vileness of my heart. Afterwards had sweet
refreshment in conversing and worshipping God, with Christian friends.

" *May* 13. Saw so much of the wickedness of my heart, that I longed
to get away from myself. I never before thought that there was so much
spiritual pride in my soul. I felt almost pressed to death with my own
vileness. O what a body of death is there in me ! Lord, deliver my soul !
I could not find any convenient place for retirement, and was greatly exercised. Rode to Hartford in the afternoon : had some refreshment and
comfort in religious exercises with Christian friends; but longed for more
retirement. O the closest walk with God is the sweetest heaven that can
be enjoyed on earth !

" *May* 14. I waited on a council of ministers convened at Hartford,
and spread before them the treatment I had met with from the rector and
tutors of Yale College ; who thought it advisable to intercede for me with
the rector and trustees, and to intreat them to restore me to my former
privileges in college.* After this, spent some time in religious exercises
with Christian friends.

" *May* 15. I rode from Hartford to Hebron; was somewhat dejected
on the road ; appeared exceeding vile in my own eyes, saw much pride and
stubbornness in my heart. Indeed I never saw such a week as this before ;
for I have been almost ready to die with the view of the wickedness of my
heart. I could not have thought I had such a body of death in me. Oh,
that God would deliver my soul ! "

The three next days (which he spent at Hebron, Lebanon,
and Norwich) he complains still of dullness and desertion,
and expresses a sense of his vileness, and longing to hide
himself in some cave or den of the earth ; but yet speaks of
some intervals of comfort and soul-refreshment each day.

" *May* 19. [At Millington] I was so amazingly deserted this morning,
that I seemed to feel a sort of horror in my soul. Alas ! when God with-
draws, what is there that can afford any comfort to the soul ! "

Through the eight days next following, he expresses more
calmness and comfort, and considerable life, fervency, and
sweetness in religion.

" *May* 28. [At New-Haven] I think I scarce ever felt so calm in my

* This application was not successful.

life; I rejoiced in resignation, and giving myself up to God, to be wholly and entirely devoted to him for ever.

"*June* 1. Had much of the presence of God in family prayer, and had some comfort in secret. I was greatly refreshed from the word of God this morning, which appeared exceedingly sweet to me; some things which appeared mysterious, were opened to me. O that the Kingdom of the dear Saviour might come with power, and the healing waters of the sanctuary spread far and wide for the healing of the nations! Came to Ripton; but was very weak. However, being visited by a number of young people in the evening, I prayed with them.

"*Lord's day, June* 6. I feel much deserted : but all this teaches me my nothingness and vileness more than ever.—June 7. Felt still powerless in secret prayer. Afterwards I prayed and conversed with some little life. God feeds me with crumbs; blessed be his name for anything. I felt a great desire that all God's people might know how mean and little and vile I am; that they might see I am nothing, that so they may pray for me aright, and not have the least dependence upon me.—June 8. I enjoyed one sweet and precious season this day; I never felt it so sweet to be nothing, and less than nothing, and to be accounted nothing.

June 12. Spent much time in prayer this morning, and enjoyed much sweetness. Felt insatiable longings after God much of the day. I wondered how poor souls do to live, that have no God. The world, with all its enjoyments, quite vanished. I see myself very helpless; but I have a blessed God to go to. I longed exceedingly to be dissolved, and to be with Christ, to behold his glory. O my weak weary soul longs to arrive at my Father's house!

Lord's day, June 13. Felt somewhat calm and resigned in the public worship: at the sacrament saw myself very vile and worthless. O that I may always lie low in the dust! My soul seemed steadily to go forth after God, in longing desire to live upon him.

June 14. Felt somewhat of the sweetness of communion with God, and the constraining force of his love ; how admirably it captivates the soul, and makes all the desires and affections to centre in God! I set apart this day for secret fastings and prayer, to intreat God to direct and bless me with regard to the great work which I have in view, of preaching the gospel—and that the Lord would return to me, and show me the light of his countenance. Had little life and power in the forenoon : near the middle of the afternoon, God enabled me to wrestle ardently in intercession for my absent friends: but just at night the Lord visited me marvellously in prayer. I think my soul never was in such an agony before. I felt no restraint; for the treasures of divine grace were opened to me. I wrestled for absent friends, for the ingathering of souls, for multitudes of poor souls, and for many that I thought were the children of God, personally, in many distant places. I was in such an agony from sun half an hour high, till near dark, that I was all over wet with sweat: but yet it seemed to me that I had wasted away the day, and had done nothing. O my dear Saviour did sweat blood for poor souls! I longed for more compassion towards them. Felt still in a sweet frame, under a sense of divine love and grace; and went to bed in such a frame, with my heart set on God.

"*June* 15. Had the most ardent longings after God, which I ever felt in my life. At noon, in my secret retirement, I could do nothing but tell my dear Lord, in a sweet calm, that he knew I desired nothing but himself, nothing but holiness; that he had given me these desires, and he only could give me the thing desired. I never seemed to be so unhinged from myself, and to be so wholly devoted to God. My heart was swallowed up in God most of the day. In the evening I had such a view of the soul being as it were enlarged, to contain more holiness, that it seemed ready to separate from my body. I then wrestled in an agony for divine blessings; had my heart drawn out in prayer for some Christian friends, beyond what I ever had before. I feel differently now from what I ever did under any enjoyments before; more engaged to live to God for ever, and less pleased with my own frames. I am not satisfied with my frames, nor feel at all more easy after such strugglings than before; for it seems far too little, if I could always be so. O how short do I fall of my duty in my sweetest moments!

"*June* 18. Considering my great unfitness for the work of the ministry, my present deadness, and total inability to do anything for the glory of God that way, feeling myself very helpless, and at a great loss what the Lord would have me to do; I set apart this day for prayer to God, and spent most of the day in that duty, but amazingly deserted most of the day. Yet I found God graciously near, once in particular; while I was pleading for more compassion for immortal souls, my heart seemed to be opened at once, and I was enabled to cry with great ardency, for a few minutes. O I was distressed to think that I should offer such dead cold services to the living God! My soul seemed to breathe after holiness, a life of constant devotedness to God. But I am almost lost sometimes in the pursuit of this blessedness, and ready to sink, because I continually fall short, and miss of my desire. O that the Lord would help me to hold out, yet a little while, until the happy hour of deliverance comes!

"*June* 19. Felt much disordered; my spirits were very low: but yet enjoyed some freedom and sweetness in the duties of religion. Blessed be God.—Lord's day, June 20. Spent much time alone. My soul earnestly wished to be holy, and reached after God; but seemed not to obtain my desire. I hungered and thirsted; but was not refreshed and satisfied. My soul rested on God, as my only portion. O that I could grow in grace more abundantly every day

"*June* 22. In the morning spent about two hours in prayer and meditation, with considerable delight. Towards night felt my soul go out in earnest desires after God, in secret retirement. In the evening, was sweetly composed and resigned to God's will ; was enabled to leave myself and all my concerns with him, and to have my whole dependence upon him. My secret retirement was very refreshing to my soul ; it appeared such a happiness to have God for my portion, that I had rather be any other creature in this lower creation, than not come to the enjoyment of God. I had rather be a beast, than a man, without God, if I were to live here to eternity. Lord, endear thyself more to me ! "

In his diary for the next seven days, he expresses a variety of exercises of mind. He speaks of great longings after God and holiness, and earnest desires for the conversion of others ; of fervency in prayer, power to wrestle with God, composure, comfort, and sweetness, from time to time ; but expresses a sense of the abomination of his heart, and bitterly complains of his barrenness, and the body of death ; and says, "he saw clearly that whatever he enjoyed, better than hell, was of free grace." He complains of falling much below the character of a child of God ; and is sometimes very disconsolate and dejected.

"*June* 30. Spent this day alone in the woods, in fasting and prayer ; underwent the most dreadful conflicts in my soul, which I ever felt, in some respects. I saw myself so vile, that I was ready to say, ' I shall now perish by the hand of Saul. I thought that I had no power to stand for the cause of God, but was almost ' afraid of the shaking of a leaf.' Spent almost the whole day in prayer, incessantly. I could not bear to think of Christians showing me any respect. I almost despaired of doing any service in the world ; I could not feel any hope or comfort respecting the heathen, which used to afford me some refreshment in the darkest hours of this nature. I spent the day in bitterness of soul. Near night I felt a little better ; and afterwards enjoyed some sweetness in secret prayer.

"*July* 1. Had some enjoyment in prayer this morning; and far more than usual in secret prayer to-night, and desired nothing so ardently as that God should do with me just as he pleased.—July 2. Felt composed in secret prayer in the morning. My desires ascended to God this day, as I was travelling : and was comfortable in the evening.

Blessed be God for all my consolation.—July 3. "My heart seemed again to sink. The disgrace I was laid under at College, seemed to damp me ; as it opens the mouths of opposers. I had no refuge but in God. Blessed be his name, that I may go to him at all times, and find him a present help.

"*Lord's day, July* 4. Had considerable assistance. In the evening I withdrew, and enjoyed a happy season in secret prayer. God was pleased to give me the exercise of faith, and thereby brought the invisible and eternal world near to my soul which appeared sweetly to me. I hoped that my weary pilgrimage in the world would be short; and that it would not be long before I was brought to my heavenly home and Father's house. I was resigned to God's will, to tarry his time, to do his work, and suffer his pleasure. I felt thankfulness to God for all my pressing desertions of late ; for I am persuaded that they have been made a means of making me more humble, and much more resigned. I felt pleased to be little, to be nothing, and to lie in the dust. I enjoyed life and consolation in pleading for the dear children of God, and the kingdom of Christ in the world : and my soul earnestly breathed after holiness, and the enjoyment of God. O come, Lord Jesus, come quickly.

"*Lord's day, July* 11. Was deserted and exceedingly dejected in the morning. In the afternoon, had some life and assistance, and felt resigned. I saw myself to be exceeding vile.

"*July* 14. Felt a degree of humble resigned sweetness: spent a considerable time in secret, giving myself up wholly to the Lord. Heard Mr. Ballamy preach towards night; felt very sweetly part of the time : longed for nearer access to God.

"*July* 19. My desires seem especially to be after weanedness from the world, perfect deadness to it, and that I may be crucified to all its allurements. My soul desires to feel itself more of a pilgrim and stranger here below; that nothing may divert me from pressing through the lonely desert, till I arrive at my Father's house.—July 20. It was sweet to give away myself to God to be disposed of at his pleasure. I had some feeling sense of the sweetness of being a pilgrim on earth.

"*July* 22. Journeying from Southbury to Ripton, I called at a house by the way, where being very kindly entertained and refreshed, I was filled with amazement and shame, that God should stir up the hearts of any to show so much kindness to such a dead dog as I ; was made sensible in some manner, how exceeding vile it is not to be wholly devoted to God. I wondered that God would suffer any of his creatures to feed and sustain me from time to time.

"*July* 29. I was examined by the Association met at Danbury, as to my learning, and also my experience in religion, and received a license from them to preach the gospel of Christ. Afterwards felt much devoted to God; joined in prayer with one of the ministers, my peculiar friend, in a convenient place, and went to bed resolving to live devoted to God all my days."

CHAPTER III.

Beginning of his Missionary Career among the Indians of North America.

"*July* 30, 1742. Rode from Danbury to Southbury ; preached there, from 1 Pet. iv. 8. And above all things have fervent charity, etc. Had much of the comfortable presence of God in the exercise. I seemed to have power with God in prayer, and power to get hold of the hearts of the people in preaching.—July 31. I was calm and composed, as well as greatly refreshed and encouraged.

"*Lord's day, Aug.* 8. n the morning I felt comfortably in secret prayer ; my soul was refreshed with the hopes of the Heathen coming home to Christ ; was much resigned to God, and thought it was no matter what became of me.—Preached both parts of the day at Bethlehem, from Job xiv. 14. If a man die, shall he live again, etc. It was sweet to me to meditate on death. In the evening, felt very comfortably, and cried to God fervently in secret prayer.

"*Aug.* 12. This morning and last night I was exercised with sore inward trials : I had no power to pray : but seemed shut out from God. I had in a great measure lost my hopes of God's sending me among the Heathen afar off, and of seeing them flock home to Christ, I saw so much of my vileness, that I wondered that God would let me live, and that people did not stone me ; much more that they would ever hear me preach ! It seemed as though I never could nor should preach any more, yet about nine or ten o'clock, the people came over, and I was forced to preach. And blessed be God, he gave me his presence and Spirit in prayer and preaching : so that I was much assisted, and spake with power from Job, xiv. 14. Some Indians cried out in great distress,* and all appeared greatly concerned. After we had prayed and exhorted them to seek the Lord with constancy, and hired an English woman to keep a kind of school among them, we came away about one o'clock and came to Judea, about fifteen or sixteen miles. There God was pleased to visit my soul with much comfort. Blessed be the Lord for all things I meet with.

"*Lord's day Aug.* 15. Felt much comfort and devotedness to God this day. At night, it was refreshing to get alone with God, and pour out my soul. Oh, who can conceive of the sweetness of communion with the

* It was near Kent, on the western borders of Connecticut, where there is a number of Indians.

blessed God, but those who have experience of it! Glory to God for ever, that I may taste heaven below.—Aug. 16. Had some comfort in secret prayer, in the morning. Felt sweetly sundry times in prayer this day ; but was much perplexed in the evening with vain conversation.—Aug. 17. Exceedingly depressed in spirit, it cuts and wounds my heart, to think how much self-exultation, spiritual pride, and warmth of temper, I have formerly had intermingled with my endeavors to promote God's work : and sometimes I long to lie down at the feet of opposers, and confess what a poor imperfect creature I have been, and still am. The Lord forgive me, and make me for the future wise as a serpent, and harmless as a dove ! Afterwards enjoyed considerable comfort and delight of soul.

"*Aug.* 18. Spent most of this day in prayer and reading. I see so much of my own extreme vileness, that I feel ashamed and guilty before God and man ; I look to myself like the vilest fellow in the land : I wonder that God stirs up his people to be so kind to me.—Aug. 19, This day, being about to go from Mr. Bellamy's at Bethlehem, where I had resided some time, I prayed with him, and two or three other Christian friends. We gave ourselves to God with all our hearts, to be his for ever : eternity looked very near to me, while I was praying. If I never should see these Christians again in this world, it seemed but a few moments before I should meet them in another world.

"*Aug.* 20. I appeared so vile to myself, that I hardly dared to think of being seen, especially on account of spiritual pride. However, to-night I enjoyed a sweet hour alone with God, [at Ripton] : I was lifted above the frowns and flatteries of this lower world ; had a sweet relish of heavenly joys ; and my soul did, as it were, get into the eternal world, and really taste of heaven. I had a sweet season of intercession for dear friends in Christ ; and God helped me to cry fervently for Zion. Blessed be God for this season.

"*Aug.* 21. Was much perplexed in the morning. Towards noon enjoyed more of God in secret ; was enabled to see that it was best to throw myself into the hands of God, to be disposed of according to his pleasure, and rejoiced in such thoughts. In the afternoon rode to New-Haven : was much confused all the way. Just at night, underwent such a dreadful conflict as I have scarce ever felt. I saw myself exceeding vile and unworthy ; so that I was guilty, and ashamed that anybody should bestow any favor on me, or show me any respect.

"*Lord's day, Aug.* 22. In the morning continued still in perplexity. In the evening enjoyed comfort sufficient to overbalance all my late distresses. I saw that God is the only soul-satisfying portion, and I really found satisfaction in him. My soul was much enlarged in sweet intercession for my fellow-men everywhere, and for many Christian friends in particular, in distant places.—Aug. 23. Had a sweet season in secret prayer: the Lord drew near to my soul and filled me with peace and divine consolation. Oh, my soul tasted the sweetness of the upper world; and was drawn out in prayer for the world, that it might come home to Christ! Had much comfort in the thoughts and hopes of the ingathering of the Heathen; was greatly assisted in intercession for Christian friends."—Aug. 25. In family prayer, God helped me to climb up near him, so that I scarce ever got nearer.

"*Aug.* 30. Felt somewhat comfortably in the morning; conversed sweetly with some friends; was in a serious composed frame; and prayed at a certain house with some degree of sweetness. Afterwards at another house, prayed privately with a dear Christian friend or two; and, I think, I scarce ever launched so far into the eternal world as then; I got so far out on the broad ocean, that my soul with joy triumphed over all the evils on the shores of mortality. I think time, and all its gay amusements and cruel disappointments, never appeared so inconsiderable to me before. I was in a sweet frame; I saw myself nothing, and my soul reached after God with intense desire. Oh, I saw what I owed to God, in such a manner, as I scarce ever did! I knew that I had never lived a moment to him as I should do; indeed, it appeared to me, that I had never done anything in Christianity: my soul longed with a vehement desire to live to God.—In the evening, sung and prayed with a number of Christians: felt the powers of the world to come in my soul, in prayer. Afterwards prayed again privately, with a dear Christian or two and found the presence of God; was somewhat humbled in my secret retirement: felt my ingratitude, because I was not wholly swallowed up in God.

"*Sept.* 1. Went to Judea, to the ordination of Mr. Judd. Mr. Bellamy preached from Matt. xxiv. 46. 'Blessed is that servant,' etc. I felt very solemn most of the time; had my thoughts much on that time when our Lord will come; that time refreshed my soul much; only I was afraid I should not be found faithful, because I have so vile a heart. My thoughts were much in eternity, where I love to dwell. Blessed be God for this solemn season. Rode home to night with Mr. Bellamy, conversed with some friends till it was very late, and then retired to rest in a comfortable frame.

"*Sept.* 2. In the afternoon, I preached from John vi. 67. Then said Jesus unto the twelve, Will ye also go away? and God assisted me in some comfortable degree; but more especially in my first prayer; my soul seemed then to launch quite into the eternal world, and to be as it were, separated from this lower world. Afterwards preached again from Isa. v. 4. What could have been done more, etc. God gave me some assistance; but I saw myself a poor worm.

"*Sept.* 4. Much out of health, exceedingly depressed in my soul, and at an awful distance from God. Towards night, spent some time in profitable thoughts on Rom. viii. 2. For the law of the spirit of life, etc. Near night, had a very sweet season in prayer; God enabled me to wrestle ardently for the advancement of the Redeemer's kingdom; pleaded earnestly for my own dear brother John, that God would make him more of a pilgrim and stranger on the earth, and fit him for singular service-ableness in the world; and my heart sweetly exulted in the Lord, in the thoughts of any distresses that might alight on him or on me, in the advancement of Christ's kingdom. It was a sweet and comfortable hour unto my soul, while I was indulged with freedom to plead, not only for myself, but also for many other souls.

" *Lord's day, Sept.* 5. Preached all day : was somewhat strengthened and assisted in the afternoon; more especially in the evening: had a sense of my unspeakable failures in all my duties. I found, alas ! that I had never lived to God in my life.—Sept. 6. Was informed that they only waited for an opportunity to apprehend me for preaching at New-Haven lately, that so they might imprison me. This made me more solemn and serious, and to quit all hopes of the world's friendship; it brought me to a further sense of my vileness, and just desert of this, and much more, from the hand of God, though not from the hand of man. Retired into a convenient place in the woods, and spread the matter before God.

" *Sept.* 7. Had some relish of divine things, in the morning. Afterwards felt more barren and melancholy. Rode to New-Haven to a friend's house, at a distance from the town ; that I might remain undiscovered and yet have opportunity to do business privately, with friends which come to commencement.

" *Sept.* 8. Felt very sweetly, when I first rose in the morning. In family prayer, had some enlargement, but not much spirituality, till eternity came up before me, and looked near ; I found some sweetness in the thoughts of bidding a dying farewell to this tiresome world. Though sometime ago I reckoned upon seeing my dear friends at commencement; yet being now denied the opportunity, for fear of imprisonment, I felt totally resigned, and as contented to spend this day alone in the woods, as I could have done, if I had been allowed to go to town. Felt exceedingly weaned from the world to-day. In the afternoon, I discoursed on divine things, with a dear Christian friend, whereby we were both refreshed. Then I prayed, with a sweet sense of the blessedness of communion with God : I think I scarce ever enjoyed more of God in any one prayer. O it was a blessed season indeed to my soul ! I know not that ever I saw so much of my own nothingness, in my life ; never wondered so, that God allowed me to preach his word. This has been a sweet and comfortable day to my soul. Blessed be God. Prayed again with my dear friend, with something of the divine presence. I long to be wholly conformed to God, and transformed into his image.

"*Sept.* 9. Spent much of the day alone; enjoyed the presence of God in some comfortable degree : was visited by some dear friends and prayed with them : wrote sundry letters to friends; felt religion in my soul while writing : enjoyed sweet meditations on some scriptures. In the evening, went very privately into town, from the place of my residence at the farms, and conversed with some dear friends ; felt sweetly in singing hymns with them : and made my escape to the farms again, without being discovered by any enemies, as I knew of. Thus the Lord preserves me continually.

"*Sept.* 10. Longed with intense desire after God ; my whole soul seemed impatient to be conformed to him, and to become 'holy, as he is holy.' In the afternoon, prayed with a dear friend privately, and had the presence of God with us ; our souls united together to reach after a blessed immortality, to be unclothed of the body of sin and death, and to enter the blessed world, where no unclean thing enters. O, with what intense desire did our souls long for that blessed day, that we might be freed from sin, and forever live to and in our God ! In the evening, took leave of that house ; but first kneeled down and prayed; the Lord was of a truth in the midst of us ; it was a sweet parting season ; felt in myself much sweetness and affection in the things of God. Blessed be God for every such divine gale of his Spirit, to speed me on in my way to the new Jerusalem ! Felt some sweetness afterwards, and spent the evening in conversation with friends, and prayed with some life, and retired to rest very late."

The next five days he appears to have been in an exceedingly comfortable frame of mind, for the most part, and to have been the subject of the like heavenly exercises as are often expressed in preceding passages of his diary ; such as, having his heart much engaged for God, wrestling with him in prayer with power and ardency; enjoying at times sweet calmness and composure of mind, giving himself up to God to be his forever with great complacence of mind ; being wholly resigned to the will of God, that he might do with him what he pleased ; longing to improve time, having the eternal world, as it were, brought nigh ; longing after God and holiness, earnestly desiring a complete conformity to him, and wondering how poor souls do to exist without God.

"*Sept.* 16. At night, enjoyed much of God, in secret prayer : felt an uncommon resignation, to be and do what God pleased. Some days past, I felt great perplexity on account of my past conduct: my bitterness, and want of Christian kindness and love. has been very distressing to my soul : the Lord forgive me my unchristian warmth, and want of a spirit of meekness !

"*Sept.* 18. Felt some compassion for souls, and mourned that I had no more. I feel much more kindness, meekness, gentleness, and love towards all mankind, than ever. I long to be at the feet of my enemies and persecutors: enjoyed some sweetness in feeling my soul conformed to Christ Jesus, and given away to him for ever."

The next day he speaks of much dejection and discouragement, from an apprehension of his own unfitness ever to do any good in preaching ; but blesses God for all dispensations of providence and grace ; finding that by all God weaned him more from the world, and made him more resigned.

The ten days following he appears to have been in great melancholy, exceedingly dejected and discouraged : speaks of his being ready to give up all for gone respecting the cause of Christ, and exceedingly longing to die ; yet had some sweet seasons and intervals of comfort, and special assistance and enlargement in the duties of religion, and in performing public services, and considerable success in them.

" *Sept.* 30. Still very low in spirits ; I did not know how to engage in any work or business, especially to correct some disorders among Christians; felt as though I had no power to be faithful in that regard. However, towards noon, I preached from Deut. viii. 2. And thou shalt remember, etc, and was enabled with freedom to reprove some things in Christians' conduct, I thought very unsuitable and irregular ; insisted near two hours on this subject."

Through this and the two following weeks, he passed through a variety of exercises ; he was frequently dejected, and felt inward distresses : sometimes sunk into the depths of melancholy ; at which turns he was not exercised about the state of his soul, with regard to the favor of God, and his interest in Christ, but about his own sinful infirmities, and unfitness for God's service. His mind appears sometimes extremely depressed with a sense of inexpressible vileness. But, in the mean time, he speaks of many seasons of comfort, and spiritual refreshment, wherein his heart was encouraged and strengthened in God, and sweetly resigned to his will ; of some seasons of very high degrees of spiritual consolation, and of his great longings after holiness, and conformity to God ; of his great fear of offending God, and of his heart being sweetly melted in religious duties ; of his longing for the advancement of Christ's kingdom, of his having at times much assistance in preaching, and of remarkable effects on the audience.

"*Lord's day, Oct.* 17. Had a considerable sense of my helplessness and inability; saw that I must be dependent on God for all I want; and especially when I went to the place of public worship. I found I could not speak a word for God, without his special help and assistance. I went into the assembly trembling, as I frequently do, under a sense of my insufficiency to do anything in the cause of God, as I ought to do. But it pleased God to afford me much assistance, and there seemed to be a considerable effect on the hearers. In the evening, I felt a disposition to praise God for his goodness to me, that he had enabled me in some measure to be faithful; and my soul rejoiced to think, that I had thus performed the work of one day more, and was one day nearer my eternal, and I trust my heavenly home. O that I may be 'faithful to the death, fullfilling as an hireling my day,' till the shades of the evening of life shall free my soul from the toils of the day ! This evening in secret prayer, I felt exceedingly solemn, and such longing desires after deliverance from sin, and after conformity to God, as melted my heart. O I longed to be 'delivered from this body of death!' I felt inward, pleasing pain, that I could not be conformed to God entirely, fully, and forever. I scarce ever preach without being first visited with inward conflicts, and sore trials. Blessed be the Lord for these trials and distresses, as they are blessed for my humbling.

"*Oct.* 18. In the morning, I felt some sweetness, but still pressed through trials of soul. My life is a constant mixture of consolations and conflicts, and will be so till I arrive at the world of spirits.—Oct. 19. "This morning and last night, I felt a sweet longing in my soul after holiness. My soul seemed so to reach and stretch towards the mark of perfect sanctity, that it was ready to break with longings.—Oct. 20. Very infirm in body, exercised with much pain, and very lifeless in divine things. Felt a little sweetness in the evening.

"*Oct.* 21. Had a very deep sense of the vanity of the world most of the day ; had little more regard to it, than if I had been to go into eternity the next hour. Through divine goodness, I felt very serious and solemn.

O, I love to live on the brink of eternity, in my views and meditations! This gives me a sweet, awful, and reverential sense and apprehension of God and divine things, when I see myself, as it were, standing before the judgment seat of Christ.

"*Oct.* 22. Uncommonly weaned from the world to-day: my soul delighted to be a stranger and pilgrim on the earth; I felt a disposition in me never to have anything to do with this world. The character given of some of the ancient people of God, in Heb. xi. 13, was very pleasing to me, 'They confessed that they were pilgrims and strangers on the earth,' by their daily practice; and O that I could always do so! Spent some considerable time in a pleasant grove, in prayer and meditation. Oh it is sweet to be thus weaned from friends, and from myself, and dead to the present world, that so I may live wholly to and upon the blessed God! Saw myself little, low, and vile in myself. In the afternoon, preached at Bethlehem, from Deut. viii. 2. God helped me to speak to the hearts of dear Christians. Blessed be the Lord for this season: I trust they and I shall rejoice on this account, to all eternity. Dear Mr. Bellamy came in while I was making the first prayer, (being returned home from a journey;) and after meeting, we walked away together, and spent the evening in sweetly conversing on divine things, and praying together, with sweet and tender love to each other, and retired to rest with our hearts in a serious spiritual frame.

"*Oct.* 23. Somewhat perplexed and confused.—Rode this day from Bethlehem to Simsbury.—Lord's day, Oct. 24. Felt so vile and unworthy, that I scarce knew how to converse with human creatures.—Oct. 25. [At Turkey Hills.] In the evening, I enjoyed the divine presence, in secret prayer. It was a sweet and comfortable season to me; my soul longed for the living God: enjoyed in sweet solemnity of spirit, and longing desire after the recovery of the divine image in my soul. 'Then shall I be satisfied when I shall awake in God's likeness,' and never before.

"*Oct.* 26. [At West Suffield.] Underwent the most dreadful distresses, under a sense of my own unworthiness. It seemed to me, that I deserved rather to be driven out of the place, than to have anybody treat me with any kindness, or come to hear me preach. And verily my spirits were so depressed at this time, (as at many others,) that it was impossible I should treat immortal souls with faithfulness. I could not deal closely and faithfully with them, I felt so infinitely vile in myself. O what dust and ashes I am, to think of preaching the gospel to others! Indeed, I never can be faithful for one moment, but shall certainly 'daub with untempered mortar,' if God do not grant me special help. In the evening, I went to the meeting-house, and it looked to me near as easy for one to rise out of the grave and preach, as for me. However, God afforded me some life and power, both in prayer and sermon; and was pleased to lift me up, and show me that he could enable me to preach. O the wonderful good-ness of God to so vile a sinner! Returned to my quarters; and enjoyed some sweetness in prayer alone, and mourned that I could not live more to God.

"*Oct.* 27. I spent the forenoon in prayer and meditation; was not a little concerned about preaching in the afternoon; felt exceedingly with-out strength, and very helpless indeed; and went into the meeting-house, ashamed to see any come to hear such an unspeakable worthless wretch. However, God enabled me to speak with clearness, power, and pungency. But there was some noise and tumult in the assembly, that I did not well like; and I endeavored to bear public testimony against it with modera-tion and mildness through the current of my discourse. In the evening, was enabled to be in some measure thankful, and devoted to God."

During the several succeeding days we have a record like this: some seasons of dejection, mourning for being so des-titute of the exercises of grace, longing to be delivered from sin, pressing after more knowledge of God, seasons of sweet consolation, precious and intimate converse with God in se-cret prayer, sweetness of Christian conversation, etc. Rode from Suffield, to Eastbury, Hebron, and Lebanon.

"*Nov.* 4. [At Lebanon.] Saw much of my nothingness most of this day: but felt concerned that I had no more sense of my insufficiency and unworthiness. O it is sweet lying in the dust! But it is distressing to feel in my soul that hell of corruption, which still remains in me. In the afternoon, had a sense of the sweetness of a strict, close and constant devotedness to God, and my soul was comforted with his consolations. My soul felt a pleasing, yet painful concern, lest I should spend some moments without God. O may I always live to God! In the evening, I was visited by some friends, and spent the time in prayer, and such con-versation as tended to our edification. It was a comfortable season to my soul: I felt an intense desire to spend every moment for God. God is unspeakably gracious to me continually. In times past, he has given me inexpressible sweetness in the performance of duty. Frequently my soul has enjoyed much of God; but has been ready to say, 'Lord, it is good to be here;' and so to indulge sloth while I have lived on the sweetness of my feelings. But of late, God has been pleased to keep my soul hungry almost continually; so that I have been filled with a kind of pleasing pain. When I really enjoy God, I feel my desires of him the more insatiable, and my thirstings after holiness the more unquenchable: and the Lord will not allow me to feel as though were fully supplied and satisfied, but keeps me still reaching forward. I feel barren and empty, as though I could not live, without more of God; I feel ashamed and guilty before him. I see that 'the law is spiritual, but I am carnal.' I do not, I cannot live to God. Oh for holiness! O for more of God in my soul! Oh this pleasing pain! It makes my soul press after God; the language of it is, ' Then shall I be satisfied, when I awake in God's likeness,' but never, never before: and consequently, I am engaged to ' press towards the mark,' day by day. O that I may feel this continual hunger, and not be retarded, but rather animated by every cluster from Canaan, to reach forward in the narrow way, for the full enjoyment and possession of the heavenly inheritance! O that I may never loiter in my heavenly journey! "

These insatiable desires after God and holiness, continued the next two days, with a great sense of his own exceeding unworthiness, and the nothingness of the things of this world.

" *Lord's day, Nov.* 7. [At Millington.] It seemed as if such an unholy wretch as I never could arrive at that blessedness, to be " holy as God is holy." At noon, I longed for sanctification and conformity to God. O that is the all, the all. The Lord help me to press after God for ever.

" *Nov.* 8. Towards night, enjoyed much sweetness in secret prayer, so that my soul longed for an arrival in the heavenly country, the blessed paradise of God. Through divine goodness, I have scarce seen the day for two months, in which death has not looked so pleasant to me, at one time or other of the day, that I could have rejoiced that the present should be my last, notwithstanding my present inward trials and conflicts. I trust the Lord will finally make me a conqueror, and more than a conqueror; and that I shall be able to use that triumphant language, ' O death where is thy sting!' And, ' O grave, where is thy victory!'

During the next ten days, the following occurs: longing and wrestling to be holy, and to live to God; a desire that every single thought might be for God; feeling guilty, that his thoughts were no more swallowed up in God: sweet solemnity and calmness of mind; submission and resignation to God; great weanedness from the world; abasement in the dust; grief at some vain conversation that was observed; sweetness from time to time in secret prayer, and in conversing and praying with Christian friends. And every day he appears to have been greatly engaged in the great business of religion, and living to God, without interruption.

" *Nov.* 19. [At New-Haven.] Received a letter from the Rev. Mr. Pemberton, of New-York, desiring me speedily to go down thither, and

consult about the Indian affairs in those parts ; and to meet certain
gentlemen there who were intrusted with those affairs. My mind was instantly seized with concern ; so I retired with two or three Christian
friends, and prayed: and indeed, it was a sweet time with me. I was
enabled to leave myself, and all my concerns with God ; and taking leave
of friends, I rode to Ripton, and was comforted in an opportunity to see
and converse with dear Mr. Mills."

In the following days, he was oppressed with the weight
of that great affair, about which Mr. Pemberton had written
to him but was enabled to " cast his burden on the Lord," and
commit himself and all his concerns to him. He continued
still in a sense of the excellency of holiness, longings after it,
and earnest desires for the advancement of Christ's kingdom
in the world and had from time to time sweet comfort in
meditation and prayer.

" *Nov.* 24. Came to New-York ; felt still much concerned about the
importance of my business ; put up many earnest requests to God for his
help and direction; was confused with the noise and tumult of the city;
but enjoyed little time alone with God: but my soul longed after him.

" *Nov.* 25. Spent much time in prayer and supplication: was examined
by some gentlemen, of my Christian experiences, and my acquaintance
with divinity, and some other studies, in order to my improvement in that
important affair of evangelizing the Heathen;* and was made sensible of
my great ignorance and unfitness for public service, I had the most
abasing thoughts of myself, I think, that ever I had; I thought myself the
worst wretch that ever lived: it hurt me, and pained my very heart, that
anybody should show me any respect. Alas! methought how sadly they
are deceived in me! how miserably would they be disappointed if they
knew my inside! O my heart! And in this depressed condition, I was
forced to go and preach to a considerable assembly before some grave
and learned ministers ; but felt such a pressure from a sense of my vileness, ignorance and unfitness to appear in public, that I was almost overcome with it; my soul was grieved for the congregation; that they should
sit there to hear such a dead dog as I preach. I thought myself infinitely
indebted to the people, and longed that God would reward them with the
rewards of his grace. I spent much of the evening alone."

* The persons referred to, were the Correspondents in New-York, New-Jersey, and
Pennsylvania, of the Society in Scotland for propagating Christian knowledge ; to whom
was committed the management of their affairs in those parts, and who were now met at
New-York.

CHAPTER IV.

Conflicts, Delays, and final settling down to Work.

"*Nov.* 26, 1742. Had still a sense of my great vileness, and endeavored as much as I could to keep alone. O what a nothing, what dust and ashes am I ! Enjoyed some peace and comfort in spreading my complaints before the God of all grace.

"*Nov.* 27. Committed my soul to God with some degree of comfort; left New York about nine in the morning; came away with a distressing sense still of my unspeakable unworthiness. Surely I may well love all my brethren ; for none of them all is so vile as I: whatever they do outwardly, yet it seems to me none is so conscious of so much guilt before God. O my leanness, my barrenness; my carnality, and past bitterness, and want of a gospel temper! These things oppress my soul. Rode from New-York, thirty miles, to White Plains, and most of the way continued lifting up my heart to God for mercy and purifying grace: and spent the evening much dejected in spirit.

"*Dec.* 1. My soul breathed after God, in sweet spiritual and longing desires of conformity to him ; my soul was brought to rest itself and all, on his rich grace, and felt strength and encouragement to do or suffer any thing that divine providence should allot me. Rode about twenty miles from Stratfield to Newtown."

During the nine days following he went a journey from Newton to Haddam, his native town ; and after staying there some days, came to Southbury. In his account of the exercises of his mind, during this time, are such things as these : frequent turns of dejection ; a sense of his vileness, emptiness, and an unfathomable abyss of desperate wickedness in his heart, attended with a conviction that he had never seen but little of it ; bitterly mourning over his barrenness, being greatly grieved that he could not live to God, to whom he owed his all ten thousand times, crying out, " My leanness my leanness !" a sense of the meetness and suitableness of his lying in the dust beneath the feet of infinite majesty ;

fervency and ardor in prayer; longing to live to God; being afflicted with some impertinent, trifling conversation that he heard; but enjoying sweetness in Christian conversation.

"*Dec.* 11. Conversed with a dear friend, to whom I had thought of giving a liberal education, and being at the whole charge of it, that he might be fitted for the gospel ministry.* I acquainted him with my thoughts in that matter, and so left him to consider of it, till I should see him again. Then I rode to Bethlehem, came to Mr. Bellamy's lodgings, and spent the evening with him in sweet conversation and prayer. We recommended the concern of sending my friend to college to the God of all grace. Blessed be the Lord for this evening's opportunity together.

"*Lord's day, Dec.* 12. I felt, in the morning, as if I had little or no power either to pray or to preach; and felt a distressing need of divine help. I went to meeting trembling; but it pleased God to assist me in prayer and sermon. I think my soul scarce ever penetrated so far into the immaterial world, in any one prayer that I ever made, nor were my devotions ever so free from gross conceptions and imaginations framed from beholding material objects. I preached with some sweetness, from Matt. vi. 33. But seek ye first the kingdom of God, etc.; and in the afternoon, from Rom. xv. 30. And now I beseech you, brethren, etc. There was much affection in the assembly. This has been a sweet Sabbath to me; and blessed be God, I have reason to think that my religion is become more spiritual, by means of my late inward conflicts. Amen. May I aways be willing that God should use his own methods with me!

"*Dec.* 13. Joined in prayer with Mr. Bellamy; and found sweetness and composure in parting with him, as he went a journey. Enjoyed some sweetness through the day; and just at night rode down to Woodbury.

"*Dec.* 14. Some perplexity hung on my mind; I was distressed last night and this morning for the interest of Zion, especially on account of the false appearances of religion, that do but rather breed confusion, especially in some places. I cried to God for help, to enable me to bear testimony against those things, which, instead of promoting, do but hin-

* BRAINERD, having now undertaken the business of a missionary to the Indians, and expecting to spend the remainder of his life among them, and having some estate left him by his father, and thinking he should have no occasion for it among them, (though afterwards, as he told me, he found himself mistaken,—set himself to think which way he might spend it most for the glory of God; and no way presenting to his thoughts, wherein he could do more good with it, than by being at the charge of deucating some young man for the ministry, he fixed upon the person here spoken of. Accordingly he was soon put to learning; and BRAINERD continued to be at the charge of his education from year to year, so long as he lived, which was till he was carried through his third year in college.

der the progress of vital piety. In the afternoon, rode down to South-bury; and conversed again with my friend about the important affair of his pursuing the work of the ministry; and he appeared much inclined to devote himself to that work, if God should succeed his attempts to qualify himself for so great a work. In the evening I preached from I Thess. IV. 8. He therefore that despiseth, etc, and endeavored, though with tenderness, to undermine false religion. The Lord gave me some assistance; but, however, I seemed so vile, I was ashamed to be seen when I came out of the meeting-house.

"*Dec.* 15. Enjoyed something of God to-day, both in secret and in social prayer; but was sensible of much barrenness and defect in duty, as well as my inability to help myself for the time to come, or to perform the work and business I have to do. Afterwards, felt much of the sweet-ness of religion, and the tenderness of the gospel-temper. I found a dear love to all mankind, and was much afraid lest some motion of anger or resentment should, some time or other, creep into my heart. Had some comforting, soul-refreshing discourse with dear friends, just as we took our leave of each other; and supposed it might be likely we should not meet again till we came to the eternal world.* I doubt not, through grace, but that some of us shall have a happy meeting there, and bless God for this season, as well as many others. Amen.

"*Dec.* 16. Rode down to Derby; and had some sweet thoughts on the road; especially on the essence of our salvation by Christ, from these words, Thou shalt call his name Jesus, etc.—Dec. 17. Spent much time in sweet conversation on spiritual things with dear Mr. Humphreys. Rode to Ripton; spent some time in prayer with dear Christian friends. —Dec. 18. Spent much time in prayer in the woods; and seemed raised above the things of the world: my soul was strong in the Lord of hosts; but was sensible of great barrenness.

"*Lord's day, Dec.* 19. At the sacrament of the Lord's supper I seemed strong in the Lord; and the world, with all its frowns and flatteries, in a great measure disappeared, so that my soul had nothing to do with them; and I felt a disposition to be wholly and for ever the Lord's. In the evening enjoyed something of the divine presence; had a humbling sense of my vileness, barrenness and sinfulness. Oh, it wounded me to think of the misimprovement of time! God be merciful to me a sinner.—Dec. 20. Spent this day in prayer, reading, and writing; and enjoyed some assistance, especially in correcting some thoughts on a certain subject; but had a mournful sense of my barrenness.

---

* It had been determined by the Commissioners, that he should go to the Indians living near the Forks of Delaware river and on Susquehannah river. Pa; which being far off, and where he would be exposed to many hardships and dangers, was the occasion of his taking leave of his friends in this manner.

"*Dec.* 21. Had a sense of my insufficiency for any public work and business, as well as to live to God. I rode over to Derby, and preached there. It pleased God to give me very sweet assistance and enlargement, and to enable me to speak with a soft, tender power and energy. We had afterwards a comfortable evening in singing and prayer. God enabled me to pray with as much spirituality and sweetness as I have done for some time; my mind seemed to be unclothed of sense and imagination, and was in a measure let into the immaterial world of spirits. This day was, I trust, through infinite goodness, made very profitable to a number of us, to advance our souls in holiness and conformity to God ; the glory be to him for ever. Amen. How blessed is it to grow more and more like God.

"*Dec.* 22. Enjoyed some assistance in preaching at Ripton ; but my soul mourned within me for my barrenness.—Dec. 23. Enjoyed, I trust, the presence of God this morning in secret. Oh, how divinely sweet is it to come into the secret of his presence, and abide in his pavilion!—Took an affectionate leave of friends, not expecting to see them again for a very considerable time, if ever in this world. Rode with Mr. Humphreys to his house in Derby; spent the time in sweet conversation; my soul was refreshed and sweetly melted with divine things. Oh that I was always consecrated to God! Near night, I rode to New-Haven, and there enjoyed some sweetness in prayer and conversation, with some dear Christian friends. My mind was sweetly serious and composed; but alas! I too much lost the sense of divine things.

"*Lord's Day, Dec.* 26. Felt much sweetness and tenderness in prayer, especially my whole soul seemed to love my worst enemies, and was enabled to pray for those that are strangers and enemies to God, with a great degree of softness and pathetic fervor. In the evening rode from New-Haven to Brantford, after I had kneeled down and prayed with a number of dear Christian friends in a very retired place in the woods, and so parted.

"*Dec.* 27. Enjoyed a precious season indeed; had a sweet melting sense of divine things, of the pure spirituality of the religion of Christ Jesus. In the evening, I preached from Matt. vi . 33. 'But seek ye first,' etc., with much freedom, and sweet power and pungency: the presence of God attended our meeting. Oh, the sweetness, the tenderness I felt in my soul! If ever I felt the temper of Christ, I had some sense of it now. Blessed be my God, I have seldom enjoyed a more comfortable and profitable day than this. Oh, that I could spend all my time for God!—Dec. 28. Rode from Brantford to Haddam. In the morning my clearness and sweetness in divine things continued : but afterwards my spiritual life sensibly declined."

The next twelve days, he was for the most part extremely dejected, and distressed and was evidently very much under the power of melancholy.   There are from day to day most bitter complaints of exceeding vileness, and corruption ; an amazing load of guilt, unworthiness, even to creep on God's earth, everlasting uselessness, fitness for nothing, etc. and sometimes expressions even of horror at the thoughts of ever preaching again.   But yet, in this time of great dejection, he speaks of several intervals of divine help and comfort.

"*Jan.* 14, 1743.   My spiritual conflicts to-day were unspeakably dreadful, heavier than the mountains and overflowing floods.   I seemed inclosed, as it were, in hell itself ; I was deprived of all sense of God, even of the being of a God ; and that was my misery.   I had no awful apprehension of God as angry.   This was distress, the nearest akin to the damned's torments, that I ever endured : their torment, I am sure, will consist much in a privation of God, and consequently of all good.   This taught me the absolute dependence of a creature upon God the Creator, for every crumb of happiness it enjoys.   Oh, I feel that, if there is no God, though I might live for ever here, and enjoy not only this, but all other worlds. I should be ten thousand times more miserable than a reptile.   My soul was in such anguish I could not eat ; but felt as I suppose a poor wretch would that is just going to the place of execution.   I was almost swallowed up with anguish, when I saw people gathering together to hear me preach.   However, I went in that distress to the house of God, and found not much relief in the first prayer : it seemed as if God would let loose the people upon me to destroy me ; nor were the thoughts of death distressing to me, like my own vileness.   But afterwards in my discourse from Deut. viii. 2. God was pleased to give me some freedom and enlargement, some power and spirituality ; and I spent the evening somewhat comfortably."

"*Jan.* 19.   [At Canterbury.]   In the afternoon preached a lecture at the Meeting-house ; felt some tenderness, and somewhat of the gospel temper ; exhorted the people to love one another, and not to set up their own frames as a standard by which to try all their brethren.   But was much oppressed, most of the day, with a sense of my own badness, inward impurity, and unspeakable corruption.   Spent the evening in tender, Christian conversation.—Jan. 20.   Rode to my brother's house between Norwich and Lebanon ; and preached in the evening to a number of people : enjoyed neither freedom nor spirituality, but saw myself exceeding unworthy.—Jan. 21.   Had great inward conflicts ; enjoyed but little comfort.   Went to see Mr. Williams of Lebanon, and spent several hours with him; and was greatly delighted with his serious, deliberate, and impartial way of discourse about religion.

"*Lord's Day Jan.* 23. I scarce ever felt myself so unfit to exist as now : saw I was not worthy of a place among the Indians, where I am going, if God permit : thought I should be ashamed to look them in the face, and much more to have any respect shown me there. Indeed I felt myself banished from the earth, as if all places were too good for such a wretch. I thought I should be ashamed to go among the very savages of Africa; I appeared to myself a creature fit for nothing, neither heaven nor earth. None know, but those who feel it, what the soul endures that is sensibly shut out from the presence of God : alas ! it is more bitter than death.

"*Jan. 26.* Preached to a pretty large assembly at Mr. Fish's meeting house : insisted on humility and steadfastness in keeping God's commands; and that through humility we should prefer one another in love, and not make our own frame the rule by which we judge others. I felt sweetly calm, and full of brotherly love : and never more free from party spirit. I hope some good will follow; that Christians will be freed from false joy, and party zeal, and censuring one another."

On Thursday, after considerable time spent in prayer and Christian conversation, he rode to New London.

"*Jan. 28.* Here I found some fallen into extravagancies; too much carried away with a false zeal and bitterness. O, the want of a gospel temper is greatly to be lamented. Spent the evening in conversing about some points of conduct in both ministers and private Christians; but did not agree with them. God had not taught them with briars and thorns to be of a kind disposition towards mankind."

On Saturday he went to East-Haddam, and spent some days there during which he speaks of feeling weanedness from the world, a sense of the nearness of eternity, special assistance in praying for the enlargement of Christ's kingdom, times of spiritual comfort, etc.

"*Feb. 2.* Preached my farewell sermon last night, at the house of an aged man, who had been unable to attend on the public worship for some time. This morning spent the time in prayer, almost wherever I went; and having taken leave of friends I set out on my journey towards the Indians; though I was to spend some time at East-Hampton, Long Island, by leave of the commissioners who employed me in the Indian affair;* and being accompanied by

* The winter was not adjudged to be a convenient season to go out into the wilderness, and enter on the hardships to which he must there be exposed.

a messenger from East-Hampton, we travelled to Lyme. On the road I felt an uncommon pressure of mind; I seemed to struggle hard for some pleasure in something here below, and seemed loth to give up all for gone; saw I was evidently throwing myself into all hardships and distresses in my present undertaking, I thought it would be less difficult to lie down in the grave; but yet I chose to go, rather than stay. Came to Lyme that night."

He waited the next two days for a passage over the sound and spent much of the time in inward conflicts and dejection, but had some comfort. On Saturday he crossed the sound and travelled to East-Hampton. And the seven following days he spent there, for the most part, under extreme dejection and gloominess of mind with great complaints of darkness, ignorance, etc. Yet his heart appears to have been constantly engaged in the great business of religion, much concerned for the interest of religion in East Hampton, and praying and laboring much for it.

"*Feb. 12.* Enjoyed a little more comfort; was enabled to meditate with some composure of mind; and especially in the evening, found my soul more refreshed in prayer, than at any time of late; my soul seemed to 'take hold of God's strength,' and was comforted with his consolations. O, how sweet are some glimpses of divine glory! how strengthening and quickening!

"*Lord's day, Feb. 13.* At noon, under a great degree of discouragement; knew not how it was possible for me to preach in the afternoon. I was ready to give up all for gone; but God was pleased to assist me in some measure. In the evening my heart was sweetly drawn out after God, and devoted to him.

"*Feb. 15.* Early in the day I felt some comfort; afterwards I walked into a neighboring grove, and felt more as a stranger on earth, I think, than ever before; dead to any of the enjoyments of the world, as if I had been dead in a natural sense. In the evening had divine sweetness in secret duty; God was then my portion, and my soul rose above those deep waters, into which I have sunk so low of late. My soul then cried for Zion, and had sweetness in so doing.

"*Feb. 17.* In the morning, found myself comfortable, and rested on God in some measure.—Preached this day at a little village belonging to East-Hampton; and God was pleased to give me his gracious presence and assistance, so that I spake with freedom, boldness, and some power. In the evening spent some time with a dear Christian friend; and felt serious, as on the brink of eternity. My soul enjoyed sweetness in lively apprehension of standing before the glorious God: prayed with my dear friend with sweetness, and discoursed with the utmost solemnity. And, truly it was a little emblem of heaven itself.—I find my soul is more refined and weaned from a dependence on my frames and spiritual feelings.

" *Feb.* 18. Felt somewhat sweetly most of the day, and found access to the throne of grace. Blessed be the Lord for any intervals of heavenly delight and composure, while I am engaged in the field of battle. Oh, that I might be serious, solemn, and always vigilant, while in an evil world ! Had some opportunity alone to-day, and found some freedom in study. O, I long to live to God !

" *Feb.* 19. Was exceeding infirm to-day, greatly troubled with pain in my head and dizziness, scarce able to sit up. However, enjoyed something of God in prayer, and performed some necessary studies. I exceedingly longed to die ; and yet, through divine goodness, have felt very willing to live, for two or three days past.

" *Lord's day, Feb.* 20. I was perplexed on account of my carelessness ; thought I could not be suitably concerned about the important work of the day, and so was restless with my easiness. Was exceeding infirm again to-day ; but the Lord strengthened me, both in the outward and inward man, so that I preached with some life and spirituality, especially in the afternoon, wherein I was enabled to speak closely against selfish religion ; that loves Christ for his benefits, but not for himself."

During the next fortnight, it appears that for the most part he enjoyed much spiritual peace and comfort. In his diary are expressed such things as these : mourning over indwelling sin, and unprofitableness ; deadness to the world ; longing after God, and to live to his glory ; heart melting desires after his eternal home ; fixed reliance on God for his help ; experience of much divine assistance, both in the private and public exercises of religion ; inward strength and courage in the service of God ; very frequent refreshment, consolation, and divine sweetness in meditation, prayer, preaching, and Christian conversation. And it appears by his account, that this space of time was filled up with great diligence and earnestness in serving God, in study, prayer, meditation, preaching and privately instructing and counselling.

" *March* 7. This morning when I arose, I found my heart go forth after God in longing desires of conformity to him, and in secret prayer found myself sweetly quickened and drawn out in praises to God for all he had done to and for me, and for all my inward trials and distresses of late. My heart ascribed glory, glory, glory to the blessed God! and bid welcome to all inward distress again, if God saw meet to exercise me with it. Time appeared but an inch long, and eternity at hand ; and I thought I could with patience and cheerfulness bear anything for the cause of God ; for I saw that a moment would bring me to a world of peace and blessedness. My soul, by the strength of the Lord, rose far above this lower world, and all the vain amusements and frightful disappointments of it. Afterwards, had some sweet meditation on Genesis v. 24. ' And Enoch walked with God,' etc. This was a comfortable day to my soul.

" *March.* 9. Endeavored to commit myself, and all my concerns to God. Rode sixteen miles to Montauk,* and had some inward sweetness on the road; but somewhat of flatness and deadness after I came there and had seen the Indians. I withdrew and endeavored to pray, but found myself awfully deserted and left, and had an afflicting sense of my vileness and meanness. However, I went and preached from Is. liii. 10. ' Yet it pleased the Lord to bruise him,' etc. Had some assistance ; and I trust somewhat of the divine presence was among us. In the evening, I again prayed and exhorted among them, after having had a season alone, wherein I was so pressed with the blackness of my nature, that I thought it was not fit for me to speak so much as to Indians."

The next day he returned to East Hampton ; was exceeding infirm in body, through the remaining part of the week but had assistance and enlargment in study and religious exercises, and inward sweetness, and breathing after God.

" *Lord's day March* 13. At noon, I thought it impossible for me to preach, by reason of bodily weakness, and inward deadness. In the first prayer, I was so weak that I could hardly stand ; but in the sermon God strengthened me, so that I spake near an hour and a half with sweet freedom, clearness, and some tender power from Gen. v. 24. ' And Enoch walked with God.' I was sweetly assisted to insist on a close walk with God, and to leave this as my parting advice to God's people here, that they should walk with God. May the God of all grace succeed my poor labors in this place '

" *March* 14. In the morning was very busy in preparation for my journey, and was almost continually engaged in ejaculatory prayer. About ten, took leave of the dear people of East-Hampton; my heart grieved and mourned, and rejoiced at the same time ; rode near fifty miles to a

---

* Montauk is in the east end of Long-Island, and was then inhabited chiefly by Indians.

part of Brook-Haven, and lodged there, and had refreshing conversation with a Christian friend."

In two days more, he reached New York ; but complains of much desertion and deadness on the road. He stayed one day in New York, and on Friday went to Mr. Dickinson's at Elizabeth Town. His complaints are the same as on the two preceding days.

"*March* 19. Was bitterly distressed under a sense of my ignorance. darkness, and unworthiness ; got alone, and poured out my complaint to God in the bitterness of my soul. In the afternoon, rode to Newark, and had some sweetness in conversation with Mr. Burr,* and in praying together. O blessed be God for ever and ever for any enlivening and quickening seasons.

"*Lord's day, March* 20. Preached in the forenoon : God gave me some assistance and sweetness, and enabled me to speak with real tenderness, love and impartiality. In the evening preached again ; and of a truth, God was pleased to assist a poor worm. Blessed be God, I was enabled to speak with life, power, and desire of the edification of God's people, and with some power to sinners. In the evening, I felt spiritual and watchful, lest my heart should by any means be drawn away from God. O when shall I come to that blessed world, where every power of my soul will be incessantly and eternally wound up in heavenly employments and enjoyments, to the highest degree ! "

On Monday, he went to Woodbridge, where he speaks of his being with a number of ministers ;† and, the day following of his travelling part of the way towards New York. On Wednesday, he came to New York. On Thursday he rode near fifty miles, from New York to North Castle. On Friday, went to Danbury. Saturday to New Milford. On the Sabbath he rode five or six miles to the place near Kent in Connecticut, called Scaticocke, where dwell a number of Indians,‡ and preached to them. On Monday being detained by the rain, he tarried at Kent. On Tuesday, he rode from Kent to

---

* Afterwards President Burr, of Nassau Hall or Princeton College.

† These ministers were the *Correspondents* who now met at Woodbridge, and gave Brainerd new directions. Instead of sending him to the Indians at the Forks at Delaware, as before intended, they ordered him to go to the Indians at Kaunaumeek; a place in the province of New York, in the woods between Stockbridge and Albany.

‡ The same Indians which he mentions in his Diary, August 12, 1742.

Salisbury. Wednesday, he went to Sheffield. Thursday, March 31, he went to Mr. Sergeant's at Stockbridge. He was dejected and very disconsolate, through the main of this journey from New Jersey to Stockbridge; and especially on the last day his mind was overwhelmed with peculiar gloom and melancholy.

CHAPTER V.

A year at Kaunaumeek.—Life in the Wilderness among Savages.—Travels, Trials, Tribulations and Triumphs.—Ordination by Presbytery at Newark, N. J.—Leaves Kaunaumeek on a Journey to New England.

"*April* 1, 1743. I rode to Kaunaumeek, near twenty miles from Stockbridge, where the Indians live with whom I am concerned, and there lodged on a little heap of straw. I was greatly exercised with inward trials and distresses all day; and in the evening, my heart was sunk, and I seemed to have no God to go to. Oh that God would help me!"

The next five days, he was for the most part in a dejected, depressed state of mind, and sometimes extremely so. He speaks of God's "waves and billows rolling over his soul;" and of his being ready sometimes to say, "Surely his mercy is clean gone forever, and he will be favorable no more;" and says, the anguish he endured, was nameless and inconceivable; but at the same time speaks thus concerning his distresses, "What God designs by all my distresses, I know not; but this I know, I deserve them all, and thousands more." He gives an account of the Indians kindly receiving him, and being seriously attentive to his instructions.

"*April* 7. Appeared to myself exceedingly ignorant, weak, helpless, unworthy, and altogether unequal to my work. It seemed to me, that I should never do any service, or have any success among the Indians. My soul was weary of my life; I longed for death, beyond measure. When I thought of any godly soul departed, my soul was ready to envy him his privilege, thinking, 'O when will my turn come? must it be years first?' But I know these ardent desires, at this and other times, rose partly for want of resignation to God under all miseries; and so were but impatience. Towards night, I had the exercise of faith in prayer, and some assistance in writing. Oh that God would keep me near him!

"*April* 8. Was exceedingly pressed under a sense of my pride, selfishness, bitterness, and party spirit, in times past, while I attempted to promote the cause of God. Its vile nature and dreadful consequences appeared in such odious colors to me, that my very heart was pained. I saw how poor souls stumbled over it into everlasting destruction, that I was constrained to make that prayer in the bitterness of my soul, 'O Lord, deliver me from blood-guiltiness.' I saw my desert of hell on this account. My soul was full of inward anguish and shame before God that I had spent so much time in conversation tending only to promote a party-spirit. I saw that I had not suitably prized mortification, self-denial, resignation under all adversities, meekness, love, candor, and holiness of heart and life; and this day was almost wholly spent in such bitter, and soul-afflicting reflections on my past frames and conduct. Of late, I have thought much of having the kingdom of Christ advanced in the world; but now I saw I had enough to do within myself. The Lord be merciful to me a sinner, and wash my soul!

"*April* 9. Remained much in the same state as yesterday, excepting that the sense of my vileness was not so quick and acute.

"*Lord's day, April* 10. Rose early in the morning, and walked out and spent a considerable time in the woods, in prayer and meditation. Preached to the Indians, both forenoon and afternoon. They behaved soberly in general; two or three in particular appeared under some religious concern; with whom I discoursed privately; and one told me, 'that her heart had cried, ever since she had heard me preach first.'

"*April* 12. Was greatly oppressed with grief and shame, reflecting on my past conduct, my bitterness and party zeal. I was ashamed, to think that such a wretch as I had ever preached. Longed to be excused from that work. And when my soul was not in anguish and keen distress, 'I felt senseless as a beast before God,' and felt a kind of guilty amusement with the least trifles; which still maintained a kind of stifled horror of conscience, so that I could not rest any more than a condemned malefactor.

"*April* 13. My heart was overwhelmed within me! I verily thought that I was the meanest, vilest, most helpless, guilty, ignorant, benighted creature living. And yet I knew what God had done for my soul, at the same time, though sometimes I was assaulted with damping doubts and fears, whether it was impossible for such a wretch as I to be in a state of grace.—April 15. In the forenoon, very disconsolate. In the afternoon, preached to my people, and was a little encouraged in some hopes that God might bestow mercy on their souls. Felt somewhat resigned to God under all dispensations of his providence.

"*April* 16. Still in the depths of distress. In the afternoon, preached to my people; but was more discouraged with them than before; feared that nothing would ever be done for them to any happy effect. I retired, and poured out my soul to God for mercy; but without any sensible relief.

Soon after came an Irishman and a Dutchman, with a design, as they said to hear me preach the next day; but none can tell how I felt, to hear their profane talk. O I longed that some dear Christian knew my distress. I got into a kind of hovel, and there groaned out my complaint to God; and withal felt more sensible gratitude and thankfulness to God, that he had made me to differ from these men, as I knew through grace he had.

"*Lord's day April,* 17. In the morning, was again distressed as soon as I awaked, hearing much talk about the world, and the things of it. I perceived that the men were in some measure afraid of me; and I discoursed about sanctifying the Sabbath, if possible to solemnize their minds; but when they were at a little distance, they again talked freely about secular affairs. O I thought what a hell it would be, to live with such men to eternity! The Lord gave me some assistance in preaching, all day, and some resignation, and a small degree of comfort in prayer, at night.

"*April* 19. In the morning, I enjoyed some sweet repose and rest in God; felt some strength and confidence in him; and my soul was in some measure refreshed and comforted. Spent most of the day in writing, and had some exercise of grace, sensible and comfortable. My soul seemed lifted above the deep waters, wherein it has been so long almost drowned; felt some spiritual longings and breathings of soul after God; and found myself engaged for the advancement of Christ's kingdom in my own soul.

"*April* 20. Set apart this day for fasting and prayer, to bow my soul before God for the bestowment of divine grace; especially that all my spiritual afflictions, and inward distresses might be sanctified to my soul. And endeavored also to remember the goodness of God to me the year past, this day being my birthday. Having obtained help of God, I have hitherto lived, and am now arrived at the age of twenty-five years. My soul was pained to think of my barrenness and deadness; that I have lived so little to the glory of the eternal God. I spent the day in the woods alone, and there poured out my complaint to God. Oh that God would enable me to live to his glory for the future!

"*April* 21. Spent the forenoon in reading and prayer, and found myself engaged; but still much depressed in spirit under a sense of my vileness, and unfitness for any public service. In the afternoon, I visited my people, and prayed and conversed with some about their souls' concerns! and afterwards found some ardor of soul in secret prayer. O that I might grow up into the likeness of God!

"*April* 22. Spent the day in study, reading, and prayer; and felt a little relieved of my burden, that has been so heavy of late. But still was in some measure oppressed; and had a sense of barrenness. O my leanness testifies against me ! my very soul abhors itself for its unlikeness to God, its inactivity and sluggishness. When I have done all, alas, what an unprofitable servant am I ! My soul groans to see the hours of the day roll away, because I do not fill them in spirituality and heavenly-minded-ness. And yet I long that they should speed their pace, to hasten me to my eternal home, where I may fill up all my moments, through eternity, for God and his glory."

On Saturday and Sunday, his melancholy again pre-vailed ; he complained of his ignorance, stupidity, and sense-lessness ; while yet he seems to have spent the time with the utmost diligence, in study, in prayer, in instructing and counseling the Indians. On Monday, he sunk into the deepest melancholy ; so that he supposed he never spent a day in such distress in his life ; not in fears of hell (which, he says, he had no pressing fear of) but a distressing sense of his own vileness. On Tuesday, he had some relief. Wednesday, he kept as a day of fasting and prayer, but in great distress. The three days next following, his mel-ancholy continued, but in a less degree, and with intervals of comfort. On the last of these days, he wrote the follow-ing letter to his brother John, then a student at Yale Col-lege.

" KAUNAUMEEK, *April* 30, 1743.
" DEAR BROTHER :

" I should tell you, ' I long to see you,' but my own experience has taught me, that there is no happiness, and plenary satisfaction to be en-joyed in earthly friends, though ever so near and dear, or in any other en-joyment, that is not God himself. Therefore, if the God of all grace be pleased graciously to afford us each his presence and grace, that we may perform the work, and endure the trials he calls us to, in a most distress-ing tiresome wilderness, till we arrive at our journey's end ; the local dis-tance, at which we are held from each other, at present is a matter of no great moment or importance to either of us. But alas ! the presence of God is what I want. I live in the most lonely melancholy desert, about eighteen miles from Albany ; for it was not thought best that I should go to Delaware River, as I believe I hinted to you in a letter from New-York, I board with a poor Scotchman ; his wife can talk scarce any English. My diet consists mostly of hasty-pudding, boiled corn, and bread baked in the ashes, and sometimes a little meat and butter. My lodging is a little heap of straw, laid upon some boards a little way from the ground; for it is a log room, without any floor, that I lodge in. My work is exceedingly hard and difficult; I travel on foot a mile and a half, the worst of ways, almost daily, and back again; for I live so far from my Indians. I have not seen an English person this month. These and many other circumstances, equally uncomfortable, attend me; and yet my spiritual conflicts and distresses, so far exceed all these, that I scarce think of them, or hardly observe that I am not entertained in the most sumptuous manner. The Lord grant that I may learn to 'endure hardness, as a good soldier of Jesus Christ!'

"As to my success here, I cannot say much as yet. The Indians seem generally kind, and well disposed towards me, are mostly very attentive to my instructions, and seem willing to be taught further. Two or three, I hope, are under some convictions ; but there seems to be little of the special workings of the divine Spirit among them yet; which gives me many a heart-sinking hour. Sometimes I hope that God has abundant blessings in store for them and me ; but at other times I am so overwhelmed with distress, that I cannot see how his dealings with me are consistent with covenant love and faithfulness: and I say, 'Surely his tender mercies are clean gone for ever.' But however, I see that I needed all this chastisement already : 'It is good for me,' that I have endured these trials, and have hitherto little or no apparent success. Do not be discouraged by my distresses. I was under great distress, at Mr. Pomroy's, when I saw you last; but 'God has been with me of a truth,' since that: he helped me sometimes sweetly at Long-Island, and elsewhere. But let us always remember, that we must through much tribulation, enter into God's eternal kingdom of rest and peace. The righteous are scarcely saved: it is an infinite wonder that we have well grounded hopes of being saved at all. For my part, I feel the most vile of any creature living ; and I am sure sometimes, there is not such another existing on this side hell. Now all you can do for me, is, to pray incessantly that God would make me humble, holy, resigned, and heavenly minded, by all my trials. 'Be strong in the Lord, and in the power of his might.' Let us run, wrestle, and fight, that we may win the prize, and obtain that complete happiness, to be 'holy, as God is holy.' So wishing and praying that you may advance in learning and grace, and be fit for special service for God, I remain your affectionate brother,

" DAVID BRAINERD.

"*Lord's day, May* 1. Was at Stockbridge to-day. In the forenoon, had some relief and assistance; though not so much as usual. In the afternoon, felt poorly in body and soul; while I was preaching, seemed to be rehearsing idle tales, without the least life, fervor, sense or comfort; and especially afterwards at the sacrament, my soul was filled with confusion, and the utmost anguish that ever I endured, under the feeling of my inexpressible vileness and meanness. It was a most bitter and distressing season to me, by reason of the view I had of my own heart, and the secret abominations that lurk there; I thought that the eyes of all in the house were upon me, and I dared not look any one in the face; for it verily seemed as if they saw the vileness of my heart, and all the sins I had ever been guilty of. And if I had been banished from the presence of all mankind, never to be seen any more, or so much as thought of, still I should have been distressed with shame; and I should have been ashamed to see the most barbarous people on earth, because I was viler, and seemingly more brutishly ignorant than they. 'I am made to possess the sins of my youth.'

"*May* 10. Was in the same state, as to my mind, that I have been in for some time; extremely oppressed with a sense of guilt, pollution, and blindness: 'The iniquity of my heels hath compassed me about: the sins of my youth have been set in order before me; they have gone over my head, as a heavy burden, too heavy for me to bear.' Almost all the actions of my life past, seem to be covered over with sin and guilt; and those of them that I performed in the most conscientious manner, now fill me with shame and confusion, that I cannot hold up my face. O, the pride, selfishness, hypocrisy, ignorance, bitterness, party zeal and the want of love, candor, meekness, and gentleness, that have attended my attempts to promote religion and virtue; and this when I have reason to hope I had real assistance from above, and some sweet intercourse from heaven! But alas, what corrupt mixtures attended my best duties!"

The next seven days, his gloom and distress continued for the most part, but he had some turns of relief and spiritual comfort. He gives an account of his spending part of this time in hard labor, to build himself a little cottage to live in amongst the Indians, in which he might be by himself; having, it seems hitherto lived with a poor Scotchman, as he observes in the letter just now given; and afterwards, before his own house was habitable, he lived in a wigwam among the Indians.

"*May* 18. My circumstances are such, that I have no comfort of any kind, but what I have in God. I live in the most lonesome wilderness; have but one single person to converse with that can speak English.*

---

* This was his interpreter, an ingenious young Indian, belonging to Stockbridge, whose name was John Wanwaumpequunnaunt. He had been instructed in the Christian religion, by Mr. Sergeant: had lived with the Rev. Mr. Williams, of Long Meadow, and been instructed by him, and understood both English and Indian very well, and wrote a good hand.

Most of the talk I hear, is either Highland Scotch, or Indian. I have no fellow-Christian to whom I may unbosom myself, or lay open my spiritual sorrows; with whom I may take sweet counsel in conversation about heavenly things, and join in social prayer. I live poorly with regard to the comforts of life: most of my diet consists of boiled corn, hasty-pudding, etc. I lodge on a bundle of straw, my labor is hard and extremely difficult, and I have little appearance of success, to comfort me. The Indians have no land to live on, but what the Dutch people lay claim to; and these threaten to drive them off. They have no regard to the souls of the poor Indians; and by what I can learn, they hate me because I come to preach to them. But that which makes all my difficulties grievous to be borne, is, that God hides his face from me.

"*May* 19. Spent most of this day in close study: but was sometimes so distressed that I could think of nothing but my spiritual blindness, ignorance, pride, and misery. O I have reason to make that prayer, 'Lord, forgive my sins of youth, and former trespasses.'

"*May* 20. Was much perplexed some part of the day; but towards night, had some comfortable meditations on Is. xl. 1. Comfort ye, Comfort ye, etc., and enjoyed some sweetness in prayer. Afterwards, my soul rose so far above the deep waters, that I dared to rejoice in God. I saw that there was sufficient matter of consolation in the blessed God."

The next nine days, his burdens were for the most part alleviated, but with variety; at some times, having considerable consolation; and at others, being more depressed. The next day, he set out on a journey to New Jersey, to consult the commissioners who employed him about the affairs of his mission.* He journey in four days; and arrived at Mr. Burr's in Newark on Thursday. In great part of his journey, he was in the depths of melancholy, under distresses like those already mentioned. On Friday, he rode to Elizabethtown; and on Saturday to New York; and from thence on his way homewards as far as White Plains. There he spent the Sabbath, and had considerable degrees of divine consolation and assistance in public services. On Monday, he rode about sixty miles to New Haven. There he attempted a reconciliation with the Faculty of the college; and spent

---

* His business with the commissioners now was, to obtain orders for them to set up a school among the Indians at Kaunaumeek, and that his interpreter might be appointed the schoolmaster, which was accordingly done.

this week in visiting his friends in those parts, and in his journey homewards, till Saturday, in a pretty comfortable frame of mind. On Saturday, in his way from Stockbridge to Kaunaumeek, he was lost in the woods, and lay all night in the open air; but happily found his way in the morning, and came to his Indians on Lord's day, June 12, and had greater assistance in preaching among them than ever before, since his first coming among them.

From this time forward he was the subject of various frames and exercises of mind: in the general, much after the same manner as hitherto, from his first coming to Kaunaumeek till he got into his own house, (a little hut, which he made chiefly with his own hands, by long and hard labor,) which was near seven weeks from this time. The great part of this time, he was dejected and depressed with melancholy; sometimes extremely; his melancholy operating in like manner as related in times past. How it was with him in those dark seasons, he himself further describes in his diary for July 2, in the following manner :—

"My soul is, and has for a long time been in a piteous condition, wading through a series of sorrows, of various kinds. I have been so crushed down sometimes with a sense of my meanness and infinite unworthiness, that I have been ashamed that any, even the meanest of my fellow-creatures, should so much as spend a thought about me ; and have wished sometimes, while traveling among the thick brakes, to drop, as one of them, into everlasting oblivion. In this case, sometimes I have almost resolved never again to see any of my acquaintance : and really thought, I could not do it and hold up my face ; and have longed for the remotest region, for a retreat from all my friends, that I might not be seen or heard of any more. Sometimes the consideration of my ignorance has been a means of my great distress and anxiety. And especially my soul has been in anguish with fear, shame, and guilt, that ever I had preached, or had any thought that way. Sometimes my soul has been in distress on feeling some particular corruptions rise and swell like a mighty torrent, with present violence! having, at the same time, ten thousand former sins and follies presented to view, in all their blackness and aggravations. And these, while destitute of most of the conveniences of life, and I may say, of all the pleasures of it; without a friend to communicate any of my sorrows to, and sometimes without **any place** of retirement, where I may unburden my soul before God, which has greatly contributed to my distress. Of late, more especially, my great difficulty has been a sort of carelessness, a kind of regardless temper of mind, whence I have been disposed to indolence and trifling : and this temper of mind has constantly been attended with guilt and shame ; so that sometimes I have been in a kind of horror, to find myself so unlike the blessed God. I have thought I grew worse under all my trials ; and nothing has cut and wounded my soul more than this. O, if I am one of God's chosen, as I trust through infinite grace I am, I find of a truth, that the righteous are scarcely saved."

It is apparent, that one main occasion of that distressing gloominess of mind which he was so much exercised with at Kaunaumeek, was reflection on his past errors and misguided zeal at college, in the beginning of the late religious commotions. And therefore he repeated his endeavors this year for reconciliation with the governors of the college, whom he had at that time offended. Although he had been at New Haven, in June, this year, and attempted a reconciliation, as mentioned already ; yet, in the beginning of July, he made another journey thither, and renewed his attempt, but still in vain.

Although he was much dejected, most of the time, yet he had many intermissions of his melancholy, and some seasons of comfort, sweet tranquility and resignation of mind, and frequent special assistance in public services, as appears in his diary. The manner of his relief from his sorrow, once in particular, is worthy to be mentioned in his own words.

"*July* 25. Had little or no resolution for a life of holiness ; was ready almost to renounce my hopes of living to God. And O how dark it looked, to think of being unholy for ever ! This I could not endure. The cry of my soul was, Psal. lxv. 3. Iniquities prevail against me. But I was in some measure relieved by a comfortable meditation on God's eternity, that he never had a beginning. Whence I was led to admire his greatness and power, in such a manner, that I stood still, and praised the Lord for his own glories and perfections ; though I was (and if I should for ever be) an unholy creature, my soul was comforted to apprehend an eternal, infinite, powerful, holy God.

"*July* 30. Just at night, moved into my own house, and lodged there that night; found it much better spending the time alone than in the wigwam where I was before.

"*Lord's Day, July* 31. Felt more comfortably than some days past. Blessed be the Lord, who has now given me a place of retirement. Oh that I may find God in it, and that he would dwell with me for ever!

"*Aug.* 1. Was still busy in further labors on my house. Felt a little of the sweetness of religion, and thought that it was worth while to follow after God through a thousand snares, deserts, and death itself. Oh that I might always follow after holiness, that I may be fully conformed to God! Had some degree of sweetness in secret prayer, though I had much sorrow.

"*Aug.* 2. Was still laboring to make myself more comfortable, with regard to my house and lodging. Labored under spiritual anxiety: It seemed to me that I deserved to be thrust out of the world; yet found some comfort in committing my cause to God It is good for me to be afflicted, that I may die wholly to this world, and all that is in it.

"*Aug.* 3. Spent most of the day in writing. Enjoyed some sense of religion. Through divine goodness I am now uninterruptedly alone; and find my retirement comfortable. I have enjoyed more sense of divine things within a few days last past, than for some time before. I longed after holiness, humility and meekness; Oh that God would enable me to ' pass the time of my sojourning here in his fear,' and always live to him!

"*Aug.* 4. Was enabled to pray much through the whole day; and through divine goodness found some intenseness of soul in the duty, as I used to do, and some ability to persevere in my supplications. I had some apprehensions of divine things which afforded me courage and resolution. It is good, I find, to persevere in attempts to pray, if I cannot pray with perseverance, i. e. continue long in my addresses to the divine Being. I have generally found, that the more I do in secret prayer, the more I have delighted to do, and have enjoyed more of a spirit of prayer: and frequently have found the contrary, when with journeying or otherwise I have been much deprived of retirement. A seasonable, steady performance of secret duties in their proper hours, and a careful improvement of all time, filling up every hour with some profitable labor, either of heart, head, or hands, are excellent means of spiritual peace and boldness before God. Christ, indeed, is our peace, and by him we have boldness of access to God; but a good conscience, void of offence, is an excellent preparation for an approach into the divine presence. There is a difference between self-confidence or a self-righteous pleasing of ourselves—as with our own duties, attainments, and spiritual enjoyments— of which good men are sometimes guilty, and that holy confidence arising from the testimony of a good conscience, which good Hezekiah had, when he says, ' Remember, O Lord, I beseech thee, how I have walked before thee in truth, and with a perfect heart.' Then, says the holy psalmist, shall I not be ashamed when I have respect to all thy commandments. Filling up our time with and for God, is the way to rise up and lie down in peace."

The next eight days, he continued for the most part in a very comfortable frame, having his mind fixed and sweetly engaged in religion ; and more than once blesses God, that he had given him a little cottage, where he might live alone, and enjoy a happy retirement, free from noise and disturbance, and could at any hour of the day lay aside all studies, and spend time in lifting up his soul to God for spiritual blessings.

"*Aug.* 13. Was enabled in secret prayer to raise my soul to God with desire and delight. It was indeed a blessed season. I found the comfort of being a Christian ; and counted the sufferings of the present life not worthy to be compared with the glory of divine enjoyments even in this world. All my past sorrows seemed kindly to disappear, and I ' remembered no more the sorrow, for joy.'—O, how kindly, and with what a filial tenderness, the soul confides in the Rock of Ages, at such a season, that he will ' never leave it, nor forsake it,' that he will cause ' all things to work together for its good ! ' I longed that others should know how good a God the Lord is. My soul was full of tenderness and love, even to the most inveterate of my enemies. I earnestly desired that they should share in the same mercy ; and loved that God should do just as he pleased with me and everything else. I felt peculiarly serious calm, and peaceful, and encouraged to press after holiness as long as I live, whatever difficulties and trials may be in my way. May the Lord always help me so to do ! Amen, and Amen.

"*Lord's day Aug.* 14. I had much more freedom in public, than in private. God enabled me to speak with some feeling sense of divine things; but perceived no considerable effect.—" Aug. 15. Spent most of the day in labor, to procure something to keep my horse on in the winter. Enjoyed not much sweetness in the morning ; was very weak in body through the day; and thought that this frail body would soon drop into the dust ; and had some very realizing apprehensions of a speedy entrance into another world. In this weak state of body, I was not a little distressed for want of suitable food. I had no bread, nor could I get any. I am forced to go or send ten or fifteen miles for all the bread I eat ; and sometimes it is mouldy and sour before I eat it, if I get any considerable

quantity. And then again I have none for some days together, for want
of an opportunity to send for it, and cannot find my horse in the woods
to go myself; and this was my case now; but through divine goodness I
had some Indian meal, of which I made little cakes, and fried them. Yet
I felt contented with my circumstances, and sweetly resigned to God. In
prayer I enjoyed great freedom; and blessed God as much for my present circumstances, as if I had been a king; and thought that I found a
disposition to be contented in any circumstances. Blessed be God."

The rest of this week, he was exceedingly weak in body,
and much exercised with pain ; yet obliged from day to day
to labor hard to procure fodder for his horse. Except some
part of the time, he was so very ill, that he was neither able
to work nor study ; but speaks of longings after holiness and
perfect conformity to God. He complains of enjoying but
little of God : yet he says, that little was better to him, than
all the world besides. In his diary for Saturday, he says, he
was somewhat melancholy and sorrowful in mind ; and adds,
"I never feel comfortably, but when I find my soul going
forth after God. If I cannot be holy I must necessarily be
miserable for ever."

"*Lord's day, Aug.* 21. Was much straitened in the forenoon exercise;
my thoughts seemed to be all scattered to the ends of the earth. At
noon, I fell down before the Lord, groaned under my vileness, barrenness,
and deadness; and felt as if I was guilty of soul murder, in speaking to
immortal souls in such a manner as I had then done. In the afternoon,
God was pleased to give me some assistance, and I was enabled to set
before my hearers the nature and necessity of true repentance. Afterwards, had some small degree of thankfulness. Was very ill and full of
pain in the evening; and my soul mourned that I had spent so much time
to so little profit.

"*Aug.* 22. Spent most of the day in study; and found my bodily
strength in a measure restored. Had some intense and passionate breathings of soul after holiness, and very clear manifestations of my utter inability to procure, or work it in myself; it is wholly owing to the power
of God. O, with what tenderness the love and desire of holiness fills
the soul! I wanted to wing out of myself to God, or rather to get a conformity to him : but, alas! I cannot add to my stature in grace one cubit.
However, my soul can never leave striving for it ; or at least groaning,
that it cannot strive for it, and obtain more purity of heart. At night I

spent some time in instructing my poor people. Oh that God would pity their souls !

"*Aug.* 23. Studied in the forenoon, and enjoyed some freedom. In the afternoon, labored abroad; endeavored to pray; but found not much sweetness or intenseness of mind. Towards night was very weary, and tired of this world of sorrow ; the thoughts of death and immortality appeared very desirable, and even refreshed my soul. Those lines turned in my mind with pleasure :

> ' Come death, shake hands; I'll kiss thy bands;
> 'Tis happiness for me to die.—
> What !—dost thou think, that I will shrink ?
> I'll go to immortality.'

In evening prayer, God was pleased to draw near my soul, though very sinful and unworthy; so that I was enabled to wrestle with God, and to persevere in my requests for grace. I poured out my soul for all the world, friends and enemies. My soul was concerned, not so much for souls as such, but rather for Christ's kingdom, that it might appear in the world, that God might be known to be God, in the whole earth. And O my soul abhorred the very thought of a party in religion ! Let the truth of God appear, wherever it is : and God have the glory for ever. Amen. This was indeed, a comfortable season. I thought I had some small taste of, and real relish for the enjoyments and employments of the upper world. O that my soul was more attempered to it !

"*Aug.* 24. Spent some time, in the morning, in study and prayer. Afterwards was engaged in some necessary business abroad. Towards night, found a little time for some particular studies. I thought, if God should say , ' Cease making any provision for this life, for you shall in a few days go out of time into eternity,' my soul would leap for joy. Oh that I may both ' desire to be dissolved, to be with Christ,' and likewise ' wait patiently all the days of my appointed time till my change come !' But, alas ! I am very unfit for the business and blessedness of heaven. Oh for more holiness!

"*Aug.* 25. Part of the day was engaged in studies ; and part in labor abroad. I find it is impossible to enjoy peace and tranquility of mind, without a careful improvement of time. This is really an imitation of God and Christ Jesus : ' My Father worketh hitherto, and I work,' says our Lord. But still if we would be like God, we must see that we fill up our time for him. I daily long to dwell in perfect light and love. In the mean time, my soul mourns that I make so little progress in grace, and preparation for the world of blessedness ; I see and know that I am a very barren tree in God's vineyard, and that he might justly say, ' Cut it down,' etc. Oh that God would make me more lively and vigorous in grace, for his own glory! Amen.

"*Lord's day, Aug.* 28. Was much perplexed with some irreligious Dutchmen. All their discourse turned upon the things of the world; which was no small exercise to my mind. O what a hell it would be to spend an eternity with such men! Well might David say, 'I beheld the transgressors, and was grieved.' But, adored be God, heaven is a place into which no unclean thing enters. O I long for the holiness of that world! Lord prepare me for it."

The next day he set out on a journey to New York. Was somewhat dejected the two first days of his journey; but yet seems to have enjoyed some degrees of the sensible presence of God.

"*Aug.* 31. Rode down to Bethlehem; was in a sweet, serious, and, I hope Christian frame, when I came there. Eternal things engrossed all my thoughts; and I longed to be in the world of spirits. O how happy is it, to have all our thoughts swallowed up in that world; to feel one's self a serious, considerate stranger in this world diligently seeking a road through it, the best, the sure road to the heavenly Jerusalem!

"*Sept.* 1. Rode to Danbury. Was more dull and dejected in spirit, than yesterday. Indeed, I always feel comfortably, when God realizes death, and the things of another world, to my mind. Whenever my mind is taken off from the things of this world, and set on God, my soul is then at rest."

He reached New York the next Monday. After tarrying there two or three days, he set out from that city towards New Haven, intending to be there at the Commencement; and, on Friday, came to Horseneck. He complains much of dullness, and want of fervor in religion; but yet, from time to time, speaks of his enjoying spiritual warmth and sweetness in conversation with Christian friends, and assistance in public services.

"*Sept. 10.* Rode six miles to Stanwich, and preached to a considerable assembly of people. Had some assistance and freedom, especially towards the close. Endeavored much afterwards in private conversation to establish holiness, humility, meekness, etc., as the essence of true religion; and to moderate some noisy sort of persons, who appeared to me to be actuated by unseen spiritual pride, Alas, into what extremes men incline to run! Returned to Horseneck; and felt some seriousness and sweet solemnity in the evening.

"*Lord's day, Sept. 11.* In the afternoon I preached from Tit. iii. 8. This is a faithful saying, and these things etc. I think God never helped me more in painting true religion, and in detecting clearly, and tenderly discountenancing false appearances of religion, wild-fire party-zeal, spiritual pride, etc., as well as a confident dogmatical spirit, and its spring, viz. ignorance of the heart. In the evening, took much pains in private conversation to suppress some confusions, which I perceived were among that people.

"*Sept. 12.* Rode to Mr. Mills' at Ripton. Had some perplexing hours ; but was some part of the day very comfortable. 'It is through great trials,' I see, ' that we must enter the gates of Paradise.' If my soul could but be holy, that God might not be dishonored, methinks I could bear sorrows.

"*Sept. 13.* Rode to New-Haven. Was sometimes dejected; not in the sweetest frame. Lodged at ****. Had some profitable Christian conversation. I find, though my inward trials were great, and a life of solitude gives them greater advantage to settle, and penetrate to the very inmost recesses of the soul; yet it is better to be alone than incumbered with noise and tumult. I find it very difficult maintaining any sense of divine things, while removing from place to place, diverted with new objects, and filled with care and business. A settled, steady business, is best adapted to a life of strict religion.

"*Sept. 14.* This day I ought to have taken my degree; [this being Commencement day] but God sees fit to deny it me. And though I was greatly afraid of being overwhelmed with perplexity and confusion, when I should see my classmates take theirs; yet, at the very time, God enabled me with calmness and resignation to say, 'the will of the Lord be done,' Indeed, through divine goodness, I have scarcely felt my mind so calm, sedate, and comfortable, for some time. I have long feared this season, and expected my humility, meekness, patience, and resignation, would be much tried;* but found much more pleasure and divine comfort, than I expected. Felt spiritually serious, tender and affectionate in private prayer with a dear Christian friend to-day.

"*Sept. 15.* Had some satisfaction in hearing the ministers discourse. It is always a comfort to me, to hear religious and spiritual conversation. O that ministers and people were more spiritual and devoted to God !

---

* His trial was the greater, in that, had it not been for the displeasure of the governors of the college, he would not only on that day have shared with his classmates in the public honors which they then received, but would have appeared at the *head* of that class; which, if he had been with them, would have been the most numerous of any that ever had graduated at that college.

Towards night with the advice of Christian friends, I offered the following reflections in writing, to the rector and trustees of the college—which are, for substance, the same that I had freely offered the rector before, and intreated him to accept—that, if possible I might cut off all occasion of offense, from those who seek occasion. What I offered is as follows :

"' Whereas I have said before several persons concerning Mr. Whittelsey, one of the tutors of Yale College, that I did not believe he had any · more grace than the chair I then leaned upon; I humbly confess, that herein I have sinned against God, and acted contrary to the rules of his word, and have injured Mr. Whittelsey. I had no right to make thus free with his character; and had no just reason to say as I did concerning him. My fault herein was the more aggravated, in that I said this concerning one who was so much my superior, and one whom I was obliged to treat with special respect and honor, by reason of the relation I stood in to him in the college. Such a manner of behavior, I confess, did not become a Christian: it was taking too much upon me, and did not savor of that humble respect, which I ought to have expressed towards Mr. Whittelsey. I have long since been convinced of the falseness of those apprehensions, by which I then justified such a conduct. I have often reflected on this act with grief; I hope on account of the sin of it; and am willing to lie low, and be abased before God and man for it. I humbly ask the forgiveness of the governors of the college, and of the whole society ; but of Mr. Whittelsey in particular. And whereas I have been accused by one person of saying concerning the reverend rector of Yale College, that I wondered he did not expect to drop down dead for fining the scholars that followed Mr. Tennent to Milford, I seriously profess, that I do not remember my saying anything to this purpose. But if I did, which I am not certain I did not, I utterly condemn it, and detest all such kind of behavior ; and especially in an undergraduate towards the rector. And I now appear to judge and condemn myself for going once to the separate meeting in New-Haven, a little before I was expelled, though the rector had refused to give me leave. For this, I humbly ask the rector's forgiveness. And whether the governors of the college shall ever see cause to remove the academical censure I lie under or no, or to admit me to the privileges I desire, yet I am willing to appear, if they think fit, openly to own, and to humble myself for those things I have herein confessed.'

"'God has made me willing to do anything that I can do, consistent with truth, for the sake of peace, and that I might not be a stumbling block to others. For this reason I can cheerfully forego, and give up what I verily believe, after the most mature and impartial search is my right, in some instances. God has given me the disposition, that, if a man has done me an hundred injuries, and I (though ever so much provoked to it) have done him only one, I feel disposed, and heartily willing, humbly to confess my fault to him, and on my knees to ask forgiveness of him; though at the same time he should justify himself in all the injuries he has done me, and should only make use of my humble confession to blacken my character the more, and represent me as the only person guilty ; yea, though he should as it were insult me, and say, 'he knew all this before, and that I was making work for repentance.' Though what I said concerning Mr. Whittelsey was only spoken in private, to a friend or two; and being partly overheard, was related to the rector, and by him extorted from my friends; yet, seeing it was divulged and made public, I was willing to confess my fault therein publicly. But I trust God will plead my cause.' "

I was witness to the very Christian spirit which Brainerd showed at that time; being then at New-Haven, and one whom he thought fit to consult on that occasion. This was my first opportunity of a personal acquaintance with him.[*] There truly appeared in him a great degree of calmness and humility; without the least appearance of rising of spirit for any ill treatment which he supposed he had suffered or the least backwardness to abase himself before them, who as he thought, had wronged him. What he did was without any objection or appearance of reluctance, even in private to his friends, to whom he freely opened himself. Earnest application was made on his behalf to the authority of the college, that he might have his degree then given him; and particular-

---

[*] [Here begins the *personal acquaintance* of these two remarkable men—the one the greatest theologian and preacher of New England, and the other the missionary saint of the Modern Church—drawn to each other and their hearts cemented by the common attraction of the Cross. Providence so arranged that, when Brainerd's brief ministry had closed, he should find an asylum and end his self-denying life in the home of the pastor of Northampton, where of all places on earth it was fitting that such a man, after such a life of solitariness and self-denial should die, attended by such gentle, Christian ministries as he there received. And the same gracious Providence that gave to New England in her colonial days these two great apostles of Christian Doctrine and Christian Life, also ordered it that the same pen which wrote the immortal *History of the Work of Redemption*, *The Freedom of the Will*, and a *Treatise on the Religious Affections*, should give to the world, BRAINERD'S BIOGRAPHY—the simple yet wondrous account of a religious experience, and of a missionary life among the Indians, in the then "wilderness" part of our land, that should be read with wonder and with tears throughout Christendom, and travel down the centuries on its blessed mission of instructive testimony. The writer has elsewhere briefly expressed his views as to the singular injustice done to Brainerd by the College authorities, as well as the eminent Christian spirit shown by him under extreme provocation.—J. M. S.]

ly by the Rev. Mr. Burr of Newark, one of the correspondents
of the honorable society in Scotland; he being sent from
New Jersey to New-Haven, by the rest of the commissioners,
for that end; and many arguments were used, but without
success. Indeed, the governors of the college were so far
satisfied with the reflections which Brainerd had made on
himself, that they appeared willing to admit him again into
college; but not to give him his degree, till he should have
remained there at least twelvemonths, which being contrary
to what the correspondents, to whom he was now engaged,
had declared to be their mind, he did not consent to it. He
desired his degree, as he thought it would tend to his being
more extensively useful; but still when he was denied it, he
manifested no disappointment or resentment. The next day
he went to Derby; then to Southbury, where he spent the
Sabbath; and speaks of some spiritual comfort, but complains much of unfixedness, and wanderings of mind in religion.

"*Sept.* 19. In the afternoon, rode to Bethlehem, and there preached.
Had some measure of assistance, both in prayer and preaching. I felt
serious, kind and tender towards all mankind, and longed that holiness
might flourish more on earth.

"*Sept.* 20. Had thoughts of going forward on my journey to my
Indians; but towards night was taken with a hard pain in my teeth, and
shivering cold; and could not possibly recover a comfortable degree of
warmth the whole night following. I continued very full of pain all night;
and in the morning had a very hard fever, and pains almost over my whole
body. I had a sense of the divine goodness in appointing this to be the
place of my sickness, among my friends, who were very kind to me. I
should probably have perished, if I had first got home to my own house
in the wilderness, where I have none to converse with but the poor, rude,
ignorant Indians. Here, I saw, was mercy in the midst of affliction. I
continued thus, mostly confined to my bed, till Friday night; very full of
pain most of the time; but through divine goodness, not afraid of death.
Then the extreme folly of those appeared to me, who put off their turning to God till a sick bed. Surely this is not a time proper to prepare
for eternity. On Friday evening my pains went off somewhat suddenly.
I was exceedingly weak, and almost fainted; but was very comfortable
the night following. These words, (Psal. cxviii. 17.) 'I shall not die,

but live,' etc., I frequently revolved in my mind, and thought we were
to prize the continuation of life, only on this account, that we may 'show
forth God's goodness and works of grace.'"

From this time he gradually recovered and in a few days
was able to go forward on his journey ; but it was not till the
Tuesday following, that he reached Kaunaumeek.   He seems,
great part of this time, to have had a very deep and lively
sense of the vanity and emptiness of all things here below,
and of the reality, nearness, and vast importance of eternal
things.

"*Oct.* 4.   This day rode home to my own house and people.   The
poor Indians appeared very glad of my return.   Found my house and all
things in safety.   I presently fell on my knees, and blessed God for my
safe return, after a long and tedious journey, and a season of sickness in
several places where I had been, and after I had been ill myself.   God
has renewed his kindness to me, in preserving me one journey more.   I
have taken many considerable journeys since this time last year, and yet
God has never suffered one of my bones to be broken, or any distressing
calamity to befal me, excepting the ill turn I had in my last journey.   I
have been often exposed to cold and hunger in the wilderness, where the
comforts of life were not to be had : have frequently been lost in the
woods ; and sometimes obliged to ride much of the night ; and once lay
out in the woods all night ; yet, blessed be God he has preserved me ! "

In his diary for the next eleven days, are great complaints
of distance from God, spiritual pride, corruption, and exceeding vileness.   He once says, his heart was so oppressed with a
sense of his pollution, that he could scarcely have the face
and impudence (as it then appeared to him) to desire that
God should not damn him forever.   And at another time, he
says, he had so little sense of God, or apprehension and relish of his glory and excellency, that it made him more disposed to kindness and tenderness towards those who are
blind and ignorant of God and things divine and heavenly.

"*Lord's day, Oct.* 16.   In the evening, God was pleased to give me a
feeling sense of my own unworthiness ; but through divine goodness such
as tended to draw me to, rather than drive me from, God.   It filled me
with solemnity.   I retired alone, (having at this time a friend with me)
and poured out my soul to God with much freedom ; and yet in anguish,
to find myself so unspeakably sinful and unworthy before a holy God.

Was now much resigned under God's dispensations towards me, though my trials had been very great. But thought whether I could be resigned, if God should let the French Indians come upon me and deprive me of life, or carry me away captive, (though I knew of no special reason then to propose this trial to myself, more than any other ;) and my soul seemed so far to rest and acquiesce in God, that the sting and terror of these things, seemed in a great measure gone. Presently after I came to the Indians, whom I was teaching to sing that evening, I received the following letter from Stockbridge, by a messenger sent on the Sabbath on purpose, which made it appear of greater importance.

"Sir—Just now we received advices from Col. Stoddard, that there is the utmost danger of a rupture with France. He has received the same from his Excellency our Governor, ordering him to give notice to all the exposed places, that they may secure themselves the best they can against any sudden invasion. We thought best to send directly to Kaunaumeek, that you may take the most prudent measures for your safety. I am, Sir, etc.'

"I thought, upon reading the contents, it came in a good season ; for my heart seemed fixed on God, and therefore I was not much surprised. This news only made me more serious, and taught me that I must not please myself with any of the comforts of life which I had been preparing. Blessed be God, who gave me any intenseness and fervency this evening I

"*Oct.* 17. Had some rising hopes, that 'God would arise and have mercy on Zion speedily.' My heart is indeed refreshed, when I have any prevailing hopes of Zion's prosperity. Oh that I may see the glorious day, when Zion shall become the joy of the whole earth I Truly there is nothing that I greatly value in this lower world."

On Tuesday, he rode to Stockbridge ; complains of being much diverted, and having but little life. On Wednesday, he expresses a solemn sense of divine things, and a longing to be always doing for God with a friendly frame of spirit.

"*Oct.* 20. Had but little sense of divine things this day. Alas, that so much of my precious time is spent with so little of God! Those are tedious days wherein I have no spirituality.—Oct. 21. Returned home to Kaunaumeek: was glad to get alone in my little cottage, and to cry to that God who seeth in secret, and is present in a wilderness.—Oct. 22. Had but little sensible communion with God. This world is a dark, cloudy mansion. O when will the Sun of Righteousness shine on my soul without intermission!

"*Lord's day, Oct.* 23. In the morning, I had a little dawn of comfort arising from hopes of seeing glorious days in the Church of God; and was enabled to pray for such a glorious day, with some courage and strength of hope. In the forenoon, treated on the glories of heaven ; in the afternoon, on the miseries of hell, and the danger of going there. Had some freedom and warmth, both parts of the day; and my people were very attentive. In the evening, two or three came to me under concern for their souls ; to whom I was enabled to discourse closely, and with some earnestness and desire. Oh that God would be merciful to their poor souls ! "

He seems, through the whole of this week, to have been greatly engaged to fill up every inch of time in the service of God, and to have been most diligently employed in study, prayer, and instructing the Indians ; and from time to time, expresses longings of soul after God, and the advancement of his kingdom, and spiritual comfort and refreshment.

" *Lord's Day, Oct.* 30. In the morning, I enjoyed some fixedness of soul in prayer, which was indeed sweet and desirable; and was enabled to leave myself with God, and to acquiesce in him. At noon, my soul was refreshed with reading Rev. iii. more especially the 11th and 12th verses. How my soul longed for that blessed day, when I should 'dwell in the temple of God,' and 'go no more out' of his immediate presence !

" *Oct.* 31. Rode to Kinderhook, about fifteen miles from my residence. While riding, I felt some divine sweetness in the thoughts of being 'a pillar in the temple of God' in the upper world, and being no more deprived of his blessed presence, and the sense of his favor, which is better than life. My soul was so lifted up to God, that I could pour out my desires to him, for more grace and further degrees of sanctification, with abundant freedom. How I longed to be more abundantly prepared for that blessedness, with which I was then in some measure refreshed! Returned home in the evening; but took an extremely bad cold by riding in the night.

" *Nov.* 1. Was very much disordered in body, and sometimes full of pain in my face and teeth; was not able to study much, and had not much spiritual comfort. Alas! when God is withdrawn, all is gone. Had some sweet thoughts, which I could not but write down, on the design, nature, and end of Christianity.

" *Nov.* 2. Was still more indisposed in body, and in much pain, most of the day. I had not much comfort ; was scarcely able to study at all ; and still entirely alone in the wilderness. But blessed be the Lord, I am not exposed in the open air ; I have a house, and many of the comforts of life, to support me. I have learned, in a measure, that all good things, relating both to time and eternity, come from God. In the evening, I had some degree of quickening in prayer: I think God gave me some sense of his presence.

"*Nov.* 3. Spent this day in secret fasting and prayer, from morning till night. Early in the morning, I had some small degree of assistance in prayer. Afterwards, read the story of Elijah the prophet, 1 Kings, xvii. xviii. and xix. chapters, and also 2 Kings, ii. and iv. chapters. My soul was much moved, observing the faith, zeal, and power of that holy man ; how he wrestled with God in prayer. My soul then cried with Elisha, 'Where is the Lord God of Elijah!' O I longed for more faith! My soul breathed after God, and pleaded with him, that a 'double portion of that spirit,' which was given to Elijah, might 'rest on me.' And that which was divinely refreshing and strengthening to my soul, was, I saw that God is the same that he was in the days of Elijah. Was enabled to wrestle with God by prayer, in a more affectionate, fervent, humble, intense, and importunate manner, than I have for many months past. Nothing seemed too hard for God to perform ; nothing too great for me to hope for from him. I had for many months entirely lost all hopes of being made instrumental of doing any special service for God in the world ; it has appeared entirely impossible, that one so vile should be thus employed for God. But at this time God was pleased to revive this hope. Afterwards read from the iii. chapter of Exodus to the xx. and saw more of the glory and majesty of God discovered in those chapters, than ever I had seen before ; frequently in the mean time falling on my knees, and crying to God for the faith of Moses, and for a manifestation of the divine glory. Especially the iii. and iv. and part of the xiv. and xv. chapters were unspeakably sweet to my soul: my soul blessed God, that he had shown himself so gracious to his servants of old. The xv. chapter seemed to be the very language which my soul uttered to God in the season of my first spiritual comfort, when I had just got through the Red Sea, by a way that I had no expectation of. O how my soul then rejoiced in God! And now those things came fresh and lively to my mind; now my soul blessed God afresh that he had opened that unthought of way to deliver me from the fear of the Egyptians, when I almost despaired of life. Afterwards read the story of Abraham's pilgrimage in the land of Canaan. My soul was melted, in observing his faith, how he leaned on God; how he communed with God ; and what a stranger he was here in the world. After that, read the story of Joseph's sufferings, and God's goodness to him; blessed God for these examples of faith and patience. My soul was ardent in prayer, was enabled to wrestle ardently for myself, for Christian friends, and for the church of God. And felt more desire to see the power of God in the conversion of souls, than I have done for a long season. Blessed be God for this season of fasting and prayer! May his goodness always abide with me, and draw my soul to him!

"*Nov.* 4. Rode to Kinderhook : went quite to Hudson's river, about twenty miles from my house; performed some business; and returned home in the evening to my own house. I had rather ride hard, and fatigue myself to get home, than to spend the evening and night amongst those who have no regard for God."

The next two days, he was very ill, and full of pain, probably through his riding in the night, after a fatiguing day's journey on Tuesday; but yet seems to have been diligent in business.

"*Nov.* 7. This morning the Lord afforded me some special assistance in prayer; my mind was solemn, fixed, affectionate, and ardent in desires after holiness; felt full of tenderness and love; and my affections seemed to be dissolved into kindness. In the evening, I enjoyed the same comfortable assistance in prayer, as in the morning: my soul longed after God, and cried to him with a filial freedom, reverence and boldness. Oh that I might be entirely consecrated and devoted to God!

"*Nov.* 10. Spent this day in fasting and prayer alone. In the morning, was very dull and lifeless, melancholy and discouraged. But after some time, while reading 2 Kings, xix. my soul was moved and affected: especially reading verse 14, and onward. I saw there was no other way for the afflicted children of God to take, but to go to God with all their sorrows. Hezekiah, in his great distress, went and spread his complaint before the Lord. I was then enabled to see the mighty power of God, and my extreme need of that power, and to cry to him affectionately and ardently for his power and grace to be exercised towards me. Afterwards, read the story of David's trials, and observed the course he took under them, how he strengthened his hands in God; whereby my soul was carried out after God, enabled to cry to him, and rely upon him, and felt strong in the Lord. Was afterwards refreshed, observing the blessed temper that was wrought in David by his trials : all bitterness and desire for revenge, seemed wholly taken away; so that he mourned for the death of his enemies; 2 Sam. i. 17. and iv. 9. *ad. fin.* Was enabled to bless God, that he had given me something of this divine temper, that my soul freely forgives, and heartily loves my enemies."

It appears by his diary for some weeks that great part of the time he was very ill and full of pain and yet obliged to be at great fatigues in labor and travelling day and night, and to expose himself in stormy and severe seasons. But he speaks of thirstings of soul after God ; of his heart being strengthened in God ; of seasons of divine sweetness and comfort ; of his heart being affected with gratitude for mercies, etc. Yet there are many complaints of lifelessness, weakness of grace, distance from God, and great unprofitableness. But still there appears a constant care from day to day, not to lose time, but to improve it all for God.

"*Lord's day*, *Nov.* 27. In the evening, I was greatly affected in reading an account of the very joyful death of a pious gentleman, which seemed to invigorate my soul in God's ways. I felt courageously engaged to pursue a life of holiness and self-denial as long as I live ; and poured out my soul to God for his help and assistance in order thereto. Eternity then seemed near, and my soul rejoiced and longed to meet it. I trust that will be a blessed day which finishes my toil here.

"*Nov.* 28. In the evening, I was obliged to spend time in company and conversation which were unprofitable. Nothing lies heavier upon me than the misimprovement of time.—Nov. 29. Began to study in Indian tongue, with Mr. Sergeant, at Stockbridge.* Was perplexed for want of more retirement. I love to live alone in my little cottage, where I can spend much time in prayer.

"*Nov.* 30. Pursued my study of Indian : but was very weak and disordered in body, and was troubled in mind at the barrenness of the day, that I had done so little for God. I had some enlargement in prayer at night. O a barn, or stable, hedge, or any other place, is truly desirable if God is there ! Sometimes, of late, my hopes of Zion's prosperity, are more raised than they were in the summer. My soul seems to confide in God that he will yet 'shew forth his salvation ' to his people, and make Zion ' the joy of the whole earth.' O how excellent is the loving-kindness of the Lord. My soul sometimes inwardly exults at the lively thoughts of what God has already done for his church, and what ' mine eyes have seen of the salvation of God ' It is sweet, to hear nothing but spiritual discourse from God's children ; and sinners ' enquiring the way to Zion,' saying, ' What shall we do ? '. Oh that I may see more of this blessed work !

"*Dec.* 1. Both morning and evening, I enjoyed some intenseness of soul in prayer, and longed for the enlargement of Christ's kingdom in the world. My soul seems of late, to wait on God for his blessing on Zion. Oh that religion might powerfully revive !—Dec. 2. Enjoyed not so much health of body, or fervor of mind, as yesterday. If the chariot-wheels

* The commissioners had directed him to spend much time this winter with Mr. Sergeant, to learn the language of the Indians ; which necessitated him very often to ride, backwards and forwards, twenty miles, through the uninhabited woods between Stockbridge and Kaunaumeek which exposed him to extreme hardship in the severe seasons of the winter.

move with ease and speed at any time, for a short space, yet, by and by, they drive heavily again. 'Oh that I had the wings of a dove, that I might fly away' from sin and corruption, and be at rest with God!

" *Dec.* 3. Rode home to my house and people. Suffered much with extreme cold.—I trust, I shall ere long, arrive safe at my journey's end, where my toils shall cease.—Lord's day, Dec. 4. Had but little sense of divine and heavenly things. My soul mourns over my barrenness. O how sad is spiritual deadness!—Dec. 5. Rode to Stockbridge. Was almost outdone with the extreme cold. Had some refreshing meditations by the way; but was barren, wandering, and lifeless, much of the day. Thus my days roll away, with but little done for God; and this is my burden.—Dec. 6. Was perplexed to see the vanity and levity of professed Christians. Spent the evening with a Christian friend, who was able, in some measure, to sympathize with me in my spiritual conflicts. Was a little refreshed to find one with whom I could converse of inward trials, etc.

" *Dec.* 7. Spent the evening in perplexity, with a kind of guilty indolence. When I have no heart or resolution for God, and the duties incumbent on me, I feel guilty of negligence and misimprovement of time. Certainly I ought to be engaged in my work and business, to the utmost extent of my strength and ability.

" *Dec.* 8. My mind was much distracted with different affections; I seemed to be at an amazing distance from God; and looking round in the world, to see if there was not some happiness to be derived from it. God, and certain objects in the world, seemed each to invite my heart and affections; and my soul seemed to be distracted between them. I have not been so much beset with the world for a long time; and that with relation to some particular objects, to which I thought myself most dead. But even while I was desiring to please myself with anything below, guilt, sorrow, and perplexity attended the first motions of desire. Indeed, I cannot see the appearance of pleasure and happiness in the world, as I used to do: and blessed be God for any habitual deadness to the world. I found no peace, or deliverance, from this distraction and perplexity of mind, till I found access to the throne of grace; and, as soon as I had any sense of God, and things divine, the allurements of the world vanished, and my heart was determined for God. But my soul mourned over my folly, that I should desire any pleasure, but only in God. God forgive my spiritual idolatry!"

The next thirteen days, he appears to have been continually in deep concern about the improvement of precious time; and there are expressions of grief, that he improved time no better; such as " O what misery do I feel, when my thoughts rove after vanity! I should be happy if always

engaged for God ! O wretched man that I am ! " etc. Speaks
of his being pained with a sense of his barrenness, perplexed
with his wanderings, longing for deliverance from sin, mourning that time passed away, and so little was done for God.
—On Tuesday, December 20, he speaks of his being visited
at Kaunaumeek, by some under spiritual concern.

"*Dec.* 22. Spent this day alone in fasting and prayer, and reading in
God's word the exercises and deliverances of his children. Had, I trust,
some exercise of faith, and realizing apprehension of divine power, grace
and holiness ; and, also, of the unchangeableness of God, that he is the
same as when he delivered his saints of old out of great tribulation. My
soul was sundry times in prayer enlarged for God's church and people.
Oh that Zion might become the 'joy of the whole earth !' It is better
to wait upon God with patience, than to put confidence in anything in
this lower world. 'My soul, wait thou on the Lord ;' for 'from him
comes thy salvation.'

"*Dec.* 23. Felt a little more courage and resolution in religion, than
at some other times.—Dec. 24. Had some assistance and longing desires
after sanctification, in prayer this day ; especially in the evening : was
sensible of my own weakness and spiritual impotency ; saw plainly ; that
I should fall into sin, if God of his abundant mercy did not 'uphold my
soul, and withhold me from evil.' Oh that God would uphold me by his
free Spirit, and save me from the hour of temptation!

"*Lord's day, Dec.* 25. Prayed much in the morning, with a feeling
sense of my own spiritual weakness and insufficiency for my duty. God
gave me some assistance in preaching to the Indians ; and especially in
the afternoon, when I was enabled to speak with uncommon plainness,
freedom, and earnestness. Blessed be God for any assistance granted to
one so unworthy. Afterwards felt some thankfulness ; but still sensible
of barrenness. Spent some time in the evening with one or two persons
under spiritual concern, and exhorting others to their duty.

"*Dec.* 26. Rode down to Stockbridge. Was very much fatigued
with my journey, wherein I underwent great hardships ; was much exposed
and very wet by falling into a river. Spent the day and evening without
much sense of divine and heavenly things ; but felt guilty, grieved, and
perplexed with wandering, careless thoughts.—Dec. 27. Had a small
degree of warmth in secret prayer, in the evening ; but, alas! had but
little spiritual life, and consequently but little comfort. Oh, the pressure
of a body of death!

This day he wrote to his brother John, at Yale college,
the following letter :

" KAUNAUMEEK, *Dec.* 27, 1743.

" DEAR BROTHER:

"I long to see you, and to know how you fare in your journey through a world of inexpressible sorrow: where we are compassed about with 'vanity, confusion, and vexation of spirit.' I am more weary of life, I think, than ever I was. The whole world appears to me like a huge vacuum, a vast empty space, whence nothing desirable, or at least satisfactory, can possibly be derived ; and I long daily to die more and more to it ; even though I obtain not that comfort from spiritual things which I earnestly desire. Worldly pleasures, such as flow from greatness riches, honors, and sensual gratifications, are infinitely worse than none. May the Lord deliver us more and more from these vanities. I have spent most of the fall and winter hitherto in a very weak state of body ; and sometimes under pressing inward trials and spiritual conflicts ; but 'having obtained help from God, I continue to this day ; ' and am now somewhat better in health, than I was some time ago. I find nothing more conducive to a life of Christianity, than a diligent, industrious, and faithful improvement of precious time. Let us then faithfully perform that business, which is allotted to us by divine Providence, to the utmost of our bodily strength, and mental vigor. Why should we sink, and grow discouraged with any particular trials and perplexities, which we are called to encounter in the world? Death and Eternity are just before us ; a few tossing billows more will waft us into the world of spirits, and we hope, through infinite grace, into endless pleasures, and uninterrupted rest and peace. Let us then 'run, with patience, the race set before us,' Heb. xii. 1, 2. And, O, that we could depend more upon the living God, and less upon our own wisdom and strength! Dear brother, may the God of all grace comfort your heart, and succeed your studies, and make you an instrument of good to his people in your day. This is the constant prayer of

" Your affectionate brother,

"DAVID BRAINERD.

" *Dec.* 28. Rode about six miles to the ordination of Mr. Hopkins. At the solemnity I was somewhat affected with a sense of the greatness and importance of the work of a minister of Christ. Afterwards was grieved to see the vanity of the multitude. In the evening, spent a little time with some Christian friends, with some degree of satisfaction ; but most of the time, I had rather have been alone.

" *Dec.* 29. Spent the day mainly in conversing with friends ; yet enjoyed little satisfaction, because I could find but few disposed to converse of divine and heavenly things. Alas, what are the things of this world, to afford satisfaction to the soul!—Near night, returned to Stockbridge ; in secret, I blessed God for retirement, and that I am not always exposed to the company and conversation of the world. O that I could live ' in the secret of God's presence ! '

"*Dec.* 30. Was in a solemn, devout frame in the evening. Wondered that earth, with all its charms, should ever allure me in the least degree. Oh, that I could always realize the being and holiness of God!— Dec. 31. Rode from Stockbridge home to my house : the air was clear and calm, but as cold as ever I felt it, or nearly. I was in great danger of perishing by the extremity of the season. Was enabled to meditate much on the road.

" *Lord's day, Jan.* 1, 1744. In the morning, had some small degree of assistance in prayer. Saw myself so vile and unworthy, that I could not look my people in the face, when I came to preach. O my meanness, folly, ignorance, and inward pollution! In the evening, had a little assistance in prayer, so that the duty was delightful, rather than burdensome. Reflected on the goodness of God to me in the past year. Of a truth God has been kind and gracious to me, though he has caused me to pass through many sorrows ; he has provided for me bountifully, so that I have been enabled, in about fifteen months past, to bestow to charitable uses about an hundred pounds New England money, that I can now remember.* Blessed be the Lord, that has so far used me as his steward, to distribute a portion of his goods. May I always remember, that all I have comes from God. Blessed be the Lord, that has carried me through all the toils, fatigues, and hardships of the year past, as well as the spiritual sorrows and conflicts that have attended it. O that I could begin this year with God, and spend the whole of it to his glory, either in life or death !

"*Jan.* 2. Had some affecting sense of my own impotency and spiritual weakness. It is nothing but the power of God that keeps me from all manner of wickedness. I see I am nothing, and can do nothing without help from above. Oh, for divine grace! In the evening had some ardor of soul in prayer, and longing desires to have God for my guide and safeguard at all times."

The following letter to his brother Israel, at Haddam, was written this day.

"KAUNAUMEEK, *Jan.* 2, 1743-4.

"MY DEAR BROTHER:

" There is but one thing that deserves our highest care and most ardent desires ; and that is, that we may answer the great end for which we were made, viz. to glorify that God, who has given us our being and all our

---

* Which was, I suppose, to the value of about £ 185 in our bills of the old tenor, as they now pass. By this, as well as many other things it is manifest that his frequent melancholy did not arise from the consideration of any disadvantage he was laid under to get a living in the world, by his expulsion from the college.

comforts, and do all the good we possibly can to our fellow-men, while we
live in the world. Verily life is not worth the having, if it be not improved for this noble end and purpose. Yet, alas, how little is this thought
of among mankind! Most men seem to live to themselves without much
regard to the glory of God, or the good of their fellow-creatures. They
earnestly desire, and eagerly pursue after the riches, the honors, and the
pleasures of life, as if they really supposed, that wealth or greatness, or
merriment, could make their immortal souls happy. But alas! what false
and delusive dreams are these! And how miserable will those ere long
be who are not awaked out of them, to see that all their happiness consists in living to God, and becoming "holy, as he is holy!" Oh, may you
never fall into the tempers and vanities, the sensuality and folly of the
present world! You are by divine Providence, left as it were alone in a
wide world, to act for yourself: be sure then to remember, that it is a
world of temptation. You have no earthly parents to be the means of
forming your youth to piety and virtue, by their pious examples, and
seasonable counsels; let this then excite you with greater diligence and
fervency to look up to the Father of mercies for grace and assistance
against all the vanities of the world. If you would glorify God, or answer his just expectations from you, and make your own soul happy in this
and the coming world, observe these few directions; though not from a
father, yet from a brother who is touched with a tender concern for your
present and future happiness.

"First: Resolve upon, and daily endeavor to practise a life of seriousness and strict sobriety. The wise man will tell you the great advantage
of such a life, Eccl. vii. 3. Think of the life of Christ; and when you can
find that he was pleased with jesting and vain merriment, then you may
indulge in it yourself.

"Again: be careful to make a good improvement of precious time.
When you cease from labor, fill up your time in reading, meditation, and
prayer; and while your hands are laboring, let your heart be employed, as
much as possible, in divine thoughts.—Further; Take heed that you faithfully perform the business which you have to do in the world, from a regard to the commands of God; and not from an ambitious desire of being
esteemed better than others. We should always look upon ourselves as
God's servants, placed in God's world, to do his work; and accordingly
labor faithfully for him; not with a design to grow rich and great, but to
glorify God, and to do all the good we possibly can.

"Again: never expect any satisfaction or happiness from the world.
If you hope for happiness in the world hope for it from God, and not from
the world. Do not think you shall be more happy if you live to such or
such a state in life, if you live to be yourself, to be settled in the world
or if you shall gain an estate in it: but look upon it that you shall then be
happy, when you can be constantly employed for God, and not for your-

self; and desire to live in this world, only to do and suffer what God allots to you.   When you can be of the spirit and temper of angels, who are willing to come down into this lower world, to perform what God commands them, though their desires are heavenly, and not in the least set on earthly things, then you will be of that temper which you ought to have, Col. iii. 2.

"Once more; never think that you can live to God by your own power or strength; but always look to, and rely on him for assistance, yea for all strength and grace.   There is no greater truth than this, that 'we can do nothing of ourselves; '(John xv. 5. and 2 Cor. iii. 5.) yet nothing but our own experience can effectually teach it us.   Indeed, we are a long time in learning, that all our strength and salvation is in God.   This is a life which I think no unconverted man can possibly live; and yet it is a life which every godly soul is pressing after, in some good measure.   Let it then be your great concern, thus to devote yourself and your all to God.

"I long to see you, that I may say much more to you than I now can for your benefit and welfare; but I desire to commit you to, and leave you with, the Father of mercies, and God of all grace; praying that you may be directed safely through an evil world, to God's heavenly kingdom.

"I am your affectionate loving brother,

"DAVID BRAINERD."

"*Jan. 3.* Was employed much of the day in writing; and spent some time in other necessary employment.   But my time passes away so swiftly that I am astonished when I reflect on it, and see how little I do.   My state of solitude does not make the hours hang heavy upon my hands.   O what reason of thankfulness have I on account of this retirement!   I find, that I do not, and it seems I cannot lead a Christian life, when I am abroad, and cannot spend time in devotion, Christian conversation, and serious meditation, as I should do.   Those weeks that I am obliged now to be from home, in order to learn the Indian tongue, are mostly spent in perplexity and barrenness, without much sweet relish of divine things; and I feel myself a stranger at the throne of grace, for want of more frequent and continued retirement.   When I return home, and give myself to meditation, prayer, and fasting, a new scene opens to my mind, and my soul longs for mortification, self-denial, humility, and divorcement from all the things of the world.   This evening, my heart was somewhat warm and fervent in prayer and meditation, so that I was loath to indulge sleep.   Continued in those duties till about midnight.

"*Jan.* 4.   Was in a resigned and mortified temper of mind, much of the day.   Time appeared a moment, life a vapor, and all enjoyments as empty bubbles, and fleeting blasts of wind.—Jan. 5.   Had a humbling and oppressive sense of my unworthiness.   My sense of the badness of my own heart filled my soul with bitterness and anguish ; which was ready to sink, as under the weight of a heavy burden. Thus I spent the evening, till late. Was somewhat intense and ardent in prayer.

"*Jan.* 6. Feeling my extreme weakness, and want of grace, the pollution of my soul, and danger of temptations on every side, I set apart this day for fasting and prayer, neither eating nor drinking from evening to evening, beseeching God to have mercy on me. My soul intensely longed that the dreadful spots and stains of sin might be washed away from it. Saw something of the power and all-sufficiency of God. My soul seemed to rest on his power and grace ; longed for resignation to his will, and mortification to all things here below. My mind was greatly fixed on divine things : my resolutions for a life of mortification, continual watchfulness, self-denial, seriousness and devotion, were strong and fixed ; my desires ardent and intense ; my conscience tender, and afraid of every appearance of evil. My soul grieved with reflection on past levity, and want of resolution for God. I solemnly renewed my dedication of myself to God, and longed for grace to enable me always to keep covenant with him. Time appeared very short, eternity near ; and a great name, either in or after life, together with all earthly pleasures and profits, but an empty bubble, a deluding dream.

"*Jan.* 7. Spent this day in seriousness, with steadfast resolutions for God, and a life of mortification. Studied closely till I felt my bodily strength fail. Felt some degree of resignation to God, with an acquiescence in his dispensations. Was grieved that I could do so little for God before my bodily strength failed. In the evening, though tired, was enabled to continue instant in prayer for some time. Spent the time in reading, meditation, and prayer, till the evening was far spent : was grieved to think that I could not watch unto prayer the whole night. But blessed be God, heaven is a place of continual and incessant devotion, though the earth is dull."

The six days following, he continued in the same happy frame of mind ; enjoyed the same composure, calmness, resignation, ardent desire, and sweet fervency of spirit, in a high degree, every day, not one excepted. Thursday, this week, he kept as a day of secret fasting and prayer.

"*Jan.* 14. This morning, enjoyed a most solemn season in prayer : my soul seemed enlarged, and assisted to pour out itself to God for grace, and for every blessing I wanted for myself, my dear Christian friends, and for the church of God ; and was so enabled to see Him who is invisible, that my soul rested upon him for the performance of everything I asked agreeable to his will. It was then my happiness to 'continue instant in prayer,' and I was enabled to continue in it for near an hour. My soul was then 'strong in the Lord, and in the power of his might.' Longed exceedingly for an angelic holiness and purity, and to have all my thoughts, at all times, employed in divine and heavenly things. O how unspeakably blessed it is, to feel a measure of that rectitude, in which we were at first created! Felt the same divine assistance in prayer sundry times in the day. My soul confided in God for myself, and for his Zion ; trusted in divine power and grace, that he would do glorious things in his church on earth, for his own glory."

The next day he speak of some glimpses which he had of the divine glories, and of his being enabled to maintain his resolutions in some measure ; but complains, that he could not draw near to God.   He seems to be filled with trembling fears lest he should return to a life of vanity, to please himself with some of the enjoyments of this lower world ; and speaks of his being much troubled, and feeling guilty, that he should address immortal souls with no more ardency and desire of their salvation.   On Monday, he rode down to Stockbridge, when he was distressed with extreme cold ; but notwithstanding, his mind was in a devout and solemn frame in his journey.   The next four days, he was very ill, probably from the cold in his journey ; yet he spent the time in a solemn manner.   On Friday evening, he visited Mr Hopkins ; and on Saturday, rode eighteen miles to Salisbury, where he kept the Sabbath, and enjoyed considerable degrees of God's gracious presence, assistance in duty, and divine comfort and refreshment, longing to give himself wholly to God, to be his forever.

"*Jan.* 23.   I think I never felt more resigned to God, nor so dead to the world, in every respect, as now ; was dead to all desire of reputation and greatness, either in life, or after death; all I longed for, was to be holy, humble, crucified to the world, etc.

"*Jan.* 24.   Near noon, rode over to Canaan.   In the evening, I was unexpectedly visited by a considerable number of people, with whom I was enabled to converse profitably on divine things ; took pains to describe the difference between a regular and irregular SELF-LOVE ; the one consisting with a supreme love to God, but the other not ; the former uniting God's glory, and the soul's happiness, that they become one common interest, but the latter disjoining and separating God's glory and man's

happiness, seeking the latter with a neglect of the former. Illustrated
this by that genuine love that is founded between the sexes ; which is
diverse from that which is wrought up towards a person only by rational
argument, or hope of self-interest. Love is a pleasing passion, it affords
pleasure to the mind where it is ; but yet, genuine love is not, nor can be
placed on any object with that design of pleasure itself."

On Wednesday he rode to Sheffield ; the next day, to Stockbridge and on Saturday, home to Kaunaumeek, though the
season was cold and stormy ; which journey was followed with
illness and pain. He spent the time while riding, in profitable
meditations, and in lifting up his heart to God ; he speaks of
assistance, comfort and refreshment ; but still complains of
barrenness, etc, His diary for the next five day is full of
bitter complaints ; he expresses himself as full of shame and
self-loathing for his lifeless temper of mind and sluggishness
of spirit, and as being in perplexity, and extremity, and appearing to himself unspeakably vile and guilty before God, on
account of inward workings of corruption he found in his
heart.

" *Feb.* 2. Spent this day in fasting and prayer ; seeking the presence and
assistance of God, that he would enable me to overcome all my corruptions, and spiritual enemies.—Feb. 3. Enjoyed more freedom and comfort than of late ; was engaged in meditation upon the different whispers
of the various powers and affections of a pious mind, exercised with a
great variety of dispensations ; and could not but write, as well as meditate,
on so entertaining a subject. I hope the Lord gave me some true sense
of divine things this day ; but alas, how great and pressing are the remains
of indwelling corruption ! I am now more sensible than ever, that God
alone is 'the author and finisher of our faith,' *i. e.* that the whole and
every part of sanctification, and every good word, work, or thought, found
in me, is the effect of his power and grace ; that, 'without him, I can do
nothing,' in the strictest sense, and that, 'he works in us to will and to do
of his own good pleasure,' and from no other motive. O how amazing
it is, that people can talk so much about men's power and goodness,
when, if God did not hold us back every moment, we should be devils
incarnate! This my bitter experience for several days last past, has
abundantly taught me concerning myself.

" *Feb.* 4. Enjoyed some degree of freedom and spiritual refreshment ;
was enabled to pray with some fervency, and longing desires of Zion's
prosperity, and my faith and hope seemed to take hold of God, for the

performance of what I was enabled to plead for. Sanctification in myself, and the ingathering of God's elect, were all my desire; and the hope of their accomplishment all my joy.

"*Lord's day*, *Feb.* 5. Was enabled in some measure to rest and confide in God, and to prize his presence and some glimpses of the light of his countenance, above my necessary food. Thought myself, after the season of weakness, temptation, and desertion I endured last week, to be somewhat like Sampson, when his locks began to grow again. Was enabled to preach to my people with more life and warmth, than I have for some weeks past.

"*Feb.* 6. This morning, my soul again was strengthened in God, and found some sweet repose in him in prayer ; longing especially for the complete mortification of sensuality and pride, and for resignation to God's dispensations, at all times, as through grace, I felt it at this time. I did not desire deliverance from any difficulty that attends my circumstances, unless God was willing. O how comfortable is this temper ! Spent most of the day in reading God's word, in writing, and prayer. Enjoyed repeated and frequent comfort and intenseness of soul in prayer through the day. In the evening, spent some hours in private conversation with my people; and afterwards felt some warmth in secret prayer.

"*Feb.* 7. Was much engaged in some sweet meditations on the powers and affections of the godly soul in the pursuit of their beloved object ; wrote something of the native language of spiritual sensation, in its soft and tender whispers; declaring, that it now feels and tastes, that the Lord is gracious ; that he is the supreme good, the only soul satisfying happiness : that he is a complete, sufficient, and almighty portion; saying: 'Whom have I in Heaven but thee ? and there is none upon earth that I desire beside,' this blessed portion. O, I feel that it is heaven to please him, and to be just what he would have me to be ! O that my soul were holy, as he is holy ! O that it were pure, even as Christ is pure ; and perfect as my Father in heaven is perfect ! These I feel are the sweetest commands in God's book, comprising all others. And shall I break them ! must I break them ! am I under the necessity of it as long as I live in the world ! O my soul, woe, woe is me, that I am a sinner, because I now necessarily grieve and offend this blessed God, who is infinite in goodness and grace ! O methinks if he would punish me for my sins, it would not wound my heart so deep to offend him : but though I sin continually, yet he continually repeats his kindness to me ! O methinks I could bear any sufferings; but how can I bear to grieve and dishonor this blessed God ! How shall I yield ten thousand times more honor to him ? What shall I do to glorify and worship this best of beings? O that I could consecrate myself, soul and body, to his service forever ! O that I could give up myself to him, so as never more to

attempt to be my own, or to have any will or affections that are not perfectly conformed to him! But, alas, alas! I find I cannot be thus entirely devoted to God ; I cannot live, and not sin. O ye angels, do ye
glorify him incessantly ; and if possible prostrate yourselves lower before
the blessed King of heaven! I long to bear a part with you ; and, if it
were possible, to help you. O when we have done all that we can, to
all eternity, we shall not be able to offer the ten thousandth part of the
homage which the glorious God deserves!' Felt something spiritual,
devout, resigned, and mortified to the world, much of the day; and
especially towards and in the evening. Blessed be God, that he enables
me to love him for himself.

"*Feb.* 8. Was in a comfortable frame of soul, most of the day;
though sensible of, and restless under spiritual barrenness. I find that
both mind and body are quickly tired with intenseness and fervor in the
things of God. O that I could be as incessant as angels in devotion and
spiritual fervor.

"*Feb.* 9. Observed this day as a day of fasting and prayer, intreating
of God to bestow upon me his blessing and grace ; especially to enable
me to live a life of mortification to the world, as well as of resignation
and patience. Enjoyed some realizing sense of divine power and goodness in prayer, several times ; and was enabled to roll the burden of myself, and friends, and Zion, upon the goodness and grace of God ; but in
the general, was more dry and barren than I have usually been of late,
upon such occasions.

"*Feb.* 10. Was exceedingly oppressed, most of the day, with shame,
grief, and fear, under a sense of my past folly, as well as present barrenness and coldness. When God sets before me my past misconduct,
especially any instances of misguided zeal, it sinks my soul into shame
and confusion, makes me afraid of a shaking leaf. My fear is such as
the prophet Jeremy complains of, Jer. xx. 10. I have no confidence to
hold up my face, even before my fellow worms ; but only when my soul
confides in God, and I find the sweet temper of Christ, the spirit of
humility, solemnity and mortification, and resignation, alive in my soul.
But, in the evening, was unexpectedly refreshed in pouring out my complaint to God; my shame and fear was turned into a sweet composure
and acquiescence in God.

"*Feb.* 11. Felt much as yesterday ; enjoyed but little sensible communion with God.—' Lord's day, Feb. 12. My soul seemed to confide in
God, and to repose itself on him ; and had intense longings after God in
prayer. Enjoyed some sweet divine assistance, in the forenoon, in preaching ; but in the afternoon, was more perplexed with shame, etc. Afterwards, found some relief in prayer ; loved, as a feeble, afflicted, despised

creature to cast myself on a God of infinite grace and goodness, hoping for no happiness but from him.

"*Feb* 13. Was calm and sedate in morning devotions; and my soul seemed to rely on God. Rode to Stockbridge, and enjoyed some comfortable meditations by the way; had a more refreshing taste and relish of heavenly blessedness, than I have enjoyed for many months past. I have many times, of late, felt as ardent desires of holiness as ever; but not so much sense of the sweetness and unspeakable pleasure of the enjoyments of heaven. My soul longed to leave earth, and bear a part with angels in their celestial employments. My soul said, 'Lord it is good to be here;' and it appeared to be better to die, than to lose the relish of these heavenly delights."

A sense of divine things seemed to continue with him, in a lesser degree, through the next day. On Wednesday, he was, by some discourse which he heard, cast into a melancholy gloom, that operated much in the same manner as his melancholy had formerly done, when he first came to Kaunaumeek; the effects of which seemed to continue in some degree the six following days.

"*Feb.* 22. In the morning, had as clear a sense of the exceeding pollution of my nature, as ever I remember to have had in my life. I then appeared to myself inexpressibly loathsome and defiled. Sins of childhood, of early youth, and such follies as I had not thought of for years together, as I remember, came now fresh to my view, as if committed but yesterday, and appeared in the most odious colors; they appeared more in number than the hairs of my head; yea, they 'went over my head as a heavy burden.' In the evening, the hand of faith seemed to be strengthened in God; my soul seemed to rest and acquiesce in him, was supported under my burdens, reading the cxxvth psalm; and found that it was sweet and comfortable to lean on God.

"*Feb.* 23. Was frequent in prayer, and enjoyed some assistance. There is a God in heaven who overrules all things for the best; and this is the comfort of my soul: 'I had fainted unless I had believed to see the goodness of God in the land of the living,' notwithstanding present sorrows. In the evening enjoyed some freedom in prayer, for myself, friends, and the church of God.

"*Feb.* 24. Was exceedingly restless and perplexed under a sense of misimprovement of time; mourned to see time pass away; felt in the greatest hurry; seemed to have everything to do, yet could do nothing, but only grieve and groan under my ignorance, unprofitableness, meanness, the foolishness of my actions and thoughts, the pride and bit-

terness of some past frames, all which at this time appeared to me in
lively colors, and filled me with shame. I could not compose my mind
to any profitable studies, by reason of this pressure. And the reason, I
judge, why I am not allowed to study a great part of my time, is, because
I am endeavoring to lay in such a stock of knowledge as shall be a self-
sufficiency.—I know it to be my indispensable duty to study, and qualify
myself in the best manner I can for public service : but this is my misery,
I naturally study and prepare, that I may 'consume it upon my lusts' of
pride and self-confidence.

" *March* 2. Was most of the day employed in writing on a divine subject. Was frequent in prayer, and enjoyed some small degree of assistance. But in the evening God was pleased to grant me divine sweetness
in prayer ; especially in the duty of intercession. I think, I never felt so
much kindness and love to those who, I have reason to think, are my enemies—though at that time I found such a disposition to think the best of
all, that I scarce knew how to think that any such thing as enmity and
hatred lodged in my soul ; it seemed as if all the world must needs be
friends—and never prayed with more freedom and delight, for myself, or
dearest friend, than I did now for my enemies.

" *March* 3. In the morning, spent an hour in prayer, with great intenseness and freedom, and with the most soft and tender affection towards
mankind. I longed that those who, It have reason to think, owe me ill
will, might be eternally happy. I seemed refreshing to think of meeting
them in heaven, how much soever they had injured me on earth ; had no
disposition to insist upon any confession from them, in order to reconciliation, and the exercise of love and kindness to them. O it is an emblem
of heaven itself, to love all the world with a love of kindness, forgiveness,
and benevolence ; to feel our souls sedate, mild and meek ; to be void of
all evil surmisings and suspicions, and scarce able to think evil of any man
upon any occasion ; to find our hearts simple, open and free, to those that
look upon us with a different eye !—Prayer was so sweet an exercise to
me, that I knew not how to cease, lest I should lose the spirit of prayer.
Felt no disposition to eat or drink, for the sake of the pleasure of it, but
only to support my nature, and fit me for divine service. Could not be
content without a very particular mention of a great number of dear
friends at the throne of grace ; as also the particular circumstances of
many, so far as they were known.

" *Lord's day, March* 4. In the morning, enjoyed the same intenseness
in prayer as yesterday morning. though not in so great a degree ; felt the
same spirit of love, universal benevolence, forgiveness, humility, resignation,
mortification to the world, and composure of mind, as then. My soul rested
in God ; and I found I wanted no other refuge or friend. While my soul
trusts in God, all things seem to be at peace with me, even the stones of

the earth; but when I cannot apprehend and confide in God, all things appear with a different aspect.

"*March 10.* In the morning, felt exceedingly dead to the world, and all its enjoyments. I thought I was ready and willing to give up life and all its comforts, as soon as called to it; and yet then had as much comfort of life as almost ever I had. Life itself now appeared but an empty bubble; the riches, honors, and common enjoyments of life appeared extremely tasteless. I longed to be perpetually and entirely crucified to all things here below, by the cross of Christ. My soul was sweetly resigned to God's disposal of me, in every regard; and I saw that nothing had happened but what was best for me. I confided in God, that he would never leave me, though I should 'walk through the valley of the shadow of death.' It was then my meat and drink to be holy, to live to the Lord, and die to the Lord. And I thought that I then enjoyed such a heaven, as far exceeded the most sublime conceptions of an unregenerate soul; and even unspeakably beyond what I myself could conceive at another time. I did not wonder that Peter said, 'Lord, it is good to be here,' when thus refreshed with divine glories. My soul was full of love and tenderness in the duty of intercession; especially felt a most sweet affection to some precious godly ministers, of my acquaintance. Prayed earnestly for dear Christians, and for those I have reason to fear are my enemies; and could not have spoken a word of bitterness, or entertained a bitter thought, against the vilest man living. Had a sense of my own great unworthiness. My soul seemed to breathe forth love and praise to God afresh, when I thought he would let his children love and receive me as one of their brethren and fellow-citizens. When I thought of their treating me in that manner, I longed to lie at their feet; and could think of no way to express the sincerity and simplicity of my love and esteem of them, as being much better than myself. Towards night was very sorrowful; seemed to myself the worst creature living; and could not pray nor meditate, nor think of holding up my face before the world. Was a little relieved in prayer, in the evening; but longed to get on my knees, and ask forgiveness of everybody that ever had seen anything amiss in my past conduct, especially in my religious zeal. Was afterwards much perplexed, so that I could not sleep quietly.

"*Lord's day, March 11.* My soul was, in some measure, strengthened in God, in morning devotion; so that I was released from trembling fear and distress. Preached to my people from the parable of the sower, Matt. xiii., and enjoyed some assistance, both parts of the day; had some freedom, affection, and fervency, in addressing my poor people; longed that God should take hold of their hearts, and make them spiritually alive. And, indeed, I had so much to say to them, that I knew not how to leave off speaking."

This was the last Sabbath in which he performed public
service at Kaunaumeek, and these the last sermons which he
ever preached there. It appears by his diary, that while he
continued with these Indians, he took great pains with them,
and did it with much discretion; but the particular manner
how has been omitted for brevity's sake.

"*March 12.* In the morning, was in a devout, tender, and loving
frame of mind; and was enabled to cry to God, I hope, with a child-like
spirit, with importunity, resignation, and composure of mind. My spirit
was full of quietness, and love to mankind; and longed that peace should
reign on the earth; was grieved at the very thoughts of fiery, angry, and intemperate zeal in religion; mourned over past follies in that regard; and
confided in God for strength and grace sufficient for my future work and
trials Spent the day mainly in hard labor, making preparation for my
intended journey.

"*March* 13. Felt my soul going forth after God sometimes; but not
with such ardency as I desired. In the evening, was enabled to continue
instant in prayer, for some considerable time together; and especially had
respect to the journey I designed to enter upon, with the leave of divine
providence, on the morrow. Enjoyed some freedom and fervency, en-
treating that the divine presence might attend me in every place where
my business might lead me; and had a particular reference to the trials
and temptations to which I apprehend I might be more eminently exposed
in particular places. Was strengthened and comforted; although I was
before very weary. Truly the joy of the Lord is strength and life.

"*March* 14. Enjoyed some intenseness of soul in prayer, repeating
my petitions for God's presence in every place where I expected to be in
my journey. Besought the Lord that I might not be too much pleased
and amused with dear friends and acquaintance, one place and another.
Near ten, set out on my journey; and near night came to Stockbridge.

"*March* 15. Rode down to Sheffield. Here I met a messenger from
East-Hampton on Long Island; who by the unanimous vote of that large
town, was sent to invite me thither, in order to settle with that people,
where I had been before frequently invited. Seemed more at a loss what
was my duty, than before; when I heard of the great difficulties of that
place, I was much concerned and grieved, and felt some desire to comply
with their request; but knew not what to do; endeavored to commit the
case to God."

The next two days, he went no further than Salisbury,
being hindered by the rain. When he came there, he was

much indisposed. He speaks of comfortable and profitable conversation with Christian friends, on these days.

"*Lord's day March* 18. [At Salisbury.] Was exceeding weak and faint, so that I could scarce walk; but God was pleased to afford me much freedom, clearness, and fervency in preaching; I have not had the like assistance in preaching to sinners for many months past. Here another messenger met me, and informed me of the vote of another congregation, to give me an invitation to come among them upon probation, for settlement.* Was somewhat exercised in mind with a weight and burden of care. Oh that God would 'send forth faithful laborers into his harvest!'"

After this he went forward on his journey to New York and New Jersey, performing it under great bodily indisposition. However, he preached several times by the way, being urged by friends, in which he had considerable assistance. He speaks of comfort in conversation with Christian friends, from time to time, and of various things in the exercises and frames of his heart, which show much of a divine influence on his mind in this journey: but yet complains of the things that he feared viz. a decline of his spiritual life, or vivacity in religion, by means of his constant removal from place to place, and want of retirement; and complains bitterly of his unworthiness, deadness, etc. He came to New York, March 28, and to Elizabethtown the Saturday following, where he waited till the commissioners came together.

"*April.* 5. Was again much exercised with weakness, and with pain in my head. Attended on the commissioners in their meeting.† Resolved to go on still with the Indian affair, if divine providence permitted; although I had before felt some inclination to go to East-Hampton, where I was solicited to go."

By the invitations which Brainerd had lately received, it appears, that it was not from necessity, or for want of oppor-

---

* This congregation was that at Millington, near Haddam. They were very earnestly desirous of his coming among them.

† The Indians at Kaunaumeek being but few in number, and Brainerd having been laboring among them about a year, and having prevailed upon them to be willing to remove to Stockbridge, to live under Mr. Sergeant's ministry; he thought he might now do more service for Christ among the Indians elsewhere, and therefore took this journey to New Jersey to lay the matter before the commissioners, who met at Elizabethtown, and determined that he should forthwith leave Kaunaumeek, and go to the Delaware Indians.

tunities to settle in the ministry amongst the English, not-withstanding the disgrace he had been laid under at college, that he was determined to forsake all the outward comforts to be enjoyed in the English settlements, to go and spend his life among the savages, and endure the difficulties and self-denials of an Indian mission. Just as he was leaving Kaun-aumeek, he had an earnest invitation to a settlement at East Hampton, Long Island, the fairest, pleasantest town on the whole island, and one of its largest and most wealthy par-ishes. The people there were unanimous in their desires to have him for their pastor, and for a long time continued in an earnest pursuit of what they desired, and were hardly brought to relinquish their endeavors, and give up their hopes of ob-taining him. Besides, the invitation which he had to Milling-ton was near his native town, and in the midst of his friends. Nor did Brainerd choose the business of a missionary to the Indians, rather than accept of those invitations, because he was unacquainted with the difficulties and sufferings which attended such a service; for he had had experience of these difficulties in summer and winter; having spent about a twelvemonth in a lonely desert among these savages, where he had gone through extreme hardships, and been the subject of a train of outward and inward sorrows which were now fresh in his mind. Notwithstanding all these things, he chose still to go on with this business; and that, although the place to which he was now going, was at a much greater distance from most of his friends, and native land.

After this he continued two or three days in New Jersey, very ill; and then returned to New York and thence into New England to his native town of Haddam, where he arrived April 14. And he continues still his bitter complaints of want of re-tirement. While he was in New York, he says thus, "Oh it is not the pleasures of the world which can comfort me! If God deny his presence, what are the pleasures of the city to me? One hour of sweet retirement where God is, is better than the whole world." And he continues to complain of his ignorance, meanness, and unworthiness.   However, he speaks of some seasons of special assistance and divine sweetness. He spent some days among his friends at East-Hampton and Millington.

"*April* 17.   Rode to Millington again; and felt perplexed when I set out; was feeble in body, and weak in faith.   I was going to preach a lecture, and feared I should never have assistance enough to get through. But, contriving to ride alone, at a distance from the company that was going, I spent the time in lifting up my heart to God.   Had not gone far before my soul was abundantly strengthened with those words, ' If God be for us, who can be against us? '   I went on, confiding in God; and fearing nothing so much as self-confidence.   In this frame I went to the house of God, and enjoyed some assistance.   Afterwards, felt the spirit of love and meekness in conversation with some friends.   Then rode home to my brother's; and, in the evening, singing hymns with friends, my soul seemed to melt; and in prayer, afterwards, enjoyed the exercise of faith, and was enabled to be fervent in spirit; found more of God's presence, than I have done any time in my late wearisome journey.   Eternity appeared very near; my nature was very weak, and seemed ready to be dissolved; the sun declining, and the shadows of the evening drawing on apace.   I longed to fill up the remaining moments all for God !   Though my body was so feeble, and wearied with preaching, and much private conversation, yet I wanted to sit up all night to do something for God. To God, the giver of these refreshments, be glory for ever and ever. Amen.

"*April* 18.   Was very weak, and enjoyed but little spiritual comfort. Was exercised with one who cavilled against original sin.   May the Lord open his eyes to see the fountain of sin in himself ! "

After this, he visited several ministers in Connecticut; and then traveled towards Kaunaumeek, and came to Mr. Sergeant's at Stockbridge.   He performed this journey in a very weak state of body.   The things he speaks of, are at some times deadness and want of spiritual comfort; at other times, resting in God, spiritual sweetness in conversation, engagedness in meditation on the road, assistance in preaching, rejoicing to think that so much more of his work was done, and he so much nearer to the eternal world.   And he once and again speaks of a sense of great ignorance and spiritual pollution.

" *April* 27 and 28. Spent some time in visiting friends, and discoursing with my people, (who were now moved down from their own place to Mr. Sergeant's,) and found them very glad to see me returned. Was exercised in my mind with a sense of my own unworthiness.

" *Lord's day, April* 29. Preached for Mr. Sergeant both parts of the day, from Rev. xiv. 4. 'These are they which were not defiled, etc.' Enjoyed some freedom in preaching, though not much spirituality. In the evening, my heart was in some measure lifted up in thankfulness to God for any assistance.—April 30. Rode to Kaunaumeek, but was extremely ill; did not enjoy the comfort I hoped for in my own house. —May 1. Having received new orders to go to a number of Indians, on Delaware river, in Pennsylvania, and my people here being mostly removed to Mr. Sergeant's, I this day took all my clothes, books, etc., and disposed of them, and set out for Delaware river ; but made it my way to return to Mr. Sergeant's, which I did this day, just at night. Rode several hours in the rain through the howling wilderness, although I was so disordered in body, that little or nothing but blood came from me."

He continued at Stockbridge the next day, and on Thursday rode to Sheffield, under a great degree of illness ; but with encouragement and cheerfulness of mind under his fatigues. On Friday, he rode to Salisbury, and continued there till after the Sabbath. He speaks of his soul's being, some part of the time, refreshed in conversation with some Christian friends, about their heavenly home, and their journey thither. At other times, he speaks of himself as exceedingly perplexed with barrenness and deadness, and has this exclamation : "O that time should pass with so little done for God !" On Monday, he rode to Sharon ; and speaks of himself as distressed at the consideration of the misimprovement of time.

" *May* 8. Set out from Sharon, in Connecticut, and traveled about forty-five miles to a place called Fishkill * and lodged there. Spent much of my time, while riding, in prayer, that God would go with me to Delaware. My heart, sometimes, was ready to sink with the thoughts of my work, and going alone in the wilderness, I knew not where ; but still it was comfortable to think that others of God's children had 'wandered about in caves and dens of the earth ;' and Abraham, when he was called to go forth, 'went out, not knowing whither he went.' Oh that I might follow after God !"

* A place in New York government, near the Hudson, on the east side of the river.

The next day, he went forward on his journey; crossed the Hudson, and traveled from the Hudson to the Delaware, about a hundred miles, through a desolate and hideous country, where were very few settlements; in which journey he suffered much fatigue and hardship. He visited some Indians on the way, and discoursed with them concerning Christianity. Was melancholy and disconsolate, being alone in a strange wilderness. On Saturday, he came to a settlement of Irish and Dutch people, about twelve miles above the Forks of Delaware.

"*Lord's day, May* 13. Rose early; felt very poorly after my long journey, and after being wet and fatigued. Was very melancholy; have scarcely ever seen such a gloomy morning in my life; there appeared to be no Sabbath; the children were all at play; I a stranger in the wilderness, and knew not where to go; and all circumstances seemed to conspire to render my affairs dark and discouraging. Was disappointed respecting an interpreter, and heard that the Indians were much scattered. O I mourned after the presence of God, and seemed like a creature banished from his sight! yet he was pleased to support my sinking soul, amidst all my sorrows; so that I never entertained any thought of quitting my business among the poor Indians; but was comforted, to think, that death would ere long set me free from these distresses. Rode about three or four miles to the Irish people, where I found some that appeared sober and concerned about religion. My heart then began to be a little encouraged: went and preached, first to the Irish, and then to the Indians; and in the evening, was a little comforted; my soul seemed to rest on God, and take courage. Oh that the Lord would be my support and comforter in an evil world!

May 14. Was very busy in some necessary studies. Felt myself very loose from all the world; all appeared 'vanity and vexation of spirit.' Seemed lonesome and disconsolate, as if I were banished from all mankind, and bereaved of all that is called pleasurable in the world; but appeared to myself so vile and unworthy, it seemed fitter for me to be here than anywhere.

"*May* 15. Still much engaged in my studies; and enjoyed more health, than I have for some time past; but was somewhat dejected in spirit with a sense of my meanness; seemed as if I could never do anything at all to any good purpose, by reason of ignorance and folly. Oh that a sense of these things might work more habitual humility in my soul!

"*May* 17. Was this day greatly distressed with a sense of my vileness; appeared to myself too bad to walk on God's earth, or to be treated with kindness by any of his creatures. God was pleased to let me see my inward pollution and corruption, to such a degree, that I almost despaired of being more holy : ' O wretched man that I am! who shall deliver me from the body of this death ?' In the afternoon, met with the Indians, according to appointment, and preached to them. And while riding to them, my soul seemed to confide in God; and afterwards had some relief and enlargement of soul in prayer, and some assistance in the duty of intercession; vital piety and holiness appeared sweet to me, and I longed for the perfection of it.

"*May* 18. Felt again somewhat of the sweet spirit of religion ; and my soul seemed to confide in God, that he would never leave me. But oftentimes saw myself so mean a creature, that I knew not how to think of preaching. Oh that I could always live to, and upon God !

"*May* 19. Was, some part of the time, greatly oppressed with the weight and burden of my work ; it seemed impossible for me ever to go through with the business I had undertaken. Towards night was very calm and comfortable ; and I think, my soul trusted in God for help.

"*Lord's day, May* 20. Preached twice to the poor Indians ; and enjoyed some freedom in speaking, while I attempted to remove their prejudices, against Christianity. My soul longed for assistance from above, all the while ; for I saw I had no strength sufficient for that work. Afterwards, preached to the Irish people; was much assisted in the first prayer, and somewhat in the sermon. Several persons seemed much concerned for their souls, with whom I discoursed afterwards with much freedom and some power. Blessed be God for any assistance afforded to an unworthy worm. Oh that I could live to him !"

Through the remainder of this week, he was sometimes ready to sink with a sense of his unworthiness and unfitness for the work of the ministry ; and sometimes encouraged and lifted above his fears and sorrows, and was enabled confidently to rely on God ; and especially on Saturday, towards night, he enjoyed calmness and composure, and assistance in prayer to God. He rejoiced, "that God remains unchangeably powerful and faithful, a sure and sufficient portion, and the dwelling-place of his children in all generations."

"*Lord's day, May* 27. Visited my Indians, in the morning, and attended a funeral among them ; was affected to see their heathenish practices. Oh that they might be ' turned from darkness to light !' Afterwards got a considerable number of them together, and preached to them ; and observed them very attentive. After this, preached to the

white people from Heb. ii. 3. How shall we escape if we neglect etc.
Was enabled to speak with some freedom and power; several people
seemed much concerned for their souls; especially one who had been
educated a Roman Catholic. Blessed be the Lord for any help.

"*May* 28. Set out from the Indians above the Forks of the Delaware,
on a journey towards Newark, in New Jersey, according to my orders.
Rode through the wilderness; was much fatigued with the heat; lodged
at a place called Black River; was exceedingly tired and worn out."

On Tuesday he came to Newark. The next day went
to Elizabethtown, and Thursday to New York, and on
Friday returned to Elizabethtown. These days were spent
in some perplexity of mind. He continued at Elizabethtown till Friday in the week following. Was enlivened, refreshed, and strengthened on the Sabbath at the Lord's
table. The ensuing days of the week were spent chiefly in
studies preparatory to his ordination; and on some of them
he seemed to have much of God's gracious presence, and of
the sweet influences of his Spirit; but was in a very weak
state of body. On Saturday he rode to Newark.

"*Lord's day, June* 10. [At Newark] in the morning was much concerned how I should perform the work of the day; and trembled at the
thoughts of being left to myself. Enjoyed very considerable assistance
in all parts of the public service. Had an opportunity again to attend on
the ordinance of the Lord's supper, and through divine goodness was refreshed in it: my soul was full of love and tenderness towards the
children of God, and towards all men; felt a certain sweetness of disposition towards every creature. At night, I enjoyed more spirituality
and sweet desire of holiness, than I have felt for some time: was afraid
of every thought and every motion, lest thereby my heart should be drawn
away from God. Oh that I might never leave the blessed God! 'Lord,
in thy presence is fullness of joy.' O the blessedness of living to God!

"*June* 11. This day the Presbytery met at Newark in order to my
ordination. Was very weak and disordered in body; yet endeavored to
repose my confidence in God. Spent most of the day alone; especially
the forenoon. At three in the afternoon preached my probation sermon,
from Acts xxvi. 17, 18. Delivering thee from the people, and from the
Gentiles, etc. being a text given me for that end. Felt not well either in
body or mind; however, God carried me through comfortably. Afterwards, passed an examination before the Presbytery. Was much tired, and
my mind burdened with the greatness of that charge I was in the most

solemn manner about to take upon me; my mind was so pressed with the weight of the work incumbent upon me, that I could not sleep this night, though very weary and in great need of rest.

"*June* 12. Was this morning further examined, respecting my experimental acquaintance with Christianity.* At ten o'clock my ordination was attended; the sermon preached by the Rev. Mr. Pemberton. At this time I was affected with a sense of the important trust committed to me; yet was composed, and solemn, without distraction; and I hope that then, as many times before, I gave myself up to God, to be for him, and not for another. O that I might always be engaged in the service of God, and duly remember the solemn charge I have received, in the presence of God, angels, and men. Amen. May I be assisted of God for this purpose.—Towards night, rode to Elizabethtown."

* Mr. Pemberton in a letter to the society in Scotland, published in the *Christian Monthly History*, writes thus. "We can with pleasure say, that Mr Brainerd passed through his ordination trial to the universal approbation of the Presbytery, and appeared uncommonly qualified for the work of the ministry. He seems to be armed with a great deal of self-denial, and animated with a noble zeal to propagate the gospel among these barbarous nations, who have long dwelt in the darkness of heathenism."

CHAPTER VI.

Enters upon a mission among the Indians at Crossweeksung.—A succinct account of his
Missionary labor and success both at Kaunaumeek and at the Forks of the Delaware,
in a Letter of Brainerd's to the Rev. Mr. Pemberton.

"*June* 13, [1744.] Spent considerable time in writing an account of
the Indian affairs to go to Scotland; some, in conversation with friends;
but enjoyed not much sweetness and satisfaction.

"*June* 14.   Received some particular kindness from friends; and
wondered, that God should open the hearts of any to treat me with kindness; saw myself to be unworthy of any favor from God, or any of my
fellow-men.   Was much exercised with pain in my head; however, I
determined to set out on my journey towards the Delaware in the afternoon; but when the afternoon came, my pain increased exceedingly; so
that I was obliged to betake myself to bed.   The night following, I was
greatly distressed with pain and sickness; was sometimes almost bereaved
of the exercise of reason by the extremity of pain.   Continued much distressed till Saturday, when I was somewhat relieved by an emetic; but
was unable to walk abroad till the Monday following, in the afternoon;
and still remained very feeble.   I often admired the goodness of God,
that he did not suffer me to proceed on my journey from this place where
I was so tenderly used, and to be sick by the way among strangers.   God
is very gracious to me, both in health and sickness, and intermingles
much mercy with all my afflictions and toils.   Enjoyed some sweetness
in things divine, in the midst of my pain and weakness.   Oh that I could
praise the Lord."

On Tuesday, June 19, he set out on his journey home,
and in three days reached his residence, near the Forks of
Delaware.*   Performed the journey under much weakness of
body; but had comfort in his soul, from day to day; and
both his weakness of body, and consolation of mind, continued through the week.

" *Lord's day, June* 24.   Extremely feeble; scarcely able to walk;
however visited my Indians, and took much pains to instruct them;
labored with some that were much disaffected to Christianity.   My mind
was much burdened with the weight and difficulty of my work.   My

*[Near where Easton, Pa., is now situated. Ed.]

whole dependence and hope of success seemed to be on God ; who alone I saw could make them willing to receive instruction, My heart was much engaged in prayer, sending up silent requests to God, even while I was speaking to them. O, that I could always go in the strength of the Lord !

"*June 25.* Was somewhat better in health than of late ; and was able to spend a considerable part of the day in prayer and close study. Had more freedom and fervency in prayer than usual of late ; especially longed for the presence of God in my work, and that the poor Heathen might be converted. And in evening prayer, my faith and hope in God were much raised. To an eye of reason, every thing that respects the conversion of the heathen, is as dark as midnight ; and yet I cannot but hope in God for the accomplishment of something glorious among them. My soul longed much for the advancement of the Redeemer's kingdom on earth. Was very fearful lest I should admit some vain thought, and so lose the sense I then had of divine things. Oh for an abiding heavenly temper !

"*June 26.* In the morning, my desires seemed to rise, and ascend up freely to God. Was busy most of the day in translating prayers into the language of the Delaware Indians ; met with great difficulty, because my interpreter was altogether unacquainted with the business. But though I was much discouraged with the extreme difficulty of that work, yet God supported me ; and especially in the evening, gave me sweet refreshment. In prayer, my soul was enlarged, and my faith drawn into sensible exercise ; was enabled to cry to God for my poor Indians ; and though the work of their conversion appeared impossible with man, yet with God I saw all things were possible. My faith was much strengthened, by observing the wonderful assistance God afforded his servants Nehemiah and Ezra, in reforming his people, and re-establishing his ancient church. I was much assisted in prayer for my dear Christian friends, and for others whom I apprehended to be Christless ; but was more especially concerned for the poor Heathen, and those of my own charge ; was enabled to be instant in prayer for them ; and hopeful that God would bow the heavens and come down for their salvation. It seemed to me, that there could be no impediment sufficient to obstruct that glorious work, seeing the living God, as I strongly hoped, was engaged for it. I continued in a solemn frame, lifting up my heart to God for assistance and grace, that I might be more mortified to this present world, that my whole soul might be taken up continually in concern for the advancement of Christ's kingdom. Earnestly desired that God would purge me more, more, that I might be as a chosen vessel to bear his name among the heathens. Continued in this frame till I fell asleep.

"*June 27.* Felt something of the same solemn concern, and spirit of prayer, which I enjoyed last night, soon after I rose in the morning. In the afternoon, rode several miles to see if I could procure any lands for the poor Indians, that they might live together, and be under better advantages for instruction.—While I was riding, had a deep sense of the greatness and difficulty of my work; and my soul seemed to rely wholly upon God for success, in the diligent and faithful use of means. Saw, with the greatest certainty, that the arm of the Lord must be revealed, for the help of these poor Heathen, if ever they were delivered from the bondage of the powers of darkness. Spent most of the time, while riding, in lifting up my heart for grace and assistance.

"*June* 28. Spent the morning in reading several parts of the holy scripture, and in fervent prayer for my Indians, that God would set up his kingdom among them, and bring them into his church. About nine, I withdrew to my usual place of retirement in the woods; and there again enjoyed some assistance in prayer. My great concern was for the conversion of the Heathen to God; and the Lord helped me to plead with him for it. Towards noon, rode up to the Indians, in order to preach to them; and, while going, my heart went up to God in prayer for them; could freely tell God, he knew that the cause in which I was engaged was not mine; but that it was his own cause, and that it would be for his own glory to convert the poor Indians; and blessed be God, I felt no desire of their conversion, that I might receive honor from the world, as being the instrument of it. Had some freedom in speaking to the Indians.

"*June* 30 My soul was very solemn in reading God's word; especially the ninth chapter of Daniel. I saw how God had called out his servants to prayer, and made them wrestle with him, when he designed to bestow any great mercy on his church. And, alas! I was ashamed of myself, to think of my dullness and inactivity, when there seemed to be so much to do for the upbuilding of Zion. O how does Zion lie waste! I longed that the church of God might be enlarged; was enabled to pray, I think, in faith; my soul seemed sensibly to confide in God, and was enabled to wrestle with him. Afterwards, walked abroad to a place of sweet retirement, enjoyed some assistance in prayer, had a sense of my great need of divine help, and felt my soul sensibly depend on God. Blessed be God, this has been a comfortable week to me.

"*Lord's day, July* 1. In the morning, was perplexed with wandering vain thoughts; was much grieved, judged and condemned myself before God. O how miserable did I feel, because I could not live to God! At ten, rode away with a heavy heart, to preach to my Indians. Upon the road I attempted to lift up my heart to God; but was infested with an unsettled wandering frame of mind; and was exceeding restless and perplexed, and filled with shame and confusion before God. I seemed to myself to be 'more brutish than any man;' and thought, none deserved to be 'cast out of God's presence' so much as I. If I attempted to lift up my heart to God, as I frequently did by the way, on a sudden, before I was aware, my thoughts were wandering 'to the ends of the earth;' and my soul was filled with surprise and anxiety, to find it thus. Thus also, after I came to the Indians, my mind was confused; and I felt nothing sensibly of that sweet reliance on God, with which my soul has been comforted in days past. Spent the forenoon in this posture of mind, and preached to the Indians without any heart. In the afternoon I felt still barren, when I began to preach; and for about half an hour, I seemed to myself to know nothing, and to have nothing to say to the Indians; but soon after, I found in myself a spirit of love, and warmth, and power, to address the poor Indians; and God helped me to plead with them, to 'turn from all the vanities of the Heathen, to the living God.' I am persuaded that the Lord touched their consciences; for I never saw such attention raised in them. When I came away from them, I spent the whole time while I was riding to my lodgings, three miles distant, in prayer and praise to God. After I had rode more than two miles, it came into my mind to dedicate myself to God again; which I did with great solemnity, and unspeakable satisfaction; especially gave up myself to him renewedly in the work of the ministry. This I did by divine grace, I hope, without any exception or reserve; not in the least shrinking back from any difficulties that might attend this great and blessed work. I seemed to be most free, cheerful, and full in this dedication of myself. My whole soul cried 'Lord, to thee I dedicate myself! O accept of me, and let me be thine forever. Lord, I desire nothing else; I desire nothing more. O come, come Lord, accept a poor worm. Whom have I in heaven but thee? and there is none upon earth that I desire beside thee.' After this, was enabled to praise God with my whole soul, that he had enabled me to devote and consecrate all my powers to him in this solemn manner. My heart rejoiced in my particular work as a missionary; rejoiced in my necessity of self-denial in many respects; and still continued to give up myself to God, and implore mercy of him, praying incessantly, every moment with sweet fervency. My nature being very weak of late, and much spent, was now considerably overcome: my fingers grew very feeble, and somewhat numb, so that I could scarcely stretch them out straight: and when I lighted from my horse, could hardly walk; my joints seemed all to be loosed. But I felt abundant strength in the inner man. Preached to the white people; God helped me much, especially in prayer. Sundry of my poor Indians, were so moved as to come to meeting also; and one appeared much concerned.

"*July* 2. Had some relish of the divine comforts of yesterday; but could not get that warmth and exercise of faith, which I desired. Had sometimes a distressing sense of my past follies, and present ignorance and barrenness; and especially in the afternoon, was sunk down under a load of sin and guilt, in that I had lived so little to God, after his abundant goodness to me yesterday. In the evening, though very weak, was enabled to pray with fervency, and to continue instant in prayer, near an hour. My soul mourned over the power of its corruption, and longed exceedingly to be washed and purged as with hyssop. Was enabled to pray for my dear absent friends, Christ's ministers, and his church ; and enjoyed much freedom and fervency, but not so much comfort, by reason of guilt and shame before God. Judged and condemned myself for the follies of the day.

"*July* 3. Was still very weak. This morning, was enabled to pray under a feeling sense of my need of help from God, and, I trust, had some faith in exercise ; and blessed be God, was enabled to plead with him a considerable time. Truly God is good to me. But my soul mourned, and was grieved at my sinfulness and barrenness, and longed to be more engaged for God. Near nine, withdrew again for prayer; and through divine goodness, had the blessed spirit of prayer; my soul loved the duty, and longed for God in it. O it is sweet to be the Lord's, to be sensibly devoted to him ! What a blessed portion is God ! How glorious, how lovely in himself ! O my soul longed to improve time wholly for God ! Spent most of the day in translating prayers into Indian.—In the evening, was enabled again to wrestle with God in prayer with fervency. Was enabled to maintain a self-diffident and watchful frame of spirit, in the evening and was jealous and afraid lest I should admit carelessness and self-confidence."

The next day, he seems to have had special assistance and fervency most of the day, but in a less degree than in the preceding day. Tuesday was spent in great bodily weakness; yet seems to have been spent in continual distress and great bitterness of spirit, in consequence of his vileness and corruption. He says, " I thought that there was not one creature living so vile as I. O my inward pollution ! O my guilt and shame before God ! I know not what to do. O I longed ardently to be cleansed and washed from the stains of inward pollution ; O, to be made like God, or rather to be made fit for God to own ! "

"*July* 6. Awoke this morning in the fear of God : soon called to mind my sadness in the evening past ; and spent my first waking minutes

in prayer for sanctification, that my soul may be washed from its exceeding pollution and defilement. After I arose, I spent some time in reading God's word, and in prayer. I cried to God under a sense of my great
indigence. I am, of late most of all concerned for ministerial qualifications, and the conversion of the heathen. Last year, I longed to be prepared for a world of glory, and speedily to depart out of this world; but
of late all my concern almost is, for the conversion of the heathen; and
for that end I long to live. But blessed be God, I have less desire to
live for any of the pleasures of the world, than I ever had. I long and
love to be a pilgrim; and want grace to imitate the life, labors, and sufferings of St. Paul among the heathen. And when I long for holiness now,
it is not so much for myself as formerly; but rather that thereby I may
become an 'able minister of the New Testament,' especially to the
heathen. Spent about two hours this morning in reading and prayer by
turns; and was in a watchful tender frame, afraid of everything that
might cool my affections, and draw away my heart from God. Was a
little strengthened in my studies; but near night was very weak and
weary.

"*July* 7. Was very much disordered this morning, and my vigor all
spent and exhausted; but was affected and refreshed in reading the sweet
story of Elijah's translation, and enjoyed some affection and fervency in
prayer; longed much for ministerial gifts and graces, that I might do
something in the cause of God. Afterwards was refreshed and invigorated,
while reading 'Alleine's first Case of Conscience,' and enabled then to
pray with some ardor of soul, and was afraid of carelessness and self-confidence, and longed for holiness.

"*Lord's day, July* 8. Was ill last night, not able to rest quietly. Had
some small degree of assistance in preaching to the Indians; and afterwards was enabled to preach to the white people with some power,
especially in the close of my discourse from Jer. iii. 23. Truly in vain is
salvation hoped for from the hills, etc. The Lord also assisted me in
some measure in the first prayer; blessed be his name. Near night,
though very weary, was enabled to read God's word with some sweet
relish of it, and to pray with affection, fervency, and I trust with faith;
my soul was more sensibly dependent on God than usual. Was watchful,
tender, and jealous of my own heart, lest I should admit carelessness and
vain thoughts, and grieve the blessed Spirit, so that he should withdraw
his sweet, kind, and tender influences. Longed to 'depart, and be with
Christ,' more than at any time of late. My soul was exceedingly united
to the saints of ancient times, as well as those now living; especially my
soul melted for the society of Elijah and Elisha. Was enabled to cry to
God with a child-like spirit, and to continue instant in prayer for some
time. Was much enlarged in the sweet duty of intercession; was

enabled to remember great numbers of dear friends, and precious souls, as well as Christ's ministers. Continued in this frame, afraid of every idle thought, till I dropped asleep.

"*July* 9. Was under much illness of body most of the day; and not able to sit up the whole day. Towards night felt a little better. Then spent some time in reading God's word and prayer; enjoyed some degree of fervency and affection; was enabled to plead with God for his cause and kingdom; and, through divine goodness, it was apparent to me, that it was his cause I pleaded for, and not my own; and was enabled to make this an argument with God to answer my requests.

"*July* 10. Was very ill and full of pain, and very dull and spiritless. In the evening, had an affecting sense of my ignorance, and of my need of God at all times to do everything for me; and my soul was humbled before God.

"*July* 11. Was still exercised with illness and pain. Had some degree of affection and warmth in prayer and reading God's word; longed for Abraham's faith and fellowship with God; and felt some resolution to spend all my time for God, and to exert myself with more fervency in his service; but found my body weak and feeble. In the afternoon, though very ill, was enabled to spend some considerable time in prayer : spent, indeed, most of the day in that exercise : and my soul was diffident, watchful, and tender, lest I should offend my blessed Friend, in thought or behavior. I am persuaded that my soul confided in, and leaned upon the blessed God. O, what need did I see myself to stand in of God at all times, to assist me and lead me ! Found a great want of strength and vigor, both in the outward and inner man."

The experiences of which he speaks in the next nine days, are very similar to those of the preceding days of this and the foregoing week ; a sense of his own weakness, ignorance, unprofitableness, and vileness ; loathing and abhorring himself ; self-diffidence ; sense of the greatness of his work, of his great need of divine help, and the extreme danger of self-confidence ; longing for holiness and humility, to be fitted for his work, and to live to God, and for the conversion of the Indians ; and these things to a very great degree.

"*July* 21. This morning, I was greatly oppressed with guilt and shame, from a sense of inward vileness and pollution. About nine, withdrew to the woods for prayer ; but had not much comfort ; I appeared to myself the vilest, meanest creature upon earth, and could scarcely live with myself ; so mean and vile I appeared that I thought I should never be able to hold up my face in heaven, if God of his infinite grace should bring me thither. Towards night my burden respecting my work among the Indians began to increase much; and was aggravated by hearing sundry things, which looked very discouraging; in particular, that they intended to meet together the next day for an idolatrous feast and dance. Then I began to be in anguish; I thought that I must in conscience go and endeavor to break them up; yet knew not how to attempt such a thing. However, I withdrew for prayer, hoping for strength from above. In prayer I was exceedingly enlarged, and my soul was as much drawn out as I ever remember it to have been in my life. I was in such anguish, and pleaded with so much earnestness and importunity, that when I rose from my knees I felt extremely weak and overcome; I could scarce walk straight; my joints were loosed; the sweat ran down my face and body; and nature seemed as if it would dissolve. So far as I could judge, I was wholly free from selfish ends in my fervent supplications for the poor Indians. I knew that they were met together to worship devils, and not God; and this made me cry earnestly, that God would now appear, and help me in my attempts to break up this idolatrous meeting. My soul pleaded long; and I thought that God would hear, and would go with me to vindicate his own cause; I seemed to confide in God for his presence and assistance. And thus I spent the evening, praying incessantly for divine assistance, and that I might not be self-dependent, but still have my whole dependence upon God. What I passed through was remarkable, and indeed inexpressible. All things here below vanished; and there appeared to be nothing of any considerable importance to me, but holiness of heart and life and the conversion of the Heathen to God. All my cares, fears, and desires, which might be said to be of a worldly nature, disappeared; and were, in my esteem, of little more importance than a puff of wind. I exceedingly longed that God would get to himself a name among the heathen; and I appealed to him with the greatest freedom, that he knew I 'preferred him above my chief joy.' Indeed, I had no notion of joy from this world; I cared not where or how I lived, or what hardships I went through, so that I could but gain souls to Christ. I continued in this frame all the evening and night. While I was asleep, I dreamed of these things; and when I waked, (as I frequently did,) the first thing I thought of was this great work of pleading for God against Satan.

"*Lord's day, July* 22. When I waked, my soul was burdened with what seemed to be before me. I cried to God, before I could get out of my bed; and as soon as I was dressed, I withdrew into the woods, to pour out my burdened soul to God, especially for assistance in my great work; for I could scarcely think of anything else. I enjoyed the same freedom and fervency as the last evening; and did with unspeakable freedom give up myself afresh to God, for life or death, for all hardships he should call me to among the heathen; and felt as if nothing could discourage me from this blessed work. I had a strong hope that God would 'bow the heavens and come down,' and do some marvellous work among the heathen. While I was riding to the Indians—three miles, my heart was continually going up to God for his presence and assistance; and hoping, and almost expecting, that God would make this the day of his power and grace amongst the poor Indians. When I came to them, I found them engaged in their frolic; but through divine goodness I persuaded them to desist; and attend to my preaching; yet still there appeared nothing of the special power of God among them. Preached again to them in the afternoon, and observed the Indians were more sober than before; but still saw nothing special among them. Hence Satan took occasion to tempt and buffet me with these cursed suggestions, There is no God, or if there be, he is not able to convert the Indians, before they have more knowledge. I was very weak and weary, and my soul borne down with perplexity; but was mortified to all the world, and was determined still to wait upon God for the conversion of the heathen, though the devil tempted me to the contrary.

"*July* 23. Retained still a deep and pressing sense of what lay with so much weight upon me yesterday; but was more calm and quiet. Enjoyed freedom and composure, after the temptations of the last evening; had sweet resignation to the divine will; and desired nothing so much as the conversion of the heathen to God, and that his kingdom might come in my own heart, and the heart of others. Rode to a settlement of Irish people, about fifteen miles south-westward; spent my time in prayer and meditation by the way. Near night preached from Matt. v. 3. Blessed are the poor in spirit, etc. God was pleased to afford me some degree of freedom and fervency. Blessed be God for any measure of assistance.

"*July* 24. Rode about seventeen miles westward, over a hideous mountain, to a number of Indians, Got together near thirty of them; preached to them in the evening, and lodged among them. Was weak, and felt in some degree disconsolate; yet could have no freedom in the thought of any other circumstances or business in life. All my desire was the conversion of the heathen; and all my hope was in God. God does not suffer me to please or comfort myself with hopes of seeing friends, returning to my dear acquaintance, and enjoying worldly comforts."

The next day, he preached to these Indians again; and then returned to the Irish settlement, and there preached to a numerous congregation. There was a considerable appearance of awakening in the congregation. Thursday he returned home, exceedingly fatigued and spent; still in the same frame of mortification to the world, and solicitous for the advancement of Christ's kingdom. On this day he writes thus : "I have felt this week, more of the spirit of a pilgrim on earth, than perhaps ever before ; and yet so desirous to see Zion's prosperity, that I was not so willing to leave this scene of sorrows as I used to be." The two remaining days of the week, he was very ill, and complains of wanderings, dullness, and want of spiritual fervency and sweetness. On the Sabbath, he was confined by illness, not able to go out to preach. After this, his illness increased upon him, and he continued very ill all the week ; and says, that " he thought he never before endured such a season of distressing weakness; that his nature was so spent, that he could neither stand, sit, nor lie with any quiet; that he was exercised with extreme faintness and sickness at his stomach ; that his mind was as much disordered as his body, seeming to be stupid, and without any kind of affections towards all objects, and yet perplexed, to think that he lived for nothing ; that precious time rolled away and he could do nothing but trifle ; and that it was a season wherein Satan buffeted him with some peculiar temptations. On Tuesday of this week he wrote the following to a friend. It indicates affections in no ordinary degree chastened and spiritual.

" FORKS OF DELAWARE, *July* 31, 1744.

"———Certainly the greatest, the noblest pleasure of intelligent creatures must result from their acquaintance with the blessed God, and with their own rational and immortal souls. O, how divinely sweet and entertaining is it, to look into our own souls, when we can find all our powers and passions united and engaged in pursuit after God ; our whole souls longing and passionately breathing after a conformity to him, and the full enjoyment of him ! Verily no hours pass away with so much divine pleasure, as those which are spent in communing with God and our own hearts. O, how sweet is a spirit of devotion, a spirit of seriousness and divine solemnity, a spirit of Gospel simplicity, love and tenderness ! O, how desirable, and how profitable to the Christian life, is a spirit of holy watchfulness, and godly jealousy over ourselves, when our souls are afraid of nothing so much as that we shall grieve and offend the blessed God, whom at such times we apprehend, or at least hope to be a Father and Friend ; whom we then love and long to please, rather than to be happy ourselves; or at least we delight to derive our happiness from pleasing and glorifying him! Surely this is a pious temper, worthy of the highest ambition and closest pursuit of intelligent creatures and holy Christians. O, how vastly superior are the pleasure, peace, and satisfaction derived from these divine frames, to that which we, alas! sometimes pursue in things impertinent and trifling! Our own bitter experience teaches us, that 'in the midst of such laughter the heart is sorrowful,' and there is no true satisfaction but in God. But, alas! how shall we obtain and retain this sweet spirit of religion and devotion! Let us follow the apostle's direction, Phil. ii. 12., and labor upon the encouragement which he there mentions, ver. 13. for it is God only can afford us this favor; and he will be sought too, and it is fit we should wait upon him for so rich a mercy. O, may the God of all grace afford us the grace and influences of his divine Spirit; and help us that we may from our hearts esteem it our greatest liberty and happiness, that 'Whether we live, we may live to the Lord, or whether we die we may die to the Lord;' that in life and death, we may be his!

"I am in a very poor state of health; I think, scarce ever poorer; but, through divine goodness, I am not discontented under my weakness, and confinement to this wilderness. I bless God for this retirement; I never was more thankful for anything, than I have been of late for the necessity I am under of self-denial in many respects. I love, to be a pilgrim and stranger in this wilderness; it seems most fit for suc.. poor, ignorant, worthless, despised creature as I. I would not change my present mission for any other business in the whole world. I may tell you freely, without vanity and ostentation, God has of late given me great freedom and fervency in prayer, when I have been so weak and feeble that my nature seemed as if it would speedily dissolve. I feel as if my all was lost, and I was undone for this world, if the poor heathen may not be converted. I feel, in general, different from what I did, when I saw you last; at least more crucified to all the enjoyments of life. It would be very refreshing to me to see you here in this desert; especially in my weak disconsolate hours; but, I think, I could be content never to see you, or any of my friends again in this world, if God would bless my labors here to the conversion of the poor Indians.

"I have much that I could willingly communicate to you which I must omit till Providence gives us leave to see each other. In the meantime, I rest

"Your obliged friend and servant,
"DAVID BRAINERD."

"*Lord's day, Aug. 5.* Am still very poor. But, though very weak, I visited and preached to the poor Indians twice, and was strengthened vastly beyond my expectations. Indeed the Lord gave me some freedom and fervency in addressing them; though I had not strength enough to stand, but was obliged to sit down the whole time. Towards night, was extremely weak, faint, sick, and full of pain. I have continued much in the same state I was in last week, through most of this, (it being now Friday,) unable to engage in any business; frequently unable to pray in the family. I am obliged to let all my thoughts and concerns run at random ; for I have not strength to read, meditate, or pray ; and this naturally perplexes my mind. I seem to myself like a man that has all his estate embarked in one small boat, unhappily going adrift, down a swift torrent. The poor owner stands on the shore, and looks, and laments his loss. But, alas! though my all seems to be adrift, and I stand and see it, I dare not lament; for this sinks my spirits more, and aggravates my bodily disorders! I am forced therefore to divert myself with trifles ; although at the same time I am afraid, and often feel as if I was guilty of the misimprovement of time. And oftentimes my conscience is so exercised, with this miserable way of spending time, that I have no peace; though I have no strength of mind or body to improve it to better purpose. O that God would pity my distressed state!"

The next three weeks, his illness was less severe ; and he was in some degree capable of business, both public and private ; though he had some turns wherein his indisposition prevailed to a great degree. He had generally also much more inward assistance, and strength of mind. He often expresses great longings for the enlargement of Christ's kingdom, especially by the conversion of the heathen to God; and speaks of this hope as all his delight and joy. He continues still to express his usual desires after holiness, living to God, and a sense of his own unworthiness. He several times speaks of his appearing to himself the vilest creature on earth ; and once says, that he verily thought there were none of God's children, who fell so far short of that holiness, and perfection in their obedience, which God requires, as he. He speaks of his feeling more dead than ever to the enjoyments of the world. He sometimes mentions the special assistance which he had at this time, in preaching to the Indians, and the appearances of religious concern among them. He speaks also of assistance in prayer for absent friends, and especially ministers and candidates for the ministry ; and of much comfort which he enjoyed in the company of some ministers who came to visit him.

"*Sept.* 1. Was so far strengthened, after a season of great weakness, that I was able to spend two or three hours in writing on a divine subject. Enjoyed some comfort and sweetness in things divine and sacred ; and as my bodily strength was in some measure restored, so my soul seemed to be somewhat vigorous, and engaged in the things of God.

"*Lord's day Sept.* 2. Was enabled to speak to my poor Indians with much concern and fervency ; and I am persuaded, that God enabled me to exercise faith in him, while I was speaking to them. I perceived that some of them were afraid to hearken to and embrace Christianity, lest they should be enchanted and poisoned by some of the powwows; but I was enabled to plead with them not to fear these ; and, confiding in God for safety and deliverance, I bid a challenge to all these powers of darkness, to do their worst on me first. I told my people that I was a Christian, and asked them why the powwows did not bewitch and poison me. I scarcely ever felt more sensible of my own unworthiness, than in this action. I saw that the honor of God was concerned in the affair ; and desired to be preserved, not from selfish views, but for a testimony of the divine power and goodness, and of the truth of Christianity, and that God might be glorified. Afterwards, I found my soul rejoice in God for his assisting grace."

After this, he went a journey into New-England, and was absent from the place of his abode, at the Forks of Delaware, about three weeks. He was in a feeble state the greater part of the time. But in the latter part of the journey, he found that he gained much in health and strength. As to the state of his mind, and his spiritual exercises, it was much with him as usual in his journeys ; excepting that the frame of his mind seemed more generally to be comfortable. In his journey, he did not forget the Indians ; but once and again speaks of his longing for their conversion.

"*Sept.* 26. Rode home to the Forks of Delaware. What reason have I to bless God, who has preserved me in riding more than four hundred and twenty miles, and has 'kept all my bones, that not one of them has been broken!' My health likewise is greatly recovered. O that I could dedicate my all to God! This is all the return I can make to him.

"*Sept.* 27. Was somewhat melancholy ; had not much freedom and comfort in prayer : my soul is disconsolate when God is withdrawn.— *Sept.* 28. Spent the day in prayer, reading, and writing. Felt some small degree of warmth in prayer, and some desires of the enlargement of Christ's kingdom by the conversion of the Heathen, and that God would make me a chosen vessel, to bear his name before them;' longed for grace to enable me to be faithful."

The next day he speaks of the same earnest desires for the advancement of Christ's kingdom by the conversion of the Indians, but complains greatly of the ill effects of the diversions of his late journey, as unfixing his mind from that degree of engagedness, fervency, and watchfullness, which he enjoyed before. The like complaints are continued the day after.

"*Oct.* 1. Was engaged this day in making preparations for my intended journey to the Susquehannah. Withdrew several times to the woods for secret duties, and endeavored to plead for the divine presence to go with me to the poor Pagans, to whom I was going to preach the gospel. Towards night rode about four miles, and met brother Byram;* who was come, at my desire, to be my companion in travel to the Indians. I rejoiced to see him; and, I trust, God made his conversation profitable to me. I saw him, as I thought, more dead to the world; its anxious cares, and alluring objects, than I was: and this made me look within myself, and gave me a greater sense of my guilt, ingratitude and misery.

"*Oct.* 2. Set out on my journey, in company with dear brother Byram, and my interpreter, and two chief Indians from the Forks of Delaware. Travelled about twenty-five miles, and lodged in one of the last houses on our road; after which there was nothing but a hideous and howling wilderness.

"*Oct.* 3. We went on our way into the wilderness, and found the most difficult and dangerous travelling, by far, that ever any of us had seen. We had scarce anything else but lofty mountains, deep valleys, and hideous rocks, to make our way through. However, I felt some sweetness in divine things, part of the day, and had my mind intensely engaged in meditation on a divine subject, Near night my beast on which I rode, hung one of her legs in the rocks, and fell down under me; but through divine goodness, I was not hurt. However, she broke her leg; and being in such a hideous place, and near thirty miles from any house, I saw nothing that could be done to perserve her life, and so was obliged to kill her, and to prosecute my journey on foot. This accident made me admire the divine goodness to me, that my bones were not broken, and the multitude of them filled with strong pain. Just at dark, we kindled a fire, cut up a few bushes, and made a shelter over our heads, to save us from the frost, which was very hard that night; and committing ourselves to God by prayer, we lay down on the ground, and slept quietly."

* Minster at a place called Rockciticus, about forty miles from Brainerd's lodgings.

The next day, they went forward on their journey, and at night took up their lodgings in the woods in like manner.

"*Oct.* 5. We reached the Susquehannah river, at a place called Opeholhaupung, and found there twelve Indian houses. After I had saluted the king in a friendly manner I told him my business, and that my desire was to teach them Christianity. After some consultation, the Indians gathered, and I preached to them. And when I had done, I asked if they would hear me again. They replied, that they would consider of it; and soon after sent me word, that they would immediately attend, if I would preach ; which I did, with freedom, both times. When I asked them again, whether they would hear me further, they replied, they would the next day. I was exceeding sensible of the impossibility of doing any thing for the poor heathen without special assistance from above ; and my soul seemed to rest on God, and leave it to him to do as he pleased in that which I saw was his own cause. Indeed, though divine goodness, I had felt somewhat of this frame most of the time while I was travelling thither, and in some measure before I set out.

"*Oct.* 6. Rose early and besought the Lord for help in my great work. Near noon, preached again to the Indians ; and in the afternoon, visited them from house to house, and invited them to come and hear me again the next day, and put off their hunting design, which they were just entering upon, till Monday. 'This night,' I trust, 'The Lord stood by me,' to encourage and strengthen my soul ; I spent more than an hour in secret retirement ; was enabled to 'pour out my heart before God,' for the increase of grace in my soul, for ministerial endowments, for success among the poor Indians, for God's ministers and people, for distant dear friends, etc. Blessed be God."

The next day, he complains of great want of fixedness and intenseness in religion, so that he could not keep any spiritual thought one minute without distraction ; which occasioned anguish of spirit. He felt amazingly guilty, and extremely miserable ; and cries out, "O, my soul, what death it is, to have the affections unable to centre in God, by reason of darkness, and consequent roving after that satisfaction elsewhere, that is only to be found here !" However, he preached twice to the Indians with considerable freedom and power ; but was afterwards damped by the objections they made against Christianity. In the evening, in a sense of his great defects in preaching, he "intreated God not to impute to him blood-guiltiness ; " but yet was at the same time enabled to rejoice in God.

"*Oct.* 8. Visited the Indians with a design to take my leave of them, supposing they would this morning go out to hunting early; but beyond my expectation and hope, they desired to hear me preach again. I gladly complied with their request, and afterwards endeavored to answer their objections against Christianity. Then they went away; and we spent the rest of the afternoon in reading and prayer, intending to go homeward very early the next day. My soul was in some measure refreshed in secret prayer and meditation. Blessed be the Lord for all his goodness."

"*Oct.* 9. We rose about four in the morning, and, commending ourselves to God by prayer, and asking his special protection, we set out on our journey homewards about five, and travelled with great steadiness till past six at night; and then made us a fire, and a shelter of barks and so rested. I had some clear and comfortable thoughts on a divine subject, by the way, towards night. In the night, the wolves howled around us; but God preserved us."

The next day, they rose early, and traveled till they came to an Irish settlement, with which Brainerd was acquainted, and lodged there. He speaks of some sweetness in divine things, and thankfulness to God for his goodness to him in this journey, though attended with shame for his barrenness. On Thursday both he and Mr. Byram preached to the people.

"*Oct.* 12. Rode home to my lodgings; where I poured out my soul to God in secret prayer, and endeavored to bless him for his abundant goodness to me in my late journey. I scarcely ever enjoyed more health, at least of later years; and God marvellously, and almost miraculously, supported me under the fatigues of the way, and traveling on foot. Blessed be the Lord who continually preserves me in all my ways."

On Saturday, he went again to the Irish settlement, to spend the Sabbath there, his Indians being gone.

"*Lord's Day, Oct.* 14. Was much confused and perplexed in my thoughts ; could not pray ; and was almost discouraged, thinking I should never be able to preach any more. Afterwards, God was pleased to give me some relief from these confusions ; but still I was afraid, and even troubled before God. I went to the place of public worship, lifting up my heart to God for assistance and grace, in my great work : and God was gracious to me, helping me to plead with him for holiness, and to ·

use the strongest arguments with him, drawn from the incarnation and sufferings of Christ for this very end, that men might be made holy. Afterwards, I was much assisted in preaching. I know not that ever God helped me to preach in a more close and distinguishing manner for the trial of men's state. Through the infinite goodness of God, I felt what I spoke ; he enabled me to treat on divine truth with uncommon clearness ; and yet I was so sensible of my defects in preaching, that I could not be proud of my performance, as at some times ; and blessed be the Lord for this mercy. In the evening I longed to be entirely alone, to bless God for help in a time of extremity ; and longed for great degrees of holiness, that I might show my gratitude to God."

The next morning, he spent some time before sunrise in prayer, in the same sweet and grateful frame of mind, that he had been in the evening before ; and, afterwards, went to his Indians, and spent some time in teaching and exhorting them.

"*Oct.* 16. Felt a spirit of solemnity and watchfulness ; was afraid I should not live to and upon God ; longed for more intenseness and spirituality. Spent the day in writing ; frequently lifting up my heart to God for more heavenly mindedness. In the evening, enjoyed sweet assistance in prayer ; thirsted and pleaded to be as holy as the blessed angels ; longed for ministerial gifts and graces, and success in my work ; was sweetly assisted in the duty of intercession ; and enabled to remember and plead for numbers of dear friends, and of Christ's ministers.

"*Oct.* 19. Felt an abasing sense of my own impurity and unholiness : and felt my soul melt and mourn, that I had abused and grieved a very gracious God, who was still kind to me, notwithstanding all my unworthiness. My soul enjoyed a sweet season of bitter repentance and sorrow, that I had wronged that blessed God, who, I was persuaded, was reconciled to me in his dear Son. My soul was now tender, devout, and solemn. And I was afraid of nothing but sin ; and afraid of that in every action and thought.

"*Oct.* 24. Near noon, rode to my people ; spent some time and prayed with them ; felt the frame of a pilgrim on ea.th; longed much to leave this gloomy mansion; but yet found the exercise of patience and resignation. And, as I returned home from the Indians, spent the whole time in lifting up my heart to God. In the evening, enjoyed a blessed season alone in prayer ; was enabled to cry to God with a childlike spirit, for the space of near an hour ; enjoyed a sweet freedom in supplicating for myself, for dear friends, ministers, and some who are preparing for that work, and for the church of God ; and longed to be as lively myself in God's service as the angels.

"*Oct.* 25. Was busy in writing. Was very sensible of my absolute dependence on God in all respects; saw that I could do nothing, even in those affairs for which I have sufficient natural faculties, unless God should smile on my attempt. 'Not that we are sufficient of ourselves, to think any thing as of ourselves,' I saw was a sacred truth.

"*Oct.* 26. In the morning, my soul was melted with a sense of divine goodness and mercy to such a vile unworthy worm. I delighted to lean upon God, and place my whole trust in him. My soul was exceedingly grieved for sin, and prized, and longed after holiness; it wounded my heart deeply, yet sweetly, to think how I had abused a kind God. I longed to be perfectly holy, that I might not grieve a gracious God; who will continue to love, notwithstanding his love is abused! I longed for holiness more for this end, than I did for my own happiness' sake; and yet this was my greatest happiness, never more to dishonor, but always to glorify the blessed God. Afterwards, rode up to the Indians, in the afternoon, etc."

The next few days, he was exercised with much disorder and pain of body, with a degree of melancholy and gloominess of mind, bitterly complaining of deadness and unprofitableness, yet longing after God.

"*Oct.* 31. Was sensible of my barrenness and decay in the things of God; my soul failed when I remembered the fervency which I had enjoyed at the throne of grace. O, I thought, if I could but be spiritual, warm, heavenly-minded, and affectionately breathing after God, this would be better than life to me! My soul longed exceedingly for death, to be loosed from this dullness and barrenness, and made for ever active in the service of God. I seemed to live for nothing, and to do no good; and O, the burden of such a life! O death, death, my kind friend, hasten, and deliver me from dull mortality, and make me spiritual and vigorous to eternity.

"*Nov.* 1. Had but little sweetness in divine things; but afterwards, in the evening, felt some life and longings after God. I longed to be always solemn, devout, and heavenly-minded; and was afraid to leave off praying, lest I should again lose a sense of the sweet things of God.

"*Nov.* 2. Was filled with sorrow and confusion in the morning, and could enjoy no sweet sense of divine things, nor get any relief in prayer. Saw I deserved that every one of God's creatures should be let loose, to be the executioners of his wrath against me; and yet therein saw I deserved what I did not fear as my portion. About noon, rode up to the Indians; and while going, could feel no desires for them, and even dreaded to say anything to them; but God was pleased to give me some freedom and enlargement, and made the season comfortable to me. In the evening, had enlargement in prayer. But, alas! what comforts and enlargements I have felt for these many weeks past have been only transient and short; and the greater part of my time has been filled up with deadness, or struggles with deadness, and bitter conflicts with corruption. I have found myself exercised sorely with some particular things that I thought myself most of all freed from. And thus I have ever found it,—when I have thought the battle was over, and the conquest gained, and so let down my watch, the enemy has risen up and done me the greatest injury.

"*Nov.* 3. I read the life and trials of a godly man, and was much warmed by it; I wondered at my past deadness; and was more convinced of it than ever. Was enabled to confess and bewail my sin before God, with self-abhorrence.—Lord's day, Nov. 4. Had, I think, some exercise of faith in prayer, in the morning; longed to be spiritual Had considerable help in preaching to my poor Indians; was encouraged with them, and hoped that God designed mercy for them."

His letter to the Rev. Mr. Pemberton of New York, giving, by request, some account of his missionary labors and success, both at Kaunaumeek and at the Forks of Delaware.

"FORKS OF DELAWARE, Nov. 5, 1744.

"REV. SIR:

"Since you are pleased to require of me some brief and general account of my conduct in the affair of my mission among the Indians; the pains and endeavors I have used to propagate Christian knowledge among them; the difficulties I have met with in pursuance of that great work; and the hopeful and encouraging appearances I have observed in any of them; I shall now endeavor to answer your demands, by giving a brief but faithful account of the most material things relating to that important affair, with which I have been and am still concerned. This I shall do with more freedom and cheerfulness, both because I apprehend it will be a likely means to give pious persons, who are concerned for the kingdom of Christ, some just apprehension of the many and great difficulties that attend the propagation of it among the poor Pagans; and consequently, it is hoped, will engage their more frequent and fervent prayers to God, that those may be succeeded, who are employed in this arduous work. Besides, I persuade myself, that the tidings of the gospel spreading among the poor heathen, will be, to those who are waiting for the accomplishment of the 'glorious things spoken of the city of our God,' as 'good news from a far country;' and that these will be so far from 'despising the day of small things,' that, on the contrary, the least dawn of encouragement and hope, in this important affair, will rather inspire their pious breasts with more generous and warm desires, that '.the kingdoms of this world, may speedily become the kingdoms of our Lord, and of his Christ.' I shall therefore immediately proceed to the business before me, and briefly touch upon the most important matters that have concerned my mission, from the beginning to this present time.

"On March 15, 1743, I waited on the Correspondents for the Indian mission at New York; and the week following, attended their meeting at Woodbridge, in New Jersey, and was speedily dismissed by them with orders to attempt the instruction of a number of Indians in a place some miles distant from the city of Albany. And on the first day of April following, I arrived among the Indians, at a place called by them Kaunaumeek, in the county of Albany, nearly twenty miles distant from the city eastward.

" The place, as to its situation, was sufficiently lonesome and unpleasant, being encompassed with mountains and woods; twenty miles distant from any English inhabitants; six or seven from any Dutch; and more than two from a family that came some time since, from the Highlands of Scotland, and had then lived, as I remember, about two years in this wilderness. In this family I lodged about the space of three months, the master of it being the only person with whom I could readily converse in those parts, except my interpreter; others understanding very little English.

"After I had spent about three months in this situation, I found my distance from the Indians a very great disadvantage to my work among them, and very burdensome to myself ; as I was obliged to travel forward and backward almost daily on foot, having no pasture in which I could keep my horse for that purpose. And after all my pains, could not be with the Indians in the evening and morning, which were usually the best hours to find them at home, and when they could best attend my instructions. I therefore resolved to remove, and live with or near the Indians, that I might watch all opportunities, when they were generally at home, and take the advantage of such seasons for their instructions.

"Accordingly I removed soon after; and, for some time, lived with them in one of their wigwams ; and, not long after, built me a small house, where I spent the remainder of that year entirely alone ; my interpreter, who was an Indian, choosing rather to live in a wigwam among his own countrymen. This way of living I found attended with many difficulties, and uncomfortable circumstances, in a place where I could get none of the necessaries and common comforts of life, (no, not so much as a morsel of bread,) but what I brought from places fifteen and twenty miles distant, and oftentimes was obliged, for some time together, to content myself without, for want of an opportunity to procure the things I needed.

"But although the difficulties of this solitary way of living are not the least, or most inconsiderable, (and doubtless are, in fact, many more and greater to those who experience, than they can readily appear to those who only view them at a distance,) yet I can truly say that the burden I felt respecting my great work among the poor Indians, the fear and concern that continually hung upon my spirit, lest they should be prejudiced against Christianity, and their minds imbittered against me, and my labors among them by means of the insinuations of some who, although they are called Christians, seem to have no concern for Christ's kingdom, but had rather (as their conduct plainly discovers) that the Indians should remain heathens, that they may with the more ease cheat, and so enrich themselves by them—were much more pressing to me, than all the difficulties that attended the circumstances of my living.

" As to the state or temper of mind in which I found these Indians, at my first coming among them, I may justly say, it was much more desirable and encouraging, than what appears among those who are altogether uncultivated. Their heathenish jealousies and suspicion, and their prejudices against Christianity, were in a great measure removed by the long-continued labors of the Reverend Mr. Sergeant among a number of the same tribe, in a place little more than twenty miles distant. Hence, these were, in some good degree, prepared to entertain the truths of Christianity, instead of objecting against them, and appearing almost entirely untractable, as is common with them at first, and as, perhaps, these appeared a few years ago. Some of them, at least, appeared very well disposed towards religion, and seemed much pleased with my coming among them.

" In my labors with them, in order to ' turn them from darkness to light,' I studied what was most plain and easy, and best suited to their capacities ; and endeavored to set before them from time to time, as they were able to receive them, the most important and necessary truths of Christianity, such as most immediately concerned their speedy conversion to God, and such as I judged had the greatest tendency, as means, to effect that glorious change in them. But especially I made it the scope and drift of all my labors, to lead them into a thorough acquaintance with these two things. First, The sinfulness and misery of the estate they were naturally in ; the evil of their hearts, the pollution of their natures; the heavy guilt they were under, and their exposedness to everlasting punishment ; as also their utter inability to save themselves, either from their sins, or from those miseries which are the just punishment of them ; and their unworthiness of any mercy at the hand of God, on account of anything they themselves could do to procure his favor, and consequently their extreme need of Christ to save them. And, secondly, I frequently endeavored to open to them the fullness, all-sufficiency, and freeness of that redemption, which the Son of God has wrought out by his obedience and sufferings, for perishing sinners; how this provision he had made, was suited to all their wants ; and how he called and invited them to accept of everlasting life freely, notwithstanding all their sinfulness, inability, unworthiness, etc.

"After I had been with the Indians several months, I composed sundry forms of prayer, adapted to their circumstances and capacities ; which, with the help of my interpreter, I translated into the Indian language ; and soon learned to pronounce their words, so as to pray with them in their own tongue. I also translated sundry psalms into their language, and soon after we were able to sing in the worship of God.

"When my people had gained some acquaintance with many of the truths of Christianity, so that they were capable of receiving and understanding many others, which at first could not be taught them, by reason of their ignorance of those that were necessary to be previously known, and upon which others depended ; I then gave them an historical account of God's dealings with his ancient professing people the Jews ; some of the rites and ceremonies they were obliged to observe, as their sacrifices, etc.; and what these were designed to represent to them ; as also some of the surprising miracles God wrought for their salvation, while they trusted in him, and sore punishments he sometimes brought upon them, when they forsook and sinned against him. Afterwards I proceeded to give them a relation of the birth, life, miracles, sufferings, death, and resurrection of Christ ; as well as his ascension, and the wonderful effusion of the holy Spirit consequent thereupon.

"And having thus endeavored to prepare the way by such a general account of things, I next proceeded to read and expound to them the gospel of St. Matthew (at least the substance of it) in course, wherein they had a more distinct and particular view of what they had before some general notion. These expositions I attended almost every evening, when there was any considerable number of them at home ; except when I was obliged to be absent myself, in order to learn the Indian language with the Rev. Mr. Sergeant. Besides these means of instruction, there was likewise an English school constantly kept by my interpreter among the Indians ; which I used frequently to visit, in order to give the children and young people some proper instructions, and serious exhortations suited to their age. The degree of knowledge to which some of them attained, was considerable. Many of the truths of Christianity seemed fixed in their minds, especially in some instances, so that they would speak to me of them, and ask such questions about them, as were necessary to render them more plain and clear to their understandings. The children, also, and young people, who attended the school, made considerable proficiency (at least some of them) in their learning ; so that had they understood the English language well, they would have been able to read somewhat readily in a psalter.

"But that which was most of all desirable, and gave me the greatest encouragement amidst many difficulties and disconsolate hours, was, that the truths of God's word seemed, at times, to be attended with some power upon the hearts and consciences of the Indians. And especially this appeared evident in a few instances, who were awakened to some sense of their miserable estate by nature, and appeared solicitous for deliverance from it. Several of them came, of their own accord, to discourse with me about their soul's concerns ; and some, with tears, inquired ' what they should do to be saved?' and whether the God that Christians served, would be merciful to those that had been frequently drunk, etc.

"And although I cannot say that I have satisfactory evidences of their being ' renewed in the spirit of their mind,' and savingly converted to God ; yet the spirit of God did, I apprehend, in such a manner attend the means of grace, and so operate upon their minds thereby, as might justly afford matter of encouragement, to hope that God designed good to them, and that he was preparing his way into their souls.

"There likewise appeared a reformation in the lives and manners of the Indians. Their idolatrous sacrifices (of which there was but one or two, that I know of, after my coming among them) were wholly laid aside. And their heathenish custom of dancing, hallooing, etc., they seemed in a considerable measure to have abandoned. And I could not but hope, that they were reformed in some measure from the sin of drunkenness. They likewise manifested a regard for the Lord's day, and not only behaved soberly themselves, but took care also to keep their children in order.

"Yet, after all, I must confess, that as there were many hopeful appearances among them, so there were some things more discouraging. And while I rejoiced to observe any seriousness and concern among them about the affairs of their souls, still I was not without continual fear and concern, lest such encouraging appearances might prove ' like a morning cloud, that passeth away.'

"When I had spent near a year with the Indians, I informed them that I expected to leave them in the spring then approaching, and to be sent to another tribe of Indians, at a great distance from them. On hearing this, they appeared very sorrowful, and some of them endeavored to persuade me to continue with them ; urging that they had now heard so much about their souls' concerns, that they could never more be willing to live as they had done, without a minister, and further instructions in the way to heaven, etc. Whereupon I told them, they ought to be willing that others also should hear about their souls' concerns, seeing those needed it as much as themselves. Yet further to dissuade me from going, they added, that those Indians, to whom I had thoughts of going (as they had heard) were not willing to become Christians as they were, and therefore urged me to tarry with them. I then told them, that they might receive further instruction without me ; but the Indians to whom I expected to be sent, could not, there being no minister near to teach them. And hereupon I advised them in case I should leave them, and be sent elsewhere, to remove to Stockbridge, where they might be supplied with land, and conveniences of living, and be under the ministry of the Rev. Mr. Sergeant : with which advice and proposal, they seemed disposed to comply.

" April 6, 1744, I was directed by the correspondents for the Indian mission, to take leave of the people, with whom I had then spent a full year, and to go, as soon as convenient, to a tribe of Indians on Delaware river in Pennsylvania.

" These orders I soon attended, and on April 29th took leave of my people, who were mostly removed to Stockbridge under the care of the Rev. Mr. Sergeant. I then set out on my journey towards Delaware ; and on May 10th met with a number of Indians in a place called Minnissinks, about a hundred and forty miles from Kaunaumeek, (the place where I spent the last year,) and directly in my way to Delaware river. With these Indians I spent some time, and first addressed their king in a friendly manner ; and after some discourse, and attempts to contract a friendship with him, I told him I had a desire (for his benefit and happiness) to instruct them in Christianity. At which he laughed, turned his back upon me, and went away. I then addressed another principal man in the same manner, who said he was willing to hear me. After some time, I followed the king into his house, and renewed my discourse to him ; but he declined talking, and left the affair to another, who appeared to be a rational man. He began, and talked very warmly near a quarter of an hour together ; he inquired why I desired the Indians to become Christians, seeing the Christians were so much worse than the Indians are in their present state. The Christians, he said, would lie, steal, and drink, worse than the Indians. It was they first taught the Indains to be drunk : and they stole from one another, to that degree, that their rulers were obliged to hang them for it, and that was not sufficient to deter others from the like practice. But the Indians, he added, were none of them ever hanged for stealing, and yet they did not steal half so much ; and he supposed that if the Indians should become Christians, they would then be as bad as these. And hereupon he said, they would live as their fathers lived, and go where their fathers were when they died. I then freely owned, lamented and joined with him in condemning the ill conduct of some who are called Christians; told him, these were not Christians in heart; that I hated such wicked practices, and did not desire the Indians to become such as these.—And when he appeared calmer, I asked him if he was willing that I should come and see them again? He replied, he should be willing to see me again, as a friend, if I would not desire them to become Christians. I then bid them farewell, and prosecuted my jour-

ney towards Delaware. And May 13th, I arrived at a place called by the
Indians Sakhauwotung, within the Forks of Delaware in Pennsylvania.

"Here also, when I came to the Indians, I saluted their king, and
others, in a manner I thought most engaging. And soon after informed
the king of my desire to instruct them in the Christian religion. After
he had consulted a few minutes with two or three old men, he told me he
was willing to hear. I then preached to those few that were present; who
appeared very attentive and well disposed. And the king in particular
seemed both to wonder, and at the same time to be well pleased with what
I taught them, respecting the divine Being, etc. And since that time he
has ever shown himself friendly to me, giving me free liberty to preach
in his house, whenever I think fit. Here therefore I have spent the
greater part of the summer past, preaching usually in the king's house.

"The number of Indians in this place is but small; most of those
that formerly belonged here, are dispersed, and removed to places farther
back in the country. There are not more than ten houses hereabouts,
that continue to be inhabited; and some of these are several miles distant from others, which makes it difficult for the Indians to meet together so frequently as could be desired. When I first began to preach here,
the number of my hearers was very small; often not exceeding twenty or
twenty-five persons; but towards the latter part of the summer, their
number increased, so that I have frequently had forty persons, or more,
at once; and oftentimes most belonging to those parts, came together to
hear me preach.

"The effects which the truths of God's word have had upon some of
the Indians in this place, are somewhat encouraging. Sundry of them
are brought to renounce idolatry, and to decline partaking of those feasts
which they used to offer in sacrifice to certain supposed unknown powers.
And some few among them have, for a considerable time, manifested a
serious concern for their souls' eternal welfare, and still continue to 'inquire the way to Zion,' with such diligence, affection, and becoming
solicitude, as gives me reason to hope that 'God who, I trust, has begun
this work in them,' will carry it on, until it shall issue in their saving conversion to himself. These not only detest their old idolatrous notions,
but strive also to bring their friends off from them. And as they are
seeking salvation for their own souls, so they seem desirous, and some of
them take pains, that others might be excited to do the like.

"In July last I heard of a number of Indians residing at a place called
Kauksesauchung, more than thirty miles westward from the place where
I usually preach. I visited them, found about thirty persons, and proposed my desire of preach'ng to them; they readily complied, and I
preached to them only twice, they being just then removing from this
place where they only lived for the present, to Susquehannah-river, where
they belonged.

" While I was preaching, they appeared sober and attentive; and were somewhat surprised, having never before heard of these things. There were two or three who suspected that I had some ill design upon them ; and urged, that the white people had abused them, and taken their lands from them, and therefore they had no reason to think that they were now concerned for their happiness ; but, on the contrary, that they designed to make them slaves, or get them on board their vessels, and make them fight with the people over the water, (as they expressed it,) meaning the French and Spaniards. However, the most of them appeared very friendly, and told me, they were then going directly home to Susquehannah, and desired I would make them a visit there, and manifested a considerable desire of further instruction. This invitation gave me some encouragement in my great work ; and made me hope, that God designed to ' open an effectual door to me ' for spreading the gospel among the poor Heathen farther westward.

" In the beginning of October last, with the advice and direction of the correspondents for the Indian mission, I undertook a journey to Susquehannah. And after three days tedious travel, two of them through a wilderness almost impassable, by reason of mountains and rocks, and two nights lodging in the open wilderness, I came to an Indian settlement on the side of Susquehannah river, called Opeholhaupung; where were twelve Indian houses, and about seventy souls, old and young.

" Here also, soon after my arrival, I visited the king, addressing him with expressions of kindness; and after a few words of friendship, informed him of my desire to teach them the knowledge of Christianity. He hesitated not long before he told me, that he was willing to hear. I then preached ; and continued there several days, preaching every day, as long as the Indians were at home. And they, in order to hear me, deferred the design of their general hunting (which they were just then entering upon) for three or four days.

" The men, I think universally, (except one) attended my preaching. Only the women, supposing the affair we were upon was of a public nature, belonging only to the men, and not what every individual person should concern himself with, could not readily be persuaded to come and hear ; but, after much pains used with them for that purpose, some few ventured to come, and stand at a distance.

" When I had preached to the Indians several times, some of them very frankly proposed what they had to object against Christianity ; and so gave me a fair opportunity for using my best endeavors to remove from their minds those scruples and jealousies they labored under : and when I had endeavored to answer their objections, some appeared much satisfied. I then asked the king if he was willing I should visit and preach to them again, if I should live to the next spring ? He replied, he should be heartily willing, for his own part, and added, he wished the young people would learn, etc. I then put the same question to the rest; some answered they would be very glad, and none manifested any dislike to it.

"There were sundry other things in their behavior, which appeared with a comfortable and encouraging aspect; that, upon the whole, I could not but rejoice I had taken that journey among them, although it was attended with many difficulties and hardships. The method I used with them, and the instructions I gave them, I am persuaded, were means, in some measure, to remove their heathenish jealousies and prejudices against Christianity; and I could not but hope, the God of all grace was preparing their minds to receive 'the truth, as it is in Jesus.' If this may be the happy consequence, I shall not only rejoice in my past labors and fatigues, but shall, I trust, also 'be willing to spend and be spent,' if I may thereby be instrumental 'to turn them from darkness to light, and from the power of Satan to God.'

"Thus, Sir, I have given you a faithful account of what has been most considerable respecting my mission among the Indians; in which I have studied all convenient brevity. I shall only now take leave to add a word or two respecting the difficulties that attend the Christianizing of these poor Pagans.

"In the first place, their minds are filled with prejudices against Christianity, on account of the vicious lives, and unchristian behavior of some that are called Christians. These not only set before them the worst examples, but some of them take pains, expressly in words, to dissuade them from becoming Christians; foreseeing, that if these should be converted to God, 'the hope of their unlawful gain,' would thereby be lost.

"Again, these poor heathens are extremely attached to the customs, traditions, and fabulous notions of their fathers. And this one seems to be the foundation of all their other notions, viz. that 'it was not the same God made them, who made the white people,' but another, who commanded them to live by hunting, etc., and not to conform to the customs of the white people. Hence, when they are desired to become Christians, they frequently reply, that 'they will live as their fathers lived, and go to their fathers when they die.' And if the miracles of Christ and his apostles be mentioned, to prove the truth of Christianity, they also mention sundry miracles, which their fathers have told them were anciently wrought among the Indians, and which Satan makes them believe were so. They are much attached to idolatry; frequently making feasts, which they eat in honor to some unknown beings, who, they suppose, speak to them in dreams; promising them success in hunting, and other affairs, in case they will sacrifice to them. They oftentimes, also, offer their sacrifices to the spirits of the dead ; who, they suppose, stand in need of favors from the living, and yet are in such a state as that they can well reward all the offices of kindness that are shown them. And they impute all their calamities to the neglect of these sacrifices.

" Furthermore, they are much awed by those among themselves, who are called powwows, who are supposed to have a power of enchanting, or poisoning them to death. or, at least, in a very distressing manner. And they apprehend, it would be their sad fate to be thus enchanted, in case they should become Christians.

" Lastly, the manner of their living is likewise a great disadvantage to the design of their being Christianized. They are almost continually roving from place to place; and it is but rare that an opportunity can be had with some of them for their instruction. There is scarce any time of the year, wherein the men can be found generally at home, except about six weeks before, and in the season of planting their corn, and about two months in the latter part of summer, from the time they begin to roast their corn, until it is fit to gather in.

" As to the hardships that necessarily attend a mission among them, the fatigues of frequent journeying in the wilderness, the unpleasantness of a mean and hard way of living, and the great difficulty of addressing 'a people of a strange language,' these I shall, at present, pass over in silence; designing what I have already said of difficulties attending this work, not for the discouragement of any, but rather for the incitement of all who 'love the appearing of the kingdom of Christ,' to frequent the throne of grace with earnest supplications, that the heathen, who were anciently promised to Christ 'for his inheritance,' may now actually and speedily be brought into his kingdom of grace, and made heirs of immortal glory.

I am, Sir,
" Your obedient, humble servant,
" DAVID BRAINERD."

The same day, Nov. 5, he set out on a journey to New York, to the meeting of the Presbytery there ; and was from home more than a fortnight. He seemed to enter on this journey with great reluctance ; fearing that the diversions of it would prove a means of cooling his religious affections, as he had found in other journeys. Yet, in this journey, he had some special seasons wherein he enjoyed extraordinary evidences and fruits of God's gracious presence. He was greatly fatigued, and exposed to cold and storms ; and when he returned from New York to New Jersey, on Friday was taken very ill, and was detained by his illness some time.

"*Nov.* 21. Rode from Newark to Rockciticus in the cold, and was almost overcome with it. Enjoyed some sweetness in conversation with dear Mr. Jones, while I dined with him. My soul loves the people of God, and especially the ministers of Jesus Christ, who feel the same trials that I do.

"*Nov.* 22. Came on my way from Rockciticus to the Delaware. Was very much disordered with a cold and pain in my head. About six at night, I lost my way in the wilderness, and wandered over rocks. and mountains, down hideous steeps, through swamps, and most dreadful and dangerous places; and, the night being dark, so that few stars could be seen, I was greatly exposed. I was much pinched with cold, and distressed with an extreme pain in my head, attended with sickness at my stomach; so that every step I took was distressing to me. I had little hope for several hours together, but that I must lie out in the woods all night, in this distressed case. But about nine o'clock, I found a house through the abundant goodness of God, and was kindly entertained. Thus I have frequently been exposed, and sometimes lain out the whole night: but God has hitherto preserved me; and blessed be his name. Such fatigues and hardships as these serve to wean me from the earth; and, I trust, will make heaven the sweeter. Formerly, when I was thus exposed to cold, rain, etc. I was ready to please myself with the thoughts of enjoying a comfortable house, a warm fire, and other outward comforts; but now these have less place in my heart, (through the grace of God,) and my eye is more to God for comfort. In this world I expect tribulation; and it does not now, as formerly, appear strange to me. I do not in such seasons of difficulty flatter myself that it will be better hereafter: but rather think how much worse it might be; how much greater trials others of God's children have endured; and how much greater are yet perhaps reserved for me. Blessed be God, that he makes the thoughts of my journey's end, and of my dissolution, a great comfort to me, under my sharpest trials; and scarce ever lets these thoughts be attended with terror or melancholy; but they are attended frequently with great joy.

"*Nov.* 23. Visited a sick man; discoursed and prayed with him. Then visited another house, where one was dead and laid out; looked on the corpse, and longed that my time might come to depart, that I might be with Christ. Then went home to my lodgings, about one o'clock. Felt poorly; but was able to read most of the afternoon."

During the next twelve days, he passed under many changes in the frames and exercises of his mind. He had many seasons of the special influences of God's Spirit, animating, invigorating, and comforting him in the ways of God and the duties of religion ; but had some turns of great dejection and melancholy. He spent much of this time in hard labor, with others, to make for himself a little cottage or hut, to live in by himself through the winter. Yet he frequently preached to the Indians, and speaks of special assistance which he had formed from time to time, in addressing himself to them ; and of his sometimes having considerable encouragement from the attention which they gave. But December 4, he was sunk into great discouragement, to see most of them going in company to an idolatrous feast and dance, after he had taken abundant pains to dissuade them from these things.

"*Dec.* 6. Having now a happy opportunity of being retired in a house of my own, which I have lately procured and moved into ; considering that it is now a long time since I have been able, either on account of bodily weakness, or for want of retirement, or some other difficulty to spend any time in secret fasting and prayer ; considering also the greatness of my work, the extreme difficulties that attend it, and that my poor Indians are now worshipping devils, notwithstanding all the pains I have taken with them, which almost overwhelms my spirit ; moreover, considering my extreme barrenness, spiritual deadness and dejection, of late ; as also the power of some particular corruptions ; I set apart this day for secret prayer and fasting, to implore the blessing of God on myself, on my poor people, on my friends, and on the church of God. At first, I felt a great backwardness to the duties of the day, on account of the seeming impossibility of performing them ; but the Lord helped me to break through this difficulty. God was pleased by the use of means, to give me some clear conviction of my sinfulness, and a discovery of the plague of my own heart, more affecting than what I have of late had. And especially I saw my sinfulness in this, that when God had withdrawn himself, then, instead of living and dying in pursuit of him, I have been disposed to one of these two things : either, first, to yield an unbecoming respect to some earthly objects, as if happiness were to be derived from them ; or, secondly, to be secretly froward and impatient, and unsuitably desirous of death, so that I have sometimes thought I could not bear to think that my life must be lengthened out. That which often drove me to this impatient desire of death, was a despair of doing any good in life ; and I chose death rather than a life spent for nothing. But now God made me sensible of my sin in these things, and enabled me to cry to him for forgiveness. Yet this was not all which I wanted, for my soul appeared exceedingly polluted, my heart seemed like a nest of vipers, or a cage of unclean and hateful birds ; and therefore I wanted to be purified 'by the blood of sprinkling, that cleanseth from all sin.' This, I hope, I was enabled to pray for in faith. I enjoyed much more intenseness, fervency, and spirituality, than I expected ; God was better to me than my fears. Towards night, I felt my soul rejoice, that God is unchangeably happy and glorious ; and that he will be glorified, whatever becomes of his creatures. I was enabled to persevere in prayer, until sometimes in the evening: at which time I saw so much need of divine help, in every respect, that I knew not how to leave off, and had forgot that I needed food. This evening, I was much assisted in meditating on Is. lii. 3. For thus saith the Lord, ye have sold yourselves for nought, etc. Blessed be the Lord for any help in the past day.

" *Dec.* 7. Spent time in prayer, in the morning ; enjoyed some freedom and affections in the duty, and had longing desires of being ' made faithful unto death.' Spent a little time in writing on a divine subject ; then visited the Indians, and preached to them ; but under inexpressible dejection. I had no heart to speak to them, and could not do it, but as I forced myself ; I knew they must hate to hear me, as having but just got home from their idolatrous feast and devil-worship. In the evening, had some freedom in prayer and meditation.

" *Dec.* 8. Have been uncommonly free this day from dejection, and from that distressing apprehension, that I could do nothing ; was enabled to pray and study with some comfort ; and especially was assisted in writing on a divine subject. In the evening, my soul rejoiced in God ; and I blessed his name for shining on my soul. O, the sweet and blessed change I then felt, when God ' brought me out of darkness into his marvellous light ! '

" *Lord's day Dec.* 9. Preached, both parts of the day, at a place called Greenwich, in New Jersey, about ten miles from my own house. In the first discourse I had scarce any warmth or affectionate longing for souls. In the intermediate season I got alone among the bushes, and cried to God for pardon of my deadness ; and was in anguish and bitterness, that I could not address souls with more compassion and tender affection. I judged and condemned myself for want of this divine temper ; though I saw I could not get it as of myself, any more than I could make a world. In the latter exercise, blessed be the Lord, I had some fervency, both in prayer and preaching ; and especially in the application of my discourse, I was enabled to address precious souls with affection, concern, tenderness, and importunity. The spirit of God, I think, was there ; as the effects were apparent, tears running down many cheeks.

"*Dec.* 10. Near noon, I preached again; God gave me some assistance, and enabled me to be in some degree faithful; so that I had peace in my own soul, and a very comfortable composure, 'although Israel should not be gathered.' Came away from Greenwich and rode home; arrived just in the evening. By the way my soul blessed God for his goodness; and I rejoiced, that so much of my work was done, and I so much nearer my blessed reward. Blessed be God for grace to be faithful.

"*Dec.* 11. Felt very poorly in body, being much tired and worn out the last night. Was assisted in some measure in writing on a divine subject: but was so feeble and sore in my breast, that I had not much resolution in my work. O, how I long for that world 'where the weary are at rest!' and yet through the goodness of God I do not now feel impatient.

"*Dec.* 12. Was again very weak; but somewhat assisted in secret prayer, and enabled with pleasure and sweetness to cry, 'Come, Lord Jesus! come, Lord Jesus! come quickly.' My soul 'longed for God, for the living God.' O, how delightful it is to pray under such sweet influences! O, how much better is this, than one's necessary food! I had at this time no disposition to eat, (though late in the morning;) for earthly food appeared wholly tasteless. O how much 'better is thy love than wine,' than the sweetest wine! I visited and preached to the Indians, in the afternoon; but under much dejection. Found my Interpreter under some concern for his soul; which was some comfort to me and yet filled me with new care. I longed greatly for his conversion; lifted up my heart to God for it, while I was talking to him; came home, and poured out my soul to God for him; enjoyed some freedom in prayer, and was enabled, I think, to leave all with God.

"*Dec.* 13. Endeavored to spend the day in fasting and prayer, to implore the divine blessing, more especially on my poor people; and in particular, I sought for converting grace for my Interpreter, and three or four more under some concern for their souls. I was much disordered in the morning when I arose; but having determined to spend the day in this manner, I attempted it. Some freedom I had in pleading for these poor concerned souls, several times; and when interceding for them, I enjoyed greater freedom from wandering and distracting thoughts, than in any part of my supplications. But, in the general, I was greatly exercised with wanderings; so that in the evening it seemed as if I had need to pray for nothing so much as for the pardon of sins committed in the day past, and the vileness I then found in myself. The sins I had most sense of, were pride, and wandering thoughts, whereby I mocked God. The former of these cursed iniquities excited me to think of writing, preaching, or converting heathens, or performing some other great work, that my name might live when I should be dead. My soul was in anguish, and ready to drop into despair, to find so much of that cursed temper. With this, and the other evil I labored under, viz. wandering thoughts, I was almost overwhelmed, and even ready to give over striving after a spirit of devotion; and oftentimes sunk into a considerable degree of despondency, and thought I was 'more brutish than any man.' Yet after all my sorrows, I trust, through grace, this day and the exercises of it have been for my good, and taught me more of my corruption, and weakness without Christ, than I knew before.

"*Dec.* 14. Near noon, went to the Indians; but knew not what to say to them, and was ashamed to look them in the face. I felt that I had no power to address their consciences, and therefore had no boldness to say anything. Was, much of the day, in a degree of despair about ever 'doing or seeing any good in the land of the living.'

"*Lord's day, Dec.* 16. Was so overwhelmed with dejection, that I knew not how to live. I longed for death exceedingly; my soul was sunk into deep waters, and the floods were ready to drown me. I was so much oppressed, that my soul was in a kind of horror; could not keep my thoughts fixed in prayer, for the space of one minute, without fluttering and distraction; and was exceedingly ashamed, that I did not live to God. I had no distressing doubt about my own state; but would have cheerfully ventured (as far as I could possibly know) into eternity. While I was going to preach to the Indians, my soul was in anguish; I was so overborne with discouragement, that I despaired of doing any good, and was driven to my wit's-end; I knew nothing what to say, nor what course to take. But at last I insisted on the evidence we have of the truth of Christianity from the miracles of Christ; many of which I set before them; and God helped me to make a close application to those who refused to believe the truth of what I taught them. Indeed, I was enabled to speak to the consciences of all, in some measure, and was somewhat encouraged, to find that God enabled me to be faithful once more. Then came and preached to another company of them; but was very weary and faint. In the evening, I was refreshed, and enabled to pray and praise God with composure and affection; had some enlargement and courage with respect to my work; was willing to live, and longed to do more for God than my weak state of body would admit of. 'I can do all things through Christ that strengthens me;' and by his grace, I am willing to spend and be spent in his service, when I am not thus sunk in dejection, and a kind of despair.

"*Dec.* 17. Was comfortable in mind, most of the day; was enabled to pray with some freedom, cheerfulness, composure, and devotion; and had also some assistance in writing on a divine subject.—Dec. 18. Went to the Indians, and discoursed to them near an hour, without any power to come close to their hearts. But at last I felt some fervency, and God helped me to speak with warmth. My interpreter also was amazingly assisted; and I doubt not but that 'the Spirit of God was upon them;' though I had no reason to think he had any true and saving grace, but was only under conviction of his lost state; and presently upon this most of the grown persons were much affected, and the tears ran down their cheeks. One old man, I suppose a hundred years old, was so much affected, that he wept, and seemed convinced of the importance of what I taught them. I staid with them a considerable time, exhorting and directing them: and came away, lifting up my heart to God in prayer and praise, and encouraged and exhorted my interpreter to 'strive to enter in at the strait gate.' Came home, and spent most of the evening in prayer and thanksgiving; and found myself much enlarged and quickened. Was greatly concerned, that the Lord's work which seemed to be begun, might be carried on with power, to the conversion of poor souls, and the glory of divine grace.

"*Dec.* 19. Spent a great part of the day in prayer to God, for the outpouring of his Spirit on my poor people; as, also, to bless his name for awakening my interpreter and some others, and giving us some tokens of his presence yesterday. And blessed be God, I had much freedom, five or six times in the day, in prayer and praise, and felt a weighty concern upon my spirit for the salvation of those precious souls, and the enlargement of the Redeemer's kingdom among them. My soul hoped in God for some success in my ministry; and blessed be his name for so much hope.

"*Dec.* 20. Was enabled to visit the throne of grace frequently this day; and through divine goodness enjoyed much freedom and fervency, sundry times; was much assisted in crying for mercy for my poor people, and felt cheerfulness and hope in my requests for them. I spent much of the day in writing; but was enabled to intermix prayer with my studies.

"*Dec.* 21. Was enabled again to pray with freedom, cheerfulness, and hope. God was pleased to make the duty comfortable and pleasant to me; so that I delighted to persevere, and repeatedly to engage in it. Towards noon, visited my people, and spent the whole time in the way to them in prayer, longing to see the power of God among them, as there appeared something of it the last Tuesday; and I found it sweet to rest and hope in God. Preached to them twice, and at two distinct places; had considerable freedom each time, and so had my interpreter. Several of them followed me from one place to the other; and I thought there was some divine influence discernible amongst them. In the evening, was assisted in prayer again. Blessed be the Lord!"

Very much the same things are expressed concerning his inward frame, exercises, and assistances on Saturday, as on the preceding days. He observes, that this was a comfortable week to him. But then concludes, "Oh, that I had no reason to complain of much barrenness! Oh that there were no vain thoughts and evil affections lodged within me! The Lord knows how I long for that world, where they rest day nor night saying, Holy, holy, holy is the Lord God Almighty!" On the following Sabbath he speaks of assistance and freedom in his public work, but as having less of the sensible presence of God, than frequently in the week past; but yet says his soul was kept from sinking in discouragement. On Monday, again, he seemed to enjoy very much the same liberty and fervency, through the day, which he enjoyed through the greater part of the preceding week. This day, he wrote the following letter to one of his intimate friends, a clergyman in New Jersey.

"FORKS OF DELAWARE, *Dec.* 24, 1744.

"REV. AND DEAR BROTHER :

"I have little to say to you about spiritual joys, and those blessed refreshments and divine consolations, with which I have been much favored in times past; but this I can tell you, that if I gain experience in no other point, yet I am sure I do in this, viz., that the present world has nothing in it to satisfy an immortal soul; and hence, that it is not to be desired for itself, but only because God may be seen and served in it. I wish I could be more patient and willing to live in it for this end, than I can usually find myself to be. It is no virtue, I know, to desire death, only to be freed from the miseries of life; but I want that divine hope which you observed, when I saw you last, was the very sinews of vital religion. Earth can do us no good, and if there be no hope of our doing good on earth, how can we desire to live in it? Yet we ought to desire, or at least to be resigned to tarry in it; because it is the will of our all-wise Sovereign. But, perhaps, these thoughts will appear melancholy and gloomy, and, consequently, will be very undesirable to you; and, therefore, I forbear to add, I wish you may not read them in the same circumstances in which I write them. I have a little more to do and suffer in a dark, disconsolate world; and then I hope to be as happy as you are.—I should ask you to pray for me, were I worthy your concern. May the Lord, enable us both to 'endure hardness as good soldiers of Jesus Christ;' and may we 'obtain mercy of God to be faithful to the death,' in the discharge of our respective trusts!

"I am your very unworthy brother,

"And humble servant,

"DAVID BRAINERD.

"*Dec.* 25. Enjoyed very little quiet sleep last night, by reason of bodily weakness, and the closeness of my studies yesterday; yet my heart was somewhat lively in prayer and praise. I was deli hted with the divine glory and happiness, and rejoiced that God was God, and that he was unchangeably possessed of glory and blessedness. Though God held my eyes waking, yet he helped me to improve my time profitably amidst my pains and weakness, in continued meditations on Luke xiii. 7. Behold, these three years I come seeking fruit, etc. My meditations were sweet; and I wanted to set before sinners their sin and danger."

He continued in a very low state, as to his bodily health, for some days, which seems to have been a great hindrance to him in his religious exercises and pursuits. But yet he expresses some degree of divine assistance, from day to day, through the remaining part of this week. He preached several times this week to his Indians; and there appeared still some concern amongst them for their souls. On Saturday, he rode to the Irish settlement, about fifteen miles from his lodgings, in order to spend the Sabbath there.

"*Lord's day, Dec.* 30. Discoursed, both parts of the day from Mark viii. 34. Whosoever will come after me, etc. God gave me very great freedom and clearness, and in the afternoon especially, considerable warmth and fervency. In the evening also, had very great clearness while conversing with friends on divine things. I do not remember ever to have had more clear apprehensions of religion in my life; but found a struggle in the evening with spiritual pride."

On Monday, he preached again in the same place with freedom and fervency; and rode home to his lodgings, and arrived in the evening, under a considerable degree of bodily illness, which continued the next two days, so that he complains much of spiritual emptiness and barrenness on those days.

"*Jan.* 3, 1745. Being sensible of the great want of divine influence, and the outpouring of God's Spirit, I spent this day in fasting and prayer, to seek so great a mercy for myself, my poor people in particular, and the church of God in general. In the morning, was very lifeless in prayer, and could get scarcely any sense of God. Near noon, enjoyed some sweet freedom to pray that the will of God might in every respect become mine; and I am persuaded, it was so at that time in some good degree. In the afternoon, I was exceedingly weak, and could not enjoy much fervency in prayer; but felt a great degree of dejection; which, I believe, was very much owing to my bodily weakness and disorder.

"*Jan.* 4. Rode up to the Indians, near noon; spent some time under great disorder: my soul was sunk down into deep waters, and I was almost overwhelmed with melancholy.—Jan. 5. Was able to do something at writing; but was much disordered with pain in my head. At night was distressed with a sense of my spiritual pollution, and ten thousand youthful, yea, and childish follies, that nobody but myself had any thought about; all which appeared to me now fresh, and in a lively view, as if committed yesterday, and made my soul ashamed before God, and caused me to hate myself.

"*Lord's day, Jan.* 6. Was still distressed with vapory disorders. Preached to my poor Indians; but had little heart or life. Towards night, my soul was pressed under a sense of my unfaithfulness. O the joy and peace that arise from a sense of 'having obtained mercy of God to be faithful!' And O the misery and anguish that spring from an apprehension of the contrary!

"*Jan.* 9. In the morning, God was pleased to remove that gloom which has of late oppressed my mind, and gave me freedom and sweetness in prayer. I was encouraged, strengthened, and enabled to plead for grace for myself, and mercy for my poor Indians; and was sweetly assisted in my intercessions with God for others. Blessed be his holy name for ever and ever, amen, and amen. Those things that of late appeared most difficult and almost impossible, now appeared not only possible, but easy. My soul was much delighted to continue instant in prayer, at this blessed season, so that I had no desire for my necessary food; even dreaded leaving off praying at all, lest I should lose this spirituality, and this blessed thankfulness to God which I then felt. I felt now quite willing to live, and undergo all trials that might remain for me in a world of sorrow; but still longed for heaven, that I might glorify God in a perfect manner. O 'come, Lord Jesus, come quickly.' Spent the day in reading a little; and in some diversions, which I was necessitated to take by reason of much weakness and disorder, In the evening, enjoyed some freedom and intenseness in prayer."

The remaining days of the week, he was feeble in body; but nevertheless continued in a comfortable frame of mind. On the Sabbath, this sweetness in spiritual alacrity began to abate; but still he enjoyed some degree of comfort, and had assistance in preaching to the Indians.

"*Jan.* 14. Spent this day under a great degree of bodily weakness and disorder; had very little freedom, either in my studies or devotions;

and in the evening, I was much dejected and melancholy. It pains and distresses me, that I live so much of my time for nothing. I long to do much in a little time ; and if it might be the Lord's will to finish my work speedily in this tiresome world, I am sure, I do not desire to live for any thing in this world ; and through grace I am not afraid to look the king of terrors in the face ; I know that I shall be afraid if God leaves me ; and therefore I think it always my duty to provide for that solemn hour. But for a very considerable time past, my soul has rejoiced to think of death in its nearest approaches, and even when I have been very weak, and seemed nearest eternity. 'Not unto me, not unto me, but to God be the glory.' I feel that which convinces me, that if God do not enable me to maintain a holy dependence upon him, death will easily be a terror to me ; but at present, I must say, 'I long to depart, and to be with Christ,' which is the best of all. When I am in a sweet resigned frame of soul, I am willing to tarry awhile in a world of sorrow. I am willing to be from home as long as God sees fit it should be so ; but when I want the influence of this temper, I am then apt to be impatient to be gone.—O, when will the day appear, that I shall be perfect in holiness, and in the enjoyment of God!

"*Jan.* 16 and 17. I spent most of the time in writing on a sweet divine subject, and enjoyed some freedom and assistance. Was likewise enabled to pray more frequently and fervently than usual , and my soul, I think, rejoiced in God ; especially on the evening of the last of these days. Praise then seemed comely, and I delighted to bless the Lord. O what reason have I to be thankful, that God ever helps me to labor and study for him ! he does but receive his own, when I am enabled in any measure to praise him, labor for him, and live to him. O, how comfortable and sweet it is, to feel the assistance of divine grace in the performance of the duties which God has enjoined on us ! Bless the Lord, O my soul !

"*Lord's day, Jan.* 27. Had the greatest degree of inward anguish, which I almost ever endured. I was perfectly overwhelmed, and so confused, that after I began to discourse to the Indians, before I could finish a sentence, sometimes I forgot entirely what I was aiming at ; or if, with much difficulty, I had recollected what I had before designed, still it appeared strange, and like something I had long forgotten, and had now but an imperfect remembrance of. I know it was a degree of distraction, occasioned by vapory disorders, melancholy, spiritual desertion, and some other things that particularly pressed upon me this morning, with an uncommon weight, the principal of which respected my Indians. This distressing gloom never went off the whole day ; but was so far removed, that I was enabled to speak with some freedom and concern to the Indians, at two of their settlements ; and I think, there was some appearance of the presence of God with us, some seriousness and seeming concern among the Indians, at least a few of them.   In the evening, this gloom continued still, till family prayer,* about nine o'clock, and almost through this, until I came near the close, when I was praying, as I usually do, for the illumination and conversion of my poor people; and then the cloud was scattered, so that I enjoyed sweetness and freedom, and conceived hopes that God designed mercy for some of them.   The same I enjoyed afterwards in secret prayer; in which precious duty I had for a considerable time sweetness and freedom, and, I hope, faith, in praying for myself, my poor Indians, and dear friends and acquaintance in New England, and elsewhere, and for the dear interests of Zion in general.   Bless the Lord, O my soul, and forget not all his benefits."

He spent the rest of this week, in dejection and melancholy; which, on Friday, rose to an extreme height This exceeding gloominess continued till Saturday evening, when he was again relieved in family prayer; and after it, was refreshed in secret, and felt willing to live and endure hardships in the cause of God and found his hopes of the advancement of Christ's kingdom, as also his hopes to see the power of God among the poor Indians, considerably raised.

" *Lora's Day Feb.* 3. In the morning, I was somewhat relieved of that gloom and confusion, with which my mind has of late been greatly exercised; and was enabled to pray with some composure and comfort. Still I went to my Indians trembling; for my soul 'remembered the wormwood and the gall' of Friday last.   I was greatly afraid that I should be obliged again to drink of that cup of trembling, which was inconceivably more bitter than death, and made me long for the grave more, unspeakably more, than for hid treasures, yea inconceivably more than the men of this world long for such treasures. But God was pleased to hear my cries, and to afford me great assistance; so that I felt peace in my own soul; and was satisfied, that if not one of the Indians should be profited by my preaching, but should all be damned, yet I should be accepted and rewarded as faithful; for I am persuaded, God enabled me to be so. Had some good degree of help afterwards, at another place; and much longed for the conversion of the poor Indians.   Was somewhat refreshed, and comfortable, towards night and in the evening. Oh, that my soul might praise the Lord for his goodness! Enjoyed some freedom, in the evening, in meditation on Luke xiii. 24. Strive to enter in at the strait gate."

* Though Brainerd now dwelt by himself in the little cottage which he had built for his own use; yet that was near to a family of white people, with whom he had lived before, and with whom he still attended family prayer.

In the next three days he was the subject of much dejection; but the three remaining days of the week seem to have been spent with much composure and comfort. On the next Sabbath, he preached at Greenwich, in New Jersey. In the evening, he rode eight miles to visit a sick man at the point of death, and found him speechless and senseless.

"*Feb.* 11. About break of day, the sick man died. I was affected at the sight; spent the morning with the mourners; and, after prayer and some discourse with them, returned to Greenwich, and preached again from Ps. lxxxix. 15. Blessed is the people that know, etc. The Lord gave me assistance; I felt a sweet love to souls, and to the kingdom of Christ; and I longed that poor sinners might know the joyful sound. Several persons were much affected. After meeting, I was enabled to discourse, with freedom and concern, to some persons, who applied to me under spiritual trouble. Left the place, sweetly composed, and rode home to my house about eight miles distant. Discoursed to friends, and inculcated divine truths upon some. In the evening, was in the most solemn frame, which I almost ever remember to have experienced. I know not that ever death appeared more real to me, or that ever I saw myself in the condition of a dead corpse, laid out, and dressed for a lodging in the silent grave, so evidently as at this time. And yet I felt exceedingly tranquil; my mind was composed and calm, and death appeared without a sting. I think, I never felt such an universal mortification to all created objects as now. O, how great and solemn a thing it appeared to die! O, how it lays the greatest honor in the dust! And O, how vain and trifling did the riches, honors, and pleasures of the world appear! I could not, I dare not, so much as think of any of them; for death, death, solemn (thought not frightful) death appeared at the door. O, I could see myself dead, and laid out, and inclosed in my coffin, and put down into the cold grave, with the greatest solemnity, but without terror! I spent most of the evening in conversing with a dear Christian friend; and blessed be God, it was a comfortable evening to us both. What are friends? What are comforts? What are sorrows? What are distresses? 'The time is short. It remains, that they which weep, be as though they wept not; and they which rejoice, as though they rejoiced not; for the fashion of this world passeth away. Oh come, Lord Jesus, come quickly. Amen.' Blessed be God for the comforts of the past day.

"*Feb.* 12. Was exceedingly weak; but in a sweet, resigned, composed frame, most of the day; felt my heart freely go forth after God in prayer. —Feb. 13. Was much exercised with vapory disorders, but still enabled to maintain solemnity, and, I think spirituality.— Feb. 14. Spent the day in writing on a divine subject; enjoyed health and free-

dom in my work; and had a solemn sense of death, as I have indeed
had every day this week, in some measure. What I felt on Monday
last, has been abiding, in some considerable degree, ever since.—Feb. 15.
Was engaged in writing most of the day. In the evening, was much assisted in meditating on that precious text, John vii. 37. Jesus stood and
cried, etc. I had then a sweet sense of the free grace of the gospel ; my
soul was encouraged, warmed and quickened. My desires were drawn
out after God in prayer; and my soul was watchful, afraid of losing so
sweet a guest as I then entertained. I continued long in prayer and
meditation, intermixing one with the other; and was unwilling to be diverted by anything at all from so sweet an exercise. I longed to proclaim
the grace I then meditated upon, to the world of sinners. O how quick
and powerful is the word of the blessed God.

" *Lord's day, Feb.* 17. Preached to the white people, my interpreter
being absent, in the wilderness upon the sunny side of a hill; had a considerable assembly, consisting of people who lived, at least many of them, not
less than thirty miles asunder. I discoursed with them all day, from John
vii. 37. Jesus stood and cried, saying, if any man thirst, etc. In the afternoon, pleased God to grant me great freedom and fervency in my discourse;
and I was enabled to imitate the example of Christ in the text, who stood
and cried. I think I was scarce ever enabled to offer the free grace of God
to perishing sinners with more freedom and plainness in my life. Afterwards, I was enabled earnestly to invite the children of God to come renewedly and, drink of this fountain of the water of life, from whence they
have heretofore derived unspeakable satisfaction. It was a very comfortable time to me, There were many tears in the assembly ; and I doubt
not but that the Spirit of God was there, convincing poor sinners of their
need of Christ. In the evening, I felt composed and comfortable, though
much tired. I had some sweet sense of the excellency and glory of God ;
my soul rejoiced that he was 'God over all blessed forever ;' but was too
much crowded with company and conversation, and longed to be more
alone with God. Oh that I could forever bless God for the mercy of this
day, who 'answered me in the joy of my heart.'

" *Lord's day, Feb.* 24. In the morning was much perplexed. My interpreter being absent, I knew not how to perform my work among the
Indians. However, I rode to them, got a Dutchman to interpret for me
though he was but poorly qualified for the business. Afterwards, I came
and preached to a few white people, from John vi. 67. Then said Jesus
unto the twelve, etc,. Here the Lord seemed to unburden me in some
measure, especially towards the close of my discourse : I felt freedom to
open the love of Christ to his own dear disciples. When the rest of the
world forsakes him, and are forsaken by him, that he calls them no more
he then turns to his own and says, Will ye also go away? I had a sense

of the free grace of Christ to his own people, in such seasons of general
apostacy, and when they themselves in some measure backslide with the
world. O the free grace of Christ, that he seasonably reminds his people
of their danger of backsliding, and invites them to persevere in their ad-
herence to himself! I saw that backsliding souls, who seemed to be
about to go away with the world, might return and welcome, to him immediately; without anything to recommend them; notwithstanding all
their former backslidings. Thus my discourse was suited to my own
soul's case; for, of late, I have found a great want of this sense and apprehension of divine grace; and have often been greatly distressed in my
own soul, because I did not suitably apprehend this 'fountain to purge
away sin;' and have been too much laboring for spiritual life, peace of
conscience, and progressive holiness, in my own strength. Now God
showed me, in some measure, the arm of all strength, and the fountain of
all grace. In the evening, I felt solemn, devout and sweet; resting on
free grace for assistance, acceptance, and peace of conscience."

During the next few days, he had frequent refreshing
influences of God's Spirit; attended with complaints of dullness, and with longings after spiritual life and holy fervency.

"*March* 6. Spent most of the day in preparing for a journey to New
England. Spent some time in prayer, with special reference to my journey. Was afraid I should forsake the Fountain of living waters, and attempt to derive satisfaction from broken cisterns, my dear friends and acquaintance, with whom I might meet in my journey. I looked to God to
keep me from this vanity, as well as others. Towards night, and in the
evening, was visited by some friends, some of whom, I trust, were real
Christians; who discovered an affectionate regard to me, and seemed
grieved that I was about to leave them; especially as I did not expect to
make any considerable stay among them, if I should live to return from
New England.* O how kind has God been to me! how has he raised up
friends in every place where his providence has called me! Friends are
a great comfort; and it is God who gives them; it is he who makes them
friendly to me. Bless the Lord, O my soul, and forget not all his benefits.

The next day, he set out on his journey and it was about
five weeks before he returned. The special design of this
journey, he declares afterwards, in his diary for March 21,
where, speaking of his conversing with a certain minister in
New England, he says, "Contrived with him how to raise

---

* It seems he had a design, by what afterwards appears, to remove and live among the
Indians on the Susquehannah river.

some money among Christian friends, in order to support a
colleague with me in the wilderness, (I having now spent
two years in a very solitary manner,) that we might be together ; as Christ sent out his disciples two and two ; and as
this was the principal concern I had in view, in taking this
journey, so I took pains in it, and hope God will succeed it,
if for his glory." He first went into various parts of New
Jersey, and visited several ministers there ; then to New
York ; and thence into New England, going to various parts
of Connecticut.　He then returned to New Jersey, and met
a number of ministers at Woodbridge, " who, " he says, " met
there to consult about the affairs of Christ's kingdom, in some
important articles."　He seems, for the most part, to have
been free from melancholy in this journey ; and many times
to have had extraordinary assistance in public ministrations,
and his preaching sometimes attended with very hopeful appearances of a good effect on the auditory.　He also had
many seasons of special comfort and spiritual refreshment, in
conversation with ministers and other Christian friends, and
also in meditation and prayer when alone.

"*April* 13.　Rode home to my own house at the Forks of Delaware ;
and was enabled to remember the goodness of the Lord, who has now
preserved me while riding full six hundred miles in this journey ; has kept
me that none of my bones have been broken.　Blessed be the Lord who
has preserved me in this tedious journey, and returned me in safety to
my own house.　Verily it is God who has upheld me, and guarded my
goings.

"*Lord's day, April* 14. Was disordered in body with the fatigues of the
late journey ; but was enabled however to preach to a considerable assembly of white people, gathered from all parts round about, with some
freedom, from Ezek. xxxiii 11.　As I live, saith the Lord God, etc.　Had
much more assistance than I expected."

This week he went a journey to Philadelphia, in order to
engage the Governor to use his interest with the chief of the
six nations, with whom he maintained a strict friendship, that
he would give him leave to live at Susquehannah, and instruct
the Indians who are within their territories.*　In his way to

* The Indians at Susquehannah are a mixed company of many nations, speaking various

and from thence, he lodged with Mr. Beaty, a young Presbyterian minister. He speaks of seasons of sweet spiritual refreshment which he enjoyed at his lodgings.

"*April* 20. Rode with Mr. Beaty to Abington, to attend Mr. Treat's
administration of the sacrament, according to the method of the church
of Scotland. When we arrived, we found Mr. Treat preaching; afterwards I preached a sermon from Matt. v. 3. Blessed are the poor in
spirit, etc. God was pleased to give me great freedom and tenderness
both in prayer and sermon; the assembly was sweetly melted, and scores
were in tears. It was, as I then hoped, and was afterwards abundantly
satisfied by conversing with them, a 'word spoken in season to many
weary souls.' I was extremely tired, and my spirits much exhausted, so
that I could scarcely speak loud; yet I could not help rejoicing in God.

"*Lord's day, April* 21. In the morning, was calm and composed
and had some thirstings of soul after God in secret duties, and longing
desires of his presence in the sanctuary and at his table; that his presence
might be in the assembly; and that his children might be entertained with
a feast of fat things. In the forenoon, Mr. Treat preached. I felt some
affection and tenderness during the administration of the ordinance. Mr.
Beaty preached to the multitude abroad, who could not half have crowded
into the meeting-house. In the season of the communion, I had comfortable and sweet apprehensions of the blissful communion of God's people,
when they shall meet at their Father's table in his kingdom, in a state of
perfection. In the afternoon, I preached abroad to the whole assembly,
from Rev. xiv. 4. These are they that follow the Lamb, etc. God was
pleased again to give me very great freedom and clearness, but
not so much warmth as before. However there was a most amazing attention in the whole assembly; and, as I was informed afterwards, this
was a sweet season to many.

"*April* 22. I enjoyed some sweetness in retirement, in the morning.
At eleven o'clock, Mr. Beaty preached, with freedom and life. Then I
preached from John vii. 37. In the last day, etc., and concluded the solemnity. Had some freedom; but not equal to what I enjoyed before; yet
in the prayer the Lord enabled me to cry, I hope with a child-like temper, with tenderness and brokenness of heart. Came home with Mr.
Beaty to his lodgings; and spent the time, while riding, and afterwards,
very agreeably on divine things.

"*April* 23. Left Mr. Beaty's and returned home to the Forks of

languages, and few of them properly of the Six Nations. But yet the country having
formerly been conquered by the Six Nations, they claim the land; and the Susquehannah
Indians are a kind of vassals to them.

Delaware ; enjoyed some sweet meditations on the road ; and was enabled to lift up my heart to God in prayer and praise."

"*April* 26. Conversed with a Christian friend with some warmth ; and felt a spirit of mortification to the world, in a very great degree. Afterwards, was enabled to pray fervently, and to rely on God sweetly, for 'all things pertaining to life and godliness.' Just in the evening, was visited by a dear Christian friend, with whom I spent an hour or two in conversation, on the very soul of religion. There are many with whom I can talk about religion; but alas! I find few with whom I can talk religion itself ; but blessed be the Lord, there are some that love to feed on the kernel, rather than the shell."

The next day, he went to the Irish settlement, before mentioned, about fifteen miles distant where he spent the Sabbath and preached with some considerable assistance, and on Monday returned in a very weak state to his own lodgings.

"*April* 30. Was scarce able to walk about, and was obliged to betake myself to bed, much of the day ; and passed away the time in a very solitary manner ; being neither able to read, meditate, nor pray, and had none to converse with in that wilderness. O how heavily does time pass away, when I can do nothing to any good purpose; but seem obliged to trifle away precious time ! But of late, I have seen it my duty to divert myself by all lawful means, that I may be fit, at least some small part of my time, to labor for God. And here is the difference between my present diversions, and those I once pursued, when in a natural state. Then I made a god of diversions, delighted in them with a neglect of God, and drew my highest satisfaction from them. Now I use them as means to help me in living to God ; fixedly delighting in him, and not in them, drawing my highest satisfaction from him. Then they were my all ; now they are only means leading to my all. And those things that are the greatest diversion, when pursued with this view, do not tend to hinder, but promote my spirituality ; and I see now, more than ever, that they are absolutely necessary.

"*May* 1. Was not able to sit up more than half the day ; and yet I had such recruits of strength sometimes, that I was able to write a little , on a divine subject. Was grieved that I could no more live to God. In the evening, had some sweetness and intenseness in secret prayer.

"*May* 2. In the evening, being a little better in health, I walked into the woods, and enjoyed a sweet season of meditation and prayer. My thoughts ran upon Ps. xvii. 15. I shall be satisfied, when I awake, with thy likeness. And it was indeed a precious text to me. I longed to preach to the whole world, and it seemed to me, they must needs all be melted in hearing such precious divine truths, as I then had a view and relish of. My thoughts were exceeding clear, and my soul was refreshed. Blessed be the Lord, that in my late and present weakness, now for many days together, my mind is not gloomy, as at some other times.

"*May.* 3. Felt a little vigor of body and mind, in the morning ; and had some freedom, strength and sweetness in prayer. Rode to, and spent some time with my Indians. In the evening, again retiring into the woods, I enjoyed some sweet meditations on Isa. liii. 1. Yet it pleased the Lord to bruise him, etc.

"*May* 7. Spent the day mainly in making preparations for a journey into the wilderness. Was still weak, and concerned how I should perform so difficult a journey. Spent some time in prayer for the divine blessing, direction, and protection in my intended journey; but wanted bodily strength to spend the day in fasting and prayer."

The next day, he set out on his journey to the Susquehannah, with his interpreter. He endured great hardships and fatigues in his way thither through a hideous wilderness; where, after having lodged one night in the open woods, he was overtaken with a northeasterly storm, in which he was almost ready to perish. Having no manner of shelter, and not being able to make a fire in so great a rain, he could have no comfort if he stopped; therefore he determined to go forward in hopes of meeting with some shelter, without which he thought it impossible to live the night through; but their horses—happening to eat poison, for the want of other food, at a place where they lodged the night before—were so sick, that they could neither ride nor lead them, but were obliged to drive them, and travel on foot: until, through the mercy of God, just at dusk, they came to a bark hut where they lodged that night. After he came to the Susquehannah, he travelled about a hundred miles on the river, and visited many towns and settlements of the Indians; saw some of seven or eight tribes, and preached to different nations, by different interpreters. He was sometimes much discouraged, and sunk in his spirits, through the opposition which appeared in the Indians to Christianity. At other times, he was encouraged by the disposition which some of these people manifested to hear, and willingness to be instructed. He here met with some who had formerly been his hearers at Kaunau-meek, and had removed hither ; who saw and heard him again with great joy. He spent a fortnight among the Indians on this river, and passed through considerable labors and hardships, frequently lodging on the ground, and sometimes in the open air. At length he felt extremely ill, as he was riding in the wilderness, being seized with an ague, followed with a burning fever, and extreme pains in his head and bowels, attended with a great evacuation of blood ; so that he thought he must have perished in the wilderness. But at last coming to an Indian trader's hut, he got leave to stay there ; and though without physic or food proper for him, it pleased God, after about a week's distress, to relieve him so far that he was able to ride. He returned homewards from Juncauta, an island far down the river ; where was a considerable number of Indians, who appeared more free from prejudices against Christianity, than most of the other Indians. He arrived at the Forks of Delaware May 30, after having rode in this journey about 340 miles. He came home in a very weak state, and under dejection of mind. However, on the Sabbath, after having preached to the Indians, he preached to the white people, with some success, from Is. liii. 10. ' Yet it pleased the Lord to bruise him,' etc., some being awakened by his preaching. The next day, he was much exercised for want of spiritual life and fervency.

"*June* 4. Towards evening, was in distress for God's presence, and a sense of divine things; withdrew myself to the woods, and spent near an hour in prayer and meditation; and I think, the Lord had compassion on me, and gave me some sense of divine things ; which was indeed refreshing and quickening to me. My soul enjoyed intenseness and freedom in prayer, so that it grieved me to leave the place.

"*June* 5. Felt thirsting desires after God, in the morning. In the evening, enjoyed a precious season of retirement; was favored with some clear and sweet meditations upon a sacred text ; divine things opened with clearness and certainty, and had a divine stamp, upon them. My soul was also enlarged and refreshed in prayer ; I delighted to continue in the duty ; and was sweetly assisted in praying for my fellow-Christians, and my dear brethren in the ministry. Blessed be the dear Lord for such enjoyments. O how sweet and precious it is, to have a clear apprehension and tender sense of the mystery of godliness, of true holiness, and of likeness to the best of beings ! O what a blessedness it is, to be as much like God, as it is possible for a creature to be like his great Creator ! Lord give me more of thy likeness ; ' I shall be satisfied, when I awake, with it.'

"*June* 6. Was engaged, a considerable part of the day, in meditation and study on divine subjects. Enjoyed some special freedom, clearness, and sweetness in meditation. O how refreshing it is, to be enabled to improve time well.''

The next day, he went a journey of near fifty miles, to Neshaminy, to assist at a sacramental occasion, to be attended at Mr. Beaty's meeting-house ; being invited thither by him and his people.

"*June* 8. Was exceedingly weak and fatigued with riding in the heat yesterday ; but being desired, I preached in the afternoon, to a crowded audience, from Is. xl. 1. ' Comfort ye, comfort ye, my people, saith your God.' God was pleased to give me great freedom, in opening the sorrows of God's people, and in setting before them comforting considerations. And, blessed be the Lord, it was a sweet melting season in the assembly.

"*Lord's day, June* 9. Felt some longing desires of the presence of God to be with his people on the solemn occasion of the day. In the forenoon Mr. Beaty preached ; and there appeared some warmth in the assembly. Afterwards, I assisted in the administration of the Lord's supper ; and towards the close of it, I discoursed to the multitude extempore, with some reference to that sacred passage, Is. liii. 10. 'Yet it pleased the Lord to bruise him.' Here God gave me great assistance in addressing sinners ; and the word was attended with amazing power ; many scores, if not hundreds, in that great assembly, consisting of three or four thousand, were much affected; so that there was a ' very great mourning, like the mourning of Hadadrimmon.' In the evening, I could hardly look anybody in the face, because of the imperfections I saw in my performances in the day past.

"*June* 10. Preached with a good degree of clearness and some sweet warmth, from Psal. xvii. 15. 'I shall be satisfied, when I awake, with thy likeness.' And blessed be God, there was a great solemnity and attention in the assembly, and sweet refreshment among God's people ; as was evident then, and afterwards.—June 11. Spent the day mainly in conversation with dear Christian friends; and enjoyed some sweet sense of divine things. O how desirable it is, to deep company with God's dear children! These are the 'excellent ones of the earth, in whom,' I can truly say, 'is all my delight.' O what delight will it afford, to meet them all in a state of perfection! Lord, prepare me for that state."

The next day he left Mr. Beaty's and went to Maidenhead, in New Jersey ; and spent the next seven days in a comfortable state of mind, visiting several ministers in those parts.

"*June* 18. Set out from New Brunswick with a design to visit some Indians at a place called Crossweeksung, in New Jersey, towards the sea.* In the afternoon, came to a place called Cranberry, and meeting with a serious minister, Mr. Macknight, I lodged there with him. Had some enlargement and freedom in prayer with a number of people.

---

* BRAINERD having when at Boston, written and left with a friend, a brief relation of facts touching his labors with the Indians, between November 5, 1744, and June 19, 1745, (with a view to connect his Narrative, addressed to Mr. Pemberton, and his Journal, in case they should ever be reprinted) concludes the same with this passage : " As my body was very feeble, so my mind was scarce ever so much damped and discouraged about the conversion of the Indians, as at this time. And in this state of body and mind I made my first visit to the Indians of New Jersey, where God was pleased to display his power and grace in the remarkable manner that I have represented in my printed Journal."

CHAPTER VII.

A wonderful Work of Grace in the Wilderness.—Publication of the First Part of Brainerd's Journal.—Interesting Services.—Revival Scenes.—A Journey to the Forks of the Delaware.—A Strange Character.—Precious Ingatherings.

[WE are now come to that part of Brainerd's life, when he had the greatest success in his labors for the good of souls and in his particular business as a missionary to the Indians. Long had he agonized in prayer, and travailed in birth for their conversion. Often had he cherished the hope of witnessing that desirable event ; only to find that hope yield to fear, and end in disappointment. But after a patient continuance in prayer, in labor, and in suffering, as it were through a long night, at length he is permitted to behold the dawning of the day. "Weeping continues for a night ; but joy comes in the morning." He went forth weeping, bearing precious seed, and now he comes rejoicing, bringing his sheaves with him. The desired event is brought to pass at last ; but at a time, in a place, and upon subjects, which scarcely ever entered into his heart.

An account of this was originally published in his JOURNAL, consisting of extracts from his Diary during one year of his residence at Crossweeksung. Those extracts are now incorporated with the rest of his Diary for the same period in regular chronological order.

The following preface by the Correspondents introduced the First Part of Brainerd's Journal to the notice of the public and is worthy of an insertion in these Memoirs.—[J. M. S.]

"The design of this publication is to give God the glory of his distinguishing grace, and gratify the pious curiosity of those who are waiting and praying for that blessed time, when the Son of God, in a more extensive sense than has yet been accomplished, shall receive ' the heathen for his inheritance, and the uttermost parts of the earth for a possession.'

" Whenever any of the guilty race of mankind are awakened to a just concern for their eternal interest, are humbled at the footstool of a sovereign God, and are persuaded and enabled to accept the offers of redeeming love, it must always be acknowledged a wonderful work of divine grace, which demands our thankful praises, But doubtless it is a more affecting evidence of almighty power, a more illustrious display of sovereign mercy, when those are enlightened with the knowledge of salvation, who have for many ages dwelt in the grossest darkness and heathenism, and are brought to a cheerful subjection to the government of our divine Redeemer, who from generation to generation had remained the voluntary slaves of ' the prince of darkness.'

" This is that delightful scene which will present itself to the reader's view, while he attentively peruses the following pages. Nothing certainly can be more agreeable to a benevolent and religious mind, than to see those that were sunk in the most degenerate state of human nature, at once, not only renounce those barbarous customs they had been inured to from their infancy, but surprisingly transformed into the character of real and devout Christians. This mighty change was brought about by the plain and faithful preaching of the gospel, attended with an uncommon effusion of the divine Spirit, under the ministry of the Reverend David Brainerd, a Missionary employed by the Honorable Society in Scotland, for propagating Christian Knowledge. And surely it will administer abundant matter of praise and thanksgiving to that honorable body, to find that their generous attempt to send the gospel among the Indian nations upon the borders of New York, New Jersey and Pennsylvania, has met with such surprising success.

" It would perhaps have been more agreeable to the taste of politer readers, if the following Journal had been cast into a different method, and formed into one connected narrative. But the worthy author amidst his continued labors, had no time to spare for such an undertaking. Besides, the pious reader will take a peculiar pleasure to see this work described in its native simplicity, and the operations of the Spirit upon the minds of these poor benighted Pagans, laid down just in the method and order in which they happened. This, it must be confessed, will occasion frequent repetitions; but these, as they tend to give a fuller view of this amazing dispensation of divine grace in its rise and progress, we trust, will be easily forgiven.

" When we see such numbers of the most ignorant and barbarous of mankind, in the space of a few months, ' turned from darkness to light, and from the power of sin and Satan unto God,' it gives us encouragement to wait and pray for that blessed time, when our victorious Redeemer shall, in a more signal manner than he has yet done, display the ' banner of his cross,' march on from ' conquering to conquer, till the king-

doms of this world are become the kingdoms of our Lord and of his Christ.'
Yea, we cannot but lift up our heads with joy, and hope that it may be
the dawn of that bright and illustrious day, when the Sun of Righteousness shall 'arise and shine from one end of the earth to the other ;'
when, to use the language of the inspired prophets, 'the Gentiles shall
come to his light, and kings to the brightness of his rising ;' in consequence of which, 'the wilderness and solitary places shall be glad, and the
desert rejoice and blossom as the rose.'

"It is doubtless the duty of all, in their different stations, and according to their respective capacities, to use their utmost endeavors to bring
forward this promised, this desired day. There is a great want of school-
masters among these christianized Indians, to instruct their youth in the
English language, and the principles of the Christian faith—for this, as
yet, there is no certain provision made ; if any are inclined to contribute to
so good a design, we are persuaded they will do an acceptable service to
the 'kingdom of the Redeemer.' And we earnestly desire the most in-
digent to join, at least, in their wishes and prayers, that this work may
prosper more and more, till the 'whole earth is filled with the glory of the
Lord.'"

"*June* 19. [At Crossweeksung,] I had spent most of my time, for
more than a year past among the Indians at the Forks of Delaware in
Pennsylvania. During that time I made two journeys to the Susquehannah to treat with the Indians on that river respecting Christianity ;
and, not having had any considerable appearance of special success in either
of those places, my spirits were depressed, and I was not a little discouraged. Hearing that there was a number of Indians at a place called
Crossweeksung, in New Jersey, nearly eighty miles southeast from the
Forks of Delaware, I determined to make them a visit, and see what
might be done towards christianizing them ; and accordingly arrived among
them, June, 19, 1745.

"I found very few persons at the place which I visited, and perceived
that the Indians in these parts were very much scattered. There were
not more than two or three families in a place ; and these small settlements, six, ten, fifteen, twenty and thirty miles, and some more from that
place. However, I preached to those few I found ; who appeared well
disposed, serious and attentive ; and not inclined to cavil and object, as the
Indians had done elsewhere. When I had concluded my discourse, I informed them, there being none but a few women and children, that I
would willingly visit them again the next day. Whereupon they readily
set out and travelled ten or fifteen miles, in order to give notice to some
of their friends at that distance. These women, like the women of
Samaria, seemed desirous that others should see the man, who had told
them what they had done in their past lives, and the misery that attended

their idolatrous ways. At night was worn out, and scarcely able to walk, or sit up. O! how tiresome is earth; how dull the body!

"*June* 20. Visited and preached to the Indians again as I proposed. Numbers were gathered at the invitations of their friends, who had heard me the day before. These also appeared as attentive, orderly and well disposed as the others; and none made any objections, as Indians in other places have usually done. Towards night preached to the Indians again, and had more hearers than before. In the evening enjoyed some peace and serenity of mind, and comfort and composure in prayer, alone; and was enabled to lift up my head with some degree of joy, under an apprehension that my redemption draws nigh. O, blessed be God, that there remains a rest to his poor weary people!

"*June* 21. Rode to Freehold to see Mr. William Tennent, and spent the day comfortably with him. My sinking spirits were a little raised and encouraged; and I felt my soul breathing after God, in the midst of Christian conversation; and in the evening was refreshed in secret prayer; saw myself a poor worthless creature, without wisdom to direct or strength to help myself. O blessed be God, who lays me under a happy, a blessed necessity of living upon himself!

"*June* 22. About noon rode to the Indians again, and next night preached to them. Found my body much strengthened, and was enabled to speak with abundant plainness and warmth. The number, which at first consisted of seven or eight persons, was now increased to nearly thirty. There was not only a solemn attention among them, but some considerable impression, it was apparent, was made upon their minds by divine truth. Some began to feel their misery, and perishing state, and appeared concerned for a deliverance from it. The power of God evidently attended the word; so that several persons were brought under great concern for their souls, and made to shed many tears, and to wish for Christ to save them. My soul was much refreshed and quickened in my work; and I could not but spend much time with them in order to open both their misery and their remedy. This was indeed a sweet afternoon to me. While riding, before I came to the Indians, my spirits were refreshed, and my soul enabled to cry to God almost incessantly, for many miles together. In the evening also, I found that the consolations of God were not small. I was then willing to live, and in some respects desirous of it, that I might do something for the dear kingdom of Christ; and yet death appeared pleasant; so that I was in some measure in a strait between two; having a desire to depart. I am often weary of this world, and want to leave it on that account; but it is desirable to be drawn, rather than driven out of it.

"*Lord's day, June* 23. Preached to the Indians, and spent the day

with them. Their number still increased; and all with one consent
seemed to rejoice in my coming among them. Not a word of opposition
was heard from any of them against Christianity, although in times past
they had been as much opposed to anything of that nature, as any Indians whatsoever. Some of them not many months before, were enraged
with my interpreter, because he attempted to teach them something of
Christianity.

"*June* 24. Preached to the Indians at their desire, and upon their
own motion. To see poor pagans desirous of hearing the gospel of
Christ, animated me to discourse to them; although I was now very
weakly, and my spirit much exhausted. They attended with the greatest
seriousness and diligence; and some concern for their souls' salvation
was apparent among them.

"*June* 27. Visited and preach'd to the Indians again. Their number
now amounted to about forty persons. Their solemnity and attention
still continued, and a considerable concern for their souls became very
apparent among numbers of them. My soul rejoiced to find, that God
enabled me to be faithful, and that he was now pleased to awaken these
poor Indians by my means. O how heart-reviving and soul-refreshing it
is to me, to see the fruit of my labors!

"*June* 28. The Indians being now gathered, a considerable number of
them, from their several and distant habitations, requested me to preach
twice a day to them; being desirous to hear as much as they possibly
could while I was with them. I cheerfully complied with their request,
and could not but admire the goodness of God, who I was persuaded, had
inclined them thus to inquire after the way of salvation. In the evening
my soul was revived, and my heart lifted up to God in prayer for my poor
Indians, myself, and friends, and the dear church of God. O how refreshing, how sweet was this! Bless the Lord, O my soul, and forget not his
goodness and tender mercy!

"*June* 29. Preached twice to the Indians; and could not but wonder
at their seriousness, and the strictness of their attention. Saw, as I
thought, the hand of God very evidently, and in a manner somewhat
remarkable, making provision for their subsistence together, in order to
their being instructed in divine things. For this day, and the day before,
with only walking a little way from the place of our daily meeting, they
killed three deer, which were a seasonable supply for their wants, and
without which they could not have subsisted together in order to attend
the means of grace. Blessed be God who has inclined their hearts to
hear. O how refreshing it is to me to see them attend, with such uncommon diligence and affection, with tears in their eyes and concern in
their hearts! In the evening, could not but lift up my heart to God in
prayer, while riding to my lodging; and, blessed be his name, had as-

sistance and freedom. O how much better than life is the presence of God!

"*Lord's day, June* 30. Preached twice this day also. Observed yet more concern and affection among the poor heathens than ever; so that they even constrained me to tarry yet longer with them, although my constitution was exceedingly worn out, and my health much impaired by my late fatigues and labors ; and especially by my late journey to Susquehannah in May last, in which I lodged on the ground for several weeks together.

"*July* 1. Preached again twice to a very serious and attentive assembly of Indians; they having now learned to attend the worship of God with Christian decency in all respects. There were now between forty and fifty persons of them present, old and young. I spent a considerable time in discoursing with them in a more private way; inquiring of them what they remembered of the great truths which had been taught them from day to day ; and may justly say, it was amazing to see how they had received and retained the instructions given them, and what a measure of knowledge some of them had acquired in a few days.

"*July* 2. Was obliged to leave these Indians at Crossweeksung, thinking it my duty as soon as my health would admit, again to visit those at the Forks of Delaware. When I came to take leave of them and to speak particularly to each of them, they all earnestly inquired when I would come again, and expressed a great desire of being further instructed. Of their own accord they agreed, that when I should come again, they would all meet and live together, during my continuance with them ; and that they would use their utmost endeavors to gather all the other Indians in these parts who were yet more remote. When I parted from them, one told me, with many tears, 'She wished God would change her heart ;' another, that 'she wanted to find Christ;' and an old man, who had been one of their chiefs, wept bitterly with concern for his soul. I then promised them to return as speedily as my health and business elsewhere would permit, and felt not a little concern at parting, lest the good impressions, then apparent upon numbers of them, might decline and wear off, when the means came to cease. Yet I could not but hope, that he, who I trusted, had begun a good work among them, and who, I knew, did not stand in need of means to carry it on, would maintain and promote it. At the same time, I must confess, that I had often seen encouraging appearances among the Indians elsewhere, prove wholly abortive, and it appeared that the favor would be too great, if God should now, after I had passed through so considerable a series of almost fruitless labors and fatigues, and after my rising hopes had been so often frustrated among these poor pagans, give me any special success in my labors with them, I could not believe, and scarcely dared to hope, that

the event would be so happy ; and scarcely ever found myself more sus-
pended between hope and fear in any affair, or at any time, than in this.

" This encouraging disposition, and readiness to receive instruction,
now apparent among the Indians, seems to have been the happy effect of
the conviction which one or two of them met with, sometime since at the
Forks of Delaware ; who have since endeavored to show their friends
the evil of idolatry. Though the other Indians seemed but little to
regard, and rather to deride, them ; yet this, perhaps, has put them into
a thinking posture of mind, or at least, given them some thoughts about
Christianity, and excited in some of them a curiosity to hear ; and so
made way for the present encouraging attention. An apprehension that
this might be the case, here, has given me encouragement that God may,
in such a manner, bless the means which I have used with the Indians
in other places; where, as yet, there is no appearance of it. If so, may
his name have the glory of it : for I have learnt, by experience, that he
only can open the ear, engage the attention, and incline the hearts of
poor benighted, prejudiced pagans to receive instruction.

" Rode from the Indians to Brunswick, nearly forty miles and lodged
there. Felt my heart drawn after God in prayer, almost all the forenoon,
especially in riding. In the evening, I could not help crying to God for
those poor Indians ; and, after I went to bed, my heart continued to go
out to God for them till I dropped asleep. O, blessed be God, that I
may pray ! "

He was now so fatigued by constant preaching to these
Indians, yielding to their importunate desires, that he found
it necessary to give himself some relaxation. He spent,
therefore, about a week in New Jersey, after he left the Indians ; visiting several ministers, and performing some necessary business, before he went to the Forks of Delaware.
Though he was weak in body, yet he seems to have been
strong in spirit. On Friday, July 12, he arrived at his own
house in the Forks of Delaware ; continuing still free from
melancholy ; from day to day enjoying freedom, assistance,
and refreshment in the inner man. But on Wednesday, the
next week, he seems to have had some melancholy thoughts
about his doing so little for God, being so much hindered by
weakness of body.

" *Lord's day, July* 14. [At Forks of Delaware.] Discoursed to the
Indians twice. Several of them appeared concerned, and were, I have
reason to think, in some measure convinced by the Divine Spirit of their

sin and misery; so that they wept much the whole time of divine service. Afterwards, discoursed to a number of white people then present.

"*July* 18. Preached to my people, who attended diligently beyond what had been common among these Indians; and some of them appeared concerned for their souls. Longed to spend the little inch of time I have in the world, more for God. Felt a spirit of seriousness, tenderness, sweetness and devotion; and wished to spend the whole night in prayer and communion with God.

"*July* 19. In the evening, walked abroad for prayer and meditation, and enjoyed composure and freedom in these sweet exercises, especially in meditation on Rev. iii, 12; 'Him that overcometh, will I make a pillar in the temple of my God.' etc. This was then a delightful theme to me, and it refreshed my soul to dwell on it. O when shall I go no more out from the service and enjoyment of the dear Redeemer! Lord hasten the blessed day!

"*Lord's day, July* 21. Preached to the Indians first; then to a number of white people present; and in the afternoon, to the Indians again. Divine truth seemed to make very considerable impressions upon several of them, and caused the tears to flow freely. Afterwards I baptized my interpreter, and his wife, who were the first whom I baptized among the Indians.

They are both persons of some experimental knowledge in religion; have both been awakened to a solemn concern for their souls; have to appearance, been brought to a sense of their misery, and undoneness in themselves; have both appeared to be comforted with divine consolations; and it is apparent that both have passed a great and I cannot but hope, a saving, change. It may perhaps be satisfactory and agreeable, that I should give some brief relation of this man's exercises and experience, since he has been with me; especially since he is employed as my interpreter to others. When I first employed him in this business, in the beginning of the summer of 1744, he was well fitted for his work, in regard to his acquaintance with the Indian and English languages, as well as with the manners of both nations; and in regard to his desire that the Indians should conform to the manners and customs of the English, and especially to their manner of living. But he seemed to have little or no impression of religion upon his mind, and in that respect was very unfit for his work; being incapable of understanding and communicating to others many things of importance, so that I labored under great disadvantages in addressing the Indians, for want of his having an experimental, as well as more doctrinal acquaintance with divine truths; and, at times, my spirits sunk, and were much discouraged under this difficulty; especially when I observed that divine truths made little or no impressions upon his mind for many weeks together. He indeed behaved soberly after

I employed him ; although before, he had been a hard drinker; and seemed honestly engaged, as far as he was capable, in the performance of his work. Especially he appeared very desirous that the Indians should renounce their heathenish notions and practices, and conform to the customs of the Christian world. But still he seemed to have no concern about his own soul, until he had been with me a considerable time.

The latter end of July, 1744, I preached to an assembly of white people, with more freedom and fervency than I could possibly address the Indians with, without their having first obtained a greater measure of doctrinal knowledge. At this time he was present, and was somewhat awakened to a concern for his soul ; so that the next day, he discoursed freely with me about his spiritual concerns, and gave me an opportunity to use further endeavors to fasten the impressions of his perishing state upon his mind. I could plainly perceive, for some time after this, that he addressed the Indians with more concern and fervency than he had formerly done.

" But these impressions seemed quickly to decline; and he remained, in a great measure, careless and secure, until some time late in the autumn of the year following ; when he fell into a weak and languishing state of body ; and continued much disordered for several weeks together. At this season, divine truth took hold of him, and made deep impressions upon his mind. He was brought under great concern for his soul ; and his exercises were not now transient and unsteady, but constant and abiding, so that his mind was burdened from day to day; and it was now his great inquiry, ' What he should do to be saved ? ' This spiritual trouble prevailed, until his sleep, in a great measure, departed from him, and he had little rest day or night; but walked about under great pressure of mind, for he was still able to walk, and appeared like another man to his neighbors, who could not but observe his behavior with wonder. After he had been for some time under this exercise, while he was striving to obtain mercy, he says there seemed to be an impassable mountain before him. He was pressing towards heaven, as he thought ; but ' his way was hedged up with thorns, so that he could not stir an inch further.' He looked this way and that way, but could find no way at all. He thought if he could but make his way through these thorns and briers, and climb up the first steep pitch of the mountain, that then there might be hope for him; but no way or means could he find to accomplish this. Here he labored for a time, but all in vain. He saw it was impossible, he says, for him ever to help himself through this insupportable difficulty. ' It signified just nothing at all for him to struggle and strive any more. ' Here, he says, he gave over striving, and felt that it was a gone case with him, as to his own power, and that all his attempts were, and for ever would be, vain and fruitless. Yet he was more calm and composed under this view of things, than he had been while striving to help himself.

"While he was giving me this account of his exercises, I was not without fears, that what he related was but the working of his own imagination, and not the effect of any divine illumination of mind. But, before I had time to discover my fears, he added, that at this time he felt himself in a miserable and perishing condition: that he saw plainly what he had been doing all his days; and that he had never done one good thing, as he expresses it. He knew he was not guilty of some wicked actions, of which he knew some others guilty. He had not been accustomed to steal, quarrel, and murder; the latter of which vices is common among the Indians. He likewise knew that he had done many things that were right; he had been kind to his neighbors, etc. 'But still, his cry was, that he had never done one good thing.' 'I knew,' said he, 'that I had not been so bad as some others in some things; and that I had done many things which folks call good; but all this did me no good now. I saw that all was bad, and that I had never done one good thing;' meaning that he had never done anything from a right principle, and with a right view, though he had done many things, that were materially good and right. 'And now, I thought,' said he, 'that I must sink down to hell; that there was no hope for me, because I never could do anything that was good;' and if God let me alone ever so long, and I should try ever so much, still I should do nothing but what is bad. This further account of his exercises satisfied me, that it was not the mere working of his imagination; since he appeared so evidently to die to himself, and to be divorced from a dependence upon his own righteousness, and good deeds, to which mankind, in a fallen state, are so much attached; and upon which they are so ready to hope for salvation.

"There was one thing more in his view of things at this time, which was very remarkable. He not only saw, he says, what a miserable state he himself was in, but he likewise saw that the world around him, in general, were in the same perishing circumstances, notwithstanding the profession which many of them made of Christianity, and the hope which they entertained of obtaining everlasting happiness. This he saw clearly, as if he was now waked out of sleep, or had a cloud taken from his eyes. He saw that the life which he had lived was the way to eternal death, that he was now on the brink of endless misery; and when he looked around he saw multitudes of others, who had lived the same life with himself, persons who had no more goodness than he, and yet dreamed that they were safe enough, as he had formerly done. He was fully persuaded, by their conversation and behavior, that they had never felt their sin and misery, as he now felt his.

"After he had been for some time in this condition, sensible of the impossibility of helping himself by anything which he could do, or of being delivered by any created arm; so that he had 'given up all for lost,' as to his own attempts, and was become more calm and composed;

then, he says, it was borne in upon his mind, as if it had been audibly spoken to him, 'There is hope, there is hope.' Whereupon his soul seemed to rest, and he in some measure satisfied, though he had no considerable joy.

" He cannot here remember distinctly any views he had of Christ, or give any clear account of his soul's acceptance of him, which makes his experience appear the more doubtful, and renders it less satisfactory to himself and others than it might be, if he could remember distinctly the apprehensions and actings of his mind at this season.—But these exercises of soul were attended and followed with a very great change in the man; so that it might justly be said he was become another man, if not a new man. His conversation and deportment were much altered; and even the careless world could not but wonder what had befallen him, to make so great a change in his temper, discourse, and behavior. Especially there was a surprising alteration in his public performances. He now addressed the Indians with admirable fervency, and scarcely knew when to leave off. Sometimes, when I had concluded my discourse and was returning homeward, he would tarry behind to repeat and inculcate what had been spoken.

" His change is abiding, and his life, so far as I know, unblemished to this day ; though it is now more than six months since he experienced this change ; in which space of time he has been as much exposed to strong drink as possible, in divers places where it has been moving as free as water; and yet has never, that I know of, discovered any hankering desire after it. He seems to have a very considerable experience of spiritual exercise, and discourses feelingly of the conflicts and consolations of a real Christian. His heart echoes to the soul-humbling doctrines of grace, and he never appears better pleased than when he hears of the absolute sovereignty of God, and the salvation of sinners in a way of mere free grace. He has lately had also more satisfaction respecting his own state ; and has been much enlightened and assisted in his work: so that he has been a great comfort to me.

" After a strict observation of his serious and savory conversation, his Christian temper, and unblemished behavior for such a length of time, as well as his experience, of which I have given an account; I think that I have reason to hope that he is 'created anew in Christ Jesus to good works.' His name is Moses Finda Fautaury. He is about fifty years of age, and is pretty well acquainted with the pagan notions and customs of his countrymen; and so is the better able now to expose them. He has, I am persuaded, already been, and I trust will yet be, a blessing to the other Indians.

"*July* 23. Preached to the Indians, but had few hearers. Those who of late are constantly at home, seem, of late, to be under some impressions of a religious nature.

"*July* 26. Preached to my people, and afterwards baptized my interpreter's children. In the evening, God was pleased to help me in prayer, beyond what I have experienced for some time. Especially, my soul was drawn out for the encouragement of Christ's kingdom, and for the conversion of my poor people; and my soul relied on God for the accomplishment of that great work. How sweet were the thoughts of death to me at this time! How I longed to be with Christ, to be employed in the glorious work of angels, and with an angel's vigor and delight! Yet how willing was I to stay awhile on earth, that I might do something, if the Lord pleased for his interest in the world. My soul, my very soul, longed for the ingathering of the poor heathen; and I cried to God most willingly and heartily. I could not but cry. This was a sweet season; for I had some lively taste of Heaven, and a temper of mind suited in some measure to the employments and entertainments of it. My soul was grieved to leave the place; but my body was weak and worn out, and it was nearly nine o'clock. I longed that the remaining part of life might be filled up with more fervency and activity in the things of God. O the inward peace, composure, and godlike serenity of such a frame! Heaven must differ from this only in degree, not in kind. Lord! ever give me this bread of life.

"*Lord's day, July* 28. Preached again, and found my people, at least some of them, more thoughtful than ever about their souls' concerns. I was told by some, that their seeing my interpreter, and others, baptized, made them more concerned than anything they had ever seen or heard before. There was, indeed, a considerable appearance of divine power among them, while the ordinance was administered. May that divine influence spread and increase more abundantly! In the evening, my soul was melted, and my heart broken with a sense of past barrenness and deadness. O how I then longed to live to God, and bring forth much fruit to his glory!—July 29. Was much exercised with a sense of vileness, with guilt and shame, before God. Discoursed to a number of my people, and gave them some particular advice and direction; being now about to leave them, for the present, in order to renew my visit to the Indians in New-Jersey. They were very attentive to my discourse, and earnestly desirous to know when I designed to return to them again."

July 31, he set out on his return to Crossweeksung, and arrived there the next day. In his way thither, he had longing desires, that he might come to the Indians there in the fullness of the blessing of the gospel of Christ, attended with a sense of his own great weakness, dependence, and worthlessness.

"*August* 2. [At Crossweeksung]. In the evening, I retired, and my soul was drawn out in prayer to God ; especially for my poor people, to whom I had sent word that they might gather together, that I might preach to them the next day. I was much enlarged in praying for their saving conversion; and scarcely ever found my desires of anything of this nature so sensibly and clearly, to my own satisfaction, disinterested, and free from selfish views. It seemed to me I had no care, or hardly any desire, to be the instrument of so glorious a work as I wished and prayed for among the Indians. If the blessed work might be accomplished to the honor of God, and the enlargement of the dear Redeemer's kingdom; this was all my desire and care ; and for this mercy I hoped, but with trembling; for I felt what Job expresses, chap. ix., 16, 'If I had called, and he had answered me, yet would I not believe that he had hearkened unto my voice.' My rising hopes, respecting the conversion of the Indians, have been so often dashed, that my spirit is, as it were, broken, and my courage wasted, and I hardly dare hope. I visited the Indians in these parts in June last, and tarried with them a considerable time, preaching almost daily : at which season, God was pleased to pour upon them a spirit of awakening, and concern for their souls, and surprisingly to engage their attention to divine truths. I now found them serious, and a number of them under deep concern for an interest in Christ. Their convictions of their sinful and perishing state were, in my absence from them, much promoted by the labors and endeavors of Rev. William Tennent; to whom I had advised them to apply for direction ; and whose house they frequented much while I was gone. I preached to them this day with some view to Rev. xxii. 17. 'And whosoever will, let him take of the water of life freely; ' though I could not pretend to handle the subject methodically among them. The Lord, I am persuaded, enabled me, in a manner somewhat uncommon, to set before them the Lord Jesus Christ as a kind and compassionate Saviour, inviting distressed and perishing sinners to accept everlasting mercy. A surprising concern soon became apparent among them. There were about twenty adult persons together; many of the Indians, at remote places, not having, as yet, had time to come since my return hither; and not above two that I could see with dry eyes. Some were much concerned, and discovered vehement longings of soul after Christ, to save them from the misery they felt and feared.

"*Lord's day, Aug.* 4. Being invited by a neighboring minister, to assist in the administration of the Lord's supper, I complied with his request, and took the Indians along with me ; not only those who were together the day before, but many more who were coming to hear me; so that there were nearly fifty in all, old and young. They attended the several discourses of the day; and, some of them, who could understand English, were much affected; and all seemed to have their concern in some measure raised. A change in their manners began to appear very visible. In the evening, when they came to sup together, they would not take a morsel until they had sent to me to come and supplicate a blessing on their food; at which time, sundry of them wept ; especially when I reminded them how they had, in times past, eat their feasts in honor to devils, and neglected to thank God for them.

"*August* 5. After a sermon had been preached by another minister, I preached, and concluded the public work of the solemnity, from John vii, 37. 'In the last day,' etc ; and, in my discourse, addressed the Indians in particular, who sat in a part of the house by themselves; at which time, one or two of them were struck with deep concern, as they afterwards told me, who had been little affected before ; and others had their concern increased to a considerable degree. In the evening, the greater part of them being at the house where I lodged, I discoursed to them ; and found them universally engaged about their souls' concerns ; inquiring ' what they should do to be saved.' All their conversation among themselves, turned upon religious matters, in which they were much assisted by my interpreter, who was with them day and night. This day there was one woman, who had been much concerned for her soul ever since she first heard me preach, in June last, who obtained comfort, I trust, solid and well grounded. She seemed to be filled with love to Christ. At the same time she behaved humbly and tenderly, and appeared afraid of nothing so much as of offending and grieving him whom her soul loved.

"*Aug.* 6. In the morning I discoursed to the Indians at the house where we lodged. Many of them were much affected, and appeared suprisingly tender; so that a few words about the concerns of their souls would cause the tears to flow freely, and produce many sobs and groans. In the afternoon, they being returned to the place where I had usually preached among them, I again discoursed to them there. There were about fifty-five persons in all; about forty that were capable of attending Divine service with understanding. I insisted on 1 John iv., 10. 'Herein is love,' etc. They seemed eager of hearing ; but there appeared nothing very remarkable, except their attention, till near the close of my discourse ; and then Divine truths were attended with a surprising influence, and produced a great concern among them. There were scarcely three in forty who could refrain from tears and bitter cries. They all as one seemed in an agony of soul to obtain an interest in Christ ; and the more I discoursed of the love and compassion of God in sending his Son to suffer for the sins of men; and the more I invited them to come and partake of his love; the more their distress was aggravated, because they felt themselves unable to come. It was surprising to see how their hearts seemed to be pierced with the tender and melting invitations of the gospel, when there was not a word of terror spoken to them.

" There was this day two persons who obtained relief and comfort ;

which, when I came to discourse with them particularly, appeared solid, rational and scriptural. After I had inquired into the grounds of their comfort, and said many things which I thought proper to them ; I asked them what they wanted that God should do further for them ? They re- plied, ‘ they wanted Christ should wipe their hearts quite clean,’ etc. So surprising were now the doings of the Lord, that I can say no less of this day, and I need say no more of it, than that the arm of the Lord was powerfully and marvelously revealed in it.

“ *Aug.* 7. Preached to the Indians from Is. liii, 3–10. There was a remarkable influence attending the word, and great concern in the assembly ; but scarcely equal to what appeared the day before ; that is, not quite so universal. However, most were much affected, and many in great distress for their souls ; and some few could neither go nor stand, but lay flat on the ground as if pierced at heart, crying incessantly for mercy. Several were newly awakened; and it was remarkable that, as fast as they came from remote places round about, the Spirit of God seemed to seize them with concern for their souls. After public service was concluded, I found two persons more who had newly met with com- fort, of whom I had good hopes ; and a third, of whom I could not but entertain some hopes, whose case did not appear so clear as the others ; so that there were now six in all, who had got some relief from their spiritual distresses ; and five, whose experience appeared very clear and satisfactory. It is worthy of remark, that those who obtained comfort first, were in general deeply affected with concern for their souls, when I preached to them in June last.

“ *Aug.* 8. In the afternoon I preached to the Indians, their number was now about sixty-five persons, men, women, and children. I discoursed upon Luke xiv. 16–23, and was favored with uncommon freedom in my discourse. There was much visible concern among them, while I was discoursing publicly ; but afterwards, when I spoke to one and another more particularly, whom I perceived under much concern, the power of God seemed to descend upon the assembly ‘ like a mighty rushing wind,’ and with an astonishing energy bore down all before it. I stood amazed at the influence, which seized the audience almost universally; and could compare it to nothing more aptly, than the irresistible force of a mighty torrent or swelling deluge, that with its insupportable weight and pressure bears down and sweeps before it whatever comes in its way. Almost all persons of all ages were bowed down with concern together, and scarcely one was able to withstand the shock of this surprising operation. Old men and women, who had been drunken wretches for many years, and some little children, not more than six or seven years of age, appeared in distress for their souls, as well as persons of middle age. It was apparent that these children, some of them at least, were not merely frightened with seeing the general concern ; but were made sensible of their danger, the badness of their hearts, and their misery without Christ, as some of them expressed it. The most stubborn hearts were now obliged to bow. A principal man among the Indians, who before was most secure and self-righteous, and thought his state good, because he knew more than the generality of the Indians had formerly done ; and who with a great degree of confidence the day before told me ' he had been a Christian more than ten years ;' was now brought under solemn concern for his soul, and wept bitterly. Another man advanced in years, who had been a murderer, a powwow or conjurer, and a notorious drunkard, was likewise brought now to cry for mercy with many tears, and to complain much that he could be no more concerned when he saw his danger so very great.

" They were almost universally praying and crying for mercy in every part of the house, and many out of doors; and numbers could neither go nor stand. Their concern was so great, each one for himself, that none seemed to take any notice of those about them, but each prayed freely for himself. I am led to think they were, to their own apprehensions, as much retired as if they had been individually by themselves, in the thickest desert ; or I believe rather that they thought nothing about anything but themselves, and their own state, and so were every one praying apart, although all together. It seemed to me that there was now an exact fulfillment of that prophecy Zech. xii, 10, 11, 12 ; for there was now 'a great mourning, like the mourning of Hadadrimmon ; '—and each seemed to ' mourn apart.' Methought this had a near resemblance to the day of God's power, mentioned Josh. x., 14; for I must say I never saw any day like it, in all respects : it was a day wherein I am persuaded the Lord did much to destroy the kingdom of darkness among this people.

" This concern, in general, was most rational and just. Those who had been awakened any considerable time, complained more especially of the badness of their hearts; and those who were newly awakened, of the badness of their lives and actions ; and all were afraid of the anger of God, and of everlasting misery as the desert of their sins. Some of the white people, who came out of curiosity to hear what 'this babbler would say' to the poor ignorant Indians, were much awakened ; and some appeared to be wounded with a view of their perishing state. Those who had lately obtained relief, were filled with comfort at this season. They appeared calm and composed, and seemed to rejoice in Christ Jesus. Some of them took their distressed friends by the hand, telling them of the goodness of Christ, and the comfort that is to be enjoyed in him ; and thence invited them to come and give up their hearts to him. I could observe some of them, in the most honest and unaffected manner, without any design of being taken notice of, lifting up their eyes to heaven, as if crying for mercy, while they saw the distress of the poor souls around them. There was one remarkable instance of awakening this day which I cannot fail to notice here.

A young Indian woman, who, I believe, never knew before that she had
a soul, nor ever thought of any such thing, hearing that there was something strange among the Indians, came to see what was the matter. In
her way to the Indians she called at my lodgings; and when I told her
that I designed presently to preach to the Indians, laughed, and seemed
to mock, but went however to them. I had not proceeded far in my discourse before she felt effectually that she had a soul; and, before I had
concluded my discourse, was so convinced of her sin and misery, and so
distressed with concern for her soul's salvation, that she seemed like one
pierced through with a dart, and cried out incessantly. She could neither
go nor stand, nor sit on her seat without being held up. After public service was over, she lay flat on the ground, praying earnestly, and would
take no notice of, nor give any answer to any who spoke to her. I hearkened to hear what she said, and perceived the burden of her prayer to be,
'Guttummaukalummeh wechaumeh kmeleh Nolah,' i. e. ' Have mercy on
me, and help me to give you my heart.' Thus she continued praying incessantly for many hours together. This was indeed a surprising day of
God's power, and seemed enough to convince an Atheist of the truth, importance, and power of God's word.

"*Aug.* 9. Spent almost the whole day with the Indians ; the former
part of it in discoursing to many of them privately, and especially to some
who had lately received comfort, and endeavoring to inquire into the
grounds of it, as well as to give them some proper instructions, cautions and
directions. In the afternoon discoursed to them publicly. They were
now present about seventy persons, old and young. I opened and applied
the parable of the sower, Matt. xiii. Was enabled to discourse with much
plainness, and found afterwards that this discourse was very instructive to
them. There were many tears among them, while I was discoursing publicly, but no considerable cry ; yet some were much affected with a few
words spoken from Matt. xii. 28. 'Come unto me all ye that labor,'etc.,
with which I concluded my discourse. But, while I was discoursing
near night to two or three of the awakened persons, a Divine influence
seemed to attend what was spoken to them in a powerful manner ; which
caused the persons to cry out in anguish of soul, although I spoke not a
word of terror ; but on the contrary, set before them the fullness and all-
sufficiency of Christ's merits, and his willingness to save all that come to him
and thereupon pressed them to come without delay. The cry of these was
soon heard by others, who, though scattered before, immediately gathered
round. I then proceeded in the same strain of gospel invitation, till they
were all melted into tears and cries, except two or three ; and seemed in
the greatest distress to find and secure an interest in the great Redeemer.
Some, who had little more than a ruffle made in their passions the day
before, seemed now to be deeply affected and wounded at heart; and the

concern in general appeared nearly as prevalent as it was the day before. there was indeed a very great mourning among them, and yet every one seemed to mourn apart. For so great was their concern, that almost every one was praying and crying for himself, as if none had been near. 'Guttummauhalummeh; guttummauhalummeh' i., e., 'Have mercy upon me; have mercy upon me;' was the common cry. It was very affecting to see the poor Indians, who the other day were hallooing and yelling in their idolatrous feasts and drunken frolics, now crying to God with such importunity for an interest in his dear Son! Found two or three persons who, I had reason to hope, had taken comfort upon good grounds since the evening before; and these, with others who had obtained comfort, were together, and seemed to rejoice much that God was carrying on his work with such power upon others.

"*Aug.* 10. Rode to the Indians, and began to discourse more privately to those who had obtained comfort and satisfaction; endeavoring to instruct, direct, caution, and comfort them. But others, being eager of hearing every word which related to spiritual concerns, soon came together one after another; and, when I had discoursed to the young converts more than half an hour, they seemed much melted with divine things, and earnestly desirous to be with Christ. I told them of the godly soul's perfect purity, and full enjoyment of Christ, immediately upon its separation from the body; and that it would be inconceivably more happy than they had ever been for any short space of time, when Christ seemed near to them in prayer or other duties. That I might make way for speaking of the resurrection of the body, and thence of the complete blessedness of the man: I said, 'But perhaps some of you will say, I love my body as well as my soul, and I cannot bear to think that my body shall lie dead, if my soul is happy.' To which they all cheerfully replied, 'Muttoh, muttoh;' before I had opportunity to prosecute what I designed respecting the resurrection; i. e. 'No, no.' They did not regard their bodies, if their souls might be with Christ. Then they appeared willing to be absent from the body, that they might be present with the Lord.

"When I had spent some time with them, I turned to the other Indians, and spoke to them from Luke xix. 10. For the son of man is come to seek, etc., I had not discoursed long, before their concern rose to a great degree; and the house was filled with cries and groans. When I insisted on the compassion and care of the Lord Jesus Christ for those that were lost, who thought themselves undone, and could find no way of escape; this melted them down the more, and aggravated their distress, that they could not find and come to so kind a Saviour.

"Sundry persons, who before had been slightly awakened, were now deeply wounded with a sense of their sin and misery. One man in particular, who was never before awakened, was now made to feel that 'the word of the Lord was quick and powerful, and sharper than any two-edged sword.' He seemed to be pierced at heart with distress; and his concern appeared most rational and scriptural, for he said that 'all the wickedness of his past life was brought fresh to his remembrance, and that he saw all the vile actions he had done formerly, as if done but yesterday.' Found one who had newly received comfort, after pressing distress from day to day. Could not but rejoice, and admire the Divine goodness in what appeared this day. There seems to be some good done by every discourse; some newly awakened every day, and some comforted. It was refreshing to observe the conduct of those who obtained comfort; while others were distressed with fear and concern; that is lifting up their hearts to God for them.

"*Lord's day, Aug.* 11. Discoursed in the forenoon from the parable of the prodigal son, Luke xv. Observed no such remarkable effect of the word upon the assembly as in days past. There were numbers of careless spectators of the white people, some Quakers and others. In the afternoon, discoursed upon a part of St. Peter's sermon, Acts ii. and at the close of my discourse to the Indians, made an address to the white people; and divine truths seemed then to be attended with power, both to English and Indians. Several of the white heathen were awakened, and could not longer be idle spectators; but found they had souls to save or lose as well as the Indians; and a great concern spread through the whole assembly. So that this also appeared to be a day of God's power, especially towards the conclusion of it, although the influence attending the word seemed scarcely so powerful now as in days past.

" The number of Indians, old and young, was now upwards of seventy; and one or two were newly awakened this day, who never had appeared to be moved with concern for their souls before. Those who had obtained relief and comfort, and had given hopeful evidences of having passed a saving change, appeared humble and devout, and behaved in an agreeable and Christian-like manner. I was refreshed to see the tenderness of conscience manifest in some of them; one instance of which I cannot but notice. Perceiving one of them very sorrowful in the morning, I inquired into the cause of her sorrow, and found the difficulty was, that she had been angry with her child the evening before, and was now exercised with fears, lest her anger had been inordinate and sinful; which so grieved her, that she waked and began to sob before daylight, and continued weeping for several hours together,

" *Aug.* 14. Spent the day with the Indians. There was one of them, who had, some time since, put away his wife, as is common amongst them, and taken another woman; and, being now brought under some serious impressions, was much concerned about that affair in particular, and seemed fully convinced of the wickedness of the practice, and earnestly desired to know what God would have him to do in his present circumstances. When the law of God respecting marriage, had been opened to them, and the cause of his leaving his wife inquired into; and when it appeared that she had given him no just occasion, by unchastity, to desert her, and that she was willing to forgive his past misconduct and to live peaceably with him for the future, and that she moreover insisted on it as her right to live with him ; he was then told, that it was his indispensable duty to renounce the woman whom he had last taken, and receive the other who was his proper wife, and live peaceably with her during life. With this, he readily and cheerfully complied ; and, thereupon, publicly renounced the woman he had last taken, and publicly promised to live with and be kind to his wife during life ; she, also, promising the same to him. Here appeared a clear demonstration of the power of God's word upon their hearts. I suppose a few weeks before, the whole world could not have persuaded this man to a compliance with Christian rules in this affair.

" I was not without fears that this proceeding might be like putting ' new wine into old bottles ; ' and that some might be prejudiced against Christianity, when they saw the demands made by it. But, the man being much concerned about the matter, the determination of it could be deferred no longer ; and it seemed to have a good rather than an ill effect among the Indians ; who generally owned that the laws of Christ were good and right, respecting the affairs of marriage. In the afternoon, I preached to them from the apostle's discourse to Cornelius, Acts x. 34. There appeared some affectionate concern among them, though not equal to what appeared in several of the former days. They still attended and heard as for their lives, and the Lord's work seemed still to be promoted and propagated among them.

" *Aug.* 15. Preached from Luke iv. 16-21. ' And he came to Nazareth,' etc. The word was attended with power upon the hearts of the hearers. There was much concern, many tears, and affecting cries among them ; and some, in a peculiar manner, were deeply wounded and distressed for their souls. There were some newly awakened who came but this week, and convictions seemed to be promoted in others. Those who had received comfort, were likewise refreshed and strengthened ; and the work of grace appeared to advance in all respects. The passions of the congregation in general were not so much moved, as in some days past ; but their hearts seemed as solemnly and deeply affected with divine truths as ever, at least in many instances, although the concern did not seem so universal, and to reach every individual in such a manner as it appeared to do some days before.

" *Aug.* 16. Spent a considerable time in conversing with sundry of the Indians. Found one who had got relief and comfort after pressing concern ; and could not but hope, when I came to discourse particularly with her, that her comfort was of the right kind. In the afternoon, I preached to them from John vi. 26-34. Toward the close of my discourse, divine truths were attended with considerable power upon the audience ; and more especially after public service was over, when I particularly addressed sundry distressed persons.

" There was a great concern for their souls spread pretty generally among them ; but especially there were two persons newly awakened to a sense of their sin and misery ; one of whom was lately come, and the other had all along been very attentive and desirous of being awakened, but could never before have any lively view of her perishing state. Now her concern and spiritual distress was such, that I thought I had never seen any more pressing. Sundry old men were also in distress for their souls ; so that they could not refrain from weeping and crying aloud ; and their bitter groans were the most convincing as well as affecting evidence of the reality and depth of their inward anguish. God is powerfully at work among them. True and genuine convictions of sin are daily promoted in many instances ; and some are newly awakened from time to time ; although some few, who felt a commotion in their passions in days past, seem now to discover, that their hearts were never duly affected. I never saw the work of God appear so independent of means, as at this time. I discoursed to the people, and spake what I suppose had a proper tendency to promote convictions ; but God's manner of working upon them, seemed so entirely supernatural, and above means, that I could scarcely believe he used me as an instrument, or what I spake as means of carrying on his work. For it appeared, as I thought, to have no connexion with, or dependence on means, in any respect. Though I could not but continue to use the means, which I thought proper for the promotion of the work, yet God seemed, as I apprehended, to work entirely without them. I seemed to do nothing, and, indeed, to have nothing to do, but to 'stand still, and see the salvation of God ;' and found myself obliged and delighted to say, ' Not unto us,' not unto instruments and means, ' but to thy name be glory.' God appeared to work entirely alone, and I saw no room to attribute any part of this work to any created arm.

"*Aug.* 17. Spent much time in private conferences with the Indians. Found one who had newly obtained relief and comfort, after a long season of spiritual trouble and distress ;—he having been one of my hearers at the Forks of Delaware for more than a year, and now having followed me here under deep concern for his soul ;—and had abundant reason to hope that his comfort was well grounded, and truly divine. Afterwards discoursed publicly from Acts viii. 29-39 ; and took occasion to treat concerning baptism, in order to their being instructed and prepared to partake of that ordinance. They were yet hungry and thirsty for the word of God, and appeared unwearied in their attendance upon it.

"*Lord's day, Aug.* 18. Preached in the forenoon to an assembly of white people, made up of Presbyterians, Baptists, Quakers, etc. Afterwards preached to the Indians, from John vi. 35-40, He that eateth my flesh, etc. There was considerable concern visible among them, though not equal to what has frequently appeared of late.

"*Aug.* 19. Preached from Isa. lv. 1. 'Ho, every one that thirsteth.' Divine truths were attended with power upon those who had received comfort, and others also. The former sweetly melted and refreshed with divine invitations ; the latter much concerned for their souls, that they might obtain an interest in these glorious gospel provisions which were set before them. There were numbers of poor impotent souls that waited at the pool for healing ; and the angel seemed, as at other times of late, to trouble the waters, so that there was yet a most desirable and comfortable prospect of the spiritual recovery of diseased perishing sinners. Near noon, I rode to Freehold, and preached to a considerable assembly, from Matt. v. 3. Blessed are the poor in spirit, etc. It pleased God to leave me to be very dry and barren ; so that I do not remember to have been so straightened for a whole twelvemonth past. God is just ; and he has made me to acquiesce in his will in this respect. It is contrary to flesh and blood to be cut off from all freedom in a large auditory, where their expectations are much raised ; but so it was with me ; and God helped me to say amen to it. Good is the will of the Lord. In the evening I felt quiet and composed, and had freedom and comfort in secret prayer.

"*Aug.* 20. Was composed and comfortable, still in a resigned frame. Travelled from Mr. Tennent's, in Freehold, to Elizabethtown. Was refreshed to see friends and relate to them what God had done and was still doing among my poor people.—Aug. 21. Spent the forenoon in conversation with Mr. Dickinson, contriving something for the settlement of the Indians together in a body, that they might be under better advantages for instruction. In the afternoon spent some time agreeably with other friends ; wrote to my brother at college ; but was grieved that time slid away, while I did so little for God.

"*Aug.* 23. In the morning was very weak, but favored with some freedom and sweetness in prayer, was comfortable and composed in mind. Afternoon, rode to Crossweeksung to my poor people.—Spent some time with the Indians in private discourse ; and afterwards, preached to them from John vi. 44-50. 'No man can come to me except,' etc. There was, as has been usual, a great attention and some affection among them. Several appeared deeply concerned for their souls, and could not but express their inward anguish by tears and cries. But the amazing divine influence, which has been so powerfully among them in general, seems at present in some degree abated; at least, in regard to its universality; though many who have obtained no special comfort, still retain deep impressions of divine things.

"*Aug.* 24. Spent the forenoon in discoursing to some of the Indians in order to their receiving the ordinance of baptism. When I had opened the nature of the ordinance, the obligations attending it, the duty of devoting ourselves to God in it, and the privilege of being in covenant with him ; numbers of them seemed to be filled with love to God, delighted with the thoughts of giving themselves up to him in that solemn and public manner, and melted and refreshed with the hopes of enjoying the blessed Redeemer. Afterwards, I discoursed publicly from 1 Thess. iv. 13-17. 'But I would not have you be ignorant,' etc. There was a solemn attention, and some visible concern and affection in the time of public service; which was afterwards increased by some further exhortations given to them to come to Christ, and give up their hearts to him, that they might be fitted to ' ascend up and meet him in the air,' when he shall ' descend with a shout, and the voice of the archangel.'

"There were several Indians newly come, who thought their state good, and themselves happy, because they had sometimes lived with the white people under gospel light, had learned to read, were civil, etc., although they appeared utter strangers to their hearts and altogether unacquainted with the power of religion, as well as with the doctrines of grace. With these I discoursed particularly after public worship; and was surprised to see their self-righteous dispositions, their strong attachment to the covenant of works for salvation, and the high value they put upon their supposed attainments. Yet after much discourse, one appeared in a measure convinced that ' by the deeds of the law no flesh living can be justified;' and wept bitterly, inquiring what he must do to be saved. This was very comfortable to others, who had gained some experimental knowledge of their own hearts ; for, before, they were grieved with the conversation and conduct of these new comers, who boasted of their knowledge, and thought well of themselves, but evidently discovered to those who had any experience of divine truths that they knew nothing of their own hearts.

"*Lord's day, Aug.* 25. Preached in the forenoon from Luke xv,. 37. A number of white people being present, I made an address to them at the close of my discourse to the Indians ; but could not so much as keep them orderly: for scores of them kept walking and gazing about, and behaved more indecently than any Indians I have ever addressed. A view of their abusive conduct so sunk my spirits, that I could scarcely go on with my work.

"In the afternoon discoursed from Rev. iii. 20 ; at which 'ime the

Indians behaved seriously, though many others were vain. Afterwards baptized twenty-five persons of the Indians: fifteen adults and ten children. Most of the adults, I have comfortable reason to hope, are renewed persons ; and there was not one of them but what I entertained some hopes of in that respect; though the case of two or three of them appeared more doubtful. After the crowd of spectators was gone, I called the baptized persons together, and discoursed to them in particular ; at the same time inviting others to attend. I reminded them of the solemn obligations they were now under to live to God ; warned them of the evil and dreadful consequences of careless living, especially after their public profession of Christianity ; gave them directions for future conduct ; and encouraged them to watchfulness and devotion, by setting before them the comfort and happy conclusion of a religious life.

" This was a desirable and sweet season indeed ! Their hearts were engaged and cheerful in duty; and they rejoiced that they had, in a public and solemn manner, dedicated themselves to God. Love seemed to reign among them ! They took each other by the hand with tenderness and affection, as if their hearts were knit together, while I was discoursing to them ; and all their deportment towards each other was such, that a serious spectator might justly be excited to cry out with admiration, ' Behold how they love one another.' Numbers of the other Indians, on seeing and hearing these things, were much affected, and wept bitterly, longing to be partakers of the same joy and comfort, which these discovered by their very countenances as well as conduct. I rode to my lodgings in the evening, blessing the Lord for this gracious visitation of the Indians, and the soul-refreshing things I had seen the day past among them ; and praying that God would still carry on his divine work among them.

" *Aug.* 26. Preached to my people from John vi. 51-55. After I had discoursed some time, I addressed them in particular, who entertained hopes that they were passed from death unto life. Opened to them the persevering nature of those consolations which Christ gives his people, and which I trusted he had bestowed upon some in that assembly showed them that such have already the beginnings of eternal life, and that their heaven shall speedily be completed.

" I no sooner began to discourse in this strain, than the dear Christians in the congregation began to be melted with affection too, and desire of the enjoyment of Christ, and of a state of perfect purity. They wept affectionately, yet joyfully ; and their tears and sobs discovered brokenness of heart, and yet were attended with real comfort and sweetness. It was a tender, affectionate, humble, and delightful meeting, and appeared to be the genuine effect of a spirit of adoption, and very far from that spirit of bondage under which they not long since labored. The influence seemed to spread from these through the whole assembly ; and there quickly appeared a wonderful concern among them. Many, who had not yet found Christ as an all-sufficient Saviour, were surprisingly engaged in seeking after him. It was indeed a lovely and very interesting assembly. Their number was now about ninety-five persons, old and young, and almost all affected with joy in Christ Jesus or with the utmost concern to obtain an interest in him.

"Being now convinced that it was my duty to take a journey far back to the Indians on the Susquehannah, it being now a proper season of the year to find them generally at home ; after having spent some hours in public and private discourse with my people, I told them that I must now leave them for the present, and go to their brethren far remote, and preach to them : that I wanted the spirit of God should go with me, without whom nothing could be done to any good purpose among the Indians—as they themselves had opportunity to see and observe by the barrenness of our meetings at sometimes, when there was much pains taken to affect and awaken sinners, and yet to little or no purpose, and asked them if they could not be willing to spend the remainder of the day in prayer for me, that God would go with me, and succeed my endeavors for the conversion of these poor souls. They cheerfully complied with the motion, and soon after I left them, the sun being about an hour and a half high at night, they began and continued praying till break of day, or very near ; never mistrusting as they tell me, till they went out and viewed the stars, and saw the morning star a considerable height, that it was later than bed time. Thus eager and unwearied were they in their devotions ! A remarkable night it was; attended, as my interpreter tells me, with a powerful influence upon those who were yet under concern, as well as those who had received comfort. These were, I trust, this day, two distressed souls brought to the enjoyment of solid comfort in him whom the weary find rest. It was likewise remarkable, that this day an old Indian, who had all his days been an idolater, was brought to give up his rattles, which they use for music in their idolatrous feasts and dances, to the other Indians, who quickly destroyed them. This was done without any attempt of mine in the affair, I having said nothing to him about it, so that it seemed to be nothing but the power of God's word, without any particular application to this sin that produced this effect. Thus God has begun ; thus he has hitherto surprisingly carried on a work of grace amongst these Indians. May the glory be ascribed to him who is the sole author of it. I went from the Indians to my lodgings, rejoicing for the goodness of God to my poor people ; and enjoyed freedom of the soul in prayer, and other duties in the evening. Bless the Lord, O my soul !"

The next day, he set out on a journey towards the Forks of Delaware, designing to go from thence to Susquehannah, before he returned to Crossweeksung. It was five days from his departure from Crossweeksung before he reached the Forks; going round by the way of Philadelphia, and waiting on the Governor of Pennsylvania, to get a recommendation from him to the chief of the Indians; which he obtained. He speaks of much rest, comfort and spiritual refreshment, in this journey, and also, a sense of his exceeding unworthiness, thinking himself the meanest creature that ever lived.

"*Lord's day, Sept.* 1. [At Forks of Delaware.] Preached to the Indians from Luke xi. 16–23. The word appeared to be attended with some power, and caused some tears in the assembly. Afterwards preached to a number of white people present, and observed many of them in tears; and some who had formerly been careless and unconcerned about religion, perhaps as the Indians. Towards night, discoursed to the Indians again, and perceived a greater attention, and more visible concern among them, than has been usual in these parts. God gave me the spirit of prayer, and it was a blessed season in that respect. My soul cried to God for mercy in an affectionate manner. In the evening also, my soul rejoiced in God.

"*Sept.* 3. Preached to the Indians from Isaiah lii. 3–6. 'He is despised and rejected of men,' etc. The Divine presence seemed to be in the midst of the assembly, and a considerable concern spread among them. Sundry persons seemed to be awakened; among whom were two stupid creatures, whom I could scarce ever before keep awake while I was discoursing to them. I could not but rejoice at this appearance of things; although at the same time, I could not but fear, lest the concern which they at present manifested, might prove like a morning cloud, as something of that nature had formerly done in these parts.

"*Sept.* 4. Rode 15 miles to an Irish settlement, and preached there from Luke xiv. 22. 'And yet there is room.' God was pleased to afford me some tenderness and enlargement in the first prayer, and much freedom as well as warmth in the sermon. There were many tears in the assembly; the people of God seemed to melt; and others seemed to be in some measure awakened. Blessed be the Lord, who lets me see his work going on in one place and another!

"*Sept.* 5. Discoursed to the Indians from the parable of the sower. Afterwards I conversed particularly with sundry persons; which occasioned them to weep, and even to cry out in an affecting manner, and seized others with surprise and concern. I doubt not but that a divine power accompanied what was then spoken. Several of these persons had been with me to Crossweeksung; and there had seen, and some of them, I trust, felt, the power of God's word, in an affecting and saving manner. I asked one of them, who had obtained comfort and given hopeful evidences of being truly religious, ' Why he now cried?' He replied, ' When he thought how Christ was slain like a lamb, and spilt his blood for sinners, he could not help crying, when he was alone;' and thereupon burst into tears, and cried again. I then asked his wife who had likewise been abundantly comforted, why she cried? She answered, 'that she was grieved that the Indians here would not come to Christ, as well as those at Crossweeksung' I asked her if she found a heart to pray for them; and whether Christ had seemed to be near her of late in prayer, as in times past; which is my usual method of expressing a sense of the divine presence. She replied 'yes, he had been near to her, and at times when she had been praying alone, her heart loved to pray so, that she could not bear to leave the place, but wanted to stay and pray longer.'

" *Sept.* 6. Enjoyed some freedom and intenseness of mind, in prayer alone ; and longed to have my soul more warmed with divine and heavenly things. Was somewhat melancholy towards night, and longed to die and quit a scene of sin and darkness, but was a little supported in prayer.—Sept. 7. Preached to the Indians from John vi., 35-39. There was not so much the appearance of concern among them as at several other times of late; yet they appeared serious and attentive.

" *Lord's day, Sept.* 8. Discoursed to the Indians in the afternoon from Acts ii. 36-39. The word of God at this time seemed to fall with weight and influence upon them. There were but few present; but most that were, were in tears; and several cried out in distressing concern for their souls. There was one man considerably awakened, who never before discovered any concern for his soul. There appeared a remarkable work of the Divine Spirit among them generally, not unlike what has been of late at Crossweeksung. It seemed as if the divine influence had spread thence to this place ; although something of it appeared here before in the awakening of my interpreter, his wife, and some few others. Several of the careless white people now present, were awakened or at least startled, seeing the power of God so prevalent among the Indians. I then made a particular address to them, which seemed to make some impression upon them, and excite some affection in them.

" There are sundry Indians in these parts, who have always refused to hear me preach, and have been enraged against those who have attended on my preaching. But of late they are more bitter than ever ; scoffing at Christianity, and sometimes asking my hearers, ' How often they have cried,' and ' Whether they have not now cried enough to do their turn,' etc. So that they have already trial of cruel workings.

" In the evening, God was pleased to assist me in prayer, and give me freedom at the throne of grace. I cried to God for the enlargement of his kingdom in the world, and in particular among my dear people; was also enabled to pray for many dear ministers of my acquaintance, both in these parts, and in New England, and also for other dear friends in New England. My soul was so engaged and enlarged in the sweet exercise, that I spent an hour in it, and knew not how to leave the mercy seat. O how I delighted to pray and cry to God! I saw that God was both able and willing to do all that I desired for myself, and his church in general. I was likewise much enlarged, and assisted in family prayer. Afterwards when I was just going to bed, God helped me to renew my petition, with ardor and freedom. O it was to me a blessed evening of prayer! Bless the Lord, O my soul.

"*Sept.* 9. Left the Indians at the Forks of Delaware, and set out on a journey towards Susquehannah river; directing my course towards the Indian town more than a hundred and twenty miles westward from the Forks. Travelled about fifteen miles, and there lodged.

"*Sept.* 13. [At Shaumoking.] After having lodged out three nights, arrived at the Indian town I aimed at on the Susquehannah, called Shaumoking; one of the places and the largest of them which I visited in May last. I was kindly received, and entertained by the Indians; but had little satisfaction by reason of the heathenish dance and revel they then held in the house where I was obliged to lodge; which I could not suppress, though I often entreated them to desist, for the sake of one of their own friends who was then sick in the house, and whose disorder was much aggravated by the noise. Alas! how destitute of natural affection are these poor uncultivated pagans! although they seem somewhat kind in their own way. Of a truth the dark corners of the earth are full of the habitations of cruelty. This town, as I observed in my diary of May last, lies partly on the east side of the river, partly on the west, and partly on a large island in it; and contains upwards of fifty houses, and nearly three hundred persons, though I never saw much more than half that number in it. They are of three different tribes of Indians, speaking three languages wholly unintelligible to each other. About one half of its inhabitants are Delawares; the others called Senakas and Tutelas. The Indians of this place, are accounted the most drunken, mischievous, and ruffianlike fellows, of any in these parts; and Satan seems to have his seat in this town in an eminent manner.

"*Sept.* 14. Visited the Delaware king; who was supposed to be at the point of death when I was here in May last, but was now recovered; discoursed with him and others, respecting Christianity; spent the afternoon with them and had more encouragement than I expected. The king appeared kindly disposed, and willing to be instructed. This gave me some encouragement that God would open an effectual door for my preaching the gospel here, and set up his kingdom in this place. This was a support and refreshment to me in the wilderness, and rendered my solitary circumstances comfortable and pleasant. In the evening, my soul was enlarged, and sweetly engaged in prayer; especially that God would set up his kingdom in this place, where the devil now reigns in the most eminent manner. I was enabled to ask this for God, for his glory, and because I longed for the enlargement of his kingdom, to the honor of his dear name. I could appeal to God with the greatest freedom, that it was his dear cause, and not my own, which engaged my heart. My soul cried ' Lord set up thy kingdom for thine own glory; glorify thyself, and I shall rejoice. Get honor to thy blessed name, and this is all I desire. Do with me just what thou wilt ; blessed be thy name forever that thou art God, and that thou wilt glorify thyself. O that the whole world would glorify thee ! O let these poor people be brought to know thee, and love thee, for the glory of thy ever dear blessed name.' I could not but hope, that God would bring in these miserable, wicked Indians ; though there appeared little human probability of it ; for they were then dancing and revelling, as if possessed by the devil. But yet I hoped, though against hope, that God would be glorified, and that his name would be glorified, by these poor Indians. I continued long in prayer and praise to God, and had great freedom, enlargement, and sweetness ; remembering dear friends in New England, as well as the people of my charge. Was entirely free from that dejection of spirit, with which I am frequently exercised Blessed be God !

" *Lord's day, Sept.* 15. Visited the chief of the Delawares again ; was kindly received by him, and discoursed to the Indians in the afternoon. Still entertained hopes that God would open their hearts, to receive the gospel ; though many of them in the place, were so drunk, from day to day, that I could get no opportunity to speak to them. Towards night, discoursed with one who understood the languages of the Six Nations, as they are usually called ; who discovered an inclination to hearken to Christianity, which gave me some hopes that the gospel might hereafter be sent to those nations far remote.

" *Sept.* 16. Spent the forenoon with the Indians, endeavoring to instruct them from house to house, and to engage them, as far as I could, to be friendly to Christianity. Towards night went to one part of the town, where they were sober, got together near fifty of them, and discoursed to them ; having first obtained the king's cheerful consent. There was a surprising attention among them, and they manifested a considerable desire of being further instructed. There were, also, one or two who seemed to be touched with some concern for their souls, who appeared well pleased with some conversation in private, after I had concluded my public discourse to them. My spirits were much refreshed with this appearance of things, and I could not but return with my Interpreter, having no other companion in this journey, to my poor hard lodgings, rejoicing in hopes that God designed to set up his kingdom here, where Satan now reigns in the most eminent manner; and found uncommon freedom in addressing the throne of grace for the accomplishment of so great and glorious a work.

"*Sept.* 17.   Spent the forenoon in visiting and discoursing to the Indians. About noon, left Shaumoking (most of the Indians going out this day on their hunting design) and traveled down the river southwestward.—Sept. 19. Visited an Indian town, called Juncauta, situate on an island in the Susquehannah. Was much discouraged with the temper and behavior of the Indians here; although they appeared friendly when I was with them the last spring, and then gave me encouragement to come and see them again. But they now seemed resolved to retain their pagan notions, and persist in their idolatrous practices.

"*Sept.* 20. Visited the Indians again at Juncauta island, and found them very busy in making preparations for a great sacrifice and dance. Had no opportunity to get them together, in order to discourse with them about Christianity, by reason of their being so much engaged about their sacrifice. My spirits were much sunk with a prospect so very discouraging; and especially seeing I had now no interpreter but a pagan, who was as much attached to idolatry as any of them ; my own interpreter having left me the day before, being obliged to attend upon some important business elsewhere, and knowing that he could neither speak nor understand the language of these Indians; so that I was under the greatest disadvantages imaginable. However, I attempted to discourse privately with some of them, but without any appearance of success ; notwithstanding I still tarried with them.

"In the evening they met together, nearly a hundred of them, and danced around a large fire, having prepared ten fat deer for the sacrifice. The fat of the inwards they burnt in the fire while they were dancing, and sometimes raised the flame to a prodigious height; at the same time yelling and shouting in such a manner, that they might easily have been heard two miles or more. They continued their sacred dance nearly all night, after which they ate the flesh of the sacrifice, and so retired each one to his own lodging. I enjoyed little satisfaction ; being entirely alone on the island as to any Christian company, and in the midst of this idolatrous revel ; and having walked to and fro till body and mind were pained and much oppressed, I at length crept into a little crib made for corn, and there slept on the poles.

"*Lord's day, Sept.* 21. Spent the day with the Indians on the island. As soon as they were well up in the morning, I attempted to instruct them, and labored for that purpose to get them together; but soon found they had something else to do, for near noon they gathered together all their powows, or conjurers, and set about half a dozen of them playing their juggling tricks, and acting their frantic distracted postures, in order to find out why they were then so sickly upon the island, numbers of them being at that time disordered with a fever and bloody flux. In this exercise they were engaged for several hours, making all the wild, ridiculous and distracted motions imaginable; sometimes singing, sometimes howling, sometimes extending their hands to the utmost stretch, and spreading all their fingers,—they seemed to push with them as if they designed to push something away, or at least keep it off at arm's-end; sometimes stroking their faces with their hands, then spirting water as fine as mist; sometimes sitting flat on the earth, then bowing down their faces to the ground; then wringing their sides as if in pain and anguish, twisting their faces, turning up their eyes, grunting. puffing, etc.

" Their monstrous actions tended to excite ideas of horror, and seemed to have something in them, as I thought, peculiarly suited to raise the devil, if he could be raised by anything odd, ridiculous, and frightful. Some of them, I could observe, were much more fervent and devout in the business than others, and seemed to chant, peep, and mutter with a great degree of warmth and vigor, as if determined to awaken and engage the powers below. I sat at a small distance, not more than thirty feet from them, though undiscovered, with my bible in my hand, resolving, if possible, to spoil their sport, and prevent their receiving any answers from the infernal world, and there viewed the whole scene. They continued their hideous charms and incantations for more than three hours, until they had all wearied themselves out; although they had in that space of time taken several intervals of rest, and at length broke up I apprehended, without receiving any answer at all.

" After they had done powwawing, I attempted to discourse with them about Christianity; but they soon scattered, and gave me no opportunity for anything of that nature. A view of these things, while I was entirely alone in the wilderness, destitute of the society of any one who so much as 'named the name of Christ,' greatly sunk my spirits, and gave me the most gloomy turn of mind imaginable, almost stripped me of all resolution and hope respecting further attempts for propagating the gospel, and converting the pagans, and rendered this the most burdensome and disagreeable Sabbath which I ever saw. But nothing, I can truly say, sunk and distressed me like the loss of my hope respecting their conversion. This concern appeared so great, and seemed to be so much my own, that I seemed to have nothing to do on earth, if this failed. A prospect of the greatest concern in the saving conversion of souls under gospel-light, would have done little or nothing towards compensating for the loss of my hope in this respect; and my spirits now were so damped and depressed that I had no heart nor power to make any further attempts among them for that purpose, and could not possibly recover my hope, resolution, and courage, by the utmost of my endeavors.

" Many of the Indians of this island understand the English language considerably well ; having formerly lived in some part of Maryland, among or near the white people ; but are very drunken, vicious, and profane, although not so savage as those who have less acquaintance with the English. Their customs, in various respects, differ from those of the other Indians upon the river. They do not bury their dead in a common form, but let their flesh consume above ground, in close cribs made for that purpose. At the end of a year, or sometimes a longer space of time they take the bones when the flesh is all consumed, and wash and scrape them, and afterwards bury them with some ceremony. Their method of charming or conjuring over the sick, seems somewhat different from that of other Indians, though in substance the same. The whole of it among these and others, perhaps, is an intimation of what seems, by Naaman's expression, 2 Kings, v. 11. to have been the custom of the ancient heathen. It seems chiefly to consist in their ' striking their hands over the diseased,' repeatedly stroking them, ' and calling upon their gods ;' except the spirting of water like a mist, and some other frantic ceremonies common to the other conjurations which I have already mentioned.

" When I was in this region in May last, I had an opportunity of learning many of the notions and customs of the Indians, as well as observing many of their practices. I then traveled more than a hundred and thirty miles upon the river, above the English settlements : and, in that journey, met with individuals of seven or eight distinct tribes, speaking as many different languages. But of all the sights I ever saw among them, or indeed anywhere else, none appeared so frightful, or so near akin to what is usually imagined of infernal powers, none ever excited such images of terror in my mind, as the appearance of one who was a devout and zealous reformer, or rather, restorer of what he supposed was the ancient religion of the Indians.

"He made his appearance in his pontifical garb, which was a coat of boar skins, dressed with the hair on, and hanging down to his toes ; a pair of bearskin stockings ; and a great wooden face painted, the one half black, the other half tawny, about the color of an Indian's skin, with an extravagant mouth, cut very much awry ; the face fastened to a bearskin cap, which was drawn over his head. He advanced towards me with the instrument in his hand, which he used for music in his idolatrous worship ; which was a dry tortoise-shell with some corn in it, and the neck of it drawn on to a piece of wood, which made a very convenient handle. As he came forward, he beat his tune with the rattle, and danced with all his might, but did not suffer any part of his body, not so much as his fingers to be seen. No one would have imagined from his appearance or actions, that he could have been a human creature, if they had not had some intimation of it otherwise. When he came near me, I could not but shrink away from him although it was then noonday, and I knew who it was; his appearance and gestures were so prodigiously frightful. He had a house consecrated to religious uses, with divers images cut upon the several parts of it. I went in, and found the ground beat almost as hard as a rock, with their frequent dancing upon it.

"I discoursed with him about Christianity. Some of my discourse he seemed to like, but some of it he disliked extremely. He told me that God had taught him his religion, and that he never would turn from it; but wanted to find some who would join heartily with him in it; for the Indians, he said, were grown very degenerate and corrupt. He had thoughts, he said, of leaving all his friends, and traveling abroad, in order to find some who would join with him; for he believed that God had some good people somewhere, who felt as he did. He had not always, he said, felt as he now did; but had formerly been like the rest of the Indians, until about four or five years before that time. Then, he said, his heart was very much distressed, so that he could not live among the Indians, but got away into the woods, and lived alone for some months. At length, he says, God comforted his heart, and showed him what he should do; and since that time he had known God, and tried to serve him; and loved all men, be they who they would, so as he never did before.

"He treated me with uncommon courtesy, and seemed to be hearty in it. I was told by the Indians, that he opposed their drinking strong liquor with all his power; and that, if at any time he could not dissuade them from it by all he could say, he would leave them, and go crying into the woods. It was manifest that he had a set of religious notions which he had examined for himself, and not taken for granted, upon bare tradition; and he relished or disrelished what ever was spoken of a religious nature, as it either agreed or disagreed with his standard. While I was discoursing, he would sometimes say 'Now that I like; so God has taught me;' etc., and some of his sentiments seemed very just. Yet he utterly denied the existence of a devil, and declared there was no such creature known among the Indians of old times, whose religion he supposed he was attempting to revive. He likewise told me, that departed souls all went southward; and that the difference between the good and the bad, was this; that the former were admitted into a beautiful town with spiritual walls; and that the latter would for ever hover around these walls, in vain attempts to get in. He seemed to be sincere, honest, and conscientious in his own way, and according to his own religious notions; which was more than I ever saw in any other pagan. I perceived that he was looked upon and derided among most of the Indians, as a precise zealot, who made a needless noise about religious matters; but I must say that there was something in his temper and disposition, which looked more like true religion, than anything I ever observed amongst other heathens.

" But alas ! how deplorable is the state of the Indians upon this river !
The brief representation which I have here given of their notions and
manners, is sufficient to show that they are ' led captive by Satan at his
will,' in the most eminent manner ; and methinks might likewise be sufficient to excite the compassion, and engage the prayers, of pious souls for
these their fellow men, who sit ' in the region of the shadow of death.'

"*Sept.* 22. Made some further attempts to instruct and Christianize
the Indians on this Island, but all to no purpose. They live so near the
white people that they are always in the way of strong liquor, as well as
of the ill examples of nominal Christians; which renders it so unspeakably
difficult to treat with them about Christianity."

Brainerd left these Indians on the 23d of September, to
return to the Forks of Delaware, in a very weak state of body
and under great dejection of mind, which continued the first
two days of his journey.

"*Sept.* 25. Rode still homeward. In the forenoon, enjoyed freedom
and intenseness of mind in meditation on Job xlii, 5, 6. ' I have heard of
thee by the hearing of the ear, but now mine eye seeth thee; wherefore I
abhor myself and repent in dust and ashes.' The Lord gave me clearness
to penetrate into the sweet truths contained in that text. It was a comfortable and sweet season to me."

"*Sept.* 26. Was still much disordered in body, and able to ride but
slowly. Continued my journey, however. Near night, arrived at the
Irish settlement, about fifteen miles from my own house. This day,
while riding, I was much exercised with a sense of my barrenness; and
verily thought there was no creature who had any true grace, but what was
more spiritual and faithful. I could not think that any of God's children
made so poor a hand of living to God.

"*Sept.* 27. Spent a considerable time in the morning in prayer and
praise to God. My mind was somewhat intense in the duty; and my
heart, in some degree, warmed with a sense of divine things. My soul
was melted to think that ' God had accounted me faithful, putting me
into the ministry.' My soul was also, in some measure, enlarged in
prayer for the dear people of my charge, as well as for other dear friends.
Afternoon, visited some Christian friends, and spent the time I think profitably; my heart was warmed and more engaged in the things of God.
In the evening I enjoyed enlargement, warmth and comfort in prayer ; my
soul relied on God for assistance and grace to enable me to do something
in his cause ; my heart was drawn out in thankfulness to God for what he
had done for his own glory among my poor people of late. I felt encouraged to proceed in his work; being persuaded of his power, and
hoping that his arm might be further revealed for the enlargement of his

dear kingdom. My soul 'rejoiced in hope of the glory of God,' in hope of the advancement of his declarative glory in the world, as well as of enjoying him in a world of glory. O, blessed be God, the living God, for ever."

He continued in this comfortable sweet frame of mind the next two days; on the following he went to his own house in the Forks of Delaware, and continued still in the same frame. The next day, he visited the Indians.

"*Oct.* 1. [At Forks of Delaware,] Discoursed to the Indians here, and spent some time in private conference with them about their souls' concerns, and afterwards invited them to accompany, or if not, to follow me to Crossweeksung as soon as they could conveniently; which invitation numbers of them cheerfully accepted."

Wednesday he spent principally in writing the meditation he had in his late journey to the Susquehannah. On Thursday he left the Forks of Delaware, reached Crossweeksung Oct. 5; and continued from day to day in a comfortable state of mind.

"*Oct.* 5. [At Crossweeksung,] Preached to my people from John xiv. 1–6. The divine presence seemed to be in the assembly. Numbers were affected with divine truths, and it was a comfort to some in particular. O what a difference is there between these, and the Indians with whom I have lately treated upon the Susquehannah! To be with those seemed to be like being banished from God and all his people; to be with these, like being admitted into his family, and to the enjoyment of his divine presence! How great is the change lately made upon numbers of those Indians, who, not many months ago, were as thoughtless and averse to Christianity as those upon the Susquehannah; and how astonishing is that grace, which has made this change!

Lord's day, Oct. 6. Preached in the forenoon from John x. 7–11. There was a considerable melting among my people; the dear young Christians were refreshed, comforted and strengthened; and one or two persons newly awakened.—In the afternoon, I discoursed on the story of the jailer, Acts xvi, and in the evening, expounded Acts xx, 1–12. There was at this time a very agreeable melting spread throughout the whole assembly. I think I scarce ever saw a more desirable affection in any number of people in my life. There was scarcely a dry eye to be seen among them; and yet nothing boisterous or unseemly, nothing that tended to disturb the public worship; but rather to encourage and excite a Christian ardor and spirit of devotion.—Those, who I have reason to hope were seriously renewed, were first affected, and seemed to rejoice much, but with brokenness of spirit and godly fear. Their exercises were much the same with those mentioned in my journal of Aug. 26, evidently appearing to be the genuine effects of a spirit of adoption.

"After public service was over, I withdrew, being much tired with the labors of the day; and the Indians continued praying among themselves for nearly two hours together; which continued exercises appeared to be attended with a blessed quickening influence from on high. I could not but earnestly wish that numbers of God's people had been present at this season to see and hear these things which I am sure must refresh the heart of every true lover of Zion's interest. To see those, who were very lately savage Pagans and idolaters, having no hope, and without God in the world, now filled with a sense of divine love and grace, and worshipping the Father in spirit and in truth, as numbers have appeared to do, was not a little affecting; and especially to see them appear so tender and humble, as well as lively, fervent, and devout in the divine service.

"*Oct.* 7. Being called by the church and people of East-Hampton, on Long Island, as a member of a council to assist and advise in affairs of difficulty in that church, I set out on my journey this morning before it was well light, and traveled to Elizabethtown, and there lodged. Enjoyed some comfort on the road in conversation with Mr. William Tennent, who was sent for on the same business."

BRAINERD prosecuted his journey with the other ministers who were sent for, and did not return till Oct. 24. While he was at East-Hampton, the importance of the business, on which the council were convened, lay with such weight on his mind, and he was so concerned for the interests of religion in that place, that he slept but little for several nights successively. In his way to and from East-Hampton, he had several seasons of sweet refreshment; wherein his soul was enlarged and comforted with divine consolations in secret retirement; and he had special assistance in public ministerial performances in the house of God; and yet at the same time a sense of extreme vileness and unprofitableness. From time to time he speaks of soul refreshments and comfort in conversation with the ministers who traveled with him, and seems to have little or nothing of melancholy until he came to the west end of Long-Island in his return. After that he was oppressed with dejection and gloominess of mind for several days together.

"*Oct.* 24. [At Crossweeksung,] Discoursed from John iv. 13, 14

There was a great attention, a desirable affection, and an unaffected melting in the assembly. It is surprising to see how eager they are to hear the word of God. I have oftentimes thought that they would cheerfully and diligently attend divine worship twenty-four hours together, if they had an opportunity so to do.

"*Oct.* 25. Discoursed to my people respecting the Resurrection, from Luke xx. 27–36. When I came to mention the blessedness which the godly shall enjoy at that season ; their final freedom from death, sin and sorrow ; their equality to the angels in their nearness to an enjoyment of Christ, some imperfect degree of which they are favored with in the present life, from whence springs their sweetest comfort ; and their being the children of God, openly acknowledged by him as such ;—I say, when I mentioned these things, numbers of them were much affected and melted with a view of this blessed state.

"*Oct.* 26. Being called to assist in the administration of the Lord's supper in a neighboring congregation, I invited my people to go with me. They in general embraced the opportunity cheerfully ; and attended the several discourses of this solemnity with diligence and affection, most of them now understanding something of the English language.

"*Lord's Day, Oct.* 27. While I was preaching to a vast assembly of people abroad, who appeared generally easy and secure enough, there was one Indian woman, a stranger, who never heard me preach before, nor ever regarded anything about religion, being now persuaded by some of her friends to come to meeting, though much against her will, was seized with distressing concern for her soul and soon after expressed a great desire of going home, more than forty miles distant, to call her husband, that he also might be awakened to a concern for his soul. Some others of the Indians appeared to be affected with divine truths this day. The pious people of the English, numbers of whom I had opportunity to converse with, seemed refreshed with seeing the Indians worship God in that devout and solemn manner with the assembly of his people ; and with those mentioned in Acts xi. 18, they could not but glorify God, saying, 'Then hath God also to the Gentiles granted repentance unto life.'

" Preached again in the afternoon, to a great assembly ; at which time some of my people appeared affected ; and, when public worship was over, were inquisitive whether there would not be another sermon in the evening, or before the sacramental solemnity was concluded ; being still desirous to hear God's word.

"*Oct.* 28. Discoursed from Matt. xxii. 1–13. I was enabled to open the scriptures, and adapt my discourse and expression to the capacities of my people, I know not how, in a plain, easy, and familiar manner, beyond all that I could have done by the utmost study : and this without any special difficulty ; yea with as much freedom as if I had been addressing a common audience, who had been instructed in the doctrines of Christianity all their days. The word of God, at this time, seemed to fall upon the assembly with a divine power and influence, especially towards the close of my discourse : there was both a sweet melting and bitter mourning in the audience. The dear Christians were refreshed and comforted, convictions revived in others, and several persons newly awakened, who had never been with us before. So much of the divine presence appeared in the assembly, that it seemed 'this was no other than the house of God and the gate of heaven.' All, who had any savor and relish of divine things, were even constrained by the sweetness of that season to say, ' Lord, it is good for us to be here ;' If ever there was among my people an appearance of the New Jerusalem, 'as a bride adorned for her husband,' there was much of it at this time ; and so agreeable was the entertainment, where such tokens of the divine presence were, that I could scarcely be willing in the evening to leave the place and repair to my lodgings. I was refreshed with a view of the continuance of this blessed work of grace among them, and with its influence upon strangers among the Indians, who had of late, from time to time, providentially come into this part of the country. Had an evening of sweet refreshing ; my thoughts were raised to a blessed eternity ; my soul was melted with desires of perfect holiness, and of perfectly glorifying God.

" *Oct.* 29. About noon, rode and viewed the Indian lands at Cranberry; was much dejected, and greatly perplexed in mind ; knew not how to see anybody again; my soul was sunk within me. Oh that these trials might make me more humble and holy. Oh that God would keep me from giving way to sinful dejection, which may hinder my usefulness. —Oct. 30. My soul was refreshed with a view of the continuance of God's blessed work among the Indians. Oct. 31. Spent most of the day in writing;—enjoyed not much spiritual comfort ; but was not so much sunk with melancholy as at other times.

" *Nov.* 1. Discoursed from Luke xxiv. briefly explaining the whole chapter, and insisting especially upon some particular passages. The discourse was attended with some affectionate concern upon some of the hearers, though not equal to what has often appeared among them.—Nov. 2. Spent the day with the Indians ; wrote some things of importance; and longed to do more for God than I did, or could do, in this present feeble and imperfect state.

" *Lord's Day, Nov.* 3. Preached to my people from Luke xvi. 17. ' And it is easier for heaven and earth,' etc., more especially for the sake of several lately brought under deep concern for their souls. There was some apparent concern and affection in the assembly ; though far less than has been usual of late. Afterwards I baptized fourteen persons ;

six adults, and eight children. One of these was nearly fourscore years of age ; and, I have reason to hope that God has brought her savingly home to himself. Two of the others were men of fifty years old, who had been singular and remarkable among the Indians for their wickedness ; one of them had been a murderer, and both notorious drunkards, as well as excessively quarrelsome ; but now I cannot but hope, that both of them have become subjects of God's special grace, especially the worst of them.* I deferred their baptism for many weeks after they had given evidence of having passed a great change, that I might have more opportunities to observe the fruits of the impressions which they had been under, and apprehended the way was now clear. There was not one of the adults whom I baptized, who had not given me comfortable grounds to hope that God had wrought a work of special grace in their hearts.

"*Nov.* 4. Discoursed from John xi, briefly explaining most of the chapter. Divine truths made deep impressions upon many in the assembly. Numbers were affected with a view of the power of Christ manifested in his raising the dead ; and especially when this instance of his power was improved to show his ability to raise dead souls, such as many of them then felt themselves to be, to a spiritual life ; as, also, to raise the dead at the last day, and dispense to them true rewards and punishments.

" There were numbers of those who had come here lately from remote places, who were now brought under deep and pressing concern for their souls. One in particular, who, not long since, came half drunk, and railed on us, and attempted to disturb us while engaged in divine worship, was now so concerned and distressed for her soul, that she seemed unable to get any ease without an interest in Christ. There were many tears and sobs and groans in the assembly in general ; some weeping for themselves, others for their friends. Although persons are, doubtless, much more easily affected now than they were in the beginning of this religious concern, when tears and cries for their souls were things unheard of among them, yet I must say, that their affection in general appeared genuine and unfeigned ; and, especially, this appeared very conspicuous in those newly awakened. So that true and genuine convictions of sin seem still to be begun and promoted in many instances. Baptized a child this day, and perceived numbers of the baptized persons affected with the administration of this ordinance, as being thereby reminded of their own solemn engagements. I have now baptized in all 47 Indians ; 23 adults, and 24 children ; 35 of them belonged to this region, and the rest to the Forks of Delaware. Through rich grace, none of them, as yet, have been left to disgrace their profession of Christianity by any scandalous or unbecoming behavior."

---

* The man mentioned in my journal of August 10, as being then awakened.

CHAPTER VIII.

Brainerd's Remarks on the Extraordinary Work of God's Grace among these Indians.

" I might now properly make many remarks on a work of grace, so very remarkable as this has been in various respects ; but shall confine myself to a few general hints only.

" 1. It is remarkable, that God began this work among the Indians at a time when I had the least hope, and, to my apprehension, the least rational prospect of seeing a work of grace propagated among them ; my bodily strength being then much wasted by a late tedious journey to the Susquehannah, where I was necessarily exposed to hardships and fatigues among the Indians ; my mind being, also, exceedingly depressed with a view of the unsuccessfulness of my labors. I had little reason so much as to hope, that God had made me instrumental in the saving conversion of any of the Indians, except my interpreter and his wife. Hence I was ready to look upon myself as a burden to the honorable society which employed and supported me in this business, and began to entertain serious thoughts of giving up my mission ; and almost resolved, I would do so at the conclusion of the present year, if I had then no better prospect of special success in my work than I had hitherto had. I cannot say that I entertained these thoughts because I was weary of the labors and fatigues which necessarily attended my present business, or because I had light and freedom in my own mind to turn any other way ; but purely through dejection of spirit, pressing discouragement, and an apprehension of its being unjust to spend money consecrated to religious uses, only to civilize the Indians, and bring them to an external profession of Christianity. This was all which I could then see any prospect of effecting, while God seemed, as I thought, evidently to frown upon the design of their saving conversion, by withholding the convincing and renewing influences of his blessed Spirit from attending the means which I had hitherto used with them for that end.

" In this frame of mind, I first visited these Indians at Crossweeksung; apprehending that it was my indispensable duty, seeing I had heard there was a number in these parts, to make some attempts for their conversion to God, though I cannot say I had any hope of success, my spirits being now so extremely sunk. I do not know that my hopes, respecting the conversion of the Indians, were ever reduced to so low an ebb, since I had any special concern for them, as at this time. Yet this was the very season in which God saw fit to begin this glorious work! Thus he 'ordained strength out of weakness,' by making bare his almighty arm, at a time when all hopes and human probabilities most evidently appeared to fail. Whence I learn, that it is good to follow the path of duty, though in the midst of darkness and discouragement.

"2. It is remarkable how God providentially, and in a manner almost unaccountable, called these Indians together, to be instructed in the great things that concerned their souls ; and how he seized their minds with the most solemn and weighty concern for their eternal salvation, as fast as they came to the place where his word was preached. When I first came into these parts in June, I found not one man at the place I visited, but only four women and a few children ; but before I had been here many days they gathered from all quarters, some from more than twenty miles distant; and when I made them a second visit in the beginning of August, some came more than forty miles to hear me. Many came without any intelligence of what was going on here, and consequently without any design of theirs, so much as to gratify their curiosity. Thus it seemed as if God had summoned them together from all quarters for nothing else but to deliver his message to them ; and that he did this, with regard to some of them, without making use of any human means ; although there was pains taken by some of them to give notice to others at remote places.

"Nor is it less surprising that they were one after another affected with a solemn concern for their souls, almost as soon as they came upon the spot where divine truths were taught them. I could not but think often, that their coming to the place of our public worship, was like Saul and his messengers coming among the prophets; they no sooner came but they prophesied ; and these were almost as soon affected with a sense of their sin and misery, and with an earnest concern for deliverance, as they made their appearance in our assembly. After this work of grace began with power among them, it was common for strangers of the Indians, before they had been with us one day, to be much awakened, deeply convinced of their sin and misery, and to inquire with great solicitude, ' What they should do to be saved?'

"3. It is likewise remarkable how God preserved these poor ignorant Indians from being prejudiced against me, and the truths I taught them, by those means that were used with them for that purpose by ungodly people. There were many attempts made by some ill-minded persons of the white people to prejudice them against, or fright them from, Christianity. They sometimes told them, that the Indians were well enough already ;—that there was no need of all this noise about Christianity;—that if they were Christians, they would be in no better, no safer, or happier state, than they were already in. Sometimes they told them, that I was a knave, a deceiver, and the like ; that I daily taught them lies, and had no other design but to impose upon them, etc. When none of these, and such like suggestions, would avail to their purpose, they then tried another expedient, and told the Indians, ' My design was to gather together as large a body of them as I possibly could, and then sell them to England for slaves ;' than which nothing could be more likely to terrify the Indians, they being naturally of a jealous disposition, and the most averse to a state of servitude perhaps of any people living.

" But all these wicked insinuations, through divine goodness over-ruling, constantly turned against the authors of them, and only served to engage the affections of the Indians more firmly to me ; for they, being awakened to a solemn concern for their souls, could not but observe, that the persons who endeavored to embitter their minds against me, were altogether unconcerned about their own souls, and not only so, but vicious and profane ; and thence could not but argue, that if they had no concern for their own, it was not likely they should have for the souls of others.

" It seems yet the more wonderful that the Indians were preserved from once hearkening to these suggestions, inasmuch as I was an utter stranger among them, and could give them no assurance of my sincere affection to, and concern for them, by anything that was past,—while the persons who insinuated these things were their old acquaintance, who had frequent opportunities of gratifying their thirsty appetites with strong drink, and consequently, doubtless, had the greatest interest in their affections. But from this instance of their preservation from fatal preju-dices, I have had occasion with admiration to say, ' If God will work, who can hinder ?'

"4. Nor is it less wonderful how God was pleased to provide a remedy for my want of skill and freedom in the Indian language, by re-markably fitting my interpreter for, and assisting him in the performance of his work. It might reasonably be supposed I must needs labor under a vast disadvantage in addressing the Indians by an interpreter; and that divine truths would undoubtedly lose much of the energy and pathos with which they might at first be delivered, by reason of their coming to the audience from a second hand. But although this has often, to my sorrow and discouragement, been the case in times past, when my inte-rpreter had little or no sense of divine things ; yet now it was quite other-wise. I cannot think my addresses to the Indians ordinarily, since the beginning of this season of grace, have lost anything of the power or pun-gency with which they were made, unless it were sometimes for want of pertinent and pathetic terms and expressions in the Indian language ; which difficulty could not have been much redressed by my personal ac-quaintance with their language. My interpreter had before gained some good degree of doctrinal knowledge, whereby he was rendered capable of understanding, and communicating, without mistakes, the intent and meaning of my discourses, and that without being confined strictly and obliged to interpret verbatim. He had likewise, to appearance, an experimental acquaintance with divine things; and it pleased God at this season to inspire his mind with longing desires for the conversion of the Indians, and to give him admirable zeal and fervency in addressing them in order thereto. It is remarkable, that, when I was favored with any special assistance in any work, and enabled to speak with more than common freedom, fervency, and power, under a lively and affecting sense of divine things, he was usually affected in the same manner almost instantly, and seemed at once quickened and enabled to speak in the same pathetic language, and under the same influence that I did. A surprising energy often accompanied the word at such seasons; so that the face of the whole assembly would be apparently changed almost in an instant, and tears and sobs became common among them.

"He also appeared to have such a clear doctrinal view of God's usual methods of dealing with souls under a preparatory work of conviction and humiliation as he never had before; so that I could, with his help, discourse freely with the distressed persons about their internal exercises, their fears, discouragements, temptations, etc. He likewise took pains day and night to repeat and inculcate upon the minds of the Indians the truths which I taught them daily; and this he appeared to do, not from spiritual pride, and an affectation of setting himself up as a public teacher, but from a spirit of faithfulness, and an honest concern for their souls.

"His conversation among the Indians has likewise, so far as I know, been savory, as becomes a Christian, and a person employed in his work; and I may justly say, he has been a great comfort to me, and a great instrument of promoting this good work among the Indians; so that whatever be the state of his own soul, it is apparent God has remarkably fitted him for this work. Thus God has manifested that, without bestowing on me the gift of tongues, he could find a way wherein I might be as effectually enabled to convey the truths of his glorious gospel to the minds of these poor benighted Pagans.

"5. It is further remarkable, that God has carried on his work here by such means and in such a manner, as tended to obviate, and leave no room, for those prejudices and objections which have often been raised against such a work. When persons have been awakened to a solemn concern for their souls, by hearing the more awful truths of God's word, and the terrors of the divine law insisted upon, it has usually in such cases been objected by some, that such persons were only frightened with a fearful noise of hell and damnation; and that there was no evidence that their concern was the effect of a divine influence. But God has left no room for this objection in the present case; this work of grace having been begun and carried on, by almost one continued strain of gospel invitation to perishing sinners. This may reasonably be guessed from a view of the passages of scripture I chiefly insisted upon in my discourses from time to time; which I have for that purpose inserted in my diary.

"Nor have I ever seen so general an awakening in any assembly in my life as appeared here while I was opening and insisting upon the parable of the great supper (Luke xiv.) in which discourse, I was enabled to set before my hearers, the unsearchable riches of gospel grace. Not that I would be understood here, that I never instructed the Indians respecting their fallen state, and the sinfulness and misery of it; for this was what I' at first, chiefly insisted upon with them, and endeavored to repeat and inculcate in almost every discourse, knowing that without this foundation, I should but build upon the sand, and that it would be in vain to invite them to Christ unless I could convince them of their need of him.

"But still this great awakening, this surprising concern, was never excited by any harangues of terror, but always appeared most remarkable when I insisted upon the compassion of a dying Saviour, the plentiful provisions of the gospel, and the free offers of divine grace, to needy, distressed sinners. Nor would I be understood to insinuate, that such a religious concern might justly be suspected as not being genuine, and from a divine influence, because produced from the preaching of terror; for this is perhaps, God's more usual way of awakening sinners, and appears entirely agreeable to scripture and sound reason. But what I meant here to observe is, that God saw fit to employ and bless milder means for the effectual awakening of these Indians, and thereby obviated the forementioned objection, which the world might otherwise have had a more plausible color of making.

"As there has been no room for any plausible objection against this work, with regard to the means; so neither with regard to the manner in which it has been carried on. It is true, persons' concern for their souls has been exceedingly great; the convictions of their sin and misery have arisen to a high degree, and produced many tears, cries, and groans; but then they have not been attended with those disorders, either bodily or mental, which have sometimes prevailed among persons under religious impressions. There has here been no appearance of those convulsions, bodily agonies, frightful screamings, swoonings, and the like, which have been so much complained of in some places; although there have been some, who, with the jailer, have been made to tremble under a sense of their sin and misery; numbers who have been made to cry out from a distressing view of their perishing state;—and some, who have been for a time, in a great measure, deprived of their bodily strength, yet without any such convulsive appearances.

"Nor has there been any appearance of mental disorders here, such as visions, trances, imaginations of being under prophetic inspiration, and the like ; or scarce any unbecoming disposition to appear remarkably affected either with concern or joy ; though I must confess, I observed one or two persons, whose concern I thought was in a considerable measure affected ; and one whose joy appeared to be of the same kind. But these workings of spiritual pride I endeavored to crush in their first appearances, and have not since observed any affection, either of joy or sorrow, but what appeared genuine and unaffected. But,

Lastly. The effects of this work have likewise been very remarkable. I doubt not but that many of these people have gained more doctrinal knowledge of divine truths, since I first visited them in June last, than could have been instilled into their minds by the most diligent use of proper and instructive means for whole years together, without such a divine influence. Their pagan notions and idolatrous practices, seem to be entirely abandoned in these parts. They are regulated, and appear regularly disposed in the affairs of marriage ; an instance whereof I have given in my journal of August 14. They seem generally divorced from drunkenness, their darling vice, the ' sin that easily besets them ; ' so that I do not know of more than two or three who have been my steady hearers, that have drunk to excess since I first visited them ; although before it was common for some or other of them to be drunk almost every day : and some of them seem now to fear this sin in particular, more than death itself. A principle of honesty and justice appears in many of them ; and they seem concerned to discharge their old debts, which they have neglected, and perhaps scarcely thought of for years past. Their manner of living, is much more decent and comfortable than formerly, having now the benefit of that money which they used to consume upon strong drink. Love seems to reign among them, especially those who have given evidences of having passed a saving change ; and I never saw any appearance of bitterness or censoriousness in these, nor any disposition to 'esteem themselves better than others,' who had not received the like mercy.

" As their sorrows under convictions have been great and pressing, so many of them have since appeared to ' rejoice with joy unspeakable, and full of glory ;' and yet I never saw anything ecstatic or flighty in their joy. Their consolations do not incline them to lightness ; but, on the contrary, are attended with solemnity, and oftentimes with tears, and an apparent brokenness of heart, as may be seen in several passages of my diary. In this respect some of them have been surprised at themselves, and have with concern observed to me, that ' when their hearts have been glad,' which is a phrase they commonly make use of to express spiritual joy, ' they could not help crying for all.'

" And now, upon the whole, I think, I may justly say, that here are all the symptoms and evidences of a remarkable work of grace among these Indians, which can reasonably be desired or expected. May the great author of this work maintain and promote the same here, and propagate it everywhere, till ' the whole earth be filled with his glory !' Amen.

" I have now rode more than three thousand miles, of which I have kept an exact account, since the beginning of March last, and almost the whole of it has been in my own proper business as a missionary, upon the design, either immediately, or more remotely, of propagating Christian knowledge among the Indians. I have taken pains to look out for a col‑ league or companion, to travel with me ; and have likewise used endea‑ vors to procure something for his support, among religious persons in New England, which cost me a journey of several hundred miles in length ; but have not, as yet, found any person qualified and disposed for this good work, although I had some encouragement from ministers and others, that it was hoped a maintenance might be procured for one, when the man should be found.

" I have likewise represented to the gentlemen concerned with this mission, the necessity of having an English school speedily set up among these Indians, who are now willing to be at the pains of gathering together in a body for this purpose. In order thereto, I have humbly proposed to them the collecting of money for the maintenance of a schoolmaster, and the defraying of other necessary charges, in the promotion of this good work ; which they are now attempting in the several congregations of Christians to which they respectively belonged.

" The several companies of Indians to whom I have preached in the summer past, live at great distances from each other. It is more than seventy miles from Crossweeksung, in New Jersey, to the Forks of Dela‑ ware in Pennsylvania ; and thence to sundry of the Indian settlements which I visited on Susquehannah, is more than a hundred and twenty miles. So much of my time is necessarily consumed in journeying, that I can have but little for any of my necessary studies, and consequently for the study of the Indian languages in particular ; and especially seeing I am obliged to discourse so frequently to the Indians at each of these places while I am with them, in order to redeem time to visit the rest. I am, at times, almost discouraged from attempting to gain any acquaintance with the Indian languages, they are so very numerous ; some account of which I gave in my diary of May last : and especially, seeing my other labors and fatigues engross almost the whole of my time, and bear ex‑ ceedingly hard upon my constitution, so that my health is much impaired. —However, I have taken considerable pains to learn the Delaware lan‑ guage, and propose still to do so, as far as my other business and bodily health will admit. I have already made some proficiency in it, though I have labored under many and great disadvantages in my attempts of that nature. It is but just to observe here, that all the pains I took to acquaint myself with the language of the Indians with whom I spent my first year, were of little or no service to me here among the Delawares ; so that my work, when I came among these Indians, was all to begin anew.

" As these poor ignorant pagans stood in need of having ' line upon line, and precept upon precept,' in order to their being instructed and grounded in the principles of Christianity ; so I preached ' publicly, and taught from house to house,' almost every day for whole weeks together, when I was with them. My public discourses did not then make up the one half of my work, while there were so many constantly coming to me with that important inquiry, ' What must we do to be saved ? ' and opening to me the various exercises of their minds. Yet I can say to the praise of rich grace, that the apparent success with which my labors were crowned, unspeakably more than compensated for the labor itself and was likewise a great means of supporting and carrying me through the business and fatigues, which, it seems, my nature would have sunk under, without such an encouraging prospect. But although this success has afforded matter of support, comfort, and thankfulness ; yet in this season I have found great need of assistance in my work, and have been much oppressed for want of one to bear a part of my labors and hardships. ' May the Lord of the harvest send forth other laborers into this part of his harvest, that those who sit in darkness may see great light ; and that the whole earth may be filled with the knowledge of himself ! ' Amen."

CHAPTER IX.

Efforts to get a Schoolmaster to instruct the Indians.—Continuance of the Good Work at Crossweeksung.—Rode more that three thousand miles in a few months in visiting different parts of his Field.—Successful attempts to teach the Assembly's Shorter Catechism to the Indians.—Amazing Changes wrought in one Year in the Character of these Indians.

ON Tuesday, Nov. 5, Brainerd left the Indians and spent the remaining part of this week in traveling to various parts of New Jersey, in order to get a collection for the use of the Indians, and to obtain a schoolmaster to instruct them. In the mean time, he speaks of very sweet refreshment and entertainment with Christian friends, and of being sweetly employed while riding, in meditation on divine subjects; his heart being enlarged, his mind clear, his spirit refreshed with divine truths, and his "heart burning within him while he went by the way, and the Lord opened to him the scriptures."

"*Lord's day, Nov.* 10. [At Elizabethtown.] Was comfortable in the morning both in body and mind; preached in the forenoon from 2 Cor. v. 20. Now then we are ambassadors for Christ, etc. God was pleased to give me freedom and fervency in my discourse; and the presence of God seemed to be in the assembly; numbers were affected, and there were many tears among them. In the afternoon, preached from Luke xiv. 22. And yet there is room. Was favored with divine assistance in the first prayer, and poured out my soul to God with a filial temper; the living God also assisted me in the sermon."

The next day he went to Newtown, Long Island, to a meeting of Presbytery. He speaks of some sweet meditations which he had while there, on Christ's delivering up the kingdom to the Father; and of his soul being much refreshed and warmed with the consideration of that blissful day.

"*Nov.* 15. Could not cross the ferry by reason of the violence of the wind; nor could I enjoy any place of retirement at the ferry-house; so that I was in perplexity. Yet God gave me some satisfaction and sweetness in meditation, and in lifting up my heart to him in the midst of company. Although some were drinking and talking profanely, which was indeed a grief to me, yet my mind was calm and composed; and I could not but bless God, that I was not likely to spend an eternity in such company. In the evening I sat down and wrote with composure and freedom ; and can say through pure grace it was a comfortable evening to my soul; an evening which I was enabled to spend in the service of God.

"*Nov.* 16. Crossed the ferry about ten o'clock, and arrived at Elizabethtown near night. Was in a calm, composed frame of mind, and felt an entire resignation, with respect to a loss I had lately sustained in having my horse stolen from me at Newtown. Had some longings of soul for the dear people of Elizabethtown, that God would pour out his Spirit upon them, and revive his work among them."

He spent the next four days at Elizabethtown, for the most part in a free and comfortable state of mind ; intensely engaged in the service of God, and enjoying at times the special assistance of his Spirit. On Thursday of this week he rode to Freehold, and spent the day under considerable dejection.

"*Nov.* 22. Rode to Mr. Tennent's, and from thence to Crossweeksung. Had but little freedom in meditation while riding ; which was a grief and burden to my soul. O that I could fill up all my time, whether, in the house or by the way, for God. I was enabled, I think, this day to give up my soul to God, and put over all his concerns into his hands; and found some real consolation in the thought of being entirely at the divine disposal, and having no will or interest of my own. I have received my all from God ; O that I could return my all to God! Surely God is worthy of my highest affections and most devoted adoration ; he is infinitely worthy that I should make him my last end, and live for ever to him. O that I might never more, in any one instance, live to myself!

"*Lord's day, Nov.* 24.* Preached both parts of the day from the story of Zaccheus, Luke xix. 1—9. In the latter exercise, when I opened and insisted upon the salvation that comes to a sinner upon his becoming a son of Abraham or a true believer, the word seemed to be attended with divine power to the hearts of the hearers. Numbers were much affected with divine truths ; former convictions were revived ; one or two persons newly awakened ; and a most affectionate engagement in divine service appeared among them universally. The impressions they were

* The second part of the journal began here.

under appeared to be the genuine effect of God's word brought home to their hearts by the power and influence of the Divine Spirit.

"*Nov.* 26. After having spent some time in private conferences with my people, I discoursed publicly among them from John v. 1—9. I was favored with some special freedom and fervency in my discourse, and a powerful energy accompanied divine truths. Many wept and sobbed affectionately, and scarcely any appeared unconcerned in the whole assembly. The influence which seized the audience, appeared gentle, and yet pungent and efficacious. It produced no boisterous commotions of the passions ; but seemed deeply to affect the heart, and excite in the persons under convictions of their lost state, heavy groans and tears : and in others, who had obtained comfort, a sweet and humble melting. It seemed like the gentle but steady showers which effectually water the earth, without violently beating upon the surface. The persons lately awakened were some of them deeply distressed for their souls, and appeared earnestly solicitous to obtain an interest in Christ ; and some of them, after public worship was over, in anguish of spirit, said, ' they knew not what to do, nor how to get their wicked hearts changed.'

"*Nov.* 28. Discoursed to the Indians publicly, after having used some private endeavors to instruct and excite some in the duties of Christianity. Opened and made remarks upon the sacred story of our Lord's transfiguration, Luke ix. 28—36. Had a principal view in insisting upon this passage of scripture to the edification and consolation of God's people. Observed some, that I have reason to think are truly such, exceedingly affected with an account of the glory of Christ in his transfiguration, and filled with longing desires of being with him, that they might with open face behold his glory. After public service was over, I asked one of them, who wept and sobbed most affectionately, What she now wanted? She replied, 'O, to be with Christ. She did not know how to stay.' This was a blessed refreshing season to the religious people in general. The Lord Jesus Christ seemed to manifest his divine glory to them, as when transfigured before his disciples ; and they were ready with the disciples universally to say, "Lord, it is good for us to be here.'

"The influence of God's word was not confined to those who had given evidence of being truly gracious ; though at this time I calculated my discourse for and directed it chiefly to such. But it appeared to be a season of Divine power in the whole assembly ; so that most were in some measure affected. One aged man, in particular, lately awakened, was now brought under a deep and pressing concern for his soul, was now earnestly inquisitive ' how he might find Jesus Christ.' God seems still to vouchsafe his divine presence, and the influence of his blessed

Spirit to accompany his word, at least in some measure, in all our meetings for divine worship.

"I enjoyed some divine comfort and fervency in the public exercise
and afterwards. While riding to my lodgings, was favored with
some sweet meditations on Luke ix. 31. 'Who appeared in glory, and
spake of his decease, which he should accomplish at Jerusalem.' My
thoughts ran with freedom; and I saw and felt what a glorious subject
the death of Christ is for glorified souls to dwell upon in their conversation. O the death of Christ! how infinitely precious!

"*Nov.* 30. Preached near night, after having spent some hours in
private conference with some of my people about their soul's concerns.
Explained and insisted upon the story of the rich man and Lazarus, Luke
xvi. 19—26. The word made powerful impressions upon many in the
assembly, especially while I discoursed of the blessedness of Lazarus in
Abraham's bosom. This I could perceive affected them much more than
what I spoke of the rich man's misery and torments; and thus it has been
usually with them. They have almost always appeared much more
affected with the comfortable than the dreadful truths of God's word.
That which has distressed many of them under conviction is, that they
found they wanted, and could not obtain, the happiness of the godly; at
least, they have often appeared to be more affected with this than with
the terrors of hell. But whatever be the means of their awakening, it is
plain, numbers are made deeply sensible of their sin and misery, the
wickedness and stubbornness of their own hearts, their utter inability to
help themselves, or to come to Christ for help, without divine assistance;
and so are brought to see their perishing need of Christ to do all for them
and to lie at the foot of sovereign mercy.

"*Lord's day, Dec.* 1. Discoursed to my people in the forenoon from
Luke xvi. 27–31. There appeared an unfeigned affection in divers
persons, and some seemed deeply impressed with divine truths. In the
afternoon, preached to a number of white people; at which time the
Indians attended with diligence, and many of them were unable to understand a considerable part of the discourse. At night discoursed to my
people again, and gave them particular cautions and directions relating to
their conduct in divers respects, and pressed them to watchfulness in their
deportment, seeing they were encompassed with those who waited for
their halting, and who stood ready to draw them into temptations of every
kind, and then to expose religion by their missteps.—Dec. 2. Was much
affected with grief that I had not lived more to God; and felt strong resolutions to double my diligence in my Master's service."

After this he went to a meeting of the Presbytery, at a
place in New Jersey called Connecticut Farms, and was ab-

sent the remainder of the week.   He speaks of some seasons
of sweetness and spiritual affection in his absence.

" *Lord's day, Dec.* 8.   Discoursed on the story of the blind man, John
ix.   There appeared no remarkable effect of the word upon the assembly
at this time.   The persons who have lately been much concerned for their
souls, seemed now not so affected nor solicitous to obtain an interest in
Christ as has been usual; although they attended divine service with
seriousness and diligence.   Such have been the doings of the Lord here
in awakening sinners, and affecting the hearts of those who are brought
to solid comfort with a fresh sense of divine things, from time to time,
that it is now strange to see the assembly sit with dry eyes and without
sobs and groans.—Dec. 9. 10. 11.   Spent most of the day in procuring
provisions in order to my setting up housekeeping among the Indians.
Enjoyed little satisfaction through the day, being very much out of my
element.   Was engaged in the same business as yesterday.   Towards
night got into my house.   Spent the forenoon in necessary labors about
my house.   In the afternoon rode out upon business; and passed the
evening with satisfaction among friends in conversation on a serious and
profitable subject.

" *Dec.* 12.   Preached from the parable of the Ten Virgins, (Matt. xxv.)
The divine power seemed in some measure to attend this discourse ; in
which I was favored with uncommon freedom and plainness of address,
and enabled to open divine truths, and explain them to the capacities of
my people in a manner beyond myself.   There appeared in many persons
an affectionate concern for their souls, although the concern in general
seemed not so deep and pressing as it had formerly done.   Yet it was refreshing to see many melted into tears and unaffected sobs; some with a
sense of divine love, and some for the want of it.

" *Dec.* 13.   Spent the day mainly in labor about my house. In the even
ing, spent some time in writing ; but was very weary and much outdone
with the labor of the day.—Dec. 14.   Rose early, and wrote by candle-
light some considerable time ; spent most of the day in writing, but was
somewhat dejected.   In the evening was exercised with pain in my head.

" *Dec.* 15.   Preached to the Indians from Luke xiii. 24-28.   Divine
truth fell with weight and power upon the audience and seemed to reach
the hearts of many.   Near night discoursed to them again from Matt.
xxv. 31-46.   At this season also the word appeared to be accompanied
with a divine influence, and made powerful impressions upon the assembly
in general, as well as upon numbers in a very special and particular
manner.   This was an amazing season of grace.   'The word of the Lord,'
this day, ' was quick and powerful, sharper than a two edged sword, and

---

* This is the third house that he built to dwell in among the Indians.   The first at
Kaunaumeek, county of Albany ; the second at the Forks of Delaware ; the third at
Crossweeksung, New Jersey.

pierced the hearts of many. The assembly was greatly affected and deeply wrought upon; yet without so much apparent commotion of the passions as appeared in the beginning of this work of grace. The impressions made by the word of God upon the audience appeared solid, rational, and deep; worthy of the solemn truths by which they were produced; and far from being the effects of any sudden fright or groundless perturbation of mind. O, how did the hearts of the hearers seem to bow under the weight of divine truths; and how evident did it now appear, that they received and felt them, 'not as the word of man, but as the word of God.' None can form a just idea of the appearance of our assembly at this time but those who have seen a congregation solemnly awed, and deeply impressed by the special power and influence of divine truths delivered to them in the name of God.

"*Dec.* 16. Discoursed to my people in the evening from Luke xi. 1–13 After having insisted some time upon the ninth verse, wherein there is a command and encouragement to ask for the divine favor, I called upon them to ask for a new heart with the utmost importunity ; as the man mentioned in the parable, on which I was discoursing, pleaded for loaves of bread at midnight. There was much affection and concern in the assembly, and especially one woman appeared in great distress for her soul. She was brought to such an agony in seeking after Christ, that the sweat ran off her face although the evening was very cold and her bitter cries were the most affecting indications of her heart.

"*Dec.* 21. My people having now attained to a considerable degree of knowledge in the principles of Christianity, I thought it proper to set up a catechetical lecture among them; and this evening attempted something in that form ; proposing questions to them agreeably to the Assembly's Shorter Catechism, receiving their answers, and then explaining and insisting as appeared necessary and proper upon each question. After this I endeavored to make some practical improvement of the whole. This was the method I entered upon. They were able readily and rationally to answer many important questions which I proposed to them; so that upon trial, I found their doctrinal knowledge to exceed my own expectations. In the improvement of my discourse, when I came to infer and open the blessedness of those who have so great and glorious a God, as had before been spoken of, 'for their everlasting friend and portion,' several were much affected, and especially when I exhorted, and endeavored to persuade them to be reconciled to God through his dear Son, and thus to secure an interest in his everlasting favor. So that they appeared not only enlightened and instructed, but affected and engaged in their soul's concern by this method of discoursing. After my labors with the Indians, I spent some time in writing some things divine and solemn; and was much wearied with the labors of the day, found that my spirits were extremely spent, and that I could do no more. I am conscious to myself that my labors are as great and constant as my nature will admit; and ordinarily I go to the extent of my strength, so that I do all I can; but the misery is I do not labor with that heavenly temper, that single eye to the glory of God, that I long for.

" *Lord's day, Dec. 22.* Discoursed upon the story of the young man in the Gospel, Matt. ix. 16–22. God made it a seasonable word, I am persuaded, to some souls. There were several of the Indians newly come here, who had frequently lived among Quakers; and, being more civilized and conformed to English manners than the generality of the Indians they had imbibed some of the Quakers' errors, especially this fundamental one, viz. That if men will but live soberly and honestly according to the dictates of their own consciences, or the light within, there is then no danger or doubt of their salvation. These persons I found much worse to deal with than those who are wholly under pagan darkness; who make no pretences to knowledge in Christianity at all, nor have any self-righteous foundation to stand upon. However, they all, except one, appeared now convinced that this sober honest life of itself was not sufficient to salvation since Christ himself had declared it so in the case of the young man. They seemed in some measure concerned to obtain that change of heart, the necessity of which I had been laboring to show them.

" This was likewise a season of comfort to some souls, and in particular to one, the same mentioned in my journal of the 16th instant, who never before obtained any settled comfort, though I have abundant reason to think she had passed a saving change some days before. She now appeared in a heavenly frame of mind, composed, and delighted with the divine will. When I came to discourse particularly with her, and to enquire of her, how she obtained relief and deliverance from the spiritual distresses which she had lately suffered; she answered in broken English,* ' Me try, me try save myself; last, my strength be all gone; (meaning her ability to save herself;) could not me stir bit further. Den last me forced let Jesus Christ alone send me hell, if he please.' I said, ' But, you was not willing to go to hell; was you?' She replied, ' Could not me help it. My heart, he would wicked for all. Could not me make him good, (meaning, she saw it was right she should go to hell, because her heart was wicked, and would be so after all she could do to mend it.) I asked her, how she got out of this case. She answered still in the same broken language, ' By by, my heart be glad desperately.' I asked her, why her heart was glad? She replied, ' Glad my heart, Jesus Christ do what he please with me. Den me tink, glad my heart

---

* In proper English, ' I tried, and tried to save myself, till at last my strength was all gone, and I could not stir any further. Then I was at last obliged to let Jesus Christ alone, to send me to hell if he pleased.

Jesus Christ send me to hell. Did not me care where he put me ; love him for all.' She could not readily be convinced, but that she was willing to go to hell if Christ was pleased to send her there ; although the truth evidently was, that her will was so swallowed up in the divine will, that she could not frame any hell in her imagination which would be dreadful or undesirable, provided it was the will of God to send her to it. Toward night discoursed to them again in the catechetical method, which I entered upon the evening before. When I came to improve the truth which I had explained to them, and to answer that question, 'But how shall I know whether God has chosen me to everlasting life ? ' by pressing them to come and give up their hearts to Christ, and thereby ' to make their election sure,' they then appeared much affected : and persons under concern were afresh engaged in seeking after an interest in him ; while some others, who had obtained comfort before, were refreshed to find that love to God in themselves, which was an evidence of his electing love to them.

" *Dec.* 23 *and* 24. Spent three days in writing with the utmost diligence. Felt in the main a sweet mortification to the world, and a desire to live and labor only for God ; but wanted more warmth and spirituality, and a more sensible and affectionate regard for the glory of God.

" *Dec.* 25. The Indians having been used on Christmas-days to drink and revel among some of the white people in these parts, I thought it proper this day to call them together and discourse to them upon divine things ; which I accordingly did from the parable of the barren fig-tree, Luke xiii, 6–9. A divine influence, accompanied the word at this season. The power of God appeared in the assembly, not by producing any remarkable crisis, but by rousing several stupid creatures, who were scarcely ever moved with any concern before. The power attending divine truths seemed to have the influence of the earthquake rather than of the whirlwind upon them. Their passions were not so much alarmed as has been common here in times past but, their judgments appeared to be powerfully convinced by the masterly and conquering influence of divine truths. The impression made upon the assembly in general, seemed not superficial, but deep and heart affecting. O how ready did they now appear universally to embrace and comply with everything which they heard and were convinced was their duty. God was in the midst of us of a truth, bowing and melting stubborn hearts ! How many tears and sobs were then to be seen and heard among us ! What liveliness and strict attention ! What eagerness and intenseness of mind appeared in the whole assembly, in the time of Divine service. They seemed to watch and wait for the droppings of God's word, as the thirsty earth for the 'former and latter rain.' Afterwards I discoursed to them on the duty of husbands and wives, from Eph. v. 22, 23. and have reason to think this was a word in season. Spent some time further in the evening in inculcating the truths on which I had insisted in my former discourse respecting the barren fig-tree ; and observed a powerful influence accompany what was spoken.

"*Dec.* 26. This evening was visited by a person under great spiritual distress ; the most remarkable instance of this kind I ever saw.*

"*Dec.* 27. Labored in my studies to the utmost of my strength, and though I felt a steady disposition of mind to live to God, and a firm conviction that I had nothing in this world to live for, yet I did not find that sensible affection in the service of God which I wanted to have. My heart seemed barren, though my head and hands were full of labor.

"*Dec.* 28. Discoursed to my people in the catechetical method on which I lately entered. In the improvement of my discourse, wherein I was comparing man's present with his primitive state, and showing from what he had fallen, and the miseries in which he is now involved, and to which he is exposed in his natural estate ; and pressing sinners to take a view of their deplorable circumstances without Christ, as also to strive that they might obtain an interest in him; the Lord, I trust, granted a remarkable influence of his blessed Spirit to accompany what was spoken ; and a great concern appeared in the assembly. Many were melted into tears and sobs ; and the impressions made upon them seemed deep and heart-affecting. In particular there were two or three persons who appeared to be brought to the last exercises of a preparatory work, and reduced almost to extremity ; being in a great measure convinced of the impossibility of their helping themselves, or of mending their own hearts ; and seemed to be upon the point of giving up all hope in themselves, and of venturing upon Christ, as poor, helpless, and undone. Yet they were in distress and anguish, because they saw no safety in so doing, unless they could do something towards saving themselves. One of these persons was the very aged woman above-mentioned, who now appeared 'weary and heavy laden' with a sense of her sin and misery, and her perishing need of an interest in Christ."

This day Brainerd wrote the following letter to his brother John, at Yale College :

CROSSWEEKSUNG, NEW JERSEY, *Dec.* 28, 1745.

"VERY DEAR BROTHER :

"I am in one continued, perpetual, and uninterrupted hurry ; and divine Providence throws so much upon me, that I do not see how it will

* [BRAINERD'S account of this remarkable conversion, and of two or three other cases, described by him in his journal, I have ventured to give in succinct form in his own words, in a separate chapter. The reader cannot fail to be deeply interested in the special operations of God's Spirit on the hearts of these untutored savages. J. M. S.]

ever be otherwise. May I obtain mercy of God to be faithful to the death!" I cannot say that I am weary of my hurry. I only want strength and grace to do more for God than I have ever yet done.

" My dear brother, the Lord of heaven, who has carried me through many trials, bless you for time and eternity, and fit you to do service for him in his church below, and to enjoy his blissful presence in his church triumphant.

"My dear brother, the time is short. O let us fill it up for God; let us count the sufferings of this present time as nothing, if we can but run our race, and finish our course with joy. O let us strive to live for God ! I bless the Lord, I have nothing to do with earth, but only to labor honestly in it for God, till I shall accomplish 'as an hireling my day.' I think I do not desire to live one minute for anything which earth can afford. Oh that I could live for none but God, till my dying moment !

> " I am your affectionate brother,
>
> " DAVID BRAINERD."

Lord's day, Dec. 29. Preached from John iii. 1-5. A number of white people were present, as is usual upon the Sabbath. The discourse was accompanied with power, and seemed to have a silent, but deep and piercing influence upon the audience. Many wept and sobbed affectionately. There were some tears among the white people, as well as the Indians. Some could not refrain from crying out ; though there were not many so exercised. But the impressions made upon their hearts appeared chiefly by the extraordinary earnestness of their attention, and their heavy sighs and tears.

" After public worship was over, I went to my house, proposing to preach again after a short season of intermission. But they soon came in, one after another, with tears in their eyes, to know ' what they should to be saved.' The divine Spirit in such a manner set home upon their hearts what I spake to them, that the house was soon filled with cries and groans. They all flocked together upon this occasion ; and those whom I had reason to think in a Christless state, were almost universally seized with concern for their souls. It was an amazing season of power among them ; and seemed as if God had bowed the heavens and come down. So astonishingly prevalent was the operation upon old as well as young, that it seemed as if none would be left in a secure and natural state, but that God was now about to convert all the world. I was ready to think then, that I should never again despair of the conversion of any man or woman living, be they who or what they would.

" It is impossible to give a just and lively description of the appearance of things at this season ; at least such as to convey a bright and adequate idea of the effects of this influence. A number might now be seen rejoicing that God had not taken away the powerful influence of his blessed Spirit from this place; refreshed to see so many striving to enter in at the strait gate; and animated with such concern for them, that they wanted to push them forward, as some of them expressed it. At the same time numbers, both of men and women, old and young, might be seen in tears; and some in anguish of spirit appearing in their very countenances, like condemned malefactors bound towards the place of execution, with a heavy solicitude sitting in their faces; so that there seemed here, as I thought, a lively emblem of the solemn day of account; a mixture of heaven and hell; of joy and anguish inexpressible.

"The concern and religious affection was such, that I could not pretend to have any formal religious exercise among them; but spent the time in discoursing to one and another, as I thought most proper and seasonable for each; and addressed them all together; and finally concluded with prayer. Such were their circumstances at this season, that I could scarcely have half an hour's rest from speaking, from about half an hour before twelve o'clock, at which time I began public worship, till after seven at night. There appeared to be four or five persons newly awakened this day and the evening before; some of whom but very lately came among us.

"*Dec.* 30. Was visited by four or five young persons, under concern for their souls; most of whom were lately awakened. They wept much while I discoursed with them; and endeavored to press upon them the necessity of flying to Christ without delay for salvation.

"*Dec.* 31. Spent some hours this day in visiting my people from house to house, and conversing with them about their spiritual concerns; endeavoring to press upon Christless souls the necessity of renovation of heart; and scarce left a house without leaving some or other of its inhabitants in tears, appearing solicitously engaged to obtain an interest in Christ.—The Indians are now gathered together from all quarters to this place, and have built them little cottages, so that more than twenty families live within a quarter of a mile of me. A very convenient situation with regard both to public and private instruction.

"*Jan.* 1, 1746. I am this day beginning a new year, and God has carried me through numerous trials and labors in the past. He has amazingly supported my feeble frame; for having obtained help of God, I continue to this day. O that I might live nearer to God this year than I did the last! The business to which I have been called, and which I have been enabled to go through, I know has been as great as nature could bear up under, and what would have sunk and overcome me quite, without special support. But alas, alas! though I have done the labors and endured the trials; with what spirit have I done the one and endured the other? How cold has been the frame of my heart oftentimes! and how little have I sensibly eyed the glory of God in all my doings and sufferings! I have found that I could have no peace without filling up all my time with labor. Thus 'necessity has been laid upon me;' yea, in that respect, I have loved to labor; but the misery is, I could not sensibly labor for God, as I would have done. May I for the future be enabled more sensibly to make the glory of God my all. Spent considerable time in visiting my people again. Found scarcely one but what was under some serious impressions respecting their spiritual concerns.

"*Jan.* 2. Visited some persons newly come among us, who had scarce ever heard anything of Christianity before, except the empty name. Endeavored to instruct them, particularly in the first principles of religion, in the most easy and familiar manner I could. There are strangers from remote parts almost continually dropping in among us, so that I have oc casion repeatedly to open and inculcate the first principles of Christianity.

"*Jan.* 4. Prosecuted my catechetical method of instructing. Found my people able to answer questions with propriety, beyond what could have been expected from persons so lately brought out of heathenish darkness. In the improvement of my discourse, there appeared some concern and affection in the assembly, and especially in those of whom I entertained hopes as being truly gracious, at least several of them were much affected and refreshed.

"*Lord's day, Jan.* 5. Discoursed from Matt. xii. 10–13. There appeared not so much liveliness and affection in divine service as usual. The same truths, which have often produced many tears and sobs in the assembly, seemed now to have no special influence upon any in it. Near night I proposed to have proceeded in my usual method of catechising ; but while we were engaged in the first prayer, the power of God seemed to descend upon the assembly in such a remarkable manner, and so many appeared under pressing concern for their souls, that I thought it much more expedient to insist upon the plentiful provision made by divine grace for the redemption of perishing sinners, and to press them to a speedy acceptance of the great salvation, than to ask them questions about doctrinal points. What was most practical, seemed most seasonable to be insisted upon, while numbers appeared so extraordinarily solicitous to obtain an interest in the great Redeemer. Baptized two persons this day ; one adult, the woman particularly mentioned in my journal of Dec. 22, and one child.

"This woman has discovered a very sweet and heavenly frame of mind from time to time, since her first reception of comfort. One morning in particular, she came to see me, discovering an unusual joy and satisfaction in her countenance ; and when I inquired into the reason of it, she replied, 'that God had made her feel that it was right for him to do what he pleased with all things ; and that it would be right if he should

cast her husband and son both into hell ; and she saw it was so right for
God to do what he pleased with them, that she could not but rejoice in
God even if he should send them into hell;' though it was apparent she
loved them dearly.   She moreover inquired whether I was not sent to
preach to the Indians by some good people a great way off.   I replied,
' Yes, by the good people in Scotland.' She answered, ' that her heart
loved those good people so the evening before, that she could not help
praying for them all night ; her heart would go to God for them.' Thus the
blessings of those ready to perish are like to come upon those pious persons who have communicated of their substance to the propagation of the
gospel.

"*Jan.* 6. Being very weak in body, I rode for my health.   While riding, my thoughts were sweetly engaged for a time upon 'the Stone cut
out of the mountain without hands, which broke in pieces all before it,
and waxed great, and became a great mountain, and filled the whole
earth ; and I longed that Jesus should take to himself his great power,
and reign to the ends of the earth.'   O how sweet were the moments
wherein I felt my soul warm with hopes of the enlargement of the Redeemer's kingdom : I wanted nothing else, but that Christ should reign
to the glory of his blessed name.

"*Jan* 8.   In the evening my heart was drawn out after God in secret ;
my soul was refreshed and quickened, and I trust faith was in exercise.
I had great hopes of the ingathering of precious souls to Christ, not only
among my own people, but others also.   I was sweetly resigned and composed under my bodily weakness ; and was willing to live or die, and desirous to labor for God to the utmost of my strength.

"*Jan* 9.   Was still very weak and exercised with vapory disorders.
In the evening enjoyed some enlargement and spirituality in prayer.   O
that I could always spend my time profitably both in health and weakness.—Jan. 10.   My soul was in a sweet, calm, and composed frame, and
my heart filled with love to all the world ; and Christian simplicity and
tenderness seemed then to prevail and reign within me.   Near night
visited a serious Baptist minister, and had some agreeable conversation
with him, and found that I could love Christ in his friends.—Jan. 11.
Discoursed in a catechetical method, as usual, of late.   Having opened
our first parent's primitive apostacy from God, and our fall in him ; I
proceeded to apply my discourse by showing the necessity we stood in of
an almighty Redeemer, and the absolute need every sinner has of an interest in his merits and mediation.   There was some tenderness and affectionate concern apparent in the assembly.

"*Lord's day, Jan.* 12.   Preached from Isaiah lv. 6.   The word of God
seemed to fall upon the audience with a divine weight and influence, and
evidently appeared to be ' not the word of man.'   The blessed Spirit, I

am persuaded accompanied what was spoken to the hearts of many ; so that there was a powerful revival of conviction in numbers who were under spiritual exercise before. Toward night catechised in my usual method. Near the close of my discourse, there appeared a great concern and much affection in the audience ; which increased while I continued to invite them to come to an all-sufficient Redeemer for salvation. The Spirit of God seems from time to time to be striving with souls here. They are so frequently and repeatedly roused, that they seem unable at present to lull themselves asleep.

"*Jan.* 13. Was visited by several persons under deep concern for their souls ; one of whom was newly awakened. It is a most agreeable work to treat with souls who are solicitously inquiring ' what they shall do to be saved.' As we are never to be ' weary in well doing,' so the obligation seems to be peculiarly strong when the work is so very desirable. Yet I must say, my health is so much impaired, and my spirits so wasted with my labors and solitary manner of living ; there being no human creature in the house with me ; that their repeated and almost incessant applications to me for help and direction, are sometimes exceedingly burdensome, and so exhaust my spirits, that I become fit for nothing at all, entirely unable to prosecute my business, sometimes for days together. What contributes much towards this difficulty is, that I am obliged to spend much time in communicating a little matter to them; there being oftentimes many things to be premised before I can speak directly to what I principally aim at; which things would readily be taken for granted, where there was a competency of doctrinal knowledge.

"*Jan.* 14. Spent some time in private conference with my people, and found some disposed to take comfort, as I thought, upon slight grounds. They are now generally awakened, and it is become so disgraceful, as well as terrifying to the conscience, to be destitute of religion, that they are in imminent danger of taking up with an appearance of grace, rather than to live under the fear and disgrace of an unregenerated state.

"*Jan.* 15. My spirits were very low and flat, and I could not but think I was a burden to God's earth ; and could scarcely look anybody in the face through shame and sense of barrenness. God pity a poor unprofitable creature.

"*Jan.* 18. Prosecuted my catechetical method of discoursing. There appeared a great solemnity and some considerable affection in the assembly. This method of instruction I find very profitable. When I first entered upon it, I was exercised with fears lest my discourses would unavoidably be so doctrinal, that they would tend only to enlighten the head, but not to affect the heart. But the event proved quite otherwise:

for these exercises have hitherto been remarkably blessed in the latter, as well as the former respects.

"*Lord's day, Jan.* 19. Discoursed to my people from Isaiah lv. 7. Toward night catechised in my ordinary method ; and this appeared to be a powerful season of grace among us. Numbers were much affected. Convictions were powerfully revived, and divers numbers of Christians refreshed and strengthened ; and one weary, heavy laden soul, I have abundant reason to hope, brought to true rest and solid comfort in Christ ; who afterwards gave me such an account of God's dealing with his soul, as was abundantly satisfying, as well as refreshing to me."*

The next day Brainerd set out on a journey to Elizabeth-town, to confer with the Correspondents at their meeting there, and enjoyed much spiritual refreshment from day to day, through this week. The things expressed at this time are such as these : serenity, composure, sweetness, and tender-ness of soul ; thanksgiving to God for his success among the Indians ; delight in prayer and praise ; sweet and profitable meditations on various divine subjects ; longing for more love, for more vigor to live to God, for a life more entirely devoted to him, that he might spend all his time profitably for God and his cause ; conversing on spiritual subjects with affection ; and lamentation for unprofitableness.

"*Lord's day, Jan.* 26. [At Connecticut Farms.] Was calm and com-posed. Was made sensible of utter inability to preach without divine help and was in some good measure willing to leave it with God to give or withhold assistance, as he saw would be most for his own glory. Was favored with a considerable degree of assistance in my public work. After public worship I was in a sweet and solemn frame of mind, thankful to God that he had made me in some measure faithful in addressing pre-cious souls, but grieved that I had been no more fervent in my work; and was tenderly affected towards all the world, longing that every sinner might be saved ; and could not have entertained any bitterness towards the worst enemy living. In the evening rode to Elizabethtown ; and while riding was almost constantly engaged in lifting up my heart to God, lest I should lose that sweet, heavenly solemnity and composure of soul which I then enjoyed. Afterwards was pleased to think that God reigneth ; and thought I could never be uneasy with any of his dispensations, but must be entirely satisfied, whatever trials he should cause me in his church to encounter. Never felt more sedateness, divine serenity, and composure

* [See the next chapter for his account of this interesting case.—J. M. S.]

of mind ; could freely have left the dearest earthly friend for the society
of angels and spirits of just men made perfect; my affections soared aloft
to the blessed Author of every dear enjoyment. I viewed the emptiness
and unsatisfactory nature of the most desirable, earthly objects, any further
than God is seen in them, and longed for a life of spirituality and inward
purity; without which I saw there could be no true pleasure.

"*Jan.* 28th. [At Crossweeksung,] The Indians in these parts, have in
times past run themselves in debt by their excessive drinking ; and some
have taken the advantage of them, and put them to trouble and charge, by
arresting sundry of them ; whereby it was supposed their hunting lands, in
great part, were much endangered, and might speedily be taken from
them. Being sensible that they could not subsist together in these parts,
in order to their being a Christian congregation, if these lands should be
taken, which was thought very likely, I thought it my duty to use my
utmost endaevors to prevent so unhappy an event. Having acquainted
the gentlemen concerned in this mission with the affair, according to the
best information I could get of it, they thought it proper to expend the
money which they had been, and still were collecting for the religious interest of the Indians, at least a part of it, for discharging their debts and
securing these lands, that there might be no entanglement lying upon
them to hinder the settlement and hopeful enlargement of a Christian congregation of Indians in these parts. Having received orders from them,
I answered, in behalf of the Indians, eighty-two pounds, five shillings,
N. Jersey currency, at eight shillings per ounce; and so prevented the
danger of difficulty in this respect.

"As God has wrought a wonderful work of grace among these Indians,
and now inclines others from remote places to fall in among them almost
continually; and as he has opened a door for the prevention of the difficulty now mentioned, which seemed greatly to threaten their religious interests as well as worldly comforts, it is to be hoped that he designs to
establish a church for himself among them, and hand down true religion to
their posterity

"*Jan.* 30. Preached to the Indians from John iii. 16, 17. There was
a solemn attention and some affection visible in the audience; especially
several persons, who had long been concerned for their souls, seemed
afresh excited and engaged in seeking after an interest in Christ. One,
with much concern, afterwards told me ' his heart was so pricked with
my preaching he knew not where to turn or what to do.'

"*Jan.* 31. This day the person whom I had made choice of and engaged
for a schoolmaster among the Indians, arrived among us, and was
heartily welcomed by my people universally. Whereupon I distributed
several dozens of primers among the children.—Feb. 1. My schoolmaster
entered upon his business among the Indians. He has generally about

thirty children and young persons in his school in the day time, and about fifteen married people in the evening school. The number of the latter sort of persons being less than it would be if they could be more constantly at home, and could spare time from their necessary employments for an attendance upon these instructions.

"Towards night enjoyed some of the clearest thoughts on a divine subject, viz., that treated of 1 Cor. xv. 13-16: But if there be no resurrection of the dead, etc., which I ever remember to have had upon any subject whatsoever; and spent two or three hours in writing them. I was refreshed with this intenseness ; my mind was so engaged in these meditations I could scarcely turn it to anything else, and indeed I could not be willing to part with so sweet an entertainment. In the evening catechised in my usual method. Towards the close of my discourse, a surprising power seemed to attend the word, especially to some persons. One man considerably in years, who had been a remarkable drunkard, a conjurer, and murderer, and was awakened some months before, was now brought to great extremity under his spiritual distress ; so that he trembled for hours together, and apprehended himself just dropping into hell, without any power to rescue or relieve himself. Divers others appeared under great concern as well as he, and solicitous to obtain a saving change.

"*Lord's day, Feb.* 2. Preached from John v. 24, 25. There appeared as usual some concern and affection in the assembly. Towards night proceeded in my usual method of catechising. Observed my people more ready in answering the questions proposed to them than ever before. It is apparent they advance daily in doctrinal knowledge. But what is still more desirable, the Spirit of God is yet operating among them ; whereby experimental, as well as speculative knowledge is propagated in their minds.

"After public worship, my bodily strength being much spent, my spirits sunk amazingly, and especially on hearing that I was generally taken to be a Roman Catholic, sent by the Papists to draw the Indians into an insurrection against the English, that some were in fear of me, and others were for having me taken up by authority and punished. Alas, what will not the devil do to bring a slur and disgrace on the work of God ! O how holy and circumspect had I need to be ! Through divine goodness I have been enabled to mind my own business in these parts as well as elsewhere ; and to let all men, and all denominations of men alone, as to their party notions, and only preached the plain and necessary truths of Christianity, neither inviting to, nor excluding from any meeting, any of any sort or persuasion whatsoever. Towards night the Lord gave me freedom at the throne of grace in my first prayer before my catechetical lecture ; and in opening the xlvth Psalm to my people, my soul confided in God ; although the wicked world should slander and persecute me, or even condemn and execute me as a traitor to my king and country. Truly, 'God is a present help in time of trouble.' In the evening my soul was in some measure comforted, having some hope that one poor soul was brought home to God this day; though the case did by no means appear clear. Oh, that I could fill up every moment of time during my abode here below in the service of my God and King.

"*Feb.* 3. My spirits were still much sunk with what I heard the day before of my being suspected to be engaged in the Pretender's interest. It grieved me, that after there had been so much evidence of a glorious work of grace among these poor Indians, as that the most carnal men could not but take notice of the great change made among them, so many poor souls should still suspect the whole to be only a Popish plot, and so cast an awful reproach on this blessed work of the divine Spirit, and at the same time wholly exclude themselves from receiving any benefit by this divine influence. This put me upon searching whether I had ever dropped anything inadvertently, which might give occasion to any to suspect that I was stirring up the Indians against the English; and could think of nothing, unless it was my attempting sometimes to vindicate the rights of the Indians, and complaining of the horrid practice of making the Indians drunk, and then cheating them out of their lands and other property. Once I remembered I had done this with too much warmth of spirit, which much distressed me ; thinking that it might possibly prejudice them against this work of grace to their everlasting destruction. God, I believe, did me good by this trial, which served to humble me, and show me the necessity of watchfulness, and of being wise as a serpent as well as harmless as a dove. This exercise led me to a throne of grace, and there I found some support; though I could not get the burden wholly removed. Was assisted in prayer, especially in the evening."

He remained still under a degree of anxiety about this affair, which continued to have the same effect upon him to cause him to reflect upon and humble himself, and frequent the throne of grace ; but soon found himself much more relieved and supported. He was this week in an extremely weak state, and obliged, as he expresses it, " to consume considerable time in diversions for his health."

"*Feb.* 5. Discoursed to a considerable number of the Indians in the evening ; at which time numbers of them appeared much affected and melted with divine things.—Feb. 8. Spent a considerable part of the day in visiting my people from house to house, and conversing with them about their soul's concerns. Divers persons wept while I discoursed to them, and appeared concerned for nothing so much as for an interest in the great Redeemer. In the evening catechised as usual. Divine truths made some impressions upon the audience ; and were attended with an affectionate engagement of soul in some.

"*Lord's day, Feb.* 9. Discoursed to my people from the story of the blind man, Matt. x. 46–52. The word of God seemed weighty and powerful upon the assembly at this time, and made considerable impressions upon many ; several in particular, who have generally been remarkably stupid and careless under the means of grace, were now awakened, and wept affectionately. The most earnest attention, as well as tenderness and affection appeared in the audience universally. Baptized three persons ; two adults and one child. The adults, I have reason to hope, were both truly pious. There was considerable melting in the assembly, while I was discoursing particularly to the persons, and administering the ordinance. God has been pleased to own and bless the administration of this as well as of his other ordinances among the Indians. There are some here who have been powerfully awakened at seeing others baptized ; and some who have obtained relief and comfort just in the season when this ordinance has been administered."

The Monday after he set out on a journey to the Forks of Delaware, to visit the Indians there. He performed the journey under great weakness, and was sometimes exercised with much pain ; but says nothing of his dejection and melancholy. He arrived at his own house at the Forks on Friday. During the week he appears from his Diary to have enjoyed a sweet composure of mind, thankfulness to God for his mercies to him and others, resignation to the divine will, and comfort in prayer and religious conversation. At the same time his heart was drawn out after God, and affected with a sense of his own barrenness, as well as with the fulness and freeness of divine grace.

"*Lord's day, February* 16. [Forks of Delaware,] Knowing that numbers of the Indians in these parts were obstinately set against Christianity, and that some of them had refused to hear me preach in times past, I thought it might be proper and beneficial to the Christian interest here, to have a number of my religious people from Crossweeksung with me to converse with them about religious matters ; hoping it might be a means to convince them of the truth and importance of Christianity, to see and hear some of their own nation discoursing of divine things, and manifesting earnest desires that others might be brought out of heathenish darkness as themselves were. For this purpose I selected half a dozen of the most serious and intelligent of those Indians, and having brought them to the Forks of Delaware, I this day met with them and the Indians of this place. Numbers of the latter probably could not have been prevailed upon to attend this meeting, had it not been for these religious Indians, who accompanied me hither, and preached to them. Some of those who had in times past been extremely averse to Christianity, now behaved soberly, and some others laughed and mocked. However the word of God fell with such weight and power that numbers seemed to be stunned, and expressed a willingness to hear me again of these matters.

"Afterwards prayed with and made an address to the white people present, and could not but observe some visible effects of the word, such as tears and sobs among them. After public worship, spent some time, and took pains to convince those that mocked of the truth and importance of what I had been insisting upon; and so endeavored to awaken their attention to divine truths. Had reason to think from what I observed then and afterwards, that my endeavors took considerable effect upon one of the worst of them. Those few Indians then present, who used to be my hearers in these parts, some having removed hence to Crossweeksung, seemed somewhat kindly disposed toward me, and glad to see me again. They had been so much attacked, however by some of the opposing Pagans, that they were almost ashamed or afraid to manifest their friendship.

"*Feb.* 17. After having spent much time in discoursing to the Indians in their respective houses, I got them together and repeated and inculcated what I had before taught them. Afterwards discoursed to them from Acts viii. 5–8. A divine influence seemed to attend the word. Several of the Indians here appeared to be somewhat awakened, and manifested earnest tears and sobs. My people of Crossweeksung continued with them day and night repeating and inculcating the truths I had taught them, and sometimes prayed and sung psalms among them; discoursing with each other in their hearing of the great things God had done for them and for the Indians from whence they came. This seemed, as my people told me, to have more effect upon them, than when they directed their discourse immediately to them. I was refreshed and encouraged, and found a spirit of prayer in the evening, and earnest longings for the illumination and conversion of these poor Indians.

"*Feb.* 18. Preached to an assembly of Irish people, nearly fifteen miles distant from the Indians.—Feb. 19. Preached to the Indians again, after having spent considerable time in conversing with them more privately. There appeared a great solemnity and some concern and affection among the Indians belonging to these parts, as well as a sweet melting among those who came with me. Numbers of the Indians here seemed to have their prejudices and aversion to Christianity removed; and appeared well disposed and inclined to hear the word of God. My heart was comforted and refreshed, and my soul filled with longings for the conversion of these poor Indians.

" *Feb.* 20. Preached to a small assembly of High Dutch people who had seldom heard the gospel preached, and were some of them at least very ignorant; but numbers of them have lately been put upon an inquiry after the way of salvation with thoughtfulness. They gave wonderful attention; and some of them were much affected under the word, and afterwards said, as I was informed, that they never had been so much enlightened about the way of salvation in their whole lives before. They requested me to tarry with them, or come again and preach to them. It grieved me that I could not comply with their request. I could not but be affected with their circumstances; for they were as ' sheep not having a shepherd,' and some of them appeared under some degree of distress for sin ; standing in peculiar need of the assistance of an experienced spiritual guide. God was pleased to support and refresh my spirits by affording me assistance this day, and so hopeful a prospect of success. I returned home rejoicing and blessing the name of the Lord ; found freedom and sweetness afterward in secret prayer and had my soul drawn out for dear friends. Oh how blessed a thing it is to labor for God faithfully and with encouragement of-success ! Blessed be the Lord forever and ever for the assistance and comfort granted this day !

" *Feb.* 21. Preached to a number of people, many of them Low Dutch. Several of the fore-mentioned High Dutch people attended the sermon, though eight or ten miles distant from their houses. Numbers of the Indians also, belonging to these parts, came of their own accord with my people from Crossweeksung, to the meeting. There were two in particular, who though the last Sabbath they opposed and ridiculed Christianity, now behaved soberly. My soul was refreshed and comforted ; and I could not but bless God, who had enabled me in some good measure to be faithful the day past. Oh how sweet it is to be spent and worn out for God.

" *Feb.* 22. Preached to the Indians. They appeared more free from prejudice and more cordial to Christianity than before ; and some of them appeared affected with divine truths. My spirits were much supported though my bodily strength was much wasted. Oh that God would be gracious to the souls of these poor Indians ! God has been very gracious to me this week. He has enabled me to preach every day; and has given me some assistance and encouraging prospect of success in almost every sermon. Blessed be his name ! Several of the white people have been awakened this week ; and numbers of the Indians much cured of prejudices and jealousies which they had conceived against Christianity, and seem to be really awakened.

"*Lord's day, Feb.* 23. Preached to the Indians from John vi. 35-37. After public service discoursed particularly with several of them, and invited them to go down to Crossweeksung, and tarry there at least for some time ; knowing that they would then be free from the scoffs and temptations of the opposing Pagans, as well as in the way of hearing divine truths discoursed of both in public and private. Obtained a promise of some of them that they would speedily pay us a visit, and attend some farther instructions. They seemed to be considerably enlightened, and much freed from their prejudices against Christianity. But it is much to be feared that their prejudices will revive again, unless they can enjoy the means of instruction here, or be removed when they may be under such advantages, and out of the way of their pagan acquaintances."

The next day Brainerd left the Forks of the Delaware to return to Crossweeksung, and spent the whole week till Saturday in his journey. He preached on the way every day except one ; and was several times greatly assisted, and had much inward comfort and earnest longings to fill up all his time in the service of God. He utters such expressions as these after preaching : "Oh that I may be enabled to plead the cause of God faithfully to my dying moment ! Oh how sweet it would be to spend myself wholly for God and his cause, and to be freed from selfish motives in my labors !"

"*March.* 1. [At Crossweeksung,] Catechised in my ordinary method. Was pleased and refreshed to see them answer the questions proposed to them with such remarkable readiness, discretion, and knowledge. Toward the close of my discourse divine truths made considerable impressions upon the audience, and produced tears and sobs in some under concern ; and more especially a sweet and humble melting in several, who I have reason to hope were truly gracious.

"*Lord's day, March* 2. Preached from John xv. 16. The assembly appeared not so lively in their attention as usual, nor so much affected with divine truths in general as has been common. Some of my people who went up to the Forks of Delaware with me, being now returned, were accompanied by two of the Indians belonging to the Forks, who had promised me a speedy visit. May the Lord meet with them here. They can scarcely go into a house now but they will meet with Christtain conversation, whereby it is to be hoped they may be both instructed and awakened.

"Discoursed to the Indians again in the afternoon, and observed among them some animation and engagedness in divine service, though not equal to what has often appeared here. I know of no assembly of Christians, where there seems to be so much of the presence of God, where brotherly love so much prevails, and where I should take so much delight in the public worship of God in general, as in my own congregation; although not more than nine months ago they were worshipping devils and dumb idols under the power of pagan darkness and superstition. Amazing change this! effected by nothing less than divine power and grace. This is the doing of the Lord, and it is justly marvellous in our eyes."

The next four days were spent in great bodily weakness, but he speaks of some seasons of considerable inward comfort.

"*March* 5. Spent some time just at evening in prayer, singing, and discoursing to my people upon divine things; and observed some agreeable tenderness and affection among them. Their present situation is so compact and commodious, that they are easily and quickly called together with only the sound of a conkshell, (a shell like that of a periwinkle), so that they have frequent opportunities of attending religious exercises publicly. This seems to be a great means, under God, of keeping alive the impressions of divine things in their minds.

"*March* 6. I walked alone in the evening, and enjoyed sweetness and comfort in prayer beyond what I have of late enjoyed. My soul rejoiced in my pilgrim state; and I was delighted with the thoughts of laboring and enduring hardness for God; felt some longing desires to preach the gospel to dear immortal souls; and confided in God, that he would be with me in my work, and that he never would leave nor forsake me to the end of my race. Oh! may I obtain mercy of God to be faithful to my dying moment.—March 7. In the afternoon went on with my work with freedom and cheerfulness, God assisted me, and enjoyed comfort in the evening.

"*March* 8. Catechised in the evening. My people answered the questions proposed to them well. I can perceive their knowledge in religion increases daily. And what is still more desirable, the divine influence which has been so remarkable among them; appears still to continue in some good measure. The divine presence seemed to be in the assembly this evening. Some who I have good reason to think are Christians indeed, were melted with a sense of divine goodness, and their own barrenness and ingratitude, and seemed to hate themselves, as one of them afterwards expressed it. Convictions also appeared to be revived in several instances; and divine truths were attended with such influence upon the assembly in general, that it might justly be called an evening of divine power.

"*Lord's day, March* 9. Preached from Luke x. 38–42. The word of God was attended with power and energy upon the audience. Numbers were affected, and concerned to obtain the one thing needful. Several who have given good evidence of being truly gracious, were much affected with a want of spirituality, and saw the need they stood in of growing in grace. The greater part of those who had been under any impressions of divine things in times past, seemed now to have those impressions revived. In the afternoon proposed to have catechised in my usual method. But while we were engaged in the first prayer in the Indian language, as usual, a great part of the assembly was so much moved and affected with divine things, that I thought it seasonable and proper to omit the proposing of questions for that time, and to insist upon the most practical truths. I accordingly did so; making a further improvement of the passage of Scripture on which I had discoursed in the former part of the day. There appeared to be a powerful divine influence in the congregation. Several who, as I have reason to think, are truly pious, were so deeply affected with a sense of their own barrenness and their unworthy treatment of the blessed Redeemer, that they looked on him as pierced by themselves, and mourned, yea, some of them were in bitterness as for a firstborn. Some awakened sinners also appeared to be in anguish of soul to obtain an interest in Christ ; so that there was a great mourning in the assembly ; many heavy groans, sobs, and tears ! and one or two newly come among us, were considerably awakened.

"*March* 10. Towards night the Indians met together, of their own accord, and sang, prayed, and discoursed of divine things among themselves; at which time there was much affection among them. Some who are hopefully gracious, appeared to be melted with divine things; and some others seemed much concerned for their souls. Perceiving their engagement and affection in religious exercises, I went among them, and prayed, and gave a word of exhortation ; and observed two or three somewhat affected and concerned, who scarce ever appeared to be under any religious impressions before. It seemed to be a day and evening of divine power. Numbers retained the warm impressions of divine things which had been made upon their minds the day before.

"My soul was refreshed with freedom and enlargement, and I hope the lively exercise of faith in secret prayer this night. My will was sweetly resigned to the divine will; my hopes respecting the enlargement of the kingdom of Christ somewhat raised; and I could commit Zion's cause to God as his own."

On Tuesday he speaks of some sweetness and spirituality

in Christian conversation. On Wednesday, complains that
he enjoyed not much comfort and satisfaction through the
day, because he did but little for God. On Thursday, spent
a considerable time in company on a special occasion, but in
perplexity, because without salutary religious conversation.

"*March* 14. Was visited by a considerable number of my people and
spent some time in religious exercises with them.—March 15. In the
evening catechised. My people answered the questions put to them with
surprising readiness and judgment, There appeared some warmth, and
a feeling sense of divine things among those who I have reason to hope
are real Christians, while I was discoursing upon peace of conscience
and joy in the Holy Ghost. These seemed quickened and enlivened in
divine service, though there was not so much appearance of concern
among those whom I have reason to think in a Christless state."

In the former part of the week following he was very ill,
and under great dejection ; being rendered unserviceable by
his illness, and fearing that he should never be serviceable
any more ; and therefore exceedingly longed for death. But
afterwards he was more encouraged, and life appeared more
desirable ; because, as he says, he " had a little dawn of hope
that he might be useful in the world." In the latter part of
this week he was somewhat relieved of his illness in the use
of means prescribed by his physician.

"*Lord's day, March* 16. Preached to my congregation from Heb. ii
1-3. Divine truths seemed to have some considerable influence upon
some of the hearers, and produced many tears, as well as heavy sighs and
sobs, among those who have given evidence of being real Christians, and
others also. The impressions made upon the audience appeared in
general deep and heart-affecting ; not superficial, noisy, and affected.
Towards night discoursed again on the Great Salvation. The word was
again attended with some power upon the audience. Numbers wept
affectionately, and to appearance, unfeignedly ; so that the Spirit of God
seemed to be moving upon the face of the assembly. Baptized the
woman particularly mentioned in my journal of last Lord's day, who now
as well as then appeared to be in a devout, humble, and excellent frame
of mind. My house being thronged with my people in the evening, I
spent the time in religious exercises with them, until my nature was
almost spent. They are so unwearied in religious exercises, and insatiable
in their thirsting after Christian knowledge, that I can sometimes scarcely
avoid laboring so as greatly to exhaust my strength and spirits.

" *March* 19. Several of the persons who went with me to the Forks of Delaware in February last, having been detained there by the dangerous illness of one of their company, returned home this day. Whereupon my people generally met together of their own accord, in order to spend some time in religious exercises ; and especially to give thanks to God for his preserving goodness to those who had been absent from them for several weeks, and recovering mercy to him who had been sick ; and that he had now returned them all in safety. As I was then absent, they desired my schoolmaster to assist them in carrying on their religious solemnity ; who tells me that they appeared engaged and affectionate in repeated prayer, singing, etc.

" *March* 22. Catechised in my usual method in the evening. My people answered questions to my great satisfaction. There appeared nothing very remarkable in the assembly, considering what has been common among us. Although I may justly say, the strict attention, the tenderness and affection, the many tears and heart-affecting sobs, appearing in numbers in the assembly would have been very remarkable, were it not that God has made these things common with us, and even with strangers soon after their coming among us from time to time. I am far from thinking that every appearance and particular instance of affection that has been among us has been truly genuine, and purely from a divine influence. I am sensible of the contrary ; and doubt not but that there has been some corrupt mixture, some chaff as well as wheat ; especially since religious concern appeared so common and prevalent here.

" *Lord's day, March* 23. There being about fifteen strangers, adult persons, come among us in the week past, several of whom had never been in any religious meeting till now, I thought it proper to discourse this day in a manner peculiarly suited to their circumstances and capacities ; and accordingly attempted it from Hosea xiii. 9. ' O Israel, thou hast destroyed thyself.' In the forenoon, I opened in the plainest manner I could, man's apostasy and ruined state, after having spoken some things respecting the being and perfections of God, and his creation of man in a state of uprightness and happiness. In the afternoon endeavored to open the glorious provision which God has made for the redemption of apostate creatures, by giving his own dear Son to suffer for them, and satisfy divine justice on their behalf. There was not that affection and concern in the assembly which has been common among us ; although there was a desirable attention appearing in general, and even in most of the strangers.

" Near sunset I felt an uncommon concern upon my mind, especially for the poor strangers, that God had so much withheld his presence and the powerful influence of his Spirit from the assembly in the exercises of the day ; and thereby withheld from them that degree of conviction which

I hoped they might have had. In this frame I visited several houses and discoursed with some concern and affection to several persons particularly; but without much appearance of success, till I came to a house where several of the strangers were. There the solemn truths on which I discoursed appeared to take effect; first upon some children, then upon several adult persons who had been somewhat awakened before, and afterwards upon several of the pagan strangers.

"I continued my discourse with some fervency, until almost every one in the house was melted into tears, and divers wept aloud, and appeared earnestly concerned to obtain an interest in Christ. Upon this numbers soon gathered from all the houses round about, and so thronged the place that we were obliged to remove to the house where we usually met for public worship. The congregation gathering immediately, and many appearing remarkably affected, I discoursed some time from Luke xix. 10. For the Son of man is come to seek, etc. endeavoring to open the mercy, compassion, and concern of Christ for lost, helpless, and undone sinners. There was much visible concern and affection in the assembly, and I doubt not but that a divine influence accompanied what was spoken to the hearts of many. There were five or six of the strangers, men and women, who appeared to be considerably awakened; and in particular one very rugged young man, who seemed as if nothing would move him, was now brought to tremble like the jailer, and weep for a long time.

"The pagans who were awakened, seemed at once to put off their savage roughness and pagan manners, and became sociable, orderly, and humane in their carriage. When they first came, I exhorted my religious people to take pains with them as they had done with other strangers from time to time, to instruct them in Christianity. But when some of them attempted something of that nature, the strangers would soon rise up and walk to other houses in order to avoid the hearing of such discourses. Whereupon some of the serious persons agreed to disperse themselves into the several parts of the settlement, so that wherever the strangers went, they met with some instructive discourse and warm addresses respecting their salvation. But now there was no need of using policy in order to get an opportunity of conversing with some of them about their spiritual concerns ; for they were so far touched with a sense of their perishing state, as made them voluntarily yield to the closest addresses which were made them respecting their sin and misery, their need of an acquaintance with, and interest in the great Redeemer.

"*March* 24. Numbered the Indians to see how many souls God had gathered together here since my coming into these parts, and found there were now about 130 persons together, old and young. Sundry of those who are my stated hearers, perhaps to the number of 15 or 20 were absent at this season. If all had been together, the number would now have been very considerable; especially considering how few were together at my first coming into this part of the country, the whole number then not amounting to ten persons.

"My people were out this day with the design of clearing some of their land, above fifteen miles distant from this settlement, in order to their settling there in a compact form, where they might be under the advantages of attending the public worship of God, of having their children taught in a school, and at the same time have a conveniency for planting; their land in the place of our present residence being of little or no value for that purpose. The design of their settling thus in a body, and cultivating their lands, of which they have done very little in their pagan state, being of such necessity and importance to their religious interest, as well as worldly comfort, I thought it proper to call them together, and show them the duty of laboring with faithfulness and industry, and that they must not now 'be slothful in business,' as they had ever been in their pagan state. I endeavored to press the importance of their being laborious, diligent, and vigorous in the prosecution of their business; especially at the present juncture, the season of planting being now near, in order to their being in a capacity of living together, and enjoying the means of grace and instruction. Having given them directions for their work, which they very much wanted, as well as for their behavior in divers respects, I explained, sang, and endeavored to inculcate upon them the cxxviith Psalm, common metre, Dr. Watts' version; and having recommended them, and the design of their going forth, to God, by prayer with them, I dismissed them to their business.

"After the Indians were gone to their work, to clear their lands, I retired by myself, and poured out my soul to God, that he would smile on their feeble beginnings, and that he would settle an Indian town, which might be a mountain of holiness. I found my soul much refreshed in these petitions, and much enlarged for Zion's interest, and for numbers of dear friends in particular. My sinking spirits were revived and raised; and I felt animated in the service to which God has called me. This was the dearest hour I have enjoyed for many days, if not weeks. I found an encouraging hope that something would be done for God; and that God would use and help me in his work. O how sweet were the thoughts of laboring for God, when I fell any spirit and courage, and had any hope that I ever should be succeeded.

"In the evening read and expounded to those of my people who were yet at home, and to the strangers newly come, the substance of the third chapter of the Acts. Numbers seemed to melt under the word; especially while I was discoursing upon ver. 19. 'Repent ye, therefore, and be converted,' etc. Several of the strangers also were affected. When I asked them afterwards: Whether they did not now feel that their hearts were wicked as I had taught them ; one of them replied, 'Yes, she felt it now.' Although before she came here, upon hearing that I taught the Indians that their hearts were all bad by nature, and needed to be changed and made good by the power of God; she had said, 'Her heart was not wicked, and she had never done anything that was bad in her life.' This, indeed, seems to be the case with them, I think, universally, in their pagan state. They seem to have no consciousness of sin and guilt, unless they can charge themselves with some gross acts of sin contrary to the commands of the second table."

The next day his schoolmaster was taken sick and he spent a great part of the remainder of this week in attending him. In his weak state, this was an almost overbearing burden ; he being obliged constantly to wait upon him from day to day, and to lie on the floor at night. His spirits sunk in a considerable degree, with his bodily strength, under this burden.

"*March* 27. Discoursed to a number of my people in one of their houses in a more private manner. Inquired particularly into their spiritual states, in order to see what impressions they were under. Laid before them the marks of a regenerate, as well as of an unregenerate state ; and endeavored to suit and direct my discourse to them severally, according as I apprehended their states to be. There was a considerable number gathered together before I finished my discourse, and several seemed much affected while I was urging the necessity and infinite importance of getting into a renewed state. I find particular and close dealing with souls in private, is often very successful.

"*March* 29. In the evening catechised as usual upon Saturday. Treated upon the benefits which believers receive from Christ at death. The questions were answered with great readiness and propriety; and those who I have reason to think, are the dear people of God, were in general sweetly melted. There appeared such a liveliness and vigor in their attendance upon the word of God, and such eagerness to be made partakers of the benefits mentioned, that they seemed not only to be 'looking for,' but 'hasting to the coming of the day of God.' Divine truths seemed to distil upon the audience with a gentle, but melting efficacy, as the refreshing 'showers upon the new mown grass.' The assembly, in general, as well as those who appear truly religious, were affected with some brief accounts of the blessedness of the godly at death ; and most of them then discovered an affectionate inclination to cry. 'Let me die the death of the righteous, and let my last end be like his;' although many were not duly engaged to obtain the change of heart that is necessary to that blessed end.

"*Lord's day, March* 30. Discoursed from Matt. xxv. 31-40. There was a very considerable moving, and affectionate melting in the assembly. I hope that there were some real, deep, and abiding impressions of divine things made upon the minds of many. There was one aged man, newly come among us, who appeared to be considerably awakened, that never was touched with any concern for his soul before. In the evening, catechised. There was not that tenderness and melting engagement among God's people, which appeared the evening before, and many other times. They answered the questions distinctly and well, and were devout and attentive in divine service.

"*March* 31. Called my people together as I had done the Monday evening before, and discoursed to them again on the necessity and importance of laboring industriously in order to their living together, and enjoying the means of grace, etc. Having engaged in a solemn prayer to God among them for a blessing upon their attempts, I dismissed them to their work. Numbers of them both men and women, seemed to offer themselves willingly to this service ; and some appeared affectionately concerned that God might go with them, and begin their little town for them ; that by his blessing it might be a place comfortable for them and theirs, with regard both to procuring the necessaries of life, and to attending on the worship of God.—Towards night, I enjoyed some sweet meditations on these words : ' It is good for me to draw near to God.' My soul, I think, had some sweet sense of what is intended in those words."

The next day he was extremely busy in taking care of the schoolmaster and in some other necessary affairs, which greatly diverted him from what he looked upon as his proper business ; but yet he speaks of comfort and refreshment at some time of the day.

"*April* 2. I was somewhat exercised with a spiritual frame of mind ; but was a little relieved and refreshed in the evening with meditation alone in the woods. But alas! my days pass away as the chaff ; it is but little I do, or can do, that turns to any account; and it is my constant misery and burden, that I am so fruitless in the vineyard of the Lord. Oh that I were a pure spirit; that I might be active for God! This I think more than anything else, makes me long that this corruptible might put on incorruption, and this mortal put on immortality. God deliver me from clogs, fetters, and a body of death, which impede my service from him."

"*April* 4. Spent the most of the day in writing on Revelation xxii.
17. 'And whosoever will,' etc. Enjoyed some freedom and encouragement in my work; and found some comfort in prayer.—April 5.
'Catechised in the evening. There appeared to be some affection and
fervent engagement in divine service through the assembly in general;
especially towards the conclusion of my discourse. After public worship,
a number of those, who I have reason to think, are truly religious, came
to my house, and seemed eager for some further entertainment upon
divine things. While I was conversing with them about their scriptural
exercises; observing to them, that God's work in the hearts of all his
children, was for substance the same ; and that their trials and temptations were also alike; and showing the obligations such were under to
love one another in a peculiar manner;—they seemed to be melted into
tenderness and affection towards each other, I thought that that particular token of their being the disciples of Christ, viz. of their having love
one towards another, had scarcely ever appeared more evident than at
this time.—After public worship, a number of my dear Christian Indians
came to my house ; with whom I felt a sweet union of soul. My heart was
knit to them; and I cannot say I have felt such a sweet and fervent love
to the brethren, for some time past. I saw in them appearances of the
same love. This gave me somewhat of a view of the heavenly state ; and
particularly of that part of the happiness of heaven which consists in the
communion of saints ; and this was affecting to me.

"*Lord's day, April* 6. Preached from Matt. vii. 21–23, 'Not every
one that saith into me, Lord, Lord,' etc. There were considerable effects
of the word visible in the audience, and such as were very desirable ;
an earnest attention, a great solemnity, many tears and heavy sighs, which
were modestly suppressed in a considerable measure, and appeared unaffected and without any indecent commotion of the passions. Numbers of
the religious people were put upon serious and close examination of their
spiritual state, by hearing that 'not every one that saith to Christ, Lord,
Lord, shall enter into his kingdom.' Some expressed fears lest they had
deceived themselves, and taken up a false hope, because they found they
had done so little of the will of his Father who is in heaven.

"There was one man brought under very great and pressing concern
for his soul; which appeared more especially after his retirement from
public worship. That, which he says gave him his great uneasiness, was
not so much any particular sin, as that he had never done the will of God
at all, but had sinned continually, and so had no claim to the kingdom of
Heaven. In the afternoon, I opened to them the discipline of Christ, in
his Church, and the method in which offenders are to be dealt with. At
which time the religious people were much affected; especially when they
heard that the offender continuing obstinate, must finally be esteemed and

treated 'as a heathen man,' and pagan, who has no part nor lot among God's visible people. Of this they seemed to have the most awful apprehensions; a state of heathenism, out of which they were so lately brought, appearing very dreadful to them. After public worship, I visited several houses, to see how they spent the remainder of the Sabbath, and to treat with them solemnly on the great concerns of their souls. The Lord seemed to smile upon my private endeavors, and to make these particular and personal addresses more effectual upon some than my public discourses.

"*April* 7. Discoursed to my people in the evening, from 1 Cor. xi. 23 –26. 'For I have received of the Lord,' etc. Endeavored to open to them the institution, nature and ends of the Lord's Supper, as well as of the qualifications and preparations necessary to the right participations of that ordinance. Numbers appeared much affected with the love of Christ, manifested in his making this provision for the comfort of his people, at a season when himself was just entering upon his sharpest sufferings."

On Tuesday he went to the meeting of the Presbytery appointed at Elizabethtown. In his way thither he enjoyed some sweet meditations. But after he came there, he was, as he expresses it, "very vapory and melancholy, and under an awful gloom which oppressed his mind." This continued until Saturday evening; when he began to have some relief and encouragement. He spent the Sabbath at Staten Island; where he preached to an assembly of Dutch and English, and enjoyed considerable refreshment and comfort, both in public and private. In the evening he returned to Elizabethtown.

"*April* 14. My spirits this day were raised and refreshed, and my mind composed; so that I was in a comfortable frame of soul most of the day. In the evening, my head was clear, my mind serene; I enjoyed sweetness in secret prayer and meditation on Psalm lxxiii. 28. 'But it is good for me to draw near to God,' etc. O how free, how comfortable, cheerful, and yet solemn, do I feel when I am in a good measure freed from those damps and melancholy glooms under which I often labor. Blessed be the Lord, I find myself relieved in this respect.

"*April* 15. My soul longed for more spirituality; and it was my burden that I could do no more for God. O, my barrenness in my daily affliction and heavy load! O how precious is time, and how it pains me to see it slide away, while I do so little to any good purpose. O that God would make me more fruitful and spiritual.

"*April* 17. Enjoyed some comfort in prayer, some freedom in meditation, and composure in my studies. Spent some time in writing in the forenoon. In the afternoon spent some time in conversation with several dear ministers. In the evening preached from Psalm lxxiii. 28. 'But it is good for me to draw near to God.' God helped me to feel the truths of my texts both in the first prayer and in the sermon. I was enabled to pour out my soul to God with great freedom, fervency and affection ; and, blessed be the Lord, it was a comfortable season to me. I was enabled to speak with tenderness, and yet with faithfulness: and divine truths seemed to fall with weight and influence upon the hearers. My heart was melted for the dear assembly ; and I loved everybody in it ; and scarcely ever felt more love to immortal souls in my life. My soul cried, ' O that the dear creatures might be saved ! O that God would have mercy upon them !'

"*Lord's day, April* 20. Discoursed, both forenoon and afternoon from Luke xxiv. explaining most of the chapter, and making remarks upon it. There was a desirable attention in the audience; though there was not so much appearance of affection and tenderness among them as had been usual. Our meeting was very full ; there being sundry strangers present who had never been with us before. Enjoyed some freedom, and, I hope, exercise of faith, in prayer in the morning, especially when I came to pray for Zion. I was free from that gloomy discouragement which so often oppresses my mind ; and my soul rejoiced in the hopes of Zion's prosperity, and the enlargement of the dear kingdom of the great Redeemer. O that his kingdom might come !

"In the evening catechised. My people answered the questions proposed to them readily and distinctly; and I could perceive that they advanced in their knowledge of the principles of Christianity. There appeared an affectionate melting in the assembly at this time. Several, who I trust are truly religious, were refreshed and quickened, and seemed by their discourse and behavior after public worship to have their 'hearts knit together in love.' This was a sweet and blessed season, like many others with which my poor people have been favored in months past. God has caused this little fleece to be repeatedly wet with the blessed dew of his divine grace, while all the earth around has been comparatively dry.

"*April* 21. Was composed and comfortable in mind most of the day and was mercifully freed from those gloomy damps with which I am frequently exercised. Had freedom and comfort in prayer several times ; and especially had some rising hopes of Zion's enlargement and prosperity. Oh, how refreshing were those hopes to my soul ! Oh, that the kingdom of the dear Lord might come. Oh, that the poor Indians might quickly be gathered in great numbers !

"*April* 22. My mind was remarkably free this day from melancholy damps and glooms, and animated in my work. I found such fresh vigor and resolution in the service of God, that the mountains seemed to become a plain before me. O blessed be God, for an interval of refreshment and fervent resolution in my Lord's work! In the evening, my soul was refreshed in secret prayer, and my heart drawn out for divine blessings ; especially for the church of God, and his interest among my own people, and for dear friends in remote places. Oh, that Zion might prosper, and precious souls be brought home to God!

"*April* 25. Of late I apprehended that a number of persons in my congregation were proper subjects of the ordinance of the Lord's supper, and that it might be seasonable speedily to administer it to them ; and having taken advice of some of the reverend correspondents in this solemn affair, I accordingly proposed and appointed the next Lord's day, with leave of divine providence, for the administration of this ordinance ; and this day, as preparatory thereto, was set apart for solemn fasting and prayer. The design of this preparatory solemnity was to implore the blessing of God upon our renewing covenant with him, and with one another, to walk together in the fear of God, in love and Christian fellowship, and to entreat that his presence might be with us in our designed approach to his table ; as well as to humble ourselves before God on account of the apparent withdrawment, at least in a measure, of that blessed influence which has been so prevalent upon persons of all ages among us ; as also on account of the rising appearance of carelessness, and vanity, and vice among some, who some time since appeared to be touched and affected with divine truths, and brought to some sensibility of their miserable and perishing state by nature. It was also designed that we might importunately pray for the peaceable settlement of the Indians together in a body ; that they might be a commodious congregation for the worship of God ; and that God would blast and defeat all the attempts that were, or might be, made against that pious design.*

"The solemnity was observed and seriously attended, not only by those who proposed at the Lord's table, but by the whole congregation universally. In the former part of the day, I endeavored to open to my people the nature and design of a fast, as I had attempted more briefly to do before, and to instruct them in the duties of such a solemnity. In the afternoon I insisted upon the special reasons there were for our engaging in these solemn exercises at this time ; both in regard of the need

"* There was at this time a terrible clamor raised against the Indians in various places in the country, and insinuations as though I was training them up to cut people's throats. Numbers wished to have them banished from these parts, and some gave out great words in order to fright and deter them from settling upon the best and most convenient tract of their own lands ; threatening to trouble them in the law ; pretending a claim to these lands themselves, although never purchased of the Indians."

we stood in of divine assistance, in order to a due preparation for that sacred ordinance upon which some of us were proposing, with leave of divine providence speedily to attend; and also in respect of the manifest decline of God's work here, as to the effectual conviction and conversion of sinners; there having been few of late deeply awakened out of a state of security. The worship of God was attended with great solemnity and reverence, with much tenderness and many tears, by those who appeared to be truly religious; and there was some appearance of divine power upon those who had been awakened some time before, and who were still under concern.

"After repeated prayer, and attendance upon the word of God, I proposed to the religious people, with as much brevity and plainness as I could, the substance of the doctrine of the Christian faith, as I had formerly done previous to their baptism; and had their renewed cheerful assent to it. I then led them to a solemn renewal of their baptismal covenant; wherein they had explicitly and publicly given up themselves to God the Father, Son and Holy Ghost, avouching him to be their God; and at the same time renouncing their heathenish vanities, their idolatrous and superstitious practices; solemnly engaging to take the Word of God, so far as it was or might be made known to them, for the rule of their lives; promising to walk together in love, to watch over themselves and one another, to lead lives of seriousness and devotion, and to discharge the relative duties incumbent on them respectively, etc. This solemn transaction was attended with much gravity and seriousness; and at the same time with the utmost readiness, freedom and cheerfulness; and a religious union and harmony of soul seemed to crown the whole solemnity. I could not but think in the evening, that there had been manifest tokens of the divine presence with us in all the several services of the day; though it was also manifest that there was not that concern among Christless souls which has often appeared there.

"*April* 26. Toward noon prayed with a dying child, and gave a word of exhortation to the bystanders, to prepare for death; which seemed to take effect upon some. In the afternoon discoursed to my people from Matthew xxvi. 26–30, of the author, the nature, and designs of the Lord's supper; and endeavored to point out the worthy receivers of that ordinance. The religious people were affected, and even melted with divine truths,—with a view of the dying love of Christ. Several others, who had been for some months under conviction of their perishing state, appeared now to be much moved with concern, and afresh engaged in seeking after an interest in Christ; although I cannot say that the word of God appeared so quick and powerful, so sharp and piercing to the assembly as it had sometimes formerly done. Baptized two adult persons; both serious and exemplary in their lives, and I hope truly religious. One of them was the man particularly mentioned in my journal of the 6th instant; who, although he was greatly distressed, because 'he had never done the will of God,' has since, it is hoped, obtained spiritual comfort upon good grounds.

"In the evening I catechised those, who were designed to partake of the Lord's supper the next day, upon the institution, nature and end of that ordinance ; and had abundant satisfaction respecting their doctrinal knowledge and fitness in that respect for an attendance upon it. They likewise appeared in general to have an affecting sense of the solemnity of this sacred ordinance, and to be humbled under a sense of their own unworthiness to approach to God in it; and to be earnestly concerned that they might be duly prepared for an attendance upon it.—Their hearts were full of love, one toward another, and that was the frame of mind which they seemed concerned to maintain and bring to the Lord's table with them. In the singing and prayer after catechising, there appeared an aggreeable tenderness and melting among them ; and such tokens of brotherly love and affection, as would even constrain one to say ' Lord, it is good to be here ;' it is good to dwell where such an heavenly influence distils.

"*Lord's day, April* 27. Preached from Tit. ii. 14, 'Who gave himself for us,' etc. The word of God at this time, was attended with some appearance of divine power upon the assembly; so that the attention and gravity of the audience were remarkable; and especially towards the conconclusion of the exercise, divers persons were much affected. Administered the sacrament of the Lord's supper to 23 persons of the Indians, the number of the men and women being nearly equal; several others to the number of five or six, being now absent at the Forks of Delaware, who would otherwise have communed with us. The ordinance was attended with great solemnity, and with a most desirable tenderness and affection. It was remarkable that in the season of the performance of the sacramental actions, especially in the distribution of the bread, they seemed to be affected in a most lively manner, as if Christ had been really crucified before them. The words of the institution, when repeated and enlarged upon in the season of the administration, seemed to meet with the same reception, to be entertained with the same free and full belief and affectionate engagement of soul, as if the Lord Jesus Christ himself had been present, and had personally spoken to them. The affections of the communicants, although considerably raised, were, notwithstanding, agreeably regulated and kept within proper bounds. So that there was a sweet, gentle, and affectionate melting without any indecent or boisterous commotion of the passions.

"Having rested sometime after the administration of the sacrament, being extremely tired with the necessary prolixity of the work, I walked from house to house, and conversed particularly with most of the communicants, and found they had been almost universally refreshed at the Lord's table, 'as with new wine.' Never did I see such an appearance of Christian love among any people in all my life. It was so remarkable, that one might well have cried with an agreeable surprise, 'Behold how they love one another.' I think there could be no greater token of mutual affection among the people of God, in the early days of Christianity, than what now appeared here. The sight was so desirable, and so well becoming the gospel, that nothing less could be said of it than that it was 'the doing of the Lord,' the genuine operation of Him, 'who is Love.'

"Toward night discoursed again on the forementioned text, Tit. ii. 14; and insisted on the immediate end and design of Christ's death, viz.: That he might redeem his people from all iniquity etc. This appeared to be a season of divine power among us. The religious people were much refreshed, and seemed remarkably tender and affectionate, full of love, joy, and peace, and desirous of being completely 'redeemed from all iniquity;' so that some of them afterwards told me that 'they had never felt the like before.' Convictions also appeared to be revived in many instances; and several persons were awakened, whom I had never observed under any religious impressions before.

"Such was the influence which attended our assembly, and so unspeakably desirable the frame of mind which many enjoyed in divine service, that it seemed almost grievous to conclude the public worship. The congregation, when dismissed, although it was then almost dark, appeared loath to leave the place and employments which had been rendered so dear to them by the benefits enjoyed, while a blessed quickening influence distilled upon them. Upon the whole, I must say, I had great satisfaction relative to the administration of this ordinance in various respects. I have abundant reason to think, that those who came to the Lord's table had a good degree of doctrinal knowledge of the nature and design of the ordinance, and that they acted with understanding in what they did.

"This competency of doctrinal knowledge, together with their grave and decent attendance upon the ordinance, their affectionate melting under it, and the sweet and Christian frame of mind which they discovered after it, gave me great satisfaction respecting my administration of it to them. O, what a sweet and blessed season was this! God himself, I am persuaded, was in the midst of his people, attending on his own ordinance. I doubt not but many, in the conclusion of the day, could say with their whole hearts, 'Verily, a day thus spent in God's house, is better than a thousand elsewhere.' There seemed to be but one heart among the pious people. The sweet union, harmony and endearing love and tenderness subsisting among them was, I thought, the most lively emblem of the heavenly world, which I had ever seen.

"*April* 28. Concluded the sacramental solemnity with a discourse upon John xiv. 15: 'If ye love me, keep my commandments.' At this time there appeared a very agreeable tenderness in the audience in general, but especially in the communicants. O, how free, how engaged and affectionate did these appear in the service of God! they seemed willing to have their ears bored to the door posts of God's house, and to be his servants forever.

"Observing numbers in this excellent frame, and the assembly in general affected, and that by a divine influence, I thought it proper to improve this advantageous season as Hezekiah did the desirable season of his great passover, 2 Chron. xxxi. in order to promote the blessed reformation begun among them; and to engage those that appeared serious and religious to persevere therein. Accordingly I proposed to them, that they should renewedly enter into covenant before God, that they would watch over themselves and one another, lest they should dishonor the name of Christ, by falling into sinful and unbecoming practices; and especially that they would watch against the sin of drunkenness, 'the sin that most easily besets them,' and, the temptations leading thereto, as well as the appearance of evil in that respect. They cheerfully complied with the proposal, and explicitly joined in that covenant; whereupon I proceeded in the most solemn manner of which I was capable, to call God to witness respecting their sacred engagements, and reminded them of the greatness of the guilt they would contract to themselves in the violation of it; as well as observed to them that God would be a terrible witness against those who should presume to do so in the great and notable day of the Lord. It was a season of amazing solemnity; and a divine awe appeared upon the face of the whole assembly in this transaction. Affectionate sobs, sighs and tears were now frequent in the audience; and I doubt not but that many silent cries were then sent up to the Fountain of grace for supplies of grace sufficient for the fulfilment of these solemn engagements. Baptized six children this day."

Tuesday, April 29, he went to Elizabethtown to attend the meeting of Presbytery and seemed to spend the time while absent from his people on this occasion, in a free and comfortable state of mind.

"*May* 3. [At Cranberry, N. J.] Rode from Elizabethtown, home to my people near Cranberry; whither they are now removed, and where I hope God will settle them as a Christian congregation. Was refreshed in lifting up my heart to God, while riding, and enjoyed a thankful frame of spirit for divine favors received the week past. Was somewhat uneasy and dejected in the evening; having no house of my own to go to in this place; but God was my support.

" *Lord's day, May* 4. My people being now removed to their lands, mentioned in my diary, of March 24, where they were then, and have since
been making provision for a compact settlement, in order to their more
convenient enjoyment of the gospel and other means of instruction, as
well as of the comforts of life; I this day visited them; being now
obliged to board with an English family at some distance from them; and
preached to them in the forenoon from Mark. iv. 5. ' And some fell upon
stony ground,' etc. Endeavored to show them the reason there was to
fear, lest many promising appearances and hopeful beginnings in religion
might prove abortive, like the seed dropped upon stony places. In the
afternoon discoursed upon Rom. viii. 9. ' Now if any man have not the spirit
of Christ, he is none of his.' I have reason to think this discourse was
peculiarly seasonable, and that it had a good effect upon some of the
hearers. Spent some hours afterwards in private conference with my
people, and labored to regulate some things which I apprehended amiss
among some of them.

" *May* 5. Visited my people again, and took care of their worldly
concerns; giving them directions relating to their business. I daily discover more and more of what importance it is likely to be to their religious interests, that they become laborious and industrious, acquainted
with the affairs of husbandry, and able in a good measure to raise the
necessaries and comforts of life within themselves; for their present
method of living greatly exposes them to temptations of various kinds.
—May 6. Enjoyed some spirit and courage in my work; was in a good
measure free from melancholy; blessed be God for freedom from this
death.

" *May* 7. Spent most of the day in writing as usual. Enjoyed some
freedom in my work. Was favored with some comfortable meditations
this day. In the evening was in a sweet composed frame of mind;
was pleased and delighted to leave all with God respecting myself for
time and eternity, and respecting the people of my charge, and dear
friends. Had no doubt but that God would take care of me and of his
own interest among my people; and was enabled to use freedom in
prayer as a child with a tender father. O, how sweet is such a frame!

" *May* 8. In the evening, was somewhat refreshed with divine things,
and enjoyed a tender melting frame in secret prayer, wherein my soul was
drawn out for the interests of Zion, and comforted with the lively hope
of the appearing of the great Redeemer. These were sweet moments; I
felt almost loath to go to bed, and grieved that sleep was necessary.
However I lay down with a tender reverential fear of God, sensible that
his favor is life, and his smiles better than all that earth can boast of,
infinitely better than life itself.

" *May* 9. Preached from John v. 40, ' And ye will not come to me,' etc., in the open wilderness; the Indians having as yet no house for public worship in this place, nor scarcely any shelter for themselves. Divine truths made considerable impressions upon the audience, and it was a season of great solemnity, tenderness and affection.

" *May* 10. Rode to Allen's-town to assist in the administration of the Lord's supper. In the afternoon, preached from Titus ii. 14 : Who gave himself for us, etc. God was pleased to carry me through, and to grant me some freedom ; and yet to deny me that enlargement and power for which I longed. In the evening my soul mourned, and could not but mourn, that I had treated so excellent a subject in so defective a manner ; that I had borne so broken a testimony for so worthy and glorious a Redeemer. If my discourse had met with the utmost applause from all the world, it would not have given me any satisfaction. O, it grieved me to think, that I had no more holy warmth and fervency, that I had been no more melted in discoursing of Christ's death and the end and design of it ! Afterwards enjoyed some freedom and fervency in family and secret prayer, and longed much for the presence of God to attend his word and ordinances the next day.

" *Lord's day, May* 11. Assisted in the administration of the Lord's supper ; but enjoyed but little enlargement ; was grieved and sunk with some things, which I thought undesirable, etc. In the afternoon went to the house of God, weak and sick in soul, as well as feeble in body, and longed that the people might be entertained and edified with divine truths, and that an honest, fervent testimony might be borne for God; but knew not how it was possible for me to do anything of that kind to any good purpose. Yet God, who is rich in mercy, was pleased to give me assistance both in prayer and preaching. God helped me to wrestle for his presence in prayer, and to tell him that he had promised, ' Where two or three are met together in his name, there he would be in the midst of them ; ' and that we were, at least some of us, so met ; and pleaded that for his truth's sake he would be with us. Blessed be God, it was sweet to my soul, thus to plead and rely on God's promises. Discoursed upon Luke ix. 30, 31 : ' And behold there talked with him two men, which were Moses and Elias, who appeared in glory, and spake of his decease, which he should accomplish at Jerusalem.' Enjoyed special freedom from the beginning to the end of my discourse without interruption. Things pertinent to the subject were abundantly presented to my view, and such a fulness of matter, that I scarce knew how to dismiss the various heads and particulars I had occasion to touch upon. Blessed be the Lord, I was favored with some fervency and power, as well as freedom ; so that the word of God seemed to awaken the attention of a stupid audience to a considerable degree. I was inwardly refreshed with the consolations of God, and could with my whole heart say, ' Though there be no fruit in the vine, etc., yet will I rejoice in the Lord.' After public service, was refreshed with the sweet conversation of some Christian friends.

"*May* 16. Near night enjoyed some agreeable and sweet conversation with a dear minister ; which was, I trust, blessed to my soul. My heart was warmed, and my soul engaged to live to God ; so that I longed to exert myself with more vigor than ever I had done in his cause ; and those words were quickening to me, ' Herein is my father glorified, that ye bring forth much fruit.' O my soul longed, and wished, and prayed to be enabled to live to God with the utmost constancy and ardor ! In the evening God was pleased to shine upon me in secret prayer, and draw out my soul after himself ; and I had freedom in supplication for myself. but much more in intercession for others; so that I was sweetly constrained to say, ' Lord, use me as thou wilt ; do as thou wilt with me ; but O, promote thine own cause ! Zion is thine ; O visit thine heritage ! Let thy kingdom come ! O let thy blessed interest be advanced in the world !' When I attempted to look to God respecting my worldly circumstances, and his providential dealings with me relative to my settling down in my congregation ; which seems to be necessary, and yet very difficult, and contrary to my fixed intentions for years past, as well as to my disposition, which has been and still is, at times especially, to go forth and spend my life in preaching the gospel from place to place, and gathering souls afar off to Jesus the great Redeemer ; I could only say, ' The will of the Lord be done; it is no matter for me.' The same frame of mind I felt with regard to another important affair, of which I have lately had some serious thoughts. I could say, with the utmost calmness and composure, ' Lord, if it be most for thy glory, let me proceed in it ; but, if thou seest it will in any wise hinder my usefulness in thy cause, oh, prevent me from proceeding; for all I want respecting this world is such circumstances as may best capacitate me to do service for God in the world.' But, blessed be God ! I enjoyed liberty in prayer for my dear flock, and was enabled to pour out my soul into the bosom of a tender Father. My heart within me was melted, when I came to plead for my dear people, and for the kingdom of Christ in general. Oh, how sweet was this evening to my soul ! I knew not how to go to bed ; and when I got to bed, longed for some way to improve time for God to some excellent purpose. Bless the Lord, O my soul !

"*May* 17. Walked out in the morning, and felt much of the same frame which I enjoyed the evening before; had my heart enlarged in praying for the advancement of the kingdom of Christ, and found the utmost freedom in leaving all my concerns with God. I find discouragement to be an exceeding hindrance to my spiritual fervency and affection ; but, when God enables me sensibly to find that I have done something for him, this refreshes and animates me, so that I could break through all hardships, and undergo any labors, and nothing seems too much either to door to suffer. But oh, what a death it is to strive and, strive; to be always in a hurry, and yet do nothing, or at least, nothing for God! Alas, alas, that time flies away, and I do so little for God!

"*Lord's day, May* 18. I felt my own utter insufficiency for my work; God made me to see that I was a child; yea, that I was a fool. I discoursed both parts of the day from Rev. iii. 20, 'Behold, I stand at the door and knock.' God gave me freedom and power in the latter part of my forenoon's discourse; although, in the former part of it, I felt peevish and provoked with the unmannerly behavior of the white people, who crowded in between my people and me; which proved a great temptation to me. But blessed be God! I got these shackles off before the middle of my discourse, and was favored with a sweet frame of spirit in the latter part of the exercise; was full of love, warmth, and tenderness in addressing my dear people. There appears some affectionate melting towards the conclusion of the forenoon exercise, and one or two instances of fresh awakening. In the intermission of public worship I took occasion to discourse to numbers, in a more private way, on the kindness and patience of the blessed Redeemer in standing and knocking, in continuing his gracious calls to sinners, who had long neglected and abused his grace; which seemed to take some effect upon several.

"In the afternoon divine truths were attended with solemnity and with some tears; although there was not that powerful awakening and quickening influence which in times past has been common in our assemblies. The appearance of the audience under divine truths was comparatively discouraging; and I was ready to fear that God was about to withdraw the blessed influence of his Spirit from us. In the evening, I was grieved that I had done so little for God. Oh that I could be 'a flame of fire' in the service of my God!

"*May* 19. Visited and preached to my people from Acts xx. 18, 19, 'And when they were come to him, he said unto them, Ye know from the first day,' etc. and endeavored to rectify their notions about religious affections; showing them on the one hand the desirableness of religious affection, tenderness, and fervent engagement in the worship and service of God, when such affection flows from a true spiritual discovery of divine glories, from a just sense of the transcendent excellence and perfections of the blessed God,—and a view of the glory and loveliness of the great Redeemer; and that such views of divine things will naturally excite us to 'serve the Lord with many tears, with much affection and fervency, and yet with all humility of mind.' On the other hand, I observed the sinfulness of seeking after high affections immediately and for their own sakes; that is, of making them the object which our eye and heart is first and principally set upon, when the glory of God ought to be that object.   Showed them, that if the heart be directly and chiefly fixed on God, and the soul engaged to glorify him, some degree of religious affection will be the effect and attendant of it.   But to seek after affection directly and chiefly ; to have the heart principally set upon that ; is to place it in the room of God and his glory.   If it be sought, that others may take notice of it, and admire us for our spirituality and forwardness in religion, it is then abominable pride ; if for the sake of feeling the pleasure of being affected, it is then idolatry and self-gratification. Labored also to expose the disagreeableness of those affections, which are sometimes wrought up in persons by the powers of fancy, and their own attempts for that purpose, while I still endeavored to recommend to them that religious affection, fervency, and devotion which ought to attend all our religious exercises, and without which religion will be but an empty name and a lifeless carcase.   This appeared to be a seasonable discourse, and proved very satisfactory to some of the religious people, who before were exercised with some difficulties relating to this point.   Afterwards took care of, and gave my people directions about their worldly affairs.

" *May* 22.   In the evening was in a frame somewhat remarkable.   I had apprehended for some days before, that it was the design of Providence that I should settle among my people here, and had in my own mind began to make provision for it, and to contrive means to hasten it, and found my heart somewhat engaged in it, hoping that I might then enjoy more agreeable circumstances of life in several respects ; and yet was never fully determined, never quite pleased with the thoughts of being settled and confined to one place.   Nevertheless I seemed to have some freedom in that respect, because the congregation with which I thought of settling, was one which God had enabled me to gather from among pagans.   For I never, since I began to preach, could feel any freedom to enter into other men's labors, and settle down in the ministry where the gospel was preached before.   I never could make that appear to be my province.   When I felt any disposition to consult my worldly ease and comfort, God has never given me any liberty in this respect, either since, or for some years before, I began to preach.   But God having succeeded my labors, and made me instrumental in gathering a church for him among these Indians, I was ready to think it might be his design to give me a quiet settlement, and a stated home of my own.   This, considering the late frequent sinking and failure of my spirits, and the need I stood in of some agreeable society, and my great desire of enjoying conveniences and opportunities for profitable studies, was not altogether disagreeable to me.   Although I still wanted to go about far and wide, in order to spread the blessed gospel among the benighted souls far remote, yet I never had been so willing to settle in any one place, for more than five years past, as I was in the preceding part of this week. But now these thoughts seemed to be wholly dashed to pieces, not by necessity, but of choice; for it appeared to me that God's dealings towards me had fitted me for a life of solitariness and hardship, and that I had nothing to lose, nothing to do with earth, and consequently nothing to lose by a total renunciation of it. It appeared to me just right that I should be destitute of house and home, and many of the comforts of life, which I rejoiced to see others of God's people enjoy. At the same time, I saw so much of the excellency of Christ's kingdom, and the infinite desirableness of its advancement in the world, that it swallowed up all my other thoughts, and made me willing, yea, even rejoice, to be made a pilgrim or hermit in the wilderness to my dying moment, if I might thereby promote the blessed interest of the great Redeemer. If ever my soul presented itself to God for his service, without any reserve of any kind, it did so now. The language of my thoughts and disposition now was 'Here I am, Lord, send me ; send me to the ends of the earth; send me to the rough, the savage pagans of the wilderness ; send me from all that is called comfort in earth, or earthly comfort ; send me even to death itself, if it be but in thy service, and to promote thy kingdom.'

" At the same time, I had as quick and lively a sense of the value of worldly comforts, as I ever had; but only saw them infinitely overmatched by the worth of Christ's kingdom, and the propagation of his blessed gospel. The quiet settlement, the certain place of abode, the tender friendship, which I thought I might be likely to enjoy in consequence of such circumstances, appeared as valuable to me, considered absolutely and in themselves, as ever before ; but considered comparatively, they appeared nothing. Compared with the value and preciousness of an enlargement of Christ's kingdom, they vanished as stars before the rising sun. Sure I am, that, although the comfortable accommodations of life appeared valuable and dear to me, yet I did surrender and resign myself, soul and body, to the service of God, and to the promotion of Christ's kingdom; though it should be in the loss of them all, I could not do any other, because I could not will or choose any other. I was constrained, and yet chose, to say, 'Farewell friends and earthly comforts, the dearest of them all, the very dearest, if the Lord calls for it ; adieu, adieu ; I will spend my life, to my latest moments, in caves and dens of the earth, if the kingdom of Christ may thereby be advanced.' I found extraordinary freedom at this time in pouring out my soul to God for his cause ; and especially that his kingdom might be extended among the Indians, far remote ; and I had a great and strong hope that God would do it. I continued wrestling with God in prayer for my dear little flock here ; and more especially for the Indians elsewhere; as well as for dear friends in one place and another until it was bed time, and I feared I should hinder the family. But, O, with what reluctancy did I feel myself obliged to consume time in sleep! I longed to be as a flame of fire, continually glowing in the divine service, and building up Christ's kingdom, to my latest, my dying moment.

"*May* 23. In the morning, was in the same frame of mind as in the evening before. The glory of Christ's kingdom so much outshone the pleasure of earthly accommodations and enjoyments, that they appeared comparatively nothing, though in themselves good and desirable. My soul was melted in secret meditation and prayer ; and I found myself divorced from any part or portion in this world ; so that in those affairs which seemed of the greatest importance to me with respect to the present life, and in those with which the tenderest feelings of the heart are most sensibly connected ; I could only say, ' the will of the Lord be done.' But just the same things, which I felt the evening before, I felt now, and found the same freedom in prayer for the people of my charge, for the propagation of the gospel among the Indians, and for the enlargement and spiritual welfare of Zion in general, and my dear friends in particular now, as I did then ; and longed to burn out in one continued flame for God. Retained much of the same frame through the day. In the evening I was visited by my brother John Brainerd ; the first visit which I have ever received from any near relative since I have been a missionary. Felt the same flame of spirit in the evening, as in the morning ; and found that it was good for me to draw near to God, and leave all my concerns and burdens with him. Was enlarged and refreshed in pouring out my soul for the propagation of the gospel of the Redeemer among the distant tribes of Indians. Blessed be God. If ever I filled up a day with study and devotion, I was enabled so to fill up this day.

"*May* 24. Visited the Indians, and took care of their secular business, which they are not able to manage themselves, without the constant care and advice of others. Afterwards discoursed to some of them particularly about their spiritual concerns. Enjoyed this day somewhat of the same frame of mind which I felt the day before.

"*Lord's day, May* 25. Discoursed both parts of the day from John xii. 44–48. ' Jesus cried and said, He that believeth on me, etc.' There was some degree of divine power attending the word of God. Several wept, and appeared considerably affected, and one, who had long been under spiritual trouble, now obtained clearness and comfort, and appeared to rejoice in God her Saviour. It was a day of grace and divine goodness; a day wherein something, I trust, was done for the cause of God among my people ; a season of comfort and sweetness to numbers of the religious people ; although there was not that influence upon the congregation which was common some months ago."

This week, at least the former part of it, he was in a very weak state, but yet seems to have been free from melancholy, which often had attended the failing of his bodily strength. He from time to time speaks of comfort and inward refreshment this week.

"*Lord's day, June* 1, 1746. Preached both forenoon and afternoon from Matt. xi. 27, 28. The presence of God seemed to be in the assembly; and numbers were considerably melted and affected under divine truths. There was a desirable appearance in the congregation in general, an earnest attention and an agreeable tenderness; and it seemed as if God designed to visit us with further showers of divine grace. I then baptized ten persons ; five adults, and five children ; and was not a little refreshed with this addition made to the church of such as I hope will be saved. I have reason to hope that God has lately, at and since our celebration of the Lord's supper, brought to himself several persons who had long been under spiritual trouble and concern; although there have been few instances of persons lately awakened out of a state of security. Those comforted of late seem to be brought in, in a more silent way; neither their concern, nor consolation being so powerful and remarkable, as appeared among those more suddenly wrought upon in the beginning of this work of grace.

"*June* 2. In the evening, enjoyed some freedom in secret prayer and meditation.—June 3. My soul rejoiced, early in the morning, to think that all things were at God's disposal. Oh, it pleased me to leave them there ! Felt afterwards much as I did on Thursday evening last, May 22, and continued in that frame for several hours. Walked out in the wilderness, and enjoyed freedom, fervency and comfort in prayer, and again enjoyed the same in the evening.

"*June* 4. Spent the day in writing, and enjoyed some comfort, satisfaction and freedom in my work. In the evening, I was favored with a sweet refreshing frame of soul in secret prayer and meditation. Prayer was now wholly turned into praise, and I could do little else but try to adore and bless the living God. The wonders of his grace displayed in gathering to himself a church among the poor Indians here, were the subject matter of my meditation, and the occasion of exciting my soul to praise and bless his name. My soul was scarcely ever more disposed to inquire, What I should render to God for all his benefits ? than at this time. Oh, I was brought into a strait, a sweet and happy strait, to know what to do : I longed to make some returns to God ; but found I had nothing to return ; I could only rejoice that God had done the work himself; and that none in heaven or earth might pretend to share the honor of it with him. I could only be glad that God's declarative glory was advanced by the conversion of these souls, and that it was to the enlargement of his kingdom in the world; but saw I was so poor that I had nothing to offer to him. My soul and body, through grace, I could cheerfully surrender to him; but it appeared to me this was rather a burden than a gift; and nothing could I do to glorify his dear and blessed name. Yet I was glad at heart, that he was unchangeably possessed of glory and blessedness. Oh, that he might be adored and praised by all his intelligent creatures to the utmost extent of their capacities! My soul would have rejoiced to see others praise him, though I could do nothing towards it myself."

"*June* 6. Discoursed to my people from part of Is. liii. The divine presence appeared to be among us in some measure.—Several persons were much melted and refreshed; and one man in particular, who had long been under concern for his soul, was now brought to see and feel, in a very lively manner, the impossibility of his doing anything to help himself, or to bring him into the favor of God, by his tears, prayers and other religious performances; and found himself undone as to any power or goodness of his own, and that there was no way left him but to leave himself with God, to be disposed of as he pleased.

"*June* 7. Being desired by the Rev. William Tennent to be his assistant in the administration of the Lord's supper, I this morning rode to Freehold to render that assistance. My people also being invited to attend the sacramental solemnity; they cheerfully embraced the opportunity, and this day attended the preparatory services with me. In the afternoon I preached from Psalm lxxiii. 28. ' But it is good for me to draw near to God,' etc. God gave me some freedom and warmth in my discourse; and I trust his presence was in the assembly. Was comfortably composed, enjoyed a thankful frame of spirit, and my soul was grieved that I could not render something to God for his benefits bestowed. O that I could be swallowed up in his praise !

"*Lord's day, June* 8. Spent much time in the morning in secret duties, but between hope and fear respecting the enjoyment of God in the business of the day then before us. Was agreeably entertained in the forenoon by a discourse from Mr. Tennent, and felt somewhat melted and refreshed. In the season of communion enjoyed some comfort; and especially in serving one of the tables. Blessed be the Lord! it was a time of refreshing to me, and I trust to many others.

" Most of my people, who had been communicants at the Lord's table, before being present at this sacramental occasion, communed with others in the holy ordinance, at the desire, and I trust to the satisfaction and comfort of numbers of God's people, who had longed to see this day, and whose hearts had rejoiced in this work of grace among the Indians, which prepared the way for what appeared so agreeable at this time. Those of my people who communed, seemed in general, agreeably affected at the Lord's table, and some of them considerably melted with the love of Christ, although they were not so remarkably refreshed and feasted at this time, as when I administered this ordinance to them in our own congregation only. A number of my dear people sat down by themselves at the last table ; at which time God seemed to be in the midst of them. Some of the bystanders were affected wi'h seeing those who had been ' aliens from the commonwealth of Israel, and strangers to the covenant of promise,' who of all men had lived ' without hope and without God in the world,' now brought near to God, as his professing people, and sealing their covenant with him, by a solemn and devout attendance upon this sacred ordinance. As numbers of God's people were refreshed with this sight, and thereby excited to bless God for the enlargement of his kingdom in the world ; so some others, I was told, were awakened by it, apprehending the danger they were in of being themselves finally cast out ; while they saw others from the east and west preparing, and hopefully prepared in some good measure, to sit down in the kingdom of God. At this season others of my people also, who were not communicants, were considerably affected ; convictions were revived in several instances ; and one, the man particularly mentioned in my journal of the 6th instant obtained comfort and satisfaction ; and has since given me such an account of his spiritual exercises, and the manner in which he obtained relief, as appears very hopeful. It seems as if He, who commanded the light to shine out of darkness, had now ' shined into his heart, and given him the light of,' and experimental ' knowledge of the glory of God in the face of Jesus Christ.'

" In the afternoon God enabled me to preach with uncommon freedom, from 2 Cor. v. 20. ' Now then we are ambassadors for Christ,' etc. Through the great goodness of God, I was favored with a constant flow of pertinent matter, and proper expressions, from the beginning to the end of my discourse. In the evening I could not but rejoice in God, and bless him in the manifestations of Grace in the day past ? O it was a sweet and solemn day and evening ! A season of comfort to the godly, and of awakening to some souls ! O that I could praise the Lord !

"*June* 9. Enjoyed some sweetness in secret duties. A considerable number of my people met together early in a retired place in the woods, and prayed, sang, and conversed of divine things ; and were seen by some religious persons of the white people to be affected and engaged, and divers of them in tears in these religious exercises. Preached the concluding sermon from Gen. v. 24. ' And Enoch walked with God,' etc God gave me enlargement and fervency in my discourse, so that I was enabled to speak with plainness and power ; and God's presence seemed to be in the assembly. Praised be the Lord, it was a sweet meeting, a desirable assembly. I found my strength renewed, and lengthened out even to a wonder, so that I felt much stronger at the conclusion than in the beginning of this sacramental solemnity. I have great reason to bless God for this solemnity; wherein I have found assistance in addressing others, and sweetness in my own soul.

"After my people had attended the concluding exercises of the sacramental solemnity, they returned home; many of them rejoicing for all the goodness of God which they had seen and felt; so that this appeared to be a profitable as well as comfortable season to numbers of my congregation. Their being present at this occasion, and a number of them communing at the Lord's table with other Christians, was, I trust, for the honor of God and the interest of religion in these parts; as numbers I have reason to think, were quickened by means of it.

"*June* 12. In the evening enjoyed freedom of mind and some sweetness in secret prayer. It was a desirable season to me; my soul was enlarged in prayer for my own dear people, and for the enlargement of Christ's kingdom, and especially for the propagation of the Gospel among the Indians, far back in the wilderness. Was refreshed in prayer for dear friends in New England and elsewhere. I found it sweet to pray at this time ; and could, with all my heart say, 'It is good for me to draw near to God.'

"*June* 13. Preached to my people upon the new creature, from 2 Cor. v. 17, 'If any man be in Christ,' etc. The presence of God seemed to be in the assembly. It was a sweet and agreeable meeting, wherein the people of God were refreshed and strengthened; beholding their faces in the glass of God's word, and finding in themselves the works and lineaments of the new creature. Some sinners under concern were also renewedly affected ; and afresh engaged for the securing of their eternal interests.

"Baptized five persons at this time, three adults, and two children. One of these was the very aged woman, of whose exercises I gave an account in my diary of Dec. 26. She now gave me a very rational, and satisfactory account of the remarkable change which she experienced some months after the beginning of her concern, which I must say appeared to be the genuine operations of the Divine Spirit, so far as I am capable of judging. Although she was become so childish through age, that I could do nothing in a way of questioning with her, nor scarcely make her understand anything that I asked her ; yet when I let her alone to go on with her own story, she could give a very distinct and particular relation of the many and various exercises of soul, which she had experienced ; so deep were the impressions left upon her mind by that influence and those exercises which she had experienced. I have great reason to think that she is born anew in her old age, she being, I presume, upwards of eighty. I had good hopes of the other adults, and trust they are such as God will own 'in the day when he makes up his jewels.' I came away from the meeting of the Indians this day, rejoicing and blessing God for his grace manifested at this season.

"*June* 14. Rode to Kingston to assist the Rev. Mr. Wales in the administration of the Lord's supper. In the afternoon preached; but almost fainted in the pulpit. Yet God strengthened me when I was just gone, and enabled me to speak his word with freedom, fervency and application to the conscience. Praised be the Lord, 'out of weakness I was made strong.' I enjoyed some sweetness in and after public worship, but was extremely tired. Oh, how many are the mercies of the Lord! 'To them that have no might he increaseth strength.'

"*Lord's day, June* 15. Was in a dejected, spiritless frame, so that I could not hold up my head, nor look anybody in the face. Administered the Lord's supper at Mr. Wales' desire, and found myself in a good measure unburdened and relieved of my pressing load, when I came to ask a blessing on the elements. Here God gave me enlargement and a tender affectionate sense of spiritual things, so that it was a season of comfort, in some measure to me, and I trust, more so to others. In the afternoon, preached to a vast multitude, from Rev. xxii. 17: 'And whoever will,' etc. God helped me to offer a testimony for himself, and to leave sinners inexcusable in neglecting his grace. I was enabled to speak with such freedom, fluency and clearness, as commanded the attention of the great. Was extremely tired in the evening, but enjoyed composure and sweetness.

"*June* 16. Preached again; and God helped me amazingly, so that this was a sweet refreshing season to my soul and others. Oh, forever blessed be God for help afforded at this time, when my body was so weak, and while there was so large an assembly to hear. Spent this afternoon in a comfortable agreeable manner."

The next day was spent comfortably. On Wednesday, he went to a meeting of ministers at Hopewell.

"*June* 19. Visited my people with two of the reverend correspondents. Spent some time in conversation with some of them upon spiritual things; and took some care of their worldly concerns.

"This day makes up a complete year from the first time of my preaching to these Indians in New Jersey. What amazing things has God wrought in this space of time, for this poor people! What a surprising change appears in their tempers and behavior! How are morose and savage pagans, in this short period, transformed into agreeable, affectionate, and humble Christians! and their drunken and pagan howlings turned into

devout and fervent praises to God ; they ‘who were sometimes in darkness are now become light in the Lord. ’   May they ‘ walk as children of
the light and of the day ! ’   And now to Him that is of power to establish
them according to the gospel, and the preaching of Christ—to God only
wise, be glory through Jesus Christ, for ever and ever, Amen.”

CHAPTER X.

Some Remarkable Cases of Conversion during the great Revival.

No. I.

"*Dec.* 26. This evening was visited by a person under great spiritual distress ; the most remarkable instance of this kind I ever saw. She was, I believe, more than fourscore years old, and appeared to be much broken and very childish through age ; so that it seemed impossible for man to instill into her any notions of divine things ; not so much as to give her any doctrinal instruction, because she seemed incapable of being taught. She was led by the hand into my house, and appeared in extreme anguish. I asked her, what ailed her ? She answered, her heart was distressed, and she feared she should never find Christ. I asked her when she began to be concerned, with divers other questions relating to her distress. To all which she answered, for substance, to this effect : That she had heard me preach many times, but never knew anything about it, never felt it in her heart, till the last Sabbath, and then it came, she said, all one as if a needle had been thrust into her heart ; since which time, she had no rest day nor night. She added, that on the evening before Christmas, a number of Indians being together at the house where she was, and discoursing about Christ, their talk pricked her heart so that she could not sit up, but fell down in her bed ; at which time she went away, as she expressed it, and felt as if she dreamed, and yet is confident she did not dream. When she was thus gone, she saw two paths ; one appeared very broad and crooked ; and that turned to the left hand. The other appeared straight and very narrow ; and that went up the hill to the right hand. She travelled, she said, for some time up the narrow right hand path, till at length something seemed to obstruct her journey, She sometimes called it darkness ; and then described it otherwise, and seemed to compare it to a block or bar. She then remembered what she had heard me say about striving to enter in at the straight gate, although she took little notice of it at the time when she heard me discourse upon that subject; and thought she would climb over this bar. But just as she was thinking of this, she came back again, as she turned it, meaning that she came to herself ; whereupon her soul was extremely distressed, apprehending that she had now termed back, and forsaken Christ, and that there was therefore no hope of mercy for her.

" As I was sensible that trances, and imaginary views of things are of dangerous tendency in religion, where sought after and depended upon ; so I could not but be much concerned about this exercise, especicially at first; apprehending this might be a design of Satan to bring a blemish upon the work of God here, by introducing visionary scenes, imaginary terrors, and all manner of mental disorders and delusions, in the room of genuine convictions of sin, and the enlightening influences of the blessed Spirit; and I was almost resolved to declare, that I looked upon this to be one of Satan's devices, and to caution my people against this and similar exercises of that nature. However, I determined first to inquire into her knowledge, to see whether she had any just views of things which might be the occasion of her present distressing concern, or whether it was a mere fright, arising only from imaginary terrors. I asked her divers questions respecting man's primitive, and more espe- ally his present state, and respecting her own heart; which she an- swered rationally, and to my surprise. I thought it next to impossible, if not altogether so, that a pagan, who was become a child through age, should in that state gain so much knowledge by any mere human instruc- tion, without being remarkably enlightened by a divine influence. I then proposed to her the provision made in the Gospel for the salvation of sin- ners, and the ability and willingness of Christ 'to save to the uttermost all, old as well as young, that come to him.' To this she seemed to give a hearty assent; but instantly replied, ' Aye, but I cannot come; my wicked heart will not come to Christ; I do not know how to come.' This she spoke in anguish of spirits, striking on her breast, with tears in her eyes, and with such earnestness in her looks, as was indeed piteous and affecting. She seems to be really convinced of her sin and misery, and her need of a change of heart. Her concern is abiding and constant, so that nothing appears why this exercise may not have a saving issue. Indeed there seems reason to hope such an issue, seeing she is so solici- tous to obtain an interest in Christ; that her heart, as she expresses it, prays day and night.

"How far God may make use of the imagination in awakening some persons under these, and similar circumstances, I cannot pretend to determine. Or whether this exercise be from a divine influence, I shall leave others, to judge. But this I must say, that its effects hitherto be- speak it to be such ; nor can it, as I see, be accounted for in any rational way, but from the influence of some spirit either good or evil. The wo- man, I am sure, never heard divine things in the manner in which she now viewed them ; and it would seem strange that she should get such a rational notion of them from the mere working of her own fancy, without some superior, or at least foreign aid. Yet I must say, I have looked upon it as one of the glories of this work of grace among the Indians, and a special evidence of it's being from a divine influence, that there has, till now been no appearance of such things, no visionary notions, trances, and imaginations, intermixed with those rational convictions of sin and solid consolations, of which numbers have been made the subjects. And might I have my desire, there had been no appearance of anything of this nature at all."

No II.

"*Lord's day, Jan.* 19. Discoursed to my people from Isaiah lv. 7. Toward night catechised in my ordinary method ; and this appeared to be a powerful season of grace among us. Numbers were much affected. Convictions were powerfully revived, and divers numbers of Christians refreshed and strengthened ; and one weary, heavy laden soul, I have abundant reason to hope, brought to true rest and solid comfort in Christ ; who afterwards gave me such an account of God's dealing with his soul, as was abundantly satisfying, as well as refreshing to me. He told me he had often heard me say, that persons must see and feel themselves utterly helpless and undone—that they must be emptied of a dependence upon themselves and of all hope of saving themselves, in order to their coming to Christ for salvation. He had long been striving after this view of things ; supposing that this would be an excellent frame of mind, to be thus emptied of a dependence upon his own goodness ; that God would have respect to this frame, would then be well pleased with him, and bestow eternal life upon him. But when he came to feel himself in this helpless, undone condition, he found it quite contrary to all his thoughts and expectations ; so that it was not the same frame, nor indeed anything like the frame after which he had been seeking. Instead of its being a good frame of mind, he now found nothing but badness in himself, and saw it was for ever impossible for him to make himself any better. He wondered, he said, that he had ever hoped to mend his own heart. He was amazed that he had never before seen, that it was utterly impossible for him by all his contrivances and endeavors to do anything in that way, since the matter now appeared to him in so clear a light. Instead of imagining now that God would be pleased with him for the sake of this frame of mind, and this view of his undone estate, he saw clearly, and felt that it would be just with God, to send him to eternal misery ; and that there was no goodness in what he then felt ; for he could not help seeing, that he was naked, sinful, and miserable, and that there was nothing in such a sight to deserve God's love or pity.

"He saw these things in a manner so clear and convincing, that it seemed to him, he said, he could convince everybody of their utter inability to help themselves, and their unworthiness of any help from God. In this frame of mind he came to public worship this evening ; and while I was inviting sinners to come to Christ naked and empty, without any goodness of their own to recommend them to his acceptance, then he thought with himself that he had often tried to come and give up his heart to Christ, and he used to hope that some time or other he should be able to do so. But now he was convinced that he could not, and that it was utterly vain for him ever to try any more; and he could not, he said, find a heart to make any further attempt, because he saw it would signify nothing at all; nor did he now hope for a better opportunity or more ability hereafter, as he had formerly done, because he saw, and was fully convinced that his own strength would for ever fail.

" While he was musing in this manner, he saw, he said, with his heart, which is a common phrase among them, something that was unspeakably good and lovely, and what he had never seen before; and ' this stole away his heart, whether he would or no.' He did not, he said, know what it was that he saw. He did not say, ' this is Jesus Christ; ' but it was such glory and beauty as he never saw before. He did not now give away his heart, as he had formerly intended and attempted to do; but it went away of itself after that glory which he then discovered. He used to make a bargain with Christ, to give up his heart to him that he might have eternal life for it. But now he thought nothing about himself, or what would become of him hereafter; but was pleased, and his mind wholly taken up with the unspeakable excellency of what he then beheld. After some time he was wonderfully pleased with the way of salvation by Christ; so that it seemed unspeakably better to be saved altogether by the mere free grace of God in Christ; than to have any hand in saving himself. The consequence of this exercise is, that he appears to retain a sense and relish of divine things, and to maintain a life of seriousness and true religion."

No. III.

" *Feb.* 9. Towards night catechised. God made this a powerful season to some. There were many affected. Former convictions appeared to be powerfully revived. There was likewise one who had been a vile drunkard remarkably awakened. He appeared to be in great anguish of soul, wept and trembled, and continued to do so till near midnight. There was also a poor heavy-laden soul, who had been long under spiritual distress, as constant and pressing as I ever saw, who was now brought to a comfortable calm, and seemed to be bowed and reconciled to the divine sovereignty, and told me she now felt and saw that it was right for God to do with her as he pleased; and that her heart felt pleased and satisfied it should be so; although of late she had often found her heart rise and quarrel with God, because he would, if he pleased, send her to hell after all she had done, or could do to save herself. She added, that the heavy burden she had lain under was now removed; that she had tried to recover her concern and distress again, fearing that the Spirit of God was departing from her, and would leave her wholly careless, but that she could not recover it; that she felt she never could do anything to save herself, but must perish for ever if Christ did not do all for her; that she did not deserved he should help her; and that it would be right if he should leave her to perish. But Christ would save her though she could do nothing to save herself, and here she seemed to rest."

No. IV.

"*March.* 9. Methinks it would have refreshed the heart of any who truly love Zion's interests, to have been in the midst of this divine influence, and seen the effects of it upon saints and sinners. The place of worship appeared both solemn and sweet, and was so endeared by a display of the divine presence and grace, that those who had any relish for divine things could not but cry, ' How amiable are thy tabernacles, O Lord of hosts ! 'After public worship was over, numbers came to my house, where we sang and discoursed of divine things ; and the presence of God seemed here also to be in the midst of us.—While we were singing the woman mentioned in my journal of February 9, who I may venture to say, if I may be allowed to say so much of any person I ever saw, was 'filled with joy unspeakable and full of glory ; ' and could not but burst forth in prayer and praises to God before us all with many tears ; crying sometimes in English, and sometimes in Indian, 'O blessed Lord ! do come, do come ! O do take me away ; do let me die and go to Jesus Christ ! I am afraid if I live I shall sin again. O do let me die now ! O dear Jesus, do come ! I cannot stay, I cannot stay ! O how can I live in this world ? do take my soul away from this sinful place ! O let me never sin any more ! O what shall I do, what shall I do, dear Jesus ! O dear Jesus ! ' In this ecstasy she continued some time, uttering these and similar expressions incessantly. The grand argument she used with God to take her away immediately was, that 'if she lived she should sin against him.' When she had a little recovered herself, I asked her, if Christ was now sweet to her soul ? Whereupon, turning to me with tears in her eyes, and with all the tokens of deep humility I ever saw in any person, she said, " I have many times heard you speak of the goodness and the sweetness of Christ, that he was better than all the world. But oh ! I knew nothing what you meant. I never believed you, I never believed you ! But now I know it is true ; ' or words to that effect. I answered, ' And do you see enough in Christ for the greatest of sinners ? ' She replied, ' O enough, enough for all the sinners in the world, if they would but come.' When I asked her, ' if she could not tell them of the goodness of Christ : '—Turning herself about to some Christless souls who stood by and were much affected, she said, ' O there is enough in Christ for you if you would but come. O strive, strive to give up your hearts to him,' etc. On hearing something of the glory of heaven mentioned, that there was no sin in that world, she again fell into the same ecstasy of joy and desire of Christ's coming, repeating her former expressions, ' O dear Lord, do let me go ! O what shall I do; what shall I do. I want to go to Christ. I cannot live. O do let me die.'

"She continued in this sweet frame for more than two hours before she was able to get home. I am very sensible that there may be great joys arising even to an ecstasy, where there is still no substantial evidence of their being well grounded. But in the present case there seemed to be no evidence wanting in order to prove this joy to be divine, either in regard to its preparatives, attendants, or consequents. Of all the persons whom I have seen under spiritual exercise, I scarcely ever saw one appear more bowed and broken under convictions of sin and misery, or what is usually called preparatory work, than this woman ; nor scarcely any who seemed to have a greater acquaintance with her own heart than she had. She would frequently complain to me of the hardness and rebellion of her heart. Would tell me that her heart rose and quarrelled with God when she thought he would do with her as he pleased, and send her to hell, notwithstanding her prayers, good frames, etc, that her heart was not willing to come to Christ for salvation, but tried every where else for help. As she seemed to be remarkably sensible of her stubbornness and contrariety to God under conviction, so she appeared to be no less remarkably bowed and reconciled to his sovereignty before she obtained any relief or comfort : something of which I have noticed in my journal of Feb. 9. Since that time she has seemed constantly to breathe the temper and spirit of the new creature : crying after Christ, not through fear of hell as before, but with strong desires after him as her only satisfied portion ; and has many times wept and sobbed bitterly, because as she apprehended, she did not and could not love him. When I have sometimes asked her why she appeared so sorrowful, and whether it was because she was afraid of hell, she would answer, ' No, I be not distressed about that, but my heart is so wicked I cannot love Christ ;' and thereupon burst into tears. But although this has been the habitual frame of her mind for several weeks together, so that the exercise of grace appeared evident to others ; yet she seemed wholly insensible to it herself, and never had any remarkable comfort and sensible satisfaction until this evening.

This sweet and surprising ecstasy appeared to spring from a true spiritual discovery of the glory, ravishing beauty, and excellency of Christ; and not from any gross imaginary notions of his human nature, such as that of seeing him in such a posture, as hanging on the cross, as bleeding and dying, as gently smiling, and the like ; which delusions some have been carried away with. Nor did it arise from sordid, selfish apprehensions of her having any benefit whatsoever conferred on her ; but from a view

of his personal excellency and transcendant loveliness ; which drew forth
these vehement desires of enjoying him which she now manifested, and
made her long, " to be absent from the body, that she might be present
with the Lord.

The attendants of this ravishing comfort were such, as abundantly discovered its spring to be divine; and that it was truly 'a joy in the Holy
Ghost.' Now she viewed divine truths as living realities, and could say,
' I know these things are so ; I feel that they are true ! ' Now her soul
was resigned to the divine will in the most tender point ; so that when I
said to her, ' What if God should take away your husband * from you who
was then very sick, how do you think you could bear that ? ' She replied,
' He belongs to God and not to me ; he may do with him just as he
pleases.' Now she had the most tender sense of the evil of sin, and discovered the utmost aversion to it, and longing to die, that she might be
delivered from it. Now she could freely trust her all with God for time
and eternity. When I questioned her, ' How she would be willing to die
and leave her little infant ; and what she thought would become of it in
that case ? ' she answered, ' God will take care of it.' Now she appeared to
have the most humbling sense of her own meanness and unworthiness,
her weakness and inability to preserve herself from sin, and to persevere
in the way of holiness, crying, ' If I live I shall sin.' I then thought that
I had never seen such an appearance of ecstasy and humility meeting in
any one person in all my life before.

" The consequents of this joy are no less desirable and satisfactory
than its attendants. She since appears to be a most tender, broken-
hearted, affectionate, devout, and humble Christian ; as exemplary in life
and conversation as any person in my congregation. May she still
grow in grace and in the knowledge of Christ ! "

No. V.

May 9. " Baptized one man this day, the conjurer, murderer, etc. mentioned in my diary of Aug. 8, 1745, and Feb 1, 1746, * who appears to be
such a remarkable instance of divine grace, that I cannot omit to give some
brief account of him here. He lived near, and sometimes attended my
meeting, at the Forks of Delaware, for more than a year together ; but
was, like many others of them, extremely attached to strong drink, and
seemed to be in no degree reformed by the means which I used with them
for their instruction and conversion. At this time he likewise murdered a
likely young Indian, which threw him into some kind of horror and desperation, so that he kept at a distance from me, and refused to hear me

* The man mentioned in my Journal of January 19.

preach for several months together, until I had an opportunity of conversing freely with him, and giving him encouragement, that his sin might be forgiven, for Christ's sake. After this he again attended my meeting sometimes.

"But that which was the worst of all his conduct, was his conjuration. He was one of those who are sometimes called powwows, among the Indians ; and, notwithstanding his frequent attendance upon my preaching, he still followed his old charms and juggling tricks, 'giving out that himself was some great one, and to him they gave heed,' supposing him to be possessed of great power. When I have instructed them respecting the miracle wrought by Christ in healing the sick, and mentioned them as evidence of his divine mission, and the truths of his doctrine ; they have quickly observed the wonders of that kind, which this man had performed by his magic charms. Hence they had a high opinion of him and his superstitious notions ; which seemed to be a fatal obstruction to some of them in regard to their receiving the Gospel. I have often thought that it would be a great favor to the design of evangelizing these Indians, if God would take that wretch out of the world ; for I had scarcely any hope of his ever becoming good. But God, whose thoughts are not as man's thoughts, has been pleased to take a much more desirable method with him ; a method agreeable to his own merciful nature, and I trust advantageous to his own interests among the Indians, as well as effectual to the salvation of the poor soul. To God be the glory of it. The first genuine concern for his soul, that ever appeared in him, was excited by seeing my interpreter and his wife baptized at the Forks of Delaware, July 21, 1745. Which so prevailed upon him, that with the invitation of an Indian who was a friend to Christianity, he followed me down to Crossweeksung, in the beginning of August following, in order to hear me preach ; and there continued for several weeks in the season of the most remarkable and powerful awakening among the Indians ; at which time he was more effectually awakened, and brought under great concern for his soul. And then he says, upon his 'feeling the word of God in his heart,' as he expresses it, his spirit of conjuration left him entirely, so that he has had no more power of that nature since, than any other man living. He also declares, that he does not now so much as know how he used to charm and conjure, and that he could not now do anything of that nature if he were ever so desirous of it.

"He continued under convictions of his sinful and perishing state, and a considerable degree of concern for his soul, all the fall and former part of the winter past ; but was not so deeply exercised until some time in January. Then the word of God took such hold upon him, that he was brought into deep distress, and knew not what to do, nor where to turn himself. He then told me, that when he used to hear me preach from time to time in the fall of the year, my preaching pricked his heart, and

made him very uneasy, but did not bring him to so great a distress, because he still hoped he could do something for his own relief; but now he
said, I drove him up in such a sharp corner, that he had no way to turn,
and could not avoid being in distress. He continued constantly under
the heavy burden and pressure of a wounded spirit, until at length he was
brought into the acute anguish and utmost agony of soul, mentioned in my
Journal of Feb. 1st. which continued that night and part of the next day.
After this he was brought to the utmost calmness and composure of mind;
his trembling and heavy burden was removed and he appeared perfectly
sedate, although he had to his apprehensions scarcely any hope of salvation.

"I observed him to appear remarkably composed; and thereupon
asked him how he did? He replied, 'It is done, it is done, it is all done
now.' I asked him what he meant! He answered, 'I can never do any
more to save myself; it is all done for ever. I can do no more.' I
queried with him, whether he could not do a little more, rather than go to
hell? He replied 'my heart is dead. I can never help myself.' I asked
him what he thought would become of him then? He answered 'I must
go to hell.' I asked him if he thought it was right, that God should send
him to hell? He replied 'Oh it is right. The devil has been in me ever
since I was born.' I asked him if he felt this when he was in such great
distress the evening before? He answered, 'No; I did not then think
it was right. I thought God would send me to hell, and that I was then
dropping into it; but my heart quarrelled with God, and would not say
it was right he should send me there; but now I know it is right, for I
have always served the devil; and my heart has no goodness in it now;
but it is as bad as ever it was,' etc. I thought I had scarcely ever seen
any person more effectually brought off from a dependence upon his own
contrivances and endeavors for salvation, or more apparently to lie at the
foot of sovereign mercy, than this man did, under these views of things.

"In this frame of mind he continued for several days, passing sentence
of condemnation upon himself, and constantly owning that it would be
right that he should be damned, and that he expected this would be his
portion for the greatness of his sins. Yet it was plain that he had a secret
hope of mercy, though imperceptible to himself, which kept him not only
from despair, but from any pressing distress; so that, instead of being
sad and dejected, his very countenance appeared pleasant and agreeable.

"While he was in this frame, he several times asked me, 'When I
would preach again?' and seemed desirous to hear the word of God
every day. I asked, 'Why he wanted to hear me preach, seeing his
heart was dead, and all was done; that he could never help himself, and
expected that he must go to hell?' He replied, , 'I love to hear you
speak about Christ for all.' I added 'But what good will that do you, if

you must go to hell at last ?—using now his own language with him, having before from time to time labored in the best manner I could to represent to him the excellency of Christ, his all-sufficiency and willingness to save lost sinners, and persons just in his case; although to no purpose, as to yielding him any special comfort. He answered, 'I would have others come to Christ, if I must go to hell myself.' It was remarkable, that he seemed to have a great love for the people of God; and nothing affected him so much as being separated from them. This seemed to be a very dreadful part of the hell to which he saw himself doomed. It was likewise remarkable, that in this season he was most diligent in the use of all the means for the soul's salvation; although he had the clearest view of the insufficiency of means to afford him help. He would frequently say, That all he did signified nothing at all ; and yet was never more constant in doing; attending secret and family prayer daily; and surprisingly diligent and attentive in hearing the word of God ; so that he neither despaired of mercy, nor yet presumed to hope upon his own doings, but used means because appointed of God in order to salvation; and because he would wait upon God in his own way.

"After he had continued in this frame of mind more than a week, while I was discoursing publicly, he seemed to have a lively soul-refreshing view of the excellency of Christ and the way of salvation by him ; which melted him into tears, and filled him with admiration, comfort, satisfaction, and praise to God. Since then, he has appeared to be a humble, devout, and affectionate Christian ; serious and exemplary in his conversation and behavior, frequently complaining of his barrenness, his want of spiritual warmth, life, and activity, and yet frequently favored with quickening and refreshing influences. In all respects, so far as I am capable of judging, he bears the marks of one ' created anew in Christ Jesus to good works.'

" His zeal for the cause of God was pleasing to me, when he was with me at the Forks of Delaware in February last. There being an old Indian at the place where I preached, who threatened to bewitch me, and my religious people who accompanied me there, this man presently challenged him to do his worst ; telling him that himself had been as great a conjurer as he; and that notwithstanding, as soon as he felt that word to his heart which these people loved, meaning the word of God, his power of conjuring immediately left him. ' And so it would you,' said he, 'if you did but once feel it in your heart ; and you have no power to hurt them, nor so much as to touch one of them,' etc. So that I may conclude my account of him, by observing, in allusion to what was said of St. Paul, that he now zealously ' defends and practically preaches the faith which he once destroyed,' or at least was instrumental of obstructing. May God have the glory of the amazing change which he has wrought in him ! "

CHAPTER XI.

Brainerd's General Remarks on the work of grace at Crossweeksung.—"Attestations" of its genuineness and power from other sources.*

"At the close of this narrative, I would make a few general remarks upon what, to me, appears worthy of notice, relating to the continued work of grace among my people.

"I. On the doctrines preached to the Indians.

"I cannot but take notice, that I have in general, ever since my first coming among the Indians in New Jersey, been favored with that assistance, which, to me, is uncommon in preaching Christ crucified, and making him the centre and mark to which all my discourses among them were directed.

"It was the principal scope and drift of all my discourses to this people, for several months together, (after having taught them something of the being and perfections of God, his creation of man in a state of rectitude and happiness, and the obligations mankind were thence under to love and honor him,) to lead them into an acquaintance with their deplorable state by nature, as fallen creatures ; their inability to extricate and deliver themselves from it ; the utter insufficiency of any external reformations and amendments of life, or of any religious performances of which they were capable, while in this state, to bring them into the favor of God, and interest them in his eternal mercy ; thence to show them their absolute need of Christ to redeem and save them from the misery of their fallen state ; to open his all-sufficiency and willingness to save the chief of sinners ;—the freeness and riches of divine grace, proposed 'without money and without price,' to all that will accept the offer ; thereupon to press them without delay, to betake themselves to him, under a sense of their misery and undone state, for relief and everlasting salvation ;—and to show them the abundant encouragement the Gospel proposes to needy, perishing, and helpless sinners in order to engage them so to do. These things, I repeatedly and largely insisted upon from time to time.

"I have oftentimes remarked with admiration, that whatever subject I have been treating upon, after having spent time sufficient to explain and illustrate the truths contained therein, I have been naturally and easily led to Christ as the substance of every subject. If I treated on

* As the General Remarks in this chapter were appended by Brainerd to his Journal which terminated June 19, 1746, we insert them here.

the being and glorious perfections of God, I was thence naturally led to discourse of Christ as the only 'way to the Father.' If I attempted to open the deplorable misery of our fallen state, it was natural from thence to show the necessity of Christ to undertake for us, to atone for our sins, and to redeem us from the power of them. If I taught the commands of God, and showed our violation of them ; this brought me in the most easy and natural way to speak of, and recommend the Lord Jesus Christ, as one who had 'magnified the law,' which we had broken, and who was 'become the end of it for righteousness, to every one that believes.' Never did I find so much freedom and assistance in making all the various lines of my discourses meet together and centre in Christ, as I have frequently done among these Indians.

"Sometimes when I have had thoughts of offering but a few words upon some particular subject, and saw no occasion, nor indeed much room, for any considerable enlargement, there has at unawares appeared such a fountain of Gospel-grace shining forth in, or naturally resulting from a just explication of it ; and Christ has seemed in such a manner to be pointed out as the substance of what I was considering and explaining ; that I have been drawn in a way not only easy and natural, proper and pertinent, but almost unavoidable to discourse of him, either in regard of his undertaking, incarnation, satisfaction, admirable fitness for the work of man's redemption, or the infinite need that sinners stand in of an interest in him ; which has opened the way for a continued strain of Gospel invitation to perishing souls, to come empty and naked, weary and heavy laden, and cast themselves upon him.

"As I have been remarkably influenced and assisted to dwell upon the Lord Jesus Christ, and the way of salvation by him, in the general current of my discourses here, and have been, at times, surprisingly furnished with pertinent matter relating to him, and the design of his incarnation ; so I have been no less assisted oftentimes in an advantageous manner of opening the mysteries of divine grace, and representing the infinite excellencies, and 'unsearchable riches of Christ,' as well as of recommending him to the acceptance of perishing sinners. I have frequently been enabled to represent the divine glory, the infinite preciousness and transcendant loveliness of the great Redeemer, the suitableness of his person and purchase to supply the wants, and answer the utmost desires of immortal souls ;—to open the infinite riches of his grace, and the wonderful encouragement proposed in the gospel to unworthy, helpless sinners ;— to call, invite, and beseech them to come and give up themselves to him, and be reconciled to God through him :—to expostulate with them respecting their neglect of one so infinitely lovely, and freely offered ;— and this in such a manner, with such freedom, pertinency, pathos, and application to the conscience, as, I am sure, I never could have made myself master of by the most assiduous application of mind. Frequently, at such seasons, I have been surprisingly helped in adapting my discourses to the capacities of my people, and bringing them down into such easy and familiar methods of expression, as has rendered them intelligible even to pagans.

"I do not mention these things as a recommendation of my own performances; for I am sure, I found, from time to time, that I had no skill or wisdom for my great work; and knew not how 'to choose out acceptable words' proper to address poor benighted pagans with. But thus God was pleased to help me, 'not to know anything among them, save Jesus Christ, and him crucified.' Thus I was enabled to show them their misery without him, and to represent his complete fitness to redeem and save them. This was the preaching God made use of for the awakening of sinners, and the propagation of this 'work of grace among the Indians.'—It was remarkable, from time to time, that when I was favored with any special freedom, in discoursing of the 'ability and willingness of Christ to save sinners,' and 'the need in which they stood of such a Saviour;' there was then the greatest appearance of divine power in awakening numbers of secure souls, promoting convictions begun, and comforting the distressed.

"I have sometimes formerly, in reading the apostle's discourse to Cornelius, (Acts x.) wondered to see him so quickly introduce the Lord Jesus Christ into his sermon, and so entirely dwell upon him through the whole of it, observing him in this point very widely to differ from many of our modern preachers; but latterly this has not seemed strange, since Christ has appeared to be the substance of the gospel, and the centre in which the several lines of divine revelation meet. Still I am sensible that there are many things necessary to be spoken to persons under pagan darkness, in order to make way for a proper introduction of the name of Christ, and his undertaking in behalf of fallen man.

"II. On the moral effects of preaching Christ crucified.

"It is worthy of remark, that numbers of these people are brought to a strict compliance with the rules of morality and sobriety, and to a conscientious performance of the external duties of Christianity, by the internal power and influence of divine truths—the peculiar doctrines of grace—upon their minds; without their having these moral duties frequently repeated and inculcated upon them, and the contrary vices particularly exposed and spoken against. What has been the general strain and drift of my preaching among these Indians, what were the truths I principally insisted upon, and how I was influenced and enabled to dwell from time to time upon the peculiar doctrines of grace, I have already observed in the preceding remarks. Those doctrines, which had the most direct tendency to humble the fallen creature; to show him

the misery of his natural state ; to bring him down to the foot of sovereign mercy, and to exalt the great Redeemer—discover his transcendent
excellency and infinite preciousness, and so to recommend him to the
sinner's acceptance—were the subject-matter of what was delivered in
public and private to them, and from time to time repeated and inculcated upon them.

" God was pleased to give these divine truths such a powerful influence
upon the minds of these people, and so to bless them for the effectual
awakening of numbers of them, that their lives were quickly reformed,
without my insisting upon the precepts of morality, and spending time in
repeated harangues upon external duties. There was indeed no room
for any kind of discourses but those which respected the essentials of religion, and the experimental knowledge of divine things, while there were
so many inquiring daily—not how they should regulate their external conduct, for that persons who are honestly disposed to comply with duty,
when known, may, in ordinary cases, be easily satisfied about, but how
they should escape from the wrath they feared, and felt a desert of,—obtain an effectual change of heart,—get an interest in Christ,—and come
to the enjoyment of eternal blessedness ? So that my great work still was
to lead them into a further view of their utter undoneness in themselves,
the total depravity and corruption of their hearts ; that there was no manner of goodness in them ; no good dispositions nor desires ; no love to
God, nor delight in his commands ; but, on the contrary, hatred, enmity,
and all manner of wickedness reigned in them. And at the same time to
open to them the glorious and complete remedy provided in Christ for
helpless perishing sinners, and offered freely to those who have no goodness of their own, no 'works of righteousness which they have done, to
recommend them to God.'

" This was the continued strain of my preaching ; this my great concern and constant endeavor, so to enlighten the mind, as thereby duly to
affect the heart, and, as far as possible, give persons a sense of feeling of
these precious and important doctrines of grace, at least, so far as means
might conduce to it. These were the doctrines, and this the method of
preaching, which were blessed of God for the awakening, and I trust, the
saving conversion of numbers of souls ;—and which were made the means
of producing a remarkable reformation among the hearers in general.

" When these truths were felt at heart, there was now no vice unre-
formed,—no external duty neglected. Drunkenness, the darling vice, was
broken off from, and scarce an instance of it known among my hearers for
months together. The abusive practice of husbands and wives in putting
away each other, and taking others in their stead, was quickly reformed ;
so that there are three or four couple who have voluntarily dismissed
those whom they had wrongfully taken, and now live together in love

and peace. The same might be said of all other vicious practices. The reformation was general ; and all springing from the internal influence of divine truths upon their hearts; and not from any external restraints, or because they had heard these vices particularly exposed, and repeatedly spoken against. Some of them I never so much as mentioned ; particularly, that of the parting of men and their wives, till some, having their conscience awakened by God's word, came, and of their own accord, confessed themselves guilty in that respect. When I at any time mentioned their wicked practices, and the sins they were guilty of contrary to the light of nature, it was not with a design, nor indeed with any hope, of working an effectual reformation in their external manners by this means for I knew, that while the tree remained corrupt the fruit would naturally be so. My design was to lead them, by observing the wickedness of their lives, to a view of the corruption of their hearts, and so to convince them of the necessity of a renovation of nature, and to excite them with the utmost diligence to seek after that great change ; which, if once obtained, I was sensible, would of course produce a reformation of external manners in every respect.

" And as all vice was reformed upon their feeling the power of these truths upon their hearts, so the external duties of Christianity were complied with, and conscientiously performed from the same internal influence ; family prayer set up, and constantly maintained, unless among some few more lately come, who had felt little of this divine influence. This duty was constantly performed, even in some families where there were none but females, and scarce a prayerless person was to be found among near an hundred of them. The Lord's day was seriously and religiously observed, and care taken by parents to keep their children orderly upon that sacred day; and this, not because I had driven them to the performance of these duties, by frequently inculcating them, but because they had felt the power of God's word upon their hearts,—were made sensible of their sin and misery, and thence could not but pray, and comply with everything which they knew to be their duty, from what they felt within themselves. When their hearts were touched with a sense of their eternal concerns, they could pray with great freedom, as well as fervency, without being at the trouble first to learn set forms for that purpose. Some of them, who were suddenly awakened at their first coming among us, were brought to pray and cry for mercy with the utmost importunity, without ever being instructed in the duty of prayer, or so much as once directed to a performance of it.

" The happy effects of these peculiar doctrines of grace, upon which I have so much insisted, upon this people plainly discover, even to demonstration, that, instead of their opening a door to licentiousness, as many vainly imagine, and slanderously insinuate, they have a directly contrary tendency ; so that a close application, a sense and feeling of them, will have the most powerful influence toward the renovation, and effectual reformation both of heart and life.

" Happy experience, as well as the word of God, and the example of Christ and his apostles, has taught me, that the very method of preaching which is best suited to awaken in mankind a sense and lively apprehension of their depravity and misery in a fallen state,—to excite them earnestly to seek after a change of heart, as to fly for refuge to free and sovereign grace in Christ as the only hope set before them, is likely to be most successful in the reformation of their external conduct.—I have found that close addresses, and solemn applications of divine truth to the conscience, strike at the root of all vice ; while smooth and plausible harangues upon moral virtues and external duties, at best are like to do no more than lop off the branches of corruption, while the root of all vice remains still untouched.

" A view of the blessed effect of honest endeavors to bring home divine truths to the conscience, and duly to affect the heart with them, has often reminded me of those words of our Lord, which I have thought might be a proper exhortation for ministers in respect of their treating with others, as well as for persons in general with regard to themselves, Cleanse first the inside of the cup and platter, that the outside may be clean also.' Cleanse, says he, the inside, that the outside may be clean. As if he had said, The only effectual way to have the outside clean, is to begin with what is within ; and if the fountain be purified, the streams will naturally be pure. Most certain it is, if we can awaken in sinners a lively sense of their inward pollution and depravity—their need of a change of heart— and so engage them to seek after inward cleansing, their external defilement will naturally be cleansed, their vicious ways of course be reformed, and their conversation and behavior become regular.

" Now, although I cannot pretend that the reformation among my people, does, in every instance, spring from a saving change of heart ; yet I may truly say, it flows from some heart-affecting view and sense of divine truths which all have had in a greater or less degree.—I do not intend, by what I have observed here, to represent the preaching of morality and pressing persons to the external performance of duty, to be altogether unnecessary and useless at any time ; and especially at times when there is less of divine power attending the means of grace; when, for want of internal influences, there is need of external restraints. It is doubtless among the things that ' ought to be done,' while 'others are not to be left undone.'—But what I principally designed by this remark, was to discover a plain matter of fact, viz. : That the reformation, the sobriety, and the external compliance with the rules and duties of Christianity, appearing among my people, are not the effect of any mere doctrinal instruction, or merely rational view of the beauty of morality, but from the internal power and influence which the soul humbling doctrines of grace have had upon their hearts.

"III. On the continuance, renewal, and quickness of the work.

"It is remarkable, that God has so continued and renewed the showers of his grace here;—so quickly set up his visible kingdom among these people; and so smiled upon them in relation to their acquirement of knowledge, both divine and human. It is now nearly a year since the beginning of this gracious outpouring of the divine Spirit among them; and although it has often seemed to decline and abate for some short space of time—as may be observed by several passages of my Journal, where I have endeavored to note things just as they appeared to me— yet the shower has seemed to be renewed, and the work of grace revived again. A divine influence seems still apparently to attend the means of grace, in a greater or less degree, in most of our meetings for religious exercises; whereby religious persons are refreshed, strengthened, and established,—convictions revived and promoted in many instances, and some few persons newly awakened from time to time. It must be acknowledged, that for some time past, there has, in general appeared a more manifest decline of this work; and the divine Spirit has seemed, in a considerable measure, withdrawn, especially with regard to his awakening influence—so that the strangers who come latterly, are not seized with concern as formerly; and some few who have been much affected with divine truths in time past, now appear less concerned. Yet, blessed be God, there is still an appearance of divine power and grace, a desirable degree of tenderness, religious affection and devotion in our assemblies.

"As God has continued and renewed the showers of his grace among this people for some time; so he has with uncommon quickness set up his visible kingdom, and gathered himself a church in the midst of them. I have now baptized, since the conclusion of my last Journal, (or the First Part,) thirty persons—fifteen adults and fifteen children. Which added to the number there mentioned, makes seventy-seven persons; whereof thirty-eight are adults, and thirty-nine children, and all within the space of eleven months past. It must be noted, that I have baptized no adults, but such as appeared to have a work of special grace wrought in their hearts; I mean such as have had the experience not only of the awakening and humbling, but in a judgment of charity, of the renewing and comfirming influences of the divine Spirit. There are many others under solemn concern for their souls who, I apprehend, are persons of sufficient knowledge, and visible seriousness, at present, to render them proper subjects of the ordinance of baptism. Yet since they give no comfortable evidence of a saving change, but only appear under convictions of their sin and misery; as the propensity in this people to abuse themselves with strong drink is naturally very great; and as some, who at present appear serious and concerned for their souls, may lose their concern, and return to this sin, and so, if baptized, prove a scandal to their profession; I have thought proper hitherto to defer their baptism.

" I likewise administered the Lord's supper to a number of persons, who I have abundant reason to think, as I elsewhere observed, were proper subjects of that ordinance, within the space of ten months and ten days, after my first coming among these Indians in New-Jersey. From the time, when, as I am informed, some of them attending an idolatrous feast and sacrifice in honor to devils, to the time when they sat down at the Lord's table, I trust to the honor of God, was not more than a full year. Surely Christ's little flock here, so suddenly gathered from among pagans, may justly say, in the language of the Church of old, ' The Lord hath done great things for us, whereof we are glad.'

" Much of the goodness of God has also appeared in relation to their acquirement of knowledge, both in religion and in the affairs of common life. There has been a wonderful thirst after Christian knowledge prevailing among them in general, and an eager desire of being instructed in Christian doctrines and manners. This has prompted them to ask many pertinent as well as important questions; the answers to which have tended much to enlighten their minds, and promote their knowledge in divine things. Many of the doctrines which I have delivered, they have queried with me about, in order to gain further light and insight into them; particularly the doctrine of predestination; and have from time to time manifested a good understanding of them, by their answers to the questions proposed to them in my catechetical lectures.

" They have likewise queried with me, respecting a proper method, as well as proper matter, of prayer, and expressions suitable to be used in that religious exercise ; and have taken pains in order to the performance of this duty with understanding. They have likewise taken pains, and appeared remarkably apt in learning to sing Psalm-tunes, and are now able to sing with a good degree of decency in the worship of God. They have also acquired a considerable degree of useful knowledge in the affairs of common life ; so that they now appear like rational creatures, fit for human society, free of that savage roughness and brutish stupidity, which rendered them very disagreeable in their pagan state.— They seem ambitious of a thorough acquaintance with the English language, and for that end frequently speak it among themselves. Many of them have made good proficiency in their acquirement of it, since my coming among them ; so that most of them can understand a considerable part, and some the substance of my discourses, without an interpreter, being used to my low and vulgar methods of expression, though they could not well understand other ministers.

"As they are desirous of instruction, and surprisingly apt in the reception of it, so divine Providence has smiled upon them with regard to the proper means in order to it. The attempts made for the procurement of a school among them have been succeeded, and a kind providence has sent them a schoolmaster of whom I may justly say, I know of 'no man like minded, who will naturally care for their state.' He has generally thirty or thirty-five children in his school : and when he kept an evening school, as he did while the length of the evenings, would admit of it, he had fifteen or twenty people, married and single.

"The children learn with surprising readiness ; so that their master tells me, he never had an English school which learned, in general, comparably so fast. There were not above two in thirty, although some of them were very small, but that learned to know all the letters in the alphabet distinctly, within three days after his entrance upon his business ; and several in that space of time learned to spell considerably. Some of them, since the beginning of Feburary last, when the school was set up, have learned so much, that they are able to read in a Psalter or Testament, without spelling.—They are instructed twice a week in the Assembly's Shorter Catechism, on Wednesday and Saturday. Some of them since the latter end of February, when they began, have learned to say it pretty distinctly by heart, considerably more than half through; and most of them have made some proficiency in it. They are likewise instructed in the duty of secret prayer, and most of them constantly attend it night and morning, and are very careful to inform their master if they apprehend that any of their little schoolmates neglect that religious exercise.

"IV. On the little appearance of false religion.

"It is worthy to be noted, to the praise of sovereign grace, that amidst so great a work of conviction—so much concern and religious affection—there has been no prevalence, nor indeed any considerable appearance of false religion, if I may so term it, or heats of imagination, intemperate zeal, and spiritual pride ; which corrupt mixtures too often attend the revival and powerful propagation of religion; and that there have been very few instances of irregular and scandalous behavior among those who have appeared serious. I may justly repeat what I formerly observed, that there has here been no appearance of 'bodily agonies, convulsions, frightful screamings, swoonings,' and the like ; and may now further add, that there has been no prevalence of visions, trances, and imaginations of any kind; although there has been some appearance of something of that nature; an instance of which I have given an account of in my diary for December 26.

"But this work of grace has, in the main, been carried on with a surprising degree of purity, and freedom from trash and corrupt mixture. The religious concern under which persons have been, has generally been

rational and just ; arising from a sense of their sins and exposedness to
the divine displeasure on account of them ; as well as their utter inability
to deliver themselves from the misery which they felt and feared. If
there has been, in any instance, an appearance of concern and perturbation of mind, when the subjects of it knew not why; yet there has been no
prevalence of any such thing ; and indeed I scarcely know of any instance
of that nature at all. It is very remarkable, that, although the concern of
many persons under convictions of their perishing state has been very
great and pressing, yet I have never seen anything like desperation attending it in any one instance. They have had the most lively sense of
their undoneness in themselves; have been brought to give up all hopes
of deliverance from themselves ; have experienced great distress and anguish of soul ; and yet, in the seasons of the greatest extremity, there has
been no appearance of despair in any of them,—nothing that has discouraged, or in anywise hindered them from the most diligent use of all proper means for their conversion and salvation. Hence it is apparent, that
there is not that danger of persons being driven into despair under spiritual trouble, unless in cases of deep and habitual melancholy, which the
world in general is ready to imagine.

" The comfort which persons have obtained after their distresses, has
likewise in general appeared solid, well grounded, and scriptural ; arising
from a spiritual and supernatural illumination of mind,—a view of divine
things, in a measure, as they are,—a complacency of soul in the divine
perfections,—and a peculiar satisfaction in the way of salvation by free
sovereign grace in the great Redeemer. Their joys have seemed to rise
from a variety of views and considerations of divine things, although for
substance the same. Some, who under conviction seemed to have the
hardest struggles and heart risings against the divine sovereignty, have
seemed, at the first dawn of their comfort, to rejoice in a peculiar manner
in that divine perfection ;—and have been delighted to think that themselves, and all things else, were in the hands of God, and that he would
dispose of them 'just as he pleased.'

"Others, who just before their reception of comfort have been remarkably oppressed with a sense of their undoneness and poverty, who
have seen themselves, as it were, falling down into remediless perdition,
have been at first more peculiarly delighted with a view of the freeness
and riches of divine grace, and the offer of salvation made to perishing
sinners ' without money, and without price.' Some have at first appeared
to rejoice especially in the wisdom of God, discovered in the way of salvation by Christ ; it then appearing to them 'a new and living way,' a way
of which they had never thought, nor had any just conceptions, until
opened to them by the special influence of the divine Spirit. Some of
them, upon a lively spiritual view of this way of salvation, have wondered

at their past folly in seeking salvation in other ways, and have wondered
that they never saw this way of salvation before, which now appeared so
plain and easy, as well as excellent to them.

" Others, again, have had a more general view of the beauty and excellency of Christ, and have had their souls delighted with an apprehension
of his divine glory, as unspeakably exceeding all of which they had ever
conceived before ; yet, without singling out any one of the divine perfections in particular ; so that although their comforts have seemed to arise
from a variety of views and considerations of divine glories, still they were
spiritual and supernatural views of them, and not groundless fancies,
which were the spring of their joys and comforts.

" Yet it must be acknowledged, that, when this work became so universal
and prevalent, and gained such general credit and esteem among the Indians as Satan seemed to have little advantage of working against it in
his own proper garb, he then transformed himself ' into an angel of light,'
and made some vigorous attempts to introduce turbulent commotions of
the passions in the room of genuine convictions of sin, imaginary and
fanciful notions of Christ, as appearing to the mental eye in a human
shape, and in some particular postures, etc. in the room of spiritual and
supernatural discoveries of his divine glory and excellency, as well as
divers other delusions. I have reason to think, that, if these things had
met with countenance and encouragement, there would have been a very
considerable harvest of this kind of converts here.

" Spiritual pride also discovered itself in various instances. Some
persons who had been under great affections, seemed very desirous from
thence of being thought truly gracious : who, when I could not but express to them my fears respecting their spiritual state, discovered their
resentments to a considerable degree upon that occasion. There also
appeared in one or two of them an unbecoming ambition of being
teachers of others. So that Satan has been a busy adversary here, as
well as elsewhere. But blessed be God, though something of this nature
has appeared, yet nothing of it has prevailed, nor indeed made any considerable progress at all. My people are now apprised of these things
are made acquainted, that Satan in such a manner ' transformed himself
into an angel of light,' in the first season of the great outpouring of the
divine Spirit in the days of the apostles ; and that something of this nature, in a greater or less degree, has attended almost every revival and
remarkable propagation of true religion ever since. They have learned
so to distinguish between the gold and dross, that the credit of the latter
' is trodden down like the mire of the streets ; ' and, as it is natural for
this kind of stuff to die with its credit, there is now scarce any appearance of it among them.

" As there has been no prevalence of irregular heats, imaginary notions, spiritual pride, and Satanical delusions among my people; so there have been very few instances of scandalous and irregular behavior among those who have made a profession, or even an appearance of serious-ness. I do not know of more than three or four such persons who have been guilty of any open misconduct, since their first acquaintance with Christianity; and not one who persists in anything of that nature. Per-haps the remarkable purity of this work in the latter respect, its freedom from frequent instances of scandal, is very much owing to its purity in the former respect, its freedom from corrupt mixtures of spiritual pride, wild fire, and delusion, which naturally lay a foundation for scandalous practices.

"May this blessed work in the power and purity of it prevail among the poor Indians here, as well as spread elsewhere, till their remotest tribes shall see the salvation of God! Amen."

[We subjoin here, in confirmation of Brainerd's own nar-rative, the following "Attestations" from ministers of emi-nence, living near the scene of his labors, and conversant with its character and results; and also from the officers of the Presbyterian Church of Freehold, N. J.—J. M. S.]

FROM REV. WILLIAM TENNENT.

"Since my dear and Rev. Brother Brainerd, has at length consented to the publication of his Journal, I gladly embrace this opportunity of testifying, that our altogether glorious Lord and Saviour, Jesus Christ, has given such a display of his almighty power and sovereign grace, not only in the ex-ternal reformation but, [in a judgment of charity,] the saving conversion of a considerable number of Indians, that it is really wonderful to all beholders! though some, alas! not-withstanding sufficient grounds of conviction to the contrary, do join with the devil, that avowed enemy of God and man, in endeavoring to prevent this glorious work, by such ways and means as are mentioned in the aforesaid Journal, to which I must refer the reader for a faithful, though very brief, account of the time when, the place where, the means by which, and manner how, this wished for work has been begun and carried on, by the great Head of the Church. This I can the more confidently do, not only because I am intimately acquainted with the author, but on account of my own personal knowledge of the matters of fact recorded in it respecting the work itself. As I live not far from the Indians, I have been much conversant with them, both at their own place, and in my own parish, where they generally convene for public worship in Mr. Brainerd's absence; and I think it my duty to acknowledge, that their conversation hath often, under God, refreshed my soul.

"To conclude, it is my opinion, that the change wrought in those savages, namely, from the darkness of paganism, to the knowledge of the pure gospel of Christ; from sacrificing to devils, to 'present themselves, body and soul, a living sacrifice to God,' and that not only from the persuasion of their minister, but from a clear heart-affecting sense of its being their reasonable service; this change I say is so great, that none could effect it but he 'who worketh all things after the good pleasure of his own will.' I would humbly hope that this is only the first fruits of a much greater harvest to be brought in from among the Indians, by him, who has promised to give his Son 'the Heathen for his inheritance, and the uttermost parts of the earth for his possession:'—who hath also declared, 'that the whole earth shall be filled with the knowledge of the Lord, as the waters cover the sea. Even so, Lord Jesus, come quickly. Amen and amen.

> "I am, courteous reader,
> "thy soul's well-wisher,
> "WILLIAM TENNENT.

"FREEHOLD, *August* 16, 1746."

FROM REV. CHARLES MACNIGHT.

"As it must needs afford a sacred pleasure to such as cordially desire the prosperity and advancement of the Redeemer's kingdom and interest in the world, to hear, that our merciful and gracious God is in very deed fulfilling such

precious promises as relate to the poor heathen, by sending
his everlasting gospel among them, which, with concurrence
of his holy Spirit, is removing that worse than Egyptian darkness, whereby the god of this world has long held them in
willing subjection; so this narrative will perhaps be more
acceptable to the world, when it is confirmed by the testimony
of such as were either eye-witnesses of this glorious dawn of
gospel-light among the benighted pagans, or personally
acquainted with those of them, in whom, in a judgment of
charity, a gracious change has been wrought. Therefore, I
the more willingly join with my brethren Mr. William
Tennent, and Mr. Brainerd, in affixing my attestation to
the foregoing narrative; and look upon myself as concerned
in point of duty both to God and his people, to do so, because
I live contiguous to their settlement, and have had frequent
opportunities of being present at their religious meetings;
where I have with pleasing wonder, beheld what I am strongly
inclined to believe were the effects of God's almighty power
accompanying his own truths; more especially, on the 8th
day of August, 1745. While the word of God was preached
by Mr. Brainerd, there appeared an uncommon solemnity
among the Indians in general; but, I am wholly unable to
give a full representation of the surprising effects of God's
almighty power which appeared among them when public
service was over. While Mr. Brainerd urged upon some of
them the absolute necessity of a speedy closure with Christ,
the holy Spirit seemed to be poured out upon them in a
plenteous measure, insomuch as the Indians present in the
wigwam seemed to be brought to the jailer's case, Acts xvi.
30, utterly unable to conceal the distress and perplexity of
their souls. This prompted the pious among them to bring
the dispersed congregation together, who soon seemed to be
in the greatest extremity. Some were earnestly begging for
mercy, under a solemn sense of their perishing condition;
while others were unable to arise from the earth, to the great
wonder of those white people that were present, one of whom

is by this means, I trust, savingly brought to Christ since. Nay, so very extraordinary was the concern which appeared among these poor Indians in general, that I am ready to conclude, it might have been sufficient to have convinced an Atheist, that the Lord was indeed in the place. I am for my part, fully persuaded that this glorious work is true and genuine, while with satisfaction I behold several of these Indians discovering all the symptoms of inward holiness in their lives and conversation. I had the satisfaction of joining with them in their service on the 11th of August, 1746: which was a day set apart for imploring the divine blessing on the labors of their minister among other tribes of Indians on the Susquehannah; in all which they conducted themselves with a very decent and becoming gravity; and as far as I am capable of judging, they may be proposed as examples of piety and godliness, to all the white people around them, which indeed is justly, 'marvelous in our eyes,' especially considering what they lately had been. Oh may the glorious God shortly bring about that desirable time, when our exalted Immanuel shall have the heathen given for his inheritance, and the uttermost parts of the earth for his possession!

"CHARLES MACNIGHT.

"CROSSWICKS, *August* 20, 1746."

FROM THE OFFICERS OF THE CHURCH OF FREEHOLD.

"We whose names are underwritten, being elders and deacons of the Presbyterian Church in Freehold, do hereby testify, that in our humble opinion, God, even our Saviour, has brought a considerable number of the Indians in these parts to a saving union with himself. Of this we are persuaded from a personal acquaintance with them; whom we not only hear speak of the great doctrines of the gospel with humility, affection, and understanding, but we see walk, as far as man can judge, soberly, righteously, and godly. We have joined with them at the Lord's supper, and do from our hearts esteem them as our brethren in Jesus. For these who were not God's people, may now be called the children of the living God ; ' it is the Lord's doing, and it is marvelous in our eyes.' Oh that he may go on 'conquering and to conquer,' until he has subdued all things to himself ! This is and shall be the unfeigned desire and prayer of,

"WALTER KER,
ROBERT CUMMINS,
DAVID RHE,
JOHN HENDERSON,
JOHN ANDERSON,
JOSEPH KER,
} *Elders.*

WILLIAM KER,
SAMUEL KER,
SAMUEL CRAIG.
} *Deacons.*

"PRESBYTERIAN CHURCH, FREEHOLD, *Aug.* 16, 1746."

CHAPTER XII.

Final stage of Brainerd's Missionary Work.—Visits the Susquehanna, and up among the Delawares.—Returns to Cranberry very much prostrated.—Continues his Work in great bodily Weakness and Suffering.

THE hardships which Brainerd had endured, had now obviously affected his constitution; and unfitted him for a life of so much toil and exposure. Of this, he appears not to have been aware, until the case had become hopeless; and unfortunately, the circumstances, in which he was placed, were calculated instead of retarding, to hasten the ravages of disease. He lived alone, in the midst of a wilderness; in a miserable hut, built by Indians; with few of the necessaries, and none of the comforts of life; at a distance from civilized society; without even a nurse or a physician. His labors, also, were sufficient to have impaired a vigorous constitution. It is not surprising, therefore, that his health was gradually, but fatally undermined.

On June 20th, as well as on the next day, he was very ill; though, with great effort, he was enabled to preach to his people on Saturday. His illness continued on the Sabbath, but he preached, notwithstanding, to his people both parts of the day; and after the public worship was ended, he endeavored to apply divine truths to the consciences of some, and addressed them personally for that end; several were in tears, and some appeared much affected. But he was extremely wearied with the services of the day, and so ill at night, that he could have no bodily rest; but remarks, that "God was his support, and that he was not left destitute of comfort in him." On Monday he continued very ill; but speaks of his mind being calm and composed, resigned to the divine dispensations, and content with his feeble state. By the account which he gives of himself, the remaining part of this week, he continued very feeble, and for the most part dejected in mind. He enjoyed no great freedom nor sweetness in spiritual things; except that for some very short spaces of time he had refreshment and encouragement, which engaged his heart on divine things; and sometimes his heart was melted with spiritual affection.

"*Lord's day, June* 29. Preached both parts of the day, from John xiv. 19: 'Yet a little while, and the world seeth me no more.' God was pleased to assist me, to afford me both freedom and power, especially towards the close of my discourse, both forenoon and afternoon. God's power appeared in the assembly, in both exercises. Numbers of God's people were refreshed and melted with divine things; one or two comforted, who had been long under distress; convictions, in divers instances, powerfully revived; and one man in years much awakened, who had not long frequented our meeting, and appeared before as stupid as a stock. God amazingly renewed and lengthened out my strength. I was so spent at noon, that I could scarce walk, and all my joints trembled; so that I could not sit, nor so much as hold my hand still; and yet God strengthened me to preach with power in the afternoon; although I had given out word to my people, that I did not expect to be able to do it. Spent some time afterward in conversing, particularly, with several persons about their spiritual state; and had some satisfaction concerning one or two. Prayed afterwards with a sick child, and gave a word of exhortation. Was assisted in all my work. Blessed be God. Returned home with more health, than I went out with; although my linen was wringing wet upon me, from a little after ten in the morning, till past five in the afternoon. My spirits also were considerably refreshed; and my soul rejoiced in hope, that I had through grace done something for God. In the evening, walked out, and enjoyed a sweet season in secret prayer and praise. But oh, I found the truth of the Psalmist's words, 'My goodness extendeth not to thee!' I could not make any returns to God; I longed to live only to him, and to be in tune for his praise and service for ever. Oh, for spirituality and holy fervency, that I might spend and be spent for God to my latest moment!

"*June* 30. Spent the day in writing; but under much weakness and disorder. Felt the labors of the preceding day; although my spirits were so refreshed the evening before, that I was not then sensible of my being spent.—July 1. In the afternoon, visited and preached to my people, from Heb. ix. 27: 'And as it is appointed unto men once to die,' etc., on occasion of some person's lying at the point of death, in my congregation. God gave me some assistance; and his word made some impressions on the audience, in general. This was an agreeable and comfortable evening to my soul ; my spirits were somewhat refreshed, with a small degree of freedom and help enjoyed in my work."

On Wednesday he went to Newark, to a meeting of the Presbytery ; complains of lowness of spirits ; and greatly laments his spending his time so unfruitfully. The remaining part of the week he spent there, and at Elizabethtown ; and speaks of comfort and divine assistance, from day to day ; but yet greatly complains for want of more spirituality.

" *Lord's day, July* 6. [At Elizabethtown.] Enjoyed some composure and serenity of mind, in the morning; heard Mr. Dickinson preach, in the forenoon, and was refreshed with his discourse; was in a melting frame some part of the time of sermon ; partook of the Lord's supper, and enjoyed some sense of divine things in that ordinance. In the afternoon I preached from Ezek. xxxiii. 11 : 'As I live, saith the Lord God,' etc. God favored me with freedom and fervency, and helped me to plead his cause beyond my own power.'

" *July* 7. My spirits were considerably refreshed and raised in the morning. There is no comfort, I find, in any enjoyment, without enjoying God, and being engaged in his service. In the evening, had the most agreeable conversation which I remember in all my life, upon God's being all in all, and all enjoyments being just that to us which God makes them, and no more. It is good to begin and end with God. Oh how does a sweet solemnity lay a foundation for true pleasure and happiness !

" *July* 8. Rode home, and enjoyed some agreeable meditations by the way.—July 9. Spent the day in writing, enjoyed some comfort and refreshing of spirit in my evening retirement.—July 10. Spent most of the day in writing. Towards night rode to Mr. Tennant's ; enjoyed some agreeable conversation ; went home in the evening, in a solemn, sweet frame of mind ; was refreshed in secret duties, longed to live wholly and only for God, and saw plainly there was nothing in the world worthy of my affection ; so that my heart was dead to all below ; yet not through dejection, as at some times, but from views of a better inheritance.

" *July* 11. Was in a calm, composed frame, in the morning, especially in the season of my secret retirement. I think, that I was well pleased with the will of God, whatever it was, or should be, in all respects of which I had then any thought. Intending to administer the Lord's supper the next Lord's day, I looked to God for his presence and assistance upon that occasion ; but felt a disposition to say, ' The will of the Lord be done,' whether it be to give me assistance, or not. Spent some little time in writing : visited the Indians, spent some time in serious conversation with them : thinking it not best to preach, many of them being absent.

"*July* 12. This day was spent in fasting and prayer by my congregation, as preparatory to the sacrament. I discoursed, both parts of the day, from Rom. iv. 25 : 'Who was delivered for our offences,' etc. God gave me some assistance in my discourses, and something of divine power attended the word; so that this was an agreeable season. Afterwards led them to a solemn renewal of their covenant, and fresh dedication of themselves to God. This was a season both of solemnity and sweetness, and God seemed to be 'in the midst of us.' Returned to my lodgings, in the evening, in a comfortable frame of mind.

"*Lord's day, July* 13. In the forenoon, discoursed on the bread of life, from John vi. 35. God gave me some assistance, in part of my discourse especially ; and there appeared some tender affection in the assembly under divine truths ; my soul also was somewhat refreshed. Administered the sacrament of the Lord's supper to thirty-one persons of the Indians. God seemed to be present in this ordinance ; the communicants were sweetly melted and refreshed, most of them. Oh how they melted, even when the elements were first uncovered! There was scarcely a dry eye among them, when I took off the linen, and showed them the symbols of Christ's broken body. Having rested a little, after the administration of the sacrament, I visited the communicants, and found them generally in a sweet loving frame ; not unlike what appeared among them on the former sacramental occasion, on April 27. In the afternoon, discoursed upon coming to Christ, and the satisfaction of those who do so, from the same verse I insisted on in the forenoon. This was likewise an agreeable season, a season of much tenderness, affection, and enlargement in divine service; and God, I am persuaded, crowned our assembly with his divine presence. I returned home much spent, yet rejoicing in the goodness of God.

"*July* 14. Went to my people, and discoursed to them from Psal. cxix. 106 : 'I have sworn, and I will perform it,' etc. Observed, 1. That all God's judgments or commandments are righteous. 2. That God's people have sworn to keep them ; and this they do especially at the Lord's table. There appeared to be a powerful divine influence on the assembly, and considerable melting under the word. Afterwards, I led them to a renewal of their covenant before God, that they would watch over themselves and one another, lest they should fall into sin and dishonor the name of Christ, just as I did on Monday, April 28. This transaction was attended with great solemnity : and God seemed to own it by exciting in them a fear and jealousy of themselves, lest they should sin against God ;

so that the presence of God seemed to be amongst us in this conclusion of the sacramental solemnity."

The next day he set out on a journey to Philadelphia; and he did not return till Saturday. He went this journey, and spent the week, under a great degree of illness of body and dejection of mind.

" *Lord's day, July* 20. Preached twice to my people from John xvii. 24: 'Father, I will that they also whom thou has given me, be with me, where I am, that they may behold my glory, which thou hast given me.' Was helped to discourse with great clearness and plainness in the forenoon. In the afternoon, enjoyed some tenderness, and spake with some influence. Numbers were in tears; and some, to appearance, in distress.

" *July* 21. Preached to the Indians, chiefly for the sake of some strangers; proposed my design of taking a journey speedily to the Susquehannah; exhorted my people to pray for me, that God would be with me in that journey; and then chose divers persons of the congregation to travel with me. Afterwards, spent some time in discoursing to the strangers, and was somewhat encouraged with them. Took care of my people's secular business, and was not a little exercised with it. Had some degree of composure and comfort in secret retirement.—July 22. Was in a dejected frame, most of the day; wanted to wear out life, and have it at an end; but had some desires of living to God, and wearing out life for him. O that I could indeed do so!"

The next day he went to Elizabethtown, to a meeting of Presbytery; and spent this, and Thursday and a part of Friday, under a very great degree of melancholy, and gloominess of mind, not through any fear of future punishment, but as being distressed with a senselessness of all good, so that the whole world appeared empty and gloomy to him. In the latter part of Friday he was greatly relieved and comforted.

" *July* 26. Was comfortable in the morning; my countenance and heart were not sad, as in days past; enjoyed some sweetness in lifting up my heart to God. Rode home to my people, and was in a comfortable, pleasant frame by the way; my spirits were much relieved of their burden, and I felt free to go through all difficulties and labors in my Master's service.

" *Lord's day, July* 27. Discoursed to my people in the forenoon, from

Luke xii. 37, on the duty and benefit of watching. God helped me in the latter part of my discourse, and the power of God appeared in the assembly. In the afternoon, discoursed from Luke xiii. 25, 'When once the master of the house is risen up,' etc. Here also I enjoyed some assistance; and the Spirit of God seemed to attend what was spoken, so that there was a great solemnity, and some tears among Indians and others.

"*July* 28. Was very weak, and scarce able to perform any business at all; but enjoyed sweetness and comfort in prayer, both morning and evening; and was composed and comfortable through the day. My mind was intense, and my heart fervent, at least in some degree, in secret duties; and I longed to spend and be spent for God.

"*July* 29. My mind was cheerful, and free from the melancholy, with which I am often exercised; had freedom in looking up to God, at various times in the day. In the evening, I enjoyed a comfortable season in secret prayer; was helped to plead with God for my own dear people, that he would carry on his own blessed work among them; was assisted also in praying for the divine presence to attend me in my intended journey to the Susquehannah; and was helped to remember dear brethren and friends in New England. I scarce knew how to leave the throne of grace, and it grieved me that I was obliged to go to bed; I longed to do something for God, but knew not how. Blessed be God for this freedom from dejection.

"*July* 30. Was uncommonly comfortable, both in body and mind; in the forenoon especially, my mind was solemn; I was assisted in my work; and God seemed to be near to me; so that the day was as comfortable as most I have enjoyed for some time. In the evening, was favored with assistance in secret prayer, and felt much as I did the evening before. Blessed be God for that freedom I then enjoyed at the throne of grace, for myself, my people, and my dear friends. It is good for me to draw near to God.

"*Aug.* 1. In the evening, enjoyed a sweet season in secret prayer; clouds of darkness and perplexing care were sweetly scattered, and nothing anxious remained. O how serene was my mind at this season! how free from that distracting concern I have often felt! 'Thy will be done,' was a petition sweet to my soul; and if God had bidden me choose for myself in any affair, I should have chosen rather to have referred the choice to him; for I saw he was infinitely wise, and could not do anything amiss, as I was in danger of doing. Was assisted in prayer for my dear flock, that God would promote his own work among them, and that God would go with me in my intended journey to the Susquehannah; was helped to remember my dear friends in New England, and my dear brethren in the ministry. I found enough in the sweet duty of prayer to have engaged me to continue in it the whole night, would my bodily state have admitted of it. O how sweet it is, to be enabled heartily to say, Lord, not my will, but thine be done.

"*Aug.* 2. Near night, preached from Matt. xi. 29, ' Take my yoke upon you, etc.' Was considerably helped; and the presence of God seemed to be somewhat remarkably in the assembly; divine truths made powerful impressions, both upon saints and sinners. Blessed be God for such a revival among us. In the evening was very weary, but found my spirits supported and refreshed.

"*Lord's day, Aug.* 3. Discoursed to my people, in the forenoon, from Col. iii. 4. and observed, that Christ is the believer's Life. God helped me, and gave me his presence' in this discourse ; and it was a season of considerable power to the assembly. In the afternoon, preached from Luke xix. 41, 42, 'And when he was come near, he beheld the city,' etc. I enjoyed some assistance ; though not so much as in the forenoon. In the evening I enjoyed freedom and sweetness in secret prayer ; God enlarged my heart, freed me from melancholy damps, and gave me satisfaction in drawing near to himself. Oh that my soul could magnify the Lord, for these seasons of composure and resignation to his will.

"*Aug.* 4. Spent the day in writing; enjoyed much freedom and assistance in my work ; was in a composed and comfortable frame, most of the day; and in the evening enjoyed some sweetness in prayer. Blessed be God, my spirits were yet up, and I was free from sinking damps ; as I have been in general ever since I came from Elizabethtown last. O what a mercy is this !

"*Aug.* 5. Towards night, preached at the funeral of one of my Christians, from Is. lvii. 2, ' He shall enter into peace, etc. I was oppressed with the nervous headache, and considerably dejected ; however, had a little freedom, some part of the time I was discoursing. Was extremely weary in the evening ; but notwithstanding, enjoyed some liberty and cheerfulness of mind in prayer ; and found the dejection that I feared, much removed, and my spirits considerably refreshed.

"*Aug.* 7. Rode to my house, where I spent the last winter, in order to bring some things I needed for my Susquehannah journey; was refreshed to see that place, which God so marvellously visited with the showers of his grace. O how amazing did the power of God often appear there ! Bless the Lord, O my soul, and forget not all his benefits.

"*Aug.* 9. In the afternoon, visited my people ; set their affairs in order, as much as possible, and contrived for them the management of their worldly business : discoursed to them in a solemn manner and concluded with prayer. Was comfortable in the evening, and somewhat fervent in secret prayer ; had some sense and view of the eternal world and found a serenity of mind. O that I could magnify the Lord for any freedom which he affords me in prayer !

"*Lord's day, Aug.* 10. Discoursed to my people, both parts of the day, from Acts iii. 19, ' Repent ye therefore,' etc. In discoursing of repentance, in the forenoon, God helped me, so that my discourse was searching ; some were in tears, both of the Indians and white people, and the word of God was attended with some power. In the intermission, I was engaged in discoursing to some in order to their baptism ; as well as with one who had then lately met with some comfort, after spiritual trouble and distress. In the afternoon, was somewhat assisted again, though weak and weary. Afterwards baptized six persons ; three adults and three children. Was in a comfortable frame in the evening, and enjoyed some satisfaction in secret prayer. I scarce ever in my life felt myself so full of tenderness, as this day.

"*Aug.* 11. Being about to set out on a journey to the Susquehannah the next day, with leave of Providence, I spent some time this day in prayer with my people, that God would bless and succeed my intended journey, that he would send forth his blessed Spirit with his word, and set up his kingdom among the poor Indians in the wilderness. While I was opening and applying part of the cxth and iid Psalms, the power of God seemed to descend on the assembly in some measure ; and while I was making the first prayer, numbers were melted, and found some affectionate enlargement of soul myself. Preached from Acts iv. 31, 'And when they had prayed the place was shaken,' etc. God helped me, and my interpreter also ; there was a shaking and melting among us ; and divers, I doubt not, were in some measure ' filled with the Holy Ghost.' Afterwards, Mr. Macnight prayed ; and I then opened the two last stanzas of the lxxiid Psalm ; at which time God was present with us ; especially while I insisted upon the promise of all nations blessing the great Redeemer. My soul was refreshed to think that this day, this blessed glorious season, should surely come ; and, I trust, numbers of my dear people were also refreshed. Afterwards prayed ; had some freedom, but was almost spent ; then walked out, and left my people to carry on religious exercises among themselves. They prayed repeatedly, and sung, while I rested and refreshed myself. Afterwards, went to the meeting, prayed with, and dismissed the assembly. Blessed be God, this has been a day of grace. There were many tears and affectionate sobs among us this day. In the evening, my soul was refreshed in prayer ; enjoyed liberty at the throne of grace, in praying for my people and friends, and the Church of God in general. Bless the Lord, O my soul."

The next day he set out on his journey to the Susque-

hannah, with six of his Christian Indians with him, whom he
had chosen out of his congregation as those he judged most
fit to assist in the business he was going upon. He took his
way through Philadelphia ; intending to go to the Susquehannah far down, where it is settled by the white people, and so
to travel up the river to the Indian habitations. This was
much farther about, yet he avoided the mountains, and hideous
wilderness, that he had encountered in the nearer ways. He
rode this week as far as Charlestown, about thirty miles westward of Philadelphia, where he arrived on Friday ; and in
his way hither, was, for the most part, in a composed, comfortable state of mind.

" *Aug.* 16. [At Charlestown.] It being a day kept by the people of
the place where I now was, as preparatory to the celebration of the Lord's
supper, I tarried ; heard Mr. Treat preach ; and then preached myself.
God gave me some good degree of freedom, and helped me to discourse
with warmth and application, to the conscience. Afterwards, I was refreshed in spirit, though much tried ; and spent the evening agreeably,
having some freedom in prayer, as well as Christian conversation.

" *Lord's day, Aug.* 17. Enjoyed liberty, composure, and satisfaction,
in the secret duties of the morning ; had my heart somewhat enlarged in
prayer for dear friends, as well as for myself. In the forenoon attended
Mr. Treat's preaching, partook of the Lord's supper, five of my people
also communicating in this holy ordinance ; I enjoyed some enlargement
and outgoing of soul in this season. In the afternoon preached from
Ezek. xxxiii. 11, ' Say unto them, as I live, saith the Lord God,' etc.
Enjoyed not so much sensible assistance as the day before ; however, was
helped to some fervency in addressing immortal souls. Was somewhat
confounded in the evening, because I thought I had done little or nothing
for God ; yet enjoyed some refreshment of spirit in Christian conversation
and prayer. Spent the evening till near midnight, in religious exercises ;
and found my bodily strength, which was much spent when I came from
the public worship, something renewed before I went to bed.

" *Aug.* 18. Rode on my way towards Paxton, on the Susquehannah.
Felt my spirits sink towards night, so that I had little comfort.—Aug. 19.
Rode forward still ; and at night lodged by the side of the Susquehannah.
Was weak and disordered both this and the preceding day, and found my
spirits considerably damped, meeting with none that I thought godly
people.

" *Aug.* 20. Having lain in a cold sweat all night, I coughed much bloody matter this morning, and was under great disorder of body, and not a little melancholy ; but what gave me some encouragement was, I had a secret hope that I might speedily get a dismission from earth, and all its toils and sorrows. Rode this day to one Chamber's, upon the Susquehannah, and there lodged. Was much afflicted in the evening, with an ungodly crew, drinking, swearing, etc. O what a hell would it be, to be numbered with the ungodly ! Enjoyed some agreeable conversation with a traveller, who seemed to have some relish of true religion.

"*Aug.* 21. Rode up the river about fifteen miles and there lodged in a family which appeared quite destitute of God. Labored to discourse with the man about the life of religion, but found him very artful in evading such conversation. O what a death it is to some, to hear of the things of God ! Was out of my element ; but was not so dejected as at some times.

"*Aug.* 22. Continued my course up the river ; my people now being with me, who before were parted from me; travelled above all the English settlements ; at night lodged in the open woods and slept with more comfort than while among an ungodly company of white people. Enjoyed some liberty in secret prayer, this evening; and was helped to remember dear friends, as well as my dear flock, and the church of God in general.

"*Aug.* 23. Arrived at the Indian town, called Shaumoking, near night, was not so dejected as formerly ; but yet somewhat exercised. Felt somewhat composed in the evening ; enjoyed some freedom in leaving my all with God. Through the great goodness of God, I enjoyed some liberty of mind ; and was not distressed with a despondency, as frequently heretofore.

"*Lord's day, Aug.* 24. Towards noon, visited some of the Delawares, and discoursed with them about Christianity. In the afternoon discoursed to the king, and others, upon divine things ; who seemed disposed to hear. Spent most of the day in these exercises. In the evening enjoyed some comfort and satisfaction ; and especially had some sweetness in secret prayer. This duty was made so agreeable to me, that I loved to walk abroad, and repeatedly engage in it. Oh, how comfortable is a little glimpse of God !

"*Aug.* 25. Spent most of the day in writing. Sent out my people that were with me, to talk with the Indians, and contract a friendship and familiarity with them, that I might have a better opportunity of treating with them about Christianity. Some good seemed to be done by their visit this day, divers appeared willing to hearken to Christianity. My spirits were a little refreshed this evening ; and I found some liberty and satisfaction in prayer.

"*Aug.* 26. About noon, discoursed to a considerable number of Indians. God helped me, I am persuaded ; for I was enabled to speak with much plainness, and some warmth and power ; and the discourse had impression upon some, and made them appear very serious. I thought things now appeared as encouraging, as they did at Crossweeks. At the time of my first visit to those Indians, I was a little encouraged ; I pressed things with all my might ; and called out my people, who were then present, to give in their testimony for God ; which they did. Towards night, was refreshed ; had a heart to pray for the setting up of God's kingdom here, as well as for my dear congregation below, and my dear friends elsewhere.

"*Aug.* 27. There having been a thick smoke in the house where I lodged all night before, whereby I was almost choked, I was this morning distressed with pains in my head and neck, and could have no rest. In the morning, the smoke was still the same ; and a cold easterly storm gathering, I could neither live within doors, nor without, a long time together. I was pierced with the rawness of the air abroad, and in the house distressed with the smoke. I was this day in great distress, and had not health enough to do anything to any purpose.

"*Aug.* 28. In the afternoon, I was under great concern of mind about my work. Was visited by some who desired to hear me preach ; discoursed to them, in the afternoon, with some fervency, and labored to persuade them to turn to God. Was full of concern for the kingdom of Christ, and found some enlargement of soul in prayer, both in secret and in my family. Scarce ever saw more clearly, than this day, that it is God's work to convert souls, and especially poor heathens. I knew, I could not touch them ; I saw I could only speak to dry bones, but could give them no sense of what I said. My eyes were up to God for help ; I could say the work was his ; and if done, the glory would be his.

"*Aug.* 29. Felt the same concern of mind, as the day before. Enjoyed some freedom in prayer, and a satisfaction to leave all with God. Travelled to the Delawares, found few at home, felt poorly ; but was able to spend some time alone in reading God's word and in prayer, and enjoyed some sweetness in these exercises. In the evening, was assisted repeatedly in prayer, and found some comfort in coming to the throne of grace.—Aug. 30. Spent the forenoon in visiting a trader, who came down the river sick ; and who appeared as ignorant as any Indian. In the afternoon spent some time in reading, writing, and prayer.

"*Lord's day, Aug.* 31. Spent much time in the morning in secret duties ; found a weight upon my spirits, and could not but cry to God with concern and engagement of soul. Spent some time also in reading and expounding God's word to my dear family which was with me, as well as in singing and prayer with them. Afterwards spake the word of God, to some few of the Susquehannah Indians. In the afternoon, felt very weak and feeble. Near night, was somewhat refreshed in mind, with some views of things relating to my great work. O how heavy is my work, when faith cannot take hold of an almighty arm, for the performance of it ! Many times have I been ready to sink in this case. Blessed be God that I may repair to a full fountain ?

"*Sept.* 1. Set out on a journey towards a place called The Great Island, about fifty miles distant from Shaumoking, on the northwestern branch of the Susquehannah. Travelled some part of the way, and at night lodged in the woods. Was exceedingly feeble this day, and sweat much the night following.

"*Sept.* 2. Rode forward ; but no faster than my people went on foot. Was very weak, on this as well as the preceding days. I was so feeble and faint, that I feared it would kill me to lie out in the open air ; and some of our company being parted from us, so that we now had no axe with us, I had no way but to climb into a young pine tree, and with my knife to lop the branches, and so made a shelter from the dew. But the evening being cloudy, and very likely for rain, I was still under fears of being extremely exposed ; sweat much in the night so that my linen was almost wringing wet all night. I scarcely ever was more weak and weary, than this evening, when I was able to sit up at all. This was a melancholy situation I was in ; but I endeavored to quiet myself with considerations of the possibility of my being in much worse circumstances, among enemies, etc.

"*Sept.* 3. Rode to the Delaware-town ; found divers drinking and drunken. Discoursed with some of the Indians about Christianity ; observed my interpreter much engaged and assisted in his work ; some few persons seemed to hear with great earnestness and engagement of soul. About noon, rode to a small town of Shauwaunoes, about eight miles distant; spent an hour or two there, and returned to the Delaware-town, and lodged there. Was scarce ever more confounded with a sense of my own unfruitfulness and unfitness for my work, than now. O what a dead, heartless, barren, unprofitable wretch did I now see myself to be ! My spirits were so low, and my bodily strength so wasted, that I could do nothing at all. At length, being much overdone, lay down on a buffalo-skin ; but sweat much the whole night.

"*Sept.* 4. Discoursed with the Indians, in the morning, about Christianity ; my interpreter, afterwards, carrying on the discourse to a considerable length. Some few appeared well disposed, and somewhat affected. Left this place, and returned towards Shaumoking ; and at night lodged in the place where I lodged the Monday night before ; was in very uncomfortable circumstances in the evening, my people being belated, and not coming to me till past ten at night ; so that I had no fire to dress any victuals, or to keep me warm, or to keep off wild beasts ; and I was scarce ever more weak and worn out in all my life. However, I lay down and slept before my people came up, expecting nothing else but to spend the whole night alone, and without fire.

" *Sept.* 5. Was exceeding weak, so that I could scarcely ride ; it seemed sometimes as if I must fall off from my horse, and lie in the open woods ; however, got to Shaumoking, towards night ; felt somewhat of a spirit of thankfulness, that God had so far returned to me; was refreshed to see one of my Christians, whom I left here in my late excursion.

" *Sept.* 6. Spent the day in a very weak state ; coughing and spitting blood, and having little appetite for any food I had with me ; was able to do very little, except discourse a while of divine things to my own people, and to some few I met with. Had, by this time, very little life or heart to speak for God, through feebleness of body, and flatness of spirits. Was scarcely ever more ashamed and confounded in myself, than now. I was sensible, that there were numbers of God's people, who knew I was then out upon a design, or at least the pretence of doing something for God, and in his cause, among the poor Indians ; and they were ready to suppose, that I was fervent in spirit ; but O the heartless frame of mind that I felt filled me with confusion ! O methought if God's people knew me, as God knows, they would not think so highly of my zeal and resolution for God, as perhaps now they do ! I could not but desire they should see how heartless and irresolute I was, that they might be undeceived, and ' not think of me above what they ought to think.' And yet I thought, if they saw the utmost of my flatness and unfaithfulness, the smallness of my courage and resolution for God, they would be ready to shut me out of their doors, as unworthy of the company or friendship of Christians.

" *Lord's day, Sept.* 7. Was much in the same weak state of body, and afflicted frame of mind, as in the preceding day; my soul was grieved, and mourned that I could do nothing for God. Read and expounded some part of God's word to my own dear family, and spent some time in prayer with them ; discoursed also a little to the pagans ; but spent the Sabbath with a little comfort.

" *Sep.* 8. Spent the forenoon among the Indians ; in the afternoon, left Shaumoking, and returned down the river, a few miles. Had proposed to have tarried a considerable time longer among the Indians upon the Susquehannah ; but was hindered from pursuing my purpose by the sickness that prevailed there, the weakly circumstances of my own people that were with me, and especially my own extraordinary weakness, having been exercised with great nocturnal sweats, and a coughing up of blood, almost the whole of the journey. I was a great part of the time so feeble and faint, that it seemed as though I never should be able to reach home ; and at the same time very destitute of the comforts, and even the necessaries of life ; at least, what was necessary for one in so weak a state. In this journey I sometimes was enabled to speak the word of God with some power, and divine truths made some impressions on divers who heard me ; so that several, both men and women, old and young, seemed to cleave to us, and be well disposed towards Christianity ; but others mocked and shouted, which damped those who before seemed friendly, at least some of them.   Yet God, at times, was evidently present, assisting me, my interpreter, and other dear friends who were with me.   God gave, sometimes, a good degree of freedom in prayer for the ingathering of souls there ; and I could not but entertain a strong hope, that the journey should not be wholly fruitless.   Whether the issue of it would be the setting up of Christ's kingdom there, or only the drawing of some few persons down to my congregation in New Jersey ; or whether they were now only being prepared for some further attempts, that might be made among them, I did not determine ; but I was persuaded, the journey would not be lost.   Blessed be God, that I had any encouragement and hope.

"*Sept.* 9.   Rode down the river, near thirty miles.   Was extremely weak, much fatigued, and wet with a thunderstorm.   Discoursed with some warmth and closeness to some poor ignorant souls, on the life and power of religion ; what were, and what were not the evidences of it. They seemed much astonished, when they saw my Indians ask a blessing, and give thanks at dinner ; concluding that a very high evidence of grace in them ; but were astonished, when I insisted that neither that, nor yet secret prayer, was any sure evidence of grace.   O the ignorance of the world !   How are some empty outward forms, that may all be entirely selfish, mistaken for true religion, infallible evidences of it.   The Lord pity a deluded world !

"*Sept.* 10.   Rode near twenty miles homeward.   Was much solicited to preach, but was utterly unable, through bodily weakness.   Was extremely overdone with the heat and showers this day, and coughed up a considerable quantity of blood.—Sept. 11.   Rode homeward ; but was very weak, and sometimes scarcely able to ride.   Had a very importunate invitation to preach at a meeting-house I came by, the people being then gathering ; but could not, by reason of weakness.   Was resigned and composed under my weakness ; but was much exercised with concern for my companions in travel, whom I had left with much regret, some lame, and some sick.—Sept. 12.   Rode about fifty miles ; and came, just at night, to a Christian friend's house, about twenty-five miles westward from Philadelphia.   Was courteously received, and kindly entertained, and found myself much refreshed in the midst of my weakness and fatigues. —Sept. 13.   Was still agreeably entertained with Christian friendship, and all things necessary for my weak circumstances.   In the afternoon, heard

Mr. Treat preach; and was refreshed in conversation with him in the evening.

"*Lord's day, Sept.* 14. At the desire of Mr. Treat and the people, I preached both parts of the day from Luke xiv. 23. And the Lord said unto the servant, go out, etc. God gave me some freedom and warmth in my discourse ; and I trust, helped me in some measure to labor in singleness of heart. Was much tired in the evening, but was comforted with the most tender treatment I ever met with in my life. My mind, through the whole of this day, was exceeding calm; and I could ask for nothing in prayer, with any encouragement of soul, but that 'the will of God might be done.'

"*Sept.* 15. Spent the whole day, in concert with Mr. Treat, in endeavors to compose a difference, subsisting between certain persons in the congregation where we now were ; and there seemed to be a blessing on our endeavors. In the evening, baptized a child; was in a calm, composed frame ; and enjoyed, I trust, a spiritual sense of divine things, while administering the ordinance. Afterwards, spent the time in religious conversation, till late in the night. This was indeed a pleasant, agreeable evening.

"*Sept.* 16. Continued still at my friend's house, about twenty-five miles westward of Philadelphia. Was very weak, unable to perform any business, and scarcely able to sit up.—Sept. 17. Rode into Philadelphia. Still very weak, and my cough and spitting of blood continued. Enjoyed some agreeable conversation with friends, but wanted more spirituality.

"*Sept.* 18. Went from Philadelphia to Mr. Treat's ; was agreeably entertained on the road ; and was in a sweet, composed frame in the evening.—Sept. 19. Rode from Mr. Treat's to Mr. Stockston's, at Princeton: was extremely weak, but kindly received and entertained. Spent the evening with some degree of satisfaction.

"*Sept.* 20. Arrived among my own people, near Cranberry, just at night; found them praying together ; went in, and gave them some account of God's dealings with me and my companions in the journey; which seemed affecting to them. I then prayed with them, and thought the divine presence was amongst us ; divers were melted into tears, and seemed to have a sense of divine things. Being very weak, I was obliged soon to repair to my lodgings, and felt much worn out, in the evening. Thus God has carried me through the fatigues and perils of another journey to the Susquehannah, and returned me again in safety, though under a great degree of bodily indisposition. Oh that my soul were truly thankful for renewed instances of mercy! Many hardships and distresses I endured in this journey, but the Lord supported me under them all."

Hitherto Brainerd had kept a constant diary, giving an

account of what passed from day to day, with very little interruption ; but henceforward his diary is very much interrupted
by his illness ; under which he was often brought so low, as
either not to be capable of writing, or not well able to bear
the burden of a care so constant as was requisite to recollect, every evening, what had passed in the day, and digest it,
and set down an orderly account of it in writing.   However,
his diary was not wholly neglected, but he took care, from
time to time, to take some notice in it of the most material
things concerning himself and the state of his mind, even till
within a few days of his death.

"*Lord's day, Sept.* 21, 1746.   I was so weak that I could not preach,
nor pretend to ride over to my people in the forenoon.   In the afternoon
rode out ; sat in my chair, and discoursed to my people from Rom. xiv.
7, 8.   For none of us liveth to himself, etc.   I was strengthened and
helped in my discourse ; and there appeared something agreeable in the
assembly,   I returned to my lodgings extremely tired, but thankful, that
I had been enabled to speak a word to my poor people, from whom I had
been so long absent.   Was enabled to sleep very little this night, through
weariness and pain.   O how blessed should I be, if the little I do were
all done with right views ! Oh that, 'whether I live, I might live to the
Lord or whether I die, I might die unto the Lord ; that, whether living
or dying, I might be the Lord's !'

"*Sept.* 27.   Spent this day as well as the whole week past, under a
great degree of bodily weakness, exercised with a violent cough, and a
considerable fever.   I had no appetite for any kind of food; and frequently brought up what I ate, as soon as it was down; oftentimes had
little rest in my bed, owing to pains in my breast and back.   I was able,
however, to ride over to my people, about two miles, every day, and take
some care of those who were then at work upon a small house for me to
reside in among the Indians.   I was sometimes scarce able to walk, and
never able to sit up the whole day, through the week.   Was calm and
composed, and but little exercised with melancholy, as in former seasons of
weakness.   Whether I should ever recover or no, seemed very doubtful ;
but this was many times a comfort to me, that life and death did not depend upon my choice.   I was pleased to think, that he who is infinitely
wise, had the determination of this matter : and that I had no trouble to
consider and weigh things upon all sides, in order to make the choice,
whether I should live or die.   Thus my time was consumed; I had little
strength to pray, none to write or read, and scarce any to meditate ; but
through divine goodness, I cou'd with great composure look death in the

face, and frequently with sensible joy. O how blessed it is, to be habitually prepared for death ! The Lord grant, that I may be actually ready also!

"*Lord's day, Sept.* 28.   Rode to my people ; and, though under much weakness, attempted to preach from 2 Cor. xiii. 5. ' Examine yourselves,' etc.   Discoursed about half an hour; at which season divine power seemed to attend the word ; but being extremely weak, I was obliged to desist ; and after a turn of faintness, with much difficulty rode to my lodgings; where betaking myself to my bed, I lay in a burning fever, and almost delirous, for several hours, till towards morning my fever went off with a violent sweat.   I have often been feverish, and unable to rest quietly after preaching, but this was the most severe, distressing turn, that ever preaching brought upon me.   Yet I felt perfectly at rest in my own mind, because I had made my utmost attempts to speak for God, and knew I could do no more.

"*Sept.* 30.   Yesterday and to-day, was in the same weak state, or rather weaker than in days past ; was scarce able to sit up half the day. Was in a composed frame of mind, remarkably free from dejection and melancholy ; as God has been pleased, in a great measure, to deliver me from these unhappy glooms, in the general course of my present weakness hitherto, and also from a peevish froward spirit.   And O how great a mercy is this !   Oh that I might always be perfectly quiet in seasons of greatest weakness, although nature should sink and fail !   Oh that I may always be able with the utmost sincerity to say, ' Lord, not my will, but thine be done ! '   This, through grace, I can say at present, with regard to life or death, ' The Lord do with me as seems good in his sight ; ' that whether I live or die, I may glorify Him, who is ' worthy to receive blessing, and honor, and dominion forever.   Amen.'

"*Oct.* 4.   Spent the former part of this week under a great degree of infirmity and disorder, as I had done several weeks before; was able, however, to ride a little every day, although unable to sit up half the day, till Thursday.   Took some care daily of some persons at work upon my house.   On Friday afternoon, found myself wonderfully revived and strengthened.   Having some time before given notice to my people, and those of them at the Forks of Delaware in particular, that I designed, with the leave of Providence, to administer the sacrament of the Lord's supper upon the first Sabbath in October on Friday afternoon I preached preparatory to the sacrament, from 2 Cor. xiii. 5; finishing what I proposed to offer upon the subject the Sabbath before.   The sermon was blessed of God to the stirring up religious affection, and a spirit of devotion, in the people of God ; and to greatly affecting one who had backslidden from God, which caused him to judge and condemn himself.   I was surprisingly strengthened in my work, while I was speaking ; but was obliged immediately after to repair to bed, being now removed into my own house among the Indians; which gave me such speedy relief and refreshment, as I could not well have lived without. Spent some time on Friday night in conversing with my people about divine things, as I lay upon my bed ; and found my soul refreshed, though my body was weak. This being Saturday, I discoursed particularly with divers of the communicants; and this afternoon preached from Zech. xii. 10. 'And I will pour on the house of David,' etc. There seemed to be a tender melting, and hearty mourning for sin, in numbers in the congregation. My soul was in a comfortable frame, and I enjoyed freedom and assistance in public service ; was myself, as well as most of the congregation, much affected with the humble confession, and apparent broken-heartedness of the forementioned backslider ; and could not but rejoice, that God had given him such a sense of his sin and unworthiness. Was extremely tired in the evening ; but lay on my bed, and discoursed to my people.

"*Lord's day, Oct* 5. Was still very weak ; and in the morning considerably afraid I should not be able to go through the work of the day; having much to do, both in private and public. Discoursed before the administration of the sacrament, from John i. 29. 'Behold the Lamb of God, that taketh away the sins of the world.' Where I considered, I. In what respects Christ is called the Lamb of God : and observed that he is so called, (1.) From the purity and innocency of his nature. (2.) From his meekness and patience under sufferings. (3.) From his being that atonement which was pointed out in the sacrifice of the lambs, and in particular by the paschal lamb. II. Considered how and in what sense he 'takes away the sin of the world :' and observed, that the means and manner, in and by which he takes away the sins of men, was his 'giving himself for them,' doing and suffering in their room and stead, etc. And he is said to take away the sin of the world, not because all the world shall actually be redeemed from sin by him ; but because, (1.) He has done and suffered sufficient to answer for the sins of the world, and so to redeem all mankind. (2.) He actually does take away the sins of the elect world. And, III. Considered how we are to behold him, in order to have our sins taken away : (1.) Not with our bodily eyes. Nor, (2.) By imagining him on the cross, etc. But by a spiritual view of his glory and goodness, engaging the soul to rely on him, etc. The divine presence attended this discourse, and the assembly was considerably melted with divine truths. After sermon, baptized two persons. Then administered the Lord's supper to near forty communicants, of the Indians, besides divers dear Christians of the white people. It seemed to be a season of divine power and grace ; and numbers seemed to rejoice in God. O the sweet union and harmony then appearing among the religious people! My soul was refreshed, and my religious friends, of the white people, with me. After the sacrament, could scarcely get home, though it was not more than twenty roods; but was supported and led by my friends, and laid on my bed; where I lay in pain till some time in the evening; and then was able to sit up and discourse with friends. O how was this day spent in prayers and praises among my dear people! One might hear them, all the morning before public worship, and in the evening, till near midnight, praying and singing praises to God, in one or other of their houses. My soul was refreshed, though my body was weak."

This week, in two days, though in a very low state, he went to Elizabethtown, to attend the meeting of the Synod there; but was disappointed by its removal to New York. He continued in a very composed, comfortable frame of mind.

" *Oct.* 11. Towards night was seized with an ague, which was followed with a hard fever, and considerable pain; was treated with great kindness; and was ashamed to see so much concern about so unworthy a creature, as I knew myself to be. Was in a comfortable frame of mind, wholly submissive, with regard to life or death. It was indeed a peculiar satisfaction to me, to think, that it was not my concern or business to determine whether I should live or die. I likewise felt peculiarly satisfied, while under this uncommon degree of disorder; being now fully convinced of my being really weak, and unable to perform my work. Whereas at other times my mind was perplexed with fears, that I was a misimprover of time, by conceiting I was sick, when I was not in reality so. O how precious is time! And how guilty it makes me feel, when I think that I have trifled away and misimproved it, or neglected to fill up each part of it with duty, to the utmost of my ability and capacity!

" *Lord's day, Oct.* 12. Was scarcely able to sit up in the forenoon; in the afternoon, attended public worship, and was in a composed, comfortable frame.—Lord's day, Oct. 19. Was scarcely able to do anything at all in the week past, except that on Thursday I rode out about four miles; at which time I took cold. As I was able to do little or nothing, so I enjoyed not much spirituality, or lively religious affection; though at some times I longed much to be more fruitful and full of heavenly affection; and was grieved to see the hours slide away, while I could do nothing for God. Was able this week to attend public worship. Was composed and comfortable, willing either to die or live; but found it hard to be reconciled to the thoughts of living useless. Oh that I might never live to be a burden to God's creation; but that I might be allowed to repair home, when my sojourning work is done!"

This week he went back to his Indians at Cranberry, to take some care of their spiritual and temporal concerns ; and was much spent with riding, though he rode but a little way in a day.

"*Oct.* 23. Went to my own house, and set things in order. Was very weak, and somewhat melancholy ; labored to do something, but had no strength ; and was forced to lie down on my bed, very solitary.—Oct. 24. Spent the day in overseeing and directing my people, about mending their fence, and securing their wheat. Found that all their concerns of a secular nature depended upon me. Was somewhat refreshed in the evening, having been able to do something valuable in the day-time. O how it pains me, to see time pass away, when I can do nothing to any purpose !—Oct. 25. Visited some of my people; spent some time in writing, and felt much better in body, than usual. When it was near night, I felt so well, that I had thoughts of expounding ; but in the evening was much disordered again, and spent the night in coughing and spitting blood.

"*Lord's day, Oct.* 26. In the morning was exceedingly weak ; spent the day, till near night, in pain, to see my poor people wandering as sheep not having a shepherd, waiting and hoping to see me able to preach to them before night. It could not but distress me, to see them in this case, and to find myself unable to attempt anything for their spiritual benefit. But towards night, finding myself a little better, I called them together to my house, and sat down, and read and expounded Matt. v. 1-16. This discourse, though delivered in much weakness, was attended with power to many of the hearers ; especially what was spoken upon the last of these verses ; where I insisted on the infinite wrong done to religion, by having our light become darkness, instead of shining before men. Many in the congregation were now deeply affected with a sense of their deficiency with respect to spiritual conversation, which might recommend religion to others, and a spirit of concern and watchfulness seemed to be excited in them. One, in particular, who had fallen in the sin of drunkenness some time before, was now deeply convinced of his sin, and the great dishonor done to religion by his misconduct, and discovered a great degree of grief and concern on that account. My soul was refreshed to see this. And though I had no strength to speak so much as I would have done, but was obliged to lie down on the bed ; yet I rejoiced to see such an humble melting in the congregation; and that divine truths, though faintly delivered, were attended with so much efficacy upon the auditory.

"*Oct.* 27. Spent the day in overseeing and directing the Indians about mending the fence round their wheat ; was able to walk with them and contrive their business, all the forenoon. In the afternoon, was visited by two dear friends, and spent some time in conversation with them. Towards night, I was able to walk out, and take care of the Indians again. In the evening, enjoyed a very peaceful frame.

"*Oct.* 28. Rode to Princeton, in a very weak state; had such a violent fever, by the way, that I was forced to alight at a friend's house, and lie down for some time. Near night, was visited by Mr. Treat, Mr. Beaty, and his wife, and another friend. My spirits were refreshed to see them; but I was surprised, and even ashamed, that they had taken so much pains as to ride thirty or forty miles to see me. Was able to sit up most of the evening; and spent the time in a very comfortable manner with my friends.

"*Oct.* 29. Rode about ten miles with my friends who came yesterday to see me; and then parted with them all but one, who stayed on purpose to keep me company, and cheer my spirits. Was extremely weak, and very feverish, especially towards night; but enjoyed comfort and satisfaction.—Oct. 30. Rode three or four miles, to visit Mr. Wales; spent some time, in an agreeable manner, in conversation; and though extremely weak, enjoyed a comfortable, composed frame of mind.—Oct. 31. Spent the day among friends, in a comfortable frame of mind, though exceedingly weak, and under a considerable fever.—Nov. 1. Took leave of friends after having spent the forenoon with them, and returned home to my own house. Was much disordered in the evening, and oppressed with my cough; which has now been constant for a long time, with a hard pain in my breast, and fever.

Lord's day, Nov. 2. Was unable to preach, and scarcely able to sit up, the whole day. Was grieved, and almost sunk, to see my poor people destitute of the means of grace; especially as they could not read, and so were under great disadvantages for spending the Sabbath comfortably. O, methought, I could be contented to be sick, if my poor flock had a faithful pastor to feed them with spiritual knowledge! A view of their want of this was more afflictive to me, than all my bodily illness.

"*Nov.* 3. Being now in so weak and low a state, that I was utterly incapable of performing my work, and having little hope of recovery, unless by much riding, I thought it my duty to take a long journey into New England, and to divert myself among my friends, whom I had not now seen for a long time. Accordingly I took leave of my congregation this day. Before I left my people, I visited them all in their respective houses, and discoursed to each one, as I thought most proper and suitable for their circumstances, and found great freedom and assistance in so doing. I scarcely left one house but some were in tears; and many were not only affected with my being about to leave them, but with the solemn addresses I made them upon divine things ; for I was helped to be fervent in spirit, while I discoursed to them.—When I had thus gone through my congregation, which took me most of the day, and, had taken leave of them, and of the school, I left home, and rode about two miles, to the house where I lived in the summer past, and there lodged. Was refreshed this evening, because I had left my congregation so well-disposed, and affected, and had been so much assisted in making my farewell addresses to them.

"*Nov.* 4. Rode to Woodbridge, and lodged with Mr. Pierson ; continuing still in a very weak state.—Nov. 5. Rode to Elizabethtown ; intending, as soon as possible, to prosecute my journey into New England. But was, in an hour or two after my arrival, taken much worse.—After this, for near a week, I was confined to my chamber, and most of the time to my bed ; and then so far revived as to be able to walk about the house ; but was still confined within doors.

" In the beginning of this extraordinary turn of disorder, after my coming to Elizabethtown, I was enabled through mercy to maintain a calm, composed, and patient spirit, as I had been before from the beginning of my weakness. After I had been in Elizabethtown about a fortnight, and had so far recovered that I was able to walk about the house, upon a day of thanksgiving kept in this place, I was enabled to recall and recount over the mercies of God, in such a manner as greatly affected me, and filled me with thankfulness and praise. Especially my soul praised God for his work of grace among the Indians, and the enlargement of his dear kingdom. My soul blessed God for what he is in himself, and adored him, that he ever would display himself to creatures. I rejoiced that he was God, and longed that all should know it, and feel it, and rejoice in it. 'Lord, glorify thyself,' was the desire and cry of my soul. O that all people might love and praise the blessed God; that he might have all possible honor and glory from the intelligent world!

" After this comfortable thanksgiving season, I frequently enjoyed freedom, enlargement, and engagedness of soul in prayer, and was enabled to intercede with God for my dear congregation, very often for every family, and every person, in particular. It was often a great comfort to me, that I could pray heartily to God for those, to whom I could not speak, and whom I was not allowed to see. But at other times, my spirits were so flat and low, and my bodily vigor so much wasted that I had scarce any affections at all."

During his confinement at Elizabethtown, Brainerd wrote the following letter to his youngest brother, then a student at Yale College.

ELIZABETHTOWN, NEW JERSEY, *Nov.* 24, 1746.

"DEAR BROTHER :

" I had determined to make you and my other friends in New England a visit, this fall ; partly from an earnest desire I had to see you and them, and partly with a view 'o the recovery of my health; which has for more than three months past, been much impaired.   In order to prosecute this design, I set out from my own people about three weeks ago and came as far as to this place; where, my disorder greatly increasing, I have been obliged to keep house ever since, until the day before yesterday; when I was able to ride about half a mile, but found myself much tired with the journey.   I have now no hopes of prosecuting my journey into New England this winter ; my present state of health will by no means admit of it.   Although I am, through divine goodness, much better than I was some days ago ; yet I have not strength now to ride more than ten miles a day, if the season were warm, and fit for me to travel in. My disorder has been attended with several symptoms of consumption ; and I have been at times apprehensive that my great change was at hand ; yet blessed be God I have never been affrighted; but, on the contrary, at times much delighted with a view of its approach.   O the blessedness of being delivered from the clogs of flesh and sense, from a body of sin and spiritual death !   O the unspeakable sweetness of being translated into a state of complete purity and perfection ! believe me, my brother, a lively view and hope of these things, will make the king of terrors himself appear agreeable.   Dear brother, let me entreat you to keep eternity in your view, and behave yourself as becomes one that must shortly ' give an account of things done in the body.'   That God may be your God, and prepare you for his service here, and his kingdom of glory hereafter, is the desire and daily prayer of

" Your affectionate loving brother,

" DAVID BRAINERD."

" In December, I had revived so far as to be able to walk abroad, and visit my friends, and seemed to be on the gaining hand with regard to my health, in the main, until Lord's day, December 21.   At which time I went to the public worship, and it being sacrament day, I labored much at the Lord's table to bring forth a certain corruption, and have it slain, as being an enemy to God and my own soul ; and could not but hope, that I had gained some strength against this, as well as other corruptions; and felt some brokenness of heart for my sin.

" After this, having perhaps taken some cold, I began to decline as to bodily health; and continued to do so, till the latter end of January, 1747. Having a violent cough, a considerable fever, an asthmatic disorder, and no appetite for any manner of food, nor any power of digestion, I was reduced to so low a state, that my friends, I believe, generally despaired of my life; and some of them, for some time together, thought I could scarce live a day.   At this time, I could think of nothing, with any application of mind, and seemed to be in a great measure void of all affection, and was exercised with great temptations ; but yet was not, ordinarily, afraid of death.

" *Lord's day, Feb.* 1.   Though in a very weak and low state, I enjoyed a considerable degree of comfort and sweetness in divine things ; and was enabled to plead and use arguments with God in prayer, I think, with a childlike spirit.   That passage of scripture occurred to my mind, and gave me great assistance, ' If ye, being evil, know how to give good gifts to your children, how much more will your heavenly Father give the holy Spirit to them that ask him?'   This text I was helped to plead, and insist upon ; and saw the divine faithfulness engaged for dealing with me better than any earthly parent can do with his child.   This season so refreshed my soul, that my body seemed also to be a gainer by it. From this time, I began gradually to amend.   As I recovered some strength, vigor, and spirit, I found at times some freedom and life in the exercises of devotion, and some longings after spirituality and a life of usefulness to the interests of the great Redeemer.   At other times, I was awfully barren and lifeless, and out of frame for the things of God; so that I was ready often to cry out, ' Oh that it were with me as in months past!'   Oh that God had taken me away in the midst of my usefulness, with a sudden stroke, that I might not have been under a necessity of trifling away time in diversions!   Oh that I had never lived to spend so much precious time, in so poor a manner, and to so little purpose! Thus I often reflected, was grieved, ashamed, and even confounded, sunk and discouraged.

" *Feb.* 24.   I was able to ride as far as Newark, (having been confined within Elizabethtown almost four months,) and the next day returned to Elizabethtown.   My spirits were somewhat refreshed with the ride, though my body was weary.

" *Feb.* 28.   Was visited by an Indian of my own congregation, who brought me letters, and good news of the sober and good behavior of my people in general.   This refreshed my soul.   I could not but soon retire ' and bless God for his goodness; and found, I trust, a truly thankful frame of spirit, that God seemed to be building up that congregation for himself.

" *March* 4.   I met with reproof from a friend, which, although I thought I did not deserve it from him, yet was, I trust, blessed of God to make me more tenderly afraid of sin, more jealous over myself, and more concerned to keep both heart and life pure and unblameable.   It likewise caused me to reflect on my past deadness and want of spirituality, and to abhor myself, and look on myself as most unworthy. This frame of mind continued the next day ; and for several days after, I grieved to think, that in my necessary diversions I had not maintained more seriousness, solemnity, heavenly affection, and conversation. Thus my spirits were often depressed and sunk; and yet, I trust, that reproof was made to be beneficial to me.

" *March* 11 being kept in Elizabethtown as a day of fasting and prayer, I was able to attend public worship; which was the first time I had been able so to do since December 21. O, how much weakness and distress did God carry me through in this space of time! But having obtained help from him, I yet live. Oh, that I could live more to his glory !

" *Lord's day, March* 15. Was able again to attend public worship, and felt some earnest desires of being restored to the ministerial work; felt, I think, some spirit and life, to speak for God.—March 18. Rode out with a design to visit my people ; and the next day arrived among them; but was under great dejection in my journey.

"On Friday morning, I rose early, walked about among my people, and inquired into their state and concerns; and found an additional weight and burden on my spirits, upon hearing some things disagreeable. I endeavored to go to God with my distresses, and made some kind of lamentable complaint ; and in a broken manner spread my difficulties before God ; but notwithstanding, my mind continued very gloomy. About ten o'clock I called my people together, and after having explained and sung a psalm, I prayed with them. There was a considerable deal of affection among them ; I doubt not, in some instances, that which was more than merely natural."

This was the last interview which he ever had with his people.

.

CHAPTER XIII.

On Friday, March 20, 1747, he left Cranberry ; little
suspecting that he saw it and his beloved people for the last
time.   On Saturday he came to Elizabethtown, enfeebled in
health, and oppressed with melancholy.   Here he continued
a considerable time, laboring under the ravages of disease,
and suffering from extreme depression of spirit.

"*March* 28.   Was taken this morning with violent griping pains.
These pains were extreme, and constant for several hours; so that it
seemed impossible for me, without a miracle, to live twenty-four hours in
such distress.   I lay confined to my bed the whole day, and in distressing
pain, all the former part of it; but it pleased God to bless means for the
abatement of my distress.   Was exceedingly weakened by this pain, and
continued so for several days following ; being exercised with a fever,
cough, and nocturnal sweats.   In this distressed case, so long as my head
was free of vapory confusions, death appeared agreeable to me.   I
looked on it as the end of toils, and an entrance into a place ' where the
weary are at rest ; ' and think I had some relish for the entertainments
of the heavenly state; so that by these I was allured and drawn, as well
as driven by the fatigues of life.   O, how happy it is, to be drawn by
desires of a state of perfect holiness !.

"*April* 4.   Was sunk and dejected, very restless and uneasy, by
reason of the misimprovement of time ; and yet knew not what to do.   I
longed to spend time in fasting and prayer, that I might be delivered
from indolence and coldness in the things of God; but, alas, I had not
bodily strength for these exercises ! O, how blessed a thing it is to enjoy
peace of conscience ! but how dreadful is a want of inward peace and
composure of soul !   It is impossible, I find, to enjoy this happiness without redeeming time, and maintaining a spiritual frame of mind.

" *Lord's day. April* 5.   It grieved me to find myself so inconceivably
barren.   My soul thirsted for grace; but, alas, how far was I from obtain-

ing what appeared to me so exceeding excellent! I was ready to despair of ever being a holy creature, and yet my soul was desirous of following hard after God; but never did I see myself so far from having apprehended, or being already perfect, as at this time. The Lord's supper being this day administered, I attended the ordinance; and though I saw in myself a dreadful emptiness, and want of grace, and saw myself as it were at an infinite distance from that purity which becomes the gospel, yet at the communion, especially at the distribution of the bread, I enjoyed some warmth of affection, and felt a tender love to the brethren; and, I think, to the glorious Redeemer, the first-born among them. I endeavored then to bring forth mine and his enemies, and slay them before him; and found great freedom in begging deliverance from this spiritual death, as well as in asking divine favors for my friends and congregation, and the church of Christ in general.

" *April* 7. In the afternoon rode to Newark, to marry the Rev. Mr. Dickinson;* and in the evening, performed that service. Afterwards rode home to Elizabethtown, in a pleasant frame, full of composure and sweetness.

" *April* 9. Attended the ordination of Mr. Tucker, † and afterwards the examination of Mr. Smith; was in a comfortable frame of mind this day, and felt my heart, I think, sometimes in a spiritual frame,

" *April* 10. Spent the forenoon in Presbyterial business. In the afternoon rode to Elizabethtown; found my brother John there; ‡ spent some time in conversation with him; but was extremely weak and outdone, my spirits considerably sunk, and my mind dejected.—April 13. Assisted in examining my brother. In the evening, was in a solemn, devout frame; but was much overdone and oppressed with a violent headache.—April 14. Was able to do little or nothing; spent some time with Mr. Byram and other friends. This day my brother went to my people. —April 15. Found some freedom at the throne of grace several times this day. In the afternoon, was very weak, and spent the time to very little purpose; yet in the evening, had, I thought, some religious warmth

---

* The late learned and very excellent Rev. Jonathan Dickinson, pastor of a church in Elizabethtown, president of the college of New-Jersey, and one of the correspondents of the honorable society in Scotland for propagating Christian knowledge. He had a great esteem for Brainerd; kindly entertained him in his house during his sickness the winter past; and after a short illness, died the ensuing October, two days before Brainerd.

† A worthy pious young man; who lived but a very short time: he died at Stratfield, in Connecticut, the December following his ordination, a little while after Brainerd's death at Northampton.

‡ This brother of his had been sent for by the correspondents, to take care of, and instruct Brainerd's congregation of Indians; he being obliged by his illness to be absent from them. He continued to take care of them till Brainerd's death: and since his death, has been ordained his successor in his mission, which continues to flourish much, under his pastoral care.

and spiritual desires in prayer. My soul seemed to go forth after God, and take complacence in his divine perfections. But, alas! afterwards awfully let down my watch, and grew careless and secure.

"*April* 16. Was in bitter anguish of soul, in the morning, such as I have scarce ever felt, with a sense of sin and guilt. I continued in distress the whole day, attempting to pray wherever I went; and indeed could not help so doing; but looked upon myself so vile, that I dared not look any body in the face ; and was even grieved, that anybody should show me any respect, or that they should be so deceived as to think I deserved it.

"*April* 17. In the evening, could not but think that God helped me to ' draw near to the throne of grace,' though most unworthy, and gave me a sense of his favor ; which gave me inexpressible support and encouragement. Though I scarcely dared to hope that the mercy was real, it appeared so great ; yet could not but rejoice, that ever God should discover his reconciled face to such a vile sinner. Shame and confusion, at times, covered me ; and then hope, and joy, and admiration of divine goodness gained the ascendant. Sometimes I could not but admire the divine goodness, that the Lord had not let me fall into all the grossest, vilest acts of sins and open scandal, that could be thought of; and felt so . much necessitated to praise God, that this was ready for a little while to swallow up my shame and pressure of spirit on account of my sins.

"*April* 20. Was in a very disordered state, and kept my bed most of the day. I enjoyed a little more comfort than in several of the preceding days. This day I arrived at the age of twenty-nine years.—April 21. I set out on my journey for New England, in order, (if it might be the will of God,) to recover my health by riding; travelled to New York, and there lodged."

This proved his final departure from New-Jersey. He travelled slowly, and arrived among his friends at East-Haddam, about the beginning of May. There is very little account in his diary of the time that passed from his setting out on his journey to May 10. He speaks of his sometimes finding his heart rejoicing in the glorious perfections of God, and longing to live to him ; but complaining of the unfixedness of his thoughts, and their being easily diverted from divine subjects, and cries out of his leanness, as testifying against him, in the loudest manner. Concerning those diversions which he was obliged to use for his health, he says, that he sometimes found he could use diversions with " singleness of heart," aiming at the glory of God ; but that he also found there was a necessity of great care and watchfulness, lest he should lose that spiritual temper of mind in his diversions, and lest they should degenerate into what was merely selfish, without any supreme aim at the glory of God in them.

"*Lord's day, May* 10. [At Had-Lime.*] I could not but feel some measure of gratitude to God at this time, wherein I was much exercised, that he had always disposed me, in my ministry, to insist on the greatest doctrines of regeneration, the new creature, faith in Christ, progressive sanctification, supreme love to God, living entirely to the glory of God, being not our own, and the like. God thus helped me to see, in the surest manner, from time to time, that these, and the like doctrines necessarily connected with them, are the only foundation of safety and salvation for perishing sinners ; and that those divine dispositions, which are consonant hereto, are that holiness, 'without which no man shall see the Lord.' The exercise of these godlike tempers—wherein the soul acts in a kind of concert with God, and would be and do everything that is pleasing to him—I saw, would stand by the soul in a dying hour ; for God must, I think, deny himself, if he cast away his own image, even the soul that is one in desires with himself.

"*Lord's day, May* 17. [At Millington.†] Spent the forenoon at home, being unable to attend public worship. At this time, God gave me such an affecting sense of my own vileness, and the exceeding sinfulness of my heart, that there seemed to be nothing but sin and corruption within me. 'Innumerable evils compassed me about ; my want of spirituality and holy living, my neglect of God, and living to myself. All the abominations of my heart and life seemed to be open to my view ; and I had nothing to say, but, 'God be merciful to me a sinner.' Towards noon, I saw, that the grace of God in Christ, is infinitely free towards sinners, and such sinners as I was. I also saw, that God is the supreme good, that in his presence is life ; and I began to long to die, that I might be with him, in a state of freedom from all sin. O how a small glimpse of his excellency refreshed my soul ! Oh how worthy is the blessed God to be loved, adored, and delighted in, for himself, for his own divine excellencies !

"Though I felt much dullness, and want of a spirit of prayer, this week, yet I had some glimpses of the excellency of divine things ; and especially one morning, in secret meditation and prayer, the excellency and beauty of holiness, as a likeness to the glorious God, was so discovered to me, that I began to long earnestly to be in that world where

---

* A parish of Haddam, in Connecticut.
† A parish of East-Haddam, in Connecticut.

holiness dwells in perfection. I seemed to long for this perfect holiness, not so much for the sake of my own happiness, although I saw clearly that this was the greatest, yea, the only happiness of the soul, as that I might please God, live entirely to him, and glorify him to the utmost stretch of my rational powers and capacities.

"*Lord's day, May* 24. [At Long-Meadow.] Could not but think, as I have often remarked to others, that much more of true religion consists in deep humility, brokenness of heart, and an abasing sense of barrenness and want of grace and holiness, than most who are called Christians, imagine; especially those who have been esteemed the converts of the late day. Many seem to know of no other religion but elevated joys and affections, arising only from some flights of imagination, or some sugges-tion made to their mind, of Christ being theirs, God loving them, and the like."

On Thursday, May 28, he came from Long-Meadow to Northampton; appearing vastly better than, by his account, he had been in the winter; indeed, so well that he was able to ride twenty-five miles in a day, and to walk half a mile; and appeared cheerful, and free from melancholy; but yet un-doubtedly, at that time, in a confirmed, incurable consump-tion.

I had much opportunity, before this, of particular informa-tion concerning him, from many who were well acquainted with him; and had myself once an opportunity of consid-erable conversation and some acquaintance with him, at New-Haven, near four years before, at the time of the Commence-ment, when he offered that confession to the rector of the col-lege, which has been already mentioned in this history; having been one whom he was pleased then several times to consult on that affair; but now I had opportunity for a more full acquaintance with him. I found him remarkably sociable, pleasant and entertaining in his conversation; yet solid, sav-ory, spiritual, and very profitable. He appeared meek, modest, and humble; far from any stiffness, moroseness, superstitious demureness, or affected singularity in speech or behavior, and seeming to dislike all such things. We enjoyed not only the benefit of his conversation, but had the comfort and advantage of hearing him pray in the family, from time to time. His manner of praying was very agreeable ; most becoming a worm of the dust, and a disciple of Christ, addressing an infinitely great and holy God, the Father of mercies ; not with florid expressions, or a studied eloquence ; not with any intemperate vehemence, or indecent boldness. It was at the greatest distance from any appearance of ostentation, and from everything that might look as though he meant to recommend himself to those that were about him, or set himself off to their acceptance. It was free also from vain repititions, without impertinent excursions, or needless multiplying of words. He expressed himself with the strictest propriety, with weight and pungency ; and yet what his lips uttered seemed to flow from the fullness of his heart, as deeply impressed with a great and solemn sense of our necessities, unworthiness, and dependence, and of God's infinite greatness, excellency, and sufficiency, rather than merely from a warm and fruitful brain, pouring out good expressions. I know not that I ever heard him so much as ask a blessing or return thanks at table, but there was something remarkable to be observed both in the matter and manner of the performance. In his prayers, he insisted much on the prosperity of Zion, the advancement of Christ's kingdom in the world, and the flourishing and propagation of religion among the Indians. And he generally made it one petition in his prayer, " that we might not outlive our usefulness."

" *Lord's day, May* 31. [At Northampton.] I had little inward sweetness in religion, most of the week past; not realizing and beholding spiritually the glory of God, and the blessed Redeemer ; from whence always arise my comforts and joys in religion, if I have any at all ; and if I cannot so behold the excellencies and perfections of God, as to cause me to rejoice in him for what he is in himself, I have no solid foundation for joy. To rejoice, only because I apprehend I have an interest in Christ, and shall be finally saved, is a poor mean business indeed."

This week, he consulted Dr. Mather, at my house, concerning his illness ; who plainly told him, that there were great evidences of his being in a confirmed consumption, and that he could give him no encouragement, that he should ever recover. But it seemed not to occasion the least discomposure in him, nor to make any manner of alteration as to the cheerfulness and serenity of his mind, or the freedom or pleasantness of his conversation.

" *Lord's day, June* 7. My attention was greatly engaged, and my soul so drawn forth, this day, by what I heard of the 'exceeding preciousness of the saving grace of God's Spirit,' that it almost overcame my body, in my weak state. I saw that true grace is exceedingly precious indeed ; that it is very rare ; and that there is but a very small degree of it, even where the reality of it is to be found ; at least I saw this to be my case. In the preceding week, I enjoyed some comfortable seasons of meditation. One morning, the cause of God appeared exceedingly precious to me. The Redeemer's kingdom is all that is valuable in the earth, and I could not but long for the promotion of it in the world. I saw, also, that this cause is God's, that he has an infinitely greater regard and concern for it, than I could possibly have ; that if I have any true love to this blessed interest it is only a drop derived from that ocean. Hence I was ready to 'lift up my head with joy ;' and conclude. 'Well, if God's cause be so dear and precious to him, he will promote it.' Thus I did, as it were, rest on God that he would surely promote that which was so agreeable to his own will ; though the time when, must still be left to his sovereign pleasure."

He was advised by physicians still to continue riding ; as what would tend, above any other means, to prolong his life. He was at a loss, for some time, which way to bend his course next ; but finally determined to ride from hence to Boston ; we having concluded that one of our family should go with him, and be helpful to him in his weak and low state.

" *June* 9. I set out on a journey from Northampton to Boston. Travelled slowly, and got some acquaintance with divers ministers on the road. Having now continued to ride for some considerable time together, I felt myself much better than I had formerly done ; and found, that in proportion to the prospect I had of being restored to a state of usefulness, so I desired the continuance of life ; but death appeared inconceivably more desirable to me than a useless life; yet, blessed be God, I found my heart, at times, fully resigned and reconciled to this greatest of afflictions, if God saw fit thus to deal with me.

" *June* 12. I arrived in Boston this day, somewhat fatigued with my journey. Observed that there is no rest, but in God ; fatigues of body, and anxieties of mind, attend us both in town and country; no place is exempted.

"*Lord's day, June* 14. I enjoyed some enlargement and sweetness in family prayer, as well as in secret exercises; God appeared excellent, his ways full of pleasure and peace, and all I wanted was a spirit of holy fervency, to live to him.—June 17. This and the two preceding days, I spent mainly in visiting the ministers of the town, and was treated with great respect by them.

"*June* 18. I was taken exceedingly ill, and brought to the gates of death by the breaking of small ulcers in my lungs, as my physician supposed. In this extremely weak state, I continued for several weeks, and was frequently reduced so low, as to be utterly speechless, and not able so much as to whisper a word. Even after I had so far revived, as to walk about the house, and to step out of doors, I was exercised every day with a faint turn, which continued usually four or five hours; at which times, though I was not so utterly speechless, but that I could say Yes, or No, yet I could not converse at all, nor speak one sentence, without making stops for breath ; and divers times this season my friends gathered round my bed to see me breathe my last, which they expected every moment, as I myself also did.

" How I was, the first day or two of my illness with regard to the exercise of reason, I scarcely know I believe I was somewhat shattered with the violence of the fever at times; but the third day of my illness, and constantly afterwards, for four or five weeks together, I enjoyed as much serenity of mind, and clearness of thought, as perhaps I ever did in my life. I think that my mind never penetrated with so much ease and freedom into divine things, as at this time ; and I never felt so capable of demonstrating the truth of many important doctrines of the gospel, as now. As I saw clearly the truth of those great doctrines which are justly styled the doctrines of grace, so I saw with no less clearness, that the essence of religion consisted in the soul's conformity to God, and acting above all selfish views, for his glory, longing to be for him, to live to him, and please and honor him in all things ; and this from a clear view of his infinite excellency and worthiness in himself, to be loved, adored, worshipped and served by all intelligent creatures. Thus I saw, that when a soul loves God with a supreme love, he therein acts like the blessed God himself who most justly loves himself in that manner. So when God's interest and his are become one, and he longs that God should be glorified, and rejoices to think that he is unchangeably possessed of the highest glory and blessedness herein, also, he acts in conformity to God. In like manner when the soul is fully resigned to, and rests satisfied and contents with the divine will, here it is also conformed to God.

" I saw further, that as this divine temper, by which the soul exalts

God, and treads self in the dust, is wrought in the soul by God's discovering his own glorious perfections in the face of Jesus Christ to it, by the special influences of the holy Spirit, so he cannot but have regard to it, as his own work ; and as it is his image in the soul, he cannot but take delight in it.   Then I saw again, that if God should slight and reject his own moral image, he must needs deny himself; which he cannot do. And thus I saw the stability and infallibility of this religion, and that those who are truly possessed of it, have the most complete and satisfying evidence of their being interested in all the benefits of Christ's redemption, having their hearts conformed to him ; and that these, these only, are qualified for the employments and entertainments of God's kingdom of glory; as none but these have any relish for the business of heaven, which is to ascribe glory to God, and not to themselves ; and that God (though I would speak it with great reverence of his name and perfection) cannot, without denying himself, finally cast such away.

"The next thing I had then to do, was to enquire, whether this was my religion ; and here God was pleased to help me to the most easy remembrance and critical review of what had passed in course of a religious nature, through several of the latter years of my life.   Although I could discover much corruption attending my best duties, many selfish views and carnal ends, much spiritual pride and self-exaltation, and innumerable other evils which compassed me about; yet God was pleased, as I was reviewing, quickly to put this question out of doubt, by showing me, that I had, from time to time, acted above the utmost influence of mere self-love; that I had longed to please and glorify him, as my highest happiness.   This review was through grace attended with a present feeling of the same divine temper of mind.   I felt now pleased to think of the glory of God, and longed for heaven, as a state wherein I might glorify God perfectly, rather than a place of happiness for myself.   This feeling of the love of God in my heart, which I trust the Spirit of God excited in me afresh, was sufficient to give me a full satisfaction, and make me long, as I had many times before done, to be with Christ.   I did not now want any of the sudden suggestions, which many are so pleased with, ' That Christ and his benefits are mine ; that God loves me,' etc, in order to give me satisfaction about my state. No, my soul now abhorred those delusions of Satan, which are thought to be the immediate witness of the Spirit, while there is nothing but an empty suggestion of a certain fact, without any gracious discovery of the divine glory, or of the Spirit's work in their own hearts.   I saw the awful delusion of this kind of confidence, as well as of the whole of that religion, from which they usually spring, or at least of which they are the attendants.   The false religion of the late day, though a day of wondrous grace, the imaginations, and impressions made only on the animal affections—together with the sudden suggestions made to the mind by Satan, transformed into an angel of light, of certain facts not revealed in scripture—and many suchlike things, I fear, have made up the greater part of the religious appearance in many places.

"These things I saw with great clearness, when I was thought to be dying. God gave me great concern for his church and interest in the world, at this time; not so much because the late remarkable influence upon the minds of people was abated, as because that false religion—those hearts of imagination, and wild and selfish commotions of the animal affections—which attended the work of grace, had prevailed so far. This was that which my mind dwelt upon, almost day and night; and this, to me, was the darkest appearance, respecting religion, in the land; for it was this, chiefly, that had prejudiced the world against inward religion. And I saw the great misery of all was, that so few saw any manner of difference between those exercises which are spiritual and holy, and those which have self-love only for their beginning, centre, and end.

"As God was pleased to afford me clearness of thought, and composure of mind, almost continually, for several weeks together, under my great weakness, so he enabled me, in some measure, to improve my time, as, I hope, to valuable purposes. I was enabled to write a number of important letters, to friends in remote places; and sometimes I wrote when I was speechless, *i. e.* unable to maintain conversation with any body; though perhaps I was able to speak a word or two so as to be heard."

Among the letters written at this period, were the following. The reader will perceive that they were written by one conscious that he was standing on the verge of the grave and realizing, in no ordinary degree, the infinite importance of eternity.

To his brother Israel, at College; written in the time of his extreme illness in Boston, a few months before his death.

" BOSTON, *June* 30, 1747.

"MY DEAR BROTHER:

"It is on the verge of eternity I now address you. I am heartily sorry that I have so little strength to write what I long so much to communicate to you. But, let me tell you, my brother, eternity is another thing than we ordinarily take it to be in a healthful state. O, how vast and boundless! O, how fixed and unalterable! O, of what infinite importance is it, that we be prepared for eternity! I have been just a dying, now for more than a week; and all around me have thought me so. I have had clear views of Eternity; have seen the blessedness of the godly, in some measure; and have longed to share their happy state ; as well as been comfortably satisfied, that through grace, I shall do so; but O, what anguish is raised in my mind, to think of eternity for those who are Christless, for those who are mistaken, and who bring their false hopes to the grave with them! The sight was so dreadful, I could by no means bear it; my thoughts recoiled, and I said, under a more affecting sense than ever before, ' Who can dwell with everlasting burnings!' O, me- thought, could I now see my friends, that I might warn them to see to it, that they lay their foundation for eternity sure. And for you, my dear brother, I have been particularly concerned; and have wondered I so much neglected conversing with you about your spiritual state at our last meeting. O, my brother, let me then beseech you now to examine, whether you are indeed a new creature? whether you have ever acted above self? whether the glory of God has ever been the sweetest and highest concern with you? whether you have ever been reconciled to all the perfections of God? in a word, whether God has been your por- tion, and a holy conformity to him your chief delight? If you cannot answer positively, consider seriously the frequent breathings of your soul ; but do not, however, put yourself off with a slight answer. If you have reason to think you are graceless, O, give yourself and the throne of grace no rest, till God arise and save. But if the case should be other- wise, bless God for his grace, and press after holiness.

" My soul longs, that you should be fitted for, and in due time go into the work of the ministry. I cannot bear to think of your going into any other business in life. Do not be discouraged, because you see your elder brothers in the ministry die early, one after another. I declare, now I am dying, I would not have spent my life otherwise for the whole world. But I must leave this with God.

" If this line should come to your hands soon after the date, I should be almost desirous you should set out on a journey to me; it may be you may see me alive; which I should much rejoice in. But if you cannot come I must commit you to the grace of God, where you are. May he be your guide and counsellor, your sanctifier and eternal portion !

" O, my dear brother, flee fleshly lusts, and the enchanting amuse- ments, as well as corrupt doctrines of the present day, and strive to live to God. Take this as the last line from

" Your affectionate dying brother,

" DAVID BRAINERD."

Letter to a young gentleman, a candidate for the ministry, for whom he had a special friendship ; written at the time of his nearness to death in Boston.

"Very dear Sir:

" How amazing it is, that the living, who know they must die, should, notwithstanding, 'put far away the evil,' in a season of health and prosperity; and live at such an awful distance from a familiarity with the grave, and the great concerns beyond it! Especially, it may justly fill us with surprise, that any whose minds have been divinely enlightened to behold the important things of eternity as they are, I say, that such should live in this manner. And yet, sir, how frequently is this the case! How rare are the instances of those who live and act, from day to day, as on the verge of eternity, striving to fill up all their remaining moments, in the service and to the honor of their great Master! We insensibly trifle away time, while we seem to have enough of it; and are so strangely amused, as in a great measure to lose a sense of the holiness and blessed qualifications necessary to prepare us to be inhabitants of the heavenly paradise. But O, dear sir, a dying bed, if we enjoy our reason clearly, will give another view of things. I have now, for more than three weeks, lain under the greatest degree of weakness; the greater part of the time, expecting daily and hourly to enter into the eternal world; sometimes have been so far gone, as to be wholly speechless, for some hours together. O, of what vast importance has a holy spiritual life appeared to me at this season! I have longed to call upon all my friends, to make it their business to live to God; and especially all that are designed for, or engaged in the service of the sanctuary. O, dear sir, do not think it enough, to live at the rate of common Christians. Alas, to how little purpose do they often converse, when they meet together! The visits, even of those who are called Christians indeed, are frequently extremely barren ; and conscience cannot but condemn us for the misimprovement of time, while we have been conversant with them. But the way to enjoy the divine presence, and to be fitted for distinguishing service for God, is to live a life of great devotion and constant self-dedication to him; observing the motions and dispositions of our own hearts, whence we may learn the corruptions that lodge there, and our constant need of help from God for the performance of the least duty. And O, dear sir, let me beseech you frequently to attend to the great and precious duties of secret fasting and prayer.

"I have a secret thought, from some things I have observed, that God may perhaps design you for some singular service in the world. O then labor to be prepared and qualified to do much for God. Read Mr. Edwards' piece on the affections, again and again ; and labor to distinguish clearly upon experiences and affections in religion, that you may make a difference between the gold and the shining dross. I say, labor here, if ever you would be an useful minister of Christ ; for nothing has put such a stop to the work of God in the late day as the false religion, and the wild affections which attend it. Suffer me, therefore, finally to entreat you earnestly to 'give yourself to prayer, to reading and meditation on divine truths;' strive to penetrate to the bottom of them, and never be content with a superficial knowledge. By this means, your thoughts, will gradually grow weighty and judicious; and you hereby will be possessed of a valuable treasure, out of which you may produce 'things new and old,' to the glory of God.

"And now, 'I commend you to the grace of God,' earnestly desiring. that a plentiful portion of the divine Spirit may rest upon you ; that you may live to God in every capacity of life, and do abundant service for him in a public one, if it be his will ; and that you may be richly qualified for the 'inheritance of the saints in light.'—I scarce expect to see your face any more in the body, and therefore entreat you to accept this as the last token of love, from

" Your sincerely affectionate dying friend,

" DAVID BRAINERD.

" P. S. I am now, at the dating of this letter, considerably recovered from what I was when I wrote it ; it having lain by me for some time, for want of an opportunity of conveyance ; it was written in Boston. I am now able to ride a little, and so am removed into the country ; but have no more expectation of recovering than when I wrote, though I am a little better for the present; and therefore I still subscribe myself,

"Your dying friend,

" D. B."

Letter to his brother John, at Bethel, the town of Christian Indians, in New-Jersey ; written likewise at Boston, when he was there on the brink of the grave.

" DEAR BROTHER :

I am now just on the verge of eternity, expecting very speedily to appear in the unseen world. I feel myself no more an inhabitant of earth, and sometimes earnestly long to 'depart and be with Christ.' I bless God. he has for some years given me an abiding conviction, that it is impossible for any rational creature to enjoy true happiness, without being entirely 'devoted to him.' Under the influence of this conviction I have in some measure acted. Oh that I had done more so! I saw both the excellency and necessity of holiness in life ; but never in such a manner as now, when I am just brought from the sides of the grave. O, my brother, pursue after holiness ; press towards this blessed mark ; and let your thirsty soul continually say, ' I shall never be satisfied till I awake in thy likeness.' Although there has been a great deal of selfishness in my views, of which I am ashamed, and for which my soul is humbled at every view; yet, blessed be God, I find I have really had, for the most part, such a concern for his glory, and the advancement of his kingdom in the world, that it is a satisfaction to me to reflect upon these years.

"And now, my dear brother, as I must press you to pursue after personal holiness, to be as much in fasting and prayer as your health will allow, and to live above the rate of common Christians; so I must entreat you solemnly to attend to your public work; labor to distinguish between true and false religion; and to that end, watch the motions of God's spirit upon your own heart. Look to him for help; and impartially compare your experiences with his word. Read Mr. Edwards on the affections; where the essence and soul of religion is clearly distinguished from false affections.* Value religious joys according to the subject-matter of them: there are many who rejoice in their supposed justification; but what do these joys argue, but only that they love themselves? Whereas, in true spiritual joys, the soul rejoices in God for what he is in himself; blesses God for his holiness, sovereignty, power, faithfulness, and all his perfections; adores God, that he is what he is, that he is unchangeably possessed of infinite glory and happiness. Now, when men thus rejoice in the perfections of God, and in the infinite excellency of the way of salvation by Christ, and in the holy commands of God, which are a transcript of his holy nature; these joys are divine and spiritual. Our joys will stand by us at the hour of death, if we can be

---

* [The extreme modesty and the delicate sensibility of the world-renowned Edwards, are touchingly disclosed in the subjoined brief note. Nothing but a high sense of duty kept him from suppressing Brainerd's reference in the way of commendation to one of his masterly treatises.—J. M.S.]

I had at first fully intended, in publishing this and the foregoing letters, to have suppressed these passages wherein my name is mentioned, and my discourse on religious affections recommended; and am sensible, that by my doing otherwise, I shall bring upon me the reproach of some. But how much soever I may be pleased with the commendations of any performance of mine, (and I confess I esteem the judgment and approbation of such a person as Brainerd worthy to be valued, and look on myself as highly honored by it,) yet I can truly say, the things that governed me in altering my forementioned determination with respect to these passages, were these two. (1.) What Brainerd here says of that discourse, shows very fully and particularly what his notions were of experimental religion, and the nature of true piety, and how far he was from placing it in impressions on the imagination, or any enthusiastical impulses, and how essential in religion he esteemed holy practice, etc. For all that have read that discourse, know what sentiments are there expressed concerning those things. (2.) I judged, that the approbation of so apparent and eminent a friend and example of inward vital religion, and evangelical piety in the height of it, would probably tend to make that book more serviceable; especially among some kinds of zealous persons, whose benefit was especially aimed at in the book; some of which are prejudiced against it, as written in too legal a strain, and opposing some things wherein the height of Christian experience consists, and tending to build men upon their own works.

then satisfied, that we have thus acted above self ; and in a disinterested manner, if I may so express it, rejoiced in the glory of the blessed God. I fear you are not sufficiently aware how much false religion there is in the world; many serious Christians and valuable ministers are too easily imposed upon by this false blaze. I likewise fear you are not sensible of the dreadful effects and consequences of this false religion. Let me tell you, it is the devil transformed into an angel of light ; it is a fiend of hell, that always springs up with every revival of religion, and stabs and murders the cause of God, while it passes current with multitudes of well meaning people for the height of religion. Set yourself, my brother, to crush all appearances of this nature, among the Indians, and never encourage any degrees of heat without light. Charge my people in the name of their dying minister, yea, in the name of him who was dead and is alive, to live and walk as becomes the gospel. Tell them how great the expectations of God and his people are from them, and how awfully they will wound God's cause, if they fall into vice ; as well as fatally prejudice other poor Indians. Always insist, that their experiences are rotten, that their joys are delusive, although they may have been rapt up into the third heavens in their own conceit by them, unless the main tenor of their lives be spiritual, watchful, and holy. In pressing these things, ' thou shalt both save thyself and those that hear thee.'

"God knows I was heartily willing to have served him longer in the work of the ministry, although it had still been attended with all the labors and hardships of past years, if he had seen fit that it should be so : but as his will now appears otherwise, I am fully content, and can with the utmost freedom say, ' The will of the Lord be done.' It affects me to think of leaving you in a world of sin ; my heart pities you, that those storms and tempests are yet before you, from which I trust, through grace, I am almost delivered. But ' God lives, and blessed be my rock ; ' he is the same almighty friend ; and will, I trust, be your guide and helper, as he has been mine.

"And now, my dear brother, ' I commend you to God and to the word of his grace,' which is able to build you up, and give you inheritance among all them that are sanctified. May you enjoy the divine presence, both in private and public ; and may 'the arms of your hands be made strong, by the right hand of the mighty God of Jacob ! ' Which are the passionate desires and prayers of

" Your affectionate dying brother,
" DAVID BRAINERD."

"At this season, also, while I was confined at Boston, I read with care and attention some papers of old Mr. Shepard's, lately come to light, and designed for the press ; and, as I was desired, and greatly urged made some corrections, where the sense was left dark, for want of a word or two. Besides this, I had many visitants, with whom, when I was able to speak, I always conversed of the things of religion; and was peculiarly assisted in distinguishing between the true and false religion of the times. There is scarcely any subject, which has been matter of controversy of late, but I was at one time or other compelled to discuss and show my opinion respecting it; and that frequently before numbers of people. Especially, I discoursed repeatedly on the nature and necessity of that humiliation, self-emptiness, or full conviction of a person's being utterly undone in himself, which is necessary in order to a saving faith, and the extreme difficulty of being brought to this, and the great danger there is of persons taking up with some self-righteous appearances of it. The danger of this I especially dwelt upon, being persuaded that multitudes perish in this hidden way; and because so little is said from most pulpits to discover any danger here: so that persons being never effectually brought to die in themselves, are never truly united to Christ, and so perish. I also discoursed much on what I take to be the essence of true religion; endeavoring plainly to describe that god-like temper and disposition of soul, and that holy conversation and behavior, which may justly claim the honor of having God for his original and patron. I have reason to hope God blessed my way of discoursing and distinguishing to some, both ministers and people; so that my time was not wholly lost."

He was much visited, while in Boston, by many persons of considerable note and character, and by some of the first rank; who showed him uncommon respect, and appeared highly pleased and entertained with his conversation. Beside being honored with the company and respect of ministers of the town, he was visited by several ministers from various parts of the country. He took all opportunities to discourse on the peculiar nature, and distinguishing characteristics of true, spiritual, and vital religion; and to bear his testimony against the various false appearances of it, consisting in, or arising from impressions on the imagination; sudden and supposed immediate suggestions of truths not contained in the scripture, and that faith which consists primarily in a person believing that Christ died for him in particular, etc. What he said was, for the most part, heard with uncommon attention and regard: and his discourses and reasonings appeared manifestly to have great weight and influence, with many with whom he conversed, both ministers and others.*

The honorable Commissioners, in Boston, of the incorporated society in London for propagating the gospel in New-England and parts adjacent, having newly had committed to them a legacy of the late reverend and famous Dr. Daniel Williams, of London, for the support of two missionaries to the heathen, were pleased, while he was in Boston, to consult him about a mission to those Indians called the Six Nations, particularly about the qualifications requisite in a missionary to those Indians.   They were so satisfied with his sentiments on this head, and had such confidence in his faithfulness, his judgment and discretion in things of this nature, that they desired him to undertake to find and recommend two persons fit to be employed in this business ; and very much left the matter with him.

Several pious and generously disposed gentlemen in Boston, moved by the wonderful narrative of his labors and success among the Indians in New-Jersey, and more especially by their conversation with him on the same subject, took opportunity to inquire more particularly into the state and necessities of his congregation, and the school among them, with a charitable intention of contributing something to promote the excellent design of advancing the interests of Christianity among the Indians.   Understanding that there was a want of Bibles for the school, three dozen Bibles were immediately procured, and 14*l.* in bills, (of the old tenor,) given over and above, beside more large benefactions made afterwards, which I shall have occasion to mention in their proper place.

Brainerd's restoration from his extremely low state in Boston, so as to go abroad again and to travel, was very un-

---

* I have had advantage for the more full information of his conduct and conversation, the entertainment he met with, and what passed relating to him while in Boston ; as he was constantly attended, during his continuance there, by one of my children, in order to his assistance in his illness.

expected to him and his friends. My daughter, who was with him, writes thus concerning him, in a letter dated June 23 ; "On Thursday, he was very ill with a violent fever, and extreme pain in his head and breast, and, at turns, delirious. So he remained till Saturday evening, when he seemed to be in the agonies of death ; the family was up with him till one or two o'clock, expecting that every hour would be his last. On Sabbath day he was a little revived, his head was better, but very full of pain, and exceeding sore at his breast, much put to it for breath. Yesterday he was better upon all accounts. Last night he slept but little. This morning he was much worse. Dr, Pynchon says, he has no hopes of his life ; nor does he think it likely that he will ever come out of the chamber ; though he says he may be able to come to Northampton."

In another letter, dated June 29, she says as follows :— "Mr. Brainerd has not so much pain, nor fever, since I last wrote, as before ; yet he is extremely weak and low, and very faint, expecting every day will be his last. He says, it is impossible for him to live ; for he has hardly vigor enough to draw his breath. I went this morning into town, and when I came home, Mr. Bromfield said, he never expected I should see him alive ; for he lay two hours, as they thought, dying ; one could scarcely tell whether he was alive or not ; he was not able to speak for some time ; but now is much as he was before. The doctor thinks he will drop away in such a turn. Mr. Brainerd says he never felt anything so much like dissolution, as that he felt to-day ; and says, he never had any conception of its being possible for any creature to be alive, and yet so weak as he is from day to day.—Dr. Pynchon says, he should not be surprised, if he should so recover as to live half a year ; nor would it surprise him if he should die in half a day. Since I began to write he is not so well, having had a faint turn again ; yet patient and resigned, having no distressing fears, but the contrary."

It was ordered in divine Providence, that the strength of

nature held out through this great conflict, so as just to escape the grave at that turn; and then he revived, to the astonishment of all who knew his case. After he began to
revive, he was visited by his youngest brother, Israel, a student at Yale College; who, having heard of his extreme illness, went from thence to Boston, in order to see him, if he
might find him alive, which he but little expected.

This visit was attended with a mixture of joy and sorrow
to Brainerd. He greatly rejoiced to see his brother, especially because he had desired an opportunity of some religious conversation with him before he died. But this meeting was attended with sorrow, as his brother brought to him
the sorrowful tidings of his sister Spencer's death at Haddam; a sister, between whom and him had long subsisted a
peculiarly dear affection, and much intimacy in spiritual
matters, and whose house he used to make his own, when he
went to Haddam, his native place. He had heard nothing of
her sickness till this report of her death. But he had these comforts, together with the tidings, viz, a confidence of her being
gone to heaven, and an expectation of his soon meeting her
there.—His brother continued with him till he left the town,
and came with him from thence to Northampton.—Concerning the last Sabbath Brainerd spent in Boston, he writes in
his diary as follows:—

"*Lord's day, July* 19. I was just able to attend public worship, being
carried to the house of God in a chaise. Heard Dr. Sewall preach, in
the forenoon; partook of the Lord's supper at this time. In this sacrament, I saw astonishing divine wisdom displayed; such wisdom, as I
saw, required the tongues of angels and glorified saints to celebrate. It
seemed to me that I never should do anything at adoring the infinite
wisdom of God, discovered in the contrivance of man's redemption, until
I arrived at a world of perfection; yet I could not help striving 'to call
upon my soul, and all within me, to bless the name of God.' In the
afternoon, heard Mr. Prince preach. I saw more of God in the wisdom
discovered in the plan of man's redemption, than I saw of any other of
his perfections through the whole day."

He left Boston the next day. But before he came away,

he had occasion to bear a very full, plain, and open testimony
against that opinion, that the essence of saving faith lies in
believing that Christ died for me in particular; and that this
is the first act of faith in a true believer's closing with
Christ. He did it in a long conference he had with a gentleman, who has very publicly and strenuously appeared to
defend that tenet. He had this discourse with him in the
presence of a number of respectable individuals who came to
visit Brainerd before he left the town, and to take their
leave of him. In this debate, he made this plain declaration,
at the same time confirming what he said by many arguments,
That the essence of saving faith was wholly left out of the
definition which that gentleman has published; and that the
faith which he had defined had nothing of God in it, nothing
above nature, nor indeed above the power of the devils; and
that all such as had this faith, and no better, though they
might have this to never so high a degree, would surely perish. He declared also, that he never had greater assurance
of the falseness of the principles of those who maintained such
a faith, and of their dangerous and destructive tendency, or a
more affecting sense of the great delusion and misery of those
who depended on getting to heaven by such a faith, while they
had no better, than he lately had when he was supposed to be
at the point to die, and expected every minute to pass into
eternity.—Brainerd's discourse at this time and the forcible
reasonings by which he confirmed what he asserted, appeared
to be greatly to the satisfaction of those present; as several
of them took occasion expressly to manifest to him, before
they took leave of him.

When this conversation, was ended, having bid an affectionate farewell to his friends, he set out in the cool of the
afternoon, on his journey to Northampton, attended by his
brother, and my daughter, who went with him to Boston;
and would have been accompanied out of the town by a number of gentlemen, besides that honorable person who gave him
his company for some miles on that occasion, as a testimony

of their esteem and respect, had not his aversion to anything of pomp and show prevented it.

"*July* 25. I arrived here, at Northampton, having set out from Boston on Monday. In this journey, I rode about sixteen miles a day, one day with another. Was sometimes extremely tired and faint on the road, so that it seemed impossible for me to proceed any further; at other times I was considerably better, and felt some freedom both of body and mind.

"*Lord's day, July*. 26. This day I saw clearly that I should never be happy, yea, that God himself could not make me happy, unless I could be in a capacity to ' please and glorify him for ever.' Take away this, and admit me in all the fine heavens that can be conceived of by men or angels, and I should still be miserable forever."

Though he had so revived as to be able to travel thus far, yet he manifested no expectation of recovery. He supposed as his physician did, that his being brought so near to death at Boston, was owing to the breaking of ulcers in his lungs. He told me that he had several such ill turns before, only not to so high a degree, but as he supposed, owing to the same cause, viz. the breaking of ulcers; that he was brought lower and lower every time; that it appeared to him, that in his last sickness he was brought as low as it was possible, and yet live; and that he had not the least expectation of surviving the next return of this breaking of ulcers; but still appeared perfectly calm in the prospect of death.

On Wednesday morning, the week after he came to Northampton, he took leave of his brother Israel, never expecting to see him again in this world; he now setting out from hence on his journey to New-Haven. When he came hither he had so much strength as to be able, from day to day, to ride out two or three miles, and sometimes to pray in the family, but from this time he gradually decayed, becoming weaker and weaker.

While he was here, his conversation from first to last was much on the same subjects as when in Boston. He spoke much of the nature of true religion in the heart and practice, as distinguished from its various counterfeits; expressing his great concern that the latter so much prevailed in many places. He often manifested his great abhorrence. of all such doctrines and principles in religion as had any tendency to Antinomianism; of all such notions, as seemed to diminish the necessity of holiness of life, or to abate men's regard to the commands of God, and a strict, diligent, and universal practice of virtue and piety, under a pretence of depreciating our works, and magnifying God's free grace. He spoke often, with much detestation of such experiences and pretended discoveries and joys, as have nothing of the nature of sanctification in them, as do not tend to strictness, tenderness, and diligence in religion, to meekness and benevolence towards mankind, and an humble behavior. He also declared, that he looked on such pretended humility as worthy of no regard, which was not manifested by modesty of conduct and conversation. He spoke often with abhorrence of the spirit and practice which appear among the greater part of separatists at this day in the land, particularly those in the eastern parts of Connecticut; in their condemning and separating from the standing ministry and churches, their crying down learning and a learned ministry, their notion of an immediate call to the work of the ministry, and the forwardness of laymen to set up themselves as public teachers and preachers. He had been much conversant in the eastern part of Connecticut, it being near his native place, when the same principles, notion, and spirit began to operate, which have since prevailed to a greater height; and had acquaintance with some of those persons who are become heads and leaders of the separatists. He had also been conversant with persons of the same class elsewhere; and I heard him say, once and again, that he knew by his acquaintance with this sort of people, that what was chiefly and most generally in repute among them as the power of godliness, was an entirely different thing from that true vital piety recommended in the scriptures, and had nothing in it of that nature. He manifested a great dislike of a disposition in persons to much noise and show in religion, and affecting to be abundant in proclaiming and publishing their own experiences.　Though at the same time he did not condemn, but approved of Christians speaking of their own experiences on some occasions, and to some persons, with due modesty and discretion.　He himself sometimes, while at my house, spake of his own experiences ; but it was always with apparent reserve, and in the exercise of care and judgment with respect to occasions, persons, and circumstances. He mentioned some remarkable things of his own religious experience to two young gentlemen, candidates for the ministry, who watched with him, each at different times, when he was very low, and not far from his end ; but he desired both of them not to speak of what he had told them till after his death.

The subject of the debate already mentioned, which he had with a certain gentleman, the day he left Boston, seemed to lie with much weight on his mind after he came hither. He began to write a letter to that gentleman, expressing his sentiments concerning the dangerous tendency of some of the tenets he had expressed in conversation, and in the writings he had published, with the considerations by which the exceeding hurtful nature of those notions is evident, but he had not strength to finish his letter.

After he came hither, as long as he lived, he spoke much of that future prosperity of Zion, which is so often foretold and promised in the scripture.　It was a theme upon which he delighted to dwell ; and his mind seemed to be carried forth with earnest concern about it, and intense desires that religion might speedily and abundantly revive and flourish. Though he had not the least expectation of recovery, yea, the nearer death advanced, and the more the symptoms of its approach increased, still the more did his mind seem to be taken up with this subject.　He told me, when near his end, that " he never in all his life had his mind so led forth in desires and earnest prayers for the flourishing of Christ's kingdom on earth, as since he was brought so exceeding low at Boston." He seemed much to wonder, that there appeared no more of a disposition in ministers and people to pray for the flourishing of religion through the world; that so little a part of their prayers was generally taken up about it, in their families, and elsewhere. Particularly, he several times expressed his wonder, that there appeared no more forwardness to comply with the proposal lately made in a memorial from a number of ministers in Scotland,* and sent over into America, for united extraordinary prayer, among Christ's ministers and people, for the coming of Christ's kingdom: and sent it as his dying advice to his own congregation, that they should practice agreeably to that proposal.†

Though he was constantly exceeding weak, yet there appeared in him a continual care well to improve time, and fill it up with something that might be profitable, and in some respect for the glory of God or the good of men; either prof-

---

* [In a tract published in 1747, urging a "visible union of God's people in extraordinary prayers," President Edwards "pealed out his trumpet-call summoning the whole Christian world to prayer" for the speedy coming of Christ's kingdom in millenial power and glory; and as a motive, an incentive, in this same tract he refers to the day of fasting and prayer kept at Northampton the year before, which was followed that same night by the utter dispersion and defeat of the French Armada under the Duke d'Anville. And Edwards adds: "This is the nearest parallel with God's wonderful works of old in the times of Moses, Joshua and Hezekiah, of any that have been in these latter ages of the world."

This tract was published and widely circulated in Scotland and in England, and produced a profound impression there, as well as throughout the infant Church in the New World, "and marked a turning point in modern history." And who can doubt that Edwards was in a measure inspired and prompted to write this masterly appeal by his intercourse with Brainerd, and his admiration of his character, and knowledge of the wonders which God had wrought by him. This very year it was that this missionary saint had gone up as in a chariot of fire from the bosom of Edwards' family, and the sacred mantle of this ascended prophet of missions had fallen upon him, and he was to continue the work, not only among the Stockbridge Indians, as he afterwards did in a personal ministry, but on a broader and more conspicuous theater in the sight and hearing of all Christendom—J M S.]

† His congregation, since this, have with great cheerfulness and unanimity fallen in with this advice, and have practised agreeably to the proposal from Scotland; and have at times appeared with uncommon engagedness and fervency of spirit in their meetings and united devotions, pursuant to that proposal. Also the Presbyteries of New York and New Brunswick, since this, have, with one consent, fallen in with the proposal, as likewise some other of God's people in those parts.

itable conversation ; or writing letters to absent friends ; or noting something in his diary; or looking over his former writings, correcting them, and preparing them to be left in the hands of others at his death ; or giving some directions concerning the future management of his people ; or employment in secret devotions. He seemed never to be easy, however ill, if he was not doing something for God, or in his service. After he came hither, he wrote a preface to a diary of the famous Mr. Shepard's, in those papers before mentioned, lately found, having been much urged to it by those gentlemen in Boston who had the care of the publication ; which diary, with his preface, has since been published.

In his diary for Lord's day, Aug 9, he speaks of longing desires after death, through a sense of the excellency of a state of perfection. In his diary for Lord's day, Aug, 16, he speaks of his having so much refreshment of soul in .the house of God, that it seemed also to refresh his body. And this is not only noted in his diary, but was very observable to others ; it was very apparent, not only that his mind was exhilarated with inward consolation, but also that his animal spirits and bodily strength seemed to be remarkably restored, as though he had forgot his illness. But this was the last time that he ever attended public worship on the Sabbath.

On Tuesday morning that week, as I was absent on a journey, he prayed with my family, but not without much difficulty, for want of bodily strength ; and this was the last family prayer that he ever made. He had been wont, till now, frequently to ride out, two or three miles; but this week, on Thursday, was the last time he ever did so.

" *Lord's day Aug.* 23. This morning I was considerably refreshed with the thought, yea, the hope and expectation of the enlargement of Christ's kingdom ; and I could not but hope, that the time was at hand, when Babylon the great would fall and rise no more. This led me to some spiritual meditations, which were very refreshing to me. I was unable to attend public worship either part of the day ; but God was pleased to afford me fixedness and satisfaction in divine thoughts. Nothing so refreshes my soul, as when I can go to God, yea, to God my exceeding joy.

When he is so sensibly to my soul, O how unspeakably delightful is this. In the week past, I had divers turns of inward refreshing ; though my body was inexpressibly weak, followed continually with agues and fevers. Sometimes my soul centred in God, as my only portion ; and I felt that I should be for ever unhappy, if He did not reign. I saw the sweetness and happiness of being his subject, at his disposal. This made all my difficulties quickly vanish.

" From this Lord's day, viz,. Aug. 23, I was troubled very much with vapory disorders, and could neither write nor read, and could scarcely live ; although through mercy, was not so much oppressed with heavy melancholy and gloominess, as at many other times."

Till this week, he had been wont to lodge in a room above stairs ; but he now grew so weak that he was no longer able to go up stairs and down. Friday, Aug. 28, was the last time he ever went above stairs ; henceforward he betook himself to a lower room.

On Wednesday, Sept. 2, being the day of our public lecture, he seemed to be refreshed with seeing the neighboring ministers who came hither to the lecture, and expressed a great desire once more to go to the house of God on that day ; and accordingly rode to the meeting and attended divine service, while the Reverend Mr. Woodbridge, of Hatfield, preached. He signified that he supposed it to be the last time he should ever attend public worship, as it proved. Indeed, it was the last time that he ever went out of our gate alive.

On the Saturday evening following, he was unexpectedly visited by his brother, John Brainerd, who came to see him from New Jersey. He was much refreshed by this unexpected visit, this brother being peculiarly dear to him, and he seemed to rejoice in a devout and solemn manner, to see him and to hear the comfortable tidings which he brought concerning the state of his dear congregation of Christian Indians. A circumstance of this visit, of which he was exceedingly glad was, that his brother brought him some of his private writings from New Jersey, and particularly his diary which he had kept for many years past.

" *Lord's day, Sept.* 6. I began to read some of my private writings, which

my brother brought me ; and was considerably refreshed with what I
found in them.—Sept. 7. I proceeded further in reading my old private
writings, and found that they had the same effect upon me as before. I
could not but rejoice and bless God for what passed long ago, which
without writing had been entirely lost.—This evening, when I was in
great distress of body, my soul longed that God should be glorified ; I
saw there was no character but this. I could not but speak to the bystanders then of the only happiness, viz,. pleasing God. O that I could
for ever live to God ! The day, I trust, is at hand, the perfect day.
O the day of deliverance from all sin !

"*Lord's day, Sept.* 13. I was much refreshed and engaged in meditation and writing, and found a heart to act for God. My spirits were
refreshed, and my soul delighted to do something for God."

On the evening following that Lord's day, his feet began
to swell ; which thenceforward swelled more and more. The
next day his brother John left him, being obliged to return
to New Jersey on some business of great importance and
necessity ; intending to return again with all possible speed,
hoping to see his brother yet once more in the land of the
living.

Brainerd having now with much deliberation, considered
of the important affair before mentioned, which was referred
to him by the honorable Commissioners in Boston, of the corporation in London for the propagation of the gospel in New
England and parts adjacent, viz., the fixing upon and recommending of two persons proper to be employed as missionaries to the Six Nations ; about this time wrote a letter recommending two young gentlemen of his acquaintance, viz.,
Mr. Elihu Spencer, of East Haddam, and Mr. Job Strong, of
Northampton. The commissioners, on the receipt of this letter
unanimously agreed to accept and employ the persons so recommended. One of them, Mr. Spencer, has been solemnly
ordained to that work, by several of the ministers of Boston,
in the presence of an ecclesiastical council convened for that
purpose ; and is now gone forth to the nation of Oneidas,
about 170 miles beyond Albany.

On Wednesday, Sept. 16, he wrote a letter to a gentleman

in Boston, (one of those charitable persons beforementioned, who appeared so forward to contribute of their substance for promoting Christianity among the Indians, relating to the growth of the Indian school, and the need of another school-master, or some person to assist the schoolmaster in instruct-ing the Indian children. These gentlemen, on the receipt of this letter, had a meeting and agreed to give 200*l*, for the sup-port of another schoolmaster: and desired the Rev. Mr. Pember-ton, of New York,(who was present at the meeting,)to procure a suitable person ; and also agreed to allow 74*l*. to defray some special charges which were requisite to encourage the mission to the Six Nations, (besides the salary allowed by the com-missioners,) which was also done on some intimations given by Brainerd.

Brainerd spent himself much in writing those letters, being exceedingly weak ; but it seemed to be much to his satisfaction that he had been enabled to do it ; hoping that it was something done for God, and which might be for the advancement of Christ's kingdom and glory. In writing the last of these letters, he was obliged to use the hand of another, not being able to write himself.

Thursday of this week, (Sept. 17,) was the last time he went out of his lodging-room. That day, he was again visited by his brother Israel, who continued with him thenceforward till his death. On that evening he was taken with something of a diarrhea, which he looked upon as another sign of his approaching death ; whereupon he expressed himself thus : " O, the glorious time is now coming ! I have longed to serve God perfectly : now God will gratify those desires ! " And from time to time, at the several steps and new symp-toms of the sensible approach of his dissolution, he was so far from being sunk or damped, that he seemed to be ani-mated, and made more cheerful, as being glad at the appear-ance of death's approach. He often used the epithet glori-ous, when speaking of the day of his death, calling it that glorious day. And as he saw his dissolution gradually approaching, he talked much about it ; and with perfect calmness spoke of a future state. He also settled all his affairs, giving directions very minutely, concerning what he would have done after his decease. And the nearer death approached, the more desirous he seemed to be of it. He several times spoke of the different kinds of willingness to die ; and represented it as an ignoble, mean kind, to be willing to leave the body, only to get rid of pain ; or to go to heaven, only to get honor and advancement there.

"*Sept.* 19. Near night, while I attempted to walk a little, my thoughts turned thus : ' How infinitely sweet it is, to love God, and be all for him ! ' Upon which it was suggested to me, ' You are not an angel, not lively and active.' To which my whole soul immediately replied, ' I as sincerely desire to love and glorify God, as any angel in heaven.' Upon which it was suggested again, ' But you are filthy, not fit for heaven.' Hereupon instantly appeared the blessed robes of Christ's righteousness, in which I could not but exult and triumph ; and I viewed the infinite excellency of God, and my soul even broke with longings, that God should be glorified. I thought of dignity in heaven ; but instantly the thought returned, ' I do not go to heaven to get honor, but to give all possible glory and praise.' O how I longed that God should be glorified on earth also ! O I was made—for eternity—if God might be glorified ! Bodily pains I cared not for ; though I was then in extremity, I never felt easier. I felt willing to glorify God in that state of bodily distress, as long as he pleased I should continue in it. The grave appeared really sweet, and I longed to lodge my weary bones in it : but Oh, that God might be glorified ! this was the burden of all my cry. oh, I knew that I should be active as an angel, in heaven ; and that I should be stripped of my filthy garments ! so that there was no objection. But, O to love and praise God more, to please him for ever ! this my soul panted after, and even now pants for while I write. O that God might be glorified in the whole earth ! ' Lord let thy kingdom come.' I longed for a spirit of preaching to descend and rest on ministers, that they might address the consciences of men with closeness and power. I saw that God ' had the residue of the Spirit ; and my soul longed that it should be ' poured from on high.' I could not but plead with God for my dear congregation, that he would preserve it, and not suffer his great name to lose its glory in that work ; my soul still longing that God might be glorified."

The extraordinary frame he was in, that evening, could not be hid. "His mouth spake out of the abundance of his heart,"

expressing in a very affecting manner much the same things
as are written in his diary. Among very many other extraordinary expressions, which he then uttered, were such as
these: " My heaven is to please God, and glorify him, and
to give all to him, and to be wholly devoted to his glory:
that is the heaven I long for ; that is my religion, and that is
my happiness, and always was ever since I suppose I had
any true religion : and all those that are of that religion shall
meet me in heaven. I do not go to heaven to be advanced,
but to give honor to God. It is no matter where I shall be
stationed in heaven, whether I have a high or low seat there ;
but to love, and please, and glorify God is all. Had I a thousand souls, if they were worth anything, I would give them
all to God ; but I have nothing to give, when all is done. It
is impossible for any rational creature to be happy without
acting all for God ; God himself could not make him happy
any other way. I long to be in heaven, praising and glorifying God with the holy angels ; all my desire is to glorify God.
My heart goes out to the burying place ; it seems to me a
desirable place ; but O to glorify God ! that is it ; that is
above all. It is a great comfort to me to think, that I have
done a little for God in the world. Oh ! it is but a very
small matter, yet I have done a little ; and I lament it, that
I have not done more for him. There is nothing in the
world worth living for, but doing good, and finishing God's
work, doing the work that Christ did. I see nothing else in
the world that can yield any satisfaction, besides living to God,
pleasing him, and doing his whole will. My greatest joy and
comfort has been, to do something for promoting the interest
of religion and the souls of particular persons : and now, in
my illness, while I am full of pain and distress, from day
to day, all the comfort I have, is in being able to do some
little service for God, either by something that I say, or by
writing or in some other way."

He intermingled with these and other like expressions,
many pathetical counsels to those who were about him, particu-

larly to my children and servants. He applied himself to some of my younger children at this time; calling them to him, and speaking to them one by one; setting before them, in a very plain manner, the nature and essence of true piety, and its great importance and necessity; earnestly warning them not to rest in anything short of a true and thorough change of heart, and a life devoted to God. He counseled them not to be slack in the great business of religion, nor in the least to delay it; enforcing his counsels with this, that his words were the words of a dying man: said he, "I shall die here, and here I shall be buried, and here you will see my grave, and do you remember what I have said to you. I am going into eternity: and it is sweet for me to think of eternity: the endlessness of it makes it sweet: but, oh, what shall I say to the eternity of the wicked! I cannot mention it, nor think of it; the thought is too dreadful. When you see my grave, then remember what I said to you while I was alive; then think with yourself, how the man who lies in that grave, counseled and warned me to prepare for death."

His body seemed to be marvellously strengthened, through the inward vigor and refreshment of his mind; so that, although before he was so weak that he could hardly utter a sentence, yet now he continued his most affecting and profitable discourse to us for more than an hour, with scarce any intermission; and said of it, when he had done, "it was the last sermon that ever he should preach."—This extraordinary frame of mind continued the next day, of which he says in his diary as follows:

"*Lord's day Sept.* 20. Was still in a sweet and comfortable frame: and was again melted with desires that God might be glorified, and with longings to love and live to him. Longed for the influences of the divine Spirit to descend on ministers, in a special manner. And oh, I longed to be with God, to behold his glory, and to bow in his presence!"

It appears by what is noted in his diary, both of this day and the evening preceding, that his mind at this time was much impressed with a sense of the importance of the work

of the ministry, and the need of the grace of God, and his
special spiritual assistance in this work. It also appeared in
what he expressed in conversation; particularly in his discourse to his brother Israel, who was then a member of Yale
College at New-Haven, prosecuting his studies for the work
fo the ministry.* He now, and from time to time, in his
dying state, recommended to his brother a life of self-denial,
of weanedness from the world, and devotedness to God, and
an earnest endeavor to obtain much of the grace of God's
Spirit, and God's gracious influences on his heart; representing the great need which ministers stand in of them, and the
unspeakable benefit of them from his own experience.
Among many other expressions, he said thus: "When
ministers feel these special gracious influences on their hearts,
it wonderfully assists them to come at the consciences of
men, and as it were to handle them; whereas, without them,
whatever reason and oratory we make use of, we do but
make use of stumps, instead of hands."

"*Sept.* 21. I began to correct a little volume of my private writings.
God, I believe, remarkably helped me in it; my strength was surprisingly
lengthened out, my thoughts were quick and lively, and my soul refreshed, hoping it might be a work for God. O how good, how sweet it
is to labor for God!

"*Sept.* 22. Was again employed in reading and correcting, and had
the same success, as the day before. I was exceeding weak; but it
seemed to refresh my soul, thus to spend time.—Sept. 23. I finished my
corrections of the little piece before-mentioned, and felt uncommonly
peaceful: it seemed as if I had now done all my work in this world, and
stood ready for my call to a better. As long as I see any thing to be
done for God, life is worth having: but oh, how vain and unworthy it is,
to live for any lower end!—this day, I indited a letter, I think, of great
importance, to the Rev. Mr. Byram in New-Jersey. Oh that God would
bless and succeed that letter, which was written for the benefit of his

* This young gentleman was an ingenious, serious, studious, and hopefully pious person; there appeared in him many qualities giving hope of his being a great blessing in his
day. But it has pleased God, since the death of his brother, to take him away also. He
died that winter, at New-Haven, January 6, 1748, of a nervous fever, after about a fortnight's illness.

church! * Oh that God would purify the sons of Levi, that his glory may be advanced! This night, I endured a dreadful turn, wherein my life was expected scarce an hour or minute together. But blessed be God, I have enjoyed considerable sweetness in divine things, this week both by night and day.

"*Sept.* 24. My strength began to fail exceedingly; which looked further as if I had done all my work; however, I had strength to fold and superscribe my letter. About two I went to bed, being weak and much disordered, and lay in a burning fever till night, without any proper rest. In the evening, I got up, having lain down in some of my clothes; but was in the greatest distress, that ever I endured, having an uncommon kind of hiccough; which either strangled me, or threw me into a straining to vomit; and at the same time was distressed with griping pains. O the distress of this evening! I had little expectation of my living the night through, nor indeed had any about me; and I longed for the finishing moment!——I was obliged to repair to bed by six o'clock; and through mercy enjoyed some rest; but was grievously distressed at turns with the hiccough.——My soul breathed after God,—' When shall I come to God, even to God, my exceeding joy?' Oh for his blessed likeness!

"*Sept.* 25. This day, I was unspeakably weak, and little better than speechless all the day; however, I was able to write a little, and felt comfortably in some part of the day. O it refreshed my soul, to think of former things, of desires to glorify God, of the pleasures of living to him! O, blessed God, I am speedily coming to thee, I hope. Hasten the day, O Lord, if it be thy blessed will, O come, Lord Jesus, come quickly. Amen.†

"*Sept.* 26. I felt the sweetness of divine things, this forenoon; and had the consolation of a consciousness that I was doing something for God.

"*Lord's day Sept.* 27. This was a very comfortable day to my soul; I think I awoke with God. I was enabled to lift up my soul to God, early this morning; and while I had little bodily strength, I found freedom to lift up my heart to God for myself and others. Afterwards, was pleased with the thought of speedily entering into the unseen world."

Early this morning, as one of the family came into the room he expressed himself thus : " I have had more pleasure this morning than all the drunkards in the world enjoy." So

---

* It was concerning the qualifications of ministers, and the examination and licensing of candidates for the work of the ministry.

† This was the last time that ever he wrote in his Diary with his own hand; though it is continued a little farther, in a broken manner; written by his brother Israel, but indited by his mouth in this his weak and dying state.

much did he esteem the joy of faith above the pleasures of
sin. He felt that morning an unusual appetite for food, with
which his mind seemed to be exhilarated, looking on it as a
sign of the very near approach of death. At this time he
also said, "I was born on a Sabbath-day; and I have reason
to think I was new-born on a Sabbath-day; and I hope I shall
die on this Sabbath-day. I shall look upon it as a favor if it
may be the will of God that it should be so: I long for the
time. O why is his chariot so long in coming? why tarry
the wheels of his chariot? I am very willing to part with
all; I am willing to part with my dear brother John, and
never to see him again, to go to be forever with the Lord.*
O, when I go there, how will God's dear church on earth be
upon my mind!"

Afterwards, the same morning, being asked how he did,
he answered, "I am almost in eternity? I long to be there.
My work is done; I have done with all my friends; all the world
is nothing to me. I long to be in heaven, praising and glorifying God with the holy angels. All my desire is to glorify God."

During the whole of these last two weeks of his life, he
seemed to continue in this frame of heart; loose from all the
world, as having finished his work, and done with all things
here below. He had now nothing to do but to die, and to
abide in an earnest desire and expectation of the happy
moment, when his soul should take its flight to a state of
perfect holiness, in which he should be found perfectly glorifying and enjoying God. He said, "That the consideration
of the day of death, and the day of judgment, had a long
time been peculiarly sweet to him." From time to time he
spoke of his being willing to leave the body and the world immediately, that day, that night, that moment, if it was the will
of God. He also was much engaged in expressing his longings

---

* He had, before this, expressed a desire, if it might be the will of God, to live till his
brother returned from New Jersey; who, when he went away, intended if possible, to
perform his journey and return in a fortnight, hoping once more to meet his brother in
the land of the living. The fortnight was now near expired, it ended the next day.

that the church of Christ on earth might flourish, and Christ's kingdom here might be advanced, notwithstanding he was about to leave the earth, and should not with his eyes behold the desirable event, nor be instrumental in promoting it.   He said to me one morning, as I came into his room, "My thoughts have been employed on the old dear theme, the prosperity of God's church on earth.   As I waked out of sleep, I was led to cry for the pouring out of God's Spirit, and the advancement of Christ's kingdom, for which the Redeemer did and suffered so much.   It is that especially which makes me long for it."   He expressed much hope that a glorious advancement of Christ's kingdom was near at hand.

He once told me, that "he had formerly longed for the outpouring of the Spirit of God and the glorious times of the Church, and hoped they were coming; and should have been willing to have lived to promote religion at that time, if that had been the will of God ; but, says he, I am willing it should be as it is ; I would not have the choice to make for myself, for ten thousand worlds."   He expressed on his death-bed a full persuasion that he should in heaven see the prosperity of the Church on earth, and should rejoice with Christ therein ; and the consideration of it seemed to be highly pleasing and satisfying to his mind.

He also still dwelt much on the great importance of the work of gospel ministers, and expressed his longings, that they might be filled with the Spirit of God.   He manifested much desire to see some of the neighboring ministers, with whom he had some acquaintance, and of whose sincere friendship he was confident that he might converse freely with them on that subject, before he died.   And it so happened, that he had opportunity with some of them according to his desire.

Another thing that lay much on his heart, from time to time, in these near approaches of death, was the spiritual prosperity of his own congregation of Christian Indians in New-Jersey; and when he spake of them, it was with peculiar tenderness ; so that his speech would be presently interrupted and drowned with tears.

He also expressed much satisfaction in the disposals of Providence, with regard to the circumstances of his death ; particularly that God had before his death given him an opportunity in Boston with so many considerable persons, ministers and others, to give in his testimouy for Gods against false religion, and many mistakes that lead to it, and promote it. He was much pleased that he had an opportunity there to lay before pious and charitable gentlemen the state of the Indians, and their necessities to so good effect, and that God had since enabled him to write to them further, concerning these affairs ; and to write other letters of importance, which he hoped might be of good influence with regard to the state of religion among the Indians, and elsewhere, after his death. He expressed great thankfulness to God for his mercy in these things. He also mentioned it as what he accounted a merciful circumstance of his death, that he should die here. When he was sick at Boston, nigh unto death, it was with reluctance he thought of dying in a place where funerals are often attended with a pomp and show, to any appearance of which he was very averse : and though it was with some difficulty he got his mind reconciled to the prospect then before him, yet at last he was brought to acquiesce in the divine will, with respect to this circumstance of his departure. However, it pleased God to order the event so as to gratify his desire which he had expressed, of getting back to Northampton, with a view particularly to a more silent and private burial. And speaking of these things, he said, "God had granted him all his desire ; " and signified, that now he could with the greatest alacrity leave the world.

"*Sept.* 28. I was able to read and make some few corrections in my private writings; but found I could not write as I had done ; I found myself sensibly declined in all respects. It has been only from a little while before noon, till about one or two o'clock, that I have been able to do any thing for some time past ; yet this refreshed my heart that I could do any thing either public or private, that I hoped was for God."

This evening he was supposed to be dying. He thought so himself, and was thought so by those who were about him. He seemed glad at the appearance of the near approach of death. He was almost speechless, but his lips appeared to move ; and one that sat very near him, heard him utter such expressions as these, " Come, Lord Jesus, come quickly. Oh why is his chariot so long in coming." After he revived, he blamed himself for having been too eager to be gone. And in expressing what he found in the frame of his mind at that time, he said, he then found an inexpressibly sweet love to those whom he looked upon as belonging to Christ beyond almost all that ever he felt before, so that it seemed, to use his own words, " like a little piece of heaven to have one of them near him." And being asked, whether he heard the prayer that was, at his desire, made with him ; he said, " Yes, he heard every word, and had an uncommon sense of the things that were uttered in that prayer, and that every word reached his heart."

On the evening of Tuesday, Sept. 29, as he lay on his bed, he seemed to be in an extraordinary frame ; his mind greatly engaged in sweet meditations concerning the prosperity of Zion. There being present here at that time two young gentlemen of his acquaintance, who were candidates for the ministry, he desired us all to unite in singing a Psalm on that subject, even Zion's prosperity. And on his desire we sung a part of the 102d Psalm. This seemed much to refresh and revive him, and gave him new strength ; so that, though before he could scarcely speak at all, now he proceeded, with some freedom of speech, to give his dying counsels to those two young gentlemen before mentioned, relating to their preparation for, and prosecution of that great work of the ministry for which they were designed ; and in particular earnestly recommended to them frequent secret fasting and prayer : and enforced his counsel with regard to this from his own experience of the great comfort and benefit of it, which said he, I should not mention, were it not that I am a dying person.

After he had finished his counsel, he made a prayer, in the audience of us all: wherein, beside praying for this family, for his brethren, and those candidates for the ministry, and for his own congregation, he earnestly prayed for the reviving and flourishing of religion in the world.—Till now he had every day sat up part of the day; but after this he never rose from his bed.

"*Sept.* 30. I was obliged to keep my bed the whole day, through weakness. However, redeemed a little time, and with the help of my brother, read and corrected about a dozen pages in my MS. giving an account of my conversion.

"*Oct.* 1. I endeavored again to do something by way of writing, but soon found my powers of body and mind utterly fail. Felt not so sweetly, as when I was able to do something which I hoped would do some good. In the evening, was discomposed and wholly delirious; but it was not long before God was pleased to give me some sleep, and fully composed my mind.* O blessed be God for his great goodness to me, since I was so low at Mr. Bromfield's on Thursday, June 18, last. He has, except those few minutes, given me the clear exercise of my reason, and enabled me to labor much for him, in things both of a public and private nature; and perhaps to do more good than I should have done if I had been well; besides the comfortable influence of his blessed Spirit, with which he has been pleased to refresh my soul. May his name have all the glory for ever and ever. Amen.

"*Oct.* 2. My soul was this day, at turns, sweetly set on God; I longed to be with him, that I might behold his glory. I felt sweetly disposed to commit all to him, even my dearest friends, my dearest flock, my absent brother, and all my concerns for time and eternity. O that his kingdom might come in the world; that they might all love and glorify him, for what he is in himself; and that the blessed Redeemer might see of the travail of his soul, and be satisfied! Oh, come Lord Jesus, come quickly! Amen."†

The next evening we expected his brother John from New Jersey, it being about a week after the time that he proposed for his return when he went away. Though our expectations

---

* From this time forward, he had the free use of his reason till the day before his death, except that at some times he appeared a little lost for a moment, when first waking out of sleep.

† Here ends his diary. These are the last words which are written in it either by his own hand, or by any other from his mouth.

were still disappointed, yet Brainerd seemed to continue unmoved, in the same calm and peaceful frame, which he had before manifested ; as having resigned all to God, and having done with his friends, and with all things here below.

On the morning of the next day, being Lord's day, Oct. 4, as my daughter Jerusha, who chiefly attended him, came into the room, he looked on her very pleasantly, and said, "Dear Jerusha, are you willing to part with me ?   I am quite willing to part with you ; I am willing to part with all my friends, I am willing to part with my dear brother John, although I love him the best of any creature living : I have committed him and all my friends to God, and can leave them with God. Though if I thought I should not see you, and be happy with you in another world, I could not bear to part with you.   But we shall spend a happy eternity together !"* In the evening, as one came into the room with a Bible in her hand, he expressed himself thus : " O that dear book ! that lovely book !

---

*[With what sorrow and grief, and yet rejoicing of spirit, did the pen of Edwards trace the following note ! This " dear child " was affianced to Brainerd, and was a kindred spirit in the highest walks of Christian experience. She had hoped to join him in his work for Christ among the poor Indians, and for years had been in training for the Lord's service. But God had a higher sphere for them both. It was, however, her privilege and joy to minister to Brainerd during his long illness in Boston and afterward at her father's house. Young, gifted in person and mind, and " uncommonly devoted to God," according to the testimony of her father, the separation of these loving kindred souls was but for a day.—J. M. S.]

Since this, it has pleased a holy and sovereign God to take away this my dear child by death, on the 14th of February, next following, after a short illness of five days, in the eighteenth year of her age. She was a person of much the same spirit with Brainerd. She had constantly taken care of and attended him in his sickness, for nineteen weeks before his death : devoting herself to it with great delight, because she looked on him as an eminent servant of Jesus Christ. In this time he had much conversation with her on the things of religion ; and in his dying state, often expressed to us, her parents, his great satisfaction concerning her true piety, and his confidence that he should meet her in heaven, and his high opinion of her, not only as a true Christian, but a very eminent saint, one whose soul was uncommonly fed and entertained with things which appertain to the most spiritual, experimental, and distinguishing parts of religion : and one who, by the temper of her mind, was fitted to deny herself for God and to do good, beyond any young woman whatsoever whom he knew. She had manifested a heart uncommonly devoted to God, in the course of her life, many years before her death ; and said on her death-bed that " she had not seen one minute for several years wherein she desired to live one minute longer, for the sake of any other good in life but doing good, living to God, and doing what might be for his glory."

I shall soon see it opened ! the mysteries that are in it and the mysteries of God's providence will be all unfolded ! "

His distemper now very apparently preyed on his vitals in an extraordinary manner ; not by the sudden breaking of ulcers in his lungs, as at Boston, but by a constant discharge of purulent matter in great quantities : so that what he brought up by expectoration, seemed to be as it were mouthfuls of almost clear pus ; which was attended with very inward pain and distress.

On Tuesday, Oct. 6, he lay, for a considerable time, as if he were dying. At which time, he was heard to utter, in broken whispers, such expressions as these : " He will come, he will not tarry. I shall soon be in glory. I shall soon glorify God with the angels." But after some time he revived.

The next day, his brother John arrived from New Jersey ; where he had been detained much longer than he intended by a mortal sickness among the Christian Indians, and by some other circumstances that made his stay with them necessary. Brainerd was affected and refreshed with seeing him, and appeared fully satisfied with the reasons of his delay ; seeing the interest of religion and the souls of his people required it.

The next day he was in great distress and agony of body, and for the greater part of the time, was much disordered as to the exercise of his reason. In the evening he was more composed, and had the use of his reason well, but the pain of his body continued and increased. He told me that it was impossible for any one to conceive of the distress which he felt in his breast. He manifested much concern lest he should dishonor God by impatience, under his extreme agony ; which was such, that he said, the thought of enduring it one minute longer was almost insupportable. He desired that others would do much in lifting up their hearts continually to God for him, that God would support him and give him patience. He signified that he expected to die that night ; but seemed to fear a longer delay : and the disposition of his mind with regard to death, appeared still the same that it had been all

along.   And notwithstanding his bodily agonies, yet the in-
interest of Zion lay still with great weight on his mind ; as
appeared by some considerable discourse he had that
evening with the Rev. Mr. Billing, one of the neighboring
ministers, who was then present, concerning the great importance of the work of the ministry.   Afterwards, when it
was very late in the night, he had much very proper and profitable discourse with his brother John, concerning his congregation in New-Jersey, and the interest of religion among the
Indians.   In the latter part of the night, his bodily distress
seemed to rise to a greater height than ever ; and he said to
those then about him, " that it was another thing to die
than people imagined ; " explaining himself to mean that
they were not aware what bodily pain and anguish is under-
gone before death.   Towards day, his eyes fixed ; and he continued lying immovable, till about six o'clock, on Friday, Oct.
9, 1747, when his soul, as we may well conclude, was received
by his dear Lord and Master, as an eminently faithful servant,
into that state of perfection of holiness, and fruition of God
for which he had so often and so ardently longed; and was
welcomed by the glorious assembly in the upper world, as
one peculiarly fitted to join them in their blessed employ and
enjoyment.

[The funeral, which occurred on the Monday following,
bore affecting testimony to the respect and esteem in which
this eminent young servant of God was held in Northampton,
and in all the regions round about. It was attended by "eight
of the neighboring ministers," (a larger show than a hundred
would be now); "a large number of gentlemen of liberal education, and a great concourse of people."

What a scene for the pencil of the artist !   What an occasion for the eloquence of the orator !   What a text for the
preacher !   On that bier lay the wasted remains of one not yet
thirty years old—as the world counts time—and yet a " leader
of the people."   And what a noble race had he accom-

plished! What eminent attainments had he made in the
divine life! What a lofty spirit of Christian heroism had he
exemplified! What a sublime example of self-sacrifice and
consecration to Christ had he set before the world! The
work done by him in the heart of the American wilderness,
and the diary written by him in the woods, among savages,
had touched the hearts and inspired the souls of tens of ,
thousands of God's children in Scotland, and in England, as
well as in our own colonies. Here were the mortal remains,
awaiting burial, of a life offered up in living sacrifice for the
glory of God and the salvation of some of the lowest of his
creatures. In all the land there was no more fitting preacher
for so solemn and affecting an occasion than JONATHAN ED-
WARDS, at whose house the worn-out missionary had died, and
who regarded him with the affection of a father, and the veneration due to extraordinary moral worth and sanctity, and
at whose obsequies his own dear child was " chief mourner."
The title of the sermon was: " Christians, when absent from
the body are present with the Lord," based on 2 Cor. v. 8.
"We are confident, I say, and willing rather to be absent
from the body, and to be present with the Lord." The sermon, in breadth, and power and manner of treatment, was
worthy of the fame of New England's greatest divine, and of
the occasion which called it forth.

As a fitting close to these memoirs, we give the concluding portion of the sermon, in which one every way competent,
gives an outline of Brainerd's life and character.—J. M. S.]

CHAPTER XIV.

President Edwards' personal estimate of Brainerd.

FROM A SERMON PREACHED AT HIS FUNERAL, OCT. 12, 1747.

" In him whose death we are now called to consider and improve, we have not only an instance of mortality, but, as we have all imaginable reason to conclude, an instance of one, who, being absent from the body, is present with the Lord. Of this we shall be convinced, whether we consider the nature of his experience at the time whence he dates his conversion, or the nature and course of his inward exercises from that time forward; or his outward conversation and practice in life ; or his frame and behavior during the whole of that long space wherein he looked death in the face.

" His convictions of sin, preceding his first consolations in Christ, as appears by a written account which he has left of his inward exercises and experiences, were exceedingly deep and thorough. His trouble and sorrow, arising from a sense of guilt and misery, were very great and long continued, but yet sound and rational ; consisting in no unsteady, violent, and unaccountable frights and perturbations of mind, but arising from the most serious consideration, and a clear illumination of the conscience to discern and consider the true state of things. The light let into his mind at conversion, and the influences and exercises to which his mind was subject at that time, appear very agreeable to reason and the gospel of Jesus Christ. The change was very great and remarkable ; yet without any appearance of strong impressions on the imagination, of sudden flights of the affections, or of vehement emotions of the animal nature. It was attended with just views of the supreme glory of the divine Being, con-

sisting in the infinite dignity and beauty of the perfections of
his nature, and of the transcendent excellency of the way of
salvation by Christ. This was about eight years ago, when
he was twenty-one years of age.

"Thus God sanctified and made meet for his use that
vessel, which he intended to make eminently a vessel of
honor in his house, and which he had made of large capacity,
having endowed him with very uncommon abilities and gifts
of nature. He was a singular instance of a ready invention,
natural eloquence, easy flowing expression, sprightly apprehension, quick discernment, and very strong memory; and yet of
a very penetrating genius, close and clear thought, and piercing judgment. He had an exact taste; his understanding
was, if I may so express it, of a quick, strong, and distinguishing scent.

"His learning was very considerable. He had a great
taste for learning, and applied himself to his studies in so
close a manner when he was at college, that he much injured
his health, and was obliged, on that account, for a while, to
leave college, throw by his studies, and return home. He
was esteemed one who excelled in learning in that society.

"He had extraordinary knowledge of men, as well as of
things, and an uncommon insight into human nature. He
excelled most whom I ever knew in the power of communicating his thoughts, and had a peculiar talent at accommodat-
ing himself to the capacities, tempers, and circumstances of
those whom he would instruct or counsel.

"He had extraordinary gifts for the pulpit. I never had
an opportunity to hear him preach; but have often heard
him pray. I think that his manner of addressing himself to
God, and expressing himself before him in that duty, almost
inimitable, such as I have very rarely known equaled. He
expressed himself with such exact propriety and pertinency,
in such significant, weighty, pungent expressions, with such
an appearance of sincerity, reverence, and solemnity, and so

great a distance from all affectations, as forgetting the presence of men, and as being in the immediate presence of a great and holy God, as I have scarcely ever known paralleled. His manner of preaching, by what I have often heard of it from good judges, was no less excellent, being clear and instructive, natural, nervous and moving, and very searching and convincing. He nauseated an affected noisiness, and violent boisterousness in the pulpit, and yet much disrelished a flat cold delivery when the subject required affection and earnestness.

" Not only had he excellent talents for the study and the pulpit, but also for conversation. He was of a social disposition; was remarkably free, entertaining, and profitable in his ordinary discourse, and discovered uncommon ability in disputing, in defending truth, and confuting error.

" He excelled in his knowledge of theology, and was truly, for one of his standing, an extraordinary divine, and above all in matters relating to experimental religion. In this, I know that I have the concurring opinion of some who are generally regarded as persons of the best judgment. According to what ability I have to judge of things of this nature, and according to my opportunities, which of late have been very great, I never knew his equal of his age and standing, for clear accurate notions of the nature and essence of true religion, and its distinctness from its various false appearances. This I suppose to be owing to the strength of his understanding; to the great opportunities which he had of observing others, both whites and Indians, and to his own great experience.

" His experiences of the holy influences of God's Spirit, were not only great at his first conversion, but they were so, in a continued course, from that time forward. This appears from a diary which he kept of his daily inward exercises, from the time of his conversion until he was disabled by the failing of his strength, a few days before his death. The change, which he looked upon as his conversion, was not only a great change of the present views, affections, and frame of his mind, but was evidently the beginning of that work of God in his heart, which God carried on, in a wonderful manner, from that time to his dying day. He abhorred the course pursued by those who live on their first evidences of piety, as though they had now finished their work, and thenceforward gradually settle into a cold, lifeless, negligent, worldly frame.

"His experiences were very different from many things which have lately been regarded by multitudes as the very height of Christian experience. When that false religion, which arises chiefly from impressions on the imagination, began first to gain a very great prevalence in the land, he was for a little while deceived with it, so as to think highly of it. Though he knew that he never had such experiences as others told of, yet he thought it was because their attainments were superior to his; and so coveted them, and sought after them, but could never obtain them. He told me that he never had what is called an impulse, or a strong impression on his imagination, in things of religion, in his life; yet owned, that during the short time in which he thought well of these things, he was tinged with that spirit of false zeal which was wont to attend them; but added, that even at this time he was not in his element, but as a fish out of water. When after a little while, he came clearly to see the vanity and perniciousness of such things, it cost him abundance of sorrow and distress of mind, and to my knowledge he afterwards freely and openly confessed the errors in conduct into which he had run, and humbled himself before those whom he had offended. Since his conviction of his error in those respects, he has ever had a peculiar abhorrence of that kind of bitter zeal, and those delusive experiences which have been the principal source of it. He detested enthusiasm in all its forms and operations, and condemned whatever in opinion or experience seemed to verge towards Antinomianism. He regarded with abhorrence the experiences of those whose first faith consists in believing that Christ died for them in particular; whose first love consists in loving God, because they suppose themselves the objects of his love, and whose assurance of their good estate arises from some immediate testimony, or suggestion, either with or without texts of Scripture, that their sins are forgiven, and that God loves them; as well as the joys of those who rejoice more in their own supposed distinction above others, in honor, privileges, and high experiences, than in God's excellence and Christ's beauty, and the spiritual pride of those laymen who set themselves up as public teachers, and decry human learning, and a learned ministry. He greatly nauseated everything like noise and ostentation in religion, and the disposition which many possess to publish and proclaim their own experiences; though he did not condemn, but approved of Christians speaking of their experiences, on some occasions, and to some persons, with modesty, discretion and reserve. He abominated the spirit and practice of the generality of the Separatists in this land. I heard him say, once and again, that he had had much intercourse with this class of people, and was acquainted with many of them in various parts of the country; and that by this acquaintance he knew that what was chiefly and most generally in repute among them, as the power of godliness, was entirely a different thing from that vital piety recommended in the Scriptures, and had nothing in it of that nature. He never was more full in condemning those things than in his last illness, and after he ceased to have any expectations of life, particularly when he had the greatest and nearest views of approaching eternity, and several times when he thought himself actually dying, and expected in a few minutes to be in the eternal world, as he himself told me.

"As his inward experiences appear to have been of the right kind, and were very remarkable as to their degrees, so were his outward behavior and practice agreeable. In his whole course, he acted as one who had indeed sold all for

Christ, had entirely devoted himself to God, had made his glory his highest end, and was fully determined to spend his whole time and strength in his service. He was animated in religion in the right way; animated not merely nor chiefly with his tongue in professing and talking, but animated in the work and business of religion. He was not one of those who contrive to shun the cross and get to heaven in the indulgence of ease and sloth. His life of labor and self-denial, the sacrifices which he made, and the readiness and constancy with which he spent his strength and substance to promote the glory of his Redeemer, are probably without a parallel in this age in these parts of the world. Much of this may be perceived by any one who reads his printed journal; but much more has been learned by long and intimate acquaintance with him, and by looking into his diary since his death, which he purposely concealed in what he published.

"As his desires and labors for the advancement of Christ's kingdom were great, so was his success. God was pleased to make him the instrument of bringing to pass the most remarkable alteration among the poor savages, in enlightening, awakening, reforming and changing their disposition and manners, and wonderfully transforming them, of which perhaps any instance can be produced in these latter ages of the world. An account of this has been given the public in his journal, drawn up by order of the Honorable Society in Scotland, which employed him. This I would recommend to the perusal of all who take pleasure in the wonderful works of God's grace, and who wish to read that which will peculiarly tend both to entertain and profit a Christian mind.

"Not less extraordinary were his constant calmness, peace, assurance and joy in God, during the long time he looked death in the face without the least hope of recovery, continuing without interruption to the last; while his distemper very sensibly preyed upon his vitals, from day to day, and often brought him to that state in which he looked upon himself and was thought by others to be dying. The thoughts of approaching death never seemed in the least to damp him, but rather to encourage him and exhilarate his mind. The nearer death approached, the more desirous he seemed to be to die. He said, not long before his death, that ' the consideration of the day of death and the day of judgment, had a long time been peculiarly sweet to him.' At another time he observed, that ' he could not but think of the propriety there was in throwing such a rotten carcase as his into the grave ; it seemed to him to be the right way of disposing of it.' He often used the epithet ' glorious,' when speaking of the day of his death, calling it ' that glorious day.' On Sabbath morning, Sept. 27, feeling an unusually violent appetite for food, and looking on it as a sign of approaching death, he said, ' he should look on it as a favor if this might be his dying day, and that he longed for the time.' He had before expressed himself desirous of seeing his brother again, whose return had been expected from New-Jersey ; but then, speaking of him, he said, ' I am willing to go, and never see him again ; I care not what I part with, to be for ever with the Lord.' Being asked that morning how he did, he answered, ' I am almost in eternity ; God knows I long to be there. My work is done ; I have done with all my friends ; all the world is nothing to me.' On the evening of the next day, when he thought himself dying, and was apprehended to be so by others, and he could utter himself only by broken whispers, he often repeated the word ' eternity,' and said, ' I shall soon be with the holy angels.' ' Jesus will come, he will not tarry.' He told me one night as he went to bed, that ' he expected to die that night,' and added, ' I am not at all, afraid, I am willing to go this night, if it be the will of God. Death is what I long for.' He sometimes expressed himself as having nothing to do but to die ; and being willing to go that minute, if it was the will of God. He sometimes used that expression, ' O why is his chariot so long in coming ? '

"He seemed to have remarkable exercises of resignation to the will of God. He once told me that he had longed for the outpouring of the Holy Spirit of God, and the glorious times of the Church, and hoped they were coming; and should have been willing to have lived to promote religion at that time, if that had been the will of God. 'But,' said he, 'I am willing it should be as it is; I would not have the choice to make for myself for ten thousand worlds.'

"He several times spoke of the different kinds of willingness to die, and mentioned it as an ignoble, mean kind of willingness to die, to be willing only to get rid of pain, or to go to heaven only to get honor and advancement there. His own longings for death seemed to be quite of a different kind, and for nobler ends. When he was first taken with one of the last and most fatal symptoms in consumption, he said, 'O, now the glorious time is coming! I have longed to serve God perfectly; and God will gratify these desires.' At one time and another, in the latter part of his illness, he uttered these expressions: 'My heaven is to please God, to glorify him, to give all to him, and to be wholly devoted to his glory; that is the heaven I long for; that is my religion; that is my happiness, and always was ever since I supposed I had any true religion. All those who are of that religion, shall meet me in heaven. I do not go to heaven to be advanced, but to give honor to God. It is no matter where I shall be stationed in heaven, whether I have a high or low seat there, but I go to love, and please, and glorify God. If I had a thousand souls, if they were worth anything, I would give them all to God; but I have nothing to give when all is done. It is impossible for any rational creature to be happy without acting all for God; God himself could not make me happy in any other way. I long to be in heaven, praising and glorifying God with the holy angels; all my desire is to glorify God. * * * My heart goes out to the burying-place, it seems to me a desirable place; but O, to glorify God! that is it! that is above all!' 'It is a great comfort to me to think that I have done a little for God in the world; it is but a very small matter; yet I have done a little, and I lament it that I have not done more for him.' 'There is nothing in the world worth living for, but doing good and finishing God's work; doing the work that Christ did. I see nothing else in the world that can yield any satisfaction beside living to God, pleasing him, and doing his whole will. My greatest joy and comfort has been to do something for promoting the interest of religion and the souls of particular persons."

"After he came to be in so low a state that he ceased to have the least expectation of recovery, his mind was peculiarly carried forth with earnest concern for the prosperity of the Church of God on earth. This seemed very manifestly to arise from a pure disinterested love to Christ, and a desire of his glory. The prosperity of Zion was a theme on which he dwelt much, and of which he spake much, and more and more the nearer death approached. He told me when near his end, that 'never, in all his life, had his mind been so led forth in desires and earnest prayers for the flourishing of Christ's kingdom on the earth, as since he was brought so exceedingly low at Boston.' He seemed much to wonder that there appeared no more of a disposition in ministers and people, to pray for the flourishing of religion through the world. Particularly he several times expressed his wonder that there appeared no more forwardness to comply with the proposal lately made from Scotland, for united extraordinary prayer among God's people, and for the coming of Christ's kingdom, and sent it as his dying advice to his own congregation, that they should practise agreeably to that proposal.

"But a little before his death, he said to me, as I came into the room, 'My thoughts have been on the old dear theme, the prosperity of God's Church on earth. As I waked out of sleep, I was led to cry for the pouring out of God's Spirit, and the advancement of Christ's kingdom, for which the dear Redeemer died and suffered so much. It is that especially which makes me long for it.'

" But a few days before his death, he desired us to sing a psalm which related to the prosperity of Zion, which he signified engaged his thoughts and desires above all things. At his desire we sung part of the 102d Psalm. When we had done, though he was so low that he could scarcely speak, he so exerted himself that he made a prayer very audibly, in which, beside praying for those present, and for his own congregation, he earnestly prayed for the reviving and flourishing of religion in the world.

" His own congregation especially lay much on his heart. He often spoke of them ; and commonly when he did so, it was with peculiar tenderness, so that his speech was interrupted and drowned with weeping.

"Thus I have endeavored to represent something of the character and behavior of that excellent servant of Christ, whose funeral is now to be attended. Though I have done it very imperfectly, yet I have endeavored to do it faithfully, and as in the presence and fear of God without flattery, which surely is to be abhorred in ministers of the gospel, when speaking ' as messengers of the Lord of hosts.'

" Such reason have we to be satisfied that the person of whom I have been speaking, now he is 'absent from the body,' is 'present with the Lord ;' not only so, but also with him now wears a crown of glory of distinguished brightness.

"Oh that the things which were seen and heard in this extraordinary person ; his holiness, heavenliness, labor and self-denial in life; his so remarkably devoting himself and his all, in heart and practice, to the glory of God ; and the wonderful frame of mind manifested, in so steadfast a manner, under the expectation of death, and under the pains and agonies which brought it on ; may excite in us all, both ministers and people, a due sense of the greatness of the work

which we have to do in the world, of the excellency and amiableness of thorough religion in experience and practice, of
the blessedness of the end of those whose death finishes such
a life, and of the infinite value of their eternal reward, when
'absent from the body and present with the Lord;' and
effectually stir us up to constant and effectual endeavors
that, in the way of such a holy life, we may at last come to
so blessed an end   Amen."